ROBERT GALBRAITH

THE RUNNING GRAVE

A *STRIKE* NOVEL

SPHERE

SPHERE

First published in Great Britain in 2023 by Sphere
This paperback edition published in 2024 by Sphere

1 3 5 7 9 10 8 6 4 2

A CIP catalogue record for this book
is available from the British Library.

ISBN 978-1-4087-3097-3

Typeset in Bembo by M Rules
Printed and bound in Great Britain by Clays Ltd, Elcograf S.p.A.

Papers used by Sphere are from well-managed forests
and other responsible sources.

Sphere
An imprint of
Little, Brown Book Group
Carmelite House
50 Victoria Embankment
London EC4Y 0DZ

An Hachette UK Company
www.hachette.co.uk

www.littlebrown.co.uk

To my goddesses,
Lynne Corbett, Aine Kiely and Jill Prewett,
Juno, Ceres and Astarte

When, like a running grave, time tracks you down . . .

Dylan Thomas
When, Like a Running Grave

It took a long time for things to go so far. It came about because things that should have been stopped were not stopped soon enough.

The I Ching or Book of Changes

PROLOGUE

All individuals are not equally fitted to consult the oracle. It requires a clear and tranquil mind, receptive to the cosmic influences hidden in the humble divining stalks.

Richard Wilhelm
*Introduction to The I Ching
or Book of Changes*

Letters between Sir Colin and Lady Edensor and their son William

13 March 2012

Will,

We were appalled to learn from your personal tutor yesterday that you've dropped out of university and joined some kind of religious movement. We're even more astounded that you didn't discuss this with us, or bother to tell us where you were going.

Unless we're being lied to by the woman who answers the phone at the headquarters of the Universal Humanitarian Church, handwritten letters are the only means of contacting members. She gave me her word that this letter would be passed to you.

1

Your mother and I don't understand why you've done this, why you didn't talk to us first, or what can have persuaded you to abandon your course and your friends. We're extremely worried about you.

Please get in touch IMMEDIATELY you receive this.

Dad

16 April 2012

Darling Will,

The lady at the church headquarters says you've received Dad's letter, but we still haven't heard from you, so we're still very worried.

We think you might be at Chapman's Farm in Norfolk. Dad and I will be at the New Inn, Roughton, this Saturday at 1 p.m. Please, Will, come and meet us, so we can talk everything over. Dad's been doing a bit of research on the Universal Humanitarian Church and it sounds like a very interesting organisation with worthy aims. We can certainly see why it would appeal to you.

We aren't trying to run your life, Will, we really do just want to see you and know that you're all right.

With lots of love,

Mum xxx

29 April 2012

Dear Will,

Yesterday, I visited the UHC's Central Temple in London and spoke to a woman who insisted that our previous letters have been passed on to you. However, as you didn't come and meet us on Saturday or send us any word, we have no means of knowing whether she's telling the truth.

I therefore feel it is necessary to state, for your benefit or for the benefit of whoever might be illegally opening your mail, that I know <u>for a fact</u> that you're at Chapman Farm, that you never leave it unaccompanied and that you've lost a substantial amount of weight. I also know that it's impossible for anyone except members of the church to visit the farm.

You're a highly intelligent individual, Will, but the fact remains that you're autistic and this isn't the first time you've been manipulated. Unless I hear back from you by phone, or in a letter written in your own handwriting, by the 5th, I will contact the police.

I've been in touch with an ex-member of the Universal Humanitarian Church whom I'd like you to meet. If the church has nothing to hide and you're remaining at Chapman Farm of your own free will, they can have no objection to you meeting us, or speaking to this individual.

Will, I repeat, unless I hear from you by the 5th of May, I will contact the police.

Dad

1 May 2012

Dear Colin and Sally,

Thank you for your letters. Everything is fine. I am very happy in the UHC and I now understand many things that I never understood before. In fact, I am not 'on the spectrum'. That's a label you've attached to me to justify the levels of control you've exerted on me all my life. I'm not your flesh object and, unlike you, I'm not motivated by money or materialist considerations.

I understand from your last letter that you've been having Chapman Farm watched. I'm an adult and the fact that you continue to treat me as an infant who should be spied on just proves how little I can trust you.

I also know exactly which 'ex-member' of the UHC you want me to meet. He's a very dangerous, malicious man who's done harm to many innocent people. I advise you to have no more contact with him.

The Drowned Prophet Will Bless All Who Worship Her.

Will

2 May 2012

Darling Will,

We were so happy to get a letter from you, but we're a little bit concerned by it, because it really doesn't sound like you, darling.

Will, please meet us. If we can meet you face-to-face, we'll be reassured that you're happy and know what you're doing. That's all we ask, a face-to-face meeting.

Darling, I want to be completely honest with you. Dad did have somebody watching Chapman Farm because he was so worried about you, but I promise that's all finished. Dad's cancelled the arrangement. Nobody's spying on you and we don't want to control you, Will. We only want to see you and hear from your own lips that you're happy and that you're acting of your own free will.

We love you, and I promise we only want the best for you.
Mum xxx

12 May 2012

Dear Colin and Sally,

    I will meet you at the Central Temple in Rupert Court, London, on 23rd May at midday. Do not bring anyone with you, especially any ex-member of the church, because they won't be admitted.

    The Drowned Prophet Will Bless All Who Worship Her.

    Will

24 May 2012

Dear Colin and Sally,

    I agreed to meet you yesterday to prove I'm completely happy and fully in control of my own choices. Both of you demonstrated high levels of egomotivity and were disrespectful to me and abusive towards people I esteem and love.

    If you contact the police or start having me watched again I will bring charges against you in court. The Church has arranged for me to be assessed by a doctor who will testify that I have full capacity and that you are the ones trying to exert undue influence on me. I have also consulted the UHC's lawyers. My trust fund is my own and as Grandpa left me that money, not you, you have no right to prevent me from using my inheritance for good.

The Drowned Prophet Will Bless All Who Worship Her.

Will

16 March 2013

Darling Will,

I know I say it in every letter, but please, please contact us. We understand and respect the fact that you want to remain with the UHC. All we want is to know that you're happy and well. Most of all, we'd like to see you in person. It's been over a year, Will. We miss you so much.

I sent your birthday present to Chapman Farm. I hope you got it all right.

Please, Will, get in touch. Nobody's going to try and persuade you to leave the UHC. All we want is your happiness. Dad deeply regrets some of the things he said when we last met. We aren't angry, Will, we just miss you desperately.

Dad's going to add his own note, but I just want to say that I love you with my whole heart and simply want to know that you're OK.

Mum xxxxxx

Will,

I sincerely apologise for what I said about the church last year. I hope you can forgive me, and that you'll get in touch. Mum misses you very much, as do I.

With love,

Dad x

Extracts from a letter from legal firm Coolidge and Fairfax to Mr Kevin Pirbright, former member of the Universal Humanitarian Church

18 March 2013

PRIVATE AND CONFIDENTIAL LEGAL
CORRESPONDENCE
NOT FOR PUBLICATION, BROADCAST OR
DISSEMINATION

Dear Sir . . .

This letter is written on the understanding that you are responsible for the blog 'Exposing the Universal Cult', which you write under the name 'Ex-UHC Member' . . .

Blog Post of April 2012: 'The Aylmerton Connection'

On 2 April 2012 you published a blog post titled 'The Aylmerton Connection'. The post contains several false and highly defamatory claims about the UHC. The opening paragraphs read:

Unbeknownst to the vast majority of its booming membership, who've been drawn to the church by its message of equality, diversity and charitable service, the Universal Humanitarian Church was born out of the Aylmerton Community, a notorious Norfolk-based commune, which in 1986 was revealed as a front for the paedophiliac activities of the Crowther family.

Most members of the Aylmerton Community were arrested along with the Crowther family, but those who were lucky

enough to escape prosecution remained on the community's
land, which they re-christened 'Chapman Farm'. This
diehard group would become the founding members of the
UHC.

Any reasonable reader would understand by this
that the UHC is, in effect, a continuation of the
Aylmerton Community under another name, and that
the UHC's activities resemble those of the Aylmerton
Community, specifically with relation to paedophiliac
activity. Both assertions are false and highly
defamatory of our clients.

Furthermore, the phrases 'lucky enough to escape
prosecution' and 'diehard group' would suggest to
the reasonable reader that those who remained on
the community's land had committed unlawful acts
similar to those for which the Crowther family and
others were jailed. There is no truth whatsoever in this
assertion, which is false and highly defamatory of the
UHC's members and Council of Principals.

The True Position
In fact, only one member of the UHC was ever part of
the Aylmerton Community: Mrs Mazu Wace, the wife
of the UHC's founder and leader, Jonathan Wace.

Mazu Wace was fifteen years old when the Aylmerton
Community was disbanded and she gave evidence
against the Crowther brothers at their trial. This is a
matter of public record and easily discoverable through
court documents and press reports of the case.

Mrs Wace has talked openly of her traumatic experiences at the Aylmerton Community, including at church groups you personally attended. Far from being 'lucky enough to escape prosecution', Mrs Wace was herself a victim of the Crowthers. The imputation that she was complicit in, or otherwise approved of, the Crowthers' vile, unlawful behaviour is highly defamatory and has caused Mrs Wace significant hurt and distress. It has also caused, and is likely to continue to cause, serious reputational harm to Mrs Wace, and to the UHC. This exposes you to significant liability.

Blog Post of 28 January 2013: 'The Great Charity Con'

On 28 January 2013, you published a post titled 'The Great Charity Con', in which you state:

> *In fact, the sole purpose of the UHC is generating money, and it is remarkably good at this. While better-known members are allowed merely to proselytise in press interviews, the rank and file are expected to be out on the streets with their collecting tins every day, and to remain outside, no matter the weather or their own state of health, for as long as it takes for them to make their 'offering'. This is the minimum one hundred pounds per day each foot soldier must return with, unless he or she wishes to face the wrath of the church's volatile enforcer Taio Wace, who is the elder of Jonathan and Mazu Wace's two sons.*

The description of Mr Taio Wace as a 'volatile enforcer' will be understood by the reasonable reader to mean that Mr Taio Wace is aggressive, unpredictable and a bully. This categorisation is highly defamatory of Mr Taio Wace and likely to cause significant reputational harm to him, as a Principal of the Church, and to the UHC itself.

You further write:

> *Where does all the money go? Good question. Visitors to the church's Chapman Farm 'retreat' will note that while ordinary members are 'enjoying' the experience of pre-mechanised farming, sleeping in unheated barns and swapping their collecting tins for hoes and horse-drawn ploughs, the accommodation offered to Principals and celebrity members is rather more comfortable.*

> *The main farmhouse has been enlarged and renovated to a distinctly 21st-century standard, complete with swimming pool, jacuzzi, gym, sauna and private cinema. Most Principals drive brand new, top-of-the-range cars and the head of the church, Jonathan Wace (known to members as 'Papa J'), is known to own property in Antigua. Visitors to the Central Temple in Rupert Court can also see the increasingly opulent fixtures and fittings, not to mention the gold-embroidered robes worn by Principals. 'Simplicity, Humility and Charity'? Try 'Venality, Duplicity and Vanity'.*

Again, any reasonable reader of this post would understand it to mean that the Council of Principals is illegally appropriating funds donated for charity and redirecting it either into their own pockets, or into luxurious accommodation or clothing for themselves. This is entirely false and highly defamatory of the Council of Principals.

The True Position

It is a matter of public record that Mrs Margaret
Cathcart-Bryce, a wealthy, long-standing church
member, donated substantial funds to the church while
alive to renovate Chapman Farm, and that when she
died in 2004, the Council of Principals was the sole
beneficiary of her will, enabling the church to purchase
suitable properties in central London, Birmingham and
Glasgow, for congregants to meet.

Your blog post contains several outright falsehoods.
Chapman Farm contains neither a jacuzzi nor a
swimming pool, and Mr Jonathan Wace does not own,
nor has he ever owned, property in Antigua. All cars
owned by the Church Principals were bought out of
their own salaries. Your assertion that church members
are required to collect one hundred pounds per day, or
they will face the 'wrath' of Mr Taio Wace, is likewise
wholly false.

The Church is open and transparent in all its
financial dealings. No monies collected for charitable
purposes were ever used to maintain or renovate
Chapman Farm, or to purchase or upgrade the
UHC headquarters in London, or to personally
benefit the Principals in any way. Again, the
suggestion that the UHC or its Council of Principals
is 'venal', 'duplicitous' and 'vain' is highly defamatory
both of the Church and its Council, and likely to
cause serious reputational damage. This increases
your liability.

ROBERT GALBRAITH

Blog Post of 23 February 2013: 'The Drowned Prophet'

On 23 February 2013, you published a post titled 'The Drowned Prophet', in which you made a series of defamatory and deeply hurtful assertions about the death by drowning in 1995 of Mr and Mrs Wace's firstborn child, Daiyu, who is considered a prophet within the UHC.

> *UHC members are well aware that while all prophets are, theoretically, equal, one is far more equal than others. The Drowned Prophet has become central to the cult of the UHC, with her own rites and separate observances. Doubtless there was an initial desire on the part of Mazu Wace to keep her dead daughter [Daiyu Wace] 'alive' in some sense, but she milks and exploits her association with the Drowned Prophet at every available opportunity. Very few of the brainwashed are brave enough to ask (even in whispers) what made a drowned 7-year-old deserving of prophet status. Still fewer dare note the strange coincidence that Jonathan Wace's first wife (always airbrushed out of UHC history) also drowned off Cromer beach.*

The assertions and insinuations contained within this paragraph could hardly be more offensive, hurtful, or defamatory of Mr and Mrs Wace, or of the UHC as a whole.

The suggestion that Mrs Wace 'milks' or 'exploits' the tragic death of her young daughter is a vile slur and highly defamatory of Mrs Wace, both as a mother and as a Principal of the church.

Moreover, a reasonable reader is likely to conclude
from your use of the phrase 'strange coincidence',
when referring to the accidental drowning of Mrs
Jennifer Wace, that there is something suspect, either
about Mrs Jennifer Wace's death, or about the fact
that Daiyu Wace met her end in a tragically similar
fashion.

The True Position
On 29 July 1995, 7-year-old Daiyu Wace drowned
in the sea off Cromer beach. As is a matter of public
record, and easily discoverable through court records
and press coverage of the inquest into her death,
Daiyu was taken to the beach in the early morning by
a church member who hadn't asked permission from
Daiyu's parents. Mr and Mrs Wace were devastated
to hear their daughter had drowned while swimming
unattended.

It is part of the belief system of the UHC that some
deceased members of the church become 'prophets'
after death. Religious belief is protected under
English law.

A true account of Mrs Jennifer Wace's tragic death
is likewise available through court records and press
accounts of the inquest. Mrs Jennifer Wace died on a
Bank Holiday afternoon in May 1988. An epileptic, she
suffered a grand mal seizure in the water and in spite
of every attempt of nearby swimmers to save her, she
drowned. Numerous witnesses gave evidence at the
inquest that Mr Jonathan Wace was not in the sea at the
time Mrs Wace drowned, and that he ran into the water

upon realising what was happening, but was too late to save his wife. Mr Wace was distraught at his first wife's untimely death, and far from wishing to 'airbrush' her out of his personal history, he has commented publicly on the fact that the tragedy deepened his burgeoning religious faith, to which he turned for solace. Any suggestion to the contrary is false, malicious and highly defamatory of Mr Jonathan Wace.

Furthermore, it is highly defamatory to describe the church as a 'cult' or to suggest that its members are 'brainwashed'. All members of the UHC attend the church of their own free will and are able to leave at any time.

In conclusion . . .

Emails between ex-UHC member Mr Kevin Pirbright and Sir Colin Edensor

Kevin Pirbright
20 March 2013
Lawyer's letter from UHC
To: Sir Colin Edensor

Dear Colin,

This morning I got a lawyer's letter from the UHC ordering me to take down my blog or they'll make me pay, take me to court etc etc, the usual thing they do to all ex-members. Good! I want this to get into court. But I haven't got money for a lawyer so I wondered if you could help me as I don't think you can get legal aid for defamation. I'm doing this for all the brainwashed, including Will. Light has to be shone on what these bastards are doing.

The book's going really well. Plus, everything they're doing against me right now is just adding new chapters!

Best,

Kevin

Sir Colin Edensor
20 March 2013
Re: Lawyer's letter from UHC
To: Kevin Pirbright

Dear Kevin,

I'd be delighted to help with lawyers' fees. I recommend my own lawyers, Rentons, who are already aware of the UHC's nefarious activities with regards to our son. Keep me posted on developments and very good news that the book's going well. I think it will make a big difference.

Sincerely,

Colin

An excerpt of an interview with actress Noli Seymour in *Zeitgeist* magazine, January 2014

I ask about the two small Chinese characters tattooed just beneath Seymour's left ear: new additions to her already extensive collection of body art.

'Oh, I got them done last month. They mean "Jinzi"; "gold", in English. It's a reference to the Golden Prophet of the Universal Humanitarian Church.'

I'd been told that Seymour won't be answering questions on her membership of the controversial UHC, but as she's brought it up, I ask what she makes of persistent negative rumours about the church.

'That isn't something Noli wants to discuss,' says Seymour's PR man, but his client ignores him.

'Oh, please,' she says, rolling those dazzling baby blues. 'There's something SO sinister about wanting to help the homeless and give kids who're carers a holiday, right? Seriously: do people not have better things to do than bash a place that does nothing but good?

'Genuinely,' she says, leaning towards me for the first time, looking earnest, 'the Universal Humanitarian Church is, like, the most progressive religion of all time. It's all integrated. It looks for universality, because that's what life is, and humanity is: the search for oneness and wholeness. That's one of the things that really attracts me about it. It's like, there are fragments of truth in all religions, but until we get a synthesis, we won't see it. So you get massive diversity there. We study every and any Holy Book. You should come to a meeting. Tons of people come out of curiosity and, like, never leave.'

Not entirely to my surprise, Seymour's PR man intervenes at this point, reminding Noli that we're here to discuss her latest movie.

Emails between Sir Colin Edensor
and his lawyer David Renton

Sir Colin Edensor
27 May 2014
Will Edensor trust fund
To: David Renton

Dear David,

I apologise for becoming heated on our call this morning. As I know you appreciate, this whole situation is taking its toll, particularly in light of Sally's recent diagnosis.

I fully appreciate that Will is over-age and that he's refusing to submit to a further psychiatric assessment, but I'm frustrated by the chicken and egg situation in which we find ourselves. You say there are no grounds on which a judge would currently rule Will to be mentally unfit. <u>He joined a dangerous cult and cut off all contact with family and former friends.</u> Surely this, in and of itself, is proof that he's unstable and provides grounds for a further assessment.

The mere fact that Dr Andy Zhou is a Principal in the UHC ought to disqualify him from treating or assessing members of the church. I appreciate that Zhou remains a practising psychologist, but one would think Zhou's membership of the UHC represents at best a glaring conflict of interest when it comes to assessing the mental health of vulnerable church members in possession of large trust funds.

As you know, I was overruled at the meeting of Will's trustees on Thursday, where the majority view was that there are no legal grounds on which to withhold funds from him. This brings the total sum of money that Will has taken out of his trust since joining the UHC to £95k. I don't believe Will ever had any intention of putting a deposit on a house or buying a car, because he's still living at Chapman Farm and there's no evidence of him taking driving lessons.

As I told you on the phone, Kevin Pirbright is willing to testify in court that wealthy individuals such as Will are given template letters to copy out in their own handwriting when applying for funds. Nobody who knows Will could possibly believe he wrote the last two letters sent to the Board of Trustees himself. I also note that he doesn't mention the Drowned Prophet when it's a question of getting his hands on cash.

I'd appreciate any advice on how to break through the impasse in which we find ourselves. I believe Sally's illness has been caused by the stress of the last two years and we both remain desperately concerned about our son.

Yours,

Colin

David Renton
27 May 2014
Re: Will Edensor trust fund
To: Sir Colin Edensor

Dear Colin,

Thank you for this. I completely understand that this is an immensely stressful situation for you and Sally, and you have my sincere sympathy, especially in the light of Sally's recent diagnosis.

While you and I might have doubts and questions about the Universal Humanitarian Church, it is a legally registered entity and has never been successfully prosecuted.

Unfortunately, I have concerns about Kevin Pirbright's credibility if we bring him before a judge. He's already been forced to retract inaccuracies in his blog posts about the UHC, and some of his allegations about the church strain credulity, particularly his accounts of the Manifestation of Prophets, which he continues to attribute to supernatural causes.

If you know of any other ex-UHC members who could be persuaded to testify as to the use of coercive control, template letters and so forth, I think we might have a case, but I'm afraid I think your chances are very slim if you proceed with Kevin as your sole witness.

I'm sorry for this gloomy prognosis, Colin. If you can track down further ex-church members, I'll be glad to rethink.

Best, David

An excerpt of an interview
with author Giles Harmon, *ClickLit*
magazine, February 2015

CL: Some readers have seen a really profound shift in your thinking on religion in this latest novel.

GH: It isn't really a shift at all. It's a development, an evolution. I'm merely a few steps further along the path than I was previously. All that's happened is that I've stumbled upon a unique way of meeting what I feel is the universal need for the divine, which doesn't bring in its wake any of the attendant evils of traditional religions.

CL: You'll be donating all royalties from *One Holy Dawn* to the Universal Humanitarian Church?

GH: I will, yes. I've been deeply impressed by the change the UHC has made in the lives of many, many vulnerable people.

CL: There was an incident at your first reading, where an ex-member of the UHC was escorted from the venue. Can you comment on that?

GH: The police told me the poor man's quite seriously mentally ill, but I don't know any more than that.

CL: Are you aware of the public comments Sir Colin Edensor has made about the UHC? Specifically, that it's a cult?

GH: That's pure nonsense. I can hardly conceive of any group less like a cult. The place is littered with intelligent professional people – doctors, writers, teachers – and the whole ethos is to freely inquire into any and all philosophies and belief systems, including atheism. I'd encourage any open-minded, intelligent person disillusioned with traditional religion to drop in on a UHC meeting, because I think they might be very surprised by what they find there.

Emails between Sir Colin Edensor and Kevin Pirbright

Sir Colin Edensor
2 March 2015
Giles Harmon's Reading
To: Kevin Pirbright

Dear Kevin,

I was extremely unhappy to read about your behaviour at Giles Harmon's book reading. I'm mystified as to how you think it will help any of us for you to stand up in public and start hurling abuse at a respected author. Given that they also publish Harmon, I wouldn't be surprised if Roper Chard terminated your contract.

Colin

Kevin Pirbright
20 March 2015
Re: Giles Harmon's Reading
To: Sir Colin Edensor

If you'd been there you'd understand exactly why I stood up and told Harman what I thought of him. These fucking rich pricks like him and Noli Seymour never see what happens at Chapman Farm. They're being used as recruitment tools and they're too fucking dumb and arrogant to realise it.

The book's stalled, so Roper Chard will probably drop me anyway. I'm dealing with a lot of stuff I think I repressed. There was a night when all the kids were given drinks that I now think must have been drugged. I'm having nightmares about the punishments. There are also big stretches of time where I can't remember anything.

I can feel the presence of the Drowned Prophet all around me. If anything happens to me, she'll have done it.

Kevin

Letters from Sir Colin and Lady Edensor to their son William

14 December 2015

Dear Will,

The doctors have now given Mum 3 months to live. I'm begging you to contact us. Mum's tormented by the idea that she might never see you again.

Dad

14 December 2015

Darling Will,

I'm dying. Please, Will, let me see you. This is my dying wish. Please, Will. I can't bear to leave this world without seeing you again. Will, I love you so very much and I always, always will. If I could hug you one more time I'd die happy.

Mum xxxxxxxxx

22

2 January 2016

Dear Will,

Mum died yesterday. The doctors thought she had longer. If you're interested in attending her funeral, let me know.

Dad

PART ONE

Ching/The Well

THE WELL. The town may be changed,
But the well cannot be changed.

The I Ching or Book of Changes

1

. . . the superior man is careful of his words
And temperate in eating and drinking.

The I Ching or Book of Changes

February 2016

Private detective Cormoran Strike was standing in the corner of a small, stuffy, crowded marquee with a wailing baby in his arms. Heavy rain was falling onto the canvas above, its irregular drumbeat audible even over the chatter of guests and his newly baptised godson's screams. The heater at Strike's back was pumping out too much warmth, but he couldn't move, because three blonde women, all of whom were around forty and holding plastic glasses of champagne, had him trapped while taking it in turns to shout questions about his most newsworthy cases. Strike had agreed to hold the baby 'for a mo' while the baby's mother went to the bathroom, but she'd been gone for what felt like an hour.

'When,' asked the tallest of the blondes loudly, 'did you realise it wasn't suicide?'

'Took a while,' Strike shouted back, full of resentment that one of these women wasn't offering to hold the baby. Surely they knew some arcane female trick that would soothe him?

27

He tried gently bouncing the child up and down in his arms. It shrieked still more bitterly.

Behind the blondes stood a brunette in a shocking pink dress, who Strike had noticed back at the church. She'd talked and giggled loudly from her pew before the service had started, and had drawn a lot of attention to herself by saying 'aww' loudly while the holy water was being poured over the sleeping baby's head, so that half the congregation was looking at her, rather than towards the font. Their eyes now met. Hers were a bright sea-blue, and expertly made up so that they stood out like aquamarines against her olive skin and long dark brown hair. Strike broke eye contact first. Just as the lopsided fascinator and slow reactions of the proud grandmother told Strike she'd already drunk too much, so that glance had told him that the woman in pink was trouble.

'And the Shacklewell Ripper,' said the bespectacled blonde, 'did you actually *physically* catch him?'

No, I did it all telepathically.

'Sorry,' said Strike, because he'd just glimpsed Ilsa, his godson's mother, through the French doors leading into the kitchen. 'Need to give him back to his mum.'

He manoeuvred past the disappointed blondes and the woman in pink and headed out of the marquee, his fellow guests parting before him as though the baby's wails were a siren.

'Oh, God, I'm sorry, Corm,' said fair-haired, bespectacled Ilsa Herbert. She was leaning up against the side talking to Strike's detective partner Robin Ellacott, and Robin's boyfriend, CID officer Ryan Murphy. 'Give him here, he needs a feed. Come with me,' she added to Robin, 'we can talk – couldn't grab me a glass of water, could you, please?'

Fucking great, thought Strike, watching Robin walk away to fill a glass at the sink, leaving him alone with Ryan Murphy who, like Strike, was well over six feet tall. There, the resemblance ended. Unlike the private detective, who resembled a broken-nosed Beethoven, with dark, tightly curling hair and a naturally surly expression, Murphy was classically good looking, with high cheekbones and wavy light brown hair.

Before either man could find a subject of conversation, they were joined by Strike's old friend Nick Herbert, a gastroenterologist, and father of the baby who'd just been assaulting Strike's eardrums. Nick, whose sandy hair had begun receding in his twenties, was now half bald.

'So, how's it feel to have renounced Satan?' Nick asked Strike.

'Bit of a wrench, obviously,' said the detective, 'but we had a good run.'

Murphy laughed, and so did somebody else, right behind Strike. He turned: the woman in pink had followed him out of the marquee. Strike's late Aunt Joan would have thought the pink dress inappropriate for a christening: a clinging, wraparound affair with a low V neckline and a hemline that showed a lot of tanned leg.

'I was going to offer to hold the baby,' she said in a loud, slightly husky voice, smiling up at Strike, who noticed Murphy's gaze sliding down to the woman's cleavage and back up to her eyes. 'I *love* babies. But then you left.'

'Wonder what you're supposed to do with a christening cake?' said Nick, contemplating the large, uncut slab of iced fruitcake that lay on the island in the middle of the kitchen, topped with a blue teddy bear.

'Eat it?' suggested Strike, who was hungry. He'd had only a couple of sandwiches before Ilsa had handed him the baby and, as far as he could see, his fellow guests had demolished most of the available food while he'd been trapped in the marquee. Again, the woman in pink laughed.

'Yeah, but are there supposed to be pictures taken first, or what?' said Nick.

'Pictures,' said the woman in pink, 'definitely.'

'We'll have to wait, then,' said Nick. Looking Strike up and down through his wire-rimmed glasses, he asked, 'How much have you lost now?'

'Three stone,' said Strike.

'Good going,' said Murphy, slim and fit in his single-breasted suit.

Fuck off, you smug bastard.

2

Six in the fifth place means . . .
The companion bites his way through the wrappings.
If one goes to him,
How could it be a mistake?

                    The I Ching or Book of Changes

Robin was sitting on the end of the double bed in the marital bedroom. The room, which was decorated in shades of blue, was tidy except for two drawers lying open at the base of the wardrobe. Robin had been acquainted with the Herberts long enough to know Nick would have left them like this: it was one of his wife's perennial complaints that he neither pushed in drawers nor closed cupboard doors.

Lawyer Ilsa was currently settled in a rocking chair in the corner, the baby already gulping greedily at her breast. As she came from a farming family, Robin was unfazed by the snuffling noises the baby was making. Strike would have found them vaguely indecent.

'It makes you so damn thirsty,' said Ilsa, who'd just gulped down most of her glass of water. Having handed Robin the empty glass she added, 'I think my mum's drunk.'

'I know. I've never met anyone happier to be a grandmother,' said Robin.

'True,' sighed Ilsa. '*Bloody* Bijou, though.'

'Bloody what?'

'The loud woman in pink! You must've noticed her, her tits are virtually hanging out of her dress. I *detest* her,' said Ilsa vehemently, 'she's *got* to be the centre of attention all the bloody time. She was in the room when I invited two other people at her chambers, and she just assumed I meant her, too, and I couldn't think of any way of telling her no.'

'Her name's Bijou?' said Robin incredulously. 'As in residence?'

'As in man-hungry pain in the arse. Her real name's Belinda,' said Ilsa, who then affected a booming, sultry voice, '"but everyone calls me Bijou".'

'Why do they?'

'Because she tells them to,' said Ilsa crossly, and Robin laughed. 'She's having an affair with a married QC, and I hope to God I don't meet him in court any time soon, because she's told us way too much about what they get up to in bed. She's quite open about trying to get pregnant by him, to get him to leave his wife ... but maybe I'm bitter ... well, I *am* bitter. I don't need women who're size eight around me, right now. This is a size sixteen,' she said, looking down at her navy dress. 'I've never been this big in my life.'

'You've just given birth and you look absolutely lovely,' said Robin firmly. 'Everyone's been saying so.'

'See, this is why I like you, Robin,' said Ilsa, wincing slightly at the enthusiastic sucking of her son. 'How're things going with Ryan?'

'Good,' said Robin.

'What's it been now? Seven months?'

'Eight,' said Robin.

'Hm,' said Ilsa, now smiling down at her baby.

'What's that mean?'

'Corm's hating it. His *face* when you and Ryan were holding hands outside the church. And I notice Corm's lost a ton of weight.'

'He had to,' said Robin, 'because his leg got so bad last year.'

'If you say so ... Ryan doesn't drink at all?'

'No, I told you: he's an alcoholic. Sober two years.'

'Ah ... well, he seems nice. He wants kids,' added Ilsa, shooting a glance at her friend. 'He was telling me so, earlier.'

'We're hardly going to start trying for a baby when we've known each other barely eight months, Ilsa.'

'Corm's never wanted kids.'

Robin ignored this comment. She knew perfectly well that Ilsa and Nick had hoped for several years that she and Strike would become more to each other than detective partners and best friends.

'Did you see Charlotte in the *Mail?*' asked Ilsa, when it became clear Robin wasn't going to discuss Strike's paternal urges or lack thereof. 'With that Thingy Dormer?'

'Mm,' said Robin.

'I'd say "poor bloke", but he looks tough enough to handle her ... mind you, so did Corm, and that didn't stop her fucking up his life as badly as she could.'

Charlotte Campbell was Strike's ex-fiancée, with whom he'd been entangled on and off for sixteen years. Recently separated from her husband, Charlotte was now featuring heavily in gossip columns alongside her new boyfriend, Landon Dormer, a thrice-married, lantern-jawed billionaire American hotelier. Robin's only thought on seeing the most recent paparazzi pictures of the couple was that Charlotte, though as beautiful as ever in her red slip dress, looked strangely blank and glassy-eyed.

There was a knock on the bedroom door, and Ilsa's husband entered.

'The consensus,' Nick told his wife, 'is that we take pictures before cutting the christening cake.'

'Well, you'll have to give me a bit longer,' said the harried Ilsa, 'because he's only had one side.'

'And in other news, your friend Bijou's trying to chat up Corm,' Nick added, grinning.

'She's not my bloody friend,' retorted Ilsa, 'and you'd better warn him she's a complete nutcase. *Ouch*,' she added crossly, glaring down at her son.

Down in the crowded kitchen, Strike was still standing beside the uncut christening cake, while Bijou Watkins, whose Christian name Strike had asked her to repeat because he hadn't believed it the first time, was subjecting him to a rapid-fire stream of gossip relating to her job punctuated by cackles of laughter at her own jokes. She spoke very loudly: Strike doubted whether there was anyone in the kitchen who wasn't able to hear her.

'... with Harkness – you know George Harkness? The QC?'

'Yeah,' lied Strike. Either Bijou imagined that private detectives routinely attended court cases, or she was one of those people who imagine that everyone is as interested in the minutiae and personalities of their profession as they are.

'... so I was on the Winterson case – Daniel Winterson? Insider trading?'

'Yeah,' said Strike, glancing around the kitchen. Ryan Murphy had disappeared. Strike hoped he'd left.

'... and we couldn't afford another mistrial, obviously, so Gerry said to me, "Bijou, I'll need you in your push-up bra, we've got Judge Rawlins ..."'

She cackled again as a few male guests looked around at Bijou, some smirking. Strike, who hadn't expected the turn the conversation had taken, found himself glancing down at her cleavage. She had an undeniably fabulous figure, small-waisted, long-legged and large-breasted.

'. . . you know who Judge Rawlins is, right? Piers Rawlins?'

'Yeah,' Strike lied again.

'Right, so, he's a real one for the ladies, so I'm walking into court like this . . .'

She pressed her breasts together with her upper arms and emitted a throaty laugh again. Nick, who'd just reappeared in the kitchen, caught Strike's eye and grinned.

'. . . and so, yeah, we were pulling out all the stops, and when the verdict came in, Gerry said to me, OK, next time it'll have to be no knickers and you just keep bending over to pick up your pen.'

She burst out laughing for the third time. Strike, who could just imagine how his two female co-workers, Robin and ex-policewoman Midge Greenstreet, would react if he started suggesting these strategies for getting information out of witnesses or suspects, settled for a perfunctory smile.

At this moment, Robin reappeared in the kitchen, alone. Strike's eyes followed her as she slid through the crowd to Nick to tell him something. He'd rarely seen Robin wear her straw-berry blonde hair up, and it suited her. Her light blue dress was far more demure than Bijou's and looked new: bought in tribute to Master Benjamin Herbert, Strike wondered, or for the benefit of Ryan Murphy? As he watched, Robin turned, saw him, and smiled over the sea of heads.

''Scuse me,' he said, cutting off Bijou mid-anecdote, 'need to talk to someone.'

He picked up two of the pre-poured glasses of champagne standing beside the christening cake and cleaved his way through the jumble of laughing, drinking friends and relatives to where Robin was standing.

'Hi,' he said. There'd been no chance to talk at the church, though they'd stood side by side at the font, jointly renouncing Satan. 'Want a drink?'

'Thanks,' said Robin, taking the glass. 'Thought you didn't like champagne?'

'Couldn't find any lager. Did you get my email?'

'About Sir Colin Edensor?' said Robin, dropping her voice. In unspoken agreement, the pair edged away from the fray into a corner. 'Yes. Funnily enough, I was reading an article about the Universal Humanitarian Church the other day. You realise their headquarters are about ten minutes from our office?'

'Rupert Court, yeah,' said Strike. 'There were girls out with collecting tins in Wardour Street last time I was there. How d'you fancy meeting Edensor with me on Tuesday?'

'Definitely,' said Robin, who'd been hoping Strike would suggest this. 'Where's he want to meet?'

'The Reform Club, he's a member. Murphy have to leave?' Strike asked casually.

'No,' said Robin, looking around, 'but he had to make a work call. Maybe he's outside.'

Robin resented feeling self-conscious as she said this. She ought to be able to talk naturally about her boyfriend with her best friend, but given Strike's lack of warmth on the rare occasions Murphy called for her at the office, she found it difficult.

'How was Littlejohn yesterday?' asked Strike.

'All right,' said Robin, 'but I don't think I've ever met anyone as quiet.'

'Makes a nice change after Morris and Nutley, doesn't it?'

'Well, yes,' said Robin uncertainly, 'but it's a bit unnerving to sit next to someone in a car for three hours in total silence. And if you say anything to him, you get a grunt or a monosyllable.'

A month previously, Strike had succeeded in finding a new subcontractor for the detective agency. Slightly older than

Strike, Clive Littlejohn, too, was ex-Special Investigation Branch, and had only recently left the army. He was large and square, with heavy-lidded eyes that gave an impression of perennial weariness, and salt-and-pepper hair that he continued to wear military short. At interview, he'd explained that he and his wife wanted a more stable life for their teenage children, after the constant upheavals and absences of army life. On the evidence of the past four weeks, he was conscientious and reliable, but Strike had to admit his taciturnity was taken to an unusual extreme, and he couldn't remember so far seeing Littlejohn crack a smile.

'Pat doesn't like him,' said Robin.

Pat was the agency's office manager, an implausibly black-haired, chain-smoking woman of fifty-eight who looked at least a decade older.

'I don't go to Pat for character judgement,' said Strike.

He'd noticed the office manager's warmth towards Ryan Murphy whenever the CID man turned up to pick Robin up from the office and didn't appreciate it. Irrationally, he felt everyone at the agency should feel as hostile to Murphy as he did.

'Sounds as though Patterson really messed up the Edensor case,' said Robin.

'Yeah,' said Strike, with an unconcealed satisfaction that stemmed from the fact that he and the head of the rival detective agency, Mitch Patterson, detested each other. 'They were bloody careless. I've been reading up on that church since I got Edensor's email and I'd say it'd be a big mistake to underestimate them. If we take the job, it might mean one of us going in under deep cover. I can't do it, the leg's too distinctive. Probably have to be Midge. She's not married.'

'Nor am I,' said Robin quickly.

'This wouldn't be like you pretending to be Venetia Hall

or Jessica Robins, though,' said Strike, referring to undercover personas Robin had adopted during previous cases.
'It wouldn't be nine-to-five. Might mean you couldn't have
contact with the outside world for a while.'

'So?' said Robin. 'I'd be up for that.'

She had a strong feeling that she was being tested.

'Well,' said Strike, who had indeed found out what he
wanted to know, 'we haven't got the job yet. If we do, we'll
have to decide who fits the bill best.'

At this moment, Ryan Murphy reappeared in the kitchen.
Robin automatically stepped away from Strike, to whom she'd
been standing close, so as to keep their conversation private.

'What're you two plotting?' asked Murphy, smiling, though
his eyes were alert.

'No plot,' said Robin. 'Just work stuff.'

Ilsa now reappeared in the kitchen, holding her finally sated,
sleeping son.

'Cake!' shouted Nick. 'Godparents and grandparents here
for pictures, please.'

Robin moved into the heart of the party as people crowded
into the kitchen from the marquee. For a moment or two,
she'd been reminded of the tensions of her former marriage:
she hadn't liked Murphy's question, nor had she appreciated
Strike pushing to find out whether she was committed to the
job as much as the single Midge.

'You hold Benjy,' said Ilsa, when Robin reached her. 'Then
I can stand behind you. I'll look thinner.'

'You're being silly, you look great,' murmured Robin,
but she accepted her sleeping godson and turned to face the
camera, which was being held by Ilsa's red-faced uncle. There
was much jostling and repositioning behind the island on
which the christening cake stood: camera phones were held
high. Ilsa's tipsy mother trod painfully on Robin's foot and

apologised to Strike instead. The sleeping baby was surprisingly heavy.

'Cheese!' bellowed Ilsa's uncle.

'It suits you!' called Murphy, toasting Robin.

Out of the corner of her eye, Robin saw a blaze of shocking pink: Bijou Watkins had found her way to Strike's other side. The flash went off several times, the baby in Robin's arms stirred but slept on, and the moment was captured for posterity: the proud grandmother's bleary smile, Ilsa's anxious expression, the light reflected on Nick's glasses so that he looked vaguely sinister, and the slightly forced smiles on the faces of both godparents, who were pressed together behind the blue icing teddy bear, Strike ruminating on what Murphy had just said, Robin noticing how Bijou leaned into her detective partner, determined to feature in the picture.

3

*To be circumspect and not to forget one's armour is
the right way to security.*

The I Ching or Book of Changes

Strike arrived back in his attic flat in Denmark Street at eight
that evening, with the gassy sensation champagne always gave
him, feeling vaguely depressed. Usually he'd have grabbed
a takeaway on the way home, but on leaving hospital after
a three-week stay the previous year he'd been given strict
instructions about weight loss, physiotherapy and giving up
smoking. For the first time since his leg had been blown off in
Afghanistan, he'd done as the doctors ordered.

Now, without much enthusiasm, he put vegetables in a
newly purchased steamer, took a salmon fillet out of the fridge
and measured out some wholegrain rice, all the time trying not
to think about Robin Ellacott, and succeeding only in so far as
he remained aware of how difficult it was not to think about
her. He might have left hospital with many good resolutions,
but he'd also been burdened with an intractable problem that
couldn't be solved by lifestyle changes: a problem that, in truth,
he'd had far longer than he cared to admit, but which he'd
finally faced only when lying in his hospital bed, watching
Robin leave for her first date with Murphy.

For several years now, he'd told himself that an affair with his detective partner wasn't worth risking his most important friendship for, or jeopardising the business they'd built together. If there were hardships and privations attached to a life lived resolutely alone in a small attic flat above his office, Strike had considered them a price well worth paying for independence and peace after the endless storms and heartache of his long, on-off relationship with Charlotte. Yet the shock of hearing that Robin was heading off for a date with Ryan Murphy had forced Strike to admit that the attraction he'd felt towards Robin from the moment she'd first taken off her coat in his office had slowly mutated against his will into something else, something he'd finally been forced to name. Love had arrived in a form he didn't recognise, which was doubtless why he'd become aware of the danger too late to head it off.

For the first time since he'd met Robin, Strike had no interest in pursuing a separate sexual relationship as a distraction from and a sublimation of any inconvenient feelings he might have for his partner. The last time he'd sought solace with another woman, beautiful as she'd been, he'd ended up with a stiletto heel puncture on his leg and a sense of grim futility. He still didn't know whether, in the event of Robin's relationship with Murphy ending, as he devoutly hoped it would, he'd force a conversation he'd once have resisted to the utmost, with a view to ascertaining Robin's own true feelings. The objections to an affair with her remained. On the other hand ('It suits you!' that prick Murphy had said, seeing Robin with a baby in her arms), he feared the business partnership might break up in any case, because Robin would decide marriage and children appealed more than a detective career. So here stood Cormoran Strike, slimmer, fitter, clearer of lung, alone in his attic, poking broccoli angrily with a wooden spoon, thinking about not thinking about Robin Ellacott.

The ringing of his mobile came as a welcome distraction. Taking salmon, rice and vegetables off the heat, he answered.

'Awright, Bunsen?' said a familiar voice.

'Shanker,' said Strike. 'What's up?'

The man on the phone was an old friend, though Strike would have been hard pressed to remember his real name. Strike's mother, Leda, had scraped the motherless and incurably criminal sixteen-year-old Shanker off the street after he'd been stabbed and brought him home to their squat. Shanker had subsequently become a kind of stepbrother to Strike, and was probably the only human being who'd never seen any flaws in the incurably flighty, novelty-chasing Leda.

'Need some 'elp,' said Shanker.

'Go on,' said Strike.

'Need to find a geezer.'

'What for?' said Strike.

'Nah, it ain't what you fink,' said Shanker. 'I ain' gonna mess wiv 'im.'

'Good,' said Strike, taking a drag on the vape pen that continued to supply him with nicotine. 'Who is he?'

'Angel's farver.'

'Whose father?'

'Angel,' said Shanker, 'me stepdaughter.'

'Oh,' said Strike, surprised. 'You got married?'

'No,' said Shanker impatiently, 'but I'm living wiv 'er mum, in' I?'

'What is it, child support?'

'Nah,' said Shanker. 'We've just found out Angel's got leukaemia.'

'Shit,' said Strike, startled. 'I'm sorry.'

'An' she wants to see 'er real dad an' we ain' got no idea where 'e is. 'E's a cunt,' said Shanker, 'just not my kind o' cunt.'

Strike understood this, because Shanker's contacts through-out the criminal world of London were extensive, and could have found a professional con with ease.

'All right, give me a name and date of birth,' said Strike, reaching for a pen and notebook. Shanker did so, then asked, ''Ow much?'

'You can owe me one,' said Strike.

'Serious?' said Shanker, sounding surprised. 'Awright, then. Cheers, Bunsen.'

Always impatient of unnecessary phone talk, Shanker then hung up and Strike returned to his broccoli and salmon, sorry to hear about the ill child who wanted to see her father, but nevertheless reflecting that it would be useful to have a favour in hand with Shanker. The small tip-offs and bits of information Strike got from his old friend, which were some-times useful when Strike needed bait for police contacts, had escalated sharply in price as Strike's agency had become more successful.

Meal made, Strike carried his plate to the small kitchen table, but before he could sit down his mobile rang for a second time. The call had been forwarded from the office landline. He hesitated before picking it up, because he had a feeling he knew who he was about to hear.

'Strike.'

'Hey, Bluey,' said a slightly slurred voice. There was a lot of background noise, including voices and music.

It was the second time Charlotte had phoned him in a week. As she no longer had his mobile number, the office line was the only way of contacting him.

'I'm busy, Charlotte,' he said, his voice cold.

'I knew you'd say that . . . 'm'in a horrible club. You'd hate it . . .'

'I'm busy,' he repeated, and hung up. He expected her to

43

call again, and she did. He let the call go to voicemail as he shrugged off his suit jacket. As he did so, he heard a rustle in his pocket and pulled out a piece of paper that shouldn't have been there. Unfolding it, he saw a mobile number and the name 'Bijou Watkins'. She must be pretty deft, he thought, to have slipped that into his pocket without him feeling it. He tore the piece of paper in half, binned it, and sat down to eat his meal.

4

Nine in the third place means:
When tempers flare up in the family,
Too great severity brings remorse.

The I Ching or Book of Changes

At eleven o'clock on the last Tuesday in February, Strike and Robin travelled together by taxi from their office to the Reform Club, a large, grey nineteenth-century building that stood on Pall Mall.

'Sir Colin's in the coffee room,' said the tailcoated attendant who took their names at the door, and led them across the vast atrium. Robin, who'd thought she looked reasonably smart in black trousers and a sweater, which would also work for her surveillance job later, now felt slightly underdressed. White marble busts stood sentinel on square plinths and large oil paintings of eminent Whigs looked benignly down from gold frames, while columns of fluted stone rose from the tiled floor to the first-floor balcony, then up to a vaulted glass ceiling.

The coffee room, which had implied a small and cosy space, proved to be an equally grand dining room, with green, red and gold walls, long windows and gilt chandeliers with frosted glass globes. Only one table was occupied, and Robin recognised their potential client at once, because she'd looked him up the previous evening.

45

Sir Colin Edensor, who'd been born into a working-class family in Manchester, had enjoyed a distinguished career in the civil service, which had culminated in a knighthood. Now patron of several charities concerned with education and child welfare, he had a quiet reputation for intelligence and integrity. Over the past twelve months his name, which had hitherto appeared only in broadsheets, had found its way into the tabloids, because Edensor's scathing remarks about the Universal Humanitarian Church had drawn fire from a wide range of people, including a famous actress, a respected author and sundry pop culture journalists, all of whom depicted Edensor as a rich man furious that his son was squandering his trust fund to help the poor.

Sir Colin's wealth had come to him through his marriage to the daughter of a man who'd made many millions from a chain of clothing stores. The couple appeared to have been happy together given that the marriage had lasted forty years. Sally had died barely two months previously, leaving behind three sons, of whom William was the youngest by ten years. Robin assumed the two men sitting with Sir Colin were his elder sons.

'Your guests, Sir Colin,' said the attendant, without actually bowing, though his tone was hushed and deferential.

'Good morning,' said Sir Colin, smiling as he got to his feet and shook hands with the detectives in turn.

Their prospective client had a thick head of grey hair and the sort of face that engenders liking and trust. There were laughter lines on his face, his mouth was naturally upturned at the corners and the brown eyes behind his gold-rimmed bi-focals were warm. His accent was still perceptibly Mancunian.

'These are Will's brothers, James and Edward.'

James Edensor, who resembled his father, except that his hair was dark brown and he looked rather less good-humoured, stood up to shake hands, whereas Edward, who had blond hair and large blue eyes, remained seated. Robin noticed a scar running down Edward's temple. A walking stick was propped against his chair.

'It's very good of you to see us,' said Sir Colin, when all had sat down. 'Would you like anything to drink?'

When Strike and Robin declined, Sir Colin cleared his throat slightly, then said,

'Well . . . I should probably start by saying I'm not sure you're going to be able to help us. As I told you over the phone, we've already tried using private detectives, which didn't go well. It might even have made things worse. However, you were highly recommended to me by the Chiswell family, who I know of old. Izzy assured me that if you didn't think you'd be able to help, you'd tell me so at once – which I thought a high compliment.'

'We certainly don't take cases we consider hopeless,' said Strike.

'In that case,' said Sir Colin, putting his fingers together, 'I'll outline the situation and you can give me your expert opinion. Yes, please, go ahead,' he added, answering Strike's unasked question as the detective reached for his notebook.

Even if he hadn't known Sir Colin's previous profession, Strike would've known he was a man well-practised in giving information in an organised, cogent fashion, so he merely readied his pen.

'I think it's best to start with Will,' said the civil servant. 'He's our youngest child and he was – I don't like to say an accident, but Sally was forty-four when she fell pregnant with him and didn't realise for quite a while. But we were delighted, once we got over the shock.'

'James and I weren't,' interjected Edward. 'Nobody likes to think their forty-something parents are up to *that* when they're not looking.'

Sir Colin smiled.

'All right, well, let's just say it was a shock all round,' he resumed. 'But we all doted on Will once he'd arrived. He was a lovely little boy. Will's always been very clever, but by the time he was six or seven we were worried there was something slightly off. He had passionate enthusiasms – obsessions, you might almost say – and disliked upsets to his routine. Things other children took in their stride unsettled him. He didn't like big groups. At children's parties he'd be found upstairs quietly reading or playing on his own. We were a little bit anxious about him, so we took him to see a psychologist and he was diagnosed as being on the mild end of the autistic spectrum. We were told it was nothing dramatic, nothing serious. The psychologist also told us he's got a very high IQ. That wasn't really a surprise: his ability to process information and his recall were both extraordinary and his reading age was at least five years ahead of his actual one.

'I'm telling you all this,' Sir Colin went on, 'because I believe Will's particular combination of abilities and quirks explain, at least partially, how the UHC was able to recruit him. There'd been a previous incident which worried us a lot, and which should have been a warning.

'When Will was fourteen he fell in with a couple of boys at school who told him they were radical socialists, waging a kind of general war on authority. Will was quite vulnerable to people who seemed to like him, because at that point he'd never had many very close friends. He bought into their philosophy of general disruption and started reading all sorts of socialist theory. Only when they convinced him to set fire to the chapel did we realise what was going on. He came within a hair's breadth of being expelled, and only a late-stage admission from a schoolmate saved him. She knew these boys were perpetuating a tease on Will for the fun of seeing how far they could persuade him to go.

'We sat him down after that, Sally and I,' said Sir Colin, 'and had a very long talk with him. It became clear to us that Will had difficulty telling when people might be duplicitous. He's quite black and white and expects other people to be as straightforward as he is, which was an irresistible temptation to the boys who put him up to arson.

'That incident aside, though, Will never got in trouble, and the older he got, the more easily he seemed to make friends. Characteristically, he went and bought books to research autism, and he could be very funny about it. By the time he came to his final year at school, Sally and I were confident he'd be fine at university. He'd already proven he could make good friends and his grades were outstanding.'

Sir Colin took a sip of coffee. Strike, who appreciated the way in which the civil servant was relating the information, posed no questions, but waited for him to continue.

'Then,' Sir Colin said, setting down his cup, 'three months before Will was due to leave for Durham, Ed was involved in a very serious car crash.'

'A lorry's brakes failed,' explained Ed. 'It crashed right through some traffic lights and hit my car.'

'God,' said Robin. 'Were you—?'

'He was in a coma for five days,' said Sir Colin, 'and had to learn to walk again. As you can imagine, all Sally's and my attention was on Ed. Sally was virtually living at the hospital.

'I blame myself for what happened next,' said Sir Colin. Both his sons made to protest, but Sir Colin said, 'No, let me say it. Will went off to university, and I wasn't checking in with him as often as I would have done. I should've asked more questions, shouldn't have taken things at face value. He mentioned people he was having drinks with, told me he'd joined a couple of societies, his coursework didn't seem a problem – but then he disappeared. Simply packed up and vanished.

'His tutor alerted us and we were extremely worried. I went up to the university myself and spoke to some of his friends, who explained that he'd been to a UHC talk held at the university, where he got talking to some members who gave him some literature to read, and asked him to attend a service, which he did. The next thing that happened was that he reappeared in his college, stripped his room and took off. Nobody has seen him since.

'We tracked him down via the temple in Rupert Court and found out he was at Chapman Farm, in Norfolk. That's where the UHC originated and it's still their largest indoctrination centre. Members aren't permitted mobile phones, so the only way to contact Will was to write to him, which we did. Eventually, under threat of the police, we managed to force the church to let us meet Will at their Central Temple in Rupert Court.

'That meeting went extremely badly. It was like talking to a stranger. Will was totally unlike himself. He met everything we said with what I now know to be standard UHC talking points and jargon, and he refused point-blank to leave the church or resume his studies. I lost my temper, which was a big mistake, because it played right into the church's hands and enabled them to paint me as his enemy. I should've done what Sally was doing: simply pour out love and show we weren't trying to control or mislead him, which of course is what the church Principals were saying about us.

'If I'd let Sally handle things, we might have had a chance of getting him out, but I was angry – angry he was throwing away his university career, and angry he'd caused so much fuss and worry when we still didn't know whether Ed was going to be wheelchair-bound for the rest of his life.'

'What year was this?' Strike asked.

'2012,' said Sir Colin.

'So he's been in there nearly four years?'

'Correct.'

'And you've only seen him once since he joined?'

'Once face to face, and otherwise only in photographs taken by Patterson Inc. Ed's seen him, though.'

'We didn't talk,' said Ed. 'I tried to approach him last year in Wardour Street and he just turned tail and ran back into the Rupert Court Temple. I've walked the area a few times since and I've spotted him from a distance, out with his collecting tin. He looks ill. Emaciated. He's the tallest of all of us and he must be several stone underweight.'

'Apparently they're chronically underfed at Chapman Farm,' said Sir Colin. 'They do a lot of fasts. I found out a lot about the inner workings of the church through a young ex-member called Kevin Pirbright. Kevin grew up in the church. He was there from the age of three.'

'Yeah,' said James, who for the last few minutes had given the impression of a man struggling to keep a guard on his tongue. '*He* had an excuse.'

There was a moment of charged silence.

'Sorry,' said James, though he didn't look it, but then, evidently unable to hold the words back, he said forcefully,

'Look, Will might have been too much of an idiot not to realise setting fire to a school chapel won't solve world poverty, but come on. *Come on.* Of all the times to join a cult, he chooses the exact moment we're waiting to find out whether Ed's going to be paraplegic for the rest of his life?'

'Will doesn't think like that,' said Ed.

'No, because he's a self-centred, monomaniacal little shit,' said James hotly. 'He knows perfectly well what he's doing and he's had plenty of opportunities to stop doing it. Don't go thinking he's some innocent halfwit,' he threw at Strike and Robin. 'Will can be bloody patronising to anyone who isn't as clever as he is and you should hear him in an argument.'

'James,' said Ed quietly, but his brother ignored him.

'My mother died on New Year's Day. One of her last conscious acts was to write a letter to Will, *begging* him to let her see him one more time. Nothing. *Nothing* back. He let her die fretting about him, desperate to see him, and he didn't turn up for the funeral, either. That was *his choice* and I'll never forgive him for it. *Never.* There. I've said it,' said James, slapping his hands to his thighs before getting to his feet. 'I'm sorry, I can't do this,' he added, and before anyone else could speak, he'd marched out of the room.

'I thought that was going to happen,' muttered Ed.

'I'm so sorry,' said Sir Colin to Strike and Robin. His eyes had become wet.

'Don't worry about us,' said Strike. 'We've seen far worse.'

Sir Colin cleared his throat again and said, with a slight tremor in his voice,

'Sally's *very* last conscious act was to beg me to get Will out ... do excuse me,' he added, as tears began to leak from beneath the bifocals and he groped for a handkerchief.

Ed struggled up to move into the seat beside his father. As he moved around the table, Strike saw he still had a pronounced limp.

'C'mon, Dad,' he said, placing a hand on Sir Colin's shoulder. ''S'all right.'

'We don't usually behave like this in public,' Sir Colin told Strike and Robin, striving for a smile as he mopped his eyes. 'It's just that Sally ... it's all still very ... very recent ...'

With what Robin felt was deplorable timing, an attendant now arrived beside their table to offer lunch.

'Yes, very good idea,' said Sir Colin huskily. 'Let's eat.'

By the time menus had been provided and food ordered, Sir Colin had regained his composure. Once the waiter was out of earshot he said,

'Of course, James is right, up to a point. Will's got a formidable intellect and he's a devil in a debate. I'm simply trying to explain that there's always been a – a worrying *naivety* allied to Will's very powerful brain. He's thoroughly well intentioned, he truly wants to make the world a better place, but he also likes certainty and rules to cleave to. Before he found the prophets of the UHC, it was socialism, and before that he was a very tiresome Cub Scout – tiresome for the Cub leaders, because he didn't like noisy games, but equally tiresome for us, with his endless good turns, and wanting to debate whether it was a good turn if it was something he'd been asked to do, or whether he had to think up his own acts of benevolence for them to qualify.

'But Will's real problem,' said Sir Colin, 'is that he doesn't see evil. It's theoretical to him, a faceless world force to be eradicated. He's utterly blind to it when he's up close.'

'And you think the UHC's evil?'

'Oh yes, Mr Strike,' said Sir Colin quietly. 'Yes, I'm afraid I do.'

'Have you tried visiting him? Arranging another meeting?'

'Yes, but he's refused. Only church members are allowed at Chapman Farm and when Ed and I tried to attend a service at the Rupert Court Temple to talk to Will, we were refused entry. It's a registered religious building, so they have a legal right to bar visitors. We deduced from the fact we weren't allowed in that the church have pictures of Will's family members and have instructed church officials to keep us out.

'As I told you on the phone, that's how Patterson Inc messed things up. They sent the same man who'd been staking out Chapman Farm to the temple. Chapman Farm has cameras all around the perimeter, so the church authorities already knew what the man looked like, and when he arrived in Rupert Court they told him they knew who he was and who he worked for, and that Will was aware I was having private detectives follow him. At that point I terminated my contract with Patterson Inc. They'd not only failed to find out any information that would help me extract Will, they'd reinforced the church's narrative against our family.'

'Will's still at Chapman Farm then, is he?'

'As far as we know, yes. He sometimes goes out collecting money in Norwich and London. He occasionally stays overnight at the Rupert Court Temple, but otherwise he's at the farm. Kevin told me recruits who don't progress to running seminars and prayer meetings usually remain in the indoctrination centres – or spiritual retreats, as the church calls them. Apparently there's a lot of hard labour at Chapman Farm.'

'How did you meet this –' Strike checked his notes '– Kevin Pirbright?'

'I contacted him through his blog about the UHC,' said Sir Colin.

'Would he be amenable to talking to us?'

'I'm sure he would have been,' said Sir Colin quietly, 'but he's dead. He was shot in August of last year.'

'Shot?' repeated Strike and Robin simultaneously.

'Yes. A single bullet to the head at home in his flat in Canning Town. It wasn't suicide,' said Sir Colin, forestalling Strike's question. 'There was no gun found at the scene. Patterson spoke to a police contact: they believe it was a drug-related killing. Apparently Kevin was dealing.'

'Were you aware of that?'

'No, but I wouldn't have been . . . I think the poor chap wanted to impress me,' said Sir Colin sadly. 'Wanted to seem more well balanced than he really was. He didn't have anyone else, because the rest of his family are still in the UHC. I never visited his flat and it was only towards the end that he admitted how much of a toll it was taking on him, writing about everything that had happened to him, trying to piece together his memories for his book about the UHC. I should've realised, I ought to have got him some kind of counselling. Should've remembered he was a damaged human being, instead of treating him as a kind of weapon to be used against the church.

'I didn't hear from him at all in the month before he was shot. Sally's illness had been declared terminal, and I'd ticked Kevin off for behaving erratically and unhelpfully: I mean, in ways that were damaging to himself, quite apart from my wish to get Will out of the UHC. He made a scene at Giles Harmon's book signing, swearing and shouting. I was constantly trying to impress upon him that those kinds of tactics could only backfire, but he was very angry, very bitter.'

'Do *you* think it was a drug-related hit?'

Ed glanced sideways at his father, who hesitated before saying,

'I was in rather an overwrought state when I heard he'd been shot and ... if I'm honest, my thoughts certainly went straight to the UHC.'

'But you've changed your mind?'

'I have, yes. They don't need guns; they've got expensive lawyers. They're expert at shutting down criticism: articles by sympathetic journalists, celebrities doing PR ... Kevin was very small fry, really, even if he'd managed to finish his book. They'd already forced him to take down every serious allegation he made on his blog, and they'd also made accusations of abuse against him.'

'What kind of abuse?'

'Sexual,' said Sir Colin. 'They claimed he'd abused his

sisters. According to a letter Kevin received from the Council of Principals, both girls had made fairly detailed allegations against him. Now, I know as well as anyone that sexual abuse is endemic. One of the charities I work with helps survivors, so I'm only too familiar with the statistics and I'm not deluded: plenty of apparently charming people do terrible things behind closed doors. Obviously, I can't discount the possibility that Kevin *did* abuse those girls, but one would have thought, if the church truly believed him guilty, they'd have informed the police, not written Kevin a threatening letter. On balance, I think it was just one more attempt to frighten him, and given what Kevin told me about the internal workings of the church, I think it likely his sisters were intimidated into signing those statements ... I wanted to attend Kevin's funeral,' Sir Colin said sadly, 'but it wasn't possible. I made enquiries: his mother, who's still inside the church, chose to bury him at Chapman Farm. I must admit, I found that very upsetting ... Kevin had fought so hard to leave ...'

Their food now arrived. Strike, who'd ordered seabass rather than the steak he really fancied, asked,

'Can anything be done legally, with regards to Will?'

'Believe me, I've tried,' said Sir Colin, picking up his knife and fork. 'Will's got a trust fund, which was left to him by Sally's father. He's now taken out half the money in there and given it to the UHC. I wanted to have him assessed by a psychiatrist, but when the church got wind of that they arranged for him to see one of their own, who gave Will a completely clean bill of health. He's of age and he's been declared mentally competent. It's a total impasse.

'I've tried to interest political contacts in the church and the way it's operating, but everyone seems afraid of taking it on, given the celebrity followers and its much-vaunted charitable work. There's one MP I strongly suspect of being a member. He agitates for them in Parliament and becomes very aggressive towards anyone who criticises them. I've tried to interest some of my press contacts in an in-depth exposé, but they're shy of being sued as well. Nobody wants to touch it.

'Kevin was keen to take the UHC to court on the grounds of their abuse of him and his family. Sally and I were more than happy to fund the case, but my lawyers felt the chances of Kevin succeeding were very slim. It wasn't just that he'd already been forced to admit to mistakes on his blog; he had some very odd beliefs.'

'Such as?'

'He was convinced the spirit world was real. As a matter of fact, he thought the UHC could conjure the dead. Patterson tried to find other people who might testify and drew a complete blank.'

'Have you ever considered taking Will back by force? Grabbing him off Wardour Street?'

'Sally and I discussed doing so, as a last resort,' Sir Colin admitted, 'but we were scared out of the idea when we found out what happened to a young man whose family did exactly that, back in 1993. His name was Alexander Graves. He came from a wealthy family, too. His father literally kidnapped him off the street when he was out collecting money. Graves was in a very poor mental state when they got him out, and a couple of days later hanged himself at the family home.

'I've read extensively about mind control in the last few years,' Sir Colin continued, his food growing cold as he talked. 'I know far more than I did in the beginning about the techniques the UHC are using, and how effective they are. Kevin told me a lot of what goes on in there and it's classic cult manipulation: restriction of information, control of thoughts and emotions and so on. I understand now why Will changed so rapidly. He's literally not in his right mind.'

'He can't be,' agreed Ed. 'Not to come when Mum was dying, not to attend her funeral. James and his wife had twin boys last year, and he's never even met them.'

'So what exactly are you looking to achieve in hiring us?' asked Strike.

Sir Colin set down his knife and fork to reach under his chair for an old black briefcase, from which he extracted a slim folder.

'Before the UHC's lawyers made Kevin bowdlerise his blog, I printed out copies. There are also two long emails from Kevin in here, which explain his family's involvement in the church and some incidents he witnessed or was involved in. He mentions people and places, and makes at least one criminal allegation about Jonathan Wace, the UHC's founder. If any of the other people Kevin mentions in these documents could be persuaded to talk, or even to testify, especially about coercion or mind control, I might be able to do something, legally. At a bare minimum, I'd like to persuade the UHC to let me see Will again.'

'But ideally, you'd like to get him out?'

'Of course,' said Sir Colin, 'but I accept that might not be realistic.

'Patterson Inc's report's in here, too, for what it's worth. They focused mainly on observing Will's movements and the comings and goings at Rupert Court and Chapman Farm. Their idea was to get abusive or intimidating behaviour on camera, or an indication from Will that he was unhappy or being coerced. A couple of their people approached him in the street, undercover, and tried to engage him in conversation, but he insisted he was perfectly happy and tried to recruit them or persuade them to hand over cash . . . so: what do you think?'

said Sir Colin, looking from Strike to Robin and back again. 'Is our case hopeless?'

Before Strike could answer, Robin had held out her hand for the documents Sir Colin had brought with him.

'No,' she said. 'We'd be very happy to help.'

5

Six in the fifth place means:
Giving duration to one's character through perseverance.
This is good fortune for a woman . . .

The I Ching or Book of Changes

'It's fine,' said Strike an hour later, in response to Robin's apology for accepting the case without consulting him. 'I'd've said it myself, but I had a mouthful of potato.'

The two partners had retired to a nearby pub after leaving the Edensors. The Golden Lion was small, Victorian and ornately decorated, and they were sitting on high leather barstools at a round table.

'I was looking at the UHC's website last night,' said Robin, who was drinking orange juice, because she needed to leave for her surveillance job shortly. 'They own a *lot* of prime real estate. That place in Rupert Court must've cost them a fortune, bang in the middle of the West End, and that's before you get to the temples and centres in Birmingham and Glasgow. *Can* they be making all that money legally?'

'Well, they're flogging self-realisation courses up and down the country at five hundred quid a day and prayer retreats at a grand a time. They've got ten thousand-odd members collecting money for them, donating a fifth of their salaries and making legacies in their favour. All that'll mount up. You'd think the Inland Revenue would be all over them, so either they're clean, or they've got a shit-hot accountant who knows how to hide the dodgy stuff. But taking cash from idiots isn't a crime, unfortunately.'

'You agree with James, do you? Will's an idiot?'

Strike took a sip of beer before answering.

'I'd say people who join cults generally have something missing.'

'What about Giles Harmon? Rich, successful writer, really clever . . .'

'I'm with Orwell,' said Strike. "Some ideas are so stupid, only intellectuals believe them" . . . you know, I can't see any way of doing this properly other than getting someone into Chapman Farm undercover.'

Robin had spent the last couple of days preparing for this very conversation.

'That means attending the Rupert Court Temple first. I've looked into it: you can't just turn up at Chapman Farm, you have to be invited there, which means being recruited at one of the temples. Whoever turns up at Rupert Court will need a fully worked-up persona with backstory, which they use from their first contact with church members, and I think they should look as though they've got a lot of money, to make them a really attractive prospect for recruitment.'

Strike, who knew perfectly well he was listening to a pitch, said, 'And I'm guessing you don't think Barclay, Shah or Littlejohn would be convincing as wealthy God-botherers.'

'Well,' said Robin, 'I doubt Barclay would last an hour before starting to take the piss out of it all. Littlejohn would be perfect if the church was a silent order—'

Strike laughed.

'—and Dev's got small kids, so he's not going to want to be away for weeks. Midge is a possibility, but she's never gone undercover before. I know I haven't, not like this,' Robin said quickly, before Strike could make that point, 'but I've never had a cover broken, not even when I was being Venetia Hall every day, in the House of Commons.'

'And what if the job lasts weeks?' said Strike.

'Then it lasts weeks,' said Robin, with a slight shrug.

It so happened that Strike had already decided Robin was the best person for the job, but he had a secondary motive for accepting her proposal. A few weeks' enforced separation while she was at Chapman Farm might just put a bit of strain on her relationship with Ryan Murphy, and there was little Strike wanted more than that. However, as he didn't want to agree too readily, lest he be suspected of an ulterior motive, he merely nodded and said, 'OK, well, that could work. It needs thinking through, though.'

'I know. I can't wear a wig at Chapman Farm, so I'm thinking of a radical haircut.'

'Really?' said Strike, without thinking. He liked her hair.

'I'll have to, I've been walking around in the vicinity of Rupert Court for a few years now. The last thing we need is anyone recognising me, especially if they've seen me coming in and out of the office.'

'OK, fair point,' said Strike, 'but no need to shave your head.'

'I'm not trying to get into the Hare Krishnas,' said Robin. 'I was thinking maybe short and a nice bold colour. A privately educated girl who wants to look a bit alternative, but not so radical it'll scare her parents into stopping footing her bills. Maybe she's had a recent bad break-up and, you know, now she wants a sense of purpose and something to fill the space where she thought a wedding was going to be.'

'You *have* given this a lot of thought,' said Strike, with a grin.

'Of course I have. I want the job.'

'Why?' asked Strike. 'Why d'you want it so much?'

'I've always been interested in mind control. We touched on it on my course at uni.'

Robin had been studying psychology before she dropped out of university. Their uncompleted degrees were one of the things she and Strike had in common.

'OK, well, that all sounds good. Work out a full cover and we can readjust the rota so you prioritise Saturday mornings at temple.'

'The only problem is clothes,' said Robin. 'I don't look like I've got loads of money, clothes-wise.'

'You always look great,' said Strike.

'Thank you,' said Robin, flushing slightly, 'but if I'm going to convince the UHC I've got a lot of money, stuff like *this,*' she held up her shoulder bag, which was six years old, 'won't cut it. I s'pose I could hire a couple of designer outfits and handbags. I've never done it, but I know you can.'

'Might be able to help with that,' said Strike, unexpectedly. 'You could borrow stuff from Pru.'

'Who?'

'My sister,' said Strike. 'Prudence. The therapist.'

'*Oh,*' said Robin, intrigued.

She'd only ever met two of Strike's eight half-siblings, and those only briefly. His family was, to say the least, complicated. Strike was the illegitimate son of a rock star he'd met only twice, and a deceased mother habitually described in the press as a super-groupie. While Robin knew Strike had finally agreed to meet his half-sister Prudence for the first time some months previously, she'd had no idea they were now on such terms that she might lend expensive clothing to his detective partner.

'I think you're about the same . . .' Strike made a vague gesture rather than say 'size'. 'I'll ask her. You might have to go round to her house to try it on.'

'No problem,' said Robin, slightly taken aback. 'That'd be great, if Prudence won't mind lending stuff to a total stranger.'

'You're not a total stranger, I've told her all about you,' said Strike.

'So ... it's going well, then?' said Robin. 'You and Prudence?'

'Yeah,' said Strike. He took another sip of beer. 'I like her a lot more than any of my father's other kids – low bar, admittedly.'

'You like Al,' said Robin.

'Vaguely. He's still pissed off at me because I wouldn't go to that bloody party for Rokeby. Where're you heading after this?'

'Taking over from Dev in Bexleyheath,' said Robin, as she checked the time on her phone. 'Actually, I should get going. What about you?'

'Afternoon off. I'll scan this stuff back at the office and email it to you,' said Strike, indicating the cardboard folder of documents Colin Edensor had handed Robin.

'Great,' said Robin. 'See you tomorrow, then.'

6

Six in the fourth place means:
A tied-up sack.
No blame, no praise.

The I Ching or Book of Changes

Robin spent the six-minute walk from the Golden Lion to Green Park station doing the thing she'd resolutely schooled herself over the past eight months not to do: thinking about Cormoran Strike in any context other than work and friendship.

The long-delayed realisation that she was in love with her work partner had burst in upon Robin Ellacott the previous year upon finding out that he was having an affair he'd carefully concealed from her. At that point, Robin had decided that the only thing to do was to fall out of love, and it was in that spirit, a few weeks later, that she'd agreed to a first date with Ryan Murphy.

Since then, she'd done her utmost to keep an inner door firmly closed on whatever she might feel for Strike, hoping love would wither and die for lack of attention. In practice, this meant turning her thoughts firmly away from him when alone, and refusing, ever, to make comparisons between him and Murphy, as Ilsa had tried to do on the day of the christening. When, in spite of her best efforts, certain unwelcome memories intruded – the way Strike had hugged her on her wedding day, or the dangerous, drunken moment outside the Ritz bar on her thirtieth birthday, when he'd moved to kiss her – she reminded herself that her detective partner was a man perfectly happy with a single life punctuated by affairs with (usually gorgeous) women. He was forty-one years old, had never married, voluntarily lived alone in a spartan attic over the office, and had a deeply entrenched tendency to erect barriers to intimacy. While some of this reserve had relaxed where Robin was concerned, she hadn't forgotten how quickly it had returned after that night at the Ritz. In short, Robin had now concluded that whatever she might once have wanted, Strike hadn't ever wanted it at all.

It was therefore a pleasure and a relief to be with Murphy, who so clearly wanted to be with her. Aside from the fact that the CID man was handsome and intelligent, they had investigative work in common, which made a very welcome contrast to the well-paid accountant she'd divorced, who'd never understood Robin's preference for what Matthew had considered an eccentric, insecure career. Robin was also enjoying having a sex life again: a sex life, moreover, that was considerably more satisfactory than that she'd had with her ex-husband.

Yet there remained something between her and Ryan that she found hard to identify. Guardedness perhaps expressed it best, and it sprung, she was sure, from the fact that each had a fractured marriage in their past. Both knew just how badly people in the most intimate relationships could hurt each other, and treated each other carefully in consequence. Wiser than she'd been during her years with Matthew, Robin made sure she didn't talk too much about Strike when with Ryan, didn't mention Strike's war record, or tell any anecdotes that cast him in too amusing or attractive a light. She and Murphy had now shared plenty of details of their respective histories, but Robin was aware that she, like Ryan, was offering an edited version. Perhaps that was inevitable, once you reached your thirties. It had been so very easy to open her heart to Matthew, whom she'd met at school: though she'd believed at the time she was telling all her secrets, she looked back and realised how little, at the time, she'd had to tell. It had taken Robin six months to talk to Ryan about the brutal rape that had ended her university career, and she'd omitted mention of the fact that a major factor in the failure of her marriage had been Matthew's persistent jealousy and suspicion of Strike. For his part, Ryan never talked much about his drinking years, and had given her what she suspected was a sanitised account of the way he and his ex-wife had split up. She assumed these things would be discussed eventually, if the relationship continued. In the meantime, a private life without jealous rows and grinding resentment made a very nice change.

All this being so, brooding on the emotional subtext of Strike's conversation could do nobody any good, and made Robin feel disloyal to Murphy. Strike probably felt safe to say things like 'you always look great' and 'I've told my sister all about you' because she was now in a steady relationship with another man. As she descended into the station, she told herself firmly that Strike was her best friend, nothing more, and forced her thoughts back onto the job in Bexleyheath.

7

*This hexagram indicates a situation in which the
principle of darkness, after having been eliminated,
furtively and unexpectedly obtrudes again from within
and below.*

The I Ching or Book of Changes

Strike had meant to return to the office once he'd finished his
pint, but the Golden Lion was so pleasant, it occurred to him
that he could just as easily read the documents provided by
Colin Edensor there, where there was also beer. He therefore
bought himself a second pint and took the first opportunity
to leave his barstool for a vacated leather bench at a lower
table, where he flipped open the folder. At the top of the pile
of paper inside was a lengthy email to Sir Colin from the late
Kevin Pirbright.

Dear Colin,

**Apologies in advance if this is long, but you asked
about my family's involvement with the Universal
Humanitarian Church and how I came to leave etc, so
here it is.**

**My mother joined the UHC when I was 3 and my sisters
were 6 and 8. It's important to say that my mother – I**

was raised to call her Louise, because the UHC forbids naming blood relationships – isn't stupid. She grew up poor and never got the chance to go to university or anything, but she's bright. She married my dad really young but he left the family when I was 1. I remember Louise being very pretty when she was younger.

I don't know when she first heard Jonathan Wace speak, but I know she fell in love with him. Loads of the women in the UHC are crazy about him. Anyway, she packed up our council house and took us off to Chapman Farm. (I've had to piece all this together from stuff my sisters told me later, because I've got no memory of our life before the UHC.)

After that, we had nowhere to go other than UHC accommodation. This is really common. People sink everything into the church, as proof of their commitment to their new lives. Some members even sell their houses and give all the money to the church.

Chapman Farm is where the UHC was founded. The five prophets are buried there and because it's in deep countryside as opposed to a city, it tends to be where members are sent for re-indoctrination if they need it. There are other centres and my older sister Becca spent three years at the one in Birmingham (she's quite high up in the church now), and Emily was allowed to go out collecting money, but Louise and I never left the farm.

The UHC teaches that normal family relationships or monogamous sexual relationships are a form of materialist possession. If you're a good person, you're spirit-bonded to everyone inside the church and you love them all just the same. Louise tried to stick to that once we were inside, but the three of us always knew she was our real mother. Most of the kids' education consisted of reading UHC tracts and memorising them, but Louise taught me, Becca and Emily things like our times tables on the sly, while we were cleaning out the chickens.

When I was very young, I literally thought Jonathan Wace was my father. We all called him 'Papa J' and I knew about family relationships because they appeared in the Bible and other holy books we studied. It was only gradually I realised I wasn't actually related to Papa J. It was really confusing for a small kid but you just went with it, because everyone else did.

Mazu Wace, Papa J's wife, grew up at Chapman Farm. She was there in the Aylmerton Community days—

Strike stopped reading, staring at the last four words.
The Aylmerton Community days.
The Aylmerton Community.
Aylmerton Community.
The rundown barns, the children running riot, the Crowther brothers striding across the yard, the strange round tower standing alone on the horizon like a giant chess piece: he saw it all again. His stoned mother trying to make daisy chains for little girls; nights in ramshackle dormitories with no locks on the door; a constant sense that everything was out of control, and a childish instinct that something was wrong, and that an undefinable danger lurked close by, just out of sight.

Until this moment, Strike had had no idea that Chapman Farm was the same place: it had been called Forgeman Farm when he'd lived there, with a motley collection of families who were working the land, housed in a cluster of rundown buildings, their activities directed by the Crowther brothers. Even though there'd been no hint of religion at the Aylmerton commune, Strike's disdain for cults sprang directly from the six months at Forgeman Farm, which had constituted the unhappiest period of his unstable and fragmented childhood. The commune had been dominated by the powerful personality of the elder Crowther brother, a rangy, round-shouldered, greasy-haired man with long black sideburns and a handlebar moustache. Strike could still visualise his mother's rapt face as Malcolm Crowther lectured the group by firelight, outlining his radical beliefs and personal philosophies. He remembered, too, his own ineradicable dislike of the man, which had amounted to a visceral revulsion.

By the time the police raided the farm, Leda had already moved her family on. Six months was the longest Leda could ever bear to remain in one place. Reading about the police action in the papers once back in London, she'd refused to believe that the community wasn't being persecuted for their pacifism, the soft drugs and their back-to-the earth philosophy. For a long time she'd insisted the Crowthers couldn't possibly have done the things for which they were eventually charged, not least because her own children told her they'd escaped unscathed. Only after reading accounts of the trial had Leda reluctantly come to accept that this had been more luck than judgement; that her pastoral fantasy had indeed been a hotbed of paedophilia. Characteristically, she'd shrugged off the whole episode as an anomaly, then continued the restless existence that meant her son and daughter, when not dumped on their aunt and uncle in Cornwall, moved constantly between different kinds of insecure housing and volatile situations of her choosing.

Strike drank a third of his fresh pint before focusing his attention once more on the page in front of him.

Mazu Wace, Papa J's wife, grew up at Chapman Farm. She was there in the Aylmerton Community days and it's like her private kingdom. I don't think she's ever visited the Birmingham or Glasgow centres and she only goes up to the London Temple occasionally. I was always terrified of Mama Mazu, as church members are supposed to call her. She looks like a witch, very white face, black hair, long pointed nose and weird eyes. She always wore robes instead of the tracksuits the rest of us had to wear. I used to have nightmares about Mazu when I was little, where she was peering in at me through keyholes or watching me from skylights.

Mazu's thing was control. It's really hard to explain to anyone who hasn't met her. She could make people do anything, even hurt themselves, and I never once saw anyone refuse. One of my earliest memories from Chapman Farm is a teenager called Jordan whipping himself across the face with a leather flail. I remember his name, because Jonathan Wace used to sing the spiritual 'Roll, Jordan, Roll' whenever he saw him. Jordan was much bigger than Mazu, and he was on his knees and his face was covered in welts, and he kept whipping himself until she said it was time to stop.

In spite of everyone telling me how good and holy Mazu was, I always thought she was a terrible person. Looking back now, hating Mazu was the beginning of me questioning the entire church, although at the time I just thought Mazu was mean, not that the entire church culture was rotten.

Mazu never liked Louise and always made sure she was given the worst jobs at the farm, outside in all weathers.

As I got older, I realised this was because Jonathan and my mother were sleeping together. Mazu never liked the women Jonathan was sleeping with.

Explaining how I woke up is complicated.

A few years after we joined the UHC, a new family moved into Chapman Farm, the Dohertys: mother, father and three kids. Deirdre Doherty got pregnant again while they were living at the farm, and gave birth to a fourth kid, a daughter Mazu called Lin. (Mazu gets naming rights over all kids born at Chapman Farm. She often asks the I Ching what the baby should be called. 'Lin' is the name of one of the hexagrams.)

I was 12 when the father, Ralph, took off in the middle of the night, taking the three oldest kids with him. We were all summoned into temple next morning, and Jonathan Wace announced that Ralph Doherty was materialist and egomotivated, whereas his wife, who'd stayed behind with Lin, was a shining example of pure spirit. I can remember us all applauding her.

I was really confused and shocked by Ralph and the kids leaving, because I'd never known anyone do it before. We were all taught that leaving the church would ruin your life, that materialist existence would literally kill you after having been pure spirit, that you'd end up going crazy and probably committing suicide.

Then, a few months after Ralph had left, Deirdre was expelled. That shocked me even more than Ralph leaving. I couldn't imagine what sin Deirdre could have committed to make the UHC force her out. Usually, if someone did something wrong, they got punished. If a person got really ill, they might be allowed to leave to get medical help, but the UHC didn't usually let people go unless they'd broken down so much they couldn't work.

Deirdre left Lin behind when she went. I should have been glad, because Lin would still be able to grow up pure spirit rather than ruining her life in the materialist world. That's how most of the members saw it, but I didn't. Although I didn't have a normal parent–child relationship with Louise, I knew she was my mother and that meant something. I secretly thought Deirdre should have taken Lin with her, and that was the first serious crack in my religious belief.

I found out why Deirdre was expelled by total accident. I was on Punishment for kicking or pushing another kid. I can't remember the details. I was tied to a tree and I was to be left there all night. Two adults went past. Electric torches are forbidden at the Farm, so I don't know who they were, but they were whispering about why Deirdre had been expelled. One was telling the other one that Deirdre had written in her journal that Jonathan Wace had raped her. (All church members over the age of nine are expected to keep journals as part of their religious practice. Higher-ups read them once a week.)

I knew what rape was, because we were taught that it was one of the terrible things that happened out in the materialist world. Inside the church, people have sex with anyone who wants it, as a way of enhancing spiritual connections. We were taught that rape was different, a violent form of materialist possession.

I can't tell you how hearing that Deirdre had accused Papa J of rape made me feel. This is how indoctrinated I was: I remember thinking I'd rather have to be tied to that tree for a full week than have heard what I'd just heard. I'd been raised to think Jonathan Wace was the closest thing to God on earth. The church teaches that allowing bad thoughts about our leader or the church itself means the Adversary is working inside you to resurrect the false self, so I tried chanting, there in the dark, which is one of the techniques you're taught to stop negative thoughts, but I couldn't forget what I'd just heard about Papa J.

From then on, I got more and more screwed up. I couldn't tell anyone what I'd overheard: for one thing, if Mazu heard me telling a story like that, God knows what she'd have made me do to myself. I tried to suppress all my bad thoughts and doubts, but the crack in my belief was getting wider and wider. I started noticing the hypocrisy, the control, the inconsistencies in the teaching. They preached love and kindness, but they were merciless on people for things they couldn't help. For instance, Lin, Deirdre's daughter, started stammering when she was really small. Mazu mocked her for it constantly. She said Lin could stop if she wanted to, and she needed to pray harder.

My eldest sister Becca was on a completely different course from the rest of us by this time, travelling round the country with Wace and helping run seminars and self-realisation courses. My other sister Emily was very envious of Becca. She sometimes got to join mission outings, but not as often as Becca did.

They both looked down on me and Louise, who were the no-hopers only fit to stay on the farm.

I got really bad acne in my teens. When UHC members go out in public, they're supposed to look groomed and attractive, but Lin, Louise and I weren't allowed out even to collect money on the street, because we didn't fit the church image, me with my acne and Lin with her stammer. Louise went grey early and looks a lot older than she is, probably from working outside all the time.

The next bit is hard to write. I now know I started planning to quit the church when I was nearly 23, but as you never celebrated birthdays in there it wasn't until I got out and found my birth records that I even knew what day I was born.

It took over a year for me to actually go, partly because I needed to get up my courage. I can't emphasise how much the church dins into you that you won't be able to survive outside, that you're bound to go crazy and kill yourself, because the materialist world is so corrupt and cruel. But the main thing holding me back was that I wanted Louise to come with me. There was something wrong with her joints. I hadn't heard of arthritis before I left the church but I think it must be that. They were swollen and I know she was in pain a lot of the time. Of course, she was told this was a sign of spiritual impurity.

One day when she and I were assigned livestock duty together, I started telling her my doubts. She started literally shaking then told me I should go to temple and pray for forgiveness. Then she started chanting to block out what I was saying. Nothing I said got through to her. In the end she just ran away from me.

I was terrified she'd tell the Principals I was having doubts and knew I needed to leave immediately, so I crawled out through a fence in the early hours of the following morning, after stealing some cash from one of the charity boxes. I genuinely feared I'd drop dead once I was outside on the dark road, alone, that the Drowned Prophet would come for me, out of the trees.

I used to hope Louise would follow me out, that me going would wake her up, but it's been nearly four years, and she's still inside.

Sorry, this has been really long, but that's the whole story – Kevin

The first email finished there. Strike picked up the second and, after fortifying himself with more beer, continued to read.

Dear Colin,

Thanks very much for your email. I don't feel brave, but I really appreciate you saying it. But you might not think it any more, once you read this.

You asked about the prophets and the Manifestations. This is really hard for me to write about, but I'll tell you as much as I can.

I was only 6 when Daiyu Wace drowned, so I haven't got very clear memories of her. I know I didn't like her. She was Mazu's princess and always got special treatment and lot more leeway than the rest of the little kids.

One of the teenage girls living at the farm took Daiyu on the vegetable run early one morning (the church sold farm produce to local shops) and they stopped off at Cromer beach on the way back. They both went in for a swim, but Daiyu got into difficulties and drowned.

Obviously, that's a huge tragedy and it's not surprising Mazu was devastated, but she went pretty weird and dark afterwards, and in hindsight, I think that's where a lot of her cruelty towards my mother and kids in general came from. She especially didn't like girls. Jonathan had a daughter from his previous marriage, Abigail. Mazu got her moved out of Chapman Farm to one of the other UHC centres after Daiyu's death.

I can't say for sure when the idea of Daiyu being a kind of deity started, but over time, Jonathan and Mazu turned her into one. They called her a prophet and claimed she'd said all these spiritually insightful things, which then became part of church doctrine. Even Daiyu's death was somehow holy, like she'd been such pure spirit she dissolved from the material world. My sister Becca used to claim Daiyu had had the power of invisibility. I don't know if Becca actually believed this, or just wanted to curry favour with Jonathan and Mazu, but the idea that Daiyu had been able to dematerialise even before she drowned got added to the myth, too.

There were already two people buried at Chapman Farm when Daiyu died. I never knew the first guy. He was an American called Rusty Andersen, who used to live on a patch of ground on the edge of the Aylmerton Community. He was an army veteran and he sounds like what you'd call a survivalist these days. Mazu and Jonathan claimed Andersen had joined the church before he died, but I don't know whether that's true. He was hit and killed by a drunk driver on the road outside the farm one night, and they buried him at the farm.

The other man buried on the land was called Alexander Graves, who died in his twenties. He was definitely part of the church. I vaguely remember him being odd and chanting all the time. Graves' family kidnapped him when he was out on the street collecting money for the UHC, but soon after they took him back to the family home, he killed himself. He'd left a will saying he wanted to be buried at the farm, so he was.

We all knew Andersen's and Graves' stories, because they were used as object lessons by Jonathan and Mazu, illustrations of the danger of leaving the farm/church.

Over time, Andersen and Graves became prophets, too – it was like Daiyu needed company. Andersen became the Wounded Prophet and Graves the Stolen Prophet, and their supposedly holy sayings became part of church doctrine, too.

The fourth prophet was Harold Coates. He was a struck-off doctor who'd been on the land since the Aylmerton Community days, too. Even though the church bans all medicines (along with caffeine, sugar and alcohol), Coates was allowed to grow herbs and treat minor injuries, because he was one of us. They made Coates the Healer Prophet almost as soon as he was buried.

The last prophet was Margaret Cathcart-Bryce, who was the filthy-rich widow of some businessman. She was over 70 when she arrived at the farm, and completely infatuated with Jonathan Wace. Her face had been lifted so many times it was tight and shiny, and she wore this big silver wig. Margaret gave Wace enough money to start doing a massive renovation of Chapman Farm, which was really run down. Margaret must have lived at the farm for 7 or 8 years before she died and left everything she had to the Council of Principals. She then became the Golden Prophet.

Once they got their hands on all of Margaret's money, they built a pool with a statue of Daiyu in the middle of it, in the new courtyard. Then they dug up the four bodies that were already buried there, and reburied them in tombs around the pool. The new graves didn't have their real names, only their prophet names. There was no tomb for Daiyu, because they never recovered her body. The inquest found she hit a rip tide near the shore and just got sucked straight out to sea. So the statue in the pool is her memorial.

All five of the prophets were incorporated into the religion, but Daiyu/The Drowned Prophet was always the most important one. She was the one who could bless you, but she'd curse you if you strayed.

This next bit is difficult for people who haven't seen the proof to understand.

Spirits are real. There is an otherworld. I know that for a fact. The UHC is evil and corrupt, but that doesn't mean some of what they believe isn't true. I've seen supernatural happenings that have no 'rational' explanation. Jonathan and Mazu are bad people and I still question whether what they were summoning were spirits or demons, but I saw them do it. Glasses shattering that nobody had touched. Objects levitating. I saw Jonathan chant, then lift a truck unaided, right off the ground. They warned us wrongdoing would result in the Adversary sending demons to the farm, and I think I saw them, once: human forms with heads of pigs.

The day of each prophet's death is marked by their Manifestation. You're not allowed to attend a Manifestation until you've turned 13, and talking about it to outsiders is absolutely forbidden. I'm not comfortable writing down details of the Manifestations. I can only tell you that I've seen absolute proof that the dead can come back. That doesn't mean I think the prophets themselves were truly holy. I only know they come back on the anniversaries of their deaths. The Manifestation of the Stolen Prophet is always pretty frightening but the Manifestation of the Drowned Prophet is the worst by far. Even knowing it's coming up changes the atmosphere at Chapman Farm.

I don't know whether the Drowned Prophet can materialise anywhere other than the farm, but I do know she and the others still exist in the otherworld and I'm afraid of calling her forth by breaking confidence around the Manifestations.

Maybe you think I'm crazy, but I'm telling the truth. The UHC is evil and dangerous, but there is another world and they've found a way into it.

Kevin

8

Nine in the fifth place means . . .
It furthers one to make offerings and libations.

The I Ching or Book of Changes

Two days after they'd taken on the Edensor case, and having given a lot of thought to how best to proceed, Strike called Robin from the office. Robin, who was having a day off, had just arrived at the hairdresser's. Having apologised to the stylist, who'd only just picked up her scissors, Robin answered.

'Hi. What's up?'

'Have you been through all the Edensor documents I sent you?'

'Yes,' said Robin.

'Well, I've been thinking about it and a good first step would be getting hold of census records, to find out who's been living at Chapman Farm in the last twenty years. If we can track down ex-UHC members, we might be able to confirm some of the claims Pirbright made about what's going on in there.'

'You can only access census records up to 1921,' said Robin.

'I know,' said Strike, who'd been perusing the National Archives online, 'which is why I'm buying Wardle a curry tonight. Want to come? I tipped him off about that tosser who's paying for everything with fake tenners, and he agreed to try and get hold of the full police report into Pirbright's shooting in return. I'm buying him curry to soften him up, because I want to persuade him to get us the census records, as well.'

'I'm sorry, I can't come,' said Robin, 'Ryan's got theatre tickets.'

'Ah,' said Strike, reaching for his vape pen. 'OK, just thought I'd ask.'

'Sorry,' said Robin.

'No problem, it's your day off,' said Strike.

'I'm actually about to have my hair cut,' said Robin, out of a desire to show that she was still working on the case, even if she couldn't meet Strike's police contact that evening.

'Yeah? What colour have you decided on?'

'Don't know,' said Robin. 'I've only just sat down.'

'OK, well, I was also going to ask whether you could come over to Prudence's tomorrow evening. She's happy to lend you some clothes.'

Unless Murphy's got tickets for the fucking opera, of course.

'That'd be great,' said Robin. 'Where does she live?'

'Strawberry Hill. I'll text you the address. We'll have to meet there, I'm tailing Bigfoot until five.'

This plan agreed, Strike hung up and sat scowling, while taking deep drags on his vape. The idea of Murphy buying theatre tickets aggravated him; it suggested a dangerous degree of effort. Eight months into the relationship, the policeman should surely have stopped pretending he'd rather watch a play than have a decent meal followed by sex. Pushing himself up from the partners' desk, Strike moved into the outer room, where the office manager, Pat, was typing away at her desk. Evidently she'd heard part of his conversation with Robin through the open door, because she asked, electronic cigarette clamped, as usual, between her teeth,

'Why d'you call him Bigfoot?'

'Because he looks like Bigfoot,' said Strike, as he filled the kettle.

The man in question was the wealthy owner of a software company, whose wife believed him to be visiting sex workers. Having been forced to share a crowded lift with him during his last bout of surveillance, Strike could testify to the fact that the target was not only extremely tall, hairy and unkempt, but smelled as though his last shower was a distant memory.

'Funny how beards come and go,' said Pat, still typing.

'It's called shaving,' said Strike, reaching for mugs.

'Ha ha,' said Pat. 'I mean fashions. Sideburns and that.'

An unwelcome memory of Malcolm Crowther sitting by the campfire at Forgeman Farm surfaced in Strike's mind: Crowther had a small girl and was encouraging her to stroke his handlebar moustache.

'Want a cup of tea?' Strike said, dismissing the mental image.

'Go on, then,' Pat replied, in the deep, gravelly voice that often caused callers to mistake her for Strike. 'That Hargreaves woman still hasn't paid her invoice, by the way.'

'Call her,' said Strike, 'and tell her we need her to settle up by the end of the month.'

'That's Monday.'

'And she's got millions.'

'Richer they are, slower they pay.'

'Some truth in that,' admitted Strike, setting down Pat's mug on her desk before returning to the inner office and closing the door.

He spent the next three hours trying to track down the absent father of Shanker's common-law stepdaughter. The man had had multiple addresses over the past five years, but Strike's research finally led him to conclude the man was now going by his middle name, probably to avoid being tracked down for child maintenance, and living in Hackney. If he was indeed the right person, he was working as a long-distance haulage driver, which doubtless suited a man keen to evade his parental responsibilities.

Having sent subcontractor Dev Shah an email asking him to put the Hackney address under surveillance and take pictures of whoever entered or left it, Strike set off for dinner with Eric Wardle.

Strike had decided a standard, cheap curry house wouldn't be sufficient to soften up his policeman friend, from whom he intended to ask a census-related favour. He'd therefore booked a table at the Cinnamon Club, which lay a short taxi ride away.

The restaurant had once been the Westminster Library, so its many white-tableclothed tables stood in a large, airy room with book-lined walls. Strike, who was first to arrive, removed his suit jacket, loosened his tie, ordered a pint and sat down to read the day's news off his phone. He realised Wardle had arrived only when the policeman's shadow fell over the table.

'Bit of a step up from the Bombay Balti,' commented the policeman, as he sat down opposite Strike.

'Yeah, well, business has been good lately,' said the latter, slipping his phone back into his pocket. 'How're you doing?'

'Can't complain,' said Wardle.

When they'd first met, Strike's friend Eric Wardle had been boyishly handsome. Though still good looking, his once full head of hair was receding, and he looked as though he'd aged by more than the six years that had actually passed. Strike knew it wasn't only hard work that had etched those grooves around Wardle's mouth and eyes; he'd lost a brother, and his wife, April, had left him six months previously, taking their three-month-old baby with her.

Talk ran along conventional lines while both perused the

menu, and only once the waiter had brought Wardle a pint did the policeman hand a folder across the table.

'That's everything I could get on the Kevin Pirbright shooting.'

'Cheers,' said Strike. 'How's our counterfeiting friend doing?'

'Arrested,' said Wardle, raising his pint in a toast, 'and I think he's going to be persuadable into dobbing in the higher-ups, as well. You might well have secured me a long-overdue promotion, so dinner's on me.'

'I'd rather you paid me in kind,' Strike replied.

'Knew you hadn't booked this place on a whim,' sighed Wardle.

'Let's order and I'll explain.'

Once they had their starters, Strike asked the favour he'd come for: Wardle's assistance in accessing census records the general public couldn't.

'Why the interest in this Chapman Farm?'

'It's the headquarters of the Universal Humanitarian Church.'

'Oh,' said Wardle. 'That place. April went to one of their meetings a few years ago. A friend of hers from yoga class got interested in it and took her along. The friend ended up joining. April only went the once, though.'

Wardle chewed and swallowed before adding,

'She was a bit weird about it, afterwards. I took the piss and she didn't like it, but I was only saying it because I never had any time for the woman who took her. She was into crystals and meditation and all that shit. You know the type.'

Strike, who well remembered Leda's intermittent phases of chanting cross-legged in front of a jade Buddha, said he did, and asked,

'April thought there was something in it, then, did she?'

'I think she got defensive because she knew how much her yoga friends got on my tits ... probably shouldn't've been an arsehole about it,' Wardle admitted, chewing morosely. 'So, which census records d'you want?'

'All from '91 onwards.'

'Bloody hell, Strike.'

'I'm trying to trace ex-members.'

Wardle raised his eyebrows.

'You want to watch yourself.'

'Meaning?'

'They've got a reputation for going hard after people who try and discredit them.'

'So I've heard.'

'What trumped-up reason do I give the census office? They don't give out information easily.'

'So far I've got coercive control, physical assaults, one allegation of rape and a good bit of child abuse.'

'Christ almighty. Why not chuck in murder and get the full set?'

'Give me time, I've only been on the case two days. Speaking of which: this shooting of Pirbright—'

'Same gun used in two previous drug-related shootings. I wasn't on the case, never heard of the bloke until you rang me, but I've looked over the stuff,' said Wardle, nodding at the file. 'Looks pretty clear cut. He'd have to have been out of his head, the state of his room. Have a look at the photo on the top.'

Strike pushed away his plate, opened the folder and took out the picture.

'Shit.'

'Yeah, there's probably some in there, underneath the rest of the crap.'

The pictures showed a small and squalid room, clothes and rubbish lying everywhere. Pirbright's body lay covered in a plastic sheet in the middle of the floor. Somebody – Strike assumed Pirbright – had scribbled words all over the walls.

'Nice example of junkie décor,' said Wardle, as the waiter returned to remove their plates.

'Anything stolen? He was supposed to have been writing a book on the UHC.'

'Looks like he was writing it on the walls,' said Wardle. 'That's the room exactly as his landlord found it. They found a bag of hash and a roll of twenties in the bottom of the wardrobe.'

'They think he was killed over a bag of hash?'

'That might've been all they left behind. He'd probably nicked gear from someone he shouldn't have, or pissed off the wrong punter.'

'Where's this place?'

'Canning Town.'

'Prints?'

'Only Pirbright's.'

'How did the killer get in and out, any idea?'

'We think they used a skeleton key to get in the front door.'

'Organised of them,' said Strike, taking out his notebook and starting to write.

'Yeah, it was fairly slick. Guy on the same floor claimed he heard Pirbright talking to someone before he let them in. Probably thought he was about to make a sale. The neighbour heard a muffled bang and Pirbright's music stopped playing. The killer must've used a silencer because otherwise half the street would've heard a shot, but it's credible the neighbour heard it, because the dividing walls in the building weren't much more than plywood. The music ending fits, too, because the bullet passed right through Pirbright and hit that old radio you can see in pieces.'

Strike scrutinised the picture of Pirbright's room again.

The shattered radio lay in fragments on a very small desk in the corner. Two leads were plugged into the socket beside it.

'Something else was there.'

'Yeah, looks like a laptop lead. Laptop was probably the only thing in the room worth nicking. Don't know what he was bothering with a radio for, if he had a laptop.'

'He was skint and he might not have been familiar with downloading music,' said Strike. 'From what I've learned about Chapman Farm, he might as well have grown up in the late eighteen hundreds, for all the experience he had with technology.'

Their curries now arrived. Strike pushed the police file aside, but kept his notebook open beside him.

'So the neighbour hears the shot and the music stopping. What then?'

'Neighbour goes and knocks on the door,' said Wardle thickly, through a mouthful of lamb pasanda, 'but gets no answer. We think the knocking spooked the killer into leaving via the window, which was found open with marks consistent with gloved hands on the outer sill.'

'How high was the window?'

'First floor, but there was an easy landing on a big communal bin directly below.'

'Nobody saw them coming out of the window?' asked Strike, who was still making notes.

'The tenants whose windows faced out back were all out or busy inside.'

'CCTV any help?'

'They got a small bit of footage of a stocky bloke in black walking away from the area, who could possibly have been carrying a laptop in a reusable shopping bag, but no clear view of the face. And that's literally all I know,' said Wardle.

Strike replaced the photograph in the police file as Wardle asked,

'Robin still seeing Ryan Murphy?'

'Yeah,' said Strike.

'You know he's an alcoholic?'

'Is he?' said Strike, masking his expression by drinking more beer. Robin told him so little about her relationship that he hadn't previously known this. Perhaps, he thought (with a leap of something strongly resembling hope), Robin didn't know, either.

'Yeah. On the wagon now, though. But he was a mean drunk. Real arsehole.'

'In what way?'

'Aggressive. Made a pass at anyone in a skirt. Tried it on with April one night. I nearly fucking punched him.'

'Seriously?'

'Oh yeah,' repeated Wardle. 'No surprise his wife walked out.'

But his expression saddened after he'd said it, remembering, perhaps, that Murphy wasn't the only person whose wife had left him.

'He's dried out now, though, has he?' asked Strike.

'Yeah,' said Wardle. 'Where are the bogs in here?'

After Wardle had left the table, Strike set down his knife and flipped open the police file again, still forking beef Madras into his mouth. He extracted the post-mortem findings on Kevin Pirbright's corpse, skipping the fatal injury to the head, and concentrating on the lines concerning toxicology. The pathologist had found a low level of alcohol in the body, but no trace of illegal drugs.

9

But in abolishing abuses one must not be too hasty.
This would turn out badly because the abuses have
been in existence so long.

The I Ching or Book of Changes

Robin's neck felt exposed and chilly as she travelled by train to Prudence's house in Strawberry Hill the following evening. She sincerely hoped the accountant would let her claim at least half the cost of her new haircut as a business expense, because it was the most expensive she'd ever had. Chin-length, with a long, graduated fringe, with the ends bleached and then dyed pale blue. After one look of shock, Murphy had beamed and told her he liked it upon meeting the previous evening, which, true or not, had made her feel slightly less self-conscious as they entered the Duke of York Theatre, to watch *The Father*.

'Blue, eh?' were Strike's first words, when Robin got into the BMW outside Strawberry Hill station. 'Looks good.'

'Thanks. I'm hoping it also says, "Hi, I've got more money than sense."'

'Maybe once you've got the posh clothes on,' said Strike, pulling out of the car park.

'How was Bigfoot?' Robin asked, as they drove past a long line of solid Edwardian villas.

'Disappointingly celibate,' said Strike. 'But for a man who's worth a couple of million, you'd think he could afford a comb.'

'You really don't like scruffiness, do you?' said Robin, amused.

'Not in people who have a choice. How hard is it to bloody wash?'

Strike took a right turn before saying,

'Dev found the bloke Shanker's after, by the way.'

'Oh good,' said Robin. While she was under no illusions about Shanker's deeply criminal nature, he happened to have once helped her escape an assault by a large murder suspect, for which she remained grateful. 'How's the little girl doing?'

'He didn't say, but hopefully seeing her dad will cheer her up ... here we go ...'

Earlier than Robin had expected, they turned into the drive of a particularly large Edwardian house, which not only made Robin feel slightly intimidated, but also made her think rue-fully of her own flimsily built flat, in which she had to endure the almost constant noise of the music from the man upstairs.

The front door opened before they reached it, revealing Strike's half-sister, who was the daughter of a well-known actress and the rock star who'd also fathered Strike. Prudence was wearing a plain black dress that looked unexceptional to Strike, but which Robin guessed would have cost the equiv-alent of her own monthly mortgage repayment.

Like Sir Colin Edensor, Prudence had the kind of face it was hard to dislike, or so thought Robin. Though not quite as beautiful as her actress mother, she was very attractive, with freckled skin and long, wavy black hair. Eyes that slanted upwards at the corners and a small, smiling mouth added a slightly Puckish look. Though by no means overweight, she was curvy, something Robin, who'd been afraid she'd be stick thin and flat-chested, saw with relief.

'Come in, come in! It's so nice to meet you,' said Prudence, beaming as she shook Robin's hand.

'You, too. My hair isn't usually like this,' Robin said, and then wished she hadn't. She'd just caught sight of her reflection in Prudence's hall mirror. 'It's all part of my cover.'

'Well, it looks great,' said Prudence, before turning to Strike and hugging him.

'Blimey, bruv, well done. There's less of you every time I see you.'

'If I'd known it would make everyone this happy, I'd've got the other leg amputated.'

'Very funny. Come on through to the sitting room. I've just opened some wine.'

She led the two detectives into a large room of exquisite taste. Beautifully proportioned, with large black and white photographs on the walls, stacked bookcases and a low, dark leather sofa on a tubular metal frame, it managed to be simultaneously stylish and welcoming.

'So,' said Prudence, gesturing Strike and Robin to the sofa and settling into a large cream armchair before pouring two extra glasses of wine, 'clothes. Do I get to ask what they're for?'

'Robin needs to look like a rich girl who's at enough of a loose end to joint a cult.'

'A *cult*?'

'Well, that's what some people would say it is,' temporised Robin. 'They've got a kind of compound in the countryside, and I'm hoping to be recruited so I can get in there.'

To both detectives' surprise, Prudence's smile disappeared and was replaced with a look of concern.

'This wouldn't be the UHC, would it?'

Startled, Robin glanced at Strike.

'That's a very swift bit of deduction,' he said. 'Why d'you think it would be them?'

'Because it started in Norfolk.'

'You've got a client who was in there,' said Strike, on a sudden hunch.

'I don't bandy around clients' identifying details, Cormoran,' said Prudence, her voice mock-stern as she pushed his glass towards him across the coffee table.

'Pity,' said Strike lightly. 'We need to find ex-members.'

Prudence looked intently at him for a moment or two, then said,

'Well, as I've got a duty of confidentiality, I can't—'

'I was being glib,' Strike reassured her. 'I'm not after a name and address.'

Prudence took a sip of wine, her expression grave. Finally, she said,

'I don't think you'll find it very easy, getting ex-members to talk. There's a lot of shame attached to having been coerced in that way, and often significant trauma.'

Seeing them face to face, Robin spotted her partner's resemblance to Jonny Rokeby for the first time. He and his half-sister shared the same defined jaw, the same spacing of the eyes. She wondered – she who had three brothers, all of the same parentage – what it felt like, to make a first acquaintance with a blood relative in your forties. But there was something more there than a faint physical resemblance between brother and sister: they appeared, already, to have established an unspoken understanding.

'All right,' said Prudence, under Strike's semi-jocular questioning, 'I *do* treat an ex-UHC member. As a matter of fact, when they first disclosed what had happened to them, I didn't think I was the right person to help them. It's specialised work, deprogramming people. Some over-indulge in things they were deprived of inside – food and alcohol, for instance. Some indulge in risky behaviours, as a reaction to being so controlled and monitored. Readjusting to a life of freedom isn't easy, and being asked to disinter things they suffered, or were forced to do, can be immensely distressing.

'Luckily, I knew of an American therapist who's worked with a lot of cult survivors, so I got in touch with him. He did a few virtual sessions with the client, which helped hugely, and I've now taken over, with some continued assistance from the American. *That's* how I know about the UHC.'

'How did the client get out?' asked Strike.

'Why? Is that what you've been hired to do, get someone out?'

Strike nodded.

'Then you need to be very careful,' said Prudence seriously. 'If they're anything like my client, they'll be exceptionally fragile and you'll do more harm than good if you're heavy-handed. You've got to understand: people in cults have been rewired. Expecting them to just snap back to normal isn't realistic.'

'How did your client manage it?'

'They ... didn't leave by choice,' said Prudence hesitantly.

'You mean they were expelled?'

'It wasn't a question of ... they had health issues,' said Prudence, 'but I can't say more than that. Suffice to say, the UHC doesn't let members leave through the front door unless they've stopped being of use. You'll need to be very careful, Robin. Have you ever read Robert Jay Lifton? *Thought Reform and the Psychology of Totalism?* Or *Combatting Cult Mind Control,* by Steven Hassan?'

Robin shook her head.

'I'll lend you my copies. I'll give them to you before you go. Being able to identify their techniques will help you resist them.'

'Robin's smart,' said Strike. 'She's not going to buy whatever they're selling.'

'Being clever's no protection, not on its own,' said Prudence. 'Restricted food, enforced chanting, rigid control over your physical environment, digging into your psyche for the places they can apply most pressure, love-bombing you one minute, tearing you down the next ... nobody's invulnerable to that, clever or not ...

'Anyway,' said Prudence, standing up, 'let's try on some clothes.'

'This is *really* kind of you, Prudence,' Robin said, as the therapist led her upstairs.

'It isn't,' said Prudence, now smiling again. 'I've been *dying* to meet you, given that you're clearly the most important person in Corm's life.'

The words gave Robin a sensation like an electric shock in the pit of her stomach.

'He's – he's really important to me, too.'

They passed the open door of a very messy bedroom, which Robin could tell belonged to a teenager even before a black-haired girl in a mini-skirt came bounding out of it, clutching a leather jacket in one hand, and a satchel in the other.

'Ooh,' she said, blinking at Robin. 'Cool hair!'

Without waiting for a response she hurried past them, running downstairs. Prudence called after her,

'Text me when you need picking up!'

'I will,' shouted the girl, and they heard her call, 'Laters, new uncle,' before the front door slammed.

'That was Sylvie,' said Prudence, leading Robin into a large bedroom of luxurious simplicity, and then into a mirrored dressing room lined with clothing racks. 'Corm said you'd need two or three outfits?'

'Ideally,' said Robin. 'I promise I'll be very careful with them.'

'Oh, don't worry about that, I've got *far* too many clothes ...

it's my weakness,' Prudence admitted, with a guilty smile. 'Sylvie's just got old enough to start borrowing stuff I can't get away with any more, so I'm kind of hanging off giving it all to charity. What size shoes do you take?'

'Six,' said Robin, 'but—'

'Perfect. Same as me.'

'—you really don't have to—'

'If you're trying to look wealthy, accessories count,' said Prudence. 'Quite exciting really, helping someone go undercover. Corm's very cagey about what you two get up to – professionally, I mean,' she added.

She began pulling out day dresses and various tops and handing them to Robin, who saw labels she could never have afforded: Valentino, Chanel, Yves Saint Laurent.

'. . . and that would *really* suit you,' Prudence said five minutes later, adding a Chloé dress to the heavy load Robin was already holding. 'Right, try it all on and see what works. You'll be completely private in here, Declan's not home for another hour.'

As the bedroom door closed behind Prudence, Robin put the pile of clothes down on the double bed, then took off her sweater and jeans, looking around at the room as she did so. From the oak floorboards and the wide mahogany sleigh bed to the sleek, modern chandelier, long gauze curtains and wall-mounted flat-screen television, everything spoke of good taste and plenty of money. Strike might be living like this, Robin thought, if he'd swallow his pride and rage, and accept his father's largesse – though, of course, she couldn't be sure it was Jonny Rokeby who'd bought this house.

Downstairs, Prudence had rejoined Strike in the sitting room, holding two books.

'For Robin,' she said, putting them on the coffee table between them.

'Cheers,' he said, as she refilled his wine glass. 'Listen, can I ask you something?'

'Go on,' said Prudence, sitting down opposite him.

'Did this client of yours ever witness supernatural events at Chapman Farm?'

'Corm, I can't talk about that.'

'I'm not going to go looking for your client,' he assured her. 'I'm just interested.'

'I've probably said too much already,' said Prudence.

'I get it,' said Strike. 'No more questions.'

Leaning forwards, he picked up *Combatting Cult Mind Control*, turned it over and read the blurb on the back.

'You've got me more worried about Robin going in there now than I was half an hour ago,' he admitted.

'Good,' said Prudence. 'Sorry, I don't mean "good, you're worried", I just think it's best she understands what she's getting into.'

'Why the hell do people join cults?' mused Strike. 'Why would anyone give over that amount of control of their lives?'

'Because they don't realise total control is where it's going to end,' said Prudence. 'It happens incrementally, step by step, after they've been offered approval and validation and a sense of purpose ... surely you can see the allure of discovering a profound truth? The key to the universe?'

Strike half-shrugged.

'OK, well, what about believing you can make a real difference to the world: alleviate suffering, cure social ills, protect the weak?'

'Why d'you need to be in a cult to do any of that?'

'You don't,' said Prudence, smiling, 'but they're very good at convincing people membership is the best possible way of achieving paradise on earth, not to mention heaven afterwards.

'The only kind of people the UHC probably couldn't do

much with, not that they'd want to recruit them in the first place, are apathetic, couch-potato types. The UHC's after idealists they can turn into evangelists, although I believe they have lower grades of recruit at Chapman Farm, just to get the actual farming done ... my poor client knows only too well that other people think they're stupid and weak-willed for having fallen for it all, which is part of the reason they feel so much shame. But the truth is, being idealistic and intellectually inquiring makes you much more vulnerable to ideologies like the UHC's ... will you two stay for dinner? It's pasta, nothing fancy.'

'You don't have to feed us as well,' said Strike.

'I want to. Please stay, Declan will be home soon. Robin seems lovely, by the way.'

'Yeah, she is,' said Strike, glancing up at the ceiling.

Upstairs, Robin had decided on her three outfits, though she still felt diffident about taking such expensive clothes away with her. She'd just got back into her own jeans and top when Prudence knocked on the door.

'Come in,' called Robin.

'Chosen?'

'Yes. If it's OK, I'd like to borrow these.'

'Great,' said Prudence, scooping up the rest of the clothes and heading back towards the rails to put them back on hangers. 'You know what?' she said, over her shoulder, 'You should just keep them. It's easier.'

'Prudence – I can't,' said Robin weakly. She knew perfectly well that the clothes she'd selected were worth at least two thousand pounds, even second-hand.

'Why not? If you'd wanted *this*,' said Prudence, holding up the Chloé dress, 'I'd've asked for it back, because Declan really likes me in it, but honestly, I easily can do without what you've chosen. I've already got too much stuff, you can see that. *Please*,' she said, as Robin opened her mouth to protest again, 'it'll be the first time any of us have been allowed to give Corm anything, even by proxy. Now let's find shoes.'

'I really don't know what to say,' Robin said, flummoxed. She was worried Strike wouldn't be happy she'd accepted the gift. As though she'd read Robin's mind, Prudence said,

'I know Corm's touchy as hell about taking anything from Dad, but none of this was bought by Jonny Rokeby, I promise. I make very good money and Declan earns a mint. Come here and choose shoes,' she added, beckoning Robin back into the dressing room. 'These look great with that dress. Try them.'

As Robin slid a foot into a Jimmy Choo pump, she asked, 'Are you close to your dad?'

'Um ...' said Prudence, now on her knees as she rifled through her boots, '... I suppose as close as you can ever be with someone like him. He's kind of juvenile. They say you remain forever stuck at the age you got famous, don't they? Which means Dad's never really aged out of his late teens. His whole mindset's instant gratification and letting other people pick up the pieces. I *am* fond of him, but he's not a parent in the usual sense, because he's never really needed to look after himself, let alone anyone else. I can see exactly why Corm's pissed off at him, though. You could hardly imagine two more different people. Try these,' she added, handing Robin a pair of boots. As Robin pulled them on, Prudence added,

'Dad's got a genuinely guilty conscience about Corm. He knows he behaved really badly. He tried to reach out a couple of years ago. I don't know exactly what was said—'

'Rokeby offered him money to meet,' said Robin baldly.

Prudence winced.

'Oh God, I didn't know that ... Dad would've thought that was generous or something ... bloody idiot ... he's so used to throwing money at problems ... Those look too tight.'

'They are, a bit,' Robin admitted, unzipping the boots again. 'You know,' she added impulsively, 'I'm really glad you and Cormoran are in touch. I think you might be ... I don't know ... what he's missing.'

'Really?' said Prudence, looking pleased. 'Because I've wanted to meet him for years. *Years.* It isn't easy, being the biracial illegitimate among the rest of them. We all get on all right, don't get me wrong, but I've always been sort of half-in, half-out of the Rokeby clan, and knowing Corm was out there, not giving a damn, making his own way ...

'Of course, he's perennially scared I'm going to start psycho-analysing him,' added Prudence, now handing Robin a pair of Manolo Blahniks. 'I've explained to him multiple times that I wouldn't be able to, even if I wanted. The relationship's too ... it's just too complicated ... he's been a kind of talisman to me for a long time. Just the idea of him. You can't be objective with somebody like that, ever ... You'll stay for dinner, won't you? I've just asked Corm.'

'I – are you sure?' said Robin, feeling slightly overwhelmed.

'God, yes, it'll be fun. Declan really likes Corm and he'll be thrilled to meet you. OK, so you're going to take these three, right?' said Prudence, setting aside another few hundred pounds' worth of footwear. 'Now let's find a handbag ...'

Downstairs in the silent sitting room, Strike was again poring over the photograph of Kevin Pirbright's room that Wardle had given him, and which he'd brought with him to show Robin. For several minutes, he'd been squinting at it, trying to make out a few things that puzzled him. Finally he glanced around and spotted exactly what he required: an antique magnifying glass lying decoratively on top of a pile of art books.

Ten minutes later, Robin reappeared in the sitting room and emitted a surprised laugh.

'What?' said Strike, looking up.

'Sherlock Holmes, I presume?'

'Don't mock it until you've tried it,' said Strike, holding out both photo and magnifying glass. 'This is Kevin Pirbright's room, as the police found it. Wardle got it for me.'

'*Oh*,' said Robin. She sat back down on the sofa beside Strike and took both picture and magnifying glass from him.

'Have a shufti at what he's written on the walls,' said Strike. 'See whether you can read any of it. That picture's all we've got, unfortunately, because I called the landlord this afternoon. Once the police had finished with it, he repainted the room.'

Robin moved the magnifying glass to and fro, trying to make out the scrawled words. She was concentrating so hard, the sound of the front door banging open made her jump.

'Hi, new uncle,' said a dark teenaged boy, poking his head into the room. He seemed disconcerted to find Robin there, as well.

'Hi, Gerry,' said Strike. 'This is my detective partner, Robin.'

'Oh,' said the boy, looking vaguely embarrassed. 'Cool. Hi.'

He disappeared again.

Robin resumed her close examination of the photo. After a minute's intense concentration, she began to read aloud.

'"*Five prophets*" . . . what's that over the mirror? Is it "*retribution*"?'

'I think so,' said Strike, shifting closer to her on the sofa, so their thighs were almost touching.

Many of the scrawls on Pirbright's walls were illegible, or too small to read from the photograph, but here and there, a word stood out.

'"*Becca*",' read Robin. '"*Sin*" . . . "*stra*" something . . . straw? "I think that's "*plot*", isn't it?'

'Yeah,' said Strike.

'"*The night before*" ... *the night before* ... I can't read the rest ...'

'Nor can I. What d'you make of that?'

Strike was pointing at something on the wall over the unmade bed. As both leaned in to look closer, Strike's hair brushed Robin's and she felt another small electric shock in the pit of her stomach.

'It looks,' she said, 'as though someone's tried to scrub something off ... or ... have they chipped away the plaster?'

'That's what I thought,' said Strike. 'Looks to me like someone's literally gouged some of the writing off the wall, but they didn't take it all. Wardle told me Pirbright's neighbour came banging on the door after hearing his music stop. Possibly that persuaded the killer to leave via the window, before they'd had time to remove the whole thing.'

'And they left that,' said Robin, looking at the last remnant of what seemed to have been a sentence or phrase.

Written in capitals and circled many times was a single, easily legible word: *PIGS*.

10

Six in the second place means:
Contemplation through the crack of the door.
Furthering for the perseverance of a woman.

The I Ching or Book of Changes

Largely because of Prudence's warnings, Strike spent the next two evenings reading *Combatting Cult Mind Control* in his attic flat. As a result, he insisted on Robin spending longer than usual on creating her undercover persona before making her first appearance at the Rupert Court Temple. While he had total confidence in Robin's ability to think on her feet, some of what he'd read, and particularly Prudence's warning that the church sought out weak places in members' psyches the better to manipulate them, had left him feeling uneasy.

'There shouldn't be any points of resemblance between your own life and Rowena's,' he told her, Rowena Ellis being the pseudonym Robin had chosen (it was always easier, especially when exhausted or caught off guard, to have a pseudonym that was vaguely familiar). 'Don't go drawing on your real past. Stick with pure fiction.'

'I know,' said Robin patiently, 'don't worry, I've thought about that already.'

'And don't change your accent too much. That's the kind of thing that slips when you're knackered.'

'Strike, *I know*,' she said, half-irritated, half-amused. 'But if I don't get in there soon, this haircut's going to have grown out and I'll have to get it redone.'

On the Friday before her planned appearance in character at the UHC's London temple, Strike insisted on testing Robin at the office by asking questions about Rowena's schooling, university career, family, friends, hobbies, pets, ex-fiancé and the details of her supposedly cancelled wedding, all of which Robin answered without pausing or hesitating. Finally, Strike asked why 'Rowena' had come to the Rupert Court Temple.

'A friend of mine showed me an interview with Noli Seymour,' said Robin, 'all about universality and diversity, so I agreed to come. It seemed interesting. I'm not committing to anything, of course!' she added, with a convincing show of nerves. 'I'm only here to have a look!'

'Bloody good,' admitted Strike, sitting back in his chair at the partners' desk and reaching for his mug of tea. 'All right: all systems go.'

So the following morning, Robin rose early in her flat in Walthamstow, ate breakfast, dressed in a pair of Valentino trousers, an Armani shirt and a Stella McCartney jacket, slung a Gucci bag over her shoulder, then set off for central London, feeling both nervous and excited.

Rupert Court, as Robin already knew, having worked in the area for years, was a narrow alleyway hung with glass lamps that connected Rupert Street and Wardour Street at the point where Chinatown and Soho converged. On one side of the passageway were various small businesses, including a Chinese reflexologist. Most of the other side was taken up by the temple. It had probably once been a nondescript commercial building housing restaurants or shops, but the lower windows and doors had been blocked up, leaving only one massive entrance. As far as Robin could see over the heads of the many people queuing patiently to get in, the heavy double doors had been given an ornate, carved and embellished frame of red and gold, the colours echoing the Chinese lanterns strung across Wardour Street behind her.

As she shuffled closer to the door with the rest of the crowd, she covertly examined her fellow temple-goers. Although there was a smattering of older worshippers, the average age seemed to be between twenty and thirty. If some looked a little eccentric – there was one young man with blue dreadlocks – most were remarkable only for their ordinariness: no fanatical glares, no vacant stares, no outré garb or strange mutterings.

Once close enough to see the entrance clearly, Robin saw that the red and gold carvings surrounding the door represented animals: a horse, a cow, a rooster, a pig, a pheasant, a dog and a sheep. She'd just had time to wonder whether this was an oblique reference to the UHC's agricultural birthplace when she spotted the dragon with bright gold eyes.

'Welcome ... welcome ... welcome ...' two smiling young women were saying, as congregants passed over the threshold. Both were wearing orange sweatshirts emblazoned with the church's logo, which comprised the letters 'UHC' displayed within two black hands which were making the shape of a heart. Robin noticed how the two women were scrutinising the approaching faces, and wondered whether they were trying to match up mental images with those they considered undesirables, like Will Edensor's family.

'Welcome!' sang the blonde girl on the right, as Robin passed her.

'Thanks,' said Robin, smiling.

The interior of the temple, of which Robin had already seen pictures online, was even more impressive in reality. The aisle leading between rows of cushioned pews was carpeted in scarlet, and led to a raised stage behind which was a large screen almost the size of a cinema's. This was currently showing a static image of tens of thousands of people wearing different colours, predominantly red and orange, standing in front of what looked like a holy building or palace in India.

Whether or not the aureate glow emanating from the walls and cornices was due to genuine gold leaf, Robin didn't know, but it reflected the light from low-hanging orbs of glass, which contained multiple bulbs, like bunches of glowing grapes. Naive figures had been hand-painted all around the upper portion of the walls, holding hands like the paper dolls Robin's mother had once taught her to cut out, as a child. Every ethnicity was represented there, and Robin was reminded of Disneyland Paris, which she'd visited in 2003 with her then boyfriend, later husband, Matthew, and the ride called 'It's a Small World', in which barges rolled mechanically around canals, and dolls from all over the world sang canned music at the visitors.

The pews were already filling rapidly, so Robin slid into an available space beside a young black couple. The man looked tense, and his partner was whispering to him. While Robin couldn't hear everything the girl was saying, she thought she caught the words, 'keep an open mind'.

On a shallow shelf attached to the pew in front of Robin lay a number of identical pamphlets, one of which she picked up.

Welcome to the Universal Humanitarian Church!
Our Mission, Our Values, Our Vision

Robin slipped the pamphlet into her bag to read later and glanced around, trying to spot Will Edensor. There was no shortage of good-looking young attendants in orange sweat-shirts bustling around the temple, showing people to seats, or chatting and joking with visitors, but there was no sign of him.

Noticing a few congregation members looking upwards, Robin now turned her attention to the ceiling. A mural had been painted there, which was of a very different style to the doll-like people painted around the walls. This looked like Disney's take on Michelangelo. Five gigantic figures in swirling robes were flying across a Technicolor dawn, and Robin deduced that these were the five prophets of whom Kevin Pirbright had written in his long email to Sir Colin Edensor.

The figure directly overhead Robin was dark-haired, bearded and wearing orange. He appeared to be bleeding from a cut on his forehead and there were bloodstains on his robes. This was surely the Wounded Prophet. Then there was a benevolent-looking old man with a white beard and blue robes who held the rod of Asclepius, a staff wrapped with a serpent: the Healer Prophet. The Golden Prophet was depicted as silver-haired woman whose yellow robes billowed out behind her; she wore a beatific expression, and was scattering jewels upon the earth.

The fourth figure was a gaunt, unsmiling young man with shadowed eyes. He wore crimson robes and, to Robin's slight consternation, had a noose around his neck, the rope flying behind him. This, Robin assumed, was the Stolen Prophet, Alexander Graves, who'd hanged himself a week after being forcibly kidnapped back by his family. She found it both strange and sinister that the church had chosen to depict him with a sunken face and the means of his destruction around his neck.

However, it was the central figure that drew most of Robin's attention. Smaller and slighter than the four others, she had long black hair, wore white robes, and even though she was depicted as airborne, she was trailing waves in her wake. The Drowned Prophet's oval face had a severe beauty, but, whether because of a trick of the light or not, the narrow eyes showed no irises, but appeared to be entirely black.

'Are you here alone?' said a voice beside Robin, who started. The young blonde woman who'd welcomed her at the door was smiling down at her.

'Yes,' said Robin, 'my friend was supposed to come with me but she's got a hangover!'

'Oh dear,' said the girl, still smiling.

'I know, I was a bit annoyed,' said Robin, with a laugh. 'She's the one who wanted to come!'

She'd planned all this, of course: best not to look too keen, too desperate to ask questions; better by far to let her clothes and several hundred pounds' worth of handbag make their own alluring impression.

'There are no accidents,' said the blonde, beaming down at Robin. 'I've learned that. No accidents. You've chosen a really auspicious day to come, as well, if this is your first visit. You'll understand once service begins.'

The blonde walked away, still smiling, as a loud bang to the rear of the temple signalled the closing of the doors. A bell rang somewhere, giving one single deep peal, and the congregation fell silent. The orange-sweatshirted attendants had retreated to standing positions along the walls.

Then, to Robin's surprise, the first notes of a well-known pop song began to play over hidden speakers: David Bowie's 'Heroes'.

The static image on the cinema screen had unfrozen and the orange-clad temple attendants began clapping in time and singing along with the song, as did some of the congregation.

Onscreen, the camera was moving through laughing people throwing coloured powders at each other, and Robin, who'd lived in multicultural London long enough to know, thought she recognised the festival of Holi. The temple lights were slowly dimming, and within a minute the only light was emanating from the cinema screen, where joyful Hindus of both sexes continued to laugh and chase each other, and rainbow colours flew through the air, and they seemed to be dancing to Bowie's song and personifying its lyrics, each of them a king or a queen who, in this glorious mass, could 'beat them', whoever they were . . .

The film cast flickering, multicoloured lights over the faces of the congregation. As the song faded out, so too did the film, to be replaced by a static image of the Hindu God Shiva, sitting cross-legged with a snake wrapped around his neck, a garland of orange flowers hanging down over his bare chest. A brilliant white spotlight now appeared on the stage, into which a man stepped, and as the brightness had made the surrounding darkness seem so deep, he appeared to have come out of thin air. Some of those watching broke into applause, including all of the beaming attendants, who also emitted a few whoops of excitement.

Robin recognised the man standing in the spotlight at once: he was Jonathan Wace, known to his adherents as 'Papa J', the founder of the Universal Humanitarian Church, making an unusual in-person appearance at one of his temples. A handsome, tall and fit-looking man in his mid-sixties, he could have passed in this light for a couple of decades younger, with his thick, dark shoulder-length hair threaded with silver, his large, dark blue eyes and square jaw with a dimple in his chin. His smile was thoroughly engaging. There was no suggestion of bombast or theatricality in the way he acknowledged the applause, but, on the contrary, a warm and humble smile, and he made a deprecatory gesture, as though to calm the excitement. He was clad in a full-length orange robe embroidered in gold thread, and wore a microphone headset, so that his voice carried easily over the two-hundred-strong crowd in front of him.

'Good morning,' he said, placing his hands together in the attitude of prayer and bowing.

'Good morning,' chorused at least half the congregation in return.

'Welcome to today's service, which, as some of you will know, is a particularly important one for members of the Universal Humanitarian Church. Today, the nineteenth of March, marks the beginning of our year. Today is the Day of the Wounded Prophet.

'This,' said Wace, gesturing towards the image onscreen, 'is the kind of image most of us associate with a divinity. Here we see Shiva, the benign and beneficent Hindu God, who contains many contradictions and ambiguities. He's an ascetic, yet also a God of fertility. His third eye gives him insight, but may also destroy.'

The image of Shiva now faded from the cinema screen, to be replaced with a blurry black and white photograph of a young American soldier.

'This,' said Wace, smiling, '*isn't* what most of us think of when imagining a holy man. This is Rusty Andersen, who as a young man in the early seventies was sent to war in Vietnam.'

The image of Rusty Andersen faded and was replaced by grainy footage of explosions and men running with rifles. Low, ominous music was now playing over the temple loudspeakers.

'Rust, as his friends called him, witnessed and endured atrocities. He was forced to commit unspeakable acts. But when the war was over . . .' The music became lighter, more hopeful. 'He went home for the last time, packed his guitar and his belongings, and went wandering in Europe.'

The screen now showed a succession of old photographs, Andersen's hair becoming longer in each one. He was busking on what looked like the streets of Rome; making the peace sign in front of the Eiffel Tower; walking with his guitar on his back through the London rain, past Horse Guards Parade.

'Finally,' said Wace, 'he arrived in a little Norfolk village called Aylmerton. There, he heard of a community living off the land, and he decided to join them.'

The screen faded to black, the music faded away.

'The community Rust joined was, sadly, not everything he hoped it would be,' said Wace, 'but a simple life, living close to nature, remained his ideal. When that first community broke up, Rust continued to live in the cabin he'd built himself, self-sufficient, self-reliant, still dealing with the trauma left by the war he'd been forced to fight.

'It was then that I met him for the first time,' said Wace, as a swell of new music filled the temple, now joyous, uplifting, and a picture of Rusty Andersen and a thirty-something Jonathan Wace filled the screen. Though Robin guessed they weren't too many years apart in age, the weather-beaten Andersen looked far older.

'He had a wonderful smile, Rust,' said Wace, with a catch in his voice. 'He held fiercely to his solitary existence, though occasionally I'd cross the fields to persuade him to come and eat with us. A new community was starting to form on the land, one that centred not only on a natural, but a spiritual life. But spirituality held no attraction for Rust. He'd seen too much, he told me, to believe in man's immortal soul or God's goodness.

'Then, one night,' said Wace, as the photograph enlarged slowly, so that Rust Andersen's face filled the entire screen, 'this broken warrior and I went walking together from dinner at the farm, back across the fields to his cabin. We were arguing, as ever, about religion and man's need for the Blessed Divinity and at last I said to Rust, "Can you know, for sure, that nothing lies beyond this life? Can you be certain that man returns to the darkness, that no divine force acts around us, or inside us? Can you not even admit the possibility of such things?"

'And Rust looked at me,' said Wace, 'and, after a long pause, replied, "I admit the possibility."

'"*I admit the possibility*,"' repeated Wace. 'The *power* of those words, from a man who'd turned resolutely away from God, from the divine, from the possibility of redemption and salvation! And as he said those astonishing words, I saw something in his face I'd never seen before. Something had awoken in him, and I knew in that moment that his heart had opened to God at last, and I, whom God had helped so much, could show him what I'd learned, what I'd seen, which made me *know* – not think, not believe, not hope, but *know* – that God is real and that help is always there, though we may not understand how to reach it, or how to even ask for it.

'Little did I realise then,' said Wace, as the music darkened again, and Andersen's smiling face began to fade from the screen, 'that Rust and I would never have that conversation, that I'd never get the chance to show him the way ... because within twenty-four hours, he was dead.'

The music stopped. The silence in the temple was now absolute.

'A car hit him out on the road outside our farm. A drunk driver killed Rust in the early hours of the following morning, while Rust was taking an early walk, which he often did, being an insomniac, and a man who thought best alone. Rust was killed instantly.'

Another picture filled the screen: of a group standing with heads bowed, over a freshly dug and covered mound of earth, outside Rust Andersen's cabin.

'We buried him at the farm, where he'd found a measure of comfort in nature and in solitude. I was distraught. It was an early test of my faith and, I freely admit, I couldn't see why the Blessed Divinity would let this happen, so soon after the possibility of Their revelation to a troubled soul like Rust. It

113

was in this state of despair that I set to work to clear out Rust's cabin . . . and on his bed, I found a letter. A letter addressed to me, in Rust's handwriting. After all these years, I still know it by heart. This is what Rust wrote, hours before his death:

Dear Jonathan,

Tonight, I prayed, for the first time since I was a little boy. It occurred to me that if there is a possibility that God is real, and that I can be forgiven, then I'd be a fool not to talk to Him. You told me he'd send me a sign if he was there. That sign has come. I won't tell you what it was, because you might think it stupid, but I knew it when it happened, and I don't believe it was coincidence.

Now I'm experiencing something I haven't felt in years: peace. Perhaps it will last, perhaps it won't, but even to have this feeling, once more before I die, has been like a glimpse of heaven.

I'm not good at talking about my feelings, as you know, and I don't even know whether I'll give you this letter, but setting all this down feels like the right thing to do. I'm going for a walk now, after a night of no sleep, but this time, for the best of reasons.

Yours,
Rust.

Beside Robin, the young black woman was wiping away tears.

'And a few short hours after that, while I slept, Rust was taken home,' said Jonathan Wace. 'He died hours after the sign he'd been given, which had caused him a night of joy and of the peace that had been denied him so long . . .

'It was only later, while I was still grieving for him, still trying to make sense of the events of that night, that I realised

Rust Andersen had died at the time of Holi, an important Hindu festival.'

Now the cinema screen behind Wace was again showing the film of joyful people in colourful robes, throwing powder at each other, laughing and dancing, packed tightly together in the street.

'Rust didn't like crowds,' said Wace. 'He wandered on from city to city after Vietnam, looking for his peace. At last, he settled on a patch of uninhabited land, and he eschewed human company. The joy of communing with other people was one he partook of sparingly and usually unwillingly, only out of need for money, or food. And as I thought about Holi, and I thought about Rust, I thought how incongruous it was that he should have returned to God at such a time ... but then I saw how wrong I was. I understood.

'Rust would find Holi in the life beyond. All that he'd missed: connection, laughter, joy, would be there for him in heaven. The Blessed Divinity had sent Rust a sign, and in taking Rust on that day, the Divinity had spoken through him to all who knew him. "Rust has no further to seek. He has achieved what he was set upon the earth to do: to gain knowledge of me, which in turn, teaches you. Celebrate the divine in the confident belief that one day, you too will find the happiness he sought."'

The riotous colours faded again from the cinema screen and a picture of many divine figures took their place, including Shiva, Guru Nanak, Jesus and Buddha.

'But what is the Blessed Divinity? Of whom am I speaking, when I speak of God? Which of these, or countless others, should you pray to? And my answer is: all, or none. The divine exists, and men have tried to draw the divine in their own image, and through their own imaginations, since the dawn of time. It doesn't matter what name you give Them. It doesn't matter what form of words you give your worship. When we see beyond the boundaries that separate us, boundaries of culture and religion, which are manmade, our vision clears, and we can at last see the beyond.

'Some of you here today are non-believers,' said Wace, smiling again. 'Some of you came out of curiosity. Some doubt, many disbelieve. Some of you might even have come to laugh at us. And why not laugh? Laughter is joyous, and joy comes from God.

'If I tell you today that I know – know beyond doubt – that there is life beyond death, and a divine force that seeks to guide and help any human who seeks it, you'll demand proof. Well, I say, you are right to ask for proof. I'd rather face an honest sceptic than a hundred who believe they know God, but are really in thrall to their own piety, their insistence that only they, and their religion, have found the right way.

'And some of you will be discouraged if I say to you that nothing on this earthly plane comes without patience and struggle. You wouldn't expect to know or understand the laws of physics in an instant. How much more complex is the originator of those physical laws? How much more mysterious?

'Yet you can take a first step, now. A first step towards proof, towards the absolute certainty I possess.

'All that's needed is to say the words the Wounded Prophet spoke, a quarter of a century ago, which gave him the sign he needed, and which led to his exultation, and his ascension to heaven. Will you say only this: "I admit the possibility"?'

Wace paused, smiling. Nobody had spoken.

'If you want a sign, speak the words now: "I admit the possibility."'

A few scattered voices repeated the words, and a titter of nervous laughter followed.

'Together, then!' said Wace, now beaming. 'Together! "*I admit the possibility!*"'

'*I admit the possibility,*' repeated the congregation, including Robin.

The attendants began applauding, and the rest of the congregation followed suit, swept up in the moment, some of them still laughing.

'Good!' said Jonathan, beaming at them all. 'And now – at the risk of sounding like the lowest of low rent magicians –' more laughter, '– I want you all to think of something. Don't speak it aloud, don't tell anyone else, just think: think of a number or a word. A number, or a word,' he repeated. 'Any number. Any word. But decide on it now, inside the temple.'

Forty-eight, thought Robin, at random.

'Soon,' said Wace, 'you'll leave this temple and go about your life. If it should happen that that word, or that number, forces itself upon your notice before midnight tonight – well, it could be coincidence, couldn't it? It could be chance. But you've just admitted the *possibility* that it is something else. You've admitted the *possibility* that the Blessed Divinity is trying to talk to you, to make Their presence known to you, through the chaos and distractions of this worldly clamour, to speak to you by the only means They have at Their disposal at this time, before you begin to learn Their language, before you're able to strip away the dross of this earthly plane, and see the Ultimate as plainly as I, and many others, do . . .

'If nothing else,' said Wace, as the images of deities on the cinema screen behind him faded, and Rust Andersen's smiling face reappeared, 'I hope the story of the Wounded Prophet will remind you that even the most troubled may gain peace and joy. That even those who have done dreadful things may be forgiven. That there is a home to which all may be called, if they only believe it is possible.'

With that, Jonathan Wace gave a little bow of the head, the spotlight vanished and, as the congregation began to applaud, the temple lamps began to glow again. But Wace had already gone, and Robin had to admire the speed with which he'd absented himself from the stage, which, indeed, gave him the air of a magician.

'Thank you, Papa J!' said the blonde girl who'd spoken to Robin earlier, mounting the stage and still applauding as she beamed around. 'And now,' she said, 'I'd like to say a word or two about the UHC's mission here on earth. We seek a fairer, more equal society and we work to empower the most vulnerable. This week,' she said, moving aside to let a new film appear on the cinema screen, 'we're collecting for the UHC's Young Carers' Project, which provides holidays for young people who're caring for chronically ill and disabled family members.'

As she talked, a number of film clips began playing, showing a group of teenagers, firstly running along a beach together, then singing around a campfire, then abseiling and canoeing.

'At the UHC we believe not only in individual spiritual enlightenment, but also in working for the betterment of conditions for marginalised people, both inside and outside the church. If you're able to do so, please consider giving a donation to our Young Carers' Project on the way out, and if you'd like to find out more about the church and our mission, don't hesitate to talk to one of the attendants, who'd be delighted to help. I'll leave you now with these beautiful images of some of our latest humanitarian projects.'

She walked off the stage. As the doors hadn't opened, most of the congregation remained seated, watching the screen. The temple lights remained dim, and David Bowie began to sing again as the stationary congregation watched further film clips, showing homeless people eating soup, beaming children raising their hands in a classroom in Africa, and adults of diverse races having some kind of group therapy.

We could be heroes, sang David Bowie, *just for one day.*

11

Six in the fifth place . . .
Shock goes hither and thither. . .
However, nothing at all is lost.

The I Ching or Book of Changes

Strike, who was eager to hear how Robin's first trip to the temple had gone, didn't receive her first few attempts to contact him because he was sitting on the Tube, with a carrier bag from Hamleys on his lap. Robin's fifth attempt to contact him finally came through when he'd left the train at Bromley South, and was on the point of pressing her number.

'Sorry,' was his first word. 'Didn't have reception. I'm on my way to Lucy's.'

Lucy was the half-sister with whom Strike had grown up, because she was his mother's child, rather than his father's. While he loved Lucy, they had very little in common, and outsiders tended to express disbelief that they were related at all, given that Lucy was small and blonde. Strike was undertaking today's visit out of a sense of duty, not pleasure, and was anticipating a difficult couple of hours.

'How was it?' he asked, setting off along the road under a sky that was threatening rain.

'Not what I expected,' admitted Robin, who'd walked several blocks away from the temple before finding a café with seats outside where, due to the chilliness of the day, she had no eavesdroppers. 'I thought it'd be a bit more fire and brimstone, but not at all, it's wall-to-wall social justice and being free to have doubts. Very slick, though – films shown on a cinema screen and David Bowie playing over the—'

'*Bowie?*'

'Yes, 'Heroes' – but the big news is that Papa J was there in person.'

'Was he, now?'

'He's very charismatic.'

'He'd need to be,' grunted Strike. 'Anyone try and recruit you?'

'Not explicitly, but a blonde woman, who I think knows how much Prudence's clothes must've cost, intercepted me on the way out. Said she hoped I'd enjoyed myself and asked whether I had any questions. I said it had all been very interesting, but I didn't show massive interest. She said she hoped she'd see me there again.'

'Playing hard to get,' said Strike, who'd just felt the first spot of icy rain on his face. 'Good call.'

'I had to bung a twenty pound note into the collecting bucket on the way out,' said Robin, 'given that I'm carrying a five hundred quid handbag. I made sure the boy on the door saw how much I was giving, though.'

'Take it out of our petty cash,' said Strike.

'And I – wow,' said Robin, half-laughing, half-startled.

'What's the matter?'

'I – nothing.'

Two young American men – tall, well-nourished, bearded and baseball-capped – had just taken a table two away from Robin. One was wearing a polo shirt, the other, a NASCAR T-shirt emblazoned with the name Jimmie Jones, and a large 48.

'Nothing important, I'll tell you later,' said Robin. 'Just

wanted to touch base. I'll let you go, if you're off to Lucy's. See you Monday.'

Strike, who didn't particularly want to forfeit the distraction of talking to Robin while he headed towards an encounter he was dreading, said goodbye, then continued walking, his feeling of foreboding growing ever deeper. Lucy had sounded thrilled that he was coming over, which made the prospect of delivering his news even less palatable.

The large magnolia tree in Lucy and Greg's front garden was, naturally, sporting no flowers on this cool March day. Strike knocked on the door, which was opened almost imme- diately by his favourite nephew, Jack.

'Bloody hell,' said Strike. 'You've grown about eight inches since I last saw you.'

'Be weird if I'd shrunk,' said Jack, grinning. 'You're thinner.'

'Yeah, well, I needed shrinking,' said Strike, wiping his feet on the doormat. 'You'll understand once you reach my age ... I got those for you, Luke and Adam,' he added, handing Jack the carrier bag.

Lucy now appeared in the hall, and on hearing these words, beamed at Strike. She'd previously expressed displeasure that he so obviously favoured her middle son.

'This is a lovely surprise,' she said, hugging her brother. 'Luke's out at football with Greg, but Adam's upstairs. Come through, I've just taken banana bread out of the oven.'

'Smells great,' said Strike, following her into the kitchen, with its glass doors overlooking a lawn. 'Give me a small bit. I'm still a stone off my target weight.'

'I'm so glad you called, because I'm a bit worried about Ted,' said Lucy, taking a couple of small plates out of the cupboard. Ted was their widowed uncle, who lived in Cornwall. 'I rang him this morning and he told me the same story he told me last time I called, word for word.'

'Think he's lonely,' said Strike, sitting down at the kitchen table.

'Maybe,' said Lucy doubtfully, 'but I've been thinking I might nip down and see him. Would you come, too?'

'Yeah, with a bit of notice,' said Strike, who was experiencing the familiar sense of constriction Lucy often gave him, whereby he was asked to commit immediately to future arrangements, and often had to deal with her irritability when he couldn't instantly fall in with her plans. Today, however, Lucy merely set a slice of banana bread down in front of him, followed shortly afterwards by a mug of tea.

'So, why the visit? Not that I'm not pleased to see you.'

Before Strike could respond, both Jack and Adam appeared, each holding an Air Storm Firetek Bow, which had been bought by Strike with the express purpose of getting Lucy's sons out into the garden while he talked to her.

'This is awesome,' said Adam to Strike.

'Glad you like it,' said Strike.

'Corm, you shouldn't have!' said Lucy, clearly delighted that he had. Given the number of times he'd forgotten his nephews' birthdays, Strike was well aware these gifts might be said to be overdue. 'Pity it's raining,' said Lucy, glancing out of the window at the garden.

'Not much,' said Strike.

'I want to try it,' said Jack, confirming his position as his uncle's favourite. 'I'll put on my wellies,' he threw at his mother, as he hurried out of the kitchen again. To Strike's relief, Adam followed his older brother.

'So, why are you here?' Lucy asked again.

'I'd rather talk once the boys can't hear us,' said Strike.

'Oh my God – are you ill?' said Lucy, in panic.

'No, of course not,' said Strike. 'I just—'

Jack and Adam came hurrying back into the kitchen, both carrying wellington boots.

'And coats, boys,' said Lucy, torn now between apprehension at what Strike was about to tell her, and the needs of her sons.

At last, when the two boys disappeared into the rain with their coats on, Strike cleared his throat.

'OK, I wanted to talk to you about a case I've just taken on.'

'Oh,' said Lucy, who looked slightly reassured. 'Why?'

'Because if we're successful, which is long odds at the moment, but if we *are,* there's a chance it'll be in the press. And if that happens, there's also a slim chance that there'll be something about us – you and me – in there. That something might be dug up.'

'Like what?' said Lucy, in a slightly brittle voice. 'They've done it all already, haven't they? "Son of super-groupie." "Notorious good-time girl Leda Strike."'

'This wouldn't just be about Mum,' said Strike.

He noticed Lucy's slight tightening of expression. She hadn't called Leda 'Mum' since she was fourteen and was explicit, these days, about the fact that she'd considered their late aunt, Joan, her true mother.

'What, then?' said Lucy.

'Well,' said Strike, 'I've been hired to investigate the Universal Humanitarian Church.'

'So?'

'So, their headquarters are where the Aylmerton Community used to be.'

Lucy slumped back in her chair as though the words had hit her physically, her expression blank. At last, she swallowed and said,

'Oh.'

'I got a hell of a shock when I realised that's where they

124

started,' said Strike. 'I only found out once we'd taken the case and—'

To his horror, Lucy had begun noiselessly crying.

'Luce,' he said, putting out a hand, but she'd withdrawn her own from the table, and now wrapped her arms around herself. This was a far worse reaction than Strike had imagined; he'd anticipated anger and resentment that he was once again exposing her to gossip at the school gates about her unorthodox past.

'Christ,' said Strike, 'I didn't—'

'Didn't what?' said Lucy, with a trace of anger, tears now trickling down her face.

'I'm sorry,' said Strike. 'I got a shock myself, when I saw—'

Lucy got to her feet and blundered towards the side where kitchen roll stood on a metal stand. Ripping off several pieces she mopped her face, took a deep breath and said, clearly fighting to regain control,

'I'm sorry. I just – I didn't expect—'

She broke down completely. Strike pushed himself up from the table and walked towards her. He half-expected her to push him away, but she let him put his arms around her and pull her close, so that she was sobbing into her brother's chest. They'd stood thus for barely a minute when the front door opened.

Lucy pushed Strike away at once, hastily wiping her face. With false gaiety she called out,

'How did it go, Luke, did you win?'

'Yeah,' called Luke back from the hall, and Strike noticed that his voice had broken since he'd last seen the boy. 'Three–one. They were pathetic.'

'Fantastic! If you're muddy, get straight in the shower,' called Lucy. 'Uncle Corm's here,' she added.

Luke made no response to this, but ran straight upstairs.

Strike's brother-in-law now entered the kitchen, his track-suit bottoms damp. Strike supposed he must coach or manage his son's team. Greg was a quantity surveyor for whom Strike entertained feelings that had never quite reached the level of liking.

'Everything all right?' he said, looking from Strike to Lucy.

'Just been talking about Ted,' said Lucy, to explain her red-dened eyes and heightened colour.

'Oh. Well, I've been telling her, it's only natural he's getting a bit forgetful,' Greg told Strike dismissively. 'What's he now, eighty-odd?'

'Seventy-nine,' said Lucy.

'Well, that's eighty-odd, isn't it?' said Greg, heading for the loaf of banana bread.

'Come through to the living room,' Lucy told Strike, pick-ing up her tea. 'We can talk it all over there.'

Greg, who evidently had no desire to talk about his uncle-in-law's well-being, made no objection at being excluded from the conversation.

The living room, with its beige three-piece suite, was unchanged since the last time Strike had been in there, except that his nephews' school photos had been updated. A large picture of Uncle Ted and Aunt Joan, dating from the eighties, stood in pride of place on a shelf. Strike well remembered the couple looking like that: Joan's hair as big as Elnett could make it, stiff in the sea breezes, Ted, the largest and strongest member of the local lifeboat men. As Strike sat down on the sofa, he felt as though he should turn the picture to face the wall before dragging up memories of the Aylmerton Community, because his aunt and uncle had dedicated so much of their lives to trying to protect the niece and nephew whom Leda dumped on them, then removed, as unpredictably as she did everything.

Having shut the door carefully on the rest of her family, Lucy sat down in an armchair and placed her mug of tea on a side table.

'I'm sorry,' she said again.

'Don't apologise,' said Strike. 'Believe me, I know.'

'Do you?' she said, with an odd note in her voice.

'It was a fucking terrible place,' said Strike. 'Don't think I've forgotten.'

'Are any of the people who were at the Aylmerton Community still there?'

'Only one, as far as I know,' said Strike. 'She claims to have been a victim of the Crowthers. She's married to the church's leader.'

'What's her name?'

'Mazu,' said Strike.

'Oh God,' said Lucy, and she covered her face with her hands again.

Horrible suspicions were now assailing Strike. He'd believed nothing more serious than feeling scared and sometimes hungry had happened to either of them at the Aylmerton Community; that they'd narrowly escaped what had later been all over the press. In his memory, he'd always been with Lucy, sticking close, trying to make sure she wasn't invited anywhere by either of the Crowther brothers. From their adjoining mattresses on the floor, brother and sister had whispered at night about how much they hated the place, about how much they wished Leda would take them away. That was all that had happened, surely? That was what he'd believed, for years.

'Luce?' he said.

'Don't you *remember* her?' said Lucy savagely, dropping her hands. 'Don't you *remember* that girl?'

'No,' said Strike truthfully.

His memory was usually excellent, but Aylmerton was a

blur to him, more feeling than fact, an ominous black memory hole. Perhaps he'd deliberately tried to forget individuals: better by far to consign the whole lot to a faceless slough that need never be waded through, now it was all over.

'You *do*. Very pale. Pointed nose. Black hair. Always wearing kind of tarty clothes.'

Something shifted in Strike's memory. He saw a pair of very brief shorts, a thin halter-neck top and straggly, dark, slightly greasy hair. He'd been twelve: his hormones hadn't yet reached the adolescent peak at which the slightest sign of unsupported breasts caused uncontainable, sometimes mortifyingly visible, excitement.

'Yeah, that rings a bell,' he said.

'So *she's* still there?' said Lucy, now breathing fast. 'At the farm?'

'Yeah. As I say, she married—'

'If *she* was a victim,' said Lucy, through clenched teeth, 'she sure as hell spread it around.'

'Why d'you say that?' said Strike.

'Because she – because she—'

Lucy was shaking. For a couple of seconds she said nothing, then a torrent of words exploded from her.

'D'you know how glad I was, knowing I was having a boy, every single time they scanned me? *Every single time*. I didn't want a girl. I knew I'd've been a lousy mother to a girl.'

'You'd've been—'

'No, I *wouldn't*,' said Lucy fiercely. 'I'd have barely let her out of my *sight*! I know it happens to boys too, I know it does, but the odds – the odds – it was only the girls at Aylmerton. Only the girls.'

Lucy continued to breathe very hard, intermittently dabbing her eyes with kitchen roll. Strike knew it was cowardice, because he could tell Lucy needed to tell him, but he didn't want to ask any more questions, because he didn't want to hear the answers.

'She took me to him,' said Lucy at last.

'To who?'

'Dr Coates,' said Lucy. 'I fell over. She must've been fifteen, sixteen. She had me by the hand. I didn't want to go. "You should see the doctor." She was half-dragging me.'

Another brief silence unrolled through the room, but Strike could feel Lucy's rage battling with her habitual reserve and her determination to pretend that the life to which Leda had subjected them was as long dead as Leda herself.

'Did he,' said Strike slowly, '*touch*—'

'He pushed four fingers inside me,' said Lucy brutally. 'I bled for two days.'

'Oh fuck,' said Strike, wiping his face with his hand. 'Where was I?'

'Playing football,' said Lucy. 'I was playing, as well. That's how I fell. You probably thought she was helping me.'

'Shit, Luce,' said Strike. 'I'm so—'

'It's not your fault, it's my so-called *mother's* fault,' spat Lucy. 'Where was she? Getting stoned somewhere? Screwing some long-haired weirdo in the woods? And that bitch Mazu shut me in with Coates, and she *knew*. She *knew*. And I saw her doing it to other little girls. Taking them to the Crowthers' rooms. That's what I talk about most in therapy, why I didn't tell anyone, why I didn't stop other little girls getting hurt—'

'You're in therapy?' blurted out Strike.

'Christ Almighty, *of course* I'm in therapy!' said Lucy, in a furious whisper, as somebody, probably Greg, now full of banana cake, walked past the sitting room door and headed upstairs. 'After that bloody childhood – aren't you?'

'No,' said Strike.

'No,' repeated Lucy bitterly, 'you don't need it, of course, so self-sufficient, so un-messed-up—'

'I'm not saying that,' said Strike. 'I'm not – bloody hell—'

'Don't,' she snapped, arms wrapped around her torso again. 'I don't want – never mind, it doesn't matter. Except it *does* matter,' she said, tears trickling down her face again, 'I can't forgive myself for not speaking up. There were other little girls being led away by that Mazu bitch, and I never said anything, because I didn't want to say what had happened to m—'

The sitting room door opened. Strike was astonished by the abrupt change in Lucy, as she wiped her face dry and straightened her back in an instant, so that when Jack entered, panting and wet-haired, she was smiling.

'These are great,' Jack told Strike, beaming, as he held up his bow.

'Glad to hear it,' said Strike.

'Jack, go dry yourself off and then you can have some banana bread,' said Lucy, for all the world as though she were perfectly happy, and for the very first time in their adult lives, it occurred to Strike that his sister's determination to cling to stability and her notion of normality, her iron-clad refusal to dwell endlessly on the awful possibilities of human behaviour, was a form of extraordinary courage.

Once the door had closed on Jack, he turned back to Lucy, and said quietly, and almost sincerely,

'I wish you'd told me this before.'

'It would've upset you. Anyway, you've always wanted to believe Leda was wonderful.'

'I haven't,' he said, now being completely honest. 'She was … what she was.'

'She wasn't fit to be a mother,' said Lucy angrily.

'No,' said Strike heavily. 'I think you're probably right, there.'

Lucy stared at him for a few seconds in blank astonishment. 'I've waited *years* to hear you say that. *Years.*'

'I know you have,' said Strike. 'Look, I know you think *I* think she was perfect, but of course I bloody don't. D'you think I look at the kind of mother you are, and remember what she was, and can't see the difference?'

'Oh Stick,' said Lucy tearfully.

'She was what she was,' repeated Strike. 'I loved her, I can't sit here and say I didn't. And she might've been a fucking nightmare in loads of ways, but I know she loved us, too.'

'*Did* she?' said Lucy, wiping her eyes with kitchen roll.

'You know she did,' said Strike. 'She didn't keep us safe, because she was so bloody naive she was barely fit to open a front door on her own. She fucked up our schooling because she hated school herself. She dragged fucking terrible men into our lives because she always thought this one was going to be the love of her life. None of it was malicious, it was just bloody careless.'

'Careless people do a lot of damage,' said Lucy, still drying her tears.

'Yeah, they do,' said Strike. 'And she did. Mostly to herself, in the end.'

'I didn't – *I didn't want her to die,*' sobbed Lucy.

'Jesus, Luce, I know you didn't!'

'I always thought one day I'd have it all out with her – and then it was too late, and she was g-gone . . . and you say she loved us, but—'

'You *know* she did,' said Strike. 'You *do,* Luce. Remember that serial story she used to make up for us? What the fuck was it called?'

'The Moonbeams,' said Lucy, still sobbing.

'The Moonbeam family,' said Strike. 'With Mummy Moonbeam and . . .'

'. . . Bombo and Mungo . . .'

'She didn't show love like most mothers,' said Strike, 'but she didn't do *anything* like other people. Doesn't mean love wasn't there. Doesn't mean she wasn't fucking irresponsible, either.'

For a couple of minutes there was silence again, but for Lucy's steadily decreasing sniffs. At last, she wiped her face with both hands and looked up, eyes red.

'If you're investigating that so-called church – what's it called?'

'The UHC.'

'Just make sure you get that bitch Mazu,' said Lucy in a low voice. 'I don't care if she was abused herself. I'm sorry, I don't. She enabled them to do it to other girls. She was pimping for them.'

Strike considered telling her that getting Mazu wasn't what he'd been hired to do, but instead said,

'If I get the opportunity, I definitely will.'

'Thank you,' mumbled Lucy, still wiping her puffy eyes. 'Then it'd be worth you taking the job.'

'Listen, there was something else I wanted to tell you,' he said, wondering, even as he heard himself say it, what the hell he was playing at. The impulse came, in a confused way, from a desire to be honest, as she'd been honest, to stop hiding from her. 'I – er – I've made contact with Prudence. You know – Rokeby's other illegitimate.'

'Have you?' said Lucy, and to his amazement – he'd hidden the burgeoning relationship from her out of fear that she'd feel jealous, or that she was being replaced – she was smiling through her tears. 'Stick, that's great!'

'Is it?' he said, thrown.

'Well, of *course* it is!' she said. 'How long have you two been in touch?'

'Dunno. A few months. She visited me in hospital when I – you know—'

He gestured with his thumb towards the lung that had been punctured by a cornered killer.

'What's she like?' said Lucy, who appeared curious and interested, but in no way resentful.

'Nice,' said Strike. 'I mean, she's not you—'

'You don't need to say that,' said Lucy, with a shaky laugh. 'I know what we went through together, I know nobody else will ever understand that. You know, Joan *always* wanted you to make it up with Rokeby.'

'Prudence isn't Rokeby,' said Strike.

'I know,' said Lucy, 'but it's still good you're seeing her. Joan would be happy.'

'I didn't think you'd take it like this.'

'Why not? I see *my* dad's other kids.'

'Do you?'

'Of course I do! I didn't want to go on about it, because—'

'You thought I'd be hurt?'

'Probably because I felt guilty that I've got a relationship with *my* dad and half-siblings, and you haven't,' said Lucy.

After a short pause, she said,

'I saw Charlotte in the paper, with her new boyfriend.'

'Yeah,' said Strike, 'well, she likes a certain lifestyle. That was always a problem, me being broke.'

'You don't wish—?'

'Christ, no,' said Strike. 'That's dead and buried.'

'I'm glad,' said Lucy. 'I'm really glad. You deserve so much better. You'll stay for lunch, won't you?'

Given the revelations of the morning, Strike felt he had no choice but to agree.

12

Strike made an uncharacteristic effort to appear cheerful while at lunch, tolerating his brother-in-law and eldest nephew with a grace he'd rarely shown before. He didn't rush away afterwards, but stayed until the rain had passed off, when the whole family went into the back garden and watched Luke, Jack and Adam play with their Firetek Bows, even feigning good humour when Luke, in what Strike refused to believe was an accident, discharged his dart into the side of his uncle's face, eliciting roars of laughter from Greg.

Only once he'd left the house did Strike allow his face to slacken, losing the determined grin he'd worn for much of the last couple of hours. Having firmly resisted Lucy's offers of a lift, he walked back to the station under a grey sky, brooding on everything he'd just heard.

Strike was a mentally resilient man who'd survived plenty of reverses in his life, not least the loss of part of his right leg. One of the tools of self-discipline he'd forged in youth and honed in the army was a habit of compartmentalisation that rarely failed him, but right now, it wasn't working. Emotions he didn't want to feel and memories he generally suppressed were closing in on him, and he, who detested anything that smacked of self-indulgence, travelled back towards Denmark Street brooding so deeply that he barely registered the passing Tube stations and realised, almost too late to disembark, that he was already at Tottenham Court Road.

By the time he arrived back at his attic flat, he felt as grimly unhappy as he'd been for a long time. In consequence, he poured himself a double whisky, refilled his vape pen, sat down at his kitchen table and stared into space while alternately downing Scotch and exhaling vapour in the direction of his draughty window.

He'd rarely felt as angry at his mother as he did this afternoon. She'd died of what had been ruled an accidental overdose when Strike was nineteen, an overdose which Strike believed to this day had been administered by her far younger husband. His reaction to the news had been to drop out of university and join the military police, a decision he knew his unconventional mother would have found both inexplicable and vaguely comical. *But why?* he demanded of the Leda in his head. *You knew I wanted order, and boundaries, and a life without endless fucking mess. If you hadn't been what you were, maybe I wouldn't be what I am. Maybe I'm reaping what you sowed, so don't you fucking laugh at the army, or me, you with your paedophile mates and the squatters and the junkies . . .*

These thoughts of Leda led inevitably to thoughts of Charlotte Campbell, because he knew that plenty of armchair psychologists, including close friends and family members, thought he'd been so irreparably damaged by Leda's parenting, he'd been inevitably drawn to a similarly chaotic and unstable woman. This had always irritated Strike, and it irritated him now as he sat with his whisky, staring out of his attic window, because it so happened that there'd been profound differences between his ex-fiancée and his late mother.

Leda had had a bottomless compassion for underdogs and an incurable optimism about human nature that had never failed her. That, indeed, had been the problem: her naive, unconquerable conviction that genuine evil was only found in the repressions of small-town respectability. She might have taken endless risks, but she wasn't self-destructive: on the contrary, she'd fully expected to live to a hundred.

Charlotte, on the other hand, was profoundly unhappy, and Strike suspected he was the only person who truly knew the depths of her misery. The surface of Charlotte's life might look glamorous and easy, because she was extraordinarily beautiful, and came from a rich and newsworthy family, but her real value to the gossip columns was her instability. There were several suicide attempts in Charlotte's past, and a long history of psychiatric evaluations. He'd seen the press pictures of her, dead-eyed in her red slip dress, and his only thought had been that she'd probably taken something to get her through another night of revelry, a supposition backed up by the fact that she'd called his office at midnight on the same night, leaving an incoherent message on the answer machine, which he'd deleted before anyone else could hear it.

Strike was well aware that Lucy, and some of his friends, believed him trapped perpetually in the shadow cast by those two dark caryatids, Leda and Charlotte. They wanted him to stride out into the sunlight, free at last, to find a less complicated woman, and a love untainted by pain. But what was a man supposed to do if he thought he might finally be ready to do that, and it was too late? Alone of the women jostling in his thoughts, Robin brought feelings of warmth, though they were tinged with a bitterness no less easier to bear because it was self-directed. He should have spoken up, should have forced a conversation about their respective feelings before Ryan Murphy swooped in and carried off the prize Strike had complacently thought was his for the taking.

Fuck this.

The sky outside the window was rapidly darkening. He got up from the table, went into his bedroom, returned to the kitchen with his notebook and laptop, and opened both. Work had always been his greatest refuge, and the sight of an email from Eric Wardle headed *Census information* at the top of his inbox felt like an immediate reward for turning away from alcohol, and back to investigation.

Wardle had done him proud. The last three censuses for Chapman Farm were attached: 1991, 2001 and 2011. Strike typed out a brief message of thanks to Wardle, then opened the first attachment, scanning the list of names provided.

After an hour and a half of online cross-referencing, and having found a bonus in the form of an interesting article about the church dating from 2005, dusk was drawing in. Strike poured himself a second whisky, sat back down at his table and contemplated the immediate results of his research: a list of names, only one of which so far had an address beside it.

He contemplated his mobile, thinking back on the days he'd occasionally called Robin at home, while she was still married. Those calls, he knew, had sometimes caused trouble, given Matthew's resentment of his wife's growing dedication to the job. It was Saturday night: Robin and Murphy might be at a restaurant, or the bloody theatre again. Strike took another swig of whisky, and pressed Robin's number.

'Hi,' she said, answering on the second ring. 'What's up?'

'Got a moment to talk? I've been digging information out of the census.'

'Oh, great – Wardle came through?'

Strike heard the rattle of what he thought might be a saucepan.

'Sure you're not busy?'

'No, it's fine, I'm cooking. Ryan's coming over for dinner, but he's not here yet.'

'I might have a couple of leads. There's a woman called Sheila Kennett who lived at Chapman Farm with her late husband until the nineties. She's knocking on a bit, but I've got an address for her in Coventry. Wondering whether you'd mind driving up there and interviewing her. Old lady – better you than me.'

'No problem,' said Robin, 'but it'll have to be week after next, because Midge is away from Wednesday and I'm covering for her.'

'OK. I've also found an article written by a journalist called Fergus Robertson, who got an ex-member of the UHC to speak to him anonymously in 2006. There are a lot of "allegeds": violence used against members, misappropriation of funds. They protect their sources, journalists, but I thought there might be stuff Robertson couldn't put in, for fear of litigation. Fancy coming with me if he agrees to talk?'

'Depends when it is,' said Robin, 'I've got a heavy week on the new stalker case, but – *ouch*—'

'You OK?'

'Burned myself – sorry, I – hang on, that's Ryan.'

He heard her walking away towards the door. Slightly despising himself, Strike hung on: he really wanted Ryan Murphy to arrive and find Robin on the phone to him.

'Hi,' he heard her say, and then came Murphy's muffled voice, and the unmistakeable sound of a kiss. 'Dinner's nearly done,' she said, and Murphy said something, Robin laughed, and said 'No, it's Strike,' while her detective partner sat frowning in front of his laptop.

'Sorry, Cormoran,' said Robin, her mouth to the receiver again, 'carry on.'

'I haven't found contact details for anyone else who lived at Chapman Farm yet, but I'll keep digging and email you what I've got,' said Strike.

'It's Saturday night,' said Robin. 'Take a break. No!' she added, laughing, and he assumed this was directed at Murphy, whose laughter he could also hear. 'Sorry,' she said again.

'No problem, I'll let you go,' he said, as she had earlier, and before she could reply, he hung up.

Thoroughly irritated at himself, Strike slapped his laptop closed and got up to examine the contents of his healthily stocked fridge. As he took out a packet of what he was starting to think of as 'more fucking fish' to check the sell-by date, his mobile rang. He returned to the table to check before answering, because if it was another call forwarded from the office phone, he wasn't going to answer: the last thing he needed right now was Charlotte. Instead, he saw an unfamiliar mobile number.

'Strike.'

'Hi,' said a bold, husky voice. 'Surprise.'

'Who's this?'

'Bijou. Bijou Watkins. We met at the christening.'

'Oh,' said Strike, a memory of cleavage and legs blotting out darker thoughts, and this, at least, was welcome. 'Hi.'

'I s'pose you've got plans,' she said, 'but I'm all dressed up and my friend I was s'posed to be meeting tonight's ill.'

'How did you get my number?'

'Ilsa,' said Bijou, with the cackle of laughter he remembered from the Herberts' kitchen. 'Told her I needed a detective, for a case I'm working on ... I don't think she believed me,' she added, with another cackle.

'No, well, she's quick like that,' said Strike, holding the

139

mobile a little further from his ear, which made the laugh slightly less jarring. He doubted he could stand that for long.

'So . . . want a drink? Or dinner? Or whatever?'

He looked down at the cellophaned tuna in his hand. He remembered the cleavage. He'd given up smoking and take-aways. Robin was cooking dinner for Ryan Murphy.

'Yeah,' he said. 'Why not?'

13

Nine at the beginning means:
The footprints run crisscross.

The I Ching or Book of Changes

The extreme taciturnity of Clive Littlejohn, the agency's newest subcontractor, was starting to grate on people other than Robin.

'There's something wrong wi' him,' Littlejohn's fellow subcontractor, Barclay, told Robin on Wednesday morning, as both sat watching the entrance to a block of flats in Bexleyheath from Barclay's car.

'Better him than Morris or Nutley,' said Robin, loyally parroting Strike's line.

'That's a low fuckin' bar,' said Barclay.

'He's doing the job OK,' said Robin.

'He just fuckin' stares,' said Barclay. 'Doesn't blink. Like a fuckin' lizard.'

'I'm pretty sure lizards blink,' said Robin. 'Wait – is that one of them?'

'No,' said Barclay, leaning forwards to squint through the windscreen at a man who'd just exited the building. 'He's fatter than ours.'

Inside the block of flats they were watching lived two brothers in their forties who, unfortunately for the agency's

141

newest investigation, closely resembled each other. One of them – a few days' surveillance hadn't yet identified which – was stalking an actress called Tasha Mayo. The police weren't taking the matter seriously enough for the client, who was starting to become, in her own words, 'freaked out'. A series of trivial incidents, at first merely irksome, had lately turned sinister with the posting of a dead bird through the woman's letter box, and then with the gluing up of the keyhole on her front door.

'I mean, I know the police are overstretched,' Tasha had told Robin, while the latter was taking down the details of the case at the office. 'I get that, and I know there's been no direct threat, but I've *told* them who I think's doing it, I've given them a physical description and where he lives and everything, because he's told me most of his life story in segments. He's always hanging around the stage door and I've signed about fifteen posters and bits of paper. Things turned nasty when I told him I hadn't got time for another selfie. And he keeps turning up places I go. I just want it to stop. Someone keyed my car last night. I've had enough. I need you to catch him in the act.'

This wasn't the first stalking case the agency had tackled, but none had yet involved dead birds, and Robin, who felt sympathetic towards the client, was hoping to catch the perpetrator sooner rather than later.

'Midge fancies her,' said Barclay, watching the suspect's window.

'Who, Tasha Mayo?'

'Aye. Did ye see that film she was in, about those two Victorian lesbians?'

'No. Was it good?'

'Fuckin' dreadful,' said Barclay. 'Hour and a half of poetry and gardening. The wife loved it. I didn't, because apparently I'm an insensitive prick.'

Robin laughed.

'Midge could be in with a shot,' Barclay went on. 'Tasha Mayo's bisexual.'

'Is she?'

'According to the wife. That'd be the wife's specialist subject on *Mastermind*: sex lives o' the stars. She's a walking fuckin' encyclopaedia on it.'

They sat in silence for a few minutes before Barclay, still staring up at the fourth floor, asked,

'Why aren't they working for a living?'

'No idea,' said Robin.

'Be handy if we could nail them on a benefits scam. Nice bit o' community service. He wouldn't have time tae go after her, then.'

'Community service would end eventually,' said Robin, sipping her coffee. 'Trouble is, I don't know how you stop someone being obsessed.'

'Punch them?' suggested Barclay, and after a moment's thought he added, 'D'ye think Littlejohn'd say something if I punched him?'

'Maybe try and find a topic of mutual interest first,' said Robin.

'It's fuckin' bizarre,' said Barclay, 'never talking. Just sitting there.'

'*That's* one of them,' Robin said, replacing her coffee in the cupholder.

A man had just left the building, walking with his hands in his pockets. Like his brother, he had an unusually high forehead, which was why Barclay had nicknamed the pair the Frankenstein brothers, which had been swiftly abbreviated to Frank One and Frank Two. Shabbily dressed in an old wind-cheater, jeans and trainers, he was heading, Robin guessed, towards the station.

'OK, I'll take him,' she said, picking up the backpack she usually took on surveillance, 'and you can stay here and watch the other one.'

'Aye, all right,' said Barclay. 'Good luck.'

Robin, who was wearing a beanie hat to cover her distinctive new haircut, followed Frank One on foot to Bexleyheath station and, after a short wait, got into the same train compartment, where she kept him under covert observation from several seats away.

After a couple of minutes, Robin's mobile rang and she saw Strike's number.

'Morning. Where are you?'

'With one of the Franks,' she said quietly. 'We're heading into London.'

'Ah. Well, I just wanted to tell you, I've persuaded that journalist I mentioned to talk to me. Fergus Robertson, meeting him later at the Westminster Arms. Have you read his article yet?'

'Yes,' said Robin, 'and I read his follow-up, too, about what the church did to him after the first one was published. They don't like criticism, do they?'

'I'd say that's an understatement,' said Strike. 'In other news, I've just spotted Will Edensor. He's collecting in Soho again today.'

'Oh wow, really?'

'Yeah. I didn't approach him, just to be on the safe side, but he looks bloody terrible. He's over six foot tall and probably weighs less than you do.'

'Did he look happy? All the temple attendants were beaming non-stop.'

'No, definitely not happy. I've also got Pat to have a look at the rota. You could go up to Coventry in the latter half of next week, if that suits you. I've got Sheila Kennett's number – the old woman who lived at Chapman Farm for years. If I text it to you, could you ring her? See whether she'd be amenable to an interview?'

'Yes, of course,' said Robin.

She'd barely returned her phone to her pocket when it rang again: Ilsa.

'Hi,' said Robin, 'what's up?'

'What the *hell* is he playing at?' said Ilsa hotly.

'What's who playing at?'

'Corm!'

'I don't—'

'He's slept with bloody Bijou Watkins! Well – I say "slept" – apparently it was standing up, against her bedroom wall.'

Robin realised she was gaping, and closed her mouth.

'He – hasn't mentioned it to me.'

'No, I'll *bet* he bloody hasn't,' said Ilsa angrily. 'She made up some bullshit reason to get his number off me, and I couldn't think of any way of not giving it to her, but I thought he'd have the *sense*, after meeting her and seeing what she's like, of not going within a *hundred miles* of her. You need to warn him: she's insane. She can't keep her bloody mouth shut, half of Chambers will have heard all the details by now—'

'Ilsa, I can't tell him who to sleep with. Or shag standing up against a bedroom wall,' Robin added.

'But she's a total *nutcase*! All she wants is a rich husband and a baby, she's completely open about it!'

'Strike's not rich,' said Robin.

'She might not realise that, after all those high-profile cases he keeps solving. You've *got* to warn him—'

'Ilsa, I can't. *You* warn him, if you want to. His sex life's hardly my business.'

Ilsa groaned.

'But why *her*, if he wants a displacement fuck?'

145

'I don't know,' said Robin, completely honestly, and then, dropping her voice, she asked, 'and what d'you mean, a "displacement fuck"?'

'Oh, please,' said Ilsa irritably. 'You know perfectly well what— shit, that's my QC, I'll have to go. Bye.'

This conversation left Robin watching Frank One's reflection in the dirty train window, prey to many conflicting emotions she wasn't sure she wanted to disentangle. A very vivid mental picture had presented itself to her while Ilsa talked, of Bijou in her shocking pink dress, long tanned legs wrapped around Strike, and it wasn't immediately possible to erase the image, especially as her imagination had given Strike quite a hairy arse.

The train stopped at last at Waterloo East. Robin followed her target on foot and then onto a Tube train, where he disembarked at Piccadilly Circus.

They were now so close to Theatreland that Robin's hopes were rising that she'd picked the right brother to follow. However, instead of heading towards Shaftesbury Avenue and the theatre where Tasha Mayo's play was showing, Frank One walked into Soho, and ten minutes later, entered a comic-book shop.

As everyone she could see through the windows was male, Robin decided she'd made herself conspicuous by following him, so she retreated a few yards and took out her phone to call the number Strike had sent her.

An out-of-breath voice, slightly cracked, either from age, smoking, or both, answered.

'Hello?'

'Hello, is that Mrs Kennett?' said Robin.

'Yes. Who's this?'

'My name's Robin Ellacott. I'm a private detective.'

'You're a what?' said the elderly woman.

'A private detective,' said Robin.

Understandably, there was a short pause.

'What d'you want?' said the voice on the end of the line suspiciously.

'I've been hired by somebody who's very concerned about a relative of theirs, who's a member of the Universal Humanitarian Church. I was hoping you might talk to me about the UHC. Just for background. You used to live at Chapman Farm, didn't you?'

'How d'you know that?' said Sheila Kennett sharply; she certainly seemed to have all her faculties.

'Just from records,' said Robin, deliberately vague: she didn't want to bandy about the fact that Strike had obtained census reports.

'That was a long time ago,' said Sheila Kennett.

'We're really just after background,' said Robin. 'I think you were there at the same time as the Pirbright family?'

'I was, yeah,' said Sheila, still sounding suspicious.

'Well, we're looking into some claims Kevin Pirbright made about the church, so we wondered whether—'

'He's dead, isn't he?'

'I – yes, he is,' said Robin.

'Yeah, I saw it in the paper. Wondered if it was our Kevin,' said Sheila. 'Have they got who did it yet?'

'Not as far as I know,' said Robin.

There was another short pause.

'All right,' said Sheila. 'I don't mind talking. I've got nothing to lose, not any more.'

'That's wonderful,' said Robin, then thought how insensitive that had sounded and added, 'I mean, thank you. You're up in Coventry, aren't you?'

'Yeah.'

'How would next Thursday suit you? A week tomorrow?'

'Yeah, all right,' said Sheila. 'Robin, did you say your name was?'

'That's right. Robin Ellacott.'

'Man's name,' said Sheila. 'Why did your parents give you a man's name?'

'I've never asked,' said Robin, with a laugh.

'Hm. All right then. What time?'

'Would midday be all right?' asked Robin, rapidly calculating the distance to Coventry.

'Yeah. All right. I'll have the kettle on.'

'Thank you so much. I'll see you then!' said Robin.

Robin texted Strike to tell him she'd arranged the interview with Sheila Kennett, then crossed the road, the better to watch the comic-book storefront.

The day was cool and cloudy, and Robin was glad of her beanie hat. She'd only just registered how close she was to the Rupert Court Temple when she spotted four young people with collecting tins, heading into Berwick Street.

Robin recognised Will Edensor at once. He looked ill and defeated, not to mention very thin. The shadows under his eyes, which Robin could see even from the other side of the street, gave him an unpleasant likeness to the image of the Stolen Prophet she'd seen on the temple ceiling. Like his companions, he was wearing an orange tabard printed with the church's logo, which was repeated on their collecting tins.

The other man in the group seemed to be giving instructions. Unlike the other three, he was overweight, and wore his hair in a straggly bob. He pointed along the street, and the two girls headed off obediently in the direction indicated, whereas Will remained where he was. His demeanour made Robin think of a donkey, used to abuse, and no longer capable of protest.

The second man turned back to Will and delivered what

looked like a lecture, through which Will nodded mechanically without making eye contact. Robin yearned to get close enough to hear what was going on, but dared not make herself recognisable to either of them. Before the lecture had finished, Frank One emerged from the comic-book shop, and Robin had no choice but to follow.

14

Nine in the second place means:
Penetration under the bed.
Priests and magicians are used in great number.

The I Ching or Book of Changes

The Westminster Arms, where Strike had agreed to meet journalist Fergus Robertson, lay close beside Westminster Abbey and the Houses of Parliament. As Strike walked towards the pub he felt small twinges of pain emanating from the back of his stump. Although his hamstring had previously been torn, it hadn't given any trouble for the last few months, largely because it was being asked to support a lot less weight. He knew exactly what had caused this mild recurrence of symptoms: the necessity of holding up Bijou Watkins, who'd expressed a loud and drunken preference for being nailed up against the bedroom wall the moment they'd entered her flat on Saturday night.

The pain in his leg turned his thoughts back to that evening. He supposed two and a half hours of mindless conversation had been justified in light of the ten minutes of frills-free sex that had followed. She'd looked better than she felt – her impressive breasts, as he'd discovered in the bedroom, were fake – but the upside of finding her obnoxious was a total absence of guilt about his lack of response to the three texts she'd sent him since, all of which had been strewn with emojis. His oldest friend, Dave Polworth, would have called that breaking even, and Strike was inclined to agree.

On entering the Westminster Arms, Strike spotted Fergus Robertson, who he'd Googled earlier, sitting in a corner at a table for two, typing on a laptop. A short, rotund and almost entirely bald man whose shining pate reflected the light hanging over the table, Robertson was currently in his shirtsleeves, vigorously chewing gum as he worked. Strike fetched himself a drink, noting a junior minister at the bar, before heading for Robertson, who kept typing until Strike arrived at the table.

'Ah,' said the journalist, looking up. 'The famous detective.'

'And the fearless reporter,' said Strike, sitting down.

They shook hands across the table, Robertson's curious blue eyes scanning Strike. He gave off an air of rough good humour. A pack of Nicorette chewing gum lay beside the laptop.

'You know Dominic Culpepper, I hear,' Robertson said, referring to a journalist who Strike disliked.

'I do, yeah. He's a tit.'

Robertson laughed.

'I heard you shagged his cousin.'

'Can't remember that,' lied Strike.

'Got a view on Brexit?'

'None whatsoever,' said Strike.

'Shame,' said Robertson. 'I need another three hundred words.'

He flipped down the screen on his laptop.

'So . . . going after the UHC, are you?' Robertson sat back in his chair, still chewing, lacing his short fingers together over a large beer belly. 'Do I get exclusive rights to the story if you find a body under the temple floor?'

'Can't guarantee that,' said Strike.

'Then what's in it for me?'

'The satisfaction of a good turn done,' said Strike.

'Do I look like a Boy Scout?'

'If I find out anything newsworthy that doesn't compromise my client,' said Strike, who'd anticipated this conversation, 'you can have it.'

'I'll hold you to that,' said Robertson, unlacing his fingers to pop another piece of nicotine gum out of its packet, shoving it in his mouth and then drinking more beer.

'You haven't been scared off writing about them, then?' said Strike.

'Not if you can get me some solid information. They're a bunch of cunts. I'd be fucking delighted to help bring them down.'

'They gave you a hard time, I gather?'

'Nearly lost my job over that piece,' said Robertson. 'Lawyers up my arse, paper shitting itself, my ex-wife getting anonymous calls to the house—'

'Really?'

'Oh, yeah. And you should've seen what the fuckers did to my Wikipedia page.'

'Got a Wikipedia page, have you?' said Strike, surprised.

'I didn't have before I tangled with them, but after my piece went out, the UHC made one for me. "Disgraced journalist Fergus Robertson." "Notorious alcoholic Fergus Robertson." "Domestic abuser F—" I never laid a finger on my ex,' added Robertson, a little defensively. 'So, yeah: if you get anything provable, I'll fucking print it and they'll rue the fucking day they went after me.'

Strike took out his notebook and pen.

'What made you look into them in the first place?'

'I started digging into the fat cats and the celebs who've joined.'

'What's in it for them?'

'For the fat cats, they get to rub shoulders with the celebs. For the latter, the UHC lines up photo ops: no work needed, just turn up an' get your picture taken with young carers or the homeless. People like Noli Seymour like to look spiritual, you know. Then you've got Dr Zhou.'

'I hadn't heard of him until I read your article.'

'Take it you don't watch breakfast TV?'

Strike shook his head.

'He's got a regular slot on one of the shows. Looks like Bruce Lee, if he'd been in a car accident. He's got a clinic in Belgravia where he sees people with more money than sense. All kinds of bullshit. Cupping. Hypnosis. Past life regression.'

'You said in the piece he was recruiting for the UHC from his clinic.'

'I think he's one of the main points of entry for the big donors. That was one of the things the UHC lawyers made me retract.'

'The ex-member you talked to for the article—'

'Poor little cow,' sighed Robertson, not unkindly. 'She was the only one I could get to talk.'

'How long was she in there?'

'Five and a half years. Tagged along to a meeting with a male schoolfriend. The friend left after the first week and she stayed. She's a lesbian,' said Robertson, 'and Daddy didn't like her liking women. The UHC was selling itself as being all about inclusivity, so you can see how she fell for it. She's from a very wealthy family. The church milked her of most of her inheritance before they spat her out again.'

'And she told you she'd been beaten?'

'Beaten, starved, made to go with men, yeah – but I couldn't get any of it corroborated, which is why every other word is "alleged".' Robertson took another sip of beer, then said, 'I couldn't use a lot of what she told me, because I knew the paper would have a massive lawsuit on its hands. 'Course, that nearly happened anyway. Should've slung the whole lot in, it would've come to the same.'

'She claimed funds were being misappropriated?'

'Yeah, mainly cash. She told me that if they were collecting on the street, they had to make a certain amount before they were allowed to stop. Bear in mind they've got people out doing that in London, Birmingham, Glasgow, Munich, San Francisco – did you know they're in Germany and the States, as well?'

'Yeah, I saw that on their website.'

'Yeah, so, she said the kids collecting have got to get a hundred quid before they're allowed to sit down or eat. She told me nobody knew where it all ended up, but old Papa J does himself very well. He's rumoured to have a property in Antigua, where the Principals go for spiritual retreats. No bloody Chapman Farm for *them*.'

'So you held some stuff back because it was too hot to print, did you?'

'Had to. I wanted to protect the source. I knew people would think she was a loon if I used everything she was claiming.'

'Would this have been supernatural stuff?'

'Already know about that, do you?' said Robertson, jaws still working hard on his nicotine gum. 'Yeah, exactly. Drowned Prophet.'

'Ex-members seem pretty scared of the Drowned Prophet.'

'Well, she comes after them if they leave, see.'

'Comes after them,' repeated Strike.

'Yeah. The membership's taught if they reveal the Divine Secrets, she'll come and get them.'

'What are the Divine Secrets?'

'She wouldn't tell me.'

Robertson now downed the rest of his beer.

'Two days after she talked to me, she saw the Drowned Prophet floating outside her bedroom window in the early hours of the morning. She rang me, hysterical, saying she'd said too much and the Drowned Prophet had come to get her, but I should still print the story. I tried to talk her down. Told her she needed a therapist, but she was having none of it. She kept saying, "There's something you don't know, there's something you don't know." Got off the phone, locked herself in her parents' bathroom and slit her wrists in the bath. She survived – just.'

'Shit,' said Strike.

'Yeah. Her father blamed me, the fucking prick – he was still being a shit to her for joining the cult and giving them all her money, so on the one side I had the source's family claiming I tipped her into suicide, and on the other, UHC threatening to bankrupt the paper for what they say are fake claims, and I'm stuck in the middle with my job hanging by a thread.'

'Where's the girl now?'

'New Zealand, last I heard. The suicide attempt panicked her family, the father finally stopped bullying her and got her some help. Packed her off to some relatives down under. Fresh start.'

'Did you put it to her that whatever supernatural stuff she'd seen in the church must've been faked?'

'Yeah, but she wouldn't have it.' Robertson now extracted a large ball of chewed gum out of his mouth, pressed it into one of the empty slots in the packet, took out a fresh piece and began chewing again. 'She swore she'd seen ghosts and magic – but they didn't call it magic, obviously. Pure spirits, that was the terminology. Pure spirits could do supernatural stuff.'

'So what was too hot to print?'

'I could use another pint,' said Robertson, pushing his empty glass towards the detective.

Strike heaved a sigh, but got back to his feet, his hamstring throbbing.

When he'd returned to the table and set down the fresh pint in front of Robertson, the journalist said,

'D'you know who Margaret Cathcart-Bryce was?'

'Rich old woman, left her entire fortune to the UHC in 2004, buried at Chapman Farm, now known as the Golden Prophet.'

'That's the one,' said Robertson. 'Well, it wasn't a good death.'

'Meaning?'

'They don't believe in medicine in the UHC. My source told me Cathcart-Bryce died in fucking agony, begging for a doctor. She said the Waces were scared that if they let one in to see her, she'd've been taken into hospital, which would've meant next of kin being alerted. They didn't want some distant relative showing up and persuading her to change her will. If I could've proved that . . . but no corroboration. You can't sling something like that in without checking it out. I tried to get hold of some of Cathcart-Bryce's relatives, but the closest she had was a great-nephew in Wales. He'd already resigned himself to the fact he wasn't getting a sniff of her money and didn't give a fuck what had happened to her. Hadn't seen the old dear in years.'

Strike made a note of all this, before asking,

'Anything else?'

'Yeah,' said Robertson. He glanced around and lowered his voice. 'Sex.'

'Go on,' said Strike.

'They called it "spirit bonding", which basically means

fucking whoever you're told to fuck. The girls prove they're above material considerations by putting out for anyone they're told to.'

'Really?' said Strike.

'It only starts happening once you're in properly. Don't want to scare them off too early. But my source told me, once they're full members, they're not supposed to refuse anyone who wants it. I went as close to talking about it as I could, in the piece – plenty of "it is rumoured" and "sources claim" – but my editor didn't want any of the better-known members suing us for saying they were raping anyone, so I had to take all that out.'

Strike made a further note before saying,

'Was your source the only ex-member you could persuade to talk?'

'Yeah,' said Robertson. 'Everyone else I tried told me to fuck off. Some of them were ashamed,' he said, taking another sip of beer, 'embarrassed they ever fell for it. They've gone back to normal lives and don't want their pasts all over the papers. You can't blame them. Others were still a real mess. There were a couple I couldn't trace. Might've died.'

'Don't s'pose you kept a list of ex-members?'

'I did, yeah,' said Robertson.

'Have you still got it?'

'Might have it somewhere ... *quid pro quo*, though, right? I get the scoop, if you get a story?'

'Absolutely.'

'All right, I'll see if I can dig it out ...'

Robertson chomped on his gum for a brief spell, before saying,

'So, when did Sir Colin Edensor hire you?'

'I don't identify my clients to journalists,' said Strike, with no change of expression.

'Worth a punt,' said Robertson, eyes twinkling. 'Edensor's been pretty vocal about the church in the last couple of years.'

'Has he?'

'I s'pose there might be some other rich kids in there, though,' said Robertson, watching Strike closely. 'Other than Will Edensor.'

'S'pose there might,' said Strike non-committally, looking over his notes. 'She told you, "There's something you don't know"? And this was something other than Cathcart-Bryce being denied a doctor, was it?'

'Yeah, she'd already told me about the old girl,' said Robertson, who now flipped open his laptop again. 'Sure you haven't got a view on Brexit? How would it affect the private detective trade, if we leave the EU?'

'Not at all,' said Strike, getting to his feet.

'So I can put down Cormoran Strike as a Brexiteer, can I?'

'You can fuck off, is what you can do,' said Strike, and he left the journalist chuckling behind him.

15

'God, it's horrible out there,' were Robin's first words to Strike
the next time they met, which was on Easter Monday.

Storm Katie was currently ravaging London, knocking
down trees and pylons, and Robin's colour was high, her hair
windblown. The windows of the office were gently rattling as
the wind howled down Denmark Street.

'I did text you, offering to catch up by phone,' said Strike,
who'd just put the kettle on.

'I was probably already on the Tube,' said Robin, tugging
off her coat and hanging it up. 'I didn't mind coming in. Quite
bracing, really.'

'You wouldn't say that if you'd got smacked in the head by a
flying bin,' said Strike, who'd just been watching plastic cones
tumbling down Charing Cross Road. 'Coffee?'

'Great,' said Robin, trying to detangle her hair with her
fingers. 'Pat got the day off?'

'Yeah. Bank holiday. One good thing about this weather,
it'll probably keep the Frank brothers in.'

159

'Hopefully,' agreed Robin. 'In other good news, I think I'm getting closer to being recruited.'

'Really?' said Strike, looking round.

'Yes. That blonde woman I met last time made a beeline for me the moment I walked in on Saturday. "Oh, I'm so glad you came back!" I told her I'd read their pamphlet and found it interesting—'

'Was it?'

'No. It's mostly generalities about self-fulfilment and changing the world. I'm still playing it cool. I told her friends of mine were trying to warn me off the UHC, telling me there were rumours circulating about the place, about it not being what it seemed.'

'What did she say to that?'

'That she was sure I wasn't closed-minded enough not to give the church a fair hearing and that she could tell I was a free thinker and a very independent person.'

'Very astute of her,' said Strike, with a smirk. 'Papa J there?'

'No. Apparently I got very lucky seeing him last time, because he doesn't often appear in person these days. We got Becca Pirbright instead – Kevin's older sister.'

'Yeah?' said Strike, as he opened the fridge and took out milk. 'What's she like?'

'Very polished and chirpy. Perfect teeth – she looks American. You definitely wouldn't know her brother was shot through the head a few months ago. If she hadn't been wearing orange robes, you'd have thought she was a motivational speaker. Pacing up and down, lots of big gestures.

'Oh, and Noli Seymour was there. The actress. That caused a bit of excitement, when she walked in. Lots of whispering and pointing.'

'Special treatment?'

'Very. One of the temple attendants went running towards

her and tried to lead her to a seat at the front. She made kind of a fuss about not taking it and sliding into a space in the middle. Very humble. She made such a fuss about being humble, everyone was looking at her by the time she took her seat.'

Strike grinned.

'I read your note about your meeting with Fergus Robertson,' Robin went on.

'Good,' said Strike, handing Robin a mug and leading the way through to the inner office. 'I wanted to talk to you about that.'

Robin thought she knew what was coming. One of the reasons she'd been so determined to battle her way through Storm Katie to talk to Strike face to face was a suspicion that he was about to suggest – notwithstanding the hours of work she'd put in to create Rowena Ellis's persona, and the expensive new haircut – that one of the subcontractors should go undercover at Chapman Farm, instead of her.

'So, you read about the spirit bonding stuff?' Strike asked, as both took their seats opposite each other at the partners' desk.

'We're using the UHC's euphemism, are we?' said Robin, eyebrows raised.

'All right, if you prefer: did you read about women being coerced into sleeping with whoever the church says they should sleep with?'

'I did, yes,' said Robin.

'And?'

'And I still want to go in.'

Strike said nothing, but stroked his chin, looking at her.

'They're using emotional coercion, not physical force,' Robin said. 'I won't be indoctrinated, will I? So that's not going to work on me.'

'But if you're shut up in there, and that's the condition of maintaining your cover—'

'If it comes to actual attempted rape, I'll leave and go straight to the police,' said Robin calmly. 'Mission accomplished: we've got something on the church.'

Strike, who'd expected this attitude, still didn't like it.

'What's Murphy's view on this?'

'What the hell's it got to do with Ryan?' said Robin, with an edge to her voice.

Recognising his strategic error, Strike said, 'Nothing.'

There was a brief silence, in which rain pounded against the window and wind whistled through the guttering.

'All right, well, I thought we should divide up these ex-members so we can work our way through them, see if any will talk,' said Strike, breaking eye contact to open a file on his computer. 'I've sent you the census names already. Robertson sent me his list last night. There was only one name I didn't already have: Cherie Gittins. He never managed to trace her, but I found out a bit about her online. She was the girl who took Daiyu Wace swimming on the day she drowned, but I can't find any trace of her after 1995.'

'Want me to have a look?' said Robin, flipping open her notebook.

'Couldn't hurt. In better news, I've found the Doherty family – the dad who left with three of the kids, and the mother who was expelled later.'

'Really?'

'Yeah, but I've had a hard "no" to an interview from the father and two of the kids. The father was bloody aggressive about it. The other kid – I say kid, they're all adults now – hasn't got back to me yet. That's Niamh, the eldest. I can't find any trace of the mother, Deirdre, and I'm wondering whether she's changed her name or gone abroad. No death certificate that I can find. I haven't had much luck with Jordan, either – that's the bloke Kevin Pirbright claims was whipped across the face with a leather flail. He's not on any of the census reports, so he must've come and gone between censuses.

'But I might have found Jonathan Wace's older daughter, Abigail. If I'm right, she switched to using her mother's maiden name, Glover, after she left the church, and she's a firefighter.'

'A literal—?'

'Hose, siren, the works, if I've got the right woman. Unmarried, no kids that I can see, and she's living in Ealing. I also think I've identified the gay girl who joined up in her teens, the one Robertson spoke to for his article.'

'Already?'

'Yeah. She's on the census for 2001 and her name's Flora Brewster. Age and dates tally. Her Facebook page is full of pictures of New Zealand and she comes from a very wealthy family. Her grandfather started a massive construction company: Howson Homes.'

'"*You'll-Be-Oh-So-Happy-in-a-Howson-Home*"?' said Robin, as the jingle from a nineties advert she didn't know she'd remembered came back to her.

'Until the dividing walls fall down, yeah. Not famous for being well built, Howson Homes.'

'Have you contacted her?'

'No, because her Facebook account's inactive; she hasn't posted anything there for over a year, but I *have* found a guy called Henry Worthington-Fields, who's a Facebook friend of hers living in London. I think it's possible he's the guy who got her into it, who only stayed a week. He talks about having an old friend the church nearly destroyed. Very angry, very bitter, dark hints about criminality. I've sent him a message, but nothing back so far. If he's willing to talk, I might be able to find out what lay behind Flora's comment to Fergus Robertson, "There's something you don't know."'

'I was thinking about that girl – Flora – after I read your

email,' said Robin. 'That makes two people who killed themselves, or tried to, right after leaving the church. It's as though they leave with invisible suicide vests on them. Then the Drowned Prophet shows up and makes them detonate it.'

'Fanciful way of putting it,' said Strike, 'but yeah, I know what you mean.'

'Did I tell you Alexander Graves is painted on the temple ceiling with a noose around his neck?'

'No, you didn't.'

'It's sick, isn't it? They're close to glorifying suicide, putting that on the ceiling. Equating it to martyrdom for the church.'

'I'd imagine it suits the UHC fine to have quitters finish themselves off. Self-solving problem.'

'But it adds weight to what Prudence said, doesn't it? About not taking Will Edensor out too quickly, not expecting him to just snap back to—'

At that moment, they heard a jingle on the landing, and the door to the outer office opened. Strike and Robin both looked round, surprised: nobody else should have been there, given that Midge was on holiday and all other subcontractors on jobs.

There in the doorway stood Clive Littlejohn, stocky and solid in his rain-speckled coat, his crewcut unchanged by the high winds. His heavy-lidded eyes blinked at the partners visible through the open inner door. Otherwise, he remained expressionless and stationary.

'Morning,' said Strike. 'Thought you were on the new client's husband?'

'Ill,' said Littlejohn.

'Is he?'

'She texted.'

'So . . . you needed something?'

'Receipts,' said Littlejohn, putting his hand into the inside of his coat and drawing out a small wad of paper, which he laid on Pat's desk.

'Right,' said Strike.

Littlejohn stood for another second or two, then turned and left the office, closing the glass door behind him.

'It's like he gets taxed per syllable,' said Robin quietly.

Strike said nothing. He was still frowning towards the glass door.

'What's the matter?' asked Robin.

'Nothing.'

'Yes, there is. Why are you looking like that?'

'How was he planning to get in? I changed the rota last night so we could have a catch-up, otherwise I'd've been tailing Frank Two and you wouldn't have had any reason to be here – especially during a near hurricane,' Strike added, as the rain thumped against the window.

'*Oh*,' said Robin, now looking blankly after Littlejohn as well. 'Did you hear keys before the door opened?'

'He hasn't got a key,' said Strike. 'Or he shouldn't have.'

Before either could say anything else, Robin's mobile rang.

'Sorry,' she said to Strike, on checking it. 'It's Ryan.'

Strike got up and headed into the outer office. His ruminations on Littlejohn's strange behaviour were disrupted by Robin's voice, and her burst of laughter. Evidently evening plans were being changed, due to the weather. Then his own mobile rang.

'Strike.'

'Hi,' said Ilsa's voice. 'How are you?'

'Fine,' said Strike, while Robin lowered her voice in the inner office, and his feeling of irritation increased. 'What's up?'

'Look, I hope you don't think I'm interfering.'

'Tell me what you've got to say, then I'll tell you if you're interfering,' said Strike, without bothering to sound too friendly.

'Well, you're about to get a call from Bijou.'

'Which you know, because—?'

'Because she just told me. Actually, she told me, and three other people I was having a conversation with.'

'And?'

'She says you haven't answered her texts, so—'

'You've called to tell me off for not answering texts?'

'God, no, the reverse!'

In the inner office, Robin was laughing at something else Ryan had said. The man simply couldn't be that fucking funny.

'Go on,' Strike said to Ilsa, striding towards the inner door and closing it rather more firmly than was necessary. 'Say your piece.'

'Corm,' said Ilsa quietly, and he could tell she was trying not to be overheard by colleagues, 'she's crazy. She's already told—'

'You've called to give me unsolicited advice on my love life, is that right?'

Robin, who'd just finished her call with Ryan, got to her feet and opened the door in time to hear Strike say,

'—no, I don't. So, yeah, don't interfere.'

He hung up.

'Who was that?' said Robin, surprised.

'Ilsa,' said Strike curtly, walking back past her and sitting back down at the partners' desk.

Robin, who suspected she knew what Ilsa had just called about, settled back into her chair without saying anything. Noticing this unusual lack of curiosity, Strike made the correct deduction that Ilsa and Robin had already discussed his night with Bijou.

'Did you know Ilsa was planning to tell me how to conduct my private life?'

'What?' said Robin, startled by both question and tone. 'No!'

166

'Really?' said Strike.

'Yes, really!' said Robin, which was true: she might have told Ilsa to talk to Strike, but she hadn't known she was going to do it.

Strike's mobile now rang for a second time. He hadn't bothered to save Bijou's number to his contacts, but, certain who he was about to hear, he answered.

'Hi, stranger,' said her unmistakeably loud, husky voice.

'Hi,' said Strike. 'How're you?'

Robin got up and walked into the next room, on the pretext of fetching more coffee. Behind her, she heard Strike say,

'Yeah, sorry about that, been busy.'

As it was Robin's determined habit these days not to think about her partner in any terms other than those of friendship and work, she chose to believe the mingled feelings of annoyance and hurt now possessing her were caused by Strike's irritability and the near slamming of the office door, while she'd been talking to Ryan. It was entirely his business if he wanted to sleep with that vile woman again, and more fool him if he didn't realise she was after him for the fortune he didn't possess, or the baby he didn't want.

'Yeah, OK,' she heard Strike say. 'I'll see you there.'

Making a determined effort to look neutral, Robin returned to the partners' desk with fresh coffee, ignoring her partner's air of truculent defiance.

16

*The line at the beginning has good fortune, the
second is favourable; this is due to the time.
The third line bears an augury of misfortune, the
fifth of illness ...*

The I Ching or Book of Changes

For the next couple of days, Strike and Robin communicated only by matter-of-fact texts, with neither jokes nor extraneous chat. Robin was more annoyed with herself for dwelling on the door slamming and the accusation that she'd been gossiping with Ilsa behind her partner's back than she was at Strike for doing either of these two things.

Strike, who knew he'd behaved unreasonably, made no apology. However, a nagging sense of self-recrimination was added to his irritation at Ilsa, and both were intensified by his second date with Bijou.

He'd known he was making a mistake within five minutes of meeting her again. While she'd roared with laughter at her own anecdotes and talked loudly about top QCs who fancied her, he'd sat in near silence, asking himself what the hell he was playing at. Determined at least to get what he'd come for, he left her flat a few hours later with a faint feeling of self-disgust and a strong desire never to set eyes on her again. The only small consolation was that his hamstring hadn't suffered this time, because he'd indicated a preference for being horizontal while having sex.

While it was hardly the first time Strike had slept with a woman he wasn't in love with, never before had he screwed someone he actively disliked. The whole episode, which he now considered firmly closed, had intensified rather than alleviated his low mood, forcing him back up against his feelings for Robin.

Little did Strike know that Robin and Murphy's relationship had suffered its first serious blow, a fact that Robin had no intention whatsoever of sharing with her business partner.

The row happened on Wednesday evening in a bar near Piccadilly Circus. Robin, who was due to leave for Coventry at five o'clock the following morning, hadn't really fancied a mid-week trip to the cinema in the first place. However, as Murphy had already bought the tickets, she felt she couldn't object. He seemed determined not to slide into a pattern whereby they merely met at each other's flats for food and sex. Robin guessed this was due to a fear of taking her for granted or getting into a rut, which she'd deduced, from oblique comments, had been a complaint of his ex-wife's.

The trigger for their argument was a casual remark of Robin's about her planned stay at Chapman Farm. It then became clear that Murphy was labouring under a misapprehension. He'd thought she'd only be gone for seven days if she managed to be recruited, and was shocked to discover that, in reality, she'd committed to an open-ended undercover job that might last several weeks. Murphy was nettled that Robin hadn't explained the situation fully, while Robin was irate at the fact he hadn't listened properly. It might not be Murphy's fault that he was bringing back unpleasant memories of her ex-husband's assumed right to dictate the limits of her professional commitment, but the comparison was unavoidable, given that Murphy seemed to think Strike had pressured Robin into doing this onerous job, and she hadn't been assertive enough to refuse.

'I happen to *want* to do it,' Robin told Murphy, speaking in an angry whisper, because the bar was crowded. The moment they should have left for the cinema had slid past twenty minutes previously, unnoticed. 'I volunteered because I know I'm the best person for the job – and for your information, Strike's been actively trying to persuade me out of it.'

'Why?'

'Because it might take so long,' said Robin, lying by omission.

'And he's going to miss you, is that what you're saying?'

'You know what, Ryan? *Sod off.*'

Indifferent to the curious looks of a group of girls standing nearby, who'd been casting the handsome Murphy sidelong glances, Robin dragged her coat back on.

'I'm going home. I've got to get up at the crack of dawn to drive to Coventry, anyway.'

'Robin—'

But she was already striding towards the door.

Murphy caught up with her a hundred yards down the road. His apology, which was fulsome, was made within sight of the cupid-topped Shaftesbury Memorial Fountain where her ex-husband had proposed, which did nothing to dispel Robin's sense of *déjà vu*. However, as Murphy gallantly took all the blame on himself, Robin felt she had no choice but to relent. Given that *Hail, Caesar!* was already half over, they went instead for a cheap Italian meal and parted, at least superficially, on good terms.

Nevertheless, Robin's mood remained low as she set off north in her old Land Rover the following morning. Yet again, she'd been forced to face the difficulty of reconciling any kind of normal personal life with her chosen line of work. She'd thought it might be easier with Ryan, given his profession, but here she was again, justifying commitments she knew he wouldn't have given a second thought to, had he been the one making them.

Her journey up the M1 was uneventful and therefore offered few distractions from her unsatisfactory musings. However, as she approached Newport Pagnell service station, where she'd been planning to stop for a coffee, Ilsa called. The Land Rover didn't have Bluetooth, so Robin waited until she was in Starbucks before ringing Ilsa back.

'Hi,' she said, trying to sound more cheerful than she felt, 'what's up?'

'Nothing, really,' said Ilsa. 'Just wondered whether Corm's said anything to you.'

'About Bijou?' said Robin, who couldn't be bothered to pretend she didn't know what Ilsa was talking about. 'Other than accusing me of talking to you behind his back, no.'

'Oh God,' groaned Ilsa. 'I'm sorry. I was only trying to warn him—'

'I know,' sighed Robin, 'but you know what he's like.'

'Nick says I should apologise, which is nice bloody solidarity from my husband, I must say. I'd like to see Nick's face if Bijou gets herself knocked up on purpose. I don't s'pose you know—?'

'Ilsa,' said Robin, cutting across her friend, 'if you're about to ask me whether I quiz Strike on his contraceptive habits—'

'You realise she told me – with five other people within earshot, incidentally – that she took a used condom out of the bin, while she was having an affair with that married QC, and inserted it inside herself?'

'Jesus,' said Robin, startled, and very much wishing she hadn't been given this information, 'well, I – I suppose that's Strike's lookout, isn't it?'

'I was trying to be a good friend,' said Ilsa, sounding frustrated. 'However much of a dickhead he is, I don't want him paying child support to bloody Bijou Watkins for the next eighteen years. She'd make a nightmarish mother, nearly as bad as Charlotte Campbell.'

By the time Robin got back in the Land Rover, she felt more miserable than ever, and it took a considerable effort of will to refocus her attention on the job in hand.

She arrived in Sheila Kennett's road at five minutes to twelve. As she locked up the Land Rover, Robin wondered how, given what Kevin Pirbright had said about church members sinking all of their money into the UHC, Sheila had managed to afford even this small bungalow, shabby though it looked.

When she rang the doorbell she heard footsteps of a speed that surprised her, given that Sheila Kennett was eighty-five years old.

The door opened to reveal a tiny old woman whose thinning grey hair was worn in a bun. Her dark eyes, of which both irises showed marked *arcus senilis,* were enormously enlarged by a pair of powerful bifocals. Slightly stooped, Sheila wore a loose red dress, navy carpet slippers, an oversize hearing aid, a tarnished gold wedding ring and a silver cross around her neck.

'Hello,' said Robin, smiling down at her. 'We spoke on the phone. I'm Robin Ellacott, the—'

'Private detective, are you?' said Sheila, in her slightly cracked voice.

'Yes,' said Robin, holding out her driving licence. 'This is me.'

Sheila blinked at the licence for a few seconds, then said,

'That's all right. Come in, then,' and moved aside for Robin to pass into the hall, which was carpeted in dark brown. The bungalow smelled slightly fusty.

'You go in there,' said Sheila, pointing Robin into the front room. 'Want tea?'

'Thank you – can I help?' asked Robin, as she watched the fragile-looking Sheila shuffling away towards the kitchen. Sheila made no answer. Robin hoped the hearing aid was turned up.

The peeling wallpaper and the sparse, shabby furniture spoke of poverty. A green sofa sat at right angles to a faded tartan chair with a matching footstool. The television was old, and beneath it sat an equally antiquated video player, while a rickety bookcase held a mixture of large-print novels. The only photograph in the room stood on top of the bookcase, and showed a 1960s wedding. Sheila and her husband, Brian, whose name Robin knew from the census reports, were pictured standing outside a registry office. Sheila, who'd been very pretty in her youth, wore her dark hair in a beehive, her full-skirted wedding dress falling to just beneath her knees. The picture was made touching by the fact that the slightly goofy-looking Brian was beaming, as though he couldn't believe his luck.

Something brushed Robin's ankle: a grey cat had just entered the room and was now staring up at her with its clear green eyes. As Robin bent to tickle it behind the ears, a tinkling sound announced the reappearance of Sheila, who was holding an old tin tray on which were two mugs, a jug and a plate of what Robin recognised as Mr Kipling's Bakewell slices.

'Let me,' said Robin, as some of the hot liquid had already spilled. Sheila let Robin lift the tray out of her hands and set it on the small coffee table. Sheila took her own mug, placed it on the arm of the tartan armchair, sat down, put her tiny feet on the stool, then said, peering at the tea tray,

'I forgot the sugar. I'll go—'

She began to struggle out of the chair again.

'That's fine, I don't take it,' said Robin hastily. 'Unless you do?'

Sheila shook her head and relaxed back into her chair. When Robin sat down on the sofa, the cat leapt up beside her and rubbed itself against her, purring.

'He's not mine,' said Sheila, watching the cat's antics. 'He's next door's, but he likes it here.'

'Clearly,' said Robin, smiling, as she ran her hand over the cat's arched back. 'What's his name?'

'Smoky,' said Sheila, raising her mug to her mouth. 'He likes it here,' she repeated.

'Would you mind if I take notes?' asked Robin.

'Write things down? That's all right,' said Sheila Kennett. While Robin took out her pen, Sheila made a kissing sound in the direction of Smoky the cat, but he ignored her, and continued to rub his head against Robin. 'Ungrateful,' said Sheila. 'I gave him tinned salmon last night.'

Robin smiled again before opening her notebook.

'So, Mrs Kennett—'

'You can call me Sheila. Why've you done that to your hair?'

'Oh – this?' said Robin self-consciously, raising a hand to the blue edges of her bob. 'I'm just trying it out.'

'Punk rock, is it?' said Sheila.

Deciding against telling Sheila she was approximately forty years out of date, Robin said,

'A bit.'

'You're a pretty girl. You don't want blue hair.'

'I'm thinking of changing it back,' said Robin. 'So . . . could I ask when did you and your husband go to live at Chapman Farm?'

'Wasn't called Chapman Farm then,' said the old lady. 'It was Forgeman Farm. Brian and me were hippies,' said Sheila,

174

blinking at Robin through the thick lenses of her glasses. 'You know what hippies are?'

'Yes,' said Robin.

'Well, that's what me and Brian was. Hippies,' said Sheila. 'Living on a commune. Hippies,' she said yet again, as though she liked the sound of the word.

'Can you remember when—?'

'Sixty-nine we went there,' said Sheila. 'When it was all starting. We grew pot. Know what pot is?'

'I do, yes,' said Robin.

'We used to smoke a lot of that,' said Sheila, with another little cackle.

'Who else was there at the beginning, can you remember?'

'Yes, I can remember all that,' said Sheila proudly. 'Rust Andersen. American, he was. Living in a tent up the fields. Harold Coates. I remember all that. Can't remember yesterday sometimes, but I remember all that. Coates was a nasty man. Very nasty man.'

'Why d'you say that?'

'Kids,' said Sheila. 'Don't you know about all that?'

'Are you talking about when the Crowther brothers were arrested?'

'That's them. Nasty people. Horrible people. Them and their friends.'

The cat's purrs filled the room as it lolled on its back, Robin stroking it with her left hand.

'Brian and me never knew what they were up to,' said Sheila. 'We never knew what was going on. We were busy growing and selling veg. Brian had pigs.'

'Did he?'

'He loved his pigs, and his chickens. Kids running around everywhere . . . I couldn't have none of my own. Miscarriages. I had nine, all told.'

'Oh, I'm so sorry,' said Robin.

'Never had none of our own,' repeated Sheila. 'We wanted kids, but we couldn't. There was loads of kids running around at the farm, and I remember your friend. Big lad. Bigger than some of the older boys.'

'Sorry?' said Robin, flummoxed.

'Your partner. Condoman Strike or something, isn't it?'

'That's right,' said Robin, looking at her curiously, and wondering whether the old lady, who might repeat herself a lot, but had seemed basically alert, was in fact senile.

'When I told Next Door you was coming to see me, she read me out an article about you and him. He was there, with his sister and his mum. I remember, because my Brian fancied Leda Strike and I could tell, and we had rows about it. Jealous. I'd see him watching her all the time. Jealous,' Sheila repeated. 'I don't think Leda would've looked at my Brian, though. He was no rock star, Brian.'

Sheila gave another cracked laugh. Doing her best to dissemble her shock, Robin said,

'Your memory's very good, Sheila.'

'Oh, I remember all what happened on the farm. Don't remember yesterday sometimes, but I remember all that. I helped little Ann give birth. Harold Coates was there. He was a doctor. I helped. She had a rough old time. Well ... she was only fourteen.'

'Really?'

'Yeah ... free love, see. It wasn't like it is now. It was different.'

'Was the baby—?'

'It was all right. Mazu, Ann called her, but Ann took off, not long after. Left her at the commune. Didn't like being a mother. Too young.'

'So who looked after Mazu?' asked Robin, 'Her father?'

'Don't know who her father was. I never knew who Ann was going with. People were sleeping with whoever. Not me and Brian, though. We were trying to have our own kids. Busy on the farm. We didn't know everything that was going on,' said Sheila, yet again. 'Police come into the farm, no warning. Somebody tipped them off. We was all questioned. My Brian was at the station for hours. They searched all the rooms. Went through all our personal things. Me and Brian left after that.'

'Did you?'

'Yeah. Awful,' said Sheila, and yet again, she emphasised, 'We didn't know. We never knew. It's not like they were doing it in the yard. We were busy with the farming.'

'Where did you go, when you left?'

'Here,' said Sheila, indicating the bungalow with her mottled hand. 'This was my mum and dad's place. Ooh, they were angry about all the things in the papers. And Brian couldn't get a job. I got one. Office clerk. I didn't like it. Brian missed the farm.'

'How long were you away, Sheila, can you remember?'

'Two years ... three years ... then Mazu wrote to us. She said it was all better and they had a good new community. Brian was good at the farming, see, that's why she wanted him ... so we went back.'

'Can you remember who was there, when you returned?'

'Don't you want a cake?'

'Thank you, I'd love one,' lied Robin, reaching for a Bakewell slice. 'Can I—?'

'No, I got them for you,' said Sheila. 'What did you just ask me?'

'About who was at Chapman Farm, when you went back there to live.'

'I don't know all the names. There was a couple of new families. Coates was still there. What did you ask me?'

'Just about the people,' said Robin, 'who were there when you went back.'

'Oh . . . Rust Andersen was still in his cabin. And the Graves boy – posh, skinny boy. He was new. He'd go up Rust's place and smoke half the night. Pot. D'you know what pot is?' she asked, again.

'I do, yes,' said Robin, smiling.

'It doesn't do some people any good,' said Sheila wisely. 'The Graves boy couldn't handle it. He went funny. Some people shouldn't smoke it.'

'Was Jonathan Wace at the farm, when you went back?' asked Robin.

'That's right, with his little girl, Abigail. And Mazu had a baby: Daiyu.'

'What did you think of Jonathan Wace?' asked Robin.

'Charming. That's what I thought, then. He took us all in. Charming,' she repeated.

'What made him come and live at the farm, d'you know?'

'No, I don't know why he came. I felt sorry for Abigail. Her mum died, then her dad brought her to the farm, and next minute she's got a sister . . .'

'And when did the whole idea of a church start up, can you remember?'

'That was because Jonathan used to give us talks about his beliefs. He had us meditating and he started making us go out on the street and collect money. People would come and listen to him talk.'

'Lots more people started coming to the farm, did they?'

'Yeah, and they were paying. Some of them were posh. Then Jonathan started going on trips, giving his talks. He left Mazu in charge. She'd grown her hair down to her waist – long black hair – and she was telling everyone she was half-Chinese, but she was never Chinese,' said Sheila scathingly. 'Her mum was

178

as white as you and me. There was no Chinese man, ever, at Chapman Farm. We never told her we knew she was lying, though. We were just happy to be back at the farm, me and Brian. What did you ask me?'

'Just about the church, and how it began.'

'Oh ... Jonathan was running courses, with his meditation and all his Eastern religions and things, and then he started taking services, so we built a temple at the farm.'

'And were you happy?' asked Robin.

Sheila blinked a few times before saying,

'It was happy sometimes. Sometimes it was. But bad things happened. Rust got hit by a car one night. Jonathan said it was a judgement, for all the lives Rust took in the war ... and then the Graves boy's family came and grabbed him off the street, when he was out in Norwich, and we heard he'd hanged himself. Jonathan told us that's what would happen to all of us, if we left. He said Alex had got a glimpse of truth, but he couldn't cope with the world outside. So that was a warning for us, Jonathan said.'

'Did you believe him?' asked Robin.

'I did then,' said Sheila. 'I believed everything Jonathan said, back then. So did Brian. Jonathan had a way of making you believe ... a way of making you want to make everything all right, for him. You wanted to look after him.'

'To look after Jonathan?'

'Yeah ... you should've seen him crying, when Rust and Alex died. He seemed to feel it worse than all the rest of us.'

'You said it was happy at the farm sometimes. Were there other times when—?'

'Nasty things started happening,' said the old lady. Her lips had started to tremble. 'It was Mazu, not Jonathan ... it wasn't Jonathan. It was her.'

'What kind of nasty things?' asked Robin, her pen poised over her notebook.

'Just ... punishments,' said Sheila, her lips still trembling. After a few seconds' silence, she said,

'Paul let the pigs out, by accident and Mazu made people hit him.'

'Can you remember Paul's surname?'

'Draper,' said Sheila, after a slight pause. 'Everyone called him Dopey. He wasn't normal. Bit retarded. They shouldn't have had him looking after the pigs. He left the gate open. Dopey Draper.'

'Do you know where he is now?'

Sheila shook her head.

'Do you remember a boy called Jordan whipping himself?'

'There was lots of times people was whipped. Yeah, I remember Jordan. Teenager.'

'Would you happen to remember his surname, Sheila?'

Sheila thought a little, then said,

'Reaney. Jordan Reaney. He was a rough sort. Been in trouble with the police.'

As Robin made a note of Jordan's surname, the cat beside her, bored of inattention, leapt lightly off the sofa and stalked out of the room.

'Everything got worse after Daiyu died,' said Sheila, unprompted. 'You know who Daiyu was?'

'Jonathan and Mazu's daughter,' said Robin. 'She drowned, didn't she?'

'That's right. Cherie took her to the beach.'

'This is Cherie Gittins?' asked Robin.

'That's right. Silly girl, she was. Daiyu bossed her around.'

'Would you happen to know what happened to Cherie after Daiyu died, Sheila?'

'Punished,' said Sheila. She now looked very distressed. 'All them who were involved were punished.'

'What d'you mean, "all of them", Sheila?'

'Cherie, and the ones who didn't stop it. The ones who

saw them leaving in the truck that morning – but they didn't know! They thought Daiyu had permission! My Brian, and Dopey Draper, and little Abigail. They was all punished.'

'Hit?' asked Robin tentatively.

'No,' said Sheila, suddenly agitated. 'Worse. It was wicked.'

'What—?'

'Never you mind,' said Sheila, her small hands balled into shaking fists. 'Least said about that . . . but they knew Brian was ill when they did it to him. He kept losing his balance. Jonathan had been telling him to go and pray in temple, and then he'd be better. But after they punished him, he was much worse. He couldn't see properly, and they still made him get up and go collecting on the street . . . and in the end,' said Sheila, her agitation increasing, 'Brian was screaming and moaning. He couldn't get out of bed. They carried him into the temple. He died on the temple floor. I was with him. He'd been quiet for a whole day, and then he died. All stiff on the temple floor. I woke up next to him and I knew he was dead. His eyes were open . . .'

The old lady began to weep. Robin, who felt desperately sorry for her, glanced around the room for a sign of a tissue.

'Tumour,' sobbed Sheila. 'That's what he had. They opened him up to find out what it was. Tumour.'

She wiped her nose on the back of her hand.

'Let me . . .' said Robin, getting up and leaving the room. In the small bathroom off the hall, which had an old pink sink and bath, she pulled off a length of toilet roll and hurried back to the sitting room to give it to Sheila.

'Thanks,' said Sheila, wiping her eyes and blowing her nose as Robin sat back down on the sofa.

'Is that when you left for good, Sheila?' Robin asked. 'After Brian died?'

Sheila nodded, tears still trickling out from behind the bifocals.

'And they threatened me, trying to stop me going. They said I was a bad person and they'd tell everyone I'd been cruel to Brian, and they said they knew I'd taken money, and they'd seen me hurting the animals on the farm ... I *never* hurt an animal, I never did ...

'*Wicked,*' she said, with a sob. '*Wicked*, they are. I thought he was so good, Jonathan. He said to me, "Brian was nearly better, Sheila, but he wasn't pure spirit yet, and that's why he died. You stopped him being pure spirit, shouting at him and not being a good wife." He *wasn't* nearly better,' said Sheila, with another sob. 'He wasn't. He couldn't see properly and he couldn't walk right, and they did terrible things to him and then they were yelling at him because he hadn't collected enough money on the street.'

'I'm so sorry, Sheila,' said Robin quietly. 'I really am. I'm so sorry.'

A loud mew pierced the silence. Smoky the cat had reappeared.

'He's after food,' said Sheila tearfully. 'It isn't time,' she told the cat. 'You'll have me in trouble with Next Door if I start giving you lunch.'

Sheila seemed exhausted. Robin, who didn't want to leave her in this state, turned the conversation gently to cats and their vagrant habits. After ten minutes or so, Sheila had regained her composure sufficiently to talk about her own cat, who'd been run over in the street outside, but Robin could tell her distress still lay close to the surface and felt it would be cruel to press for further reminiscences.

'Thank you so much for talking to me, Sheila,' she said at last. 'Just one last question, if you don't mind. Do you know when Cherie Gittins left Chapman Farm? Would you have any idea where she is now?'

'She left not long after Brian died. I don't know where she

went. It was her fault it all happened!' she said, with a resurgence of anger. 'It was all her fault!'

'Is there anything I can do for you, before I go?' asked Robin, returning her notebook to her bag. 'Maybe call your neighbour? It might be good to have some company.'

'Are you going to stop them?' asked Sheila tearfully, ignoring Robin's suggestion.

'We're going to try,' said Robin.

'*You need to stop them*,' said Sheila fiercely. 'We were hippies, Brian and me, that's all. Hippies. We never knew what it was all going to turn into.'

17

*For youthful folly it is the most hopeless thing to
entangle itself in empty imaginings.
The more obstinately it clings to such unreal fantasies,
the more certainly will humiliation overtake it.*

The I Ching or Book of Changes

'You got a hell of a lot out of her,' said Strike. 'Excellent work.'

Robin, who was sitting in the parked Land Rover eating a tuna sandwich she'd bought from a nearby café, hadn't been able to resist calling Strike after leaving Sheila. He sounded considerably less grumpy than the last time they'd spoken.

'Awful, though, isn't it?' she said. 'Nobody getting her poor husband any medical help.'

'Yeah, it is. Trouble is, he made the choice not to go to hospital, didn't he? So it'd be very hard to make a criminal charge stick. It's not like Margaret Cathcart-Bryce, who was actively asking for a doctor.'

'Allegedly asking,' said Robin. 'We've got no corroboration for that.'

'Yeah, that's the problem,' said Strike, who was currently standing in the street outside the Frank brothers' block of flats. 'What we really need is something criminal that had multiple eyewitnesses who're prepared to stand up in court and talk, which I'm starting to think is going to be a bloody tall order.'

184

'I know,' said Robin. 'I can't see Sheila's accounts of beatings and whippings being believed after all this time without corroboration. I'll start looking for Paul Draper and Jordan Reaney, though.'

'Great,' said Strike. 'With luck, they can confirm their own and each other's assaults – oh, here he comes.'

'Who?'

'One of the Franks. I can't tell them apart.'

'Frank One's got a bit of a squint and Frank Two's balder.'

'It's Two, then,' said Strike, watching the man. 'Hope he's heading for central London, otherwise I'll have to get Dev to take over from me early. I'm interviewing the Facebook friend of housing heiress Flora Brewster at six. He called me last night.'

'Oh, great. Where are you meeting him?'

'The Grenadier pub, Belgravia,' said Strike, setting off after his target, who was heading for the station. 'His choice. Apparently it's near his place of work. He also claims we've got a mutual friend.'

'Probably a client,' said Robin. The number of very rich Londoners who'd come to the agency for help had been steadily increasing, year on year, and they'd recently done jobs for a couple of billionaires.

'So that's all Sheila said, is it?' asked Strike.

'Er – yes, I think so,' said Robin. 'I'll write up my notes and email them to you.'

'Great. Well, I'd better go, we're heading for a train. Safe travels.'

'OK, bye,' said Robin, and hung up.

She sat for a moment, contemplating the last bit of her sandwich, which was very dry, before putting it back into its paper bag and reaching instead for a yoghurt and a plastic spoon. Her slight hesitation before answering Strike's last question was due to the fact that she'd omitted mention of his presence at the Aylmerton Community as a boy. Robin assumed that Strike didn't want to talk about that, given that he hadn't revealed it himself.

Unaware how close he'd come to a conversation he definitely didn't want to have, Strike spent the journey into London feeling slightly less disgruntled at the world after restoring friendly relations with Robin. His mood was further elevated, though for less sentimental reasons, when Frank Two led him to Notting Hill, then made his way to the very terrace of pastel-coloured houses where their client, actress Tasha Mayo, lived.

'He's been skulking behind parked cars, looking up at her windows,' Strike told Dev Shah an hour later, when the latter turned up to take over surveillance. 'I've taken a few pictures. He hasn't glued up any keyholes yet.'

'Probably waiting for night time,' said Shah. 'More romantic.'

'Have you spoken to Littlejohn lately?' Strike asked.

'"Spoken",' repeated Shah, musingly. 'No, I don't think you could call it speaking. Why?'

'What d'you think of him?' said Strike. 'Off the record?'

'Weird,' said Shah flatly, looking directly at his boss.

'Yeah, I'm starting to—'

'Here she is,' said Shah.

The door of the actress's house had opened and a slight, short-haired blonde stepped out onto the pavement, a holdall over her shoulder. She set off at a brisk walk in the direction of the Tube, reading something off her phone as she went. The younger Frank took off in pursuit, his mobile raised: he seemed to be filming her.

'Creepy fucker,' were Shah's last words before setting off, leaving Strike free to proceed to the Grenadier.

Henry Worthington-Fields' chosen venue for his meeting with Strike was a pub the detective had visited years previously, because it had been a favourite of Charlotte's and her well-heeled friends. The smartly painted frontage was red, white and blue; flower baskets hung beside the windows and a scarlet guard's box stood outside the door.

The interior was exactly as Strike remembered it: military prints and paintings on the walls, highly polished tables, red leather benches and hundreds of banknotes in different currencies pinned up on the ceiling. The pub was supposed to be haunted by a soldier who'd been beaten to death after being discovered cheating at cards. The money left by visitors was to pay the ghost's debt, but this hadn't worked, as the spectral soldier continued to haunt the pub – or so the tourist-friendly story went.

Aside from a couple of Germans, who were discussing the banknotes on the ceiling, the clientele was English, the men mostly dressed in suits or the kinds of coloured chinos favoured by the upper classes, the women in smart dresses or jeans. Strike ordered himself a pint of zero-alcohol beer and sat down to drink it while reading Fergus Robertson's article about the forthcoming Brexit referendum off his phone, glancing up regularly to see whether his interviewee had yet arrived.

Strike guessed Henry Worthington-Fields' identity as soon as he entered the pub, mainly because he had the wary look common to those about to speak to a private detective. Henry was thirty-four years old, though he looked younger. Tall, thin and pale, with a mop of wavy red hair, he wore horn-rimmed glasses, a well-tailored, single-breasted pin-striped suit and a flamboyant red tie patterned with horseshoes. He looked as though he worked either in an art gallery, or as a salesman of luxury goods, either of which would have fitted with the Belgravia location.

Having bought himself what looked like a gin and tonic, Henry peered at Strike for a second or two, then approached his table.

'Cormoran Strike?' His voice was upper class and very slightly camp.

'That's me,' said Strike, holding out a hand.

Henry slid onto the bench opposite the detective.

'I thought you'd be, like, hiding behind a newspaper. Eyeholes cut out or something.'

'I only do that when I'm following someone on foot,' said Strike, and Henry laughed: a nervous laugh, which went on a little longer than the joke warranted.

'Thanks for meeting me, Henry, I appreciate it.'

'That's OK,' said Henry.

He took a sip of gin.

'I mean, when I got your message, I was kind of freaked out, like, *who is this guy?* But I looked you up, and Charlotte told me you're a good person, so I—'

'Charlotte?' repeated Strike.

'Yeah,' said Henry. 'Charlotte Ross? I know her from the antiques shop where I work – Arlington and Black? She's redecorating her house, we've found a couple of really nice pieces for her. I knew from looking you up that you two used to – so I rang her – she's lovely, she's, like, one of my favourite clients – and I said, "Hey, Charlie, should I talk to this guy?" or whatever, and she said, "Yeah, definitely", so – yeah – here I am.'

'Great,' said Strike, determinedly keeping both tone and expression as pleasant as he could make them. 'Well, as I said in my message, I noticed you've been quite outspoken about the UHC on your Facebook page, so I—'

'Yeah, so, OK,' said Henry, shifting uncomfortably in his seat, 'I need to say – I wanted to say, like, before we get into

188

it – it's kind of a condition, actually – you won't go after Flora, will you? Because she's still not right. I'm only talking to you so she doesn't have to. Charlotte said you'd be OK with that.'

'Well, it's not really Charlotte's call,' said Strike, still forcing himself to sound pleasant, 'but if Flora's having mental health problems—'

'She is, she's never been right since she left the UHC. But I really feel, like – well, somebody needs to hold the UHC accountable,' said Henry. 'So I'm happy to talk, but only if you don't go near Flora.'

'Is she still in New Zealand?'

'No, it didn't work out, she's back in London, but – seriously – you can't talk to her. Because I think it might tip her over the edge. She can't stand talking about it any more. Last time she told anyone what happened she tried to kill herself, afterwards.'

Notwithstanding Henry's fondness for Charlotte (gay men, in Strike's experience, were the most likely to see no flaw in his beautiful, funny and immaculately dressed ex), Strike had to respect Henry for his wish to protect his friend.

'OK, agreed. So: have you ever had direct contact with the UHC yourself?'

'Yeah, when I was eighteen. I met this guy in a bar, and he said I should come along to Chapman Farm, to do a course. Yoga and meditation and stuff. He was hot,' Henry added, with yet another nervous laugh. 'Good-looking older guy.'

'Did he talk about religion at all?'

'Not like – more like spirituality, you know? He made it sound interesting and cool. Like, he was talking about fighting, like, materialism and capitalism, but he also said you could learn – I know this sounds crazy, but kind of learn ... not magic, but to make things happen with your own power, if you studied enough ... I'd just finished school, so ... I thought

I'd go along and see what it was about and – yeah, I asked Flora to come with me. We were school friends, we were at Marlborough together. We were kind of like – we were both gay or whatever, and we were into stuff nobody else was, so I said to Flora, "Come with me, we'll just do a week there, it'll be a laugh." It was just, like, something to do in the holidays, you know?'

'Are you all right with me taking notes?'

'Er . . . yeah, OK,' said Henry. Strike took out his notebook and pen.

'So, you were approached in a bar – where was this, London?'

'Yeah. It isn't there any more, the bar. It wasn't far from here, actually.'

'What was the man called who invited you, can you remember?'

'Joe,' said Henry.

'Was this a gay bar?'

'Not a *gay* bar,' said Henry, 'but the guy who ran it was gay, so, yeah . . . it was a cool place, so I thought, like, this guy, Joe, must be cool, too.'

'And this was in 2000?'

'Yeah.'

'How did you and Flora travel to Chapman Farm?'

'I drove, thank God,' added Henry fervently, 'because then I had the car there, so I could get away. Most of the other people had come on a minibus, so they had to wait for the minibus to take them back. I was really fucking glad I took my car.'

'And what happened when you got there?'

'Er – well, you had to check in all your stuff and they gave you these tracksuits to wear, and after we changed, they made us all sit down in this barn, or whatever, and Flora and I were looking sideways at each other, and we were, like, cracking up. We were thinking, "What the fuck have we done, coming here?"'

'Then what happened?'

'Then we went to this big communal meal, and before the food arrived, they played "Heroes", by David Bowie. Over speakers. Yeah, and then ... he came in. Papa J.'

'Jonathan Wace?'

'Yeah. And he talked to us.'

Strike waited.

'And, I mean, you can see how people fall for it,' said Henry uneasily. 'While he was talking, it was like, he was saying, people chase things, all their lives, that never make them happy. People die miserable, and frustrated, and they never, kind of, realise it was all there for them to find. Like, the true way, or whatever. But he said, people get, like, buried in all this materialistic bullshit ... and he was really ... he's got something,' said Henry. 'He wasn't, like, some big shouty guy – he wasn't what you'd think. Flora and I felt like – we discussed it, afterwards – he was, like, one of us.'

'What d'you mean by that?'

'Like, he got what it's like, to be ... what it feels like, not to be ... like, to be different, you know? Or maybe you don't, I don't know,' Henry added, with a laugh and a shrug. 'But Flora and I weren't taking the piss any more, we kind of ... yeah, anyway, we went off to our dormitories. Separate, obviously. They put men and women in different dorms. It was kind of like being back in boarding school, actually,' said Henry, with another little laugh.

'Next day, they woke us up at, like, 5 a.m. or something, and we had to go and do meditation before breakfast. Then, after we'd eaten, we got split into separate groups. I wasn't with Flora. They split up people who knew each other.

'And after that it was, like, really intense. You hardly had a minute to think and you were never alone. There were always UHC people with you, talking to you. You were either in a lecture, or you were chanting in the temple, or you were helping work the land, or feeding the livestock, or making stuff to sell on the street, or cooking, and people were constantly reading UHC literature to you … oh yeah, and there were discussion groups, where you all sat around and listened to one of the UHC people talk and you asked questions. You had activities until, like, 11 o'clock at night, and you were so tired at the end of the day, you could hardly think, and then it all started at 5 a.m. again.

'And they taught you these techniques that – like, if you had a negative thought, like, about the church, or about anything, really, you had to chant. They called it killing the false self, because, like, the false self is going to struggle against the good, because it's been indoctrinated by society to think certain things are true, when they're not, and you've got to fight your false self constantly to keep your mind open enough to accept the truth.

'It was just a couple of days, but it felt like a month. I was so tired, and really hungry most of the time. They told us that was deliberate, that fasting sharpens perception.'

'And how did you feel about the church, while all this was going on?'

Henry drank more gin and tonic before saying,

'For the first couple of days, I was thinking, *I can't wait for this to fucking end*. But there were a couple of guys in there, proper members, who were really friendly and helped me do stuff, and they seemed really happy – and it was, like – it was a different world, you kind of lost – lost your bearings, I s'pose. Like, they're constantly telling you how great you are, and you started wanting their approval,' said Henry uncomfortably. 'You couldn't help it. And all this talk about pure spirit – they made it sound like you'd be a superhero or something, once you were pure spirit. I know that sounds insane, but – if you'd been there – it didn't sound insane, the way they were talking.

'On the third day, Papa J gave another big speech in the temple – it wasn't the kind of temple like they've got now, because this was before the really big money started coming in. The farm temple was just another barn, then, but they'd made it the nicest building and painted the inside with all these different symbols across religions, and put an old bit of carpet down where we all sat.

'Papa J talked about what will happen if the world doesn't wake up, and basically the message was: normal religions divide, but the UHC unites, and when people unite across cultures, and when they become the highest version of themselves, they'll be an unstoppable force and they can change the world. And there were loads of black and brown people at Chapman Farm, as well as white people, so that seemed, like, proof of what he was saying. And I – you just believed him. It sounded – there was nothing there you could, like, disagree with – ending poverty and all that, and becoming your highest self – and Papa J was just, like, someone you'd want to hang out with. Like, he was really warm and he seemed – he was, like, the dad you'd have if you could choose, you know?'

'So what changed your mind? Why did you leave, at the end of the week?'

The smile faded off Henry's face.

'Something happened and it kind of . . . kind of altered how I felt about them all.

'There was this really heavily pregnant woman at the farm. I can't remember her name. Anyway, she was with our group one afternoon when we were ploughing, with Shire horses, and it was bloody hard work, and I kept looking at her and thinking, *should she be doing this?* But, you know, I was eighteen, so what did I know?

'And we'd just finished up the last bit we were supposed to be doing, and she kind of doubled over. She was kneeling in the earth in her tracksuit, and clutching her belly. I was terrified, I thought she was going to, like, give birth there and then.

'And one of the other members knelt down beside her, but he didn't help her or anything, he just started chanting loudly in her face. And then the others started chanting. And I was watching this, and I was thinking, "Why aren't they helping her up?" But I was kind of ... paralysed,' said Henry, looking shamefaced. 'It was, like – this is how they do things here and maybe ... maybe it'll work? So I didn't – but she was looking really ill, and finally one of them ran off towards the farmhouse, while everyone else was still chanting at her.

'And the guy who'd gone to get help came back with Wace's wife.'

For the first time, Henry hesitated.

'She's ... she was creepy. I liked Wace at the time, but there was something about her ... I couldn't see why they were together. Anyway, when she reached us, everyone stopped chanting, and Mazu stood over this woman and just ... *stared at her.* She didn't even speak. And the pregnant woman just looked terrified and she kind of struggled up, and she still looked like she was in a load of pain or was going to pass out, but she staggered off with Mazu.

'And none of the others would look me in the eye. They acted like nothing had happened. I looked for the pregnant woman at dinner that evening, but she wasn't there. I didn't actually see her again, before I left.

'I wanted to talk to Flora about what had happened, but I couldn't get near enough and obviously she was in a different dormitory at night.

'Then, on the last night, we had another talk from Papa J, in the temple. They turned out all the lights and he stood in front of this big water trough, which was lit up inside, like, with underwater lights, and he made the water do stuff. Like, it rose up when he commanded it to, and made spiral shapes, and then he parted it and made it come back together . . .

'It spooked me,' said Henry. 'I kept thinking, "It's got to be a trick," but I couldn't see how he was doing it. Then he made the water make a face, a human face. One girl screamed. And then all the water settled down again and they put on the temple lights, and Papa J said, "We had a spirit visitor at the end, there. They come, sometimes, especially if there are many Receptives gathered together." And he said he thought the new intake must be particularly receptive for that to happen.

'And then we were asked whether we were ready to be reborn. And people walked forwards one by one and got into the trough, went under the water and were pulled out again, and everyone was clapping and cheering, and Papa J hugged them, and they went to stand beside the wall with the other members.

'I was shitting myself,' said Henry. 'I can't even explain – it was, like, the pressure to join, and to have all these people approve of you, was really intense, and everyone was watching, and I didn't know what was going to happen if I said no.

'And then they called Flora forwards, and she just walked straight to the trough, got in, went under, was pulled out and she went to stand against the wall, beaming.

'And I swear, I didn't know if I was going to have the strength to say no, but *thank God* there was this girl ahead of me, a black girl with a tattoo of the Buddha on the back of her neck, and I've never forgotten her, because if she hadn't been there . . . so, they called her name, and she said, "No, I don't want to join." Like, really loud and clear. And the atmosphere just turned to *ice*. Everyone was, like, glaring at her. And Papa

J was the only one who was still smiling, and he gave her this whole spiel about how he knew the material world had a strong allure, and basically, he was implying she wanted to go and work for Big Oil or something, instead of saving the world. But she didn't budge, even though she got kind of tearful.

'And then they called my name, and I said, "I don't want to join, either." And I saw Flora's face. It was like I'd slapped her.

'Then they called the last two people forwards, and they both joined.

'Then, while everyone's cheering and clapping all the new members, Mazu came up to me and the girl who'd said no and said, "You two come with me," and I said, "I want to speak to Flora first, I came with her," and Mazu said, "She doesn't want to talk to you." Flora was already being led off with all the members. She didn't even look back.

'Mazu took us back to the farmhouse and said, "The minibus won't be leaving until tomorrow, so you'll have to stay here in the meantime," and she showed us this little room with no beds, and bars over the window. And I said, "I came in a car," and I said to the girl, "D'you want a lift back to London?" and she agreed, so we went . . .

'Sorry, I really need another drink,' said Henry weakly.

'It's on me,' said Strike, getting to his feet.

When he'd returned to the table with a fresh gin and tonic for Henry, he found the younger man wiping the lenses of his glasses with his silk tie, looking shaken.

'Thanks,' he said, putting his glasses back on, accepting the glass and taking a large swig. 'God, just talking about it . . . and I was only there a week.'

Strike, who'd made extensive notes on everything Henry had just said, now flipped back a couple of pages.

'This pregnant woman who collapsed – you never saw her again?'

'No,' said Henry.

'What did she look like?' asked Strike, picking up his pen again.

'Er . . . blonde, glasses . . . I can't really remember.'

'Did you ever see violence used against anyone at Chapman Farm?'

'No,' said Henry, 'but Flora definitely did. She told me, when she got out.'

'Which was when?'

'Five years later. I heard she was home, and I called her. We met up for a drink, and I was really shocked at how she looked. She was so thin. She looked really ill. And she wasn't right. In the head.'

'In what way?'

'God, just in – in *every* way. She'd talk kind of normally for a bit, then she'd start laughing at nothing. Like, this really artificial laugh. Then she'd try and stop, and she said to me "That's me putting on my happy face", and – I don't know if it was something they were forced to do, like, laugh if they felt sad or whatever, but it was fucking freaky. And she kept chanting. It was like she had no control over herself.

'I asked her why she'd left and she told me bad things had gone down, but she didn't want to talk about them, but after she'd had two drinks she, like, started spilling all this stuff. She said she'd been flogged, with a belt, and she told me about the sex stuff, like, she had to sleep with whoever they told her to, and she kept laughing and trying to stop herself – it was horrible, seeing her like that. And after a third drink,' said Henry, dropping his voice, 'she said she'd seen the Drowned Prophet kill somebody.'

Strike looked up from his notebook.

'But she wouldn't say – like, she didn't give me details,' said Henry quickly. 'It might've been something she – not imagined, but – I mean, she wasn't right. She was fucking terrified after she'd said it, though. She was drunk,' said Henry, 'she'd got rat-arsed on three drinks. She hadn't had alcohol for five years, so obviously . . .'

'Didn't she tell you who'd been killed?'

'No, the only thing she said was that more people than her had witnessed it. She said something like, "Everyone was there." Then she got really, properly panicky, and told me she hadn't meant it, and I should forget it, that the Drowned Prophet would come for her next, because she'd talked. I said, "It's OK, I know you were just joking . . . "'

'Did you believe that? That it was a joke?'

'No,' said Henry uncertainly, 'she definitely wasn't joking, but – like, nobody's reported anything like that, have they? And if there were a load of witnesses, you'd think someone would have gone to the police, wouldn't you? Maybe the church made it look like someone had been killed, to scare people?'

'Maybe,' said Strike.

Henry now checked the time on his watch.

'I'm actually supposed to be somewhere in twenty minutes. Is that—?'

'Just a couple more questions, if you don't mind,' said Strike. 'This Joe individual, who recruited you. Did you see much of him, once you were at the farm?'

'He was kind of around,' said Henry. 'But I never really got to talk to him again.'

'What was he doing in a bar? Alcohol's forbidden by the church, isn't it?'

'Yeah,' said Henry. 'I don't know . . . maybe he was drinking a soft drink?'

'OK . . . were there a lot of children around, at the farm?'

'Quite a few, yeah. There were some families staying there.'

'Can you remember a man called Harold Coates? He was a doctor.'

'Er . . . maybe,' said Henry. 'Kind of an old guy?'

'He'd have been fairly old by then, yes. Did you ever see him around the kids?'

'No, I don't think so.'

'OK, well, I think that's everything,' said Strike, now pulling a business card out of his wallet. 'If you remember anything else, anything you'd like to tell me, give me a ring.'

'I will,' said Henry, taking the card before gulping down the rest of his second gin and tonic.

'I appreciate you meeting me, Henry, I really do,' said Strike, getting to his feet to shake hands.

'No problem,' said Henry, also standing. 'I hope I've been some use. I've always felt so shit about having taken Flora there in the first place, so . . . yeah . . . that's why I agreed to talk to you. Well, bye then. Nice meeting you.'

As Henry walked towards the door, a dark woman entered the pub, and with anger and a sense of absolute inevitability, Strike recognised Charlotte Ross.

18

Thunder and wind: the image of DURATION.
Thus the superior man stands firm
And does not change his direction.

The I Ching or Book of Changes

Strike had suspected Charlotte was on her way from the moment Henry had mentioned their mutual connection. Heads were turning; Strike had watched this happen for years; she had the kind of beauty that ran through a room like an icy breeze. As she and Henry made exclamations of surprise (on Henry's side, probably genuine) and exchanged pleasantries at the door, Strike gathered up his things.

'Corm,' said a voice behind him.

'Hello, Charlotte,' he said, with his back to her. 'I'm just leaving.'

'I need to talk to you. Please. For five minutes.'

'Afraid I've got to be somewhere.'

'Corm, *please*. I wouldn't ask if it wasn't – *please*,' she said again, more loudly.

He knew she was capable of making a scene if she didn't get what she wanted. She was a newsworthy woman, and he, too, was now of interest to the papers, and he feared that, if such a scene happened, there would be gossip, and maybe a leak to a journalist.

'OK, I'll give you five minutes,' he said coldly, sitting back down with the last inch of his non-alcoholic beer.

'Thank you,' she said breathlessly, and immediately departed for the bar, to buy herself a glass of wine.

She returned within a couple of minutes, shrugged off her black coat to reveal a dark green silk dress, which was cinched at the waist with a heavy black belt, then took the seat Henry had just vacated. She was thinner than he'd ever seen her, though as beautiful as ever, even at the age of forty-one. Her long dark hair fell to beneath her shoulders; her mottled green eyes were fringed with thick, natural lashes, and if she was wearing make-up, it was too subtle to see.

'I knew you'd be here, as you've probably gathered,' she said, smiling, willing him to smile back, to laugh at her cunning. 'I suggested this pub to Hen. He's lovely, isn't he?'

'What d'you want?'

'You've lost a ton of weight. You look great.'

'What,' Strike repeated, 'do you want?'

'To talk.'

'About . . .'

'This is difficult,' said Charlotte, taking a sip of wine. 'OK? I need a moment.'

Strike checked his watch. Charlotte glared at him over the rim of her wine glass.

'OK, fine. I've just found out I've got cancer.'

Whatever Strike had expected, it wasn't that. As unpalatable and possibly unjustified as the suspicion might have been, he found himself wondering whether she was lying. He knew her to be not only highly manipulative, but reckless – sometimes self-destructively so – in pursuit of what she wanted.

'I'm sorry to hear that,' he said formally.

She looked at him, her colour slowly rising.

'You think I'm lying, don't you?'

'No,' said Strike. 'That'd be a fucking despicable thing to lie about.'

'Yes,' said Charlotte, 'it would. Are you going to ask me what kind, or how—?'

'I thought you were about to tell me,' said Strike.

'Breast,' she said.

'Right,' said Strike. 'Well. I hope you're OK.'

Tears filled her eyes. He'd seen her cry hundreds of times, out of distress, certainly, but also from rage, and being thwarted, and he wasn't moved.

'That's all you've got to say?'

'What else can I say?' he said. 'I *do* hope you're OK. For your kids' sake, apart from anything else.'

'And that's ... that's *it*?' whispered Charlotte.

Once, she might have started screaming, indifferent to the presence of witnesses, but he could tell she knew that tactic would be unwise now that he wasn't bound to her.

'Charlotte,' he said in a low voice, leaning towards her to make sure he wasn't overheard, 'I don't know how many different ways I can make this clear to you. We're done. I wish you well, but we're finished. If you've got cancer—'

'So you *do* think I'm lying?'

'Let me finish. If you've got cancer, you should be focusing on your health and your loved ones.'

'My loved ones,' she repeated. 'I see.'

She sat back against the leather bench and wiped her eyes with the back of her hand. A couple of men at the bar were watching. Perhaps Charlotte, too, had sensed she had an audience, because she now covered her face with her hands and began to sob.

For fuck's sake.

'When were you diagnosed?' he asked her, to stop her crying.

202

She looked up at once, mopping her sparkling eyes.

'Last week. Friday.'

'How?'

'I went for a routine check on Tuesday, and . . . yeah, so they phoned me on Friday, and told me they'd found something.'

'And they already know it's cancer?'

'Yes,' she said, too fast.

'Well, as I say . . . I hope you're OK.'

He made to get up, but she reached across the table and grabbed his wrist tightly.

'Corm, please hear me out. Seriously. Please. *Please.* This is life and death. I mean, that makes a person . . . you remember,' she whispered, staring into his eyes, 'after you got your leg blown off . . . I mean, my God . . . it makes you realise what's important. After that, you wanted me. Didn't you? Wasn't I the only person in the world you wanted, then?'

'Did I?' said Strike, looking into her beautiful face. 'Or did I just take what was on offer, because it was easiest?'

She recoiled, letting go of his wrist.

All relationships have their own agreed mythology, and central to his and Charlotte's had been their shared belief that at the lowest point of his life, when he was lying in a hospital bed with half his leg and his military career gone, her return had saved him, giving him something to hold on to, to live for. He knew he'd just shattered a sacred taboo, desecrating what was for her not only a source of pride, but the foundation of her certainty that, however much he might deny it, he continued to love the woman who'd been generous enough to love a mutilated man now career-less and broke.

'I hope you'll be OK.'

He got to his feet before she could recover herself enough to retaliate, and walked out, half expecting a beer glass to hit him on the back of the head. By a happy stroke of providence, a vacant black cab slid into view as he stepped out onto the pavement and, barely two minutes after he'd left her, he was speeding away, back towards Denmark Street.

19

Nine at the top means:
The standstill comes to an end.

The I Ching or Book of Changes

'. . . a conspiracy so vast, it is literally unseeable, because we live within it, because it forms our sky and our earth, and so the only way – *the only way* – to escape, is to step, quite literally, into a different reality, the *true reality*.'

It was Saturday morning. Robin had been sitting in the Rupert Court Temple for three quarters of an hour. Today's speaker was the man she'd seen lecturing Will Edensor in Berwick Street, who'd introduced himself as Papa J's son, Taio. This had earned him a smattering of applause, in which Robin joined while recalling Kevin Pirbright's description of Taio as the UHC's 'volatile enforcer'.

Taio, who wore his hair in a dark, straggly bob, had the same large blue eyes as his father, and might also have had Jonathan's square jaw, had he not been carrying several stone of extra weight, which had added a second chin below the first. He put Robin in mind of an overfed rat: his nose was long and pointed and his mouth unusually small. Taio's speech was forceful and didactic, and while there were occasional murmurs of agreement from the congregation as he talked, nobody wept and nobody laughed.

In the front row of the temple sat the well-known novelist Giles Harmon, who Robin had recognised when he passed her in the entrance. A short man who wore his silver hair dandyishly long, Harmon had fine, almost delicate features, and carried himself self-consciously, like a man expecting to be watched. He'd been accompanied into the temple by a striking man of around forty, who had black hair, Eurasian features and a deep scar running down from the side of his nose, which was slightly crooked, to his jaw. The pair had moved up the aisle slowly, waving to acquaintances and temple attendants. Unlike Noli Seymour, the two men made no show of humility, but smiled approvingly as temple-goers made way for them, and moved a row back.

Get on with it, Robin thought wearily, as Taio continued to talk. Ryan had stayed over the previous evening, and after sex there'd been a lot of talk, primarily about the risks of going undercover. Robin was neither ignorant nor arrogant enough to think she stood in no need of advice, but her last thought before falling asleep was, *thank God I didn't tell you about the spirit bonding.*

At long last, Taio Wace wound up his talk. The applause, while respectable, wasn't as enthusiastic as it had been for either his father or Becca Pirbright. The temple lights brightened, and David Bowie began to sing again. Robin was deliberately slow to rise from her seat, fumbling over her Gucci handbag, hoping the blonde attendant was going to approach her again. Giles Harmon passed, nodding grandly to the left and right. His taller companion remained near the stage, the centre of a knot of people.

Robin lingered in the aisle, smiling vaguely, looking up at the Prophets painted on the ceiling as though it was the first time she'd seen them. She was almost directly beneath the Drowned Prophet in her white robes, with her malevolent black eyes, when a familiar voice said,

'Rowena?'

'Hi!' said Robin. The blonde who'd previously approached her had appeared, beaming as before and holding a pile of pamphlets that were thicker than those that usually lay on the shelves on the backs of the pews. 'It's so great you're here again!'

'I know,' said Robin, smiling back, 'I don't seem to be able to stay away, do I?'

As the blonde laughed, Robin became aware of someone standing immediately behind her. Turning, she found herself almost eye to eye with Taio Wace, and experienced a spasm of dislike. She couldn't remember ever having felt such a strong, immediate antipathy to a man, and it took every ounce of her self-discipline to smile back at him, wide-eyed and friendly, and say,

'That was so inspiring. Your talk, I mean. I really loved it.'

'*Thank* you,' he said, smiling complacently as he placed a hand lightly on her back. 'Very glad you enjoyed it.'

'This is Rowena, Taio,' said the blonde. 'I feel like she's—'

'*Very* much a Receptive,' said Taio Wace, his hand still resting lightly on Robin's bra strap. 'Yes, that's obvious.'

Robin felt a strong impulse to hit his arm away, but stood her ground, smiling.

'Would you be interested in coming to one of our retreats?' Taio asked.

'That's exactly what I was going to say!' said the blonde, beaming.

'What would that involve?' said Robin, every nerve protesting against the continuing pressure of Taio Wace's hand on her back.

'A week of your time,' he said, gazing into her eyes. 'At Chapman Farm. To explore things a little more deeply.'

'Oh, wow,' said Robin, 'that sounds interesting . . .'

'I think you'd find it very stimulating,' said Taio.

'It's really great,' the blonde assured Robin. 'Just to be with nature, and explore ideas and meditate . . .'

'Wow,' said Robin, again.

'Could you get time off work?' asked Taio, his hand still on Robin's back.

'I'm actually kind of between jobs at the moment,' said Robin.

'Perfect timing!' trilled the blonde.

'When would this be?' asked Robin.

'We've got a minibus leaving from outside Victoria Station at 10 a.m. next Friday,' said the blonde. 'We've actually got three groups coming to Chapman Farm that day. Here . . .'

She offered Robin one of the pamphlets in her hands.

'That's all the information you'll need, what to bring . . .'

'Thanks so much,' said Robin, smiling. 'Yes, I'd love to come!'

Taio Wace slid his hand down to the small of Robin's back before breaking contact.

'We'll see you on Friday, then,' he said, and moved away.

'This is so great,' said the blonde, embracing Robin, who laughed in surprise. 'You wait. Honestly, I've just got a feeling about you. You're going to go pure spirit really fast.'

Robin headed for the exit. Another female temple attendant was pressing one of the pamphlets on a thin, brown-skinned young man in glasses and a Spiderman T-shirt. The tall, handsome man with the scarred face was now chatting to one of the charity collectors on the door. As Robin made to pass him, his eyes flickered from her face to the pamphlet in her hand, and he smiled.

'Looking forward to seeing you at the farm,' he said, holding out a large, dry hand. 'Dr Zhou,' he added, in a tone that said *but of course, you knew that.*

'Oh, yes, I can't wait,' said Robin, smiling at him.

She was back on Wardour Street before she let her face relax from its fixed smile. After glancing over her shoulder to make sure there were no temple attendants in her vicinity, Robin pulled her mobile out of her handbag and called Strike.

'Third time lucky . . . I'm in.'

PART TWO

Shêng/Pushing Upward

Within the earth, wood grows:
The image of PUSHING UPWARD.
Thus the superior man of devoted character
Heaps up small things
In order to achieve something high and great.

The I Ching or Book of Changes

20

'Right then,' said Midge, who'd been back from her holiday in California for a week, but whose dark tan, which emphasised her grey eyes, showed no sign of fading. She smoothed out a map on the partners' desk. 'Here it is. Chapman Farm.'

It was Wednesday morning, and Strike had lowered the blinds in the inner office, to block out the watery April sunshine, which dazzled without warming. A desk lamp shone onto the map, on which were marked many annotations in red ink.

Barclay, Midge and Dev had spent the previous seven days rotating between London and Norfolk, making a careful survey of the environs of the UHC's base while ensuring that the cameras didn't pick up any individual face too often. Midge had used a couple of different wigs. They'd also affixed false number plates on each of their vehicles to drive around the farm's perimeter.

'These,' said Midge, pointing at a series of red crosses the three subcontractors had added to the periphery of Chapman

Farm's land, 'are cameras. They're serious about security. The whole perimeter's under surveillance. But there –' she pointed at a circled red mark, which was on the edge of a patch of woodland '– is the blind spot. Barclay found it.'

'You're sure?' said Strike, looking around at the Scot, who was drinking tea out of a Celtic mug, in what was usually Strike's chair.

'Aye,' said Barclay, leaning forwards to point. 'The two cameras either side are fixed tae trees, an' they're a wee bit too far apart. They've noticed it's nae properly covered, because they've fortified it. Extra barbed wire. The ground inside the fence was covered in nettles an' brambles, as well.'

'"Was"?' said Robin.

'Aye. I've cut a path through it. That's how I confirmed they can't see anything there: naebody came to tell me to get oot an' I was there a couple of hours. I got in over the barbed wire, nearly fuckin' castrated meself – ye're welcome – an' cut it all back. There's a wee clearing there now, hard by the road. If I hadnae done it,' Barclay told Robin, 'ye'd have had to explain why you keep gettin' covered in stings and lacerations.'

'Bloody good going,' said Strike.

'Thanks, Sam,' said Robin, warmly.

'Last thing we did was check what happens when they *do* see someone coming in over the perimeter fence, on the security camera,' said Midge, pointing to a circled blue cross. 'I climbed over the fence here. Five minutes later, I had a guy running towards me holding a scythe. I acted dumb. A rambler who thought the farm might have a nice shop. He believed me. The farm's up a track off a local walk, Lion's Mouth. Beauty spot.'

'OK,' said Strike, now lifting a realistic-looking plastic rock off a chair onto the desk, 'this is going to be at the blind spot, right by the perimeter fence.'

He opened it to show Robin the contents.

'Pencil torch and pen and paper, just in case they don't give you any inside. You write us a note, put it back in the rock and place it in the spot where the cameras can't see you. We collect it every Thursday evening at nine, put in a return message you can read on the spot, then tear up.

'If you skip a Thursday letter, one of us stays in the vicinity and keeps checking the rock. If we haven't heard from you by Saturday evening, we come in the front.'

'Too soon,' said Robin. 'Make it Sunday.'

'Why?'

'Because if I'm worried about hitting every Thursday dead-line, I'm at risk of messing up. I just want a bigger margin.'

'What instructions have they given you?' Midge asked Robin.

'No phones or any electronic devices. They say you can check them in when—'

'Don't take them,' said Midge and Barclay simultaneously.

'No, you definitely don't want the UHC having possession of your phone,' agreed Strike. 'Leave it here, in the office safe. House keys, as well. Take nothing in there that ties you to your real life.'

'And I'm to bring a waterproof coat,' said Robin, 'three changes of underwear, and that's it. You're given tracksuits to wear when you arrive, and you leave your daywear in a locker. No alcohol, sugar, cigarettes or drugs, prescription or otherwise—'

'They make you leave medication?' said Barclay.

'The body will heal itself if the spirit is pure enough,' said Robin, straight-faced.

'Fuck's sake,' muttered Barclay.

'Face it, the UHC doesn't want people who need medi-cation,' said Strike. 'No diabetic's going to stand up to that starvation regime for long.'

'And no toiletries. Those are all provided,' said Robin.

'You can't even take your own deodorant?' said Midge indignantly.

'They don't want you reminded of your life outside,' said Robin. 'They don't want you thinking of yourself as an individual.'

A few seconds' silence followed this remark.

'You're gonnae be all right, are ye?' said Barclay.

'Yes, I'll be fine. But if anything goes wrong, I've got you lot, haven't I? And my trusty rock.'

'Dev's going to drive up there tonight and put the rock in position,' said Strike. 'You might have to feel around a bit to find it. We want to make it look like it's been there forever.'

'Right,' said Barclay, slapping his thighs before getting to his feet, 'I'm off tae take over from Littlejohn. Frank One should be ready for a bit o' light stalking once he's had his lunch.'

'Yeah, I should go relieve Dev,' said Midge, checking her watch. 'See what Bigfoot's up to.'

'Has he met anyone yet?' said Robin, who'd been buried so deep in her preparation for Chapman Farm, and research on ex-UHC members, that she hadn't had time to read the Bigfoot file.

'He's been to Stringfellows,' said Midge dismissively, 'but the wife's not going to get half his business just because he had a lap dance ... not that I'm really arsed about her getting it, snotty cow.'

'We're Team Client, even if they're bastards,' said Strike.

'I know, I know,' said Midge, heading for the outer office, where her leather jacket was hanging up, 'but you get bored of helping out people who've never done a day's bloody work in their lives.'

'When I find a starving orphan who can afford to hire us, I'll pass them straight to you,' said Strike.

Midge returned a sardonic salute, then said to Robin,

'If I don't see you before you go in, good luck.'

'Thanks, Midge,' said Robin.

'Aye, best o' luck,' said Barclay. 'An' if the worst comes tae the worst, an' ye're on the verge of gettin' brainwashed, take a rusty nail and dig it intae the palm of your hand. Worked for Harry Palmer in the *The Ipcress File*.'

'Good advice,' said Robin. 'I'll try and smuggle one in.'

The two subcontractors left the office.

'I had something else to tell you,' Robin told Strike, now sitting down on her usual side of the partners' desk. 'I think I've found Jordan Reaney. The guy who was forced to whip himself across the face with the leather flail? He was using his middle name at Chapman Farm. His real name's Kurt.'

She typed 'Kurt Reaney' and swung the screen of her PC round to face Strike, who was confronted with the mugshot of a heavily tattooed man. An ace of spades was inked onto his left cheek, and a tattooed tiger covered his throat.

'He was sentenced to ten years for armed robbery and aggravated assault. Kurt Jordan Reaney,' said Robin, rolling her chair around the desk to contemplate the mugshot alongside Strike. 'He'll have been in his late teens when Sheila knew him, which fits. I've trawled through all the usual online records, and got as many addresses for him as I can find. There's a gap in online records from '93 to '96, then he reappears in a flat in Canning Town. We know the UHC Jordan was frightened of the police, because Kevin Pirbright said that's what Mazu was threatening him with, while she was making him whip himself.'

'Sounds like our guy,' said Strike, 'but you can't just ring up a bloke in jail.'

'Maybe a letter?' said Robin, though without much conviction.

'"Dear Mr Reaney, having seen your mugshot, you strike me

as the kind of bloke who'd very much like to help a criminal investigation ...'"

Robin laughed.

'What about next of kin?' said Strike.

'Well, there's a woman with the same surname living at his last address.'

'I'll try and get at him through her. What about the other kid who got beaten up?' said Strike. 'The one with the low IQ?'

'Paul Draper? Haven't found any trace of him yet. Cherie Gittins seems to have vanished off the face of the earth too.'

'OK, I'll keep digging on them while you're at Chapman Farm. I've left a message at Abigail Glover's fire station, as well.'

'Wace's daughter?'

'Exactly.'

Strike now moved to the door separating the inner office from the outer, where Pat sat typing, and closed it.

'Listen,' he said.

Robin braced herself, trying not to look exasperated. Murphy had said 'listen' in exactly that tone on Friday night, five minutes after ejaculating, and immediately before embarking on his prepared speech about the risks of going under deep cover.

'I wanted to tell you something, before you go in there.'

He looked serious, but hesitant, and Robin felt a tiny electric shock in the pit of her stomach, just as she had when Prudence said Robin was the most important person in Strike's life.

'There's a slight chance – *very* slight, actually, but it's still better you know – that someone in there might say something about me, so I wanted to forewarn you, so you don't look shocked and give yourself away.'

Now Robin knew what was coming, but said nothing.

'I was at the Aylmerton Community for six months, with

my mum and Lucy, back in 1985. I'm not saying people will remember *me*, I was just a kid, but my mother was a minor celebrity. Well, she'd been in the papers, anyway.'

For a few seconds, Robin debated what best to say, and decided on honesty.

'Actually, Sheila Kennett remembered you and your mum. I didn't want to say anything,' she added, 'unless you told me yourself.'

'Ah,' said Strike. 'Right.'

They looked at each other.

'Fucking terrible place,' said Strike bluntly, 'but nothing happened to me in there.'

He'd unintentionally placed a slight emphasis on the word 'me'.

'I've got another reason for telling you this,' said Strike. 'That Mazu woman. Don't trust her.'

'I won't, she sounds really—'

'No, I mean, don't assume there's any sense of – ' he groped for the right word '– you know – *sisterhood* there. Not when it comes to spirit bonding. If she wants to take you to some bloke—'

There came a knock on the door.

'What?' called Strike, with a trace of impatience.

Pat's monkeyish face appeared, scowling. She said to Strike, in her deep, gravelly voice,

'There's a woman on the phone, wanting to talk to you. Name of Niamh Doherty.'

'Put her through,' said Strike at once.

He moved around to his side of the desk, and the phone began to ring within seconds.

'Cormoran Strike.'

'Hello,' said a tentative woman's voice. 'Er – my name's Niamh Doherty? You left a message with my husband, asking whether I'd answer some questions about the Universal Humanitarian Church?'

'I did, yes,' said Strike. 'Thanks very much for getting back to me.'

'That's all right. Can I ask why you want to talk to me?'

'Yes, of course,' said Strike, eyes on Robin's. 'My agency's been hired to investigate claims about the church made by an ex-member. We're after corroboration, if we can get it.'

'Oh,' said Niamh. 'Right.'

'This would be an off-the-record chat,' Strike assured her. 'Just for background. I understand you were pretty young when you were there?'

'Yes, I was there from ages eight to eleven.'

There was a pause.

'Have you tried my father?' Niamh asked.

'Yes,' said Strike, 'but he declined to talk.'

'He would . . . I understand if you can't say, but why are you trying to corroborate these claims? Are you working for a newspaper, or—?'

'No, not a newspaper. Our client's got a relative inside the church.'

'Oh,' said Niamh, 'I see.'

Strike waited.

'All right,' said Niamh at last, 'I don't mind talking to you. Actually, if you could manage tomorrow, or Friday—'

'Tomorrow would be no problem,' said Strike, who had his own reasons for favouring Thursday.

'Thank you, that'd be great, because I'm off work – we've just moved house. And, it's a bit cheeky to ask this, but would you mind coming to me? I'm not far from London. Chalfont St Giles.'

'No problem whatsoever,' said Strike, reaching for a pen to take down her address.

When he'd hung up, Strike turned to Robin.

'Fancy a trip to Chalfont St Giles with me tomorrow?'

'She's agreed to talk?'

'Yep. Be good if you heard what she's got to say, before you go in.'

'Definitely,' said Robin, getting to her feet. 'Would you mind if I go home now, then? I've got a few things to sort out before I leave for Chapman Farm.'

'Yeah, no problem.'

Once Robin had left, Strike sat down at his computer, his spirits rather higher than they'd been on waking up. He'd just scuppered the possibility of Robin spending the whole of her last free day before going undercover with Ryan Murphy. If his actions recalled, however faintly, Charlotte Ross's machinations with regard to himself, his conscience remained surprisingly untroubled as he Googled pleasant places to have lunch in Chalfont St Giles.

21

The danger of heaven lies in the fact that one cannot
climb it . . . The effects of the time of danger are
truly great.

The I Ching or Book of Changes

The village Strike and Robin entered the following morning,
which lay an hour from London, had a sleepy English prettiness. As they drove past half-timbered buildings overlooking
a village green, Strike, who'd accepted Robin's offer to drive
his BMW, looked out at the stone grey Norman tower of the
parish church, and spotted a sign proclaiming that they were
in Buckinghamshire's best kept village.

'None of this will come cheap,' he commented, as they
turned off the High Street into Bowstridge Lane.

'We're here,' said Robin, coming to a halt beside a square,
detached house of tawny brick. 'We're ten minutes early,
should we wait or—?'

'Wait,' said Strike, who had no desire to hurry through the
interview. The longer it took, the more likely Robin would
want something to eat before returning to London. 'You all
packed and ready for tomorrow?'

'I've put my waterproof coat and underwear in a holdall, if
you can call that packing,' said Robin.

What she didn't tell Strike was that she'd realised for the first time yesterday that she wouldn't be able to take contraceptive pills with her into Chapman Farm. Having checked the small print on the pamphlet she'd been given, they were specifically listed as banned medications. Nor was she about to tell Strike that she and Murphy had had something close to an argument the previous evening, when Murphy had announced that he'd taken the day off to spend it with her, as a surprise, and she'd told him she was driving off to Buckinghamshire with Strike.

Strike's mobile rang. Caller ID was withheld.

'Strike.'

'Hi,' said a female voice. 'This is Abigail Glover.'

Strike mouthed 'Jonathan Wace's daughter' at Robin before turning his mobile to speakerphone so that she could hear what was going on.

'Ah, great,' he said. 'You got the message I left at the station?'

'Yeah,' she said. 'Woss this about?'

'About the Universal Humanitarian Church,' said Strike.

Absolute silence followed these words.

'Are you still there?' asked Strike.

'Yeah.'

'I was wondering whether you might be willing to talk to me,' said Strike.

More silence: Strike and Robin were looking at each other. At last a single monosyllable issued from the phone.

'Why?'

'I'm a private—'

'I know 'oo you are.'

Unlike her father's, Abigail's accent was pure working-class London.

'Well, I'm trying to investigate some claims made about the church.'

''Oose claims?'

'A man called Kevin Pirbright,' said Strike, 'who's now

223

dead, unfortunately. Did he ever make contact with you? He was writing a book.'

There was another silence, the longest yet.

'You working for a newspaper?' she asked suspiciously.

'No, for a private client. I wondered whether you'd be happy to talk to me. It can be off the record,' Strike added.

Yet another lengthy silence followed.

'Hello?'

'I dunno,' she said at last. 'I'll need to fink about it. I'll call you back if I . . . I'll call you later.'

The line went dead.

Robin, who realised she'd been holding her breath, exhaled.

'Well . . . I can't say I'm surprised. If I were Wace's daughter, I wouldn't want to be reminded of it, either.'

'No,' agreed Strike, 'but she'd be very useful, if she was happy to talk . . . I left a message for Jordan Reaney's wife yesterday, after you left, by the way. Tracked her down to her place of work. She's a manicurist at a place called Kuti-cles with a K.'

He checked the time on the dashboard.

'We should probably go in.'

When Strike pressed the doorbell they heard a dog barking, and when the door opened, a wire-haired fox terrier came flying out of the house so fast he flew right past Strike and Robin, skidded on the paved area in the front of the house, turned, ran back and began jumping up and down on its hind legs, barking hysterically.

'Calm *down*, Basil!' shouted Niamh. Robin was taken aback by her youth: she was in her mid-twenties, and for the second time lately, Robin found herself comparing her own flat to somebody else's house. Niamh was short and plump, with shoulder-length black hair and very bright blue eyes, and was wearing jeans and a sweatshirt with a quotation by

Charlotte Brontë printed on the front: *I would always rather be happy than dignified.*

'Sorry,' Niamh said to Strike and Robin, before saying, 'Basil, *for God's sake,*' seizing the dog by its collar and dragging it back inside. 'Come in. Sorry,' she repeated over her shoulder, as she dragged the overexcited dog along the wooden floorboards towards a kitchen at the end of the hall, 'we moved in last Sunday and he's been hyper ever since ... get *out,*' she added, forcibly pushing the dog out into the garden through a back door, which she closed firmly on him.

The kitchen was farmhouse style, with a purple Aga and plates displayed on a dresser. A scrubbed wooden table was surrounded by purple-painted chairs, and the fridge door was covered in a child's paintings, mostly blobs of paint and squiggles, which were held up with magnets. There was also – and this, Robin thought, explained how a twenty-five-year-old came to find herself living in such an expensive house – a picture of Niamh in a bikini, arm in arm with a man in swimming trunks, who looked at least forty. A smell of baking was making Strike salivate.

'Thanks very much for seeing us, Mrs—'

'Call me Niamh,' said their hostess, who, now that she didn't have a fox terrier to manage, looked nervous. 'Please, sit down, I've just made biscuits.'

'You've just moved in and you're baking?' said Robin, smiling.

'Oh, I love baking, it calms me down,' said Niamh, turning away to grab oven gloves. 'Anyway, we're pretty much straight now. I only took a couple of days off because I had leave owed to me.'

'What d'you do for a living?' asked Strike, who'd taken the chair nearest the back door, at which Basil was now whining and scratching, eager to get back in.

'Accountant,' said Niamh, now lifting cookies off the baking tray with a spatula. 'Tea? Coffee?'

By the time the two detectives and Niamh had their mugs of tea, and the biscuits were sitting on a plate in the middle of the table, Basil's whines had become so piteous that Niamh let him back into the room.

'He'll settle,' she said, as the dog zoomed around the table, tail wagging furiously. 'Eventually.'

Niamh sat down herself, making unnecessary adjustments to the sleeves of her sweatshirt.

'Who's the artwork by?' Robin asked, pointing at the blobby creations on the fridge, and trying to put Niamh more at ease.

'Oh, my little boy, Charlie,' said Niamh. 'He's two. He's with his dad this morning. Nigel thought it would be easier for me to talk to you without Charlie here.'

'I take it that's Nigel?' asked Robin, smiling as she pointed at the beach picture.

'Yes,' said Niamh. She seemed to feel something needed explaining. 'I met him at my first job. He was actually my boss.'

'How lovely,' said Robin, trying not to feel judgemental. Given Nigel's hair loss, the couple looked more like father and daughter in the picture.

'So,' said Strike, 'as I said on the phone, we're after background on the Universal Humanitarian Church. Is it OK if I take notes?'

'Yes, fine,' said Niamh nervously.

'Could we start with what year you and your family went to Chapman Farm?' asked Strike, clicking out the nib of his pen.

'1999,' said Niamh.

'And you were eight, right?'

'Yes, and my brother Oisin was six and my sister Maeve was four.'

226

'What made your parents join, do you know?' asked Strike.

'It was Dad, not Mum,' said Niamh. 'He was always a bit, um ... it's hard to describe. When we were little he was politically quite far left, but he's about as far right as you can go these days. I actually haven't spoken to him for three years ... he just got worse and worse. Weird ranting phone calls, temper tantrums. Nigel thinks I'm better off without contact with him.'

'Was your family religious?' asked Strike.

'Not before the UHC. No, I just remember Dad coming home one evening, incredibly excited, because he'd been to a meeting and got talking to Papa J, who converted him on the spot. It was like Dad had found the meaning of life. He was going on and on about a social revolution. He'd brought home a copy of Papa J's book, *The Answer*. Mum just ... went along with it,' said Niamh sadly. 'Maybe she thought everything would be better inside the church, I don't know.

'She told us it'd be fun. We cried about leaving home, and all our friends, she told us not to do it in front of Dad, because he'd be upset. Anything for an easy life, that was Mum ... we hated it, though, from the moment we got there. No clothes of our own. No toys. I can remember Maeve sobbing for the cuddly bunny she used to take to bed every night. We'd taken it to the farm, but everything was locked up, the moment we arrived, including Maeve's bunny.'

Niamh took a sip of tea, then said,

'I don't want to be hard on Mum. From what I can remember, she had a tough time with Dad's mood swings and how erratic he was. She wasn't very strong, either. She'd had some kind of heart condition since childhood. I remember her as very passive.'

'Are you still in contact with her?' asked Robin.

Niamh shook her head. Her eyes had become damp.

'I haven't seen her since we left her behind at Chapman

Farm, in 2002. She stayed behind, with our younger sister. That's actually part of the reason I said I'd see you,' said Niamh. 'I'd just like to know … if you happened to find out what happened to her … I wrote to the church a few years ago, trying to find out where she was, and I got a letter back saying she left in 2003. I don't know whether it's true. Maybe she couldn't find us after we got out, because Dad took us to Whitby, where we'd never lived before, and he changed our surname. Maybe she didn't want to find us, I don't know, or possibly Dad told her to stay away. I think he might have heard from her, though, or from the UHC, after we left, because he got a few letters that made him really angry. Maybe they were forwarded from our old address. Anyway, he'd tear them up really small so we couldn't read them. We were forbidden from ever mentioning Mum, after we left Chapman Farm.'

'What made your father take you away, do you know?' asked Strike.

'I only know what he was saying as he dragged us out of there. It was night-time. We had to climb out over fences. We all wanted Mum to come with us – we were begging Dad to let us fetch her, and Maeve was calling for her, and Dad hit her. He told us Mum was a slut,' said Niamh miserably, 'which was just *mad*, because in the church, the women are supposed to … I mean, they're shared, between all the men. But Dad must've thought Mum wasn't joining in with all that, which just – it beggars belief, it really does, but it's *so* typical of him. He thought he could join the church and just have the bits he liked, and leave the rest, which was idiotic: the church is completely anti-marriage. Everyone's supposed to sleep around. From what I heard him telling our uncle afterwards, he didn't believe Lin was his … I really hate saying all this, because from what I remember of Mum, she was quite – you know – prim. I don't think she'd have *wanted* to sleep with people other than

Dad. The whole thing's so ... so bizarre,' said Niamh bleakly. 'You can't explain, to people who don't understand about the UHC. I usually tell people my mum died when I was eleven. It's just easier.'

'I'm so sorry,' said Robin, who really couldn't think of anything else to say.

'Oh, I'm all right,' said Niamh, who no longer looked young, but far older than her years. 'Compared to Oisin and Maeve, I've done fine. They've never got over the UHC. Maeve's always at the doctor's, constantly signed off sick from work, on tons of different medication. She binge eats, she's got really big and she's never had a stable relationship. And Oisin drinks far too much. He's had kids with two different girls already, and he's only twenty-three. He works really menial jobs, just to get drinking money. I've tried to help, to look after both of them a bit, because I'm the only one who made it through the whole thing kind of intact, and I've always felt guilty about that. Both of them are angry at me. "It's all right for you, you married a rich old man." But I coped better, right from the moment we got out. I could remember our pre-church life, so the change wasn't such a shock. I caught up at school quicker than the other two and I'd had Mum around longer ... but to this day, I can't stand David Bowie. The UHC used to play "Heroes" all the time, to get people revved up. It doesn't even have to be that song. Just the sound of his voice ... when Bowie died, and they were playing his music non-stop on the radio, I hated it ...'

'Would you happen to have any photographs of your mother?' Strike asked.

'Yes, but they're very old.'

'Doesn't matter. We're just trying to tie names to faces at the moment.'

'They're upstairs,' said Niamh. 'Shall I—?'

'If you wouldn't mind,' said Strike.

Niamh left the kitchen. Strike helped himself to a biscuit.

'Bloody nice,' he said, through a mouthful of chocolate chips.

'Don't give him any,' said Robin, as Basil the dog placed his front paws on Strike's leg. 'Chocolate's really bad for dogs.'

'She says you can't have any,' Strike told the fox terrier, cramming the rest of the biscuit into his mouth. 'It's not my decision.'

They heard Niamh's returning footsteps, and she reappeared.

'That's Mum,' she said, passing a faded Polaroid to Strike.

He guessed it had been taken in the early nineties. Fair-haired Deirdre Doherty looked up at him, wearing a pair of square-framed glasses.

'Thanks,' said Strike, making a note. 'Would you be all right with me taking a picture of this? I won't take the original.'

Niamh nodded and Strike took a photograph on his mobile.

'So you were at Chapman Farm for three years?' Strike asked Niamh.

'That's right – not that I knew it until we got out, because there are no clocks or calendars in there.'

'Really?' said Robin, thinking of her Thursday night appointments with the plastic rock.

'No, and they never celebrated birthdays or anything. I can remember walking through the woods and thinking, "Today could be my birthday. I don't know." But the people running the place must have known our dates of birth, because certain things happened when you reached different ages.'

'What kind of things?' asked Strike.

'Well, up to the age of nine, you slept in a mixed dormitory. Then you went into a single-sex dormitory, and you had to start keeping a journal for the church elders to read. Obviously, you didn't say what you were really thinking. I soon found out if I wrote one thing I'd learned and one thing I'd enjoyed, I'd be OK. "Today I learned more about what the false self is,'" she said, adopting a flat voice, "'and ways of fighting my false self. I understand that the false self is the bad part of me that wants bad things. It is very important to defeat the false self. I enjoyed dinner tonight. We had chicken and rice and there were songs.'"

Beneath the table, Basil had finally settled down, his woolly head resting on Robin's foot.

'Then, when you turned thirteen, you moved into the adult dorms,' Niamh continued, 'and you started attending Manifestations and training to go pure spirit. The children who'd been raised in the church told me pure spirits get special powers. I remember fantasising at night that I'd go pure spirit really fast, and blast apart the walls of the dormitories and grab Mum, Oisin and Maeve and fly away with them ... I don't know whether I thought that was really possible ... after you'd been in there a while, you did start to believe mad things.

'But I can't tell you how you go pure spirit,' said Niamh, with a wry smile, 'because I was only eleven when we left.'

'So what was the routine, for younger kids?' asked Strike.

'Rote learning of church dogma, lots of colouring in, and sometimes going to the temple to chant,' said Niamh. 'It was incredibly boring and we were very heavily supervised. No proper teaching. Very occasionally we were allowed to go and play in the woods.

'I remember this one day – ' Niamh's tone lightened a little, '– in the woods, Oisin and I found a hatchet. There was this big old tree with a hollow in it. If you climbed up high enough into its branches, you could see down into the hollow. One day Oisin got a long branch and started poking around inside the trunk, and he saw something at the bottom.

'It was about that big,' Niamh held her hands a foot apart, 'and the blade was sort of rusty-looking. It'll have been used for chopping wood, but Oisin was convinced it had blood on it. We couldn't get it out, though. We couldn't reach.

'We didn't tell anyone. You learned never to tell anyone anything, even if it was innocent, but we made up this whole story in secret about how Mazu had taken a naughty child into the woods and killed them there. We half-believed it, I think. We were all terrified of Mazu.'

'You were?' said Robin.

'God, yes,' said Niamh. 'She was ... like nobody I've ever met, before or since.'

'In what way?' asked Strike.

Niamh gave an unexpected shudder, then a half-ashamed laugh.

'She ... I always thought of her as, like, a really big spider. You don't want to know what it might do to you, you just know you don't want to be near it. That's how I felt about Mazu.'

'We've heard,' said Strike, 'that there were beatings and whippings.'

'They kept the children away from anything like that,' said Niamh, 'but sometimes you'd see grown-ups with bruises or cuts. You learned never to ask about it.'

'And we know one boy was tied to a tree in the dark overnight,' said Robin.

'Yes, that – that was quite a common punishment, for children, I think,' said Niamh. 'Kids weren't supposed to talk about what had happened to them if they were taken away to be disciplined, but of course people whispered about it, in the dorms. I never got a bad punishment, personally,' Niamh added. 'I toed the line and I made sure Oisin and Maeve did, too. No, it wasn't so much what actually happened to you, as what you were afraid *might* happen. There was always this feeling of lurking danger.

'Mazu and Papa J could both do supernatural – I mean,

obviously, they *weren't* supernatural things, I know that now, but I believed it at the time. I thought they both had powers. Both of them could make objects move, just by pointing at them. I saw him levitate, as well. All the adults believed it was real, or they acted as if they did, so, of course, we did, too. But the worst thing for the children was the Drowned Prophet. You know about her?'

'We know a bit,' said Robin.

'Mazu used to tell us stories about her. She was supposed to have been this perfect little girl who never did anything wrong and was marked for this important destiny. We were taught that she'd drowned on purpose, to prove that spirit is stronger than flesh, but that she came back to Chapman Farm in the white dress she drowned in, and appeared in the woods where she used to play – and we saw her,' said Niamh quietly. 'A couple of times at night I saw her, standing in the trees, staring towards our dormitory.'

Niamh shuddered.

'I know it must have been a trick, but I had nightmares about it for years afterwards. I'd see her outside my bedroom window in Whitby, soaking wet in her white dress, with long black hair like Mazu's, staring in at me, because we'd all been bad and left Chapman Farm. All the kids at Chapman Farm were petrified of the Drowned Prophet. "She's listening. She'll know if you're lying. She'll come and find you, in the dark." That was enough to scare us all into good behaviour.'

'I'm sure it was,' said Robin.

Strike now reached into his breast pocket and pulled out a folded list.

'Could I go through some names with you, and see whether you remember any of these people?' he asked Niamh, who nodded. However, she showed no sign of recognition of the first half-dozen names Strike read out.

'Sorry, it's so long ago, and unless they were in our dormitory . . .'

The first name Niamh recognised was that of Kevin Pirbright, and Robin could tell from her reaction that she didn't know he was dead.

'Kevin Pirbright, yes! I remember him and his sister, Emily. They were nice. And they had an older sister, Becca, who came back not long after we'd arrived.'

'What d'you mean, "came back"?' asked Strike, his pen at the ready.

'She'd been at the Birmingham centre for three years. She'd been kind of fast-tracked by Papa J, as a future church leader. She was really bossy. A big favourite of Papa J's and Mazu's. I didn't like her much.'

Strike kept reading out names, but Niamh kept shaking her head until Strike said 'Flora Brewster'.

'Oh, yes, I think I remember her. She was a teenager, right? I helped her make her first corn dolly – they make them a lot, at Chapman Farm, to sell in Norwich.'

Strike continued working his way down the list of names.

'Paul Draper? He'd have been older than you. A teenager, as well.'

'No, can't remember a Paul.'

'Jordan Reaney? Also a teenager.'

'No, sorry.'

'Cherie Gittins?'

'No. I mean, they *might* have been there, but I can't remember them if they were.'

'Margaret Cathcart-Bryce?'

'Oh God, yes, I remember her,' said Niamh at once. 'She was really strange and stretched-looking, she'd had so much work done on her face. She was one of the rich women who used to visit the farm all the time. There was another one who liked grooming the horses, and some of the others took "yoga" with Papa J, but Margaret was the richest of the lot.'

Strike kept reading out names, but the only one Niamh recognised was that of Harold Coates.

'He was a doctor, wasn't he?'

'That's right,' said Strike. 'Did you used to see much of him?'

'I didn't, but Maeve did. She kept getting nervous rashes. He used to treat her.'

Strike made a note of this, his face expressionless.

'D'you remember Jonathan Wace's daughter?' asked Robin.

'Well, no,' said Niamh, looking confused. 'She was dead.'

'Sorry, not Daiyu – I mean his elder daughter, Abigail.'

'Oh, did he have another one?' said Niamh, surprised. 'No, I never met her.'

'OK,' said Strike, having made a final note, 'that's been helpful, thank you. We're trying to establish a timeline, find out who was there, and when.'

'I'm sorry I don't remember more,' said Niamh.

Cups of tea finished, they all rose from the table, Robin disengaging her foot carefully from Basil.

'If,' said Niamh tentatively, 'you find out anything about Mum, will you let me know?'

'Of course,' said Strike.

'Thank you. Since having Charlie, I think about Mum such a lot . . . Oisin and Maeve say they don't care, but I think it would mean a lot to them, too, if we could find out what happened to her . . .'

Strike, Robin noticed, looked unusually severe as the three of them headed down the hall, even allowing for the natural surliness of his resting expression. At the front door, Robin thanked Niamh for her time and the biscuits. Basil stood panting beside them, tail wagging, evidently convinced he might yet wheedle fun and treats out of the strangers.

Strike now turned to his partner.

'You go on. I'd like a private word with Niamh.'

Though surprised, Robin asked no questions, but left. When the sound of her footsteps had disappeared, Strike turned back to Niamh.

'I'm sorry to ask this,' he said quietly, looking down at her, 'but has your younger sister ever talked to you about what Harold Coates did, to cure her rashes?'

'I think he gave her some cream, that's all,' said Niamh, looking nonplussed.

'She's never talked about anything else that happened, when he was treating her?'

'No,' said Niamh, fear now dawning in her face.

'How old's your sister now – twenty-one?'

'Yes,' said Niamh.

'Harold Coates was a paedophile,' said Strike, and Niamh gasped and clapped her hands to her face. 'I think you should ask her what happened. She's probably in need of more help than anti-depressants, and it might be a relief to have someone else know.'

'Oh my God,' whispered Niamh through her fingers.

'I'm sorry,' repeated Strike. 'It won't be much consolation, I know, but Maeve was far from the only one.'

22

Nine at the top means:
Look to your conduct and weigh the favourable signs.

The I Ching or Book of Changes

'Fancy some lunch while we debrief?' said Strike, once he was back in the car. 'Niamh recommended a good place just round the corner,' he lied. In fact, he'd found the Merlin's Cave restaurant online, the previous day.

Robin hesitated. Having taken the day off, Murphy would be expecting her back as soon as possible, to spend their last few hours together. Yet their slightly tense phone conversation of the previous evening, in which Murphy had just refrained from becoming openly annoyed, had irked her. Her boyfriend, who supposedly wanted her as well prepared as possible before going undercover, had resented her speaking to a last witness before she went in, and his behaviour was all too reminiscent of her marriage.

'Yes, OK,' said Robin. 'I can't hang around too long, though, I – er – told Ryan I'd be back.'

'Fair enough,' said Strike, happy to have gained lunch. Hopefully, the service would be slow.

Merlin's Cave, which stood on the village green, was a country pub with a timbered and red brick façade. Strike and

Robin were shown to a table for two in a pleasant restaurant area, with glass windows overlooking a rear garden.

'If I drive back,' said Strike, as they sat down, 'you can drink. Last chance for alcohol before Chapman Farm.'

'I'm not bothered, I can have a drink later,' said Robin.

'Murphy's OK with you drinking in front of him, is he?'

Robin looked up from the menu the waitress had just handed her. She didn't remember ever telling Strike that Murphy was an alcoholic.

'Yes, he's fine with it. Did Ilsa—?'

'Wardle,' said Strike.

'Oh,' said Robin, looking back down at the menu.

Strike had no intention of relaying what Wardle had said about Murphy's behaviour when still a drinker, largely because he knew how he'd make himself look to Robin, by saying it. Nevertheless, he said,

'What made him give up?'

'He says he just didn't like himself, drunk,' said Robin, preferring to keep looking at the menu, rather than Strike. She had a suspicion that Strike was looking for a way to impart information she probably wouldn't want to hear. Given Strike's recent irritation at what he considered Ilsa's meddling, she thought it grossly hypocritical for him to start questioning her about Murphy's past.

Sensing the slight increase in froideur from across the table, Strike probed no further. When both had ordered food, and Strike had asked for bread, he said,

'So, what did you make of Niamh?'

Robin lowered her menu.

'Well, apart from feeling really sorry for her, I thought she gave us a few interesting things. Especially that photograph of her mother. From Henry Worthington-Fields' description of the pregnant woman he saw collapsing, while ploughing—'

'Yeah, I think that was Deirdre Doherty,' said Strike, 'and now we know she had a heart condition which, along with hard manual labour and a fourth pregnancy, would seem ample grounds for fainting, or whatever she did.'

'But we know she survived the fainting fit, got through the birth OK and lived for another two years, at least,' said Robin.

The waitress now set down Robin's water, Strike's zero-alcohol beer and a basket of bread. Strike took a roll (the diet could be resumed once Robin was at Chapman Farm) and waited until the waitress was out of earshot, before saying,

'You think Deirdre's dead?'

'I don't *want* to think so,' said Robin, 'but it's got to be a possibility, hasn't it?'

'And the letters her husband kept tearing up?'

'They might not have had anything to do with Deirdre at all. I can't believe it would have been *that* hard to track her family down, if she really did leave Chapman Farm in 2003. And don't you find it fishy that she left her youngest daughter behind when she was so-called expelled?'

'If Kevin Pirbright was right, and Lin was Jonathan Wace's daughter, Wace might not have been prepared to give her up.'

'If Kevin Pirbright was right,' said Robin, 'Lin was a product of rape, and if Deirdre was prepared to write it in her journal that Wace had raped her, she was a real danger to him and to the church.'

'You think Wace murdered her, buried her at Chapman Farm and then told everyone he'd expelled her in the night, to avoid a DNA test? Because all Wace had to do was say the sex was consensual, get a few cult members to state on the record that Deirdre walked happily into his bedroom of her own free will, and it'd be very hard to get a conviction. As you've just pointed out, Deirdre stayed at Chapman Farm, even after the rest of her family took off. That wouldn't look great in court.

Nor would the fact that her husband thought she was a slut and didn't want anything more to do with her.'

Catching the expression on Robin's face, Strike added,

'I'm not saying I think any of those arguments would be fair or valid. I'm just being realistic about Deirdre's odds of convincing a jury.'

'Why did she write about the rape in her journal at all?' asked Robin. 'She knew the journal would be read by a higher-up, which doesn't really tally with the way Niamh described her mother. It doesn't feel like the act of a passive woman.'

'Maybe she was desperate,' said Strike. 'Maybe she hoped the journal was going to be read by someone she thought would help her.' He took a bite of bread, then said, 'I'll keep trying to track Deirdre down while you're at the farm. She'd be a bloody good witness, if we can find her.'

'Of course, she needn't have been murdered,' said Robin, still following her own train of thought. 'If she had a weak heart before going to Chapman Farm and was made to work without adequate food, she could have died of natural causes.'

'If that happened, and they didn't register the death, we've got a crime. Trouble is, to prove it, we need a body.'

'It's farmland,' said Robin. 'She could have been buried anywhere, over acres.'

'And we're not going to get the authority to dig up all the fields on an evidence-free hunch.'

'I know,' said Robin. 'There's also that thing about no calendars and watches—'

'Yeah, I was going to talk to you about that,' said Strike.

'Even if we manage to find people who're prepared to talk, they're going to have credibility problems,' Robin continued. '"When did this happen?" "I have literally no idea." It'd make faking alibis a piece of cake. Only the people at the top know what time of day it is – literally.'

'Yeah, but the more immediate problem is, you're going to have to find a way of keeping track of the days without anyone knowing you're doing it.'

'I'll think of something,' said Robin, 'but if you could put dates and days of the week on your notes to me, that'll help keep me orientated.'

'Good thinking,' said Strike, pulling out his notebook and making a note to this effect.

'And,' said Robin, feeling slightly awkward about asking this, 'if I put the odd note for Ryan in the rock, along with my report for you, would you mind passing it on?'

'No problem,' said Strike, making a further note, his expression impassive. 'Do me a return favour, though: if you get a chance to get the blood-stained hatchet out of the hollow tree, be sure and take it.'

'OK, I'll try,' said Robin, smiling.

'Do your family know what you're about to do, by the way?'

'No details,' said Robin. 'I've just said I'll be undercover for a bit. I haven't told them where I'm going. Ryan's going to call them with updates ... I really hope Abigail Glover decides to talk to you,' Robin added, again keen to get off the subject of Murphy, 'because I'd love to hear some more background on her father. There isn't much about Wace's past out there, have you noticed?'

'Yeah, I have, though I note he doesn't mind people knowing he was educated at Harrow.'

'No, but after that it all gets sketchy, doesn't it? His father was a "businessman", but no detail on what kind of business, and his first wife dies tragically, he finds religion and founds the UHC. That's basically it.'

Their food arrived. Strike, who was still abstaining from chips, looked so enviously at Robin's that she laughed.

'Have some. I only ordered them because I'm going to be on starvation rations from tomorrow.'

'No,' said Strike gloomily, 'I still need to get another stone off.'

He'd just cut into his chicken breast when his mobile rang again, this time, from an unknown London number. Setting down his knife and fork again, he answered.

'Hello?'

'Oh – 'iya,' said a woman's voice. 'Are you Cameron Strike?'

'That's me,' said Strike, who rarely bothered to correct the mistake. 'Who's this?'

'Ava Reaney. You left a message for me to call you?'

'Yes,' said Strike, scribbling *Reaney wife* on his notebook and turning it to face Robin. 'I did. I was actually wondering whether you could get a message to your husband for me, Mrs Reaney.'

'To Jordan? Wha' for?' said the voice suspiciously. There was a lot of background noise, including pop music. Strike assumed Ava Reaney was at her nail salon.

'I'm trying to find as many people as I can who've lived at Chapman Farm,' said Strike.

'What – that cult place?' asked Ava Reaney.

'That's the one. I think your husband was there in the nineties?'

''E was, yeah,' she said.

'So, could you—?'

'No,' she said. 'We've split up.'

'Oh. Sorry to hear that,' said Strike.

''E's inside,' said Ava.

'Yeah, I know,' said Strike, 'which is why—'

''E's a bastard. I'm divorcing 'im.'

'Right,' said Strike. 'Well, could anyone else take a message to him, to see whether he'd be prepared to talk to me about the UHC?'

'I can ask 'is sister, if you want,' said Ava. 'She's going

up next week. Hey, are you that bloke what caught the Shacklewell Ripper?'

'I am, yeah,' said Strike.

'It *is* 'im,' Ava said loudly, apparently to somebody standing nearby, before saying, 'So you're after people from the UHT are you? No,' she corrected herself, 'that's milk, innit?'

'Did Jordan ever talk to you about his time in there?' asked Strike.

'Not much. 'E gets nightmares abou' it, though,' she added, with a certain malicious satisfaction.

'Really?' said Strike.

'Yeah. Abou' the pigs. 'E's frightened of pigs.'

She laughed, and so did the unknown person standing near her.

'OK, well, if you wouldn't mind asking Jordan's sister to give him my message – you've got my phone number, haven't you?'

'Yeah, I will. OK. See ya.'

Strike hung up.

'Apparently Jordan Reaney has nightmares about pigs, dating from his time in Chapman Farm.'

'Really?'

'Yeah . . . D'you know much about them?'

'What, pigs? Not really.'

'Shame. I look to you for farming expertise.'

'The boars can be really aggressive,' said Robin, 'I know that. Our local vet got badly injured by one when I was at school. It slammed him up against metal railings – he had some nasty bites and broken ribs.'

Strike's mobile now buzzed with the arrival of a text. Robin glimpsed a lot of emojis before her partner swiped the phone off the table and returned it to his pocket.

She deduced, correctly, that the text was from Bijou

Watkins. For a moment or two, she considered passing on Ilsa's warning about Bijou's bedroom behaviour, but given Strike's reaction the last time someone tried to interfere with his new relationship, she decided against it. After all, this was the last time she was going to see her business partner for a while, and she preferred not to part on bad terms.

23

Nine at the beginning means:
Fellowship with men at the gate.

The I Ching or Book of Changes

At half past nine the following day, Robin walked out of Victoria Station into the cool, overcast morning. For a moment, she stood with her half-empty holdall over her shoulder, looking around at taxis, swarming commuters and buses, and experienced a moment of panic: there was no minibus, and she groped in her pocket for the UHC pamphlet, to check she had the right station and time, even though she knew perfectly well she did. However, just as she found the pamphlet, she spotted an orange-tabarded woman holding up a sign with the church's heart-hands logo on it, and recognised Becca Pirbright, Kevin's older sister, who'd led the second temple service Robin had attended.

Though Robin had previously compared Becca to a motivational speaker, it now struck her that she was more like an idealised notion of a Girl Guide: pretty and neat, with thick-lashed dark eyes, glossy brown hair and a creamy-skinned, oval face, which dimpled when she smiled. Beckoning hesitant arrivals to gather around her, she projected a cheery natural authority.

Beside Becca stood a short, heavy-set young man who had

a low forehead, dark eyes, fuzzy dark hair and an underbite. As Robin looked at him, she noticed a slight tic in his right eye; it began to wink, apparently uncontrollably, and he hastily raised a hand to cover it. He too was wearing an orange tabard, and held a clipboard. Seven or eight people with backpacks and bags had already congregated around the pair by the time Robin joined the group.

'Hi,' she said.

'Hello!' said Becca. 'Are you one of us?'

'I think so,' said Robin. 'Rowena Ellis?'

The young man with the clipboard marked off the name.

'Great! I'm Becca, and this is Jiang. He's going to be our driver.'

'Hi,' said Robin, smiling at Jiang, who merely grunted.

The name 'Jiang' made Robin wonder whether the young man was another son of Jonathan Wace's, although he didn't resemble the church leader in the slightest.

Robin's fellow initiates were an eclectic bunch. She recognised the young, brown-skinned man in glasses who'd worn a Spiderman T-shirt in the temple, but the others were unfamiliar. They included a pink-faced man who looked to be in his late sixties and had the air of a professor, with his tweed jacket and wispy white hair; two teenaged girls who seemed inclined to giggle, one of whom was plump, with bright green hair, the other pale, blonde and much-pierced. An atmosphere of nervous tension hung over the group, which suggested people waiting to turn over their papers in an important exam.

By five to ten, the group had swelled to twenty people and everybody's name had been checked off. Becca led the group across the busy road and up a side street, to a smart white minibus with the UHC logo on its side. Robin found herself a window seat directly behind the two teenaged girls. The spectacled young man sat beside her.

'Hi, I'm Amandeep,' he said.

'Rowena,' said Robin, smiling.

As the minibus pulled away from the pavement, Becca picked up a microphone and turned, kneeling on a front seat, to address the newcomers.

'So, good morning! I'm Becca Pirbright, and I've been blessed to be a member of the Universal Humanitarian Church since I was eight years old. I'm going to be giving you a brief rundown on what you can expect during your week's retreat, and then I'll be happy to answer any questions you've got! Let's just get out of London, so I'm not arrested for not wearing my seat belt!' she said, and there was a little titter of laughter as she turned to take her seat again.

As they drove through London, quiet conversations broke out inside the minibus, but there seemed to be an unspoken agreement that these should be kept respectfully low, as though they were already inside a religious space. Amandeep told Robin he was doing a PhD in engineering, Robin told him about her cancelled wedding and her imaginary career in PR, and most of the bus heard the sixty-something man announce that he was a professor of anthropological philosophy called Walter Fernsby. Becca, Robin noticed, was observing the passengers in a mirror positioned directly over the windscreen, which was angled to watch the seats rather than the road. The slight movement of Becca's right shoulder suggested that she was making notes.

When the minibus reached the M11, Becca turned on her microphone again and, speaking to the passengers in the angled mirror, she said,

'Hi! So, now we're fully on our way, I'll give you some idea what to expect when we reach Chapman Farm, which has a really important place in our church's history. Have any of you read Papa J's book *The Answer?*'

Most passengers raised their hands. Robin deliberately hadn't read Jonathan Wace's book prior to entry into the church, because she wanted both a pretext for questions, and to present herself as someone who still needed to be convinced of the church's truths.

'Well, as those who've read *The Answer* will know, we follow the teachings of the five prophets, who are all buried or memorialised at Chapman Farm.

'Your stay at the farm will focus on what we like to call the three "S"s: study, service and spiritual practice. You'll be undertaking a wide range of activities, some of them practical tasks out in the fresh air, others focusing on your spiritual needs. We find that people learn a lot about themselves, perhaps even more than they learn about us, during these retreats.

'To get you started, I'm going to pass back some questionnaires. Please fill them in as best you can – I'm passing out pens, too. We're coming up to a nice straight bit of motorway, so hopefully nobody will get motion sickness!'

There was another ripple of nervous laughter. Becca passed a pile of stapled questionnaires to one of the people behind her, and a handful of pens, which were then passed around the passengers, who took one of each.

Robin noticed as she took a pen that it had been numbered. She glanced down the list of questions on the paper. She'd half-expected a medical questionnaire, but instead saw what she quickly realised was a kind of personality test. The person answering was supposed to mark a series of statements 'strongly agree', 'somewhat agree', 'somewhat disagree' or 'strongly disagree', and to write their name at the top of the page.

1 *Once I make up my mind, I seldom change it.*
2 *I prefer to work at my own pace.*
3 *I have many friends and acquaintances.*

4 *People like to come to me with their problems.*
5 *I gain satisfaction from achieving my goals.*

The questionnaire ran over ten sides of paper. Many of the statements were reworded versions of those that had gone before. Robin set to work, answering in the persona of Rowena, who was both more gregarious and more concerned about other people's approval than her creator. The two teen-aged girls in the seat in front were giggling as they compared answers.

It took forty minutes for the first completed questionnaire to be passed back to Becca. Robin handed in her own shortly afterwards, but deliberately kept hold of her pen, to see what happened. When at last all the questionnaires had been handed in, Becca took to the microphone again.

'I'm missing pens ten and fourteen!' she said gaily, and Robin made a show of realising she'd absent-mindedly put pen ten into her pocket. Pen fourteen was located rolling under a seat.

'We're going to have a quick bathroom break here,' said Becca over the microphone, as the minibus turned into a Shell service station. 'You've got thirty minutes. Don't be late back to the minibus, please!'

As Robin descended the minibus steps, she saw Becca was flicking through the questionnaires.

Having visited the bathroom, Robin walked back towards the car park. Knowing what lay ahead, she felt a strong desire to buy chocolate, even though she wasn't hungry. Instead, she examined the front pages of newspapers in the shop. The ever-nearing Brexit referendum dominated them.

'Well, I hope you're all feeling relieved!' said Becca merrily into the microphone, after everyone had got back onto the bus, eliciting another little laugh from her passengers. 'We've got just over an hour left until we arrive at Chapman Farm, so I'm going to say a little bit more about what you should expect there, and then give you the opportunity to ask any questions.

'As you probably know, one of the UHC's priorities is to effect meaningful change in the materialist world.'

'Amen to that!' said Walter Fernsby, the professor of philosophy, which made many of his companions laugh again.

'Our main charitable concerns,' continued the smiling Becca, 'are homelessness, addiction, climate change and social deprivation. All these issues are, of course, inter-related, and are ills generated by a capitalist, materialistic society. This week, you'll be joining us in our efforts to, quite literally, change the world. You might think your contribution too small to matter, but our teaching is that every single act of mercy or generosity, every minute of time given to better the world, or to help another human being, has its own spiritual power which, if harnessed, can bring about almost miraculous transformations.

'And this change won't merely be external. An internal change takes place when we commit to lives of service. We become more than we've ever dreamed we could be. I've personally witnessed people coming into their full spiritual power, shedding all materialism, becoming capable of extraordinary acts.

'On arrival at Chapman Farm you'll be divided into small groups. I can promise you, you won't be bored! Groups rotate through different activities. You'll attend temple and lectures, but you'll also be crafting objects that we sell for charity and looking after the animals we keep at the farm, who are part of our commitment to ethical farming and a life in harmony with nature. You may even be asked to do some cooking and cleaning: acts of simple caretaking which prove commitment to our community and care of our brothers and sisters within the church.

'Now, does anyone have any questions for me?'

Half a dozen hands shot into the air.

'Yes?' said Becca, smiling at the plump, green-haired girl.

'Hi – um – how quickly do most people go pure spirit?'

'I get asked that question *every single time!*' said Becca, and the passengers laughed along with her. 'OK, so – the answer is, there is no answer. I'm not going to lie to you: for most people, it takes a while, but there are definitely individuals for whom it happens fast. The founder of the church, whom we call Papa J – but he's exceptional – he was showing signs of being pure spirit aged thirteen or fourteen, although if you read *The Answer,* you'll know he didn't yet realise why he could do things most people can't. Yes?' she said, to the blonde teenager sitting beside the first questioner.

'Do we get to choose our groups?'

'I'm afraid not,' said Becca kindly. 'We want you all to have the best possible individual experience during the retreat, which means we tend to put people who know each other into different groups.'

Robin saw the teenaged girls glance at each other, crest-fallen, as Becca went on,

'Don't worry, you'll still see each other! You'll be sharing a dormitory at night. But we want you to have an individual experience that you can process in your own, unique way . . . yes?' she said, to Walter the professor.

'If we have a specific skill set that might be useful to the church, should we declare it? So we can be of more use?'

'That's a great question,' said Becca. 'We have some very gifted individuals within the church – I'm talking about artists, doctors, scientists – who initially undertake what, in the materialist world, would be considered quite menial tasks, knowing that this is a step towards enlightenment. That said, we do assess individual members once they've completed what

251

we call Service, so as to place them where they can best serve the church and its broader mission.

'Yes, the gentleman in the glasses?'

'What do you say to people who claim the UHC is actually a cult?' asked Amandeep.

Becca laughed. Robin didn't see even a split second of consternation.

'I'd say the church definitely attracts slurs and negative attention. The question we should be asking is, why? We're arguing for equality across races, we want redistribution of wealth. I'll just say, judge for yourselves, after a week. Keep an open mind, and don't let the mainstream media, or people with a vested interest in the status quo, tell you what truth is. You're on the threshold of seeing truths that, honestly, will amaze you. I've seen it hundreds of times now. Sceptics come along out of curiosity. Some of them are actively hostile, but they can't believe it, when they see what we're really about . . . yes?'

'Will Papa J be at Chapman Farm, when we're there?'

The questioner was a middle-aged woman with what looked like home-dyed ginger hair and large, round glasses.

'You're Marion, aren't you?' said Becca, and the questioner nodded. 'Papa J moves between our temples and centres, but I believe he's going to be dropping into Chapman Farm this week, yes.'

'*Oh!*' sighed Marion, beaming as she pressed her hands together, as though in prayer.

24

*The dark force possesses beauty but veils it. So must
a man be when entering the service of a king.*

The I Ching or Book of Changes

The minibus had driven through Norwich and arrived in countryside. After half an hour's travel along lanes bordered by hedgerows, Robin finally saw the sign for Lion's Mouth, a narrow, tree-lined road. Robin, who'd memorised the map with the subcontractors' annotations, spotted cameras placed discreetly in trees to the right.

Not long after entering Lion's Mouth, they turned up a well-maintained track. Electric gates opened at the minibus's approach. The bus drove up a short driveway until it reached a car park, in which two identical minibuses were already parked. Ahead lay a long, one-storey edifice of light brick which, in spite of its Gothic windows, appeared recently built, and far away, on the horizon beyond the farm, Robin spotted a tall, circular tower that looked like the rook of a chess-playing giant.

The passengers disembarked, carrying their holdalls and rucksacks. Becca led them inside, where they found a room that resembled the changing room of an upmarket gym. Opposite the door was a wall of lockers. To the right was a counter, behind which stood a smiling black woman with long braids, wearing an orange tracksuit. On the left-hand side were a series of changing cubicles.

'All right, everyone!' said Becca. 'Line up here to receive your tracksuits from Hattie!'

'OK, everyone, listen, please!' said the attendant, clapping her hands. 'When I've given you a tracksuit, footwear, pyjamas, bag and locker key, you change in the cubicle. Put your waterproof coat, underwear and pyjamas in your UHC bag. Then put your day clothes, jewellery, phones, money, credit cards, etc into the bag you've brought with you, and put it in the locker! I'll ask you to sign a chit, to show which locker's yours, and you'll hand me back the key.'

Robin joined the line and soon, equipped with white cotton pyjamas, a slightly worn pair of trainers, a size medium orange tracksuit and a bag made of hessian with the church's logo stamped on it, proceeded into a cubicle and changed.

Having put on her tracksuit and trainers, and stuffed her pyjamas, underwear and coat into the hessian bag, Robin placed her holdall into the locker – she'd brought no credit cards, as they were all in Robin Ellacott's name, only a purse containing cash – handed her key back to the woman with braids and signed a chit to say her possessions were in locker 29.

'Just a quick check,' said the attendant, and she rifled through Robin's hessian bag to check the contents, then directed her with a nod to sit on a bench with the others who'd already changed.

The blonde teenager was now tearfully demanding why Hattie wanted her to remove the many studs and hoops from her ears and nose.

'This was clearly stated in your pamphlet,' said the attendant calmly, 'no jewellery. It's all down there in black and white, honey. Just put it in the locker.'

The girl looked around for support, but none came.

Eventually she began tugging out the bits of metal, eyes full of tears. Her green-haired friend watched, and Robin thought she seemed torn between sympathy and a desire to blend in with the silent watchers on the bench.

'Wonderful!' said Becca, once everyone was clad in their orange tracksuits, and had their hessian bags over their shoulders. 'OK, everyone, follow us!'

The group rose, bags over their shoulders, and followed Becca and Jiang through a second door, which opened onto a path leading between square buildings of pale brick. Multicoloured pictures of children's handprints had been stuck to the windows of the building to the left.

'Some of our classrooms!' Becca called over her shoulder, 'and the children's dormitories!'

At that moment, a procession of small children, all dressed in miniature orange tracksuits, appeared out of one of the classrooms, led by two women. The new recruits paused to let the children pass into the opposite building, and the children gazed at them, round-eyed. Robin noticed that all of their hair had been cropped close to their heads.

'Aww,' said the green-haired teenager, as the children disappeared. 'Suh-*weet*!'

As the group passed through the archway at the end of the path, Robin heard gasps from those directly ahead of her, and when she, too, emerged into the paved courtyard beyond the arch, she understood why.

They were facing an enormous five-sided building built of ruddy stone. White marble columns stood either side of a flight of broad white marble steps, which led up to a pair of golden doors, currently closed, but which had a similar, ornate scarlet and gold carved surround to the entrance to the temple in Rupert Court, featuring the same animals, but on a far larger scale.

In front of the temple, in the centre of the courtyard, were four plain stone sarcophagi, which had been positioned around a central fountain and pool, like rays of the sun. In the middle of the pool stood the statue of a little girl, whose long hair swirled around her, as though in water, whose face was tilted to look upwards and whose right arm was raised to the skies. The fountain spouting behind her made the surface of the surrounding pool dimple and sparkle.

'Our temple,' said Becca, smiling at the looks of surprise and awe on the newcomers' faces, 'and our prophets.'

She led them now towards the pool, where both she and Jiang knelt quickly, dipped a finger into the water and dabbed it onto their foreheads. Together they said,

'The Drowned Prophet will bless all who worship her.'

Robin didn't look to see how her fellow initiates reacted to this unusual behaviour, because she was primarily interested in memorising the layout of the buildings. The building on the left-hand side of the courtyard looked like the original farmhouse. Originally a plain, undistinguished house with walls covered in rounded flints, it had clearly been enlarged and substantially renovated, with extra wings and a reworked entrance with double doors, on which a pair of dragons had been carved.

Facing the farmhouse on the other side of the courtyard were four much plainer buildings that Robin thought looked like more dormitories.

'All right,' said Becca, 'the women are going to follow me and the men, follow Jiang. We'll reconvene by the pool.'

Becca led the women into the dormitory on the centre right.

The interior reminded Robin of a large, old-fashioned sanatorium. Rows of metal-framed beds stood upon shining tiled floors. The walls were painted a stark white. A large copper bell hung from the middle of the ceiling, which was connected to a thick rope whose end dangled beside the entrance.

'Choose any bed that doesn't already have pyjamas on it,' said Becca, 'and put your bags into the boxes under your beds. You'll find journals on your pillows!' she called after the women who were already striding away from her, to find their sleeping places. 'We ask you to record your thoughts and impressions daily! This is a way of measuring spiritual progress, and also a means of helping the Principals guide you better on your journey with us. Your journals will be collected in and read every morning! Please write your name clearly on the front of the journal, and please *do not tear out pages*.'

Most of the women had gravitated naturally towards the far end of the dormitory, where there were windows overlooking woods, but Robin, who wanted a bed as close as possible to the door, spotted one by the wall and, by dint of walking faster than anyone else, managed to secure it by placing her pyjamas on the pillow. Her blank journal had a pencil tied to it with a length of string. Glancing around, she saw three or four small wooden tables supporting the kind of sturdy, crank-turned, desktop pencil sharpeners she'd used at primary school. Having put her hessian bag into the wicker box under the bed, she wrote the name Rowena Ellis on the front of her journal.

'If anyone needs the loo,' called Becca, pointing through a door leading to a communal bathroom, 'it's right through there!'

Though she felt in no need of the toilet, Robin took the opportunity to examine the communal bathroom, which had a row of toilets and a row of showers. Tampons and sanitary towels lay in packets in open baskets. Windows were set high over the handbasins.

When all the women who wished to do so had used the bathroom, Becca led the group back into the courtyard, where they were reunited with the men.

'This way,' said Becca, leading the group on.

As they walked around the temple, they passed a few church members walking in the opposite direction, all of whom beamed and said hello. Among them was a teenaged girl, sixteen at most, who had long, fine mousey hair, sun-bleached at the ends, and enormous dark blue eyes in a thin, anxious face. She smiled automatically at the sight of the newcomers, but Robin, glancing back, saw the smile disappear from the girl's face as though a switch had been flicked.

Behind the temple was a smaller courtyard. To the left lay what appeared to be a small library built of the same red stone as the temple, its doors standing open, a couple of people in orange tracksuits sitting at tables inside, reading. There were also older buildings, including barns and sheds which looked as though they'd been there for decades. A newer building lay ahead, which, while not as grand as the temple, must still have cost a huge amount of money. It was long and broad, made of brick and timber, and when Becca led them inside, it proved to be a spacious dining hall with a beamed ceiling, and many trestle tables standing on a flagged stone floor. At one end was a stage, with what Robin supposed would be called a high table standing on it. Sounds of clanging, and a faint, depressing smell of cooking vegetables, proclaimed the close proximity of a kitchen.

Around forty orange-tracksuited people were already sitting at a trestle table, and Robin, remembering that minibuses had also brought recruits from cities other than London, supposed she was looking at more newcomers. Sure enough, Becca told her own group to join those already seated, then moved aside to have a quiet conversation with a few of her fellow members.

Now Robin spotted Will Edensor, who was so tall and thin that his tracksuit hung off him. A few inches of hairy ankle were visible between the top of his trainer and the hem of the trousers. He wore a fixed smile as he stood in silence, apparently waiting for instructions. Beside Will stood pointy-nosed, straggly haired Taio Wace, who was far fatter than all the other church members. Becca and Jiang were consulting clipboards and notes, and talking quietly among themselves.

'Walter Fernsby,' said a loud voice in Robin's ear, which made her jump. 'We haven't met yet.'

'Rowena Ellis,' said Robin, shaking the professor's hand.

'And you?' Fernsby said to the plump green-haired girl.

'Penny Brown,' said the girl.

'All right, everyone, if I could have your attention!' said a loud voice, and silence fell as Taio Wace stepped forwards. 'For those of you who don't know me, I'm Taio, son of Jonathan Wace.'

'Oooh,' said Marion, the ginger-haired, middle-aged woman. 'He's his *son*?'

'You're going to be split into five groups,' said Taio, 'which may change as your stay progresses, but for now, these will be your workmates as you begin your Week of Service.

'The first group will be Wood.'

Taio began to call out names. As first the Wood Group, and then the Metal Group, were formed and led away by a church member, Robin noticed that those in charge were not only dividing people who evidently knew each other, but also mixing together the occupants of the three minibuses. Will Edensor departed the dining hall at the head of the Water Group.

'Fire group,' said Taio. 'Rowena Ellis—'

Robin stood up and took her place beside Taio, who smiled.

'Ah,' he said. 'You came.'

Robin forced herself to smile back at him. His pale, pointed nose and small mouth reminded her more than ever of an albino rat.

Taio continued reading out names until Robin was standing with eleven others, including the ginger-haired, bespectacled Marion Huxley, and Penny Brown, the teenager with short green hair.

'Fire Group,' said Taio, handing his clipboard to Becca, 'you'll come with me.'

From the slight flicker of surprise on Becca's face, Robin had the feeling this hadn't been the plan, and she hoped very much that Taio's decision to lead Fire Group had nothing to do with her.

Taio led his group out of the dining hall and turned right.

'Laundry,' he said, pointing at the brick building behind the dining hall.

Ahead was open farmland. Orange figures dotted the fields, which stretched as far as the eye could see, and Robin saw two Shire horses in the distance, ploughing.

'Chickens,' said Taio dismissively, as they turned left along a track bordered by cow parsley and passed a gigantic coop in which both speckled and brown hens were strutting and scratching. 'Back there,' he said, jerking a thumb over his shoulder, 'we've got pigs and beehives. These,' he added, pointing ahead at a collection of smaller brick buildings, 'are the crafting workshops.'

'Oooh, fun,' said green-haired Penny happily.

Taio opened the door of the second building. The noise of sewing machines met them.

Two young women and a man were sitting at the far end of the room, using the machines to make what looked like small, floppy pouches, until Robin realised that the small group of people sitting at the nearer table were filling them with stuffing and turning them into small, cuddly turtles. The workers looked around at the opening of the door, smiling. They were sitting a chair apart, leaving space for each of the newcomers to sit between two church members.

'Fire Group, called to service,' said Taio.

A friendly looking man in his early forties got to his feet, holding a half-stuffed turtle.

'Wonderful!' he said. 'Take a seat, everyone!'

Robin found herself a space between a very pretty girl who looked Chinese, and was sitting a little further from the table than everyone else, due to the fact that she was in late pregnancy, and a middle-aged white woman whose head was entirely shaven, only a tiny amount of grey stubble poking through. Her eyebags were purple, and the joints of her hands were, Robin noticed, very swollen.

'I'll see you all at dinner,' said Taio. His eyes lingered on Robin as he shut the door.

'Welcome!' said the activity leader brightly, looking round at the newcomers. 'We're making these for street sales. All proceeds will be going to our Homes for Humanity project. As you're probably aware . . .'

As he began talking about homelessness statistics, and the ways in which the church was trying to alleviate the problem, Robin took covert stock of the room. Large, framed signs hung on the walls, each containing a short declarative sentence: *I Admit the Possibility; I Am Called to Service; I Live to Love and Give; I Am Master of My Soul; I Live Beyond Mere Matter.*

'. . . delighted to say our London hostels have now taken nearly a thousand people off the street.'

'Wow!' said green-haired Penny.

'And in fact, we have a beneficiary of the scheme here with us,' said the activity leader, indicating the pregnant Chinese girl. 'Wan was in a very bad situation, but she found our hostel,

261

and now she's a valued member of the Universal Humanitarian family.'

Wan nodded, smiling.

'All right, so, you'll find stuffing and empty skins beside you. Once your box is full, carry it back to our machinists and they'll seal up our turtles for us.'

Robin reached into the box between herself and Wan, and set to work.

'What's your name?' the shaven-headed woman asked Robin in a quiet voice.

'Rowena,' said Robin.

'I'm Louise,' said the woman, and Robin remembered that Kevin Pirbright's mother had been called Louise.

She wondered why Louise's head was shaved. In the outside world, she'd have assumed she'd been through chemotherapy, but the UHC's spiritual beliefs made that unlikely. Louise's skin was weathered and chapped; she looked as though she spent most of her life out of doors.

'You're fast,' she added, watching Robin begin to stuff the toy turtle. 'Where are you from?'

'Primrose Hill, in London,' said Robin. 'Where do you—?'

'That's a nice area. Have you got family?'

'A younger sister,' said Robin.

'Are both your parents alive?'

'Yes,' said Robin.

'What do they do?'

'My dad's a hedge fund manager. My mum's got her own business.'

'What kind of business?'

'She provides external HR support to companies,' said Robin.

Louise was working slowly, due to the stiffness of her hands. Her fingernails, Robin noticed, were all broken off. All around the table, the church members were talking to the newcomer to their right, and from what Robin could hear of the conversations, they were running very much along the lines of hers and Louise's: quick-fire questions intended to elicit a lot of personal information. In very brief pauses in Louise's questioning, she overheard Marion Huxley telling her neighbour that she was a widow, who'd run an undertakers with her husband.

'You're not married?' Louise asked Robin.

'No . . . I was going to be, but we called it off,' said Robin.

'Oh, that's a pity,' said Louise. 'What made you interested in the UHC?'

'It was actually a friend of mine,' said Robin. 'She wanted to go, but then she let me down and I ended up attending the temple on my own.'

'That wasn't a coincidence,' said Louise, just as the blonde had said, on Robin's first visit to the temple. 'Most pure spirits were called like that, by what feels like chance. Do you know the fable of the blind turtle? The blind turtle who lives in the depths of the ocean and surfaces once every hundred years? The Buddha said, imagine there was a yoke floating on the ocean, and he asked what the chances that the old, blind turtle would surface at exactly the point that meant his neck would pass through the yoke. That's how hard it is to find enlightenment for most people . . . you're a good worker,' Louise said again, as Robin completed her fourth stuffed turtle. 'I think you'll go pure spirit really fast.'

On Robin's other side, Wan had begun to tell her neighbour the parable of the blind turtle, too. She wondered whether she dared ask Louise why her head was shaved, but decided it might be too personal a question to start with, so instead she said,

'How long have you—?'

But Louise spoke across her, as though she hadn't heard.

'Did you have to take time off your job to come to Chapman Farm?'

'No,' said Robin, smiling. 'I'm not actually working at the moment.'

25

The correct place of the woman is within;
the correct place of the man is without.

The I Ching or Book of Changes

The late afternoon sun pierced Strike's retinas through the sides of his sunglasses as he walked along Sloane Avenue, ready to take over surveillance of Bigfoot. His thoughts were entirely with Robin as he wondered what was happening right now at Chapman Farm, how she was finding her new environment and whether she'd be able to find the plastic rock hidden just inside the perimeter fence.

As Strike approached his destination, Shah, who'd been watching the large hotel called the Chelsea Cloisters, walked away, which was usual procedure for a handover when facing a many-windowed building, from which people might be watching the street. However, a minute later, Strike received a call from the now out-of-sight subcontractor.

'Hi, what's up?'

'He's been in there an hour and a half,' said Shah. 'It's chock-full of sex workers. Eastern European, mainly. I wanted a word about Littlejohn, though.'

'Go on.'

'Did he tell you he worked at Pattersons for a couple of months, before coming to us?'

'No,' said Strike, frowning. 'He didn't.'

'A guy I used to know there, who's now head of security at a City bank, told me yesterday Littlejohn was working for them. The guy resigned before Littlejohn left. He heard he was sacked. No details.'

'Very interesting,' said Strike.

'Yeah,' said Dev. 'He's definitely ex-army, is he?'

'Yeah, ex-SIB, I checked his references,' said Strike. 'His story was he hadn't worked for a couple of months before he came to us. OK, thanks. I'll talk to him.'

Strike was on the point of slipping his mobile back into his pocket when it vibrated, and he saw another emoji-strewn text from Bijou.

Hey strong and silent international man of mystery 👤 🔍 Fancy a "get together" some time this week? 💣 💕 Just bought a new bra and suspender belt and nobody to show them to 😣 😣 Can send pics if you like 😊 ♥ 😊

'Christ,' muttered Strike, returning his mobile to his pocket and taking out his vape pen instead. This would be the second text from Bijou he'd ignored. Two shags did not, in Strike's view, necessitate a formal notice of termination, although he suspected most of the women he knew would have disagreed.

Across the street, a couple of teenaged girls emerged from the Chelsea Cloisters, wearing what looked like pyjamas with their trainers. Talking together, they passed out of sight, returning half an hour later with chocolate bars and bottles of water, and disappeared back inside the large brick and stone building.

Afternoon had shaded slowly into early evening before Strike's target emerged from the building, unknowingly filmed by Strike. As hairy and unkempt as ever, Bigfoot walked off along the street, apparently texting someone.

Evidently one of the advantages of owning your own software company was both the time and means to spend hours of a workday at a hotel. As Strike followed Bigfoot back towards Sloane Square, the detective's mobile rang again.

'Strike.'

'Hi,' said a female voice. 'It's Abigail Glover again. We spoke yesterday.'

'Ah, yes,' said Strike, surprised, 'thanks for getting back to me.'

'I just wanna bit more info,' said Abigail. 'I'm not agreeing to anyfing.'

'Fair enough,' said Strike.

'Who are you working for?'

'Can't disclose that, I'm afraid,' said Strike. 'Client confidentiality.'

'You mentioned that guy Pirbright.'

'Yes. As I said, I've been hired to investigate claims Kevin was making about the church.'

Bigfoot had slowed down and now withdrew into a doorway to read another text. Pretended to be equally absorbed in his own phone conversation, Strike also stopped walking, and feigned interest in passing traffic.

'Pirbright was writing a book, wasn' 'e?' said Abigail.

'How d'you know that?'

'He told me, when he phoned me at work.'

Strike had a hunch he knew exactly what was bothering Abigail.

'I haven't been hired to help finish Pirbright's book.'

When she didn't respond, he said,

'Our client's trying to get a relative out of the UHC. Pirbright told the client about certain incidents he witnessed while in the church, and the client wants to find out how much truth, or otherwise, there was in Pirbright's claims.'

'Oh,' said Abigail. 'I see.'

Bigfoot had set off again. Strike followed, mobile still clamped to his ear.

'I'm not looking to identify ex-church members, or expose their identities,' he reassured Abigail. 'It'll be down to individual witnesses to decide whether they want to go on the record—'

'I don't,' said Abigail quickly.

'I understand,' said Strike, 'but I'd still like to talk to you.'

Up ahead, Bigfoot had stopped again, this time to talk to a slim, dark teenage girl who was heading in the direction of the hotel he'd just left. Strike hastily turned his mobile to camera and took a couple of pictures. When he'd placed the phone back to his ear, Abigail was talking.

'. . . weekend?'

'Great,' said Strike, hoping she'd just agreed to meet him. 'Where would you—?'

'Not at my flat, my lodger's bloody nosy. I'll meet you at seven on Sunday in the Forester on Seaford Road.'

26

*The Joyous is the lake . . . it is a sorceress; it is
mouth and tongue.
It means smashing and breaking apart . . .*

The I Ching or Book of Changes

Robin had no idea how long she'd stuffed toy turtles, but at
a guess, it was a couple of hours. During that time her fake
identity had been so thoroughly tested that she could only be
glad she'd devoted so many hours to bringing Rowena to life.
When Louise asked, Robin was able to give the names of both
her imaginary parents' imaginary cats.

She might have worried that Louise's meticulous questioning of her indicated suspicion of her bona fides, except for the
fact that all the new recruits, as far as she could hear, were
being subjected to similar interrogations. It was as though the
established members had been given a rota of questions to ask,
and Robin had a feeling that the most important parts of what
she'd told Louise would have been memorised, and passed in
due course to somebody else.

The room in which Fire Group was making the toys
became progressively stuffier as they worked, and the relentless
questioning had left so little time to think, that Robin was
relieved when Becca came to the door, smiling and letting in
a cool breeze.

'Thank you for your service,' she told the group, pressing her hands together as though in prayer, and bowing. 'Now, please follow me!'

Everyone trooped after Becca, back past the chicken coop, inside which Wood Group was ushering the hens back into their shed. Seeing the low-hanging sun, Robin realised she must have spent longer with the toy turtles than she'd imagined. There were no longer people in orange dotted over the fields, nor could she see the two Shire horses.

Becca now led them to what Robin guessed was the oldest part of the farm. Ahead lay an old stone sty, and beyond it, a muddy acre of field, where pigs were roaming. Robin could see a couple of teenagers in bee-keeping hats and gloves, tending to the hives. Tethered at a wall nearby stood the two massive horses, still wearing harnesses, their bodies steaming in the cooling air.

'As I explained to some of you on the minibus,' said Becca, 'this is still a working farm. One of our central tenets is to live in harmony with nature, and commit to ethical food production and sustainability. I'm going to hand you over to Jiang now, who'll instruct you.'

Jiang, the minibus driver, now moved forwards.

'OK, you – you – you – you,' muttered Jiang, pointing at four people at random, 'you find wellingtons in the shed, you get the buckets of swill, you get the pigs back in the sty.'

Robin noticed as he spoke that Jiang had several missing teeth. Like Louise, his skin was coarse and chapped, giving him the appearance of being outside in all weathers. As he began to give instructions, his tic recurred; as his right eye began its uncontrollable winking again, he clapped his hand over it and pretended to be rubbing it.

'You four,' said Jiang, pointing at Robin and three others, 'you get the harness off the horses, then you rub them down and brush their feathers. The rest will clean the harness when it comes off.'

Jiang gave the grooming group brushes and combs and left them to their job, disappearing into the stable, while behind them, those trying to entice the pigs into the sty called and cajoled, shaking their buckets of food.

'Did he say *feathers*?' asked green-haired Penny, puzzled.

'He means the hair over their hooves,' Robin explained.

A yell from the field made them all look round: widowed Marion Huxley had slipped in the mud and fallen. The pigs had charged those holding the buckets: country-born Robin, whose uncle was a farmer, could have told them they should have put the food in the trough and opened the gate between sty and field, rather than trying to lead the pigs in, Pied Piper style.

There was pleasure in doing a physical task, and not being bombarded with questions. The harness they removed from the horses was very heavy; Robin and Penny struggled to take it into the stable where some of their group sat waiting to clean it. The Shire horses stood over eighteen hands each, and took a lot of grooming; Robin had to stand on a crate to reach their broad backs and their ears. She was becoming increasingly hungry. She'd wrongly assumed they'd be given something to eat upon arrival.

By the time the inept pig-wranglers had succeeded in persuading their temporary charges back into their sty and both the horses and their harness had been cleaned to Jiang's satisfaction, the red sun was sinking slowly over the fields. Becca now returned. Robin hoped she was about to announce dinner; she felt hollow with hunger.

'Thank you for your service,' said the smiling Becca, putting her hands together and bowing as before. 'Now follow me to temple, please!'

271

Becca led them back past the dining hall, the laundry and the library, then into the central courtyard, where the Drowned Prophet's fountain was glinting red and orange in the sunset. Fire Group followed Becca up the marble steps and through doors that now stood open.

The interior of the temple was every bit as impressive as the outside. Its inner walls were of muted gold, with many scarlet creatures – phoenixes, dragons, horses, roosters and tigers – cavorting together as unlikely playmates. The floor was of shining black marble and the benches, which were cushioned in red and appeared to be of black lacquer, were arranged around a central, raised pentagon-shaped stage.

Robin's eyes travelled naturally upwards, towards the high ceiling. Halfway up the high walls, the space narrowed, because a balcony ran all the way around the temple, behind which were regularly spaced, shadowy arched recesses, which reminded Robin of boxes at a theatre. The five painted prophets in their respective robes of orange, scarlet, blue, yellow and white stared down at worshippers from the ceiling.

A woman in long, amber-beaded orange robes was standing on the raised stage, waiting for them. Her eyes were shadowed by the long curtains of black hair that fell to below her waist; only the long, pointed nose was clearly visible. Only as Robin drew nearer did she see that one of the woman's very dark, narrow eyes was set noticeably higher than the other, giving her a strange lopsided stare, and for reasons Robin couldn't have explained, a tremor passed through her, such as she might have experienced on glimpsing something pale and slimy watching her from the depths of a rockpool.

'Nǐ hǎo,' she said, in a deep voice. 'Welcome.'

She made a wordless gesture of dismissal at Becca, who left, closing the temple doors quietly behind her.

'Please, sit down,' said the woman to Fire Group, indicating benches directly in front of her. When all the recruits had taken their seats, she said,

'My name is Mazu Wace, but church members call me Mama Mazu. My husband is Jonathan Wace—'

Marion Huxley let out a tiny sigh.

'—founder of the Universal Humanitarian Church. You have already rendered us service – for which I thank you.'

Mazu pressed her hands together, prayer style, and bowed as they'd just seen Becca do. The crookedly set, shadowed eyes were darting from face to face.

'I'm about to introduce you to one of the meditation techniques we use here to strengthen the spiritual self, because we cannot fight the ills of the world until we are able to control our false selves, which can be as destructive as anything we may encounter outside.'

Mazu began to pace in front of them, her robes fanning out behind her, glittering in the light from hanging lanterns. Around her neck, on a black cord, she wore a flat mother-of-pearl fish.

'Who here has sometimes been prey to shame, or guilt?'

Everyone raised their hands.

'Who here sometimes feels anxious and overwhelmed?'

All put their hands up again.

'Who sometimes feels hopeless in the face of world issues like climate change, wars and rising inequality?'

The entire group raised their hands for a third time.

'It's perfectly natural to feel those things,' said Mazu, 'but such emotions hamper our spiritual growth and our ability to effect change.

'I'm now going to teach you a simple meditation exercise,' said Mazu. 'Here in the church, we call it the joyful meditation. I want you all to stand up ...'

They did so.

'Spread out a little – you should be at least an arm's length apart . . .'

There was some shuffling.

'We begin with arms hanging loose by your sides . . . now, slowly . . . slowly . . . raise your arms, and as you do so, take in a deep breath and hold it, while your hands join over your head.'

When everyone had clasped their hands over their heads, Mazu said,

'And exhale, slowly lowering your arms . . . and now smile. Massage your jaw as you do so. Feel the muscles' tightness. Keep smiling!'

A tiny gust of nervous laughter passed through the group.

'That's good,' said Mazu, staring down at them all, and she smiled again, as humourlessly as before. Her skin was so pale, her teeth looked yellow by contrast. 'And now . . . I want you to laugh.'

Another ripple of laughter ran through the group.

'That's it!' said Mazu. 'It doesn't matter if you're faking at first. Just laugh. Come on, now!'

A couple of recruits forced faked laughs, which elicited real ones from their companions. Robin could hear her own fake laughter over the apparently sincere giggles of green-haired Penny.

'Come on now,' said Mazu, looking down at Robin. 'Laugh for me.'

Robin laughed more loudly, and catching the eye of a mousey-haired youth who was determinedly, though very insincerely, guffawing, found herself amused and broke into real laughter. The infectious sound made her neighbours join in, and soon, Robin doubted whether there was a single person not genuinely laughing.

'Keep it up!' said Mazu, waving her hand around at them, as though conducting an orchestra. 'Keep laughing!'

For how long the group laughed, Robin didn't know; perhaps only five minutes, perhaps ten. Every time she found her face aching, and reverted to forced chuckles, she found genuine laughter overtaking her once more.

At last, Mazu raised a single finger to her lips and the laughing stopped. The group stood, slightly breathless, still grinning.

'You feel that?' said Mazu. 'You have control over your own moods and your own state of mind. Grasp that, and you have placed your foot on the path that leads to pure spirit. Once there, you'll unlock power you never knew you had ...

'And now we kneel.'

The command took everyone by surprise, but all obeyed and instinctively closed their eyes.

'Blessed Divinity,' intoned Mazu, 'we thank you for the wellspring of joy you have placed in all of us, which the materialist world tries so hard to extinguish. As we explore our own power, we honour yours, which lies forever beyond our full understanding. Each of us is spirit before flesh, containing a fragment of the force that animates the universe. We thank you for today's lesson and for this moment of gladness.

'And now, rise,' said Mazu.

Robin got to her feet with the others. Mazu descended from the stage, the train of her robes rippling over the black marble steps, and led them towards the closed temple doors. As she approached them, she pointed a pale finger at the handles. They turned of their own accord and the doors slowly opened. Robin assumed someone else had opened them from outside, but there was nobody there.

27

Thunder comes resounding out of the earth:
The image of ENTHUSIASM.
Thus the ancient kings made music
In order to honour merit,
And offered it with splendour
To the Supreme Deity . . .

The I Ching or Book of Changes

'*Did you see that?*' breathed Penny in Robin's ear, as they descended the temple steps. 'She opened the doors without touching them!'

'I know,' said Robin, carefully astonished. 'What *was* that?'

She was certain the door opening must have been a trick, using some kind of a hidden mechanism, but the thing had looked unnervingly convincing.

Ahead, in the otherwise deserted courtyard, stood Becca Pirbright. Glancing back, Robin saw that Mazu had retreated inside the temple again.

'How was the Joyful Meditation?' Becca asked.

There was a small chorus of 'it was great's and 'amazing's.

'Before we go to dinner – ' *thank God,* thought Robin, '– I'd like to just say a word about another of our spiritual practices at the UHC.

'This,' said Becca, gesturing towards the statue in the pool, 'is the Drowned Prophet, who in life was called Daiyu Wace. I actually had the privilege of knowing her, and I witnessed her performing extraordinary spiritual feats.

'Each of our prophets, when alive, exemplified a principle of our church. The Drowned Prophet teaches us, firstly, that death may come to any of us, at any time, so we should hold ourselves always in spiritual readiness to rejoin the spirit world. Secondly, her self-sacrifice shows us the importance of obedience to the Blessed Divinity. Thirdly, she proves the reality of life after death, because she continues to move between the earthly and spiritual planes.

'Whenever we pass her pool, we kneel, anoint ourselves with her water, and acknowledge her teachings by saying, "The Drowned Prophet will bless all who worship her." By which we do not mean that Daiyu is a goddess. She merely embodies the pure spirit and the higher realm. I invite you now to kneel at the pool and anoint yourselves before dinner.'

Tired and hungry as they were, nobody refused.

'The Drowned Prophet will bless all who worship her,' muttered Robin.

'All right, Fire Group, follow me!' Becca said, smiling, when all had made the tribute to the Drowned Prophet, and she led them back towards the dining hall, Robin aware of the cool spot of water on her forehead as the breeze hit it.

Fire Group was the last to enter the room. Robin estimated that a hundred people were already sitting at the tables, although there was no sign of any small children, who presumably had been fed earlier. Free spaces were dotted about, so the members of her group were forced to split up and find places wherever they could. Robin scanned the room for Will Edensor, finally spotting him at a crowded table which had no free spaces, so she took a seat between two strangers instead.

'Here for your Week of Service?' said a smiling young man with wavy blond hair.

'Yes,' said Robin.

'I thank you for your service,' he said immediately, pressing his hands together and performing a little bow.

'I – don't know what to say back to that,' said Robin, and he laughed.

'The response is, "And I for yours."'

'With the bow?' asked Robin, and he laughed again.

'With the bow.'

Robin pressed her hands together, bowed and said,

'And I for yours.'

Before either could speak again, music started from hidden speakers: David Bowie's 'Heroes'. The blond-haired man whooped and got to his feet, as did nearly everyone else. Cheers broke out, as Jonathan and Mazu Wace entered the room, hand in hand. Robin spotted Marion Huxley, the undertaker's widow, pressing her hands to her face as though she'd just seen a rock star. Jonathan waved at the excited church members, while Mazu wore a gracious smile, the train of her robes sliding over the paved floor. There were many cries of 'Papa J!' as the pair climbed up to the top table, where Taio Wace and Becca Pirbright were already sitting. Glancing around, Robin saw Jiang sitting in front of his clean tin plate among the ordinary members. The similarity of Jiang's and Mazu's narrow, dark eyes made Robin suspect that he was, at the very least, Taio's half-brother. As she watched, Jiang's eye began to twitch uncontrollably again, and he concealed it swiftly with his hand.

Mazu took her seat at the top table, but Jonathan walked in front of it, hands raised, gesturing for the church members to settle down. Robin was once again struck by his striking good looks, and how little he looked like a man in his mid-sixties.

'Thank you,' he said with his self-deprecating smile, wearing a wireless microphone that amplified his voice over hidden speakers. 'Thank you . . . it's good to be home.'

Will Edensor, who was easy to spot given his height, was smiling and cheering with the rest of the room, and for a moment, remembering Will's dying mother, she found herself completely in sympathy with James Edensor, who'd called Will an idiot.

'We shall replenish our material bodies, and then we'll talk!' said Jonathan.

More cheers and more applause followed. Jonathan took his seat between Mazu and Becca Pirbright.

Kitchen workers now appeared from a side door, wheeling along large metal vats, from which they ladled food onto the tin plates. The four at the top table, Robin noticed, were being brought china plates already full of food.

When her turn came, Robin received a dollop of brown sludge that seemed to comprise overcooked vegetables, followed by a ladleful of noodles. The vegetables had been flavoured with too much turmeric and the noodles had an overcooked, gluey consistency. Robin ate as slowly as she could, trying to fool her stomach into believing it had consumed more calories than it had, because she knew the nutritional value of what they were eating was very low.

Robin's two young male neighbours kept up a steady stream of chat, asking her name, where she was from and what had attracted her to the church. She soon found out that the young man with wavy blond hair had been at the University of East Anglia, which had hosted one of Papa J's meetings. The other, who was wearing a buzz cut, had been to one of the church-run addiction centres and been recruited there.

'Have you seen anything, yet?' the latter asked Robin.

'You mean the tour of the—?'

'No,' he said, 'I mean – you know. Pure spirit.'

'Oh,' said Robin, cottoning on. 'I saw Mazu make the temple doors open, just by pointing at them.'

'Did you think it was a trick?'

'Well,' said Robin cautiously, 'I don't know. I mean, it could have—'

'It's not a trick,' said the young man. 'You think it is at first, then you realise it's real. You should see the things Papa J can do. You wait. You think at first it must all be a load of bull, then you start seeing what it means, being pure spirit. It blows your effing mind. Have you read *The Answer*?'

'No,' said Robin, 'I—'

'She hasn't read *The Answer*,' said the man with the buzz cut, leaning forwards to address Robin's other neighbour.

'Oh, dude, you've got to read *The Answer*,' said the blond man, laughing. 'Wow.'

'I'll lend you my copy,' said the man with the buzz cut. 'Only I want it back, because Papa J's written something in there for me, OK?'

'OK, thanks very much,' said Robin.

'Wow,' he said, shaking his head and laughing, 'Can't believe you haven't read *The Answer*. Like, it gives you the tools and it explains – I can't do it as well as Papa J, you need to read his actual words. But I can tell you first-hand, there's life after death, and a spiritual war raging here on earth, and if we can win—'

'Yeah,' said the wavy blond young man, who now looked serious. '*If* we win.'

'We have to,' said the other intensely. 'We *have* to.'

Through a gap between the two diners opposite her, Robin spotted the shaven-headed Louise, who was eating very slowly, and kept glancing up at the top table, ignoring the chatter of those on either side of her. There were many other

280

middle-aged women dotted around the hall, Robin saw, and most of them looked like Louise, as though they'd long since abandoned any interest in their appearance, their faces deeply lined and their hair cropped short, though none of them were entirely shaven-headed like Louise. Watching her, Robin remembered what Kevin had said about his mother being in love with Jonathan Wace. Had the feeling survived all these years of servitude? Had it been worth the loss of her son?

One of the people who came to clear away the plates was the teenaged girl Robin had noticed earlier, with the long, mousey, sun-bleached hair and large, anxious eyes. When the plates had been cleared away, more kitchen workers appeared with stacks of metal bowls on their trolleys. These proved to be full of stewed apple, which Robin found very bitter, doubtless because refined sugar was forbidden by the church. Nevertheless, she ate it all, while her neighbours talked across her of holy war.

Robin had no idea what time it was. The sky outside the window was black, and it had taken a long time to dish out food for a hundred people. Finally the bowls, too, were cleared away, and somebody dimmed the overhead lights, though leaving the top table spot lit.

At once, those at the trestle tables began clapping and cheering again, some of them even banging their tin water mugs on the table. Jonathan Wace stood up, walked around the table, his microphone switched back on, and once again calmed the crowd by making a dampening motion with his hands.

'Thank you, my friends. Thank you ... I stand before you tonight with both hope and fear in my heart. Hope and fear,' he added, looking solemnly around.

'I want to tell you, firstly, that this church, this community of souls, which now stretches across two continents—'

There were a few more whoops and cheers.

'—represents the single biggest spiritual challenge to the Adversary that the world has ever seen.'

The room applauded.

'I feel its power,' said Jonathan, holding his clenched fist to his heart. 'I feel it when I speak to our American brothers and sisters, I feel it in when I spoke earlier this week at our Munich temple, I felt it today when I re-entered this place, and when I went to temple to purify. And I want to single out some individuals this evening, who give me hope. With individuals like these on our side, the Adversary should rightly tremble . . .'

Wace, who was carrying no notes, now called out several names, and as each person was identified, they either screamed or shouted, bounding to their feet while those sitting around them cheered and clapped.

'. . . and last, but never least,' said Wace, 'Danny Brockles.'

The young man with the buzz cut beside Robin jumped to his feet so fast he hit her hard on the elbow.

'Oh my God,' he was saying, over and over again, and Robin saw that he was crying. 'Oh my God.'

'Come up here, all of you,' said Jonathan Wace. 'Come on . . . everyone, show your appreciation for these people . . .'

The dining hall rang with further cheers and shouts. All those called had burst into tears and seemed overcome to have been recognised by Wace.

Wace began talking about each member's achievements. One of the girls had collected more money on the street than anyone else, over a four-week period. Another girl had recruited a dozen new members to the Week of Service. When finally Jonathan Wace reached Danny Brockles, the younger man was sobbing so hard that Wace walked to him and embraced him, while Brockles cried into the church leader's shoulder. The watchers, by now cheering wildly, got to their feet to give Danny and Wace a standing ovation.

'Tell us what you did this week, Danny,' said Wace. 'Tell everyone why I'm so proud of you.'

'I c-c-can't,' sobbed Danny, completely overcome.

'Then I'll tell them,' said Wace, turning to face the crowd. 'Our addiction services centre in Northampton was threatened with closure by agents of the Adversary.'

A storm of booing broke out. The news about the addiction centre seemed to have been unknown to everyone but the top table.

'Wait – wait – wait,' said Jonathan, making his usual calming gestures with his left hand, while holding Danny's arm with his right. 'Becca took Danny along, to explain how much it had helped him. Danny stood up in front of those materialists and spoke so eloquently, so powerfully, that he ensured the service's continuation. He did that. *Danny did that.*'

Wace raised Danny's arm into the air. A storm of cheers ensued.

'With people like Danny with us, should the Adversary be afraid?' shouted Jonathan, and the screams and applause grew even louder. Jonathan was crying now, tears flooding down his face. This show of emotion caused a level of hysteria in the hall that Robin started to find almost unnerving, and it continued even after the six selected people had resumed their seats, until at last, mopping his eyes and making his calming gesture, Jonathan managed to make himself heard again, his voice now slightly hoarse.

'And now ... with regret ... I must bring you bulletins from the materialist world ...'

A hush fell over the hall as Jonathan began to speak.

He told of the continuing war in Syria, and described the atrocities there, then spoke of massive corruption among the world's political and financial elites. He spoke of the outbreak of Zika in Brazil, which was causing so many babies to be miscarried or born severely disabled. He described individual instances of appalling poverty and despair he'd witnessed while attending church-run projects in both the UK and America, and as he told of these injustices and disasters, he might have been describing things that had befallen his own family, so deeply did they seem to touch him. Robin remembered Sheila Kennett's words: *he had a way of making you want to make everything all right, for him . . . you wanted to look after him . . . he seemed to feel it worse than all the rest of us.*

'That, then, is the materialist world,' Jonathan said at last. 'And if our task seems overwhelming, it is because the Adversary's forces are powerful . . . desperately powerful. The inevitable End Game approaches, which is why we fight to hasten the coming of the Lotus Way. Now, I ask you all to join me in meditation. For those who have not yet learned our mantra, the words are printed here.'

Two girls in orange tracksuits mounted the stage, holding large white boards, on which were printed: *Lokah Samastah Sukhino Bhavantu.*

'A deep breath, raising the arms,' said Jonathan, and though the benches at the tables were cramped, every arm was slowly raised, and there was a universal intake of breath. 'And exhale,' said Jonathan quietly, and the room breathed out again.

'And now: *Lokah Samastah Sukhino Bhavantu. Lokah Samastah Sukhino Bhavantu. Lokah Samastah Sukhino Bhavantu . . .*'

Robin caught the pronunciation of the mantra from her neighbours. A hundred people chanted, and chanted, and chanted some more, and Robin began to feel a strange calm creeping over her. The rhythm seemed to vibrate inside her, hypnotic and soothing, with Jonathan's the only distinguishable voice among the many, and soon she didn't need to read the words off the board, but was able to repeat them automatically.

At last, the first bars of David Bowie's 'Heroes' blended with the voices of the crowd, at which point the chants became cheers, and everyone jumped to their feet, and began embracing. Robin was pulled into a hug with the elated Danny, then by her blond neighbour. The two young men embraced each other, and now the entire crowd was singing along to Bowie's song and clapping in time. Tired and hungry though she was, Robin smiled as she clapped and sang along with the rest.

28

This hexagram is composed of the trigram Li above,
i.e., flame, which burns upward, and Tui below, i.e.,
the lake, which seeps downward . . .

The I Ching or Book of Changes

Strike had to change the rota to accommodate his interview
with Abigail Glover on Sunday evening. Only then did he
see that Clive Littlejohn was off work for four days. As Strike
wanted to see Littlejohn's reaction in person when he asked
why he hadn't disclosed his previous employment at Patterson
Inc, he decided to postpone their chat until it could be done
face to face.

Strike spent Saturday afternoon at Lucy's, because she'd persuaded their Uncle Ted to come for a short visit. There was no
doubt that Ted had aged considerably since their aunt's death.
He seemed to have shrunk, and several times lost the thread
of conversation. Twice, he called Lucy 'Joan'.

'What d'you think?' Lucy whispered to Strike in the
kitchen, where he'd gone to help her with coffee.

'Well, I don't think he thinks you *are* Joan,' said Strike
quietly. 'But yeah . . . I think we should get him looked at by
someone. Someone who can assess him for dementia.'

'It'd be his GP, wouldn't it?' said Lucy. 'First?'

'Probably,' said Strike.

'I'll ring and see if I can make an appointment for him,' said Lucy. 'I know he'll never leave Cornwall, but it'd be so much easier to look after him here.'

Guilt, which wasn't entirely due to the fact that Lucy did considerably more looking after Ted than he did, prompted Strike to say, 'If you make the appointment, I'll go down to Cornwall and go with him. Report back.'

'Stick, are you serious?' said Lucy, astonished. 'Oh my God, that would be *ideal.* You're about the only person who could stop him cancelling.'

Strike travelled back to Denmark Street that evening with the now familiar faint depression dogging him. Talking to Robin, even on work matters, tended to lift his mood, but that option wasn't open to him and might not be possible for weeks. Another text from Bijou, which arrived while he was making himself an omelette, caused him nothing but irritation.

So are you undercover somewhere you can't get texts or am I being ghosted? 👻 😵

He ate his omelette at the kitchen table. Once finished, he picked up his mobile with a view to dealing with at least one problem quickly and cleanly. After thinking for a few moments, and dismissing any idea of ending what, in his view, had never started, he typed:

Busy, no time for meet ups for foreseeable future

If she had any pride, he thought, that would be the end of the matter.

He spent most of a chilly Sunday on surveillance, handing over to Midge at four o'clock, then drove out to Ealing for his meeting with Abigail Glover.

The Forester on Seaford Road was a large pub with an exterior featuring wooden columns, window baskets and green tiled walls, its sign showing a stump with an axe sticking out of it. Strike ordered himself the usual zero-alcohol beer and took a corner table for two beside the wood-panelled wall.

Twenty minutes passed, and Strike had started to wonder whether Abigail had changed her mind about meeting him, when a tall and striking woman entered the bar, wearing gym gear with a coat hastily slung over it. The only picture he'd found of Abigail online had been small and she'd been wearing overalls, surrounded by fellow fire fighters who were all male. What hadn't been captured by the photograph was how good looking she was. She'd inherited her father's large, dark blue eyes and firm, dimpled chin, but her mouth was fuller than Wace's, her pale skin flawless and her high cheekbones could have been those of a model. He knew her to be in her mid-thirties, but her hair, which was tied back in a ponytail, was already grey. Strangely, it not only suited her, it made her look younger, her skin being fine and unlined. She nodded greetings to a couple of men at the bar, then spotted him and strode, long-legged, towards his table.

'Abigail?' he said, getting to his feet to shake hands.

'Sorry I'm late,' she said. 'Timekeeping's not me strong point. They call me "the late Abigail Glover" at work. I was in the gym, I lost track of time. 'S my stress buster.'

'No problem, I'm grateful you agreed to—'

'D'you wanna drink?'

'Let m—'

''S'OK, I'll get me own.'

She shrugged off her coat, revealing a Lycra top and leggings. One of the men she'd already greeted at the bar wolf-whistled. Abigail gave him the finger with one hand, which elicited gales of laughter, while rummaging in her gym bag for her purse.

Strike watched her buying a drink. Her rear view showed a lot of muscle, which made him reflect that his own daily exercises weren't having nearly such a dramatic effect. She was almost as broad across the back as the man nearest her, who evidently found her very attractive, though she didn't seem to return his interest. He wondered whether she was gay, then wondered whether wondering this was offensive.

Having secured her drink, Abigail returned to Strike's table, sat down opposite him and took a large gulp of white wine. One of her knees was jogging up and down.

'Sorry we couldn't do this at me flat. Patrick, my lodger, 'e's a pain in the arse about the UHC. 'E'd get overexcited if he knew *you* was investigatin' 'em.'

'Has he been your lodger long?' asked Strike, purely to make conversation.

'Free years. 'E's all right, really. 'E got divorced an' needed a room an' I needed rent. On'y, ever since I told 'im where I grew up 'e's been bangin' on, "you should write a book abou' your child'ood, make some proper money." Wish I'd never said nuffing to 'im about it. I just 'ad too much wine one night. I'd been out to a bloody terrible 'ouse fire where a woman an' two kids died.'

'Sorry to hear that,' said Strike.

''S the job,' said Abigail, with a slight shrug, 'but sometimes it gets to you. That one did – arson – the farver did it 'imself, tryna work an insurance scam on 'is shop, downstairs. 'E got out all right, bastard ... I 'ate it when there's kids involved. We got the younger one out alive, but it was too late. Smoke in'alation done for 'im.'

'What made you join the fire service?'

'Adrenaline junkie,' she said with a fleeting grin, her knee still bouncing up and down. She took another gulp of wine. 'I got outta Chapman Farm an' I just wan'ed to fuckin' *live*, wan'ed to see some action and do somefing wiv a *point* to it, instead of makin' effing corn dollies to sell for starvin' kids in Africa – if that's where the money even wen'. Doubt it. But I never 'ad much education. I 'ad to study for GCSEs when I got out. Scraped free of 'em. Older'n all the other kids in the class. Still, I was one o' the lucky ones. Least I know 'ow to read.'

As she picked up her glass again, a bearded man passed their table.

'Been on Tinder, 'ave you, Ab?'

'Fuck off,' said Abigail coldly.

The man smirked, but didn't move away.

'Baz,' he said, holding out his hand to Strike.

'Terry,' said Strike, shaking it.

'Well, you watch yourself, Terry,' said Baz. 'She goes froo men like diarrhoea.'

He swaggered away.

'Bastard,' muttered Abigail, looking over her shoulder. 'Wouldna come in 'ere if I'd known *'e'd* be 'ere.'

'Work mate?'

'No, 'e's a friend of Patrick's. I wen' out for a drink wiv 'im a coupla times an' then I told 'im I didn' wanna see 'im again, an' 'e was pissed off. Then Patrick gets drunk wiv 'im and blabs stuff abou' what I told 'im abou' the UHC, and now, whenever that arsehole sees me, 'e uses it to ... s'my fault,' she said angrily. 'I should've kep' me mouf shut. When men 'ear ...'

Her voice trailed away and she took another gulp of wine. Strike, who assumed Baz had been told about the church's spirit bonding practices, wondered for the first time how young girls were when they were expected to join in.

'Well, as I said on the phone, this talk's strictly off the record,' said the detective. 'Nothing's going to be published.'

'Unless you bring the church down,' said Abigail.

'You might be overestimating my capabilities.'

She was rapidly emptying her wine glass. After considering him for a moment or two out of her dark blue eyes she said, a little aggressively,

'Fink I'm a coward, do yah?'

'Probably the last thing I was thinking,' said Strike. 'Why?'

'Don' you fink I should try'na to expose 'em? Write one of them bloody misery books? Well,' she said, before Strike could respond, 'they've got far better lawyers than I can afford on a fire fighter's salary, an' I get enough grief about the UHC, just from people like *that* arsehole knowing.'

She jabbed an angry finger at Baz, who was now standing alone at the bar.

'I won't be publicising anything,' Strike assured her. 'I only want to—'

'Yeah, you said on the phone,' she interrupted, 'an' I wanna say somefing about that Kevin Pirbright bloke what rang me. There was this one fing 'e said an' it really bloody upset me.'

'What was that?'

'It was abou' me mum,' said Abigail, 'an' 'ow she died.'

'How did she die, if you don't mind me asking?' said Strike, though he already knew.

'She drowned, off Cromer beach. She was epileptic. She 'ad a fit. We was swimming back to the beach, racin' each other. I looked round when it was shallow enough, and I fort I'd won, but . . . she'd disappeared.'

'I'm sorry,' said Strike, 'that sounds extremely traumatic. How old were you?'

'Seven. But that bloody Kevin guy, on the phone . . .'e wanted me to say my father drowned 'er.'

Abigail drained her glass before saying forcefully,

''S *not true*. My farver wasn' even in the water when it 'appened, 'e was buying ice cream. He come sprintin' back when 'e 'eard me screamin'. 'E an' anuvver man dragged Mum back onto the sand. Dad tried to give her mouf-to-mouf, but it was too late.'

'I'm sorry,' said Strike again.

'When Pirbright said Dad killed 'er … it was like 'e was taking somefing … it's about the only good fing I've ever 'ad to 'old onto, from before Chapman Farm, that they loved each ovver, an' if I 'aven't got that, then it's *all* shit, you know?'

'Yes,' said Strike, who'd had to work so hard to hold onto the good in his memories of his own mother, 'I do.'

'Pirbright kept sayin', "'E killed her, didn' 'e? 'E *did*, didn' 'e?" An' I was saying, "No, 'e fuckin' didn'" an' I ended up telling 'im to fuck off and I 'ung up. It shook me right up, 'im finding me and ringing me at work,' said Abigail, with an air of faint surprise at her own reaction. 'I 'ad a couple of really bad days, after.'

'I'm not surprised,' said Strike.

''E said 'e'd been dropped by 'is publisher. Seemed to fink, if I give 'im enough gory details, 'e'd be able to get another deal. You've read 'is book, 'ave you?'

'There isn't one,' said Strike.

'What?' said Abigail, frowning. 'Was 'e lying?'

'No, but his laptop was stolen, presumably by his killer.'

'Oh … yeah. I 'ad the police call me, after 'e got shot. They'd found the station number in 'is room. I didn' understand at first. I fort 'e'd shot 'imself. 'E sounded weird on the phone. Unstable. Then I seen in the paper 'e was dealing drugs.'

'That's what the police think,' said Strike.

'It's ev'rywhere,' said Abigail. 'That's the on'y fing the UHC gets right, no drugs. I've dragged enough junkies outta shitholes they set on fire by accident, I should know.'

She glanced around. Baz was still standing at the bar.

'I'll get it,' said Strike.

'Oh. Cheers,' she said, surprised.

When Strike returned with a fresh glass of wine, she thanked him, then said,

'So 'ow d'you know abou' these allegations 'e made about the church, if there was no book?'

'Pirbright was emailing our client. D'you mind if I take notes?'

'No,' she said, but she looked edgy as he drew out his notebook.

'I just want to make one thing clear,' said Strike. 'I believe your mother's death was an accident. I'm only asking the following questions to make sure I've covered everything. Was there a life insurance policy on her?'

'No. We was broke after she died. She was always the one wiv the steady job.'

'What did she do?'

'Anyfing – worked in shops, did a bit of cleaning. We moved around a lot.'

'Did your parents own property?'

'No, we always rented.'

'Couldn't either of your parents' families have helped out, financially?' asked Strike, remembering the old Harrovian background.

'My farver's parents emigrated to Souf Africa. 'E didn' get on wiv 'em. Probably 'cause they sent 'im to 'Arrow, but 'e turned out a grifter. I fink 'e used to weasel bits of money out of 'em, but they got sick of 'im.'

'Was he ever employed?'

'Not properly. There was a few dodgy schemes, get-rich-quick stuff. It was all gettin' by on the accent and the charm. I remember a luxury car business what went bust.'

'And your mother's family?'

'Workin' class. Skint. My muvver was very pretty but I

fink my farver's family fort she was rough – probably annuver reason they didn' approve. She was a dancer when they met.'

Well aware that the word 'dancer' might not necessarily imply the Royal Ballet, Strike chose not to enquire further.

'How soon after your mother died did your father take you to Chapman Farm?'

'Coupla monfs, I fink.'

'What made him move there, d'you know?'

'Cheap place to live.' Abigail swigged more wine. 'Off the grid. 'Ide from 'is debts. An' it was a group wiv a power what-sit at the top ... vacuum ... you know abou' that? Abou' the people 'oo was at Chapman Farm, before the church started?'

'Yeah,' said Strike, 'I do.'

'I only found ou' after I left. There was still a few of 'em there, when we arrived. My farver got rid of anyone 'e didn't want, but 'e kept people 'oo'd be useful.'

'Took charge immediately, did he?'

'Oh yeah,' said Abigail, unsmiling. 'If 'e'd been a businessman or somefing ... but that was too ordinary for 'im. But 'e knew 'ow to make people wanna do fings, an' 'e was good at spotting talent. 'E kept the creepy old guy 'oo said 'e was a doctor, an' this couple 'oo knew 'ow to run the farm, an' there was this guy called Alex Graves, 'oo my farver kept because 'is family was rich. An' *Mazu,* of course,' said Abigail, with contempt. ''E kept *'er.* The police shouldn' of let *any* of 'em stay behind,' she added fiercely, before taking another large gulp of wine. 'It's like cancer. You've gotta cut the 'ole fing out, or you'll jus' be back where you started. Sometimes, you get sumfing worse.'

She'd already drunk most of her second glass of wine.

'Mazu's Malcolm Crowther's daughter,' she added. 'She's the spit of 'im.'

'Really?'

'Yeah. When I got out, I looked 'em up. An' I found out

what the ovver bruvver did, too, an' I fort, "Ah, thass where she learned it all. 'Er uncle.'"

'What d'you mean "learned it all"?' asked Strike.

'Gerald was a kids' magician before 'e wen' to live at the farm.'

Another memory came back to Strike at that moment, of the fatter of the two Crowther brothers showing little girls card tricks by firelight, and in that moment he felt nothing but sympathy for Abigail's comparison of the community to cancer.

'When you say "that's where she learned it all"—?'

'Slate – no, sleight, is it? – of 'and? She was good at it,' said Abigail. 'I'd seen magicians on the telly, I knew what she mus' be up to, but the ovver kids fort she could really do magic. They didn' call it magic, though. Pure spirit,' said Abigail, her lip curling.

She glanced over her shoulder in time to see Baz leaving the pub.

'Good,' she said, getting up immediately. 'Wan' anuvver beer?'

'No, you're all right,' said Strike.

When Abigail had returned with her third wine and sat down again, Strike asked,

'How soon after you moved into Chapman Farm was your sister born?'

'She was never born.'

Strike thought she must have misunderstood him.

'I'm talking about when Daiyu—'

'She wasn' my sister,' said Abigail. 'She was already there when we arrived. Mazu 'ad 'er wiv Alex Graves.'

'I thought—?'

'I know what you fort. After Alex died, Mazu pretended Daiyu was my farver's.'

'Why?'

'Because Alex's family tried to get custody of 'er, after 'e killed 'imself. Mazu didn' wanna give Daiyu up, so she an' my farver cooked up the story that Daiyu was really 'is. Alex's family took it to court. I remember Mazu going berserk when she gotta legal letter sayin' she 'ad to provide Daiyu's DNA samples.'

'This is interesting,' said Strike, who was now taking rapid notes. 'Were the samples ever taken?'

'No,' said Abigail, ''cause she drowned.'

'Right,' said Strike, looking up. 'But Alex Graves thought Daiyu was his?'

'Oh, yeah. 'E made a will and named Daiyu as the sole bene – ben – what's it?'

'Beneficiary?'

'Yeah ... tole you I never 'ad no education,' Abigail muttered. 'Should read more, prob'ly. Sometimes I fink abou' tryin' to do a course, or somefing.'

'Never too late,' said Strike. 'So there was a will, and Daiyu stood to get everything Graves had to leave?'

'Yeah. I 'eard Mazu an' my farver talkin' abou' it.'

'Did he have much to give?'

'Dunno. 'E looked like an 'obo, but 'is family was wealfy. They used to come an' see 'im at the farm sometimes. The UHC weren' as strict abou' visitors then, people could still jus' drive in. The Graves was posh. My farver 'ad Graves' sister eatin' out of 'is 'and. Chubby girl. My farver'd try an' get in wiv anyone 'oo 'ad money.'

'So after Daiyu died, your stepmother—'

'Don' call her that,' said Abigail sharply. 'I never use the word "muvver" for that bitch, not even wiv "step" in front of it.'

'Sorry,' said Strike. 'Mazu, then – she presumably inherited all Graves had left?'

'I s'pose,' said Abigail, with a shrug. 'I was shunted off to the Birming'am centre not long after Daiyu died. Mazu always 'ated the bloody sight of me, she wasn' gonna let me stay if *'er* daughter was dead. I ran away from the street in Birming'am when I was out collectin' for the church. The day's takings paid for a coach ticket to London an' my mum's mum. It's 'er flat I live in now. She left it to me, bless 'er.'

'How old were you when you left the church?'

'Sixteen,' said Abigail.

'Have you had any contact with your father since?'

'None,' said Abigail, 'which is jus' the way I like it.'

'He never tried to find you or contact you?'

'No. I was a Deviate, wasn' I? Thass what they call people that leave. He couldn' 'ave a daughter 'oo was a Deviate, not the 'Ead of the Church. 'E was probably as 'appy to see the back of me as I was of 'im.'

Abigail drank more wine. Her pale cheeks were becoming pink.

'Y'know,' she said abruptly, 'before the church, I liked 'im. Prob'ly loved 'im. I always liked being one of the lads, an' 'e'd mess around wiv me, an' chuck a ball around and whatever. 'E was cool wiv me being a tomboy and everyfing, but after Mazu, 'e changed. She's a fuckin' sociopath,' said Abigail viciously, 'an' she changed 'im.'

Strike chose not to respond to this comment. He knew, of course, that alchemical changes of personality were possible under a strong influence, especially in those whose characters weren't fully formed. However, by Abigail's own account, Wace had been a charismatic, amoral chancer even when married to his first wife; his second, by the sounds of it, had merely been the ideal accomplice in his ascent to the status of Messiah.

''E started telling me off for all the stuff Mazu didn' like about me,' Abigail went on. 'She told 'im I was boy mad. I was on'y eight. I just liked playing football . . . and then 'e told me I couldn't call 'im "Dad" any more, I 'ad to say Papa J, like everyone else.

'It's a man's world,' said Abigail Glover, throwing back her head, 'an' women like Mazu, they know where the power is, an' they play the game, they wanna make sure the men are 'appy, an' then the men'll let 'em 'ave a bit of power themselves. She made all the girls do . . . stuff she didn' 'ave to do. *She* didn' do it. She was up there' Abigail raised one hand horizontally, as high as it would go, 'an' we were down there,' she said, pointing at the floor. 'She trod on all of us so she could be the fuckin' queen.'

'She felt differently about her own daughter, though?' said Strike.

'Oh, yeah,' said Abigail, taking another glug of wine. 'Daiyu was a spoiled brat – but that don' mean . . . what 'appened to 'er . . . it was bloody terrible. She was annoyin', but – I was upset, too. Mazu didn' fink I cared, but I did. It brought it all back, what 'appened to Mum, an' all. I fuckin' 'ate the sea,' Abigail muttered. 'Can't even watch *Pirates of the* fuckin' *Caribbean*.'

'Would it be OK to go back over what happened to Daiyu?' asked Strike. 'I'll understand if you'd rather not.'

'We can, if you wan',' said Abigail, 'but I was at the farm when it 'appened, so I can' tell you much.'

Her tongue was much looser now. Strike guessed she hadn't eaten anything between gym and pub: the wine was having a definite effect, large framed though she was.

'Do you remember the girl who took Daiyu to the beach that morning?'

'I remember she was blonde, an' a bit older than me, but I couldn' pick 'er out of a line-up now. You didn' 'ave friends, you weren' s'posed to get close to people. They used to call it material possession or somefing. Sometimes I'd get people tryna smarm up to me because I was my farver's daughter, but they soon realised that didn' count for nuffin. If I'd put in a good word for anyone, Mazu'd prob'ly make sure they were punished.'

'So you've got no idea where Cherie Gittins is now?'

'That was 'er name, was it? I fort it was Cheryl. No, I dunno where any of 'em are.'

'I've heard,' said Strike, 'that Cherie drove the truck out of Chapman Farm past you and two other people, on the morning Daiyu drowned.'

'The 'ell d'you know that?' said Abigail, seeming more unnerved than impressed.

'My partner interviewed Sheila Kennett.'

'Bloody 'ell, is old Sheila still alive? I'd've fort she was long gone. Yeah, me an' this lad called Paul an' Sheila's 'usband was all on early duty – you 'ad to feed the livestock an' collect eggs an' start breakfast. That girl Cherie an' Daiyu come past us in the van, off to do the vegetable run. Daiyu waved at us. We was surprised, but we fort she 'ad permission to go. She got to do a ton of stuff the rest of the kids didn'.'

'And when did you find out she'd drowned?'

'Near lunchtime. Mazu 'ad already gone fuckin' berserk, findin' out Daiyu 'ad gone off wiv Cherie, an' we was in the shit, the ones 'oo'd seen 'em go by an' not stopped 'em.'

'Was your father upset?'

'Oh, yeah. I remember 'im cryin'. 'Uggin' Mazu.'

'Cried, did he?'

'Oh, yeah,' said Abigail dourly. ''E can turn on the water-works like no man you ever met ... but I don't fink 'e liked Daiyu much, really. She wasn' 'is, an' men don' never feel the same abou' kids that aren' theirs, do they? We've got a guy at work, the way 'e talks abou' 'is stepson ...'

'I've heard you were all punished – Cherie, and the three of you who saw the truck go past?'

'Yeah,' said Abigail. 'We were.'

'Sheila's still very upset about her husband being punished. She thinks whatever was done to him contributed to his poor health.'

'It won't 'ave bloody 'elped,' said Abigail in a clipped voice. 'Sheila told your partner what 'appened to us, did she?'

'No,' said Strike, who judged it better not to lie.

'Well, if Sheila's not talkin', I'm not,' said Abigail. 'That's the sorta fing that Pirbright bloke wanted off me. Find out all the sala – salaysh – all the dirty fuckin' details. I'm not diggin' it all up again, so people can picture me on my fuckin' – forget that.'

Abigail's voice was very slightly slurred now. Strike, who wasn't entirely without hope that he might yet get details of the punishment she'd suffered, turned a fresh page in his notebook and said,

'I've heard Cherie spent a lot of time with Daiyu.'

'Mazu palmed Daiyu off on older girls a lot, yeah.'

'Did you attend the inquest into Daiyu's death?'

'Yeah. Brian 'ad died by then, poor bastard, but me an' Paul 'ad to give evidence, because of seeing 'em pass in the van. I 'eard Cheryl did a runner after it was over – don't blame 'er. Mazu o'ny let 'er stay alive that long 'cause of the inquest. Once that was over, she was on borrowed time.'

'D'you mean that as a figure of speech?'

'No, I mean it for real. Mazu would've killed 'er. Or made 'er kill 'erself.'

'How would she do that?'

'You'd understand if you'd met 'er,' muttered Abigail.

'Did she make you do things? I mean, things to hurt yourself?'

'All the fuckin' time.'

'Didn't your father intervene?'

'I stopped goin' to 'im or talkin' to 'im abou' any of it. No point. There was one time, in Revelation—'

'What's that?'

'You 'ad to say things you were ashamed of an' get purified. So, this one girl said she masturbated an' I laughed. I was prob'ly twelve or somethin'. Mazu made me smack my head off the temple wall until I was near enough concussed.'

'What would have happened if you'd refused?'

'Somefing worse,' said Abigail. 'It was always best to take the first offer.'

She looked at Strike with an odd mixture of defiance and defensiveness.

'Thass the sorta fing Patrick wants me to put in my book. Tell the 'ole world I was treated like shit, so people like fuckin' Baz can throw it back in my face.'

'I'm not going to publicise any of this,' Strike reassured her. 'I'm just looking for confirmation – or not – of things Pirbright told my client.'

'Go on, then. What else did 'e say?'

'He claimed there was a night when all the children were given drugged drinks. He was younger than you, but I wondered whether you ever heard of anyone being drugged?'

Abigail snorted, twirling her empty glass between her fingers.

'You weren' allowed coffee, or sugar, or booze – nuffin'. You weren' even given paracetamol. 'E was babbling to me on the phone abou' people flyin'. 'E'd probably rather fink it was drugs they slipped 'im, than 'e was tricked by some of Mazu's bullshit magic tricks, or 'e was crackin' up.'

Strike made a note.

'OK, this next one's odd. Kevin thought Daiyu could turn herself invisible – or said that one of his sisters believed she could.'

'What?' said Abigail, half-laughing.

'I know,' said Strike, 'but he seemed to attach significance to this. I wondered whether she went missing at any point, prior to her death.'

'Not that I remember ... but I wouldn't've put it past 'er to claim she could be invisible. Make 'erself out t'be magic, like 'er muvver.'

'OK, this next question's also odd, but I wanted to ask you about pigs.'

'Pigs?'

'Yeah,' said Strike. 'It might mean nothing, but they keep cropping up.'

''Ow?'

'Sheila Kennett says Paul Draper got beaten for letting some escape, and Jordan Reaney's wife says he used to have nightmares about pigs.'

''Oo's Jordan Reaney?'

'You can't remember him?'

'I ... oh, maybe,' she said slowly. 'Was 'e the tall one who overslept, who should've been on the truck?'

'What truck?'

'If 'e's the one I'm thinkin' of, he should've been with Cheryl – Cherie – on the vegetable run, the morning Daiyu drowned. If 'e'd gone, there wouldn' of been room for Daiyu. It was a small flatbed truck. On'y room for two up front.'

'I don't know whether he was supposed to be on the vegetable run,' said Strike, 'but according to Pirbright, Reaney was forced to whip himself across the face with a leather flail by Mazu, for some unspecified crime she seemed to think merited the police.'

'I toldja, that sorta fing 'appened all the time. An' why's Reaney's wife talkin' for 'im? Is 'e dead?'

'No, in jail for armed robbery.'

'Waste of a gun,' muttered Abigail. ''E knows where Mazu is.'

'Kevin Pirbright also wrote the word "pigs" on his bedroom wall.'

'Sure 'e wasn' talkin' abou' the police?'

'He might've been, but "pigs" might also have been a reminder to himself, about something he wanted to include in his book.'

Abigail looked down at her empty glass.

'Another one?' suggested Strike.

'Tryna get me drunk?'

'Repaying you for giving me your time.'

'Charmer. Yeah, fanks,' she said.

When Strike returned with her fourth drink, Abigail took a gulp, then sat in silence for nearly a minute. Strike, who suspected she wanted to talk more than perhaps she realised, waited.

'All righ',' she said suddenly, ''ere it is: if you wanna know the troof. If people 'oo were at Chapman Farm in the nineties are 'aving nightmares about pigs, it won' be because fuckin' farm animals got out.'

'Why, then?'

'"The pig acts in the abysmal."'

'Sorry?'

''S from the I Ching. Know what that is?'

'Er – a book of divination, right?'

'Mazu said it was an orac – whass the word?'

'Oracle?'

'Yeah. That. But I found out, after I left, she wasn' usin' it properly.'

Given that he wasn't talking to Robin, who was familiar with his views on fortune telling, Strike decided not to debate whether it was possible to use an oracle properly.

'What d'you mean by—?'

'It's s'posed to be, like, used by the person 'oo's after – y'know – guidance, or wisdom, or shit. You count out yarrow stalks, then you look up the meaning of the 'exa-fing you've made, in the I Ching. Mazu likes anyfing Chinese. She pretends to be 'alf Chinese. My arse, she is. Anyway, she wouldn' let anyone else touch the stalk fings. She gave readings, an' she rigged it.'

'How?'

'She used it to decide punishments an' stuff. She'd say she'd consult the I Ching to find out 'oo was tellin' the truth. See, if you're pure spirit, the *divine vibration*' (Abigail's voice was full of scorn) 'works froo you, so if you do somefing like the I Ching – or cards, or crystals, or wha'ever – they'll work, but not fr'anyone 'oo's not as pure.'

'And where do pigs come in?'

''Exa-fing – gram – twenny-nine,' said Abigail. 'The Abyss. It's one o' the worst 'exagrams to get. "*Water is the image associated with the Abysmal; of the domestic animals, the pig is the one that lives in mud and water.*" I still know it off by fuckin' 'eart, I 'eard it so often. So if 'exagram twenny-nine came up – an' it came up *far* more often than it should've done, because there are sixty-fuckin'-four diff'rent 'exagrams – you was a filfy liar: you was a pig. An' Mazu made you crawl around on all fours, until she said it was time to get up again.'

'This happened to you?'

'Oh, yeah. Bleedin' 'ands and knees. Crawlin' through mud . . . on the night after Daiyu drowned,' said Abigail, her eyes glassy, 'Mazu made me, old Brian Kennett, Paul Draper, that Jordan guy an' Cherie strip naked an' crawl round the yard in fuckin' pig masks, wiv everyone watching. For free days an' free nights, we 'ad to stay naked and on all fours, an' we 'ad to sleep in the pigsty wiv the real pigs.'

'Jesus Christ,' said Strike.

'So now you fuckin' know,' said Abigail, who seemed half-furious, half-shaken, 'an' you can put it in a fuckin' book an' make a ton of money out of it.'

'I've already told you,' said Strike, 'that isn't going to happen.'

Abigail dashed angry tears out of her eyes. They sat in silence for a couple of minutes until, abruptly, Abigail threw back the last of her fourth glass of wine and said,

'Come ou'side wiv me, I wanna fag.'

They left the pub together, Abigail's gym bag and coat slung over her shoulder. It was cold outside, with a stiff breeze blowing. Abigail drew her coat more closely around herself, leaned up against the brick wall, lit a Marlboro Light, inhaled deeply, and blew the smoke up at the stars. She seemed to regain her composure as she smoked. When Strike said,

'I had you figured as a keep-fit buff,' she answered dreamily, eyes on the sky,

'I am. When I'm workin' ou', I'm workin' out. An' when I'm partyin', I'm partyin' 'ard. An' when I'm workin', I'm fuckin' good at it . . . There isn' enough time in the world,' she said, looking sideways at him, 'to *not* be at Chapman Farm. Y'know what I mean?'

'Yeah,' said Strike. 'I think I do.'

She looked at him, a little blearily, and she was so tall they were almost eye to eye.

'You're kinda sexy.'

'And you're definitely drunk.'

She laughed and pushed herself off the wall.

'Should've eaten after the gym . . . shoulda drunk some water. See ya, Crameron – Cormarion – wha'ever your fucking name is.'

And with a gesture of farewell, she walked away.

29

Thus in all his transactions the superior man
Carefully considers the beginning.

The I Ching or Book of Changes

Strike arrived back in Denmark Street a little after ten, having done some food shopping on the way. After a joyless dinner of grilled chicken and steamed vegetables, he decided to move down into the deserted office to pursue the train of thought engendered by his interview with Abigail Glover. He told himself this was because it was easier to work at the PC than at his laptop, but was dimly aware of a desire to sit at the partners' desk, where he and Robin often faced each other.

The familiar sounds of traffic grumbling past on Charing Cross Road mingled with occasional shouts and laughter from passers-by as Strike opened the folder on his computer in which he'd already saved the account of Daiyu Wace's drowning he'd found in the British Library archives, which gave him access to decades' worth of press reports, including those in local papers.

The child's death had merited only brief mentions in the nationals, though not all of them had carried the story. However, north Norfolk papers the *Lynn Advertiser* and the *Diss Express* had printed fuller reports. Strike now re-read them.

Daiyu Wace had drowned early in the morning of 29 July

1995, during what was described as an impromptu swim with a seventeen-year-old girl described as her babysitter.

The *Lynne Advertiser*'s article carried pictures of the two girls. Even allowing for the blurry effect of newsprint, Daiyu was distinctly rabbity in appearance, with an overbite emphasised by a missing tooth, dark, narrow eyes and long, shining hair. Cherie Gittins' picture showed a teenaged girl with crimped blonde curls and what looked like an affected smile.

The facts given in both papers were identical. Cherie and Daiyu had decided to take a swim, Daiyu had got into difficulties, Cherie had tried to reach her, but the child had been pulled out of reach by a powerful current. Cherie had then exited the water and tried to raise the alarm. She'd hailed passers-by Mr and Mrs Heaton of Garden Street, Cromer, and Mr Heaton had hurried off to alert the coastguard while Mrs Heaton remained with Cherie. Mr Heaton was quoted as saying that he and his wife had seen 'a hysterical young woman running towards us in her underwear' and that they'd realised something was very amiss upon spotting the pile of discarded child's clothing lying on the pebbles a short distance away.

Strike, who was Cornish-born, with an uncle in the coastguard, knew more about tides and drowning than the average person. A rip current such as Daiyu appeared to have swum into could have carried away a seven-year-old child with ease, especially as she'd have had neither the strength nor, presumably, the knowledge that she should swim parallel to the shore to escape the danger, rather than trying to fight a force that would challenge even a powerful and experienced sea bather. The article in the *Diss Express* concluded by quoting a life-guard who gave precisely that advice to those unlucky enough to find themselves in a similar situation. Strike also knew that the gases that cause bodies to rise to the surface form far more slowly in cold water. Even in late July, the early morning North Sea would have been very chilly, and if the small body had been dragged out into deep water and sank to the sea bed, it might soon have been stripped by crustaceans, fish and sea lice. Strike had heard such stories as a child from his uncle.

Nevertheless, Strike found certain incongruities in the story. While neither local journalist made an issue of this, it seemed odd, to say the least, that the two girls had visited the beach before sunrise. Of course, there might have been an innocent, undisclosed reason, such as a dare or a bet. Sheila Kennett had suggested that Daiyu had the whip hand in the relationship with the older girl. Perhaps Cherie Gittins had been too weak-willed to resist the pressure of the cult leaders' child, who'd been determined to paddle no matter the hour and the temperature. Cherie's simpering smile didn't suggest a strong personality.

While the sky darkened outside the office window, Strike made a fresh search of the newspaper archives, this time looking for reports into Daiyu's inquest. He found one dated September 1995 in the *Daily Mirror*. Certain features of the case had clearly piqued the national newspaper's interest.

CHILD RULED 'LOST AT SEA'

A verdict of 'lost at sea' was delivered today at the Norwich Coroner's Office, where an inquest was held into the drowning of 7-year-old Daiyu Wace of Chapman Farm, Felbrigg.

Unusually, the inquest was held in the absence of a body.

Head of the local coastguard, Graham Burgess, told the court that in spite of an extensive search, it had proved impossible to find the little girl's remains.

'There was a powerful current near the beach that morning, which could have carried a small child a long distance,' Burgess told the court. 'Most drowning victims rise to the surface or wash ashore eventually, but sadly a minority remain unrecoverable. I'd like to offer the service's sincere condolences to the family.'

17-year-old Cherie Gittins (pictured), a friend of Daiyu's family, took the primary schooler for an early morning swim on 29th July, after the pair had delivered farm vegetables to a local shop.

'Daiyu was always nagging me to take her to the beach,' a visibly distressed Gittins told the coroner, Jacqueline Porteous. 'I thought she just wanted a paddle. The water was really cold, but she just dived right in. She was always really brave and adventurous. I was worried, so I went after her. One minute she was laughing, then she disappeared – went under and didn't come up.

'I couldn't reach her, I couldn't even see where she was. The light was bad because it was so early. I went back to the beach and I was screaming and shouting for help. I saw Mr and Mrs Heaton walking their dog. Mr Heaton went to phone the police and the coastguard.

'I never wanted any harm to come to Daiyu. This has been the worst thing that's ever happened to me and I'll never get over it. I just want to apologise to Daiyu's parents. I'm so, so sorry. I'd give absolutely anything if I could bring Daiyu back.'

Giving evidence, Muriel Carter, owner of a beachside café, said she saw Gittins taking the child down to the beach, shortly before sunrise.

'They had towels with them and I thought it was a

silly time to be going swimming, that's why it stuck in my mind.'

Interviewed after the inquest, bereaved mother Mrs Mazu Wace (24) said:

'I never dreamed anyone would take my child without permission, let alone take her swimming in the sea, in the dark. I'm still praying we'll find her and be able to give her a decent burial.'

Mr Jonathan Wace (44), father of the dead girl, said:

'This has been an appalling time and of course, it's been made far worse by the uncertainty, but the inquest has given us some sense of closure. My wife and I are sustained by our religious faith and I'd like to thank the local community for their kindness.'

Strike reached for the notebook that was still in his pocket from his interview with Abigail Glover, re-read the *Mirror* article and made a note of a couple of points that struck him as interesting, along with the names of the witnesses mentioned. He also scrutinised the new picture of Cherie Gittins, which seemed to have been taken outside the coroner's court. She looked much older here, her eyelids heavier, the previously babyish contours of her face more defined.

Strike sat in thought for a few more minutes, vaping, then made another search of the newspaper archives, now looking for information relating to Alex Graves, the man who, if Abigail was to be believed, was Daiyu's biological father.

It took twenty minutes, but Strike finally found Graves' obituary notice in a copy of *The Times*.

> **Graves, Alexander Edward Thawley**, *passed away at home, Garvestone Hall, Norfolk, on 15th June 1993, after a long illness. Beloved son of Colonel and Mrs Edward*

Graves, and dearly missed brother of Phillipa. Private funeral.
No flowers. Donations if wished to The Mental Health
Foundation. 'Say not the struggle naught availeth.'

As Strike would have expected, the carefully worded
obituary concealed more than it revealed. The 'long illness'
surely referred to mental health problems given the suggestion for donations, while the 'private funeral', for which no
date was given, had presumably been held at Chapman Farm,
where Graves had been buried according to the wish he'd
stated in his will. Nevertheless, the obituary-writer had been
determined to state that Garvestone Hall was 'home'.

Strike Googled Garvestone Hall. Although it was a private
residence, there were numerous pictures of the house online,
due to its medieval origins. The stone mansion had hexag-
onal towers, rectangular leaded windows and spectacular
gardens, which featured topiary, statuary, intricately laid-out
flowerbeds and a small lake. The grounds, Strike read, were
occasionally opened to the public to raise money for charity.

Exhaling nicotine vapour in the silent office, Strike wondered again how much money Graves, who according to
Abigail had looked like a hobo, had left the girl he believed
was his daughter.

The sky outside the office window was a deep, velvety
black. Almost absent-mindedly, Strike Googled 'drowned
prophet UHC'.

The top hit led to the website of the UHC, but a number of
idealised pictures of Daiyu Wace also appeared. Strike clicked
on 'images' and scrolled slowly down through many identical
pictures of Daiyu as she appeared in the Rupert Court Temple,
with her white robes and her flying black hair, stylised waves
trailing behind her.

Towards the bottom of the page, however, Strike saw a

picture that caught his attention. This showed Daiyu as she'd looked in life, although in far more sinister form. The accomplished pencil and charcoal drawing had turned the rabbity face skeletal. Where there should have been eyes, there were empty sockets. The picture was taken from Pinterest. Strike clicked on the link.

The drawing had been posted by a user calling themselves Torment Town. The page had only twelve followers, which didn't surprise Strike in the slightest. All Torment Town had posted were drawings that had the same nightmarish quality as the first.

A small, long-haired, naked child lay in the foetal position on the ground, face hidden, with two cloven feet standing either side. The image was surrounded by two hairy, clawed hands making a heart, a clear parody of the UHC symbol.

The same hairy hands formed their heart around a drawing of a naked man's lower body, although the erect penis had been replaced by a spiked club.

A gagged woman was depicted with one of the clawed hands throttling her, the letters UHC drawn onto both dilated pupils.

Daiyu appeared repeatedly, sometimes only her face, sometimes full length, in a white dress that dripped water onto the floor around her bare feet. The eyeless, rabbity face stared in through windows, the dripping corpse floated across ceilings and peered out from between dark trees.

A loud bang made Strike start. A bird had hit the office window. For two seconds, he and the raven blinked at each other and then, in a blur of black feathers, it had gone.

Heart rate now slightly elevated, Strike returned his attention to the images on Torment Town's page. He paused on the most complex picture yet: a meticulously rendered depiction of a group standing around a black five-sided pool. The figures around the pool were hooded, their faces in shadow, but Jonathan Wace's face was illuminated.

Over the water hovered the spectral Daiyu, looking down at the water below, a sinister smile on her face. Where Daiyu's reflection should have been, there was a different woman, floating on the surface of the water. She was fair haired and wore square-framed glasses, but like Daiyu she had no eyes, only empty sockets.

30

. . . a princess leads her maids-in-waiting like a shoal
of fishes to her husband and thus gains his favour.

The I Ching or Book of Changes

The women in the dormitory were woken at 5 a.m. as usual by the ringing of the large copper bell on Robin's fourth morning at Chapman Farm. After the same scant breakfast of watery porridge they'd eaten every day so far, new recruits were asked to remain in the dining hall, because their groups were to be reconfigured.

Every member of Fire Group other than Robin left to join other groups. Her new companions included the professor, Walter Fernsby, Amandeep Singh, who'd worn the Spiderman T-shirt in temple, and a young woman with short, spiky black hair called Vivienne.

''Owzit going?' she said, on joining the others.

In spite of her best efforts to drop her aitches, Robin noticed, as Vivienne exchanged remarks with the others, that her accent was really irremediably upper middle class.

Robin was almost certain the newly formed groups were no longer randomly selected. Fire Group now seemed to consist only of university-educated people, most of whom clearly had money or came from well-off families. Metal Group, by contrast, contained some of the people who'd had most difficulty

with daily tasks, including bespectacled, ginger-haired widow
Marion Huxley, and a couple of recruits whom Robin had
already heard complain of fatigue and hunger, like green-
haired Penny Brown.

After the re-sorting of the groups, the day proceeded in
the same way as the previous ones. Robin and the rest of Fire
Group were ushered through a mixture of tasks, some physical, some spiritual. After feeding the pigs and putting fresh
straw in the chickens' nesting boxes, they were taken to their
third lecture on church doctrine, which was conducted by
Taio Wace, then had a chanting session in the temple, during
which Robin, already tired, entered a pleasant, trance-like
state which left her with a feeling of increased well-being. She
could now recite *Lokah Samastah Sukhino Bhavantu* without
needing to check the words or pronunciation.

After temple, they were led to a new crafting workshop.

'Fire Group, called to service,' said Becca Pirbright as they
entered a slightly larger space than that in which the toy turtles had been made. The walls were hung with many different
kinds of woven and plaited corn dollies: stars, crosses, hearts,
spirals and figures, many of them finished with ribbons. In
a far corner of the room, two church members – Robin recognised the woman who'd stood at the reception desk when
they arrived, and the pregnant Wan – were working on a
large straw sculpture. Piles of straw also lay on a long central
table, in front of every seat. At the head of the table stood
Mazu Wace in her long orange robes, with the mother-of-
pearl fish around her neck, holding a leatherbound book.

'*Nǐ hǎo*,' she said, gesturing for Fire Group to take their
seats.

There were fewer permanent church members seated at the
table than at the turtle-making session. Among them was the
teenage girl with long, fine mousey hair and large blue eyes

whom Robin had already noticed. Robin deliberately selected a seat beside her.

'As you know,' said Mazu, 'we sell our handiwork to raise funds for the church's charitable projects. We have a long tradition of making corn dollies at Chapman Farm and grow our own straw specifically for this purpose. Today you'll be making some simple Glory Plaits,' said Mazu, walking to the wall and pointing at a flat, plaited corn dolly with wheat heads fanning out of the bottom. 'Regular members will help, and once you're working properly, I'll read you today's lesson.'

'Hi,' Robin said to the teenage girl beside her, as Mazu began leafing through the book, 'I'm Rowena.'

'I'm L-L-Lin,' stammered the girl.

Robin knew at once that the girl must be the daughter of Deirdre Doherty, who'd been (if Kevin Pirbright was to be believed) the product of Jonathan Wace's rape.

'That looks hard,' Robin said, watching Lin's thin fingers working the straw.

'It isn't r-r-really,' said Lin.

Robin noticed Mazu glance up irritably from her book at the sound of Lin's voice. Although Lin hadn't looked at Mazu, Robin was certain she'd registered her reaction, because she began showing Robin what to do without words. Robin remembered Kevin Pirbright writing in his email to Sir Colin that Mazu had mocked Lin for her stammer since childhood.

Once everyone had set to work in earnest, Mazu said,

'I'm going to talk to you this morning about the Golden Prophet, whose life was a beautiful lesson. The Golden Prophet's mantra is *I Live to Love and Give*. The following words were written by Papa J himself.'

She dropped her gaze to the open book in her hands and now Robin saw *The Answer, by Jonathan Wace* printed on its spine in gold leaf.

'"There was once a worldly, materialistic woman who married with the sole aim of living what the bubble world considers a fulfilled, successful li—"'

'Are we allowed to ask questions?' interrupted Amandeep Singh.

Robin sensed an immediate tension among the regular church members.

'I usually take questions at the end of the reading,' said Mazu coolly. 'Were you going to ask what the "bubble world" is?'

'Yeah,' said Amandeep.

'That's about to be explained,' said Mazu, with a tight, cold smile. Looking back at her book, she continued reading.

'"We sometimes call the materialist world the 'bubble world' because its inhabitants live inside a consumer-driven, status-obsessed and ego-saturated bubble. Possession is key to the bubble world: possession of things and possessiveness of other human beings, who are reduced to flesh objects. Those who can see beyond the gaudy, multicoloured walls of the bubble are deemed strange, deluded – even mad. Yet the bubble world's walls are fragile. It takes just one glimpse of Truth for them to burst, and so it was with Margaret Cathcart-Bryce.

'"She was a rich woman, vain and selfish. She had doctors operate upon her body, the better to ape the youth so venerated within the bubble world, which lives in terror of death and decay. She had no children by choice, for fear that it would spoil her perfect figure, and she amassed great wealth without giving away a penny, content to live a life of material ease that other bubble-dwellers envied for its trappings."'

Robin was carefully folding the hollow straws under Lin's silent direction. Out of the corner of her eye, she saw the pregnant Wan massaging one side of her swollen belly.

'"Margaret's sickness was one of false self,"' read Mazu. '"This is the self that craves external validation. Her spiritual self had been untended and neglected for a very long time. Her awakening came after her husband's death by what the world calls chance, but which the Universal Humanitarian Church recognises as part of the eternal design.

"'Margaret came to hear one of my talks. She told me, later, that she'd attended because she had nothing better to do. Of course, I was well aware that people often attended my meetings purely to have something new to talk about at fashionable dinner parties. Yet I've never scorned the company of the rich. That in itself is a form of prejudice. All judgement based on a person's wealth is bubble thinking.

"'So I spoke at the dinner and the attendees nodded and smiled. I didn't doubt that some would write me cheques to support our charitable work at the end of the evening. It would cost them little and perhaps give them a sense of their own goodness.

"'But when I saw Margaret's eyes fixed upon me, I knew that she was what I sometimes call a sleepwalker: one who has great unawakened spiritual capacity. I hurried through my talk, eager to speak to this woman. I approached her at the conclusion of our talk and with a few short sentences, I'd fallen as deeply in love as I'd ever done in my life.'"

Robin wasn't the only person who glanced up at Mazu at these words.

"'Some will be shocked to hear me talk of love. Margaret was seventy-two years old, but when two sympathetic spirits meet, so-called physical reality dissolves into irrelevance. I loved Margaret instantly, because her true self called to me from behind the masklike face, pleading for liberation. I had already undertaken sufficient spiritual training to see with a clarity physical eyes cannot. Beauty that is of the flesh will always wither, whereas beauty of the spirit is eternal and unchange—'"

The door of the workshop opened. Mazu looked up. Jiang Wace entered, squat and sullen in his orange tracksuit. At the sight of Mazu, his right eye began to flicker and he hastily covered it.

'Doctor Zhou wants to see Rowena Ellis,' he muttered.

'That's me,' said Robin, holding up her hand.

'All right,' said Mazu, 'go with Jiang, Rowena. I thank you for your service.'

'And I for yours,' said Robin, putting her hands together and bowing her head towards Mazu, which earned her another cold, tight smile.

31

Nine in the fifth place . . .
One should not try an unknown medicine.

The I Ching or Book of Changes

'You catch on quick,' said Jiang, as he and Robin walked back past the chicken coop.

'What d'you mean?' asked Robin.

'Knowing the right responses,' said Jiang, again rubbing the eye with the tic, and Robin thought she detected a hint of resentment. 'Already.'

To their left lay the open fields. Marion Huxley and Penny Brown were staggering over the deeply rutted earth, leading the Shire horses in their endless ploughing, a pointless exercise, given that the field was already ploughed.

'Metal Group,' said Jiang with a snigger. Confirmed in her impression that this morning's group reconfiguration had been a ranking exercise, Robin merely asked,

'Why does Dr Zhou want to see me?'

'Medical,' said Jiang. 'Check you're ready to fast.'

They passed the laundry and dining hall, and then the older barns, one of which had a cobwebbed padlock on the door.

'What do you keep in there?' Robin asked.

'Junk,' said Jiang. Then, making Robin jump, he bellowed, 'Oi!'

Jiang was pointing at Will Edensor, who was crouching in the shade of a tree off the path and appeared to be comforting a child of maybe two, who was crying. Will Edensor jumped up as though he'd been scalded. The little girl, whose white hair hadn't been shaved like that of the other children, but stood out around her head like a dandelion clock, raised her arms, imploring Will to pick her up. A group of nursery age were toddling about behind him among more trees, under the supervision of shaven-headed Louise Pirbright.

'Are you on child duty?' Jiang shouted at Will.

'No,' said Will. 'She just fell over, so I—'

'You're committing *materialist possession*,' shouted Jiang, and specks of spittle issued from his mouth. Robin was sure her presence was making Jiang more aggressive, that he was enjoying asserting his authority in front of her.

'It was only because she fell over,' said Will. 'I was going to the laundry and—'

'Then go to the *laundry*!'

Will hurried off on his long legs. The little girl attempted to follow him, tripped, fell and cried harder than ever. Within a few seconds, Louise had scooped the child up and retreated with her into the trees where the rest of the little ones were roaming.

'He's been warned,' said Jiang, heading off again. 'I'm going to have to report that.'

He seemed to take pleasure in the prospect.

'Why isn't he allowed near children?' asked Robin, hurrying to keep up with Jiang as they rounded the side of the temple.

'Nothing like that,' said Jiang quickly, answering an unspoken question. 'But we've got to be careful about who works with the little ones.'

'Oh, right,' said Robin.

'Not because of – it's spiritual,' growled Jiang. 'People get ego hits from materialist possession. It interferes with spiritual growth.'

'I see,' said Robin.

'You've got to kill the false self,' said Jiang. 'He hasn't killed his false self yet.'

They were now crossing the courtyard. When they crouched down at the pool of the Drowned Prophet between the tombs of the Stolen and Golden Prophets, Robin picked up a tiny pebble lying on the ground and hid it in her left hand before dipping the forefinger of her right into the water, anointing her forehead and intoning 'The Drowned Prophet will bless all who worship her.'

'You know who she was?' Jiang asked Robin, as he stood up and pointed at the statue of Daiyu.

'Er – her name was Daiyu, wasn't it?' said Robin, still with the tiny pebble held in her closed hand.

'Yeah, but d'you know who she was? To *me*?'

'Oh,' said Robin. She'd already learned that the naming of family relationships was frowned upon at Chapman Farm, because it suggested a continuing allegiance to materialist values. 'No.'

'My sister,' said Jiang in a low voice, smirking.

'Can you remember her?' said Robin, careful to sound awed.

'Yeah,' said Jiang. 'She used to play with me.'

They proceeded towards the entrance of the farmhouse. As Jiang drew a little ahead of her to push open the dragon-orna-mented doors of the farmhouse, Robin stowed the tiny pebble out of sight down the front of her sweatshirt, inside her bra.

There was a motto inlaid in Latin in the stone floor just inside the doors of the farmhouse: STET FORTUNA DOMUS. The hallway was wide, pristinely clean and immaculately decorated, the white walls covered in Chinese art, including framed silk panels and carved wooden masks. A scarlet-carpeted stairway curved up to the first floor. A number of closed doors, all painted in glossy black, led off the hall, but Jiang led Robin past all of these and turned right, into a corridor that led into one of the new wings.

At the very end of the corridor, he rapped on another glossy black door and opened it.

Robin heard a woman's laughter, and as the door opened she saw actress Noli Seymour leaning up against an ebony desk and apparently lost in merriment about something Dr Zhou had just said to her. She was a dark, elfin young woman with cropped hair, wearing what Robin recognised as head-to-toe Chanel.

'Oh, hello,' she said through her laughter. Robin had the impression Noli vaguely recognised Jiang, but couldn't remember his name. Jiang's hand had again leapt to his winking eye. 'Andy's just making me *roar* . . . I had to come down here to get my treatments,' she pouted slightly, 'seeing as he's *abandoned* us in London.'

'Abandoned *you*? Never,' said Zhou, in his deep voice. 'Now, you'll stay for the night? Papa J's back.'

'Is he?' squealed Noli, clapping her hands to her face in delight. 'Oh my God, I haven't seen him in weeks!'

'He says you can take your usual room,' said Zhou, pointing upstairs. 'The membership will be delighted to see you. Now, I have to assess this young lady,' he said, pointing at Robin.

'All right, darling,' said Noli, offering her face to be kissed. Zhou clasped her hands, pecked her on each cheek, and Noli walked out past Robin in a cloud of tuberose, winking as she passed and saying:

'You're in *very* safe hands.'

The door closed on Noli and Jiang, leaving Robin and Dr Zhou alone.

The luxurious, meticulously tidy room smelled of sandal-wood. A red and gold art deco rug lay on the dark polished floorboards. Floor-to-ceiling shelves of the same ebony as the rest of the furniture carried leatherbound books and also what Robin recognised as hundreds of journals of the kind lying on her bed, their spines labelled with the names of their owners. Behind the desk were more shelves carrying hundreds of tiny brown bottles arranged with precision and labelled in minus-cule handwriting, a collection of antique Chinese snuff bottles and a fat golden Buddha, sitting cross-legged on a wooden plinth. A black leather examination couch stood beneath one of the windows, which looked out onto a part of the property screened from the courtyard by trees and bushes. Here, Robin saw three identical cabins built of timber, each of which had sliding glass doors, and which hadn't been shown to any of the new recruits as yet.

'Please, sit down,' said Zhou, smiling as he gestured Robin to the chair opposite his desk, which like the desk was made of ebony, and upholstered in red silk. Robin registered how comfortable it was as she sank into it: the chairs in the work-shop were of hard plastic and wood, and the mattress of her narrow bed very firm.

Zhou was wearing a dark suit and tie and a pristine white shirt. Pearls shone discreetly in the buttonholes of his cuffs. Robin assumed he was biracial because he was well over six feet tall – the Chinese men she was used to seeing in Chinatown, near the office, were generally much shorter – and he was undeniably handsome, with his slicked-back black hair and high cheekbones. The scar running down from nose to jaw hinted at mystery and danger. She could understand why Dr Zhou attracted television viewers, even though she personally found the sleekness and slight but detectable aura of self-importance unappealing.

Zhou flipped open a folder on his desk and Robin saw several sheets of paper, with the questionnaire she'd completed on the bus lying on top.

'So,' said Zhou, smiling, 'how are you finding life in the church so far?'

'Really interesting,' said Robin, 'and I'm finding the meditation techniques incredible.'

'You suffer from a little anxiety, yes?' said Zhou, smiling at her.

'Sometimes,' said Robin, smiling back.

'Low self-esteem?'

'Occasionally,' said Robin, with a little shrug.

'I think you've recently had an emotional blow?'

Robin wasn't sure whether he was pretending to intuit this about her, or admitting that some of the hidden sheets of paper contained the biographical details she'd confided in church members.

'Um ... yes,' she said, with a little laugh. 'My wedding got called off.'

'Was that your decision?'

'No,' said Robin, no longer smiling. 'His.'

'Family disappointed?'

'My mum's quite ... yes, they weren't happy.'

'I promise, you'll live to be very glad you didn't go through with it,' said Zhou. 'Much societal unhappiness stems from the unnaturalness of the married state. Have you read *The Answer*?'

'Not yet,' said Robin, 'although one of the church members offered to lend me his copy, and Mazu was just ...'

Zhou opened one of the desk drawers and took out a pristine paperback copy of Jonathan Wace's book. The image on the front was of a bursting bubble, with two hands making the heart shape around it.

'Here,' said Zhou. 'Your own copy.'

'Thank you so much!' said Robin, feigning delight while wondering when on earth she was supposed to have time to read, in between the lectures, the work and the temple.

'Read the chapter on materialist possession and egomotivity,' Zhou instructed her. 'Now ...'

He extracted a second questionnaire, this one blank, and took a lacquered fountain pen out of his pocket.

'I'm going to assess your fitness to fast – what we call purification.'

He took down Robin's age, asked her to step onto scales, noted down her weight, then invited her to sit down again so he could take her blood pressure.

'A little low,' said Zhou, looking at the figures, 'but it's nearly lunchtime ... nothing to worry about. I'm going to listen to your heart and lungs.'

While Zhou pressed the cold head of the stethoscope to her back, Robin could feel the tiny pebble she'd tucked inside her bra sticking into her.

'Very good,' said Zhou, putting the stethoscope away, sitting and making a note on the questionnaire before continuing his questions on pre-existing health conditions.

'And where did you get that scar on your forearm?' he asked.

Robin knew at once that the eight-inch scar, which was currently covered by the long sleeves of her sweatshirt, must have been reported by one of the women in the dormitory where she undressed at night.

'I fell through a glass door,' she said.

'Really?' said Zhou, for the first time showing some disbelief.

'Yes,' said Robin.

'It wasn't a suicide attempt?'

'God, no,' said Robin, with an incredulous laugh. 'I

326

tripped down some stairs and put my hand right through a glass panel in a door.'

'Ah, I see ... you were having regular sex with your fiancé?'

'I – yes,' said Robin.

'Were you using birth control?'

'Yes. The pill.'

'But you've come off it?'

'Yes, the instructions said—'

'Good,' said Zhou, still writing. 'Synthetic hormones are exceptionally unhealthy. You should put nothing unnatural in your body, ever. The same goes for condoms, caps ... all disrupt the flow of your qi. You understand qi?'

'In our lecture, Taio said it's a sort of life force?'

'The vital energy, composed of Yin and Yang,' said Zhou, nodding. 'You have a slight imbalance already. Don't worry,' he said smoothly, still writing, 'we'll address it. Have you ever had an STD?'

'No,' lied Robin.

In fact, the rapist who'd ended her university career had given her chlamydia, for which she'd been given antibiotics.

'Do you orgasm during sex?'

'Yes,' said Robin. She could feel a blush rising in her face.

'Every time?'

'Pretty much,' said Robin.

'Your typology test places you in the decant Fire-Earth, which is to say, Gift-Bearer-Warrior,' went on Zhou, looking up at her. 'That's a very auspicious nature.'

Robin didn't feel particularly flattered by this assessment, not least because she'd answered as the fictional Rowena, rather than herself. She also had a feeling 'Gift-Bearer' might be a synonym for financial target. However, she said with enthusiasm,

'That's so interesting.'

'I devised the typology test myself,' said Zhou, with a smile. 'We find it very accurate.'

'What type are you?' asked Robin.

'Healer-Mystic,' said Zhou, evidently pleased to be asked, as had been Robin's intention. 'Each quintant corresponds to one of our prophets and one of the five Chinese elements. You may have noticed that we name our groups for the elements. However,' said Zhou seriously, now sitting back in his chair, 'you mustn't think I subscribe to any one rigid tradition. I favour a synthesis of the best of world medicine. Ayurvedic practices have much to recommend them, but as you've seen, I don't disdain the stethoscope or blood pressure gauge. However, I have no truck with Big Pharma. A global protection racket. Not a single cure to their names.'

Rather than challenging this statement, Robin settled for looking mildly confused.

'True healing is only possible from the spirit,' said Zhou, placing a hand on his chest. 'There's ample evidence of the fact, but of course, if the whole world subscribed to the UHC healing philosophy, those companies would lose billions in revenue.

'Are your parents still together?' he asked, with another swift change of subject.

'Yes,' said Robin.

'You have siblings?'

'Yes, a sister.'

'Do they know you're here?'

'Yes,' said Robin.

'Are they supportive? Happy for you to explore your spiritual growth?'

'Er – they're a bit – I think,' said Robin, with another little laugh, 'they think I'm doing it because I'm depressed.

Because of the wedding being cancelled. My sister thinks it's a bit weird.'

'And you, do you think it's weird?'

'Not at all,' said Robin defiantly.

'Good,' said Zhou. 'Your parents and sister currently regard you as their flesh object. It will take time to reorientate yourself to a healthier pattern of bonding.

'Now,' he said briskly, 'you are fit to undergo a twenty-four-hour fast, but we need to address this qi imbalance. These tinctures,' he said, getting to his feet, 'are very effective. All natural. I mix them myself.'

He chose three small brown bottles from the shelf, poured Robin a glass of water, added two drops from each bottle, swilled the glass then handed it over to her. Wondering whether it was reckless to drink something of which she didn't know the ingredients, though reassured by the tiny quantities, Robin finished it all.

'Good,' said Zhou, smiling down at her. 'Now, if you have negative thoughts, you know what to do, yes? You have your chanting meditation and your joyful meditation.'

'Yes,' said Robin, smiling as she set the empty glass back on the desk.

'All right then, you're fit to fast,' he said, in a tone that was a clear dismissal.

'Thanks so much,' said Robin, getting up. 'Can I ask —' she pointed at the timber cabins visible through the study window '— what are those? We didn't see them on our tour.'

'Retreat Rooms,' said Zhou. 'But they're for use only by full church members.'

'Oh, I see,' said Robin.

Zhou showed her to the door. Robin was unsurprised to find Jiang waiting for her in the corridor. She'd already learned that the only permissible reason to be left unattended was to visit the bathroom.

'It's lunchtime,' said Jiang, as they walked back through the farmhouse.

'Good,' said Robin. 'I'm fasting tomorrow, better build up my strength.'

'Don't say that,' said Jiang severely. 'You shouldn't prepare for fasting, except spiritually.'

'Sorry,' said Robin, intentionally sounding cowed. 'I didn't mean – I'm still learning.'

When they stepped out into the courtyard they found it full of church members heading towards the dining hall. There was something of a crowd around the pool of the Drowned Prophet as people waited to ask for her blessing.

'Actually,' Robin said to Jiang, 'I might just nip to the bathroom before lunch.'

She left before he could protest, heading into the women's dormitory, which was deserted. Having used the bathroom, she hurried to her bed. To her surprise, a second object lay on her pillow beside her nightly journal: a very old, dog-eared copy of the same paperback she held in her hands. Opening it, she saw a flamboyant handwritten inscription inside.

To Danny, Martyr-Mystic,
my hope, my inspiration, my son.
With love always, Papa J

Robin remembered Danny Brockles' insistence that she return the book to him, so she placed her own copy of *The Answer* on the bed and picked up his to take it to lunch. She then dropped to her knees, extracted the tiny pebble from the yard from her bra and placed it carefully beside three others, which she'd hidden between the bedframe and mattress. She'd have known it was Tuesday without this method of counting the passing days, but she also knew that if her fatigue and hunger worsened, checking the number of pebbles she'd collected might be her only recourse for keeping track of the passing days.

32

*The superior man is on his guard against what is not
yet in sight and on the alert for what is not yet within
hearing . . .*

The I Ching or Book of Changes

Clive Littlejohn returned to work on Wednesday. Strike texted
him at nine to say he wanted a face-to-face talk at one o'clock
at the office, once both had handed over their separate surveillance jobs to other subcontractors.

Unfortunately, this plan went awry. At ten past nine, shortly
after Strike had taken up position outside the Frank brothers'
block of flats in Bexleyheath, Barclay called him.

'Ye on the Franks?'

'Yeah,' said Strike.

'Aye, well, I thought ye should know: it's both o' them,' said
Barclay. 'Not jus' the younger one. I've been looking at the
pictures I took outside her house last night an' it was the older
one who was skulkin' around there at midnight. They're in it
taegether. Pair o' fuckin' freaks.'

'Shit,' said Strike.

They'd just taken on another case of possible marital infidelity, so the news that they'd need double the manpower on
the Franks was unwelcome.

'You're off today, right?' said Strike.

'Aye,' said Barclay. 'Dev's on the new cheatin' wife an' Midge is tryin' tae talk tae that sex worker you photographed talking tae Bigfoot.'

'All right,' said Strike, briefly considering but rejecting the idea of asking Barclay to forgo his day off, 'thanks for letting me know. I'll look at the rota, see how we can keep both under surveillance going forwards.'

Immediately after Barclay had hung up, Strike received a text from Littlejohn, saying that Bigfoot, who rarely went into his office, had chosen today to drive out to the company in Bishop's Stortford, which lay forty miles away from where Strike was currently standing. Much as Strike had wanted to look Littlejohn in the face when asking him about the omission of Patterson Inc from his CV, he now decided it would be quickest and cleanest to do the job by phone, so called Littlejohn back.

'Hi,' said Littlejohn, on answering.

'Forget the meeting at one,' Strike told him. 'We can talk now. Wanted to ask you why you didn't tell me you worked for Mitch Patterson for three months, before coming to me.'

The immediate response to these words was silence. Strike waited, watching the Franks' windows.

'Who told you that?' said Littlejohn at last.

'Never mind who told me. Is it true?'

More silence.

'Yeah,' said Littlejohn at last.

'Mind telling me why you didn't mention it?'

The third long pause didn't improve Strike's temper.

'Listen—'

'I got the heave ho,' said Littlejohn.

'Why?'

'Patterson didn't like me.'

'Why didn't he?'

'Dunno,' said Littlejohn.

'Did you fuck up?'

'No ... personality clash,' said Littlejohn.

You haven't got a fucking personality, though.

'There was a row, was there?'

'No,' said Littlejohn. 'He just told me he didn't need me any more.'

Strike was certain there was something he wasn't being told.

'There's another thing,' he said. 'What were you doing at the office on Easter Monday?'

'Receipts,' said Littlejohn.

'Pat was off. It was a bank holiday. Nobody should've been at the office.'

'I forgot,' said Littlejohn.

Strike stood with his phone pressed to his ear, thinking. His gut was issuing a warning, but his brain reminded him they wouldn't be able to cover all present cases without Littlejohn.

'I need this job,' said Littlejohn, speaking unprompted for the first time. 'The kids are getting settled. I've got a mortgage to pay.'

'I don't like dishonesty,' said Strike, 'and that includes lying by omission.'

'I didn't want you thinking I couldn't handle the work.'

Still frowning, Strike said,

'Consider this a verbal warning. Any more hiding anything from me, and you're out.'

'Understood,' said Littlejohn. 'I won't.'

Strike hung up. Difficult as it was to find new subcontractors of the required quality, he thought he might need to start looking again. Whatever lay behind Littlejohn's failure to mention his time at Patterson Inc, Strike's experience in managing people, inside the army and out, had taught him that where there was one lie, there were almost certain to be more.

The phone in his hand now rang. Answering, he heard Pat's deep, gravelly voice.

'I've got a Colonel Edward Graves on the phone for you.'

'Put him through,' said Strike, who'd left a message for Alexander Graves' parents on an old-fashioned answering machine on Monday morning.

'Hello?' said an elderly male voice.

'Good morning, Colonel Graves,' said Strike. 'Cormoran Strike here. Thanks for calling me back.'

'You're the detective, yes?'

The voice, which was distinctly upper class, was also suspicious.

'That's right. I was hoping I could talk to you about the Universal Humanitarian Church and your son, Alexander.'

'Yes, so you said in your message. Why?'

'I've been hired by someone who's trying to get a relative out of the church.'

'Well, we can't advise them,' said the colonel bitterly.

Deciding not to tell Graves that he already knew how badly wrong the plan to extract Alexander had gone, Strike said,

'I also wondered whether you'd be prepared to talk to me about your granddaughter, Daiyu.'

In the background, Strike heard an elderly female voice, though the words were indistinguishable. Colonel Graves said 'Gimme a minute, Baba,' before saying to Strike,

'We hired a detective ourselves. Man called O'Connor. Do you know him?'

'No, I'm afraid not.'

'Might have retired ... all right. We'll talk to you.'

Taken aback, Strike said,

'That's very good of you. I understand you're in Norfolk?'

'Garvestone Hall. You can find us on any map.'

'Would next week suit you?'

Colonel Graves agreed that it would, and a meeting was arranged for the following Tuesday.

As Strike was putting his phone back into his pocket, he saw a sight he hadn't expected. Both Frankenstein brothers had just emerged from their block of flats, as shabbily dressed as ever, wearing wigs that partially disguised their high foreheads, yet easily recognisable to Strike, who'd become familiar with both their limited stock of clothing and their slightly shambling walks. Intrigued by this paltry effort at disguise, Strike followed them to a bus stop, where after a ten-minute wait, the brothers boarded the number 301 bus. They ascended to the upper deck while Strike remained on the lower, texting Midge to say the Franks were on the move, and that he'd let her know where to meet him to take over surveillance.

Forty-five minutes later, the Franks disembarked at the Beresford Square stop in Woolwich, Strike in pursuit, his eyes on the backs of the badly fitting wigs. After walking for a while, the brothers paused to don gloves, then entered a Sports Direct. Strike had a hunch that the decision not to go to a sports shop nearer their home was part of the same misguided attempt at subterfuge that had made them don wigs, so after texting Midge their current location, he followed them into the shop.

While he hadn't classified either of the brothers as geniuses, he was rapidly revising his estimate of their intelligence downwards. The younger brother kept glancing up at the security cameras. At one point his wig slipped and he straightened it. They ambled with studied nonchalance around the store, picking up random objects and showing them to each other, before making their way to the climbing section. Strike now started taking photos.

After a whispered conversation, the Franks selected a heavy length of rope. A muttered disagreement then ensued, apparently over the merits of two different mallets. Finally they selected a rubber one, then headed for the checkout, paid for the goods, then ambled out of the store, unwieldy packages under their arms, Strike in pursuit. Shortly afterwards, the brothers came to rest in a McDonald's. Strike felt it inadvisable to follow them in there, so he skulked on the street watching the entrance. He'd just texted Midge to update her when his phone rang yet again, this time from an unknown number.

'Cormoran Strike.'

'Yeah,' said an aggressive male voice. 'What d'you want?'

'Who's this?' Strike asked. He could hear background clanging and male voices.

'Jordan Reaney. My sister says you've been pestering my fucking family.'

'There's been no pestering,' said Strike. 'I called your ex-wife to see wheth—'

'She's not my fucking ex, she's me wife, so why're you pestering her?'

'There was no pestering,' repeated Strike. 'I was trying to get a message to you, because I wanted to talk to you about the UHC.'

'The fuck for?'

'Because I'm conducting an investi—'

'You keep the fuck away from my wife and my sister, all right?'

'I've got no intention of going near either of them. Would you be prepar—?'

'I've got nuffing to fucking say about nuffing, all right?' said Reaney, now almost shouting.

'Not even pigs?' asked Strike.

'What the fuck – why pigs? Who's talked about fucking pigs?'

'Your wife told me you have nightmares about pigs.'

A presentiment made Strike move the mobile slightly away from his ear. Sure enough, Reaney began to bellow.

'THE FUCK DID SHE TELL YOU THAT FOR? I'LL FUCKING BREAK YOUR LEGS IF YOU GO TALKING TO MY FUCKING WIFE AGAIN, YOU FUCKING COCKSUCKING—'

There ensued a series of loud bangs. Strike surmised that Reaney was bashing the handset of the prison phone against the wall. A second man yelled, 'OI, REANEY!' Scuffling noises followed. The line went dead.

Strike put his mobile back into his pocket. For a full ten minutes he stood vaping and thinking, watching the door of the McDonald's. Finally, he pulled out his phone again and called his old friend Shanker.

'Awright Bunsen?' said the familiar voice, answering after a couple of rings.

'How's Angel?' asked Strike.

'Started treatment last week,' said Shanker.

'Did she get to see her dad?'

'Yeah. He didn't wanna – cunt – but I persuaded 'im.'

'Good,' said Strike. 'Listen, I need a favour.'

'Name it,' said Shanker.

'It's about a guy called Kurt Jordan Reaney.'

'And?'

'I was hoping we could talk about that face to face,' said Strike. 'Would you be free later today? I can come to you.'

Shanker being amenable, they agreed to meet later that afternoon in an East End café well known to both of them, and Strike hung up.

33

Slight digressions from the good cannot be avoided . . .

The I Ching or Book of Changes

Having handed over surveillance of the Franks to Midge, Strike took the Tube to Bethnal Green station. He'd gone barely ten yards along the road when his ever-busy phone vibrated in his pocket. Drawing aside to let other people pass, he saw yet another text from Bijou Watkins.

You less busy yet? Cos here's what you're missing. 💕 🍎 😊

She'd attached two photographs of herself in lingerie, taken with a mobile in the mirror. Strike gave these only a cursory glance before closing then deleting the message. He had no intention of ever meeting her again, but those photographs might tend to weaken his resolve, because she looked undeniably fabulous in a bright red bra, suspender belt and stockings.

Pellicci's, which lay on Bethnal Green Road, was an East End institution: a small, century-old Italian-run café where the art deco wooden panels gave the incongruous feeling of eating chips in a compartment on the Orient Express. Strike chose a corner seat with his back to the wall, ordered coffee, then reached for an abandoned copy of the *Daily Mail* a previous diner had left lying on the table beside his.

Skipping the usual discussion of the Brexit referendum, he paused on page five, where there was a large picture of Charlotte with Landon Dormer, both of them holding glasses of champagne and laughing. The caption informed him that Charlotte and her boyfriend had attended a fundraising dinner for Dormer's charitable foundation. The story below hinted at a possible engagement.

Strike studied this picture far longer than he'd looked at Bijou's. Charlotte was wearing a long, clinging gold dress and looked entirely carefree, one thin arm resting on Dormer's shoulder, her long black hair styled in waves. Had she lied about having cancer, or was she putting on a brave face? He scrutinised the lantern-jawed Dormer, who also looked untroubled. Strike was still examining the picture when a voice above him said,

'Wotcha, Bunsen.'

'Shanker,' said Strike, tossing the paper back onto the neighbouring table and extending a hand, which Shanker shook before sitting down.

Gaunt and pale, Shanker had grown a beard since Strike had last seen him, which disguised most of the deep scar that gave him a permanent sneer. He was wearing ill-fitting jeans and a baggy grey sweatshirt. Tattoos covered his wrists, knuckles and neck.

'You ill?' he demanded of Strike.

'No, why?'

'You've lost weight.'

'That's intentional.'

'Oh, right,' said Shanker, now rapidly clicking his fingers, a tic he'd had as long as Strike had known him.

'Want anything?' said Strike.

'Yeah, I could do a coffee,' said Shanker. Once this had been ordered, Shanker asked, 'What d'you want wiv Reaney, then?'

'D'you know him personally?'

'I know 'oo 'e is,' said Shanker, whose extensive knowledge of organised crime in London would have shamed the Met. 'Used to run wiv the Vincent firm. I 'eard about the job 'e got banged up for. Silly cunts nearly killed that bookie.'

'Would you happen to know where he is?'

'Yeah, HMP Bedford. Got a couple of mates in there right now, as it goes.'

'I was hoping you'd say that. Reaney's got information that might help one of our investigations, but he isn't being cooperative.'

Shanker seemed unsurprised at the turn the conversation had taken. The waitress now set down Shanker's coffee in front of him. Strike thanked her, as Shanker seemed to have no intention of doing it, then waited until she'd moved away before asking,

'How much?'

'Nah, you can 'ave this one on me. You 'elped me out wiv Angel's fing.'

'Cheers, Shanker. Appreciate it.'

'That it?'

'Yeah, but I wanted your opinion about something else.'

'I want somefing to eat, then,' said Shanker, looking around restlessly. 'Wait there.'

'The menu's here,' said Strike, pushing the card towards Shanker. He had longstanding knowledge of his companion's usual way of getting what he wanted, which was to demand, then threaten, irrespective of whether his request was possible to fulfil. Shanker brushed the menu away.

'Wanna bacon roll.'

Having ordered, Shanker turned back to Strike.

'What else?'

'There was a shooting last year in Canning Town. Guy by the name of Kevin Pirbright, shot through the head with the same make of gun used in two previous drug-related shootings. The police found drugs and cash in his flat. Their theory is, he ran afoul of a local dealer, but personally, I think they're working backwards from the gun that was used.

'The dead guy grew up in a church,' Strike continued. 'I doubt he'd know where to get his hands on drugs, let alone start dealing in quantities to disrupt local drug lords. I wondered what your take was – professionally speaking.'

'What kinda gun?'

'Beretta 9000.'

'Popular shooter,' said Shanker with a shrug.

'It's your manor, Canning Town. Have you heard anything about a young bloke getting shot in his flat?'

Shanker's roll arrived. Once again, Strike thanked the waitress in the absence of any recognition from Shanker. The latter took a large mouthful of bacon roll, then said,

'Nope.'

Strike knew perfectly well that if the hit on Pirbright had been carried out by a colleague of Shanker's, the latter was hardly likely to admit it. On the other hand, he'd have expected some retaliatory aggression if Strike seemed to be prodding around in Shanker's associates' affairs, which wasn't forthcoming.

'So you think—?'

'Frame-up, innit,' said Shanker, still chewing. 'Sure it's not some bent pig?'

Strike, who was inured to Shanker's tendency to attribute half the wrongdoing in London to corrupt police, said,

'Can't see why the force would want this particular bloke dead.'

'Could've 'ad somefing on a pig, couldn' 'e? Me auntie still finks it was a copper what shot Duwayne.'

Strike remembered Shanker's cousin Duwayne who, like Pirbright, had been shot, his killer never caught. Doubtless it was easiest for Shanker's aunt to lay one more death at the Met's door, given that her other son had died in a high-speed chase with police. At least half of Shanker's sprawling family were engaged in some level of criminal activity. As Duwayne had been in a gang from the age of thirteen, Strike thought there were plenty of people more likely to have executed him than the police, an opinion he was tactful enough not to express.

'The people Pirbright had stuff on definitely weren't police.'

He was trying to convince himself he didn't want a bacon roll. Shanker's smelled very good.

'Reaney's scared of pigs,' Strike said. 'The animal, I mean.'

'Yeah?' said Shanker, mildly interested. 'Don't fink we're gonna be able to smuggle a pig into Bedford, Bunsen.'

As Strike laughed, his mobile rang yet again and he saw Lucy's number.

'Hi Luce, what's up?'

'Stick, Ted's got a GP appointment for a week Friday.'

'OK,' said Strike. 'I'll be there.'

'Really?' said Lucy, and he heard her incredulity that, for once, he wasn't saying he'd check his diary or being irritable about being asked to commit to a date.

'Yeah, I told you, I'll be there. What time?'

'Ten o'clock.'

'OK, I'll get down there Thursday,' said Strike, 'and I'll ring Ted and tell him I'm coming with him.'

'This is so good of you, Stick.'

'No, it's not,' said Strike, whose conscience continued to

trouble him after Lucy's recent revelations. 'Least I can do. Listen, I'm in the middle of something. I'll call you later, OK?'

'Yes, of course.'

Lucy rang off.

'Everyfing awright?' asked Shanker.

'Yeah,' said Strike, slipping his phone back in his pocket. 'Well, my uncle might have dementia, I don't know. My mum's brother,' he added.

'Yeah?' said Shanker. 'Sorry to 'ear that. Fuckin' bitch, dementia. My old man 'ad it.'

'Didn't know that,' said Strike.

'Yeah,' said Shanker. 'Early onset. Last time I saw 'im, 'e never 'ad a clue 'oo I was. Mind you, 'e 'ad that many kids, he could 'ardly remember 'oo I was even when 'e weren't senile, randy old fucker. Why 'aven't you 'ad any kids?' asked Shanker, as though the thought had only just occurred to him.

'Don't want them,' said Strike.

'You don' wan' kids?' said Shanker, his tone suggesting this was akin to not wanting to breathe.

'No,' said Strike.

'You miserable bastard,' said Shanker, contemplating Strike with incredulity. 'Kids is wha' it's all abou'. Fuckin' 'ell, look at your mum. You free was everyfing to 'er.'

'Yeah,' said Strike automatically. 'Well—'

'You should see fuckin' Alyssa, wiv Angel bein' ill. That's fuckin' love, man.'

'Yeah – well, give her my best, OK? And Angel.'

Strike got to his feet, bill in his hand.

'Cheers for this, Shanker. I'd better get going. Got a lot of work on.'

Having paid for the coffees and the bacon roll, Strike headed back up Bethnal Green Road, lost in not entirely productive thought.

You free was everyfing to 'er.

Strike never thought of Leda as having had three children, but his old friend had reminded him of the existence of somebody whom Strike probably thought about once a year at most: the much younger half-brother who'd been the product of his mother's marriage to her killer. The boy, who'd been given the predictably eccentric name Switch by his parents, had been born shortly before Strike left for Oxford University. The latter had felt literally nothing for the squalling baby, even as a beaming Leda insisted her older son hold his brother. Strike's most vivid memory of that time was his own feeling of dread at leaving Leda in the squat with her increasingly erratic and aggressive husband. The baby had been merely an additional complication, forever tainted in Strike's eyes by being Whittaker's son. His half-brother had just turned one when Leda died, and had then been adopted by his paternal grandparents.

He felt no curiosity about Switch's current whereabouts and no desire to meet or know him. As far as he knew, Lucy felt the same way. But then Strike corrected himself: he didn't know how Lucy felt. Perhaps Switch was one of the half-siblings with whom she maintained contact, hiding this from the elder brother who'd arrogantly assumed he knew everything about her.

Strike re-entered Bethnal Green station, burdened with guilt and unease. He'd have called Robin had she been available, not to bore her with his personal problems, but to let her know Shanker was prepared to help loosen Jordan Reaney's tongue, that Shanker, too, thought the police were wrong about Pirbright's murder, and that the Frank brothers had gone out in disguise to buy rope. Once again, the fact that she was unavailable, and likely to be so for the foreseeable future, made him realise just how much the sound of her voice generally raised his spirits. He was ever more conscious of how much he, the most self-sufficient of men, had come to rely on the fact that she was always there, and always on his side.

34

It is a question of a fierce battle to break and
to discipline the Devil's Country, the forces of
decadence.
But the struggle also has its reward. Now is the time
to lay the foundations of power and mastery for the
future.

The I Ching or Book of Changes

Robin was craving solitude, sleep and food, but the routine at Chapman Farm was designed to give as little of all three as possible, and some recruits were starting to show the strain. Robin had witnessed green-haired Penny Brown being berated by Taio Wace for dropping some of the large pile of clean folded sheets she'd been carrying across the courtyard. Becca Pirbright ushered Fire Group quickly onwards towards the pig pen, but not in time to prevent them seeing Penny break down in sobs.

In subtle and not so subtle ways, an apocalyptic note began to creep into the critiques of materialism and social inequality with which new recruits were being bombarded. The lack of contact with the outside world served to heighten the sense of being in a bunker, with church members delivering regular bulletins on the horrors of the Syrian war and the slow death of the planet. A sense of increasing urgency permeated these briefings: only the awoken could possibly head off global catastrophe, because the bubble people were continuing, selfishly and apathetically, to hasten humanity's doom.

Papa J and the UHC were now openly described as the world's best hope. Though Wace hadn't appeared since the first dinner, Robin knew he was still present at the farm because church members made frequent mention of the fact in hushed, reverent voices. The infrequency of his appearances seemed to fuel rather than quench his followers' adoration. Robin assumed he was holed up in the farmhouse, eating separately from the mass of members who, in spite of the church's stated allegiance to organically produced and ethically sourced food, ate meals largely composed of cheap dehydrated noodles, with small amounts of protein coming in the form of processed meat and cheese.

On Wednesday morning, Mazu Wace, who unlike her husband was often to be seen gliding through the courtyard, conducted a joint session in the temple with Fire Group and Wood Group. A circle of lacquered chairs had been placed on the central pentagon-shaped stage, and when all had taken their seats, Mazu gave a brief speech about the need for spiritual death and rebirth which, she said, could only take place once past pain and delusion had been accepted, healed or renounced. She then invited the group members to share injustices or cruelties perpetuated on them by family members, partners or friends.

After some prompting, people began to volunteer their stories. A young member of Wood Group called Kyle, who was thin and nervy-looking, gave a detailed account of his father's furious reaction on hearing that his son was gay. As he told the group how his mother had sided with her husband against him, he broke down and cried. The rest of the group murmured support and sympathy while Mazu sat in silence, and when Kyle had finished his story, she summarised it while eradicating any words relating to familial relationships, substituting the terms 'flesh object' and 'materialist possession', then said,

'Thank you for being brave enough to share your story, Kyle. Pure spirits are untouchable by materialist harms. I wish you a hasty death of the false self. When that's gone, your hurt and your suffering will depart, also.'

One by one, the other group members began to talk. Some were clearly struggling with profound hurt caused by outside relationships, or the lack of them, but Robin couldn't avoid the suspicion that some were dredging up and even exaggerating trauma, so as to fit in better with the group. When invited by Mazu to contribute, Robin told the story of her cancelled wedding and her family's disappointment, and admitted that her fiancé's abandonment had left her bereft, particularly as she'd given up her job to go travelling with him once they were husband and wife.

Those in the circle, many of whom were already tearful after sharing their own stories, offered commiseration and sympathy, but Mazu told Robin that placing importance on professions was to connive at systems of control perpetuated within the bubble world.

'A sense of identity based on jobs, or any of the trappings of the bubble world, is inherently materialist,' she said. 'When we firmly reject the cravings of the ego and begin nourishing the spirit, hurts disappear and the true self can emerge, a self that will no longer care if flesh objects pass out of its life.'

Mazu turned last to a skinny girl with a heart-shaped face who'd remained conspicuously silent. Her arms were folded tightly across her chest and her legs were crossed, the upper foot hooked behind her lower.

'Would you like to share with the group how you've suffered through materialist possession?'

In a voice that shook slightly, the girl replied:

'I haven't suffered anything.'

Mazu's dark, crooked eyes contemplated her.

'Nothing at all?'

'No, nothing.'

Robin judged the girl to be in her late teens. Her face was reddening slightly under the censorious scrutiny of the circle.

'My family's never done me any harm,' she said. 'I know some people here have had really awful things happen to them, but I haven't. I haven't,' she repeated, with a shrug of her stiff shoulders.

Robin could feel the group's animosity towards the girl as surely as if they'd declared it openly, and willed her not to speak again, to no avail.

'And I don't think it's right to call, like, parents loving their kids "materialist possession",' she blurted out. 'I'm sorry, but I don't think it is.'

Several group members, including Amandeep, now spoke up at once. Mazu intervened, and gestured to Amandeep to continue alone.

'There's a power dynamic in all conventional family structures,' he said. 'You can't deny there isn't coercion and control, even if it's well intentioned.'

'Well, little children need boundaries,' said the girl.

Most of the group now spoke up simultaneously, some of them clearly angry. Vivienne, the girl with spiky black hair who was usually at pains to sound as working class as possible, spoke loudest, and others fell silent to let her carry on.

'What you call "boundaries" is the justification for abuse, right, in my family's case it *was* abuse, and when you say fings like that, you don't just invalidate the experiences of people who've been 'armed, *actively 'armed*, by their parents' desire to control them –' Kyle was vigorously nodding '– you're perpetuating and propping up the same damn systems of control that some of us are trying to escape, OK? So you 'aven't suffered, well, bully for you, but maybe listen and learn from people who have, *OK*?'

There was much muttering in agreement. Mazu said nothing, letting the group deal with the dissident themselves. For the first time, Robin thought she saw a genuine smile on the woman's face.

The girl with the heart-shaped face was openly ostracised that afternoon by other members of Fire Group. Robin, who wished she could have muttered some words of kindness or support, copied the majority and ignored her.

Their twenty-four-hour fast began on Wednesday evening. Robin received only a cup of hot water flavoured with lemon at dinner time. Looking around at the other recruits, she realised that only Fire, Wood and Earth groups were undertaking the fast; Metal and Water groups had been served the usual slop of boiled vegetables and noodles. Robin thought it unlikely that Metal and Water groups could have failed Dr Zhou's physical assessment en masse. From muttered comments uttered by her fellow fasters, some of whom were sitting nearby, Robin gathered they saw themselves as worthier than those being fed, seeming to consider the forthcoming twenty-four hours of enforced starvation a badge of honour.

Robin woke next day, which was the last of her seven-day retreat, after a few hours' sleep that had been disrupted by the gnawing hunger pains in her stomach. Tonight was the night she was supposed to find the plastic rock at the boundary of the farm, the thought of which made her feel simultaneously excited and scared. She hadn't yet attempted to leave her dormitory by night, and was apprehensive not only about being intercepted on the way to the woods, but finding her way to the right spot in the dark.

After breakfast, which for the three fasting groups consisted of another cup of hot water with lemon, all recruits were reunited for the second time since being sorted into groups on arrival, then led by church members into the left wing of the farmhouse. Inside was an empty, stone-paved room, in the middle of which was a steep wooden staircase leading into the basement.

Below lay a wood-panelled room that Robin thought must run almost the length of the farmhouse above. Two doors on the left-hand side showed the basement space extended even further than was currently visible. There was a stage at the opposite end from the staircase, in front of a screen almost as large as the one in the Rupert Court Temple. Subdued lighting came from spotlights and the floor was covered in rush matting. The recruits were instructed to sit down on the floor facing the stage, and Robin was irresistibly reminded of being back at primary school. Some of the recruits had difficulty complying with the order, including Walter Fernsby, who nearly toppled over onto his neighbour as he lowered himself in stiff and ungainly fashion onto the floor.

Once everyone was seated, the lights overhead were extinguished, leaving the stage spot lit.

Into the spotlight onstage stepped Jonathan Wace, clad in his long orange robes, handsome, long-haired, dimple-chinned and blue-eyed. Spontaneous applause broke out, not just from the church attendants, but also among the recruits. Robin could see the thrilled, blushing face of widowed Marion Huxley, who had such an obvious crush on Wace, through a gap to her left. Amandeep was one of those applauding hardest.

Jonathan smiled his usual self-deprecating smile, gestured

to settle the crowd down, then pressed his hands together, bowed and said,

'I thank you for your service.'

'And I for yours,' chorused the recruits, bowing back.

'That's no mere form of words,' said Wace, smiling around at them all. 'I'm sincerely grateful for what you've given us this week. You've sacrificed your time, energy and muscle power to help us run our farm. You've helped raise funds for our charitable work and begun to explore your own spirituality. Even if you go no further with us, you will have done real and lasting good – for us, for yourselves and for victims of the materialist world.

'And now,' said Wace, his smile fading, 'let's talk about that world.'

Ominous organ music began to play over hidden speakers. The screen behind Wace came to life. The recruits saw moving clips of heads of state, wealthy celebrities and government officials pass in succession across the screen as Wace began talking about the recently leaked confidential documents from an offshore law firm: the Panama Papers, which Robin had seen in the news before coming to Chapman Farm.

'Fraud ... kleptocracy ... tax evasion ... violation of international sanctions ...' said Wace, who was wearing a microphone. 'The world's grubby materialist elite stands exposed in all their duplicity, hiding the wealth, a fraction of which could solve most of the world's problems ...'

Onscreen, incriminated kings, presidents and prime ministers smiled and waved from podia. Famous actors beamed from red carpets and stages. Smartly suited businessmen waved away questions from journalists.

Wace began to talk fluently and furiously of hypocrisy, narcissism and greed. He contrasted public pronouncements with private behaviour. The eyes of the hungry, exhausted audience followed him as he strode backwards and forwards onstage. The room was hot and the rush-covered floor uncomfortable.

Next, a melancholy piano played over footage of homeless people begging at the entrances to London's most expensive stores, then of children swollen-bellied and dying in Yemen, or torn and maimed by Syrian bombs. The sight of a small boy covered in blood and dust, shocked into an almost cataleptic state as he was lifted into an ambulance, made Robin's eyes fill with tears. Wace, too, was crying.

Choral voices and kettle drums accompanied catastrophic footage of climate change and pollution: glaciers crumbling, polar bears struggling between melting ice floes, aerial views of the decimation of the rainforest, and now these images were intercut with flashbacks of the plutocrats in their cars and their boardrooms. Maimed children being carried from collapsed buildings were contrasted with images of celebrity weddings costing millions; selfies from private planes were followed by heartrending images of Hurricane Katrina and the Indian Ocean tsunami. The shadowy faces around Robin were stupefied and in many cases tearful, and Wace was no longer the mild-spoken, self-deprecating man they'd first met, but was shouting in fury, raging at the screen and the world's venality.

'And all of this, all of it, could be stopped if only enough people could be woken from the slumber in which they are walking to their doom!' he bellowed. *'The Adversary and his agents stalk the world, which must awake from its slumber or perish! And who will wake them, if we don't?'*

The music slowly died away. The images faded from the screen. Now Wace stood breathless, apparently spent by his long speech, his face tearstained, his voice hoarse.

'You,' he said weakly, stretching out his hands to those seated on the floor in front of him, 'were called. You were chosen. And today you have a choice. Rejoin the system, or stand apart. Stand apart and *fight*.

'There will now be a short break,' said Wace, as the lights began to brighten. 'No – *no*,' he said, as a smattering of applause broke out. 'There's nothing to be happy about in what I've just shown you. Nothing.'

Cowed, the applauders desisted. Robin was desperate for a breath of fresh air, but as Wace disappeared, church attendants opened a door on the left onto a second panelled, windowless room, in which cold food had been laid out.

The new space was comparatively cramped. The door onto the lecture room had been closed, increasing the feeling of claustrophobia. Fasters were directed to a table bearing flasks of hot water and lemon slices. Some recruits chose to sit down with their backs against the wall while eating their sandwiches or sipping their hot water. Queues formed for two more doors leading to toilets. Robin was certain they'd been in the lecture room for the entire morning. The girl with the heart-shaped face, who'd challenged Mazu the previous day in the temple, was sitting in a corner with her head in her arms. Robin was concerned about Walter, the philosophy professor, who appeared unsteady on his feet, his face white and sweaty.

'Are you all right?' she asked him quietly as he leaned up against the wall.

'Fine, fine,' he said, smiling while clutching his mug. 'The spirit remains strong!'

Eventually, the door to the lecture room was opened again. It was already dark, and people stumbled and whispered apologies as they tried to find a free place to sit.

When at last all were settled back on the floor, Jonathan Wace stepped out into the spotlight once more. Robin was glad to see him smiling. She really didn't want to be harangued any further.

'You've earned a reprieve,' said Wace, to a ripple of relieved laughter from his audience. 'It's time to meditate and chant. Take up a comfortable position. A deep breath. Raise your arms over your head on an in breath ... lower them slowly ... release the breath. And: *Lokah Samastah Sukhino Bhavantu* ... *Lokah Samastah Sukhino Bhavantu* ...'

Thought was impossible while chanting; Robin's feelings of fear, guilt and horror gradually subsided; she felt herself dissolving into the deafening chant, which echoed off the wooden walls, taking on its own power, existing independently of the chanters, a disembodied force that vibrated within the walls and within her own body.

The chanting went on longer than they'd ever chanted before. She could feel her mouth becoming dry and was dimly aware that she felt close to fainting, but somehow the chant sustained her, holding her up, enabling her to bear the hunger and the pain.

At long last Wace called a halt, smiling down at them all, and Robin, though weak, and uncomfortably hot, was left with the feeling of well-being and euphoria chanting always gave her.

'You,' said Wace quietly, his voice now more hoarse and cracked than ever, 'are remarkable.'

And in spite of herself, Robin felt an irrational pride in Wace's approval.

'Extraordinary people,' said Wace, walking up and down in front of them again. 'And you have no idea of it, do you?' he said, smiling down into the upturned faces. 'You don't realise what you are. A truly remarkable group of recruits. We've noticed it from the moment you arrived. Church members have told me, "These are special. These might be the ones we've been waiting for."

'The world teeters on a precipice. It's ten to midnight and Armageddon beckons. The Adversary may be winning, but the Blessed Divinity hasn't given up on us yet. The proof? They sent you to us – and with you, we might have a chance.

'They have spoken to you already, by the means at Their disposal, through the noise of the materialist world. That's why you're here.

'But you've breathed pure air this week. The clatter has died away and you see and hear more clearly than you have. Now is the time for a sign from the Divinity. Now is the moment for you to truly see. To truly understand.'

Wace dropped to his knees. He closed his eyes. As the recruits watched, transfixed, he said in a ringing voice,

'Blessed Divinity, if it pleases You, send us Your messenger. Let the Drowned Prophet come to us, here, and prove there is life after death, that the pure spirit lives independently of the material body, that the reward for a life of service is life eternal. Blessed Divinity, I believe these people are worthy. Send Daiyu to us now.'

The silence in the dark, hot room was total. Wace's eyes were still closed.

'Blessed Divinity,' he whispered, 'let her come.'

A collective gasp issued from the watchers.

The transparent head of a girl had appeared out of thin air on stage. She was smiling.

Alarmed, Robin looked over her shoulder, looking for a projector, but there was no beam of light and the wall was solid. She faced the front again, her heart beating rapidly.

The smiling spectral figure was growing a body. She had long black hair and wore a long white dress. She raised a hand and waved childishly at the crowd. A few people waved back. Most looked terrified.

Wace opened his eyes.

'You came to us,' he said.

Daiyu turned slowly to face him. They could see right through her, to Wace kneeling behind her, smiling through his tears.

'Thank you,' Wace told her, through a sob. 'I don't call you back for selfish reasons, you know that ... although seeing you ...'

He swallowed.

'Daiyu,' he whispered, 'are they ready?'

Daiyu turned slowly back to face the crowd. Her eyes travelled over the recruits. She smiled and nodded.

'I thought so,' said Wace. 'Go well, little one.'

Daiyu raised a hand to her mouth and appeared to blow a kiss to the recruits. Slowly, she began to fade from sight, until for a brief moment only her face shone in the darkness. Then she vanished.

The watchers were utterly still. Nobody spoke, nobody turned to their neighbour to talk of what they'd just seen. Wace got to his feet, wiping his eyes on the sleeve of his robe.

'She returns from Paradise when she knows we need her. She humours her foolish Papa J. She realises you're too special to let slip away. Now,' said Wace quietly, 'please follow me to temple.'

35

Nine at the top . . .
One attains the way of heaven.

The I Ching or Book of Changes

The recruits got to their feet as the lights went up. Wace descended and walked through them, pausing here and there to greet certain people by name, even though he'd never been introduced to them. Those who were so honoured looked stunned.

'Rowena,' he said, smiling at Robin. 'I've heard wonderful things about you.'

'Thank you,' said Robin weakly, letting him clasp both her hands in his.

People around Robin looked at her with envy and increased respect as Wace walked on, leading the way back up the stairs into the farmhouse.

The recruits followed him. As Robin neared the top of the stairs, she saw sunset through the windows: they'd spent the entire day in the dark, stuffy room. She was aching with hunger, and her body was sore from physical labour and from sitting on the uncomfortable floor.

Then the sound of loud rock music reached her ears, blasting out of speakers in the courtyard. Church members had formed two lines, making a path between farmhouse and temple, and were singing and clapping along with the song. As Robin emerged into the damp evening air the chorus began.

I don't need no one to tell me 'bout heaven
I look at my daughter, and I believe . . .

Robin walked with her fellow recruits between the rows of singing church members. Spots of rain hit her and she heard thunder rumbling over the music.

Sometimes it's hard to breathe, Lord,
At the bottom of the sea, yeah yeah . . .

Wace led the recruits up the steps into the temple, which was now illuminated by many lamps and candles.

The central pentagonal stage had become a five-sided pool. Robin realised that the pool had been there all along, beneath a heavy black lid. The water beneath looked jet black due to the dark sides. Mazu stood facing them, reflected as though in a dark mirror. She was no longer wearing orange, but a long white robe matching that of her daughter on the ceiling above. Now Wace climbed the steps to stand beside her.

The rock song finished after everyone, church members as well as recruits, had entered the temple. The doors closed with a loud bang. Those who'd led the recruits into the farmhouse instructed them in whispers to remain standing facing the pool, then filed into the surrounding seats.

Hollow with hunger, aching, sweaty and emotionally wrung out, Robin could only think that the cool water looked inviting. It would be wonderful to sink beneath the surface, to experience a few moments of solitude and peace.

'Tonight,' said Jonathan Wace, 'you have a free choice. Remain with us, or rejoin the materialist world. Which of you will step forwards and enter the pool? Be reborn tonight. Cleanse yourself of the false self. Step out of the purifying water as your true self. Which of you is prepared to take this first, essential step towards pure spirit?'

Nobody moved for a second or two. Then Amandeep pushed past Robin.

'I will.'

The watching church members exploded into cheers and applause. Jonathan and Mazu held out their arms, beaming. Amandeep walked forwards, ascended the steps at the side of the pool, and Jonathan and Mazu gave him unheard instructions. He took off his trainers and socks, then stepped forwards into the pool, sank briefly beneath the surface before reappearing, his glasses askew, but laughing. The cheers and applause of the church members echoed around the temple as Jonathan and Mazu helped the sodden Amandeep climb out on the other side, his tracksuit now heavy with water. He collected his trainers and socks and was led away by a pair of church members through a door at the back of the temple.

Kyle was the next into the pool. He received the same rapturous reaction when he re-emerged from the pool.

Robin decided she didn't want to wait any longer, and sidled through the other recruits to reach the front of the group.

'I want to join,' she said, to a further eruption of cheers.

She walked forwards, climbed the steps and took off her socks and trainers. At a sign from Jonathan, she stepped into the surprisingly deep pool and let herself sink into the cold water. Her feet found the bottom and she pushed upwards again, and the glorious silence was shattered as she broke the surface to loud clapping and shouts of approval.

Jonathan Wace helped her out. Now weighed down in her soaking wet tracksuit, hair in her eyes, Robin was handed her socks and trainers by a smiling Taio Wace, who escorted her personally to the back of the temple and through a door into an anteroom where Amandeep and Kyle were already dressed in clean, dry tracksuits and towelling off their hair, both evidently elated. More clean, folded tracksuits lay waiting on wooden benches that ran around the walls. Opposite lay a door that Robin knew must lead outside.

'Here,' said the smiling Taio, handing Robin a towel. 'Take a tracksuit and change.'

Amandeep and Kyle both looked courteously away as Robin peeled off her top, very conscious that her underwear, too, was soaking wet, but Taio watched openly, smirking.

'How many more d'you think will join?' Amandeep asked Taio.

'We'll see,' said Taio, not taking his eyes off Robin as she sat down, trying to remove her wet tracksuit bottoms and pull on dry ones without anyone seeing how translucent her pants had become. 'We need all the people we can get. This is a fight of good against evil, pure and simple ... better get back,' Taio added, as Robin, now dressed, began pulling on her socks.

'I can't believe this,' said the breathless Amandeep, as the door closed behind Taio. 'I came here thinking, "This place is crazy. It's a cult." I was gonna write an article for my student paper. And now ... I've joined the damn cult.'

He began to laugh uncontrollably and so did Kyle and Robin.

Over the next half hour, more and more people entered the room in a similar condition of near hysterical laughter. Walter Fernsby came in, a little tottery and shaken, followed immediately by Penny Brown, whose green hair was plastered around her face like algae. Marion Huxley appeared, shivering, apparently disorientated, but also inclined to giggle. Soon the changing room was packed with people excitedly discussing the materialisation of Daiyu in the basement, and their own pride at having joined the church.

Then came ten minutes when nobody else appeared. After taking a quick, silent headcount, Robin estimated that there were half a dozen hold-outs, including the girl with the heart-shaped face who'd refused to criticise her family to Fire Group, and Penny's blonde friend. Indeed, Penny was looking around anxiously, no longer laughing. A further ten minutes passed, and then a door to the outside was opened by Will Edensor.

'This way,' he said, and he led the new church members out of the temple and towards the dining hall.

It was dark now and gooseflesh crept up Robin's body and under her still-wet hair. Penny Brown was still looking around anxiously for the friend who'd come with her to Chapman Farm.

The newly joined church members entered the dining room to a standing ovation from the church members who'd left the temple ahead of them. Evidently there'd been a lot of activity during the hours the recruits had been shut away in the basement beneath the farmhouse, because scarlet and gold paper lanterns of the kind that swung in the breeze in Wardour Street had been strung from the rafters and an appetising smell of cooked meat filled the air. Kitchen workers were already moving between the tables, wheeling their enormous metal vats.

Robin dropped into the nearest free seat and gulped down some of the tap water already poured in a plastic cup in front of her.

'Congratulations,' said a quiet voice behind her, and she saw shaven-headed Louise, who was pushing along a vat of what smelled like chicken curry, which she now ladled onto Robin's tin plate, adding a couple of spoonfuls of rice.

'Thank you,' said Robin gratefully. Louise smiled weakly, then moved away.

Although it wasn't the best curry in the world, this was certainly the most appetising and filling meal Robin had been given since her arrival at Chapman Farm, and contained by far the most protein. She was eating fast, so desperate for calories she couldn't pace herself. Once the curry was finished she was given a bowl of yoghurt mixed with honey, which was the best thing she'd tasted all week.

An air of festivity filled the hall. There was far more laughter than usual and Robin guessed that this comparative feast was the reason. Robin now noticed that Noli Seymour had joined the top table, dressed in orange robes, and for the first time Robin realised that the actress must be a church Principal. Beside Noli sat two middle-aged men, also in orange robes. Upon enquiry, the young man sitting beside Robin told her that one was a multi-millionaire who'd made his fortune in packaging, and the other was an MP. Robin stored up both men's names for her letter to Strike.

Jonathan and Mazu Wace entered the dining hall to renewed cheers after most people had finished eating. There was no sign of the girl with the heart-shaped face, or the other recruits who hadn't entered the pool, and Robin wondered where they'd gone, whether they were being held somewhere without food, and whether the Waces' prolonged absence had been due to a last attempt at persuasion.

She dreaded the prospect of another Wace speech, but instead music started up out of loudspeakers again as the Waces took their seats, and with a wave of his hand, Wace seemed to indicate that informality was now permitted, that the party should begin. An old REM song blasted across the dining hall, and some church members, now full of meat for the first time in who knew how long, got up to dance.

It's the end of the world as we know it
And I feel fine . . .

36

Nine in the third place means:
A halted retreat
Is nerve-wracking and dangerous.

The I Ching or Book of Changes

The party had been going on for at least two hours. Jonathan Wace had descended from the top table to screams of excitement, and begun to dance with some of the teenage girls. The packaging millionaire also got up to dance, moving like somebody whose joints needed oiling, and inserting himself into the group around Wace. Robin remained sitting on her wooden bench, forcing a smile but wanting nothing more than to get back to the dormitory. The ingestion of a proper meal after her fast, the loud music, the ache of her muscles after a long day sitting on the hard floor: all were exacerbating her exhaustion.

At last she heard the opening bars of 'Heroes' and knew the evening was about to end, as surely as if she'd heard the start of 'Auld Lang Syne'. She was careful to sing along and look happy, and was rewarded when at last everyone began to file back to the dormitories through the rain that had begun to fall while they were eating, except for the drudges like Louise who were left behind to clean up the tables.

In spite of her bone-deep tiredness, that part of Robin's

mind that kept reminding her why she was there told her that tonight would be her best opportunity to find the plastic stone. Everyone at the farm had just enjoyed an atypically filling meal and would be more likely to fall asleep quickly. Sure enough, the women around her undressed quickly, pulling on pyjamas, scribbling in their journals, then falling into bed.

Robin made a brief entry in her own journal then put on her pyjamas too, leaving on the underwear that was still slightly damp. Glancing around to make sure nobody was watching, she got into bed with her socks and trainers still on, hiding her tracksuit under the covers. After ten minutes, the lights, which were controlled by a master switch somewhere, finally went out.

Robin lay in the darkness, listening to the rain, forcing herself to stay awake even though her eyelids kept drooping. Soon snores and slow, heavy breathing could be heard over the patter on the windows. She daren't wait too long, nor did she dare try and extricate her waterproof jacket from under her bed. Trying not to rustle her sheets, she succeeded in pulling her tracksuit back on over her pyjamas. Then, slowly and carefully, she slid out of bed and crept towards the dormitory door, ready to tell anyone who woke that she was on her way to the bathroom.

She opened the door cautiously. There were no electric lights in the deserted courtyard, although Daiyu's pool and fountain glinted in the moonlight and a single lit window shone from the upper floor of the farmhouse.

Robin felt her way around the side of the building and along the strip of ground between the women's and men's dormitories, her hair becoming rapidly wetter in the rain. By the time she reached the end of the passage her eyes had somewhat acclimatised to the darkness. Her objective was the patch of dense woodland visible from the dormitory's window, which lay beyond a small field which none of the recruits had yet entered.

Trees and shrubs had been planted at the end of the passage-way between the dormitories, which screened the field from view. As she made her way carefully through this thicket, trying not to trip over roots, she saw light and paused between bushes.

She'd found more Retreat Rooms, such as she'd seen from Dr Zhou's office, screened from the dormitories by careful planting. Through the bushes, she could see light shining from behind curtains which had been pulled across the sliding glass doors of one of them. Robin feared that someone might be about to walk out of it, or peer outside. She waited for a minute, pondering her options, then decided to risk it. Leaving the shelter of the trees, she crept on, passing within ten yards of the cabin.

It was then that she realised there was no danger of anyone leaving the Retreat Room immediately. Rhythmic thumps and grunts were issuing from it, along with small squeals that might have been pleasure or pain. Robin hurried on.

A five-bar gate separated the field from the planted area where the Retreat Rooms stood. Robin decided to climb this rather than attempt to open it. Once she'd reached the other side she set off at a jog, the wet ground squelching beneath her feet, consumed by barely controlled panic. If there were night vision cameras covering the farm, she'd be detected any moment; the agency might have taken a careful survey of the perimeter, but they'd had no way of knowing what surveillance technology was used inside. Her rational self kept telling her she'd seen no sign of cameras anywhere, yet the fear dogged her as she hurried towards the deeper darkness that was the wood.

Reaching the shelter of the trees was a relief, but now another kind of fear gripped her. She seemed to see again the smiling, transparent form of Daiyu as she'd appeared in the basement a few hours previously.

It was a trick, she told herself. *You know it was a trick.*

But she didn't understand how it had been done, and it was only too easy to believe in ghosts when struggling blindly through overgrown woodland, nettles and over more twisted roots, with the crack of twigs underfoot sounding as loud as gunshots in the still of the night and rain beating down on the tree canopy overhead.

Robin couldn't tell whether she was going in the right direction, because in the absence of any passing cars she couldn't be sure where the road was. She blundered on for ten minutes until, with a whoosh and a sweep of light, a car did indeed pass on the road to her right and she realised she was some twenty yards from the perimeter.

It took her nearly half an hour to find the small clearing Barclay had cut just inside the perimeter wall, with its heavy reinforcement of barbed wire. Crouching down, she groped around on the ground and at long last her fingers felt something unnaturally warm and smooth. She lifted the plastic rock out of the patch of weeds where it had lain and pulled the two halves apart with shaking hands.

Turning on the pencil torch, she saw the pen, paper and a note in Strike's familiar handwriting, and her heart leapt as though she'd seen him in person. She'd just removed his message when she heard voices in the wood behind her.

Terrified, Robin turned off the torch and flung herself flat to the ground in the nearest patch of nettles, shielding her face as best she could with her arms, certain the pounding of her heart would be audible to whoever had followed her. Expecting a shout or a demand to show herself, she heard nothing at all except footsteps. Then a girl spoke.

'I th-th-thought I saw a light just then.'

Robin lay very still and closed her eyes, as though that would somehow make her less visible.

'Moonlight on the wire, probably,' said a male voice. 'Go on. What did you want to—?'

'I n-n-need you to m-m-make me increase again.'

'Lin . . . I can't.'

'You've g-g-got to,' said the girl, who sounded on the verge of tears. 'Or I-I-I'll have t-t-t-t-to go with him again. I c-c-can't, Will. I c-c-c-c—'

She started to cry.

'Shh!' said Will frantically.

Robin heard a rustle of fabric and murmuring. She guessed that Will had put his arms around Lin, whose sobs now sounded muffled.

'Why c-c-c—'

'You know why,' he whispered.

'They're g-g-g-going to send me t-t-to Birmingham if I d-d-don't go with him and I c-c-can't leave Qing, I w-w-won't—'

'Who says you're going to Birmingham?' said Will.

'M-M-M-M-Mazu, if I d-d-d-don't go with h-h-h—'

'When did she tell you that?'

'Y-y-y-yesterday, but if I'm increasing m-m-maybe she w-w-won't m-m-m—'

'Oh God,' said Will, and Robin had never heard the two syllables more freighted with despair.

There was more silence and faint sounds of movement.

Please don't be having sex, Robin thought, eyes tightly closed as she lay among the nettles. *Please, please don't.*

'Or c-c-c-could d-d-do w-w-what Kevin d-d-did,' said Lin, her voice thick with tears.

'Are you insane?' said Will harshly. 'Be damned forever, annihilate our spirits?'

'I w-w-won't leave Qing!' wailed Lin. Again Will frantically hushed her. There was another lull, in which Robin thought she could hear kissing of a comforting rather than passionate nature.

She should have foreseen that somebody other than the Strike and Ellacott Detective Agency might be aware of the blind spot on the cameras and the useful cover of the woods. She was now dependent for her own safe return to the dormitory on whatever the couple decided to do next. Petrified that one of them might stray closer to the spot where she lay, because another passing car would undoubtedly reveal her bright orange tracksuit, she had no choice but to remain curled up among the nettles. How she was going to explain the mud and grass stains on her clean tracksuit was a problem she'd worry about if she ever got safely out of the woods.

'Can't you tell Mazu you've got something – what's that thing you had?'

'Cystitis,' sobbed Lin. 'She w-w-won't believe m-m-me.'

'OK,' said Will, 'then – then – you'll have to pretend to be ill with something else. Ask to see Dr Zhou.'

'B-b-but I'll have to g–g-get better in the end – *I can't leave Qing!*' wailed the girl again, and Will, now clearly scared out of his wits, said,

'For God's sake don't shout!'

'*Why* won't you just m-m-make me increase again?'

'I can't, you don't understand, I can't—'

'You're sc-sc-scared!'

Robin heard rapidly receding footsteps and was certain the girl was running away, Will in pursuit, because his voice sounded further away when he spoke again.

'Lin—'

'If you're not g-g-going to make m-m-me increase—'

The voices became indistinguishable. Robin continued to lie still in her hiding place, heart thumping, ears straining to hear what was going on. The couple were still arguing, but she couldn't make out what they were saying any more. How long she lay and listened, she didn't know. Another car swished past. At last, the voices and footsteps died away.

Robin lay where she was for a further five minutes, scared the couple was going to return, then gingerly sat back up again.

Strike's note was still crumpled up in her hand. She took a few deep breaths, then turned the torch back on, smoothed out the letter and read it.

Thursday 14th April

Hope all's going well in there. Dev's going to drop this off and he'll be in the vicinity until Saturday, checking on the rock until you've put a note in. If nothing arrives, we'll see you Sunday.

I've met Abigail Glover, Jonathan Wace's daughter. Some very interesting stuff. She claims Daiyu wasn't Wace's daughter, but Alexander Graves'. Apparently when she died, there was a custody battle for her going on between the Waces and Graves' parents. Abigail witnessed and suffered plenty of violence in there, and was personally shut in the pigsty, naked, for three nights after Daiyu drowned, but isn't keen on testifying, unfortunately.

On Tuesday I'm meeting Alexander Graves' parents. Will let you know how that goes.

Still trying to trace Cherie Gittins, the girl who took Daiyu swimming. I've been looking into Daiyu's death and I've got questions. Anything you can find out in there would be helpful.

Might also have found a way of persuading Jordan Reaney to talk to me — Shanker's got mates inside with him.

Littlejohn is worrying me. He didn't tell me he worked for Patterson for 3 months before coming to us. Trying to find a replacement.

The Franks remain freaks and might be planning a kidnapping.

Look after yourself. Any time you want to come out, say the word. We'll batter down the door if necessary.

Sx

Robin wasn't sure why the note had made her cry, but a tear now dropped down onto the paper. The connection with her outside life had affected her like medicine, fortifying her, and the offer to batter down the door and the single kiss beside Strike's initial felt like a hug.

Now she took out the pen, propped the small pile of paper on her knee and began to write, clumsily, with the torch held in her left hand.

All going well. Tonight I joined the church. Total submersion in the pool in the temple.

Will Edensor's here and I've just overheard a conversation between him and Lin, Deirdre Doherty's daughter. She was begging him to make her 'increase' again, to stave off having to sleep with 'him'. No idea who 'him' is. Lin even suggested leaving but Will sounds completely indoctrinated, says it would mean damnation. I can't be certain, but if she's already had a child in here it might be Will's. If so, I'm sure she'll have been underage when she gave birth, because she doesn't look very old now.

No violence witnessed as yet but the sleep deprivation and underfeeding is real.

Tonight I saw the spirit of Daiyu materialise out of thin air, moving and waving at us all. Jonathan W conjured her. No idea how it was done but I have to say it was effective and I think it convinced nearly everyone.

Robin paused, trying to remember anything else Strike might think significant. She was now shivering with cold and so tired she could barely think.

I think that's everything, sorry there isn't more. Hopefully now I'm a real church member I'll start seeing the bad stuff.
Sounds like a good idea to get rid of Little John when you can.
Robin x

She folded up her note, put it inside the safe rock and replaced the rock where she'd found it. Then, with a heavy heart, she tore Strike's note into tiny pieces, and began to make her way back through the trees towards the distant farm, strewing pieces of the note into different patches of nettles as she went.

However, she was so tired she'd lost her sense of direction. Soon she found herself in a dense clump of trees she definitely didn't remember coming through. Panic started to rise in her again. Finally she forced her way between two trunks tangled with creepers, took a few steps across a small clearing and then, with a shriek she couldn't prevent, fell over something hard and sharp.

'Shit,' Robin moaned, feeling for her lower leg. She'd cut herself, though thankfully there was no tear in her trousers. Groping around, she found the thing she'd tripped over: it appeared to be a broken stump or post in the ground. She stood up, and as she did so, she saw by the moonlight that there were several broken posts set in a rough circle. They were definitely manmade and looked unnervingly ritualistic, set amid the surrounding wilderness. Robin remembered Kevin Pirbright's story of being tied to a tree overnight as punishment when he was twelve. Had there once been posts here, to which an entire group of children could be tied? If so, they appeared to be no longer in use, because they were rotting quietly away in the depths of the wood.

Now limping slightly, Robin set off again and at long last, with the aid of a fleeting spell of moonlight, found the edge of the wood.

Only as she was walking back across the dark, damp field towards the farm did she remember that she hadn't written a note for Murphy. Far too tired and shaken to go back now, she decided she'd write him an apology next week. Fifteen minutes later, she was climbing the five-bar gate. She passed the now dark and silent Retreat Rooms and, with profound relief, slipped back inside the dormitory undetected.

PART THREE

Chien/Obstruction

OBSTRUCTION means difficulty.
The danger is ahead.
To see the danger and to know how to stand still,
that is wisdom.

              The I Ching or Book of Changes

37

*Through resoluteness one is certain to encounter
something.*
*Hence there follows the hexagram of COMING TO
MEET.*

The I Ching or Book of Changes

If the receipt of Robin's letter from Chapman Farm didn't have
quite the same effect on Strike as his had on her, the absence
of a note for Ryan Murphy cheered him enormously, a fact
he concealed from Dev Shah when the latter confirmed that
there'd been only one letter inside the plastic rock when he'd
checked before dawn.

'Well, good to know she's OK,' was Strike's only comment,
after reading Robin's message at the partners' desk. 'And that's
a pretty bloody big piece of information she's got already. If
Will Edensor's fathered a kid in there, we've got a partial
explanation of why he's not leaving.'

'Yeah,' said Dev. 'Fear of prosecution. Statutory rape, isn't
it? Gonna tell Sir Colin?'

Strike hesitated, frowning as he rubbed his chin.

'If the kid's definitely Will's he'll have to know eventually,
but I'd rather get a bit more information first.'

'Underage is underage,' said Dev.

Strike had never seen Shah look that uncompromising before.

'I agree. But I'm not sure you can judge what goes on in there by normal standards.'

'Fuck normal standards,' said Dev. 'Keep your dick in your pants around kids.'

There was a short, charged silence, following which Dev announced that he needed to get some sleep, having been up all night in the car, and departed.

'What's upset him?' enquired Pat, as the glass door closed rather harder than necessary and Strike emerged from the inner office with an empty mug in his hand.

'Sex with underage girls,' said Strike, moving towards the sink to wash up the mug before heading out for more surveillance on Bigfoot. 'Not Dev,' he added.

'Well, I knew *that*,' said Pat.

How Pat could know that, Strike didn't ask. Dev was easily the most handsome subcontractor employed by the agency and Strike knew from experience that their office manager's sympathies were most readily engaged by good-looking men. An association of ideas led him to say,

'Incidentally, if Ryan Murphy calls, tell him there's no note for him from Robin this week.'

Something in Pat's sharp glance made Strike say,

'There wasn't one in the rock.'

'All right, I'm not accusing you of burning it,' snapped Pat, turning back to her typing.

'Everything all right?' asked Strike. While he doubted anyone had ever compared Pat to a ray of eternal sunshine, he couldn't offhand remember her being this tetchy without provocation.

'Fine,' said Pat, e-cigarette waggling as she scowled at her monitor.

Strike decided the politic course was to wash his mug in silence.

'Well, that's me off to watch Bigfoot,' he said. As he turned to get his coat, his eye fell on a small pile of receipts on Pat's desk.

'Those Littlejohn's?'

'Yeah,' said Pat, her fingers moving rapidly over the keys.

'Mind if I have a quick look?'

He shuffled through them. There was nothing unusual or extravagant in there; indeed, if anything, they were on the sketchy side.

'What d'you think of Littlejohn?' Strike asked Pat, setting the receipts back down beside her.

'What d'you mean, what do I think of him?' she said, glaring up at him.

'Exactly what I said.'

'He's all right,' said Pat, after a moment or two. 'He's fine.'

'Robin told me you don't like him.'

'I thought he was a bit quiet when he started, that's all.'

'Got chattier, has he?' said Strike.

'Yeah,' said Pat. 'Well – no – but he's always polite.'

'You've never noticed him doing anything odd? Behaving strangely? Lying about anything?'

'No. Why're you asking me this?' said Pat.

'Because if you had, you wouldn't be the only one,' said Strike. He was now intrigued: Pat had never before shown the slightest inclination to pull her punches when judging anyone: client, employee or, indeed, Strike himself.

'He's fine. Doing the job OK, isn't he?'

Before Strike could answer, the phone on Pat's desk rang.

'Oh, hello Ryan,' she said, her tone far warmer.

Strike decided it was time to leave, and did so, closing the glass door quietly behind him.

The next few days yielded little progress in the UHC case. There was no word from Shanker on a possible interview with Jordan Reaney. Cherie Gittins remained unfindable on every database Strike consulted. Of the witnesses to Cherie and Daiyu's early morning swim, the café owner who'd seen Cherie taking the child down to the beach while carrying towels had died five years previously. He'd tried to contact Mr and Mrs Heaton, who'd seen the hysterical Cherie running up the beach after Daiyu disappeared beneath the waves, and who were still living at an address in Cromer, but nobody ever answered their landline, no matter what time of day Strike tried it. He toyed with the idea of driving on to Cromer after visiting Garvestone Hall, but as the agency was already stretched with its current cases, and he was already planning to go down to Cornwall later in the week, he decided against sacrificing another few hours on the road merely to find an unoccupied house.

His drive to Norfolk on a sunny Tuesday morning was uneventful until, on a flat, straight stretch of the A11, Midge called him about the most recently acquired case on the agency's books, a case of presumed marital infidelity in which the husband wanted the wife watched. The client had been taken on so recently that no nickname had been assigned to either client or target, although Strike understood who Midge was talking about when she said without preamble,

'I've caught Mrs What's-Her-Name in the act.'

'Already?'

'Yeah. Got pictures of her coming out of the lover's flat this morning. Visiting her mother, my arse. Maybe I should've strung it out a bit. We're not going to make much out of this one.'

'Good word of mouth, though,' said Strike.

'Shall I get Pat to notify the next on the waiting list?'

'Let's give it a week,' said Strike, after a slight hesitation. 'The Frank job needs twice the manpower now we know it's both of them. Listen, Midge, while I've got you – is there anything up with Pat and Littlejohn?'

'What d'you mean?'

'There hasn't been a row or anything?'

'Not that I know of.'

'She was a bit odd when I asked her what she thought of him, this morning.'

'Well, she doesn't like him,' said Midge. 'None of us do,' she added, with her usual candour.

'I'm putting out feelers for a replacement,' said Strike, which was true: he'd emailed several contacts in both the police and the army for possible candidates the previous evening. 'OK, good work on Mrs Thing. I'll see you tomorrow.'

He drove on through the relentlessly flat landscape, which was having its usual lowering effect on his mood. The Aylmerton Community had forever tainted Norfolk in his mind; he found no beauty in the seeming immensity of the sky pressing down upon the level earth, nor for its occasional windmills and marshy wetlands.

His satnav guided him along a series of narrow, winding country lanes, until he finally saw his first signpost to Garvestone. Three hours after he'd left London, he entered the tiny village, passing a square-towered church, school and village hall in rapid succession and finding himself out the other side barely three minutes later. A quarter of a mile beyond Garvestone he spotted a wooden sign directing him up a track to his right to the hall. Shortly thereafter, he was driving through the open gates towards what had once been home to the Stolen Prophet.

38

Six at the top . . .
Not light but darkness.
First he climbed up to heaven,
Then he plunged into the depths of the earth.

The I Ching or Book of Changes

The drive was bordered with high hedges, so Strike saw little of the surrounding gardens until he reached the gravel forecourt in front of the hall, which was an irregular but impressive building of grey-blue stone, with Gothic windows and a front door of solid oak reached by a flight of stone steps. He paused for a few seconds after leaving the car to take in the immaculate green lawns, the topiary lions and the water garden glimmering in the distance. Then a door creaked and a croaky but powerful male voice said,

'Hello thah!'

An elderly man had come out of the house and now stood leaning on a mahogany stick at the top of the stone steps to the front door. He was wearing a shirt under his tweed blazer, and the blue and maroon regimental tie of the Grenadier Guards. Beside him stood an immensely fat yellow Labrador, wagging its tail but evidently deciding to wait for the newcomer to climb the steps rather than descend to greet him.

'Can't get down the damn steps any more without help, sorry!'

'No problem,' Strike said, the gravel crunching beneath his feet as he approached the front door. 'Colonel Graves, I presume?'

'How d'yeh do?' said Graves, shaking hands. He had a thick white moustache and a slight overbite, faintly reminiscent of a rabbit or, if you were being unkind, of the standard impersonation of an upper-class twit. The eyes blinking behind the lenses of his steel-rimmed glasses were milky with cataracts, and a large, flesh-coloured hearing aid protruded from one ear.

'Come in, come in – here, Gunga Din,' he added. Strike took the last exhortation to be an invitation to the fat Labrador now sniffing at the hems of his trousers, rather than himself.

Colonel Graves shuffled along ahead of Strike into a large hall, cane thudding loudly on the dark polished floorboards, the panting Labrador bringing up the rear. Victorian oil portraits of what Strike didn't doubt were ancestors looked down upon the two men and the dog. The place had an aged, serene beauty enhanced by the light flooding through a large leaded window over the stairs.

'Beautiful house,' said Strike.

'M'grandfather bought it. Beerocracy. Brewery's long gone, though. Graves Stout, ever heard of it?'

'Afraid not.'

'Went out of business in 1953. Still got a couple of bottles in the cellar. Nasty stuff. M'father made us drink it. Foundation of the family's fortune and what have yah. Hyar we are,' said the colonel, by now panting as loudly as his dog as he pushed open a door.

They entered a large drawing room of homely upper-class comfort, with deep sofas and armchairs of faded chintz, more leaded windows looking out onto the splendid gardens and a dog's bed made of tweed, into which the Labrador flopped with an air of having had more than his day's worth of exercise.

Three people were sitting around a low table laden with tea

things and what looked like a home-baked Victoria sponge. In an armchair sat an elderly woman with thin white hair, who was dressed in navy blue and pearls. Her hands were trembling so much that Strike wondered whether she had Parkinson's disease. A couple in their late forties were sitting side by side on the sofa. The balding man's heavy eyebrows and prominent Roman nose gave him the look of an eagle. His tie, unless he was pretending to be something he wasn't, which Strike thought unlikely in this context, proclaimed that he'd once been a Royal Marine. His wife, who was plump and blonde, was wearing a pink cashmere sweater and a tweed skirt. Her bobbed hair was tied back in a velvet bow, a style Strike hadn't seen since the eighties, while her ruddy, broken-veined cheeks suggested a life led largely out of doors.

'M'wife, Barbara,' said Colonel Graves, 'our daughter, Phillipa, and her husband, Nicholas.'

'Good morning,' said Strike.

'Hello,' said Mrs Graves. Phillipa merely nodded at Strike, unsmiling. Nicholas made no sound or gesture of welcome.

'Siddown,' said the colonel, gesturing Strike to an armchair opposite the sofa. He lowered himself slowly into a high-backed chair with a grunt of relief.

'How d'you take your tea?' Mrs Graves asked.

'Strong, please.'

'Good man,' barked the colonel. 'Can't stand weak tea.'

'I'll do it, Mummy,' said Phillipa, and indeed, Mrs Graves' hands were trembling so much, Strike thought it advisable she didn't handle boiling water.

'Cake?' the unsmiling Phillipa asked him, once she'd passed his tea.

'I'd love some,' said Strike. Sod the diet.

Once everyone had been served, and Phillipa had sat down again, Strike said,

'Well, I'm very grateful for this chance to talk to you. I understand this can't be easy.'

'We've been assured you're not a sleaze hound,' said Nicholas.

'Good to know,' said Strike drily.

'No offence,' said Nicholas, though his manner was that of a man who didn't particularly mind being offensive and might even pride himself on it, 'but we thought it important to check you out.'

'Do we have your assurance we're not going to be dragged into the tabloids?' said Phillipa.

'You do seem to make a habit of popping up there,' said Nicholas.

Strike could have pointed out that he'd never given the press an interview, that most of the journalistic interest he'd aroused had been due to solving criminal cases, and that it was hardly within his control whether the press became interested in his investigation. Instead he said,

'At the moment, the risk of press interest is slight to non-existent.'

'But you think it might all be dragged up?' Phillipa pressed him. 'Because our children don't know anything about all this. They think their uncle died of natural causes.'

'It was so long ago now, Pips,' said Mrs Graves. Strike thought she seemed a little nervous of her daughter and son-in-law. 'It's been twenty-three years. Allie would have been fifty-two now,' she added quietly, to nobody.

'If we can stop another family going through what we did,' said Colonel Graves loudly, 'we'll be delighted. One has an obligation,' he said, with a look at his son-in-law that, in spite of his cloudy eyes, was pointed. Turning stiffly in his chair to address Strike he said, 'What d'yeh want to know?'

'Well,' said Strike, 'I'd like to start with Alexander, if that's all right.'

'We always called him Allie, in the family,' said the colonel.

'How did he become interested in the church?'

'Long story,' said Colonel Graves. 'He was ill, yeh see – but we didn't realise f'ra long time. What did they call it?' he asked his wife, but it was his daughter who answered.

'Manic depression, but they've probably got another fancy word for it, these days.'

Phillipa's tone suggested scepticism of the psychiatric profession and all its ways.

'When he was younger,' said Mrs Graves tremulously, 'we just thought he was *naughty*.'

'Problems all through school,' said Colonel Graves, nodding ruminatively. 'Expelled from Rugby, in the end.'

'Why was that?' asked Strike.

'Drugs,' said Colonel Graves gloomily. 'I was stationed out in Germany at the time. We brought him out to join us. Put him into the international school to do his A-levels, but he didn't like it. Huge rows. Missed his friends. "Why's Pips allowed to stay in England?" I said, "Pips hasn't been caught smoking marriage-huana in her dorm, that's why." I was hopin',' said the colonel, 'bein' around the military, y'know – might show him another way. I'd always hoped . . . but there y'are.'

'His granny volunteered to have Allie stay with her, in Kent,' said Mrs Graves. 'She always loved Allie. He was to finish his A-levels at the local college, but next thing we heard, he'd taken orf. Granny was out of her mind with worry. I flew back to England to help look for him and found him staying with one of his old schoolfriends, in London.'

'Tom Bantling,' said Colonel Graves, nodding lugubriously. 'Both of 'em holed up in a basement, doin' drugs all day. Tom sorted himself out in the end, mind you,' he added with a sigh. 'OBE now . . . trouble was, y'see, by the time Baba found him, Allie had turned eighteen. One couldn't make him come home, or do anything he didn't want to.'

'How was he supporting himself?' asked Strike.

'He had some money his other grandmother left him,' said Mrs Graves. 'She left some to you, too, didn't she, darling?' she added to Phillipa. 'You used yours to buy Bugle Boy, didn't you?'

Mrs Graves gestured towards a bow-fronted cabinet on which many silver-framed photographs stood. After a second's confusion Strike realised his attention was being directed to one of the largest pictures, which featured a stout, beaming teenaged Phillipa in full hunting garb, sitting on top of a gigantic grey horse, presumably Bugle Boy, hounds milling behind them. Her hair, which was dark in the photograph, was tied back in what looked like the same velvet bow she was wearing today.

'So Allie had enough money to live on without working?' Strike said.

'Yerse, until he burned through it all,' said Colonel Graves, 'which he did in about twelve months. Then he signed on for the whatchamacallit – dole. I decided to leave th'army. Didn't want to leave Baba hyar on her own, tryin' to sort him out. It was startin' to be obvious there was something very wrong.'

'He was showing definite signs of mental illness by then, was he?'

'Yes,' said Mrs Graves, 'he was getting very paranoid and strange. Funny ideas about the government. But the awful thing is, one didn't really think of it as mental illness at the time, because he'd always been a bit—'

'Told us he was getting messages from God,' said Colonel Graves. 'Thought it was the drugs. We thought, if only he'd just stop smoking that bloody marriage-huana ... he fell out with Tom Bantling, and after that he stayed on other people's sofas until they got annoyed and kicked him out. Tried to keep tabs on him, but sometimes we didn't know where he was.'

'Then he got himself into *awful* trouble, in a pub. Nick was with him, weren't you?' Mrs Graves said to her son-in-law. 'They were at school together,' she explained to Strike.

'I was trying to talk sense into him,' said Nicholas, 'when some fella bumped inter him, an' he lashed out with a beer glass. Cut the chap's face. Stitches. He was charged.'

'Quite right, too,' barked the colonel. 'Couldn't argue with that. We got him a lawyer, personal friend of ours, and Danvers fixed up a psychiatrist.'

'Allie only agreed because he was terrified of prison,' said Mrs Graves. 'That was a real fear of his, being locked up. I think that's why he never liked boarding school.'

Phillipa gave the slightest of eye rolls, unnoticed by her parents, though not by Strike.

'So the psychiatrist fella diagnosed this manic what-have-you,' said Colonel Graves, 'and put him on pills.'

'And he said Allie *mustn't* smoke pot any more,' said Mrs Graves. 'We got Allie cleaned up for court, got him a haircut and so on, and he looked *marvellous* in his suit. And the judge was really very nice and basically said he thought Allie would do best with community service. And at the time,' sighed Mrs Graves, 'we thought him getting arrested was a blessing in disguise, didn't we, Archie? Not that we wanted some poor chap to be hurt, of course.'

'And he came back here to live, did he?' Strike asked.

''Sright,' said Colonel Graves.

'And his mental state improved?'

'Yes, it was *much* better,' said Mrs Graves. 'And you loved having him home, didn't you, Pips?'

'Hm,' said Phillipa.

'It was like having him back to how he was when he was a little boy,' said Mrs Graves. 'He was really awfully sweet and funny ...'

Tears swam in her eyes.

''Pologise,' she whispered, fumbling in her sleeve for a handkerchief.

Colonel Graves assumed the stolid, wooden expression of the average upper-class Englishman when confronted with a show of open emotion. Nicholas took refuge in sweeping cake crumbs off his jeans. Phillipa merely stared stonily at the teapot.

'What community service was Allie given?' asked Strike.

'Well, that's where she got her claws into him, y'see,' said Colonel Graves heavily. 'Community project fifty minutes up the road, in Aylmerton. Cleanin' up litter and so on. There were a couple of people there from Chapman Farm, and *she* was one of 'em. Mazu.'

The name changed the atmosphere in the room. Though the sunshine continued to flood in through the leaded windows, it seemed, somehow, to darken.

'He didn't tell us he'd met a gel at first,' said the colonel.

'But he was spending longer than he needed to in Aylmerton,' said Mrs Graves. 'Coming home very late. We could smell alcohol on his breath again, and we knew he wasn't supposed to be drinking on his medication.'

'So there was another row,' said Colonel Graves, 'and he blurted out that he'd met someone, but he said he knew we wouldn't like her, and that's why he took her to the pub instead of comin' hyar. And I said, "Watcha talkin' about, we wouldn't like her? How d'yeh know? Bring her over to meet us. Bring her for tea!" Tryin' to make him happy, y'know. So he did. He brought her hyar ...'

'He'd made it sound as though Mazu was a farmer's

daughter, before he brought her t'meet us. Nothin' wrong with that. But I could tell she wasn't a farmer's daughter, moment I laid eyes on her.'

'We'd never met any of his gelfriends before,' said Mrs Graves. 'Bit of a shock.'

'Why was that?' asked Strike.

'Well,' said Mrs Graves, 'she was very young and—'

'Filthy,' said Phillipa.

'—bit grubby,' said Mrs Graves. 'Long black hair. Skinny, with dirty jeans and a sort of smock.'

'Didn't talk,' said Colonel Graves.

'Not a word,' said Mrs Graves. 'Just sat next to Allie, where Nick and Pips are sitting now, clinging to his arm. We tried to be nice, didn't we?' she said plaintively to her husband, 'But she just stared at us through her hair. And Allie could tell we didn't like her.'

'*Nobody* could've bloody liked her,' said Nicholas.

'You met her too?' asked Strike.

'Met her later,' said Nicholas. 'Made my bloody flesh crawl.'

'It wasn't shyness,' said Mrs Graves. 'I could've understood shyness, but that's not why she didn't say anything. One had a sense, of real . . . *badness*. And Allie got defensive – didn't he, Archie? – "You think I like her because I'm mental." Well, of *course* we didn't think that, but we could tell she was encouraging the – the unstable part of him.'

'It was obvious she was the stronger personality,' said Colonel Graves, nodding.

'She can't have been more than sixteen, and Allie was twenty-three when he met her,' said Mrs Graves. 'It's very hard to explain. From the outside, it looked . . . I mean, *we* thought she was too young for him, but Allie was . . .'

Her voice trailed away.

'*Bloody* hell, Gunga,' said Nicholas angrily.

The stench of the old dog's fart had just reached Strike's nostrils.

'The hell are you feeding him?' Phillipa demanded of her parents.

'He had some of our rabbit last night,' said Mrs Graves apologetically.

'You spoil him, Mummy,' snapped Phillipa. 'You're too soft on him.'

Strike had the feeling this disproportionate anger wasn't really about the dog.

'When did Allie move to the farm?' he asked.

'Quite soon after we had them over for tea,' said Mrs Graves.

'And he was still on the dole at this point?'

'Yerse,' said the colonel, 'but there's a family trust. He'd been able to apply for funds from it, since he'd turned eighteen.'

Strike now took out his notebook and pen. Phillipa's and Nicholas' eyes followed these movements closely.

'He started applying for money the moment he moved in with Mazu, but the trustees weren't going to give him money just to fritter away,' said the colonel. 'Then Allie turned up here one day out of the blue to tell us Mazu was pregnant.'

'He said he wanted money to get baby things, and make Mazu comfortable,' said Mrs Graves.

'Daiyu was born in May 1988, right?' asked Strike.

'That's right,' said Mrs Graves. The tremor in her hands was making every sip of tea risky. 'Born at the farm. Allie rang us up, and we drove over right away, to see the baby. Mazu was lying in a filthy bed, nursing Daiyu, and Allie was very thin and jittery.'

'As bad as he'd been before he was arrested,' said Colonel Graves. 'Orf his medication. Told us he didn't need it.'

'We'd taken presents for Daiyu, and Mazu didn't even thank us,' said his wife. 'But we kept visiting. We were worried about

Allie, and about the baby, too, because the living conditions were quite unsanitary. Daiyu was very sweet, though. Looked just like Allie.'

'Spittin' image,' said the colonel.

'Except dark, and Allie was fair,' said Mrs Graves.

'Would you happen to have a picture of Allie?' asked Strike.

'Nick, could you—?' asked Mrs Graves.

Nicholas reached behind him and extracted a framed photo from behind the one of Phillipa sitting on the large grey horse.

'That's Allie's twenty-second,' said Mrs Graves, as Nicholas passed the picture over the tea things. 'When he was all right, before . . .'

The picture showed a group, at the centre of which stood a young man with a narrow head, blond hair and a distinctly rabbity face, though his lopsided grin was endearing. He greatly resembled the colonel.

'Yes, Daiyu was very like him,' said Strike.

'How would *you* know?' said Phillipa coldly.

'I saw a photo of her in an old news report,' Strike explained.

'I always thought she was just like her mother, personally,' said Phillipa.

Strike was scanning the rest of the group in the photograph. Phillipa was there, dark haired and stocky as she was in the hunting photograph, and beside her stood Nick, his hair military short, with his right arm in a sling.

'Injured on exercises?' Strike asked Nicholas, passing the photograph back.

'What? Oh, no. Just a stupid accident.'

Nicholas took the photograph back from Strike and replaced it carefully, hiding it again behind the one of his wife on her magnificent hunter.

'D'you remember Jonathan Wace coming to live at the farm?' asked Strike.

'Oh, yes,' said Mrs Graves, quietly. 'We were completely taken in. Thought he was the best thing about the place, didn't we, Archie? And you liked him, didn't you, Pips?' she said timidly. 'At first?'

'He was politer than Mazu, that's all,' said the unsmiling Phillipa.

'Fella seemed intelligent,' said Colonel Graves. 'One realised later it was all an act, but he was charmin' when you first met him. Talked about the sustainable farming they were going to do. Made it sound quite worthy.'

'I looked him up,' said Nicholas. 'He wasn't lying. He *had* been to Harrow. Big in the drama society, apparently.'

'He told us he was keeping an eye on Allie, Mazu and the baby,' said Mrs Graves. 'Making sure they were all right. We thought he was a *good* thing, at the time.'

'Then the religious stuff started creepin' in,' said Colonel Graves. 'Lectures on Eastern philosophy and what have yeh. Thought it was harmless at first. We were far more concerned about Allie's mental state. The letters to the trustees kept comin', clearly dictated by someone else. Passin' himself orf as a partner in the farming business, y'know. Balderdash, but hard to disprove. They got a fair bit out of the trust, one way or another.'

'Every time we visited the farm, Allie was worse,' said Mrs Graves, 'and we could tell there was something between Mazu and Jonathan.'

'Only time she ever cracked a smile was when Wace was around,' said Colonel Graves.

'And she'd started treating Allie *awf'ly*,' said Mrs Graves. '*Spiteful*, y'know. "Stop babbling." "Stop making a fool of yourself." And Allie was chanting and fasting and whatever else Jonathan was making him do.'

'We wanted Allie to see another doctor, but he said

medicines were poison, and he'd be fine as long as kept his spirit pure,' said Colonel Graves. 'Then, one day, Baba visited – you two were with her, werencha?'

'Yes,' said Phillipa stiffly. 'We'd just got back from our honeymoon. We took photos of the wedding with us. I don't know why. It's not as though Allie was interested. And there was a row.

'They claimed to be offended we hadn't asked Daiyu to be a flower girl,' she said, with a little laugh. 'Such nonsense. We'd sent Allie and Mazu invitations, but we knew they wouldn't come. Jonathan wouldn't let Allie leave the farm by then, except to collect money on the street. The flower girl thing was just an excuse to wind Allie up and make him think we all hated him and his child.'

'Not that we *wanted* her as a flower girl,' said Nicholas. 'She was—'

His wife shot him a look and he fell silent.

'Allie was making no sense at all that day,' said Mrs Graves desperately. 'I said to Mazu, "He's got to see someone. He's got to see a doctor."'

'Wace told us Allie just needed to clear his ego, and balls like that,' said Nicholas. 'And I bloody well let him have it. Told him, if he wanted to live like a pig that was his business, and if he wanted to spout crap at credulous morons who'd pay for the pleasure, fine, but the family had bloody well had enough of it. And I said to Allie, "If you can't see this for the bollocks it is, then you're even more of a fool than I thought you were, you need your head sorted out, now get in the bloody car—"'

'But he wouldn't come,' said Mrs Graves, 'and then Mazu said she was going to take out a restraining order against us. She was pleased there'd been a row. It's what she wanted.'

'That's when we decided somethin' had to be done,' said Colonel Graves. 'I hired O'Connor, the detective chappie I told you about on th'phone. Brief was to dig inter Mazu and Wace's backgrounds, get somethin' we could use against them.'

'Did he get anything?' asked Strike, his pen poised.

'Got a bit on the gel. Found out she was born at Chapman Farm. He thought she was one of the Crowthers' children – yeh know about that business? Mother was dead. She'd left the gel at the farm and gawn orf to work as a prostitute in London. Drug overdose. Pauper's grave.

'Wace was clearly a wastrel, but no criminal convictions. Parents were in South Africa. His first wife's death seemed to have been a pure accident. So we thought: desperate times call for desperate measures. We had O'Connor watchin' the farm. We knew Allie sometimes went inter Norwich to collect money.

'We grabbed him orf the street, me, m'brother-in-law and Nick,' Colonel Graves continued. 'Bundled him into the back of the car and drove him back hyar. He was goin' berserk. We dragged him inside, into this room, and kept him here all afternoon and most of the night, tryin' to talk some sense into him.'

'He just kept chanting and telling us he had to go back to temple,' said Mrs Graves hopelessly.

'We called the local GP,' said the colonel. 'He didn't come until late the next day. Young fella, new at the practice. Moment he walked in, Allie pulled himself together enough to say we'd kidnapped him and were forcin' him to stay here. Said he wanted to go back to Chapman Farm and begged the chap to get the police.

'Moment the doctor left, Allie started screamin' and throwing around furniture – if that bloody GP could've seen him like *that* – and while he was chucking things around, his shirt came untucked and we saw marks on his back. Bruising and welts.'

'I said to him, "What have they done to you, Allie?"' said Mrs Graves tearfully, 'But he wouldn't answer.'

'We got him upstairs again, into his old room,' said Colonel Graves, 'and he locked the door on us. I was worried he was goin' to climb out of the window so I went out onto the lawn to keep watch. Worried he'd jump, y'see, tryin' to get back to Chapman Farm. I was there all night.

'Early next mornin', two police officers came round. Tipped orf by the GP we were holdin' a man against his will. We explained what was goin' on. We wanted emergency services out to see him. The police said they needed to meet him first, so I went upstairs to get him. Knocked. No answer. Got worried. Nick and I broke down the door.'

Colonel Graves swallowed, then said quietly,

'He was dead. Hanged himself with a belt, orf a hook on the back of the door.'

There was a brief silence, broken only by the fat Labrador's snores.

'I'm sorry,' said Strike. 'Appalling for you all.'

Mrs Graves, who was now wiping her eyes with a lace handkerchief, whispered,

'Excuse me.'

She got to her feet and shuffled out of the room. Looking cross, Phillipa followed.

'One looks back,' said the old man quietly, once his daughter had closed the door behind her, 'and thinks "What could we've done diff'rently?" If I had to do it all again, I think I'd still've forced him into that car, but driven him straight to a hospital. Got him sectioned. But he was terrified of being locked up. I thought he'd never forgive us.'

'And it might have ended the same way,' said Strike.

'Yerse,' said Colonel Graves, looking directly at the detective. 'I've thought that since, too. Out of his mind. We were too late, by the time we got hold of him. Should've acted years before.'

'There was a post-mortem, I take it?'

Colonel Graves nodded.

'No surprises on cause of death, but we wanted a professional view on the marks on his back. The police went to th'farm. Wace and Mazu claimed he'd done it to himself, and other church members backed them up.'

'They claimed he whipped himself?'

'Said he felt sinful and was mortifyin' his own flesh ... couldn't pour me another cup of tea, couldja, Nick?'

Strike watched Nicholas fiddling with the hot water and tea-strainer and wondered why some people resisted teabags. Once the colonel was provided with a refilled cup, Strike asked,

'Can you remember the names of these people who saw Allie whipping himself?'

'Not any more. Load of shysters. Coroner's report was inconclusive. They thought it was possible Allie'd done it to himself. Hard t'get past eyewitnesses.'

Strike made a note, then said,

'I've heard Allie made a will.'

'Right after Daiyu was born,' said Colonel Graves, nodding. 'They used a solicitor in Norwich, not the firm th'family's always used.'

The old man glanced at the door through which his wife and daughter had disappeared, then said in a lower voice,

'In it, Allie stipulated that, if he died, he wanted to be buried at Chapman Farm. Made me think Mazu already expected him to die young. Wanted control of him, even in death. Damn' near broke m'wife's heart. They shut us out of the funeral. Didn't even tell us when it was happenin'. No goodbye, nothin'.'

'And how was Allie's estate left?'

'Everythin' went to Daiyu,' said Colonel Graves.

'There wasn't much to leave, presumably, as he'd got through his inheritance?'

'Well, no,' said Colonel Graves with a sigh, 'as a matter of fact, he had some stocks and shares, rather valuable ones, left to him by m'uncle, who never married. Allie was named after him, so he, ah –' Colonel Graves glanced at Nicholas '– yerse, well, he left it all to Allie. We think Allie either forgot he had the shares, or was too unwell to know how to turn them into cash. We weren't in any hurry to remind him about them. Not that we were stintin' Mazu and the baby! The family trust was always there for anythin' the child needed. But yerse, Allie had a lot of investments he hadn't touched, and they were steadily accruin' in value.'

'Can I ask what they were worth?'

'Quarter of a million,' said Colonel Graves. 'Those went straight to Daiyu when Allie died – and she was also in line to inherit this place,' said Colonel Graves.

'Really?'

'Yerse,' said Colonel Graves, with a hollow laugh. 'None of us saw that comin'. Lawyers wanted to go through everything after Allie died, and they dug out the entail. I'm certain m'grandfather meant the house was t'go to the eldest son in every generation. That's what was usual at the time, y'know – the place has come down from m'grandfather to m'father and then to me – nobody had checked the paperwork in decades, never needed to. But when Allie died, we dug the papers out, and blow me down, it said "eldest child". 'Course, over generations, the first child had always been a son. Maybe m'grandfather didn't imagine a gel coming first.'

The sitting room door opened and Mrs Graves and Phillipa returned to the room. Phillipa assisted her mother to resume

her seat while Strike was still writing down the details of
Daiyu's considerable inheritance.

'I understand you tried to get custody of Daiyu, after Allie
died?' he asked, looking up again.

''S'right,' said Colonel Graves. 'Mazu was refusin' to let us
see her. Then she married Wace. Well, I was *damned* if Allie's
daughter was goin' to grow up there to be whipped and abused
and all the rest of it. So, we initiated custody proceedin's.
We got O'Connor back on the case and he tracked down a
couple of people who'd been for meditation sessions at the
farm, who said the children at the farm were bein' neglected,
underweight and runnin' round in inadequate clothin', no
schoolin' and so on.'

'Is this when Mazu started claiming Wace was Daiyu's real
father?' said Strike.

'Know that already, do yeh?' said the colonel approvingly.
'Huh. Trust a Red Cap. Trust th'army!' he said, with a smirk
at his son-in-law, who looked ostentatiously bored. 'Yerse, they
started claiming she hadn't been Allie's child at all. If we got
her back, they lost control of those shares, y'see? So we thought,
"Fine, let's prove who the father was," and pressed for a DNA
sample. We were still tryin' to get the DNA when the call came
through. It was Mazu. She said, "She's dead."' Colonel Graves
mimed putting down an invisible telephone receiver. '*Click* . . .
We thought she was being malicious. Thought maybe she'd
taken Daiyu somewhere and hidden her – playin' a game, d'yeh
see? But next day we saw it in the newspapers. Drowned. No
body. Just swept out to sea.'

'Did you attend the inquest?' asked Strike.

'Damn right we did,' said Colonel Graves loudly. 'They
couldn't stop us goin' to the coroner's court.'

'Were you there for the whole thing?'

'All of it,' said Colonel Graves, nodding. 'All of them

arrivin' to watch, in their robes and what have you. Wace and Mazu turned up in a brand-new Mercedes. Coroner was concerned about the lack of a body. She would be, of course. Hardly usual. It was the coroner's neck on the block if she got it wrong. But the coastguard confirmed they'd had a strong rip tide around there for a few days.

'They brought in an expert witness chap, search and rescue type, who said bodies can sink in cold water and not come up for a long time, or get caught up in somethin' on the seabed. Yeh could see the coroner was relieved. Made it all nice and easy. And witnesses had seen the gel, Cherie, takin' her down onto the beach. The retarded boy—'

'It's "learning disability" these days, Archie,' said Nicholas, who seemed to enjoy correcting his father-in-law, after his crack about the army's superiority to the navy. 'Can't say things like that.'

'Comes t'the same thing, doesn't it?' said Colonel Graves irritably.

'You're lucky you don't have to deal with the bloody education system any more,' said Nicholas. 'You'd be in a lot of trouble there for callin' a spade a spade.'

'Was the witness called Paul Draper?' asked Strike.

'Can't remember the name. Short boy. Vacant look. Seemed scared. Thought he was in trouble, y'know, because he'd seen the gel Cherie drivin' Daiyu out of the farm.'

'The people who saw the van leaving the farm *did* get in trouble,' said Strike. 'They were punished for not stopping it.'

'Well, that'll all have been part of the Waces' act, won't it?' said the colonel, frowning at Strike. 'Probably told the gel to make sure people saw them leavin', so they could give the witnesses hell afterwards. Pretend they weren't behind it.'

'You think the Waces ordered Cherie to drown her?'

'Oh, yerse,' said the old soldier. 'Yerse, I do. She was worth a quarter of a million, dead. And they didn't give up hope of gettin' their hands on this house, either, until we'd spent more money on lawyers to shake 'em orf.'

'Tell me about Cherie,' said Strike.

'Feather-brained,' said Colonel Graves at once. 'Blubbed a lot in the witness box. Guilty conscience. Clear as day. I don't say the gel ackshly pushed Daiyu under. Just took her there in the dark, where they knew there was a strong current, and let nature take its course. Wouldn't be difficult. Why were they swimmin' at all, that time in the mornin'?'

'Did you by any chance put O'Connor onto Cherie Gittins?'

'Oh yerse. He tracked her down to a cousin's house in Dulwich. "Cherie Gittins" wasn't her real name – she was a runaway. Real name was Carine Makepeace.'

'That,' said Strike, making another note, 'is extremely useful information.'

'Goin' t'find her?' said the colonel.

'If I can,' said Strike.

'Good,' said Colonel Graves. 'She got the wind up when O'Connor approached her. Took off next day and he wasn't able to find her again – but she's the one who really knows what happened. She's the key.'

'Well,' said Strike, looking over his notes, 'I think that's everything I had to ask. I'm very grateful for your time. This has been extremely helpful.'

'I'll see you out,' said Phillipa, getting unexpectedly to her feet.

'G'bye,' said the colonel, holding out his hand to Strike. 'Keep us posted if you turn up anythin', what?'

'I will,' Strike assured him. 'Thanks very much for the tea and cake, Mrs Graves.'

'I do hope you find something,' said Allie's mother earnestly.

The elderly Labrador woke up at the sound of footsteps and

lolloped after Strike and Phillipa as they left the room. The latter maintained her silence until they'd descended the steps onto the gravel forecourt. The dog waddled past them until he reached an immaculate stretch of lawn, upon which he crouched and set about producing a turd remarkable for its size.

'I want to say something to you,' said Phillipa.

Strike turned to look at her. Wearing the same kind of flat pumps favoured by the late Princess Diana, Phillipa was a full eight inches shorter than he was, and had to throw her head back to look at him with her chilly blue eyes.

'Nothing good,' said Phillipa Graves, 'can come of you digging around into Daiyu's death. *Nothing.*'

Strike had met other people during his detective career who'd expressed similar sentiments, but he'd never managed to muster any sympathy for them. Truth, to Strike, was sacrosanct. Justice was the only other value he held as high.

'What makes you say that?' he asked, as politely as he could manage.

'*Obviously*, the Waces did it,' said Phillipa. 'We know that. We've always known it.'

He looked down at her, as baffled as he'd have been on meeting an entirely new species.

'And you don't want to see them in court?'

'No,' said Phillipa defiantly. 'I simply *don't care*. All I want *is to forget about the whole bloody thing.* My whole childhood – my whole *life*, before he killed himself – was *Allie, Allie, Allie.* Allie's naughty, Allie's ill, where's Allie, what shall we do about Allie, Allie's had a baby, what shall we do about Allie's baby, let's throw more money at him, now it's Allie and Daiyu, you *will* invite them to your wedding, won't you, darling, poor Allie, crazy Allie, *dead Allie.*'

Strike wouldn't have been surprised to learn it was the first time Phillipa Graves had ever said these things. Her face had turned red and she was shaking slightly, not like her mother, but because every muscle was knotted with rage.

'And no sooner has he gone than it's *Daiyu, Daiyu, Daiyu*. They hardly noticed *my* first child being born, it was still Allie, all Allie – and Daiyu was a *horrible* child. We're not supposed to say it, Nick and I, oh no, I was supposed to stand aside, *all over again,* for that *vile woman's child,* and pretend I loved her and wanted her to come *here,* to *our* family home, and inherit it. You think you're going to be doing something wonderful, don't you, proving they did it? Well, I'll tell you what that will achieve. *Allie, Allie, Allie* for the family, all over again, masses of publicity, my children asked at school all about their murdered cousin and their uncle the suicide – *The Stolen Prophet* and *the Drowned Prophet,* I know what they call them – it'll be books, probably, if you prove they drowned her, not just the newspapers – and my children will have to have Allie hanging over them forever, too. And you think, if you prove they killed her, it'll stop that damned church? Of course it won't. The UHC isn't going anywhere, whatever *you* might think. So idiots want to go there and be whipped by the Waces – well, it's their choice, isn't it? Who are you *actually* helping?'

The front door of Garvestone Hall opened again. Nick walked slowly down onto the gravel, frowning slightly. He was a fit-looking man, Strike saw now: almost as tall as the detective.

'Ev'rythin' all right, Pips?'

Phillipa turned to her husband.

'I'm just telling him,' she said furiously, 'how *we* feel.'

'You agree with your wife, do you, Mr – sorry, I don't know your surname,' said Strike.

'Delaunay,' said Nicholas coldly, placing a hand on his wife's shoulder. 'Yes, I do. The potential repercussions to our family could be severe. And after all,' he said, 'there's no bringing Daiyu back, is there?'

'On the contrary,' said Strike. 'My information is, the church brings her back regularly. Well, thanks for your time.'

He heard the slam of the oak front door over the sound of his starting engine. The Labrador, forgotten on the lawn, watched Strike reverse the car then pull away, its tail still vaguely wagging.

39

Six in the fourth place means:
The finest clothes turn to rags.
Be careful all day long.

The I Ching or Book of Changes

Robin's first five days as a fully committed member of the Universal Humanitarian Church had brought a couple of challenges.

The first was trying to disguise the dirty state of her tracksuit on the morning after her trip into the woods. By good fortune, she was sent with a few others to collect eggs before the sun rose and was able to fake a slip and fall in the chicken coop, which justified the stains. A couple of eagle-eyed church members asked her over breakfast about the nettle stings on her neck and cheek, and she'd told them she thought she might be allergic to something. The unsympathetic response was that ills of the material body reflected the state of the spirit within.

Shortly after breakfast that day, Jonathan Wace left the premises, taking with him several people, including Danny Brockles. All church Principals other than Mazu and Taio also departed. The church members staying behind gathered in the car park to bid Papa J farewell. Wace drove away in a silver Mercedes, while those accompanying him followed in a trail of lesser cars, the crowd behind them cheering and applauding.

That afternoon, two minibuses brought church members who'd been relocated from the Birmingham and Glasgow centres.

Robin was interested in these new arrivals, because Kevin Pirbright had said church members in need of re-indoctrination were sent back to Chapman Farm. Rebellious or dissatisfied people would surely be inclined to talk more freely about the church, so Robin intended to keep an eye on them with a view to inveigling them into conversation.

The newcomer who interested Robin most was the second shaven-headed person she'd seen at Chapman Farm: a sallow-skinned, virtually bald young woman who had very thick eyebrows. She looked grumpy and seemed disinclined to return greetings from people at Chapman Farm, to whom she seemed a familiar figure. Unfortunately, the shaven-headed woman and the other relocated church members were immediately assigned low-status jobs such as laundry and livestock care, whereas Robin was now being fast-tracked through increasingly demanding lectures on church doctrine.

Tuesday afternoon brought the second serious challenge Robin had faced, which made her realise her preparation for going undercover hadn't been quite as complete as she'd thought.

All new members were collected together and taken once more into the basement room that ran beneath the farmhouse. Robin had started to dread this room, because she'd come to associate it with hours of particularly intense indoctrination. These sessions always seemed to happen in the late afternoon, when energy levels were lowest and hunger at its peak, and the windowless room became claustrophobic and hot. Agreeing with any proposition put to them was the easiest way for members to speed release from the hard floor and the insistent voice of whoever was lecturing them.

This afternoon it was the perennially cheerful Becca who stood waiting for them on the stage in front of the large screen, which was currently blank.

'I thank you for your service,' Becca said, putting her hands together and bowing.

'And I for yours,' chorused the seated church members, also bowing.

A young man then started handing out pens and paper, which was a most unusual occurrence. These basic means of self-expression were ruthlessly controlled at Chapman Farm, even down to the pencils tied firmly to the journals. The pens were numbered, as they'd been on the minibus.

'This afternoon, you'll be taking an important step in freeing yourselves from materialist possession,' said Becca. 'Most of you will have somebody back in the materialist world who'll be expecting communication from you at this time.'

The screen behind Becca now lit up, showing printed words.

Key Components of Materialist Possession.

- Assumed ownership based on biology.
- Abuse (physical, emotional, spiritual).
- Anger at actions/beliefs that challenge materialism.
- Attempts to disrupt spiritual development.
- Coercion disguised as concern.
- Demand for emotional service/labour.
- Desire to direct your life's course.

'I want each of you now to think of the person or people who most strongly demonstrate the seven key signs of materialist possession towards you. A good measure is to ask yourself who'll be angriest that you've dedicated yourself to the Universal Humanitarian Church.

'Vivienne,' said Becca, pointing at the girl with the spiky black hair, who always determinedly tried to sound less middle class than she really was. 'Who demonstrates the key signs most strongly in *your* life?'

'My muvver and stepfather, definitely,' said Vivienne at once. 'All seven points.'

'Walter?' said Becca, pointing at him.

'My son,' said Walter promptly. 'Most of those points would apply. My daughter would be far more understanding.'

'Marion?' said Becca, pointing to the ginger-haired middle-aged woman who always became pink and breathless at the mere mention of Jonathan Wace, and whose roots were slowly turning silver.

'I suppose . . . my daughters,' said Marion.

'Materialist bonds are hard to sever,' said Becca, now walking up and down on stage in her long orange robes and wearing her tight, cold smile, 'but they're the ties that bind you closest to the bubble world. It's impossible to become pure spirit until you've dissolved these connections and rid yourself of the cravings of the false self.'

The image on the screen behind Becca changed to show a scribbled letter. All names had been blacked out.

'This is an example of a case of extreme materialist possession, which was sent to one of our members by a supposedly loving family member, a few years ago.'

There was silence in the room as the group read the words onscreen.

We got your letter the same day. ████████ *was admitted to hospital with a massive stroke, brought on by the stress she's been under following* ████████'s *death, and by totally avoidable worry about you. Given the important work you're*

*doing saving the world from Satan, you probably don't give
a shit whether* ███████ *lives or dies, but I thought I'd just
let you know the consequences of your actions. As for screwing
any more money out of* ███████ *,unfortunately for you I've
now got Power of Attorney, so consider this letter an invitation
for you and the UHC to go fuck yourselves.*

███████████

'It's all in there, isn't it?' said Becca, looking up at the screen.
'Emotional blackmail, materialist obsession with money,
sneering at our mission, but most importantly, duplicity. The
elderly family member in question hadn't suffered a stroke at
all and the writer of the letter was found to be embezzling
money out of their account.'

A mingled groan and sigh issued from most of the people
sitting on the hard, rush-covered floor. Some shook their
heads.

'I want you to think now of the person or people who are
most likely to try these kinds of tactics on you. You're going to
write them a calm, compassionate letter clearly setting out why
you've decided to join the church. Here,' said Becca, as the
image on the screen changed again, 'are some of the phrases
we find most effective in explaining the spiritual journey
you've begun in ways that materialists can grasp. However,
you should feel free to write the letter in any way that feels
authentic to you.'

Panic now rose in Robin. Who the hell was she to send a
letter to? She was afraid the UHC might check, to make sure
both addressee and address were genuine. The recruits hadn't
been given envelopes: clearly, the letters would be read before
being sent. Rowena's fictional parents were the most obvious
recipients for the letter, but their non-existence would surely
be exposed instantly once she put down a traceable address.

'Can I help?' said a quiet voice beside Robin.

Becca had noticed that Robin wasn't writing and had stepped through the people sitting on the floor to talk to her.

'Well, I'd like to write to my parents,' said Robin, 'but they're on a cruise. I can't even remember the name of their ship.'

'Oh, I see,' said Becca. 'Well, you've got a sister, haven't you? Why don't you write to your parents, via her?'

'Oh, that's a good idea,' said Robin, who could feel sweat rising beneath her sweatshirt. 'Thanks.'

Robin bent her head over the letter, wrote *Dear Theresa,* then looked back up at the screen, pretending to be looking for phrases to copy down, but actually trying to think of a solution to her dilemma. She'd unthinkingly given Theresa a job in publishing and now wished she'd made her a student, because a hall of residence might have been harder to check for her presence. Hoping to make it as hard as possible for the UHC to decide definitively that Theresa didn't exist, Robin wrote:

I can't remember when you said you were moving, but hopefully –

Robin thought rapidly. A nickname seemed safest, because it could apply to anyone who might be actually living at the random address she was about to write down. Her eyes fell on the back of Walter the professor's balding head.

- Baldy will send this on if you've already left.

Robin looked back up at the screen. Most of a template letter was there, ready to be copied.

Letter of Declaration of UHC Membership

Dear X,

[As you know] I've just completed a week's retreat at the Universal Humanitarian Church. I've [really enjoyed it/found it very inspiring/gained a huge amount] so I've decided to stay on and [pursue my spiritual growth/explore further self-development/help with the church's charitable projects].

Robin dutifully copied out a version of this paragraph, then moved to the second.

Chapman Farm is a closed community and we don't use electronic devices because we find them disruptive to a meditative spiritual environment. However, letters are passed on to members, so if you'd like to, write to me here at Chapman Farm, Lion's Mouth, Aylmerton, Norfolk, NR11 8PC.

Robin copied this out, then looked up once more. There were a few final bits of advice about the letters' contents, and how to terminate them.

Do not use phrases like 'don't worry about me', which may lay you open to emotional blackmail.

When signing off, avoid pet familial terms such as 'mum' or 'granny', and terms such as 'love'. Use your given name, no diminutives or nicknames, which demonstrate continuing acceptance of materialist possession.

Write the address to send the letter to on the back of the page.

Robin now wrote:

Please can you let our parents know I'm staying, because I know they're on their cruise. It's great to have a sense of purpose again and I'm learning so much. Rowena.

Turning the page over, she jotted down a street she knew from surveillance work existed in Clapham, picked a house number at random, then invented a postcode of which only SW11 was likely to be accurate.

Looking up, she saw that most people had finished writing. Putting up her hand, she passed her finished letter to the smiling Becca and waited for everybody else to complete the task. Finally, when all letters, paper and pens had been collected in, they were permitted to rise and file back upstairs.

As Robin stepped out into the courtyard, she saw Dr Andy Zhou hurrying towards the farmhouse's carved double doors, carrying what looked like a medical case. He had an abstracted, anxious air that contrasted strongly with his usual suavity. As those who'd been writing their template letters crowded around the pool of the Drowned Prophet to pay their usual respects on passing, Robin hung back, watching Zhou. The doors to the farmhouse opened and she caught a glimpse of an elderly Indian woman. Zhou stepped over the threshold and vanished from sight, the doors closing behind him. Robin, who was living in daily expectation of hearing that the pregnant Wan had gone into labour, wondered whether that explained Zhou's haste.

'The Drowned Prophet will bless all who worship her,' she muttered when her turn at the pool side came, dabbing cold water on her forehead as usual, before falling into step with Kyle, Amandeep and Vivienne. Vivienne was saying,

'. . . probably be really angry, like I give a toss. Seriously, they could both be in a textbook under "false self". It's only since I've been in 'ere I've, like, started to fully process what they've done to me, y'know?'

'Totally,' said Kyle.

The letter writers were some of the earliest to arrive in the dining hall and consequently had a choice of seats. Robin, who saw every meal as an opportunity to collect information, because it was the one time all church members mingled, chose to sit down beside a knot of church members having a whispered conversation. They were so deeply engrossed, they didn't immediately notice when Robin sat down beside them.

'. . . says Jacob's really bad, but I think Dr Zhou—'

The speaker, a young black man with short dreadlocks, broke off. To Robin's exasperation, Amandeep, Kyle and Vivienne had followed her to the table. The last's loud voice had alerted the whisperers to their presence.

'—then they can go to 'ell, frankly,' Vivienne was saying.

'We don't use that expression,' said the man with dreadlocks sharply to Vivienne, who turned pink.

'Sorry, I didn't mean—'

'We don't wish hell on anyone,' said the young man. 'UHC members don't want to swell the Adversary's ranks.'

'No, of course not,' said Vivienne, now scarlet. 'I'm really sorry. Actually, I need the bathroom . . .'

Barely a minute later, the shaven-headed, grumpy-looking young woman who'd been recently relocated from another UHC centre entered the rapidly filling hall. After glancing around, she headed for Vivienne's vacated space. Robin thought she saw the idea of telling her the seat was already taken cross Kyle's mind, but after opening his mouth he closed it again.

'Hi,' said the always talkative Amandeep, holding out a hand to the woman in glasses. 'Amandeep Singh.'

'Emily Pirbright,' muttered the woman, returning his handshake.

'Pirbright? Whoa – is Becca your sister?' said Amandeep.

Robin understood Amandeep's surprise, because the two young women didn't resemble each other in the slightest. Aside from the contrast between Becca's well-groomed, glossy bob and Emily's almost bald head, the latter's perpetual expression of bad temper formed a greater contrast to Becca's apparently unquenchable cheeriness.

'We don't use words like "sister",' said Emily. 'Haven't you learned that yet?'

'Oh, yeah, sorry,' said Amandeep.

'Becca and I used to be flesh objects to each other, if that's what you mean,' said Emily coldly.

The group of established church members who'd been whispering when Robin sat down had now subtly angled their bodies away from Emily. It was impossible not to draw the conclusion that Emily was in some form of disgrace and Robin's interest in her doubled. Fortunately for her, Amandeep's incorrigible sociability swiftly reasserted itself.

'So you grew up here at the farm?' he asked Emily.

'Yeah,' said Emily.

'Is Becca older or—?'

'Older.'

Robin thought Emily was conscious of her silent shunning by the group beside her.

'That's another old flesh object of mine, look,' she said.

Robin, Amandeep and Kyle looked in the direction Emily was pointing and saw Louise wheeling the usual vat of noodles along, ladling them out onto plates at the next table. Louise glanced up, met Emily's eyes, then returned stolidly to her work.

'What, is she your—?'

Amandeep caught himself just in time.

A few minutes later, Louise reached their table. Emily waited until Louise was on the point of dropping a ladleful of noodles onto her plate before saying loudly,

'And Kevin was younger than Becca and me.'

Louise's hand shook: hot noodles slid off Emily's plate into her lap.

'*Ouch!*'

Expressionless, Louise moved on down the line.

Scowling, Emily picked the noodles out of her lap, put them back on her plate, then deliberately speared the only chunks of fresh vegetable out of what Robin was sure was tinned tomato, set them aside and began to eat the rest of her meal.

'Don't you like carrot?' asked Robin. Meals were so scant at Chapman Farm, she'd never before seen anyone fail to clear their plate.

'What's it to you?' said Emily aggressively.

Robin ate the rest of her meal in silence.

40

*... the most sacred of human feelings, that of
reverence for the ancestors.*

The I Ching or Book of Changes

Strike made the long trip to St Mawes on Thursday by train
and ferry. His uncle was so surprised and delighted to see him
that Strike knew Ted had forgotten he was coming, in spite
of the fact that he'd called that morning to tell his uncle what
time he'd be arriving.

The house where the fastidious Joan had once presided was
dusty, although Strike was pleased to see the fridge was well
stocked with food. Strike understood that Ted's neighbours
had been rallying around, making sure he had enough to eat
and checking in with him regularly. This increased Strike's
guilt about not doing more to support Ted, whose conversation was rambling and repetitive.

The visit to the GP the following morning did nothing to
allay Strike's concerns.

'He asked Ted what date it is and he didn't know,' Strike
told Lucy by phone after lunch. Strike had left Ted with a
mug of tea in the living room, then slipped out into the back
garden on the pretext of vaping and was now pacing the small
patch of lawn.

'Well, that's not too serious, is it?' said Lucy.

'Then he told Ted an address and made him say it back, which Ted did fine, and he told Ted he was going to ask him to repeat the address a few minutes later, but Ted couldn't.'

'Oh no,' said Lucy.

'He asked if Ted could remember a recent news story and Ted said "Brexit", no problem. Then he told him to fill in the numbers on a picture of a clock. Ted did that OK, but then he had to mark in the hands to make it say ten to eleven, and Ted was lost. Couldn't do it.'

'Oh shit,' Lucy whispered, disconsolate. 'So what's the diagnosis?'

'Dementia,' said Strike.

'Was Ted upset?'

'Hard to say. I've got the impression he knows something's up. He told me yesterday he's forgetting things a lot and it's worrying him.'

'Stick, what are we going to do?'

'I don't know,' said Strike. 'I wouldn't give good odds on him remembering to turn the cooker off at night. He left the hot tap running an hour ago, just walked away and forgot it. It might be time for sheltered housing.'

'He won't want that.'

'I know,' said Strike, who now paused in his pacing to contemplate the strip of sea just visible from Ted's back garden. Joan's ashes had been strewn there from Ted's old sailing boat and some irrational part of him sought guidance from the distant, glittering ocean. 'But I'm worried about him living alone if he goes downhill much further. The stairs are steep and he's not too steady on his feet.'

The call ended with no definite plan for Ted's future in place. Strike returned to the house to find his uncle fast asleep in an armchair, so removed himself quietly to the kitchen to look at emails on the laptop he'd brought down from London.

A message from Midge sat at the top of his inbox. She'd attached a scanned copy of the letter Robin had put in the plastic rock the previous evening.

The first paragraph dealt with the disgruntled Emily Pirbright's return to the farm and Robin's so far unrealised hope of getting information out of her. The second paragraph described the basement session in which the new recruits had to write to their families, and concluded,

> . . . so can one of you please write a letter from Theresa, acknowledging the letter saying I've joined the church? Make her sound worried, they'll expect that.
>
> Other news: someone in the farmhouse might be ill, possibly called Jacob. Saw Dr Zhou hurrying in there looking worried. No further details as yet, will try and find out more.
>
> This afternoon we had our first Revelation. We all sat in a circle in the temple. The last time we did that, it was to talk about how much we'd suffered in the outside world. This was very different. The people who were called on had to take a chair in the middle and confess things they were ashamed of. When they did, they got abused and shouted at. They all ended up in tears. I didn't get called, so I'll probably get it next time. Mazu led the Revelation session and was definitely enjoying herself.
>
> Nothing new on Will Edensor. I see him from a distance sometimes but no conversation. Lin still around. There was talk of her going to Birmingham, can't remember if I said.
>
> Think that's everything. I'm so tired. Hope all well with you
>
> x

Strike read the letter through twice, taking particular note of the 'I'm so tired' at the end. He had to admire Robin's resourcefulness in thinking up a way of obfuscating her relatives' whereabouts at short notice, but like her, felt he should have foreseen the necessity for a safe address for mail. Strike also wondered whether there'd been a letter for Murphy this week, but could think of no way of asking without arousing the suspicions of Pat and the other subcontractors. Instead, he texted Midge to ask her to write the letter from Theresa, as he feared his own handwriting looked too obviously masculine.

As Ted's snores were still emanating from the sitting room, Strike opened his next email, which was from Dev Shah.

Having spent hours the previous day searching online records for Cherie Gittins under her birth name of Carine Makepeace, Strike had at last succeeded in finding her birth certificate and death certificates for both her father, who'd died when she was five, and the cousin in Dulwich with whom she'd stayed after fleeing Chapman Farm. However, Cherie's mother, Maureen Agnes Makepeace, née Gittins, was still alive and living in Penge, so Strike had asked Shah to pay her a visit.

Visited Ivychurch Close this morning, Shah had written. **Maureen Makepeace and her flat are both falling apart. She looks & talks like a heavy drinker, v aggressive. Neighbour called out to me as I was approaching the front door. He hoped I was from the council, because there've been arguments over bins, noise, etc. Maureen says she's had no contact with her daughter since the latter ran away, aged 15.**

Inured as he was to leads petering out in this way, Strike was nevertheless disappointed.

He made himself a mug of tea, resisted a chocolate biscuit, and sat back down in front of his laptop while Ted's snores continued to rumble through the open door.

The difficulty he was having tracing Carine/Cherie was making Strike commensurately more interested in her. He now began Googling combinations and variations of the two names he knew for certain the girl had used. Only when he returned to the British Library's newspaper archive did he finally get a hit on the name 'Cherry Makepeace' in a copy of the *Manchester Evening News* dated 1999.

'*Gotcha,*' he muttered, as two mugshots appeared onscreen, one showing a young man with long hair and extremely bad teeth, the other, a tousle-haired blonde who, beneath the heavy eyeliner, was clearly recognisable as Cherie Gittins of Chapman Farm.

The news story described a robbery and stabbing committed by Isaac Mills, which was the name of the young man with the bad teeth. He'd stolen morphine, temazepam, diazepam and cash from a pharmacy before knifing a customer who'd tried to intervene. The victim had survived, but Mills had still been sentenced to five years' imprisonment.

The report concluded:

> Cherry Makepeace, 21, also known as Cherry Curtis, drove Mills to the pharmacy on the day of the robbery and waited for him outside. Makepeace claimed she was unaware of Mills' intention to rob the pharmacy and didn't know he possessed a knife. She was convicted of aiding and abetting a criminal and received a six-month sentence, suspended for three years.

Strike jotted down the names Carine/Cherie/Cherry along with the surnames Gittins/Makepeace/Curtis. Where the last of these had come from, he had no idea; perhaps she'd simply pulled it out of thin air. The regular name changes suggested someone keen not to be found, but Strike tended to believe that Colonel Graves' assessment of Cherie as 'feather-brained' and 'easily influenced' had been correct, given her dumbstruck look in the *Manchester Evening News* photo.

He now navigated to the Pinterest page of Torment Town, with its eerie drawings of Daiyu Wace and grotesque parodies of the UHC logo. Torment Town hadn't responded to the message Strike had sent them, over which he'd taken more trouble than the few words might have suggested.

Amazing pictures. Do you draw from imagination?

A particularly loud snore from the sitting room made Strike turn off his laptop, feeling guilty. He'd soon need to make his way back to Falmouth for the overnight train. It was time to wake Ted so they could have a last chat before leaving him, once more, to his loneliness.

41

One is courageous and wishes to accomplish one's task, no matter what happens.

The I Ching or Book of Changes

The account of Revelation that Robin had sent Strike had been brief and to the point, partly because she'd had neither time nor energy to go into details while exhausted, crouching among nettles in the dark and pausing regularly to listen out for footsteps, but it had shaken her more than she'd liked to admit in her letter. Mazu had encouraged those in the circle to use the filthiest and most abusive words they could find when berating those confessing, and Robin thought she was unlikely ever to forget the sight of Kyle doubled over in his chair, sobbing, while others screamed 'pervert' and 'faggot' in response to his admission that he continued to feel shame about being gay.

When Kyle's time in the hot seat had concluded, Mazu had told him calmly he'd be more resilient for having undergone Revelation, that he'd faced 'externalisation of his inner shame', and congratulated the group for doing what she knew had been difficult for them, too. Yet the facial expressions of those shouting abuse at Kyle were still seared on Robin's memory: they'd been given permission to be as vile as they liked, irrespective of their true feelings about Kyle or homosexuality, and she was disturbed by the gusto with which they'd participated, even knowing that their own turn in the middle of the circle would come.

Robin was rapidly learning that at Chapman Farm, practices that in the outside world would be considered abusive or coercive were excused, justified and disguised by a huge amount of jargon. The use of slurs and offensive language during Revelation was justified as part of PRT, or Primal Response Therapy. Whenever a question was posed about contradictions or inconsistencies in church doctrine, the answer was almost always that they would be explained by an HLT (Higher-Level Truth), which would be revealed when they had progressed further along the path to pure spirit. A person putting their own needs above those of the group was deemed to be in the grip of EM (egomotivity), one who continued to prize worldly goods or status was a BP, or bubble person, and leaving the church was 'going DV', meaning, becoming a Deviate. Terms such as false self, flesh object and materialist possession were now employed casually among the new members, who'd begun to reframe all past and present experience in the church's language. There was also much talk of the Adversary, who was not only Satan, but also all temporal power structures, which were populated by the Adversary's agents.

The intensity of indoctrination crept up even further during Robin's third week at the farm. New members were regularly bombarded with dreadful images and statistics about the outside world, sometimes for hours at a time. Even though Robin knew this was being done to create a sense of urgency with regard to the war the UHC was supposedly waging on the Adversary, and to bind recruits more closely to the church as the world's only hope, she doubted anyone of normal empathy could fail to feel distressed and anxious after being forced to look at hundreds upon hundreds of images of starving and wounded children, or learning the statistics on people trafficking and world poverty, or hearing how the rainforest would be entirely destroyed within another two decades. It was difficult not to agree that the planet was on the brink of collapse, that humanity had taken terrible wrong turns and that it would face an awful reckoning unless it changed its ways. The anxiety induced by this constant bombardment of dreadful news was such that Robin welcomed the times recruits were led to the temple to chant on the hard floor, where she experienced the blessed relief of not thinking, of losing herself in the collective voice of the group. Once or twice, she found herself muttering *Lokah Samastah Sukhino Bhavantu* even when nobody around her was chanting.

Her only real bulwark against the onslaught of indoctrination was to remind herself, constantly, what she was at the farm to do. Unfortunately, her third week inside the church yielded very little in the way of useful information. Emily Pirbright and Will Edensor remained impossible to engage in conversation due to the unacknowledged system of segregation in place at the farm. In spite of Will's wealth and Emily's almost lifelong membership of the church, both were currently acting as farmhands and domestic servants, whereas Robin continued to spend most of her time in the temple or the lecture room. Nevertheless, she tried to keep a covert eye on both of them, and her observation led her to a couple of deductions.

The first was that Will Edensor was trying, as far as he dared, to maintain personal contact with the white-haired toddler Robin had previously seen him comforting. She was now almost certain that Qing was the daughter he'd had with Lin Doherty, a conclusion reinforced when she spotted Lin cuddling the child in the shadow of some bushes near the farmhouse. Will and Lin were both in clear breach of the church's teaching on materialist possession, and risking severe penalties if their ongoing quest to maintain a parental relationship with their daughter was made known to Mazu, Taio and Becca, who were currently reigning supreme at Chapman Farm in the absence of Jonathan Wace.

Still more intriguingly, Robin had noticed definite signs of tension and possibly dislike between the Pirbright sisters. She hadn't forgotten that Becca and Emily had accused their dead brother of sexually abusing them, yet she'd seen no signs of solidarity between the pair. On the contrary, whenever they found themselves in close proximity, they made no eye contact and generally removed themselves from each other's vicinity as quickly as possible. Given that church members usually made a point of greeting each other as they passed in the yard, and an elaborate courtesy was observed when it came to opening doors for each other, or ceding to each other when it came to vacant spaces in the dining hall, this behaviour definitely couldn't be attributed to fear of succumbing to materialist possession. Robin wondered whether Becca was afraid of being tarnished by the faint aura of disgrace which hung over the shaven-headed Emily, or whether there was another, more personal, source of animosity. The sisters seemed united in one thing only: disdain for the woman who'd brought them into the world. Not once did Robin see any sign of warmth towards or even acknowledgement of Louise from either of her daughters.

Robin was still keeping track of the days with the tiny pebbles she picked up daily. The approach of her third Thursday at the farm brought the now familiar mixture of excitement and nerves, because while she craved communication from the outside world, the nocturnal journey to the plastic rock remained nerve-wracking.

When the lights went out, she dressed beneath the covers again, waited for the other women to fall silent, and for the usual snorers to prove they'd fallen asleep, then got quietly out of bed.

The night was cold and windy, a stiff breeze blowing across the dark field as Robin crossed it, and she entered the woods to the sound of trees creaking and rustling around her. To her relief, she found the plastic rock more easily than she'd done previously.

When Robin opened the rock she saw a letter from Strike, a note in Ryan's handwriting, and, to her delight, a small bar of Cadbury's Dairy Milk. Easing herself behind a tree, she ripped the wrapping off the chocolate and devoured it in a few bites, so hungry she couldn't slow down to savour it. She then turned on the torch and opened Ryan's letter.

Dear Robin,

It was great to hear from you, I was getting worried. The farm sounds bizarre, although being a country girl you're probably not hating it as much as I would.

Not much news this end. Work's busy. Currently on a new murder case but it lacks something without the involvement of a hot female private detective.

I had a long phone conversation with your mother last night. She's worried about you, but I talked her down.

My sister in San Sebastian wants us to go over there in July because she's gagging to meet you. There'd be worse ways of celebrating you getting out of that place.

Anyway, I'm really missing you, so please don't join up and never come back.

Love, Ryan xxx

PS Your plants are still alive.

In spite of her recent ingestion of chocolate, this letter didn't do much to lift Robin's spirits. Hearing that Ryan and her mother were worried about her did nothing to calm the guilt and fear the UHC was busy inculcating in her.

Nor could she think of things like summer holidays right now, when every day seemed to last a week.

She now turned to Strike's note.

Thursday 28th April

Very good job on your quick thinking re: your sister. Midge has written a letter back to you from 14 Plympton Road NW6 2JJ (address will be on letter). It's Pat's sister's place (she's got a different surname from Pat, so no easily discoverable connection – could be Theresa's landlady). She'll alert us if you write back, we'll collect the letter and Midge can respond again.

I've met the Graves family. Turns out Alex Graves had a quarter of a million to leave, which Mazu inherited when Daiyu died. Colonel Graves is convinced the Waces and Cherie were in cahoots over the drowning. I've had no luck tracing Cherie Gittins in spite of a couple of possible leads. Her life post–farm definitely suggests she had something to hide: several name changes and a brush with the law in the form of a pharmacy-robbing boyfriend.

Not much other news. The Franks have gone quiet. Still trying to find a replacement for Littlejohn. Wardle might know someone and I'm trying to fix up an interview.

Don't forget: the moment you've had enough, say the word and we'll come and get you out.

Sx

Unlike Ryan's note, Strike's brought a measure of comfort, because Robin had been fretting about what she was going to do to keep the fiction of Theresa alive. She tugged the top off the biro with her teeth and began to write back to Strike, apologising for the lack of concrete information but saying that she didn't want to leave the farm until she had something Sir

Colin could use against the church. Having finished her note with thanks for the chocolate, she dashed off a quick message for Ryan, enclosed both with the torch and the pen in the plastic rock, then tore up their letters and the chocolate wrapper. Instead of scattering the fragments in the wood, she slid a hand beneath the barbed wire and dropped them onto the road, where the breeze immediately carried them away. Robin watched the white specks disappearing into the darkness, and felt envious of them for escaping Chapman Farm.

She then made her way back through the whispering woods, shivering slightly in spite of the fact that she was wearing pyjamas under her tracksuit, and set back off across the field.

42

Robin had almost reached the five-bar gate when she heard voices and saw lanterns swinging down the passage between the men's and women's dormitories. Terrified, she ducked down behind the hedge, certain that her empty bed had been discovered.

'. . . check Lower Field and the woods,' said a voice she thought she recognised as Taio's.

'He won't've got that far,' said a second male voice.

'Do as you're fucking told,' said Taio. 'You two do the Retreat Rooms, all of them.'

A man climbed over the five-bar gate, his lantern swinging, barely ten feet from where Robin was crouching. The lamplight darted towards and away from her as he set off, and she saw the short dreadlocks of the black man who'd told Vivienne off for using the phrase 'go to hell'.

'*Bo!*' he bellowed, striding off towards the woods. 'Bo, where are you?'

431

Such was Robin's panic it took her a few seconds to compute that they weren't looking for her after all, but her situation remained perilous. The women surely wouldn't sleep through this shouting for long, and if the searchers entered her dormitory to look for the unknown Bo, they'd soon discover there were two people missing, not one. Waiting for the voices and lights of the search party to recede, Robin climbed quickly over the five-bar gate, then had to crouch down behind more bushes as Jiang emerged from the nearest Retreat Room, also holding a lantern. Once he'd stomped off into the darkness, she crept to the rear wall of the women's dormitory before realising that more people with lanterns were hurrying across the courtyard, meaning she had no chance of entering through the door unseen.

She moved as quickly and quietly as possible through the trees and bushes at the rear of the dormitories, aiming for the older part of the farm, which offered many hiding places, and soon found herself at the rear of the dilapidated barn that was always locked. Her familiarity with old farm buildings made her feel her way along the rear until her fingers found exactly what she was hoping for: a gap where a plank of wood had rotted away and the one next to it could be pushed inwards sufficiently to make a gap large enough for her to squeeze inside, snagging her hair and scraping her body painfully.

The air inside the barn was dank and musty, but there was more light inside than she'd expected, due to a gap in the roof through which moonlight was streaming. This illuminated an old tractor, broken farming tools, stacks of crates and bits of fencing. Something, doubtless a rat, scurried away from the intruder.

Lanterns were now passing outside the barn, casting slivers of gold through the gaps in the wooden plank walls. Voices close and distant were still shouting, 'Bo? *Bo!*'

Robin remained where she was, scared of moving in case she knocked something over. Now she noticed a mound of personal belongings almost as tall as she was, heaped in a corner and covered in thick dust. There were clothes, handbags, wallets, shoes, cuddly toys and books, and Robin was horribly reminded of a picture she'd seen of the mound of shoes belonging to the gassed at Auschwitz.

The searchers outside had moved on. Full of curiosity about these old belongings, Robin climbed carefully over an upended wheelbarrow to examine them. After three weeks of seeing nothing but orange tracksuits and trainers, of reading nothing but church literature, it was strange to see different kinds of clothing and shoes, not to mention the old child's picture book with its vivid colours.

There was something disturbing, even eerie, about the mound of old possessions, thrown away with what seemed like casual contempt. Robin noticed a single stack-heeled shoe which once, perhaps, a teenage girl had coveted and treasured, and a cuddly toy rabbit, its face covered in cobwebs. Where were their owners? After a minute or two, a possible explanation occurred to her: anyone leaving the farm by stealth, at night, would be forced to leave the belongings they'd left in the lockers.

She reached for an old handbag lying close to the top of the heap. A cloud of dust rose into the air as she opened it. There was nothing inside except an old white LRT bus ticket. She replaced the handbag and as she did so, noticed the rusty edge of a rectangular red biscuit tin with *Barnum's Animals* printed on it. She'd loved those biscuits when she was little, but hadn't thought about them for years. Seeing the packaging in this strange context reminded her poignantly of the safety of her family home.

'BO!' bellowed a voice just outside the barn, causing the

unseen rat to scratch and scrabble in the shadows. Then, somewhere in the distance a female voice shrieked,

'I'VE GOT HIM!'

Robin heard a confusion of voices, some expressing relief, others demanding to know how Bo had 'got out', and decided her best option was to emerge from the barn and present herself as having been looking for Bo all along.

She'd taken a couple of steps back towards the gap in the rear wall before she stopped dead, looking back at the dusty pile of old belongings, seized by the urge to look in that *Barnum's Animals* biscuit tin. Chilly, nervous and exhausted as she was, it took several moments for her to work out why her subconscious was telling her the tin's presence at the farm was strange. Then she realised: there was a total prohibition on sugar here, so why would anybody have brought biscuits to the place? In spite of the urgent need to join the searchers outside before her absence was noticed, Robin climbed quickly back over the wheelbarrow and pulled the tin out of the pile.

The lid showed the image of four caged circus animals and balloons, along with '85th Anniversary' written inside a gold circle. She prised it off, expecting the tin to be empty because it was so light, but on the contrary: a number of faded Polaroids lay inside. Unable to see what they showed in the dim light, Robin took them out and stuffed them inside her bra, as she did daily with her date-marking pebbles. She then replaced the lid, re-inserted the tin where she'd found it, hurried to the gap in the rear wall of the barn and squeezed back outside.

Judging from the distant noise coming from the courtyard, almost everyone at the farm was now awake. Robin set off at a jog, passing the dining hall and temple, and joined the throng, who were mostly in pyjamas, at a moment when everyone's attention was on Mazu Wace, who was standing between the tombs of the Stolen and Golden Prophets in her long orange robes. Beside her stood Louise Pirbright, who was holding a struggling toddler in a nappy, whom Robin guessed to be the errant Bo. Other than the child's whimpers, there was complete silence. Mazu barely needed to raise her voice for everyone in the crowd to hear her.

'Who was on child dorm duty?'

After a small hesitation, two teenage girls sidled to the front of the crowd, one with short fair hair, the other, long dark twists. The latter was crying. Robin, who was watching through the thicket of heads in front of her, saw both girls fall to their knees as though they'd rehearsed the movement and crawl towards Mazu's feet.

'Please, Mama . . .'

'We're so sorry, Mama!'

When they reached the hem of Mazu's robes she lifted them slightly, and watched, her expression blank, as the two girls wept and kissed her feet.

Then she said sharply, 'Taio.'

Her elder son pushed his way through the watching crowd.

'Take them to the temple.'

'Mama, *please,*' wailed the fair-haired girl.

'Come on,' said Taio, grabbing the arms of the two girls and dragging them forcibly to their feet. Robin was most disturbed by the way the girl with the twists tried to cling on to Mazu's leg, and the utter coldness of Mazu's expression as she watched her son drag them away. Nobody asked what was going to happen to the girls; nobody spoke or even moved.

As Mazu turned back to the watching crowd, Louise said,

'Shall I put Bo back to—?' but Mazu said,

'No. You – ' she pointed at Penny Brown '– and you,' she said to Emily Pirbright, 'take him back to the dormitory and stay there.'

435

Penny went to lift the little boy out of Louise's arms, but he clung to Louise. The latter prised him off and handed him over. His screams receded as Penny and Emily hurried away through the arch that led to the children's dormitory.

'You may go back to bed,' said Mazu to the watching crowd. She turned and walked towards the temple.

None of the women looked at each other or spoke as they filed back into their dormitory. Robin grabbed her pyjamas off her bed, then hurried off into the bathroom and locked herself into a cubicle before pulling the Polaroids out of her bra to examine them.

All were faded, yet Robin could still just make out the images. The uppermost picture showed the figure of a naked, chubby dark-haired young woman – possibly a teenager – wearing a pig mask, her legs spread wide. The second showed a different, blonde young woman being penetrated from behind by a squat man, both in pig masks. The third showed a stringy-looking man with a skull tattooed on his bicep sodomising a smaller man. Robin rifled hastily through the pictures. In total, four naked people were pictured in various sexual combinations in a space Robin didn't recognise, but which looked like an outhouse, possibly even the barn she'd just left. They wore pig masks in every image.

Robin shoved the pictures back inside her bra and left it on as she stripped off her tracksuit. She then left the cubicle, turned out the bathroom light and returned to her bed. As she settled down to sleep at last, a distant scream pierced the silence, emanating from the temple.

'Please no – please no, Mama – no, please, please!'

If anyone in the surrounding beds had also heard it, none of them made a sound.

43

Six days after Robin, unbeknownst to Strike, had found the old Polaroids in the rusty biscuit tin, he held an afternoon team meeting attended by everyone at the detective agency apart from Littlejohn, who was on surveillance. Strike had opted to hold the meeting in the otherwise deserted basement room of his favourite local pub, which until recently had been called the Tottenham, but had now become the Flying Horse. As an Arsenal fan, Strike thoroughly approved of the rebrand. While waiting for his subcontractors to join him, he checked Pinterest to see whether Torment Town had responded to his message, but there was no change to the page.

'I'm no' complainin', but why're we doing this here?' asked Barclay ten minutes later. The Glaswegian was the last to arrive in the red carpeted room and, as he had the evening off, had stopped at the upstairs bar to buy himself a pint.

'In case Littlejohn decides to come back to the office,' said Strike.

'We're gonnae be plottin' his downfall, are we?'

'He might not be working for us for much longer, so there's no need for him to know any more of our business,' said Strike.

437

'I'm interviewing Wardle's mate tomorrow and if that goes well, Littlejohn's out.'

Shah, Midge and Barclay all said, 'Good.' Pat, Strike noticed, remained silent.

'Where's he now?' asked Midge.

'On the Franks,' said Strike.

'Speakin' of which, I've got somethin' on them,' said Barclay, reaching into the inside pocket of his jacket for two sheets of paper which, when unfolded, proved to be photocopied news articles. 'I've been wonderin' whether we could get them on a benefits scam an' I ended up findin' this.'

He pushed the papers towards Strike. Both news items were small, though one featured a headshot of the older brother. The surname given wasn't the one the Frank brothers were currently living under, though the forenames remained the same.

'The younger one was done fer flashin',' Barclay told Shah and Midge, while Strike was reading. 'Got a suspended sentence. The older one's supposedly the younger one's carer. No idea what's s'posed to be wrong wi' him.'

'And the older one's been done for stalking,' said Strike, now reading the second article, 'of another actress. Judge let him off with a suspended sentence, because he's his brother's carer.'

'Typical,' said Midge angrily, banging her glass down on the table to the slight consternation of Shah, who was sitting beside her. 'If I saw that once, I saw it *fifty fookin' times* when I was in the force. Men like them get cut too much fookin' slack, and everyone'll act surprised when one of the fookers is charged with rape.'

'Good job finding this, Barclay,' said Strike. 'I think—'

Strike's mobile rang and he saw Littlejohn's number. He answered.

'Just seen Frank One posting something in an envelope through the client's front door,' said Littlejohn. 'I've sent you video.'

'Where is he now?'

'Walking away.'

'OK, I'll call the client and warn her. Stay on him.'

'Righto.'

Littlejohn hung up.

'Frank One's just posted something through the client's letter box,' Strike told the rest of the team.

'More dead birds?' asked Midge.

'Not unless they'd fit in an envelope. I think we should tip off the police that the Franks have got form under previous names. A visit from Plod might make them back off. I'll take care of that,' Strike added, making a note. 'What's the latest on Bigfoot?'

'He was back at Chelsea Cloisters yesterday,' said Shah.

'That young girl you photographed him with in the street isn't going to give us anything,' Midge told Strike. 'I got talking to her in a sandwich place up the road. Thick East European accent, very nervous. They tell those girls they're coming to London to get modelling contracts, don't they? I was hoping she might fancy a nice press payday for selling him out, but I think she'd be too scared to talk.'

'One of us needs tae get intae that place, posing as a punter,' said Barclay.

'I'd have thought the pictures of him going in and out of there would be enough for his wife,' said Shah.

'She thinks he'll explain it away somehow,' said Strike, who'd received a tetchy email that morning from the client. 'She's after something he can't wriggle out of.'

'Like wha', a picture of him actually bein' sucked off?' said Barclay.

'Couldn't hurt. Might be better to get in the building as some kind of tradesman or safety inspector, instead of a punter,' said Strike. 'More freedom to move around and maybe catch him coming out of a room.'

There followed a discussion as to which detective should undertake the job, and possible covers. Shah, who'd successfully posed as an international art dealer during a previous case, was finally assigned the job.

'Bit of a comedown, heating engineer,' he said.

'We'll get you fake ID and documentation,' said Strike.

'So, are we going to take a new case from the waiting list yet?' asked Midge.

'Give it a bit longer,' said Strike. 'Let's make sure we've got a replacement for Littlejohn first.'

'Who's off tae visit the plastic rock tomorrow?' asked Barclay.

'I am,' said Strike.

'She must be nearly ready to come out,' said Midge. 'It's a month now.'

'She hasn't got anything Edensor can use against the church yet,' said Strike. 'You know Robin: no half measures. OK, I think that's everything. I'll let you know about the Littlejohn replacement as soon as I do.'

'Can I have a word?' Shah asked Strike, as the others headed for the door.

'Yeah, of course,' said Strike, sitting back down. To his surprise, the subcontractor now took a copy of *Private Eye* out of his back pocket.

'Have you read this?'

'No,' said Strike.

Shah flicked through the magazine, then handed it across the table. Strike saw a column circled in pen.

Andrew 'Honey Badger' Honbold QC, UK slebs' favourite defamation litigator and self-proclaimed moral arbiter, may soon be in desperate need of his own services. Honey Badger's longstanding preference for pretty young juniors is, of course, entirely avuncular. However, a mole at Lavington Court Chambers informs the *Eye* that a curvaceous young brunette has been spreading tales of the Badger's prowess and stamina in a context other than the courtroom. The legal lovely has even been heard predicting the imminent demise of the Badger's marriage to the saintly Lady Matilda.

Stalwarts of the London charity circuit, the Honbolds have been married for 25 years and have four children. A recent *Times* profile emphasised the personal probity of the UK's most prominent anti-sleaze brief.

'I've seen close up the effect slurs and insinuations have on undeserving people,' thundered the Honey Badger, 'and I personally would strengthen the existing defamation laws to protect the innocent.'

The indiscreet lady in the case is now rumoured to be bestowing her favours upon one Cormoran Strike, the increasingly newsworthy private detective. Has she been getting tips on hidden cameras and microphones? If so, the Hon Honbold QC had better hope slurs and insinuations are all he has to deal with.

'Fuck,' said Strike. He looked up at Shah and could find nothing better to do than repeat *'fuck'*.

'Thought you should know,' said Shah.

'It was a one-night – no, two-night stand. She never said a word to me about this Honbold.'

'Right,' said Shah. 'Well, y'know – he's not popular with the papers, so I think they might run with this story.'

'I'll sort it,' said Strike. 'She's not dragging me into her mess.'

But he was well aware he'd already been dragged into Bijou's mess, and Shah looked as though he was thinking exactly the same thing.

They parted outside the Flying Horse, Shah returning to the office to finish some paperwork, leaving Strike consumed with rage and self-recrimination outside the pub. He'd had enough experience of both kinds of misfortune to know that there was a vast difference between feeling yourself a victim of random strokes of fate and having to accept that your troubles had been brought about by your own folly. He'd been warned by Ilsa that Bijou was mouthy and indiscreet, and what had he done? Fucked her a second time. After avoiding the spotlight for years, giving testimony in court cases only in a full beard, refusing every offer of a press interview and ending a previous relationship with a woman who'd wanted him to pose with her at high-profile events, he'd knowingly bedded a loudmouth with, it turned out, a well-known married lover in the background.

He called Bijou's number, but reached voicemail. After leaving a message telling her to ring him as soon as possible, he called Ilsa.

'Hi,' she said, sounding cold.

'Calling to apologise,' said Strike, which was only partially true. 'I shouldn't have bitten your head off. I know you were only trying to look out for me.'

'Yes, I was,' said Ilsa. 'All right, apology accepted.'

'Well, you've been proven right in spades,' said Strike. 'I'm in today's *Private Eye*, linked to her and to her married boyfriend.'

'Oh shit, not Andrew Honbold?' said Ilsa.

'You know him?'

'Only slightly.'

'The *Eye's* implying that in addition to shagging her, I've been helping her bug Honbold's bedroom.'

'Corm, I'm sorry – she's been trying to get him to leave his wife for ages. She's completely open about it.'

'I can't see Honbold marrying her if he thinks she's put a private detective on him. Where is she right now, d'you know?'

'She'll be at Lavington Court Chambers,' said Ilsa.

'OK, I'll go and wait for her there,' said Strike.

'Is that wise?'

'It'll be easier to put the fear of God into her in person than over the phone,' said Strike grimly, already heading towards the Tube station.

44

A man must part company with the inferior and superficial. The important thing is to remain firm.

The I Ching or Book of Changes

This, Strike thought, was the first time he'd been glad that Robin was currently at Chapman Farm. He'd done something bloody stupid, and while the consequences were likely to be more severe for himself than the agency as a whole, he preferred Robin to remain in ignorance of the mess he'd got himself into.

Having looked up the address, Strike made the short journey on the Central line, exiting the Tube at Holborn and heading for Lincoln's Inn. He then took up a position behind a tree in the gardens from which he could watch the neo-classical façade of Lavington Court Chambers, and waited.

He'd been there for an hour, watching a few people enter, and more leave the building, when his mobile rang. Expecting to see Bijou's number, he instead saw Shanker's.

'Wotcha, Bunsen, just callin' to say you're in, wiv Reaney. Twenny-eighth of May. Couldn't do nuffin' earlier.'

'Cheers, Shanker, that's great news,' said Strike, still keeping his eyes trained on the entrance of Bijou's building. 'He knows I'm coming, right?'

'Oh, yeah, 'e knows,' said Shanker. 'An' you'll 'ave a bit of security there, to make sure 'e's cooperating.'

'Even better,' said Strike. 'Thanks a lot.'

'Awright, 'appy 'untin',' said Shanker, and rang off.

Strike had just put his mobile back in his pocket when the door of Lavington Court Chambers opened and Bijou descended the steps wearing a bright red coat, setting off in the direction of the Tube station. Strike let her get a head start, then followed. As he walked, he took out his mobile and called her number again. She took her phone out of her bag, still walking, looked at it, then put it back in the bag without answering.

As he wanted to put some distance between himself and Lavington Court Chambers to reduce the possibility of being seen by Bijou's work colleagues, Strike continued to walk fifty yards behind his quarry until she entered narrow Gate Street. Here, she slowed down, took out her mobile again, apparently to read a recently received text, and finally came to a halt to send a reply. Strike sped up, and when she'd again put her mobile back into her bag, called her name.

She looked round, and was clearly horrified to see who had called her.

'I'd like a word, in there,' he said grimly, pointing to a pub called the Ship, which was tucked away in a pedestrian-only alleyway visible between two buildings.

'Why?'

'Have you read today's *Private Eye*?'

'I – yes.'

'Then you know why.'

'I don't—'

'Want to be seen with me? Then you should've answered your phone.'

She looked as though she'd have liked to refuse to go with him, but let him lead her into the alleyway. When he held open the door of the Ship, she walked in past him, her expression cold.

'I'd rather go upstairs,' she said.

'Fine by me,' said Strike. 'What d'you want to drink?'

'I don't care – red wine.'

Five minutes later he joined her upstairs in the low-ceilinged, dimly lit Oak Room. She'd taken off her coat to reveal a tight red dress, and was sitting in a corner with her back to the room. Strike set her wine on the table before sitting down opposite her, holding a double whisky. He didn't intend to stay long enough for a pint.

'You've been shooting your mouth off about me.'

'No, I haven't.'

'"A mole at Lavington Court Chambers—"'

'I know what it said!'

'You need to make it very clear to this Honbold individual that I never gave you any advice on surveillance.'

'I've already told him that!'

'Seen the article, has he?'

'Yes. And the *Mail* have been on to him. And the *Sun*. But he's going to deny everything,' she added, her bottom lip trembling.

'I'll bet he is.'

Strike watched unsympathetically as Bijou dug in her pockets for a tissue and blotted her eyes carefully so as not to disturb her make-up.

'What are you going to do when journos turn up at your flat?' he asked.

'Tell them I never slept with him. It's what Andrew wants.'

'You're going to deny you ever slept with me, as well.'

She said nothing. Suspecting he knew what lay behind her silence, he said,

'I'm not going to be collateral damage in all this. We met at a christening, that's all. If you still think Honbold's going to be spurred into leaving his wife out of jealousy that we're screwing, you're deluded. I doubt he'd touch you with a barge-pole after this.'

'You *bastard*,' she croaked, still mopping her eyes and nose. 'I *liked* you.'

'You were playing a little game that blew up in your face, but I'm not going to get caught in the crossfire, so understand now, there'll be consequences if you try and save face by saying we're having an affair.'

'Are you *threatening* me?' she whispered over the damp tissue.

'It's a warning,' said Strike. 'Delete the texts you sent me and take my number off your phone.'

'Or?'

'Or there'll be consequences,' he repeated. 'I'm a private detective. I find out things about people, things they think they've hidden very effectively. Unless there's nothing in your past you'd mind seeing printed in the *Sun*, I'd think long and hard about using me to try and leverage a proposal out of Honbold.'

She was no longer crying. Her expression had hardened, but he thought she'd gone slightly paler beneath her foundation. Finally she took out her mobile, deleted his contact details, the texts they'd exchanged and the photos she'd sent him. Strike then did the same on his own phone, downed his whisky in one and stood up again.

'Right,' he said, 'blanket denials all round and this should blow over.'

He left the Ship feeling no qualms whatsoever about the tactics he'd just employed, but consumed with fury at her and himself. Time would tell whether he was going to find the *Mail* at his own door, but as he walked back towards Holborn

Tube station, he vowed to himself that this would be the last time, ever, he risked his own privacy or career for a pointless affair undertaken to distract him from thoughts of Robin Ellacott.

45

*But every relationship between individuals bears
within it the danger that wrong turns may be
taken . . .*

The I Ching or Book of Changes

Robin had had to carry around the Polaroids she'd found for
a week before placing them in the plastic rock on Thursday
night. She didn't dare hide them anywhere in the dormitory,
but the awareness of them close to her skin was an ever-
present source of anxiety in case one slipped out from under
her tracksuit top. Her fourth trip into the woods and back
again was mercifully uneventful, and she returned safely to
her bed undetected, deeply relieved to have got rid of the
photographs.

The following evening, after a day of lectures and chanting,
Robin returned to the dormitory with the other women to
find scarlet tracksuits lying on their beds, instead of orange.

'Why the colour change?' said widowed Marion Huxley
blankly. Marion, whose ginger hair had now grown out to
reveal an inch of silver, often asked rather basic questions, or
spoke when others might have remained silent.

''Aven't you finished reading *The Answer* yet?' snapped
spiky-haired Vivienne. 'We must've entered the Season of the
Stolen Prophet. Red's his colour.'

'Very good, Vivienne,' called Becca Pirbright, smiling from a few beds away, and Vivienne visibly preened herself.

But there was something else on Robin's bed beside her folded scarlet tracksuit: a box of hair colour remover with a slip of paper lying on top of it, with what she recognised as a quotation from *The Answer* printed on it.

> The False Self craves that which is artificial and
> unnatural.
> The True Self craves that which is genuine and natural.

Robin glanced across the dormitory and saw green-haired Penny Brown also examining a box of hair colour remover. Their eyes met; Robin smiled and pointed towards the bathroom and Penny, smiling back, nodded.

To Robin's surprise, Louise was standing at the sink, carefully shaving her head in the mirror. Their eyes met briefly. Louise dropped her gaze first. Having towelled off her now completely bald pate, she left the bathroom without speaking.

'People were telling me,' whispered Penny, 'that she's been shaved for, like, *a year.*'

'Wow,' said Robin. 'D'you know why?'

Penny shook her head.

Tired as she was, and resentful that she had to give up valuable sleeping time to removing her blue hair dye, Robin was nevertheless glad for the opportunity to talk freely to another church member, especially one whose daily routine differed so markedly from her own.

'How're you doing? I've barely seen you since we were in Fire Group together.'

'Great,' said Penny. 'Really great.'

Her round face was slimmer than it had been on arrival at

the farm and there were shadows beneath her eyes. Side by side at the bathroom mirror, Robin and Penny opened the boxes and began to apply the product to their hair.

'If this is the start of the Season of the Stolen Prophet,' said Penny, 'we'll be seeing a proper Manifestation soon.'

She sounded both excited and frightened.

'It was incredible, seeing the Drowned Prophet appear, wasn't it?' said Robin.

'Yes,' said Penny. 'That's what really – I mean, once you've seen that, there's no going back to normal life, is there? Like, the proof.'

'Absolutely,' said Robin. 'I felt the same.'

Penny looked disconsolately at her reflection, with her green hair now covered in a thick white paste.

'It was growing out anyway,' she said, with an air of trying to convince herself she was happy to be doing what she was doing.

'So what have you been up to?' asked Robin.

'Um, loads of stuff,' said Penny. 'Cooking, working on the vegetable patch. I've been helping with Jacob as well. And we had a really good talk this morning, on spirit bonding.'

'Really?' said Robin. 'I haven't had that yet ... how's Jacob doing?'

'He's *definitely* getting better,' said Penny, evidently under the impression that Robin knew all about Jacob.

'Oh, good,' said Robin. 'I heard he wasn't too well.'

'I mean, he hasn't been, obviously,' said Penny. Her manner was somewhere between anxious and cagey. 'It's like, difficult, isn't it? Because someone like that, they can't understand about the false self and the pure spirit, and that's why they can't heal themselves.'

'Right,' said Robin, nodding, 'but you think he's getting better?'

'Oh yeah,' said Penny. 'Definitely.'

'It's nice of Mazu to have him in the farmhouse,' said Robin, subtly probing.

'Yeah,' said Penny again, 'but he couldn't be in the dormitory with all his problems.'

'No, of course not,' said Robin, carefully feeling her way. 'Dr Zhou seems so nice.'

'Yeah, it's really lucky Jacob's got Dr Zhou, because it'd be a nightmare if he was on the outside,' said Penny. 'They euthanise people like Jacob out there.'

'D'you think so?' asked Robin.

'Of course they do,' said Penny, in disbelief at Robin's naivety. 'The state doesn't want to look after them, so they're just quietly done away with by the NHS – the Nazi Hate Squad, Dr Zhou calls it,' she added, before looking anxiously in the mirror at her hair and saying, 'How long d'you think it's been on? It's hard to know, without a watch or anything . . .'

'Maybe five minutes?' said Robin. Seeking to capitalise on Penny's mention of the lack of watches, and encourage the girl to share anything negative she might have noticed about the UHC, she said lightly,

'Funny, having to get our dye out. Mazu's hair can't be naturally that black, can it? She's in her forties and she hasn't got a single bit of grey.'

Penny's demeanour changed instantly.

'Critiquing people's looks is pure materialist judgement.'

'I'm not—'

'Flesh is unimportant. Spirit is all-important.'

Her tone was didactic, but her eyes were fearful.

'I know, but if it doesn't matter what we look like, why have we got to take out our hair dye?' said Robin reasonably.

'Because – it was on the bit of paper on the box. The true self is natural.'

Now looking alarmed, Penny scurried away into a shower cubicle and closed the door behind her.

When she estimated that twenty minutes had passed, Robin stripped off her tracksuit, showered the product out of her hair, dried herself, checked in the mirror that all traces of blue dye were gone, then returned to the dark dormitory in her pyjamas.

Penny remained hidden in her shower cubicle throughout.

46

*An individual finds himself in an evil environment to
which he is committed by external ties.
But he has an inner relationship with a superior
man . . .*

The I Ching or Book of Changes

The routine of the higher-level recruits changed with the
arrival of the Season of the Stolen Prophet. They were no
longer spending entire mornings watching footage of war
atrocities and famine in the farmhouse basement but were
given more lectures on the nine steps to pure spirit: admission,
service, divestment, union, renunciation, acceptance, purification, mortification and sacrifice. They were given practical
advice on how to achieve steps one to six, which could be
worked on concurrently, but the rest were shrouded in mystery, and only those who were judged to have successfully
mastered the first half dozen were deemed worthy to learn
how to achieve the last three.

Robin also had to endure a second Revelation session.
For the second time, she escaped sitting in the hot seat in the
middle of the circle, although Vivienne and the elderly Walter
were less fortunate. Vivienne was attacked for her habit of
changing her accent to disguise her moneyed background and
accused of arrogance, self-centredness and hypocrisy until she

was reduced to heaving sobs, while Walter, who'd admitted to a long-running feud with an ex-colleague at his old university, was berated for egomotivity and materialist judgement. Alone of those who'd so far been subjected to Primal Response Therapy, Walter didn't cry. He turned white, but nodded rhythmically, almost eagerly, as the circle threw insults and accusations at him.

'Yes,' he muttered, blinking furiously behind his glasses, 'yes ... that's true ... it's all true ... very bad ... yes, indeed ... false self ...'

Meanwhile the bottoms of the medium-sized tracksuits Robin was given once a week kept sliding down from her waist, because she'd lost so much weight. Other than the irritation of having to constantly pull them up again, this didn't trouble her nearly as much as the awareness that she was slowly becoming institutionalised.

When she'd first arrived at Chapman Farm, she'd registered her own tiredness and hunger as abnormal, and noticed the effects of claustrophobia and group pressure during lectures in the basement. Gradually, though, she'd stopped noticing her exhaustion, and had adapted to making do with less food. She was alarmed to find the unconscious habit of chanting under her breath becoming more frequent and she'd even caught herself thinking in the church's language. Pondering the question of why the unknown Jacob, who was clearly too ill to be useful to the church, was being kept at Chapman Farm, she found herself framing the possibility of his departure as a 'return to the materialist world'.

Unnerved by what she was still objective enough to recognise as partial indoctrination, Robin tried a new strategy to maintain her objectivity: trying to analyse the methods the church was using to force acceptance of its world view.

She noted the way duress and leniency were applied to

church members. Recruits were so grateful for any let-up in the constant pressure to listen, learn, work or chant that they showed disproportionate gratitude for the smallest rewards. When older children were permitted to run into the woods at the perimeter for unsupervised leisure time, they took off with the kind of glee Robin imagined children in the outside world might have displayed on being told they were going to Disneyland. A kind word from Mazu, Taio or Becca, five minutes of unsupervised time, an extra scoop of noodles at dinner: these triggered feelings of warmth and delight that showed just how normalised enforced obedience and deprivation had already become. Robin was aware that she, too, was beginning to crave the approval of church elders, and that this craving was rooted in an animalistic urge for self-protection. The regular re-sorting of the groups and the ever-present threat of ostracism prevented any feeling of real solidarity developing between members. Those giving lectures had impressed upon all of them that the pure spirit saw no human being as better or more loveable than any other. Loyalty was supposed to flow upwards, towards the divine and the heads of the church, but never sideways.

Yet her strategy of objectively analysing the church's means of indoctrination was only partially successful. Kept in a permanent state of tiredness, it was a constant effort to reflect on how obedience was compelled, rather than simply complying. Finally, Robin hit upon the trick of imagining herself telling Strike what she was up to. This forced her to discard all church jargon, because he wouldn't understand or, more likely, would mock it. The idea of Strike laughing at what she was having to do – though she did him the credit of doubting he'd find Revelation amusing – was a better means of keeping a foothold in the reality that lay outside Chapman Farm, and even broke the chanting habit, because she trained herself to imagine Strike grinning at her when she found herself doing it. Not once did it occur to Robin that she might have imagined talking to Murphy, or any of her female friends, rather than Strike. She was desperately looking forward to his next letter, partly because she wanted to hear his opinion on the Polaroids she'd placed in the plastic rock the previous Thursday, but also because the sight of his handwriting proved he was real, not just a useful figment of her imagination.

The journey across the dark field and through the woods the following Thursday was her easiest so far, because the route through the trees was becoming familiar. When she opened the plastic rock and turned on the torch, she saw the longest letter from Strike yet, and two Cadbury's Flakes. Only as she began unwrapping one of these and easing herself into position behind a tree, to make sure her torchlight wasn't visible to anyone who might be looking through the woods from the farm, did she realise there was no note from Ryan. Too nervous and ravenous to worry about that now, she began gobbling down the chocolate while reading Strike's letter.

Hi,

Your last was very interesting indeed. The tin you described dates from 1987. Assuming the person who took the Polaroids owned the tin, and assuming the tin was taken to the farm when new, it got there before the church started, which might suggest our amateur pornographer was there in the commune days, even if his models arrived later. Could be the Crowthers, Coates, Wace himself, Rust Andersen, or someone we don't know about. I'm inclined to discount the Crowthers or Coates, because they specialised in pre-pubescents. The blonde girl's hair looks like Cherie Gittins', though obviously there could have been more than one blonde, curly haired girl there. I also wondered about the boy with the tattoo on his arm. Shanker's

457

got me a date with Jordan Reaney, so I'll ask him if he's got any skulls up his sleeve.

Other news: Frank One posted a birthday card through the client's door. Hard to prosecute over that, but Barclay's found out one brother's a flasher and the other one's got previous for stalking. I called Wardle and I think/hope the police are going to pay them a visit.

We're still lumbered with Littlejohn, unfortunately. Wardle recommended an ex-copper and I interviewed him, but he's taken a job with Patterson instead. Says the pay's better. News to me, Dev says they pay less than we do. Maybe he just thought I was a dick.

Pat's in a bad mood.

Murphy apologises for the lack of letter, he's had to go up north. Sends his best.

Take care of yourself in there and any time you want to leave, we're ready.

S x

Robin now unwrapped the second chocolate bar, propped the pile of blank paper on her knee and began to write back, pausing regularly to take more bites of Flake and try and recall everything she needed to tell Strike.

Having apologised for not having anything new on Will Edensor, she continued:

I told you about the two girls who let the little boy escape. Both have had their heads shaved. It's clearly a punishment, which means Louise and Emily Pirbright have been punished, too, but I don't yet know why. I haven't been able to talk to Emily Pirbright again. Two nights ago I also saw the back of the black girl, whose bed's a couple away from mine. It had weird marks on it as if she'd been dragged along the floor.

I haven't had any opportunity to talk to her. The trouble is, everyone in here shuns/avoids people who've been told off or punished, so it's very obvious if you make overtures to them.

I've heard more about Jacob from a girl who's been helping look after him. She says he's getting better (not sure that's true) and that people 'like him' are euthanised in the materialist —

Catching herself, Robin crossed the word out.

— ~~materialist~~ outside world. She also said people like Jacob don't really understand about the false self and the pure spirit so they can't heal themselves. Will keep an ear out for more.

We're now in the middle of a lot of lectures on how you become pure spirit. There are nine steps and the third is when you start committing a lot of money to the church, to divest yourself of materialism. I'm a bit worried about what's going to happen when they expect me to start setting up bank transfers, given that they think I can afford £1k handbags.

I don't want to come out yet —

Robin paused here, listening to the rustling leaves, her back sore from leaning against the knobbly bark of the tree, her backside and thighs damp from the wet grass. What she'd written was a lie: she very much wanted to leave. The thought of her flat, her comfortable bed and a return to the office were incredibly tempting, but she was certain staying would provide opportunities to find something incriminating against the church that would be impossible from the outside.

— because I haven't really got anything Colin Edensor can use. Hopefully I'll get something this week. I swear I'm trying.

Still haven't had to do Revelation. I'll feel happier once I've got that out of the way.

R x

PS Please keep the chocolate coming.

47

Nine at the beginning means:
When ribbon grass is pulled up, the sod comes with it.

The I Ching or Book of Changes

Strike waited to read Robin's most recent dispatch from Chapman Farm before finishing an interim report for Sir Colin Edensor. The question that was vexing him most was whether or not to reveal the possibility that Will had fathered a child with an underage girl at Chapman Farm. The overheard conversation Robin had mentioned didn't, in Strike's view, rise to the standard of proof, and he was wary of increasing Sir Colin's anxiety without being certain of his facts. He therefore omitted mention of Will's alleged paternity, and concluded:

Proposed Next Steps

We now have RE's eyewitness account of physical coercion and injuries, plus her first-hand experience of underfeeding, enforced lack of sleep and a 'therapeutic' technique I think legitimate psychologists would agree is abusive. RE believes she may yet uncover evidence of more serious/criminal activity at Chapman Farm. Given that none of the church members RE and I have interviewed so far are willing to testify against the

*church, or likely to be credible witnesses given the length
of time they've been out, I recommend RE staying
undercover for the present.*

*I'll be interviewing another ex-member of the UHC on the
twenty-eighth of May and am actively searching for more.
Identifying the subjects of the photographs RE found is a
priority, as they suggest sexual abuse has been used as a
form of discipline.*

If you have any questions, please get in touch.

Having emailed the password-protected report to Sir
Colin, Strike drank the last of his mug of tea, then sat for a
few moments staring out of the window of his attic kitchen,
contemplating several of his current dilemmas.

As he'd foreseen, the *Private Eye* article had led to phone
calls from three different journalists, all of whose publications
had tangled with Andrew Honbold QC in court and were
consequently eager to wring as much newsprint as possible
out of his extra-marital affair. On Strike's instructions, Pat had
responded with a one-line statement denying any involvement
with Honbold or anyone associated with him. Honbold himself had issued a statement vehemently denying the *Eye* story
and threatening legal action. Bijou's name hadn't appeared in
the press, but Strike had a nasty feeling that there might yet
be further repercussions from his ill-advised dalliance, and
was keeping a weather-eye out for any opportunistic journalist
who might be watching the office.

Meanwhile he still hadn't managed to track down any of the
former church members he was most eager to talk to, remained
saddled with Littlejohn and was plagued by worries about his
Uncle Ted, whom he'd called the previous evening and who
appeared to have forgotten that he'd seen his nephew recently.

Strike turned his attention back to the laptop lying open on his kitchen table. More in hope than in expectation, he navigated to Torment Town's Pinterest page, but there were no additional pictures, nor was there any response to his enquiry as to whether the artist drew from imagination.

He'd just got to his feet to wash up his mug when his mobile rang with a call transferred from the office. He picked up and had barely got his name out when a furious, high-pitched voice said,

'*I've had a fucking live snake posted through my front door!*'

'What?' said Strike, completely nonplussed.

'A fucking *SNAKE!* One of those *total fuckers* has put a fucking *snake* through my letter box!'

In rapid succession Strike realised that he was talking to the actress the Franks were stalking, that he'd momentarily forgotten her name, and that his team must have fucked up very badly indeed.

'Did this happen this morning?' he said, dropping back into his kitchen chair and opening the rota on his laptop to see who was on the Franks.

'I don't know, I've only just fucking found it in my sitting room, it could've been here for *days!*'

'Have you called the police?'

'What's the *point* in calling the police? This is what I'm paying *you* to stop!'

'I appreciate that,' said Strike, 'but the immediate problem is the snake.'

'Oh, *that's* all right,' she said, thankfully no longer shouting. 'I've put it in the bath. It's only a corn snake. I used to have one, I'm not *scared* of them. Well,' she added heatedly, 'I'm not scared of them until I see them slithering out from beneath the sofa when I didn't know they were there.'

'Don't blame you,' said Strike, who'd just found out that

Barclay and Midge were currently on the Franks. 'It'd be good to get an approximate idea of when you think it might have arrived, because we're keeping the brothers under constant surveillance and they haven't been anywhere near your front door since the older one dropped your birthday card in. I've seen the video and there definitely wasn't a snake in his hand.'

'So you're telling me I've got a *third* nutter after me?'

'Not necessarily. Were you in last night?'

'Yes, but—'

She broke off.

'*Oh.* Actually, I *do* remember hearing the letter flap last night.'

'What time?'

'Must've been around ten. I was having a bath.'

'Did you check to see whether anything had been put through the door?'

'No. I kind of registered there was nothing there when I went downstairs to get a drink. I thought I must have mistaken a noise outside for the letter box.'

'D'you need help getting rid of the snake?' asked Strike, who felt this was the least he could do.

'No,' she sighed, 'I'll call the RSPCA or something.'

'All right, I'll contact the people I've got tailing the brothers, find out where they were last night at ten and get back to you. Glad to hear you're not too shaken up, Tasha,' he added, her name having just come back to him.

'Thank you,' she said, mollified. 'OK, I'll wait to hear back.'

When she'd hung up, Strike called Barclay.

'You were on Frank One overnight, right?'

'Yeah,' said Barclay.

'Where was he around ten?'

'At home.'

'You sure?'

'Aye, and so was his brother. Frank Two hasn't been oot at all these last few days. Mebbe he's ill.'

'Neither of them been near what's–her–name's house lately?'

'Frank One took a stroll round there on Monday. Midge was on him.'

'Right, I'll call her. Thanks.'

Strike rang off and phoned Midge.

'He definitely didn't post anything through the front door,' said Midge, when Strike explained why he was calling. 'Just lurked on the opposite pavement, watching her windows. He's been at home the last few days and so's his brother.'

'So Barclay said.'

'She can't have *another* stalker, can she?'

'That's exactly what she just asked me,' said Strike. 'Could be some deluded fan's idea of a surprise gift, I s'pose. Apparently she used to own a corn snake.'

'I don't care how many snakes you've owned, you don't want one posted through your bloody door at night,' said Midge.

'I agree. Have you seen any coppers visiting the Franks yet?'

'Nope,' said Midge.

'OK, I'll get back to the client. This might mean keeping someone on her house for a bit, as well as the Franks.'

'Bloody hell. Who'd have thought this pair of freaks would turn out to be so labour intensive?'

'Not me,' admitted Strike.

After he'd hung up the phone he reached for his vape pen, frowning slightly as he inhaled nicotine, lost in thought for a minute. He then turned his attention back to the weekly rota.

Littlejohn and Shah had both had the previous evening off. Bigfoot's extramarital activities were confined to daylight hours and he went home nightly to his suspicious, irritable wife. Strike was still asking himself whether the idea he'd just had was ludicrous, when his mobile rang again, forwarded from the office as before. Expecting his actress client, he realised too late that he was talking to Charlotte Campbell.

'It's me. Don't hang up,' she said quickly. 'It's in your best interests to hear what I've got to say.'

'Say it, then,' said Strike irritably.

'A journalist from the *Mail* called me. They're trying to run some sleazy profile of you, saying you sleep with female clients. Like father, like son, that kind of thing.'

Strike could feel the tension gripping every part of his body.

'I told her I didn't believe you'd ever sleep with a client, that you're very honourable and that you've got strict ethics about that kind of thing. And I said you're nothing like your father.'

Strike couldn't have said what he was feeling, except a dim surprise mixed with some ghostly vestige of what he'd once felt for her, resurrected by the sorrowful voice he'd sometimes heard at the end of their worst fights, when even Charlotte's ineradicable love of conflict left her spent and atypically honest.

'I know they've been to a few of your exes as well,' said Charlotte.

'Who?' said Strike.

'Madeline, Ciara and Elin,' said Charlotte. 'Madeline and Elin have both said they've never hired a private detective and refused to give any other comment. Ciara says she just laughed when the *Mail* called her, then hung up.'

'How the hell did they know I was with Elin?' said Strike, more to himself than Charlotte. That affair, which had ended acrimoniously, had been conducted with what he'd thought was complete discretion on both their parts.

'Darling, people talk,' sighed Charlotte. 'You should know that, seeing as it's your job to make them. But I just wanted you to know, nobody's cooperating and I've done what I could. You and I were together longest, so – so that should count for something.'

Strike tried to find something to say and finally mustered a 'Well – thanks.'

'That's all right,' said Charlotte. 'I know you think I want to ruin your life, but I don't. I *don't*.'

'I never thought you wanted to ruin my life,' said Strike, now rubbing his face with his hand. 'I just thought you didn't mind messing with it a bit.'

'What d'you—?'

'Shit-stirring,' said Strike. 'With Madeline.'

'Oh,' said Charlotte. 'Yeah . . . I did do that, a bit.'

The answer forced a reluctant laugh out of Strike.

'How are you?' he said. 'How's your health?'

'I'm fine.'

'Really?'

'Yes. I mean, they've caught it early.'

'OK, well, thanks for doing what you could with the *Mail*. I'll just have to hope they haven't got enough to run with.'

'Bluey,' she said urgently, and his heart sank.

'What?'

'Could we have a drink? Just a drink. To talk.'

'No,' he said wearily.

'Why not?'

'Because,' he said, 'it's over. I've told you this, repeatedly. We're through.'

'And we can't even stay friends?'

'Jesus Christ, Charlotte, we were never friends. That was the whole trouble. We were *never* fucking friends.'

'How can you say—?'

'Because it's true,' he said forcefully. 'Friends don't do to each other what we did. Friends have each other's backs. They want each other to be OK. They don't rip each other apart every time there's a problem.'

Her breathing was ragged in his ear.

'You're with Robin, aren't you?'

'My love life's none of your business any more,' said Strike. 'I said it in the pub the other week, I wish you well, but I don't—'

Charlotte hung up.

Strike replaced the mobile on his kitchen table and reached for his vape again. Several minutes passed before he was able to subdue his disordered thoughts. Finally, he returned his attention to the rota on the screen in front of him, his eyes fixed on the name Littlejohn, and after some further rumination, picked up his mobile again, and once again called Shanker.

48

... the inferior man's wickedness is visited upon himself. His house is split apart. A law of nature is at work here.

The I Ching or Book of Changes

Shortly after midday on Tuesday, Strike was to be found rising up the escalator at Sloane Square station, prepared to take over surveillance on Bigfoot, who was once again indulging in his favourite pastime at the large hotel full of sex workers. Among the small, framed posters on the escalator walls, many of which were advertising West End shows and grooming products, Strike noticed several featuring a flattering headshot of 'Papa J', the UHC's heart-shaped logo and the legend *Do you admit the possibility?*

The detective had just emerged from the station into the rainy street when his mobile rang and he heard Shah's voice, which was oddly thickened.

'I'b god hib.'

'You've what?'

'God hib on cambra, coming ouddob a room, girl behind hib in stoggings and nudding else – fug, sorry, I'b bleeding.'

'What's happened?' said Strike, though he thought he knew.

'He punjed be in da fugging face.'

Five minutes later, Strike entered the Rose and Crown on

Lower Sloane Street to find his best-looking subcontractor sitting in a corner with a split lip, a puffy left eye and a swollen nose, a pint on the table in front of him.

'Id fine, id nod broggen,' said Shah, gesturing to his nose and forestalling Strike's first question.

'Ice,' was Strike's one word response, and he headed for the bar, returning with a zero-alcohol beer for himself, a glass of ice and a clean beer towel he'd cadged from the curious barmaid. Shah tipped the ice onto the towel, wrapped it up and pressed the bundle to his face.

'Cheerd. Der you go,' Shah said, pushing his mobile across the table. The screen was smashed, but the picture of Bigfoot was sharp and clear behind the broken glass. He was caught in the act of yelling, mouth wide open, fist raised, a near-naked girl looking terrified behind him.

'Now, that,' said Strike, 'is what I call evidence. Excellent work. Heating engineer ruse worked, then?'

'Didn' deed id. Followed a fat bloke inside, ride after Bigfood. Hug around in de corridor. Caud hib coming out. He'd quig on hid feet for a big lad.'

'Bloody well done,' said Strike. 'Sure you don't want to see a doctor?'

'Doe, I'll be fine.'

'I'll be happy to see the back of this case,' said Strike. 'Midge is right, the client's a pain in the arse. S'pose she'll get her multi-million settlement now.'

'Yeah,' said Shah. 'New case, den? Ob the waiting list?'

'Yeah,' said Strike.

'Even wid the Franks being a three-perdon job now?'

'Heard about the snake, did you?'

'Yeah, Barglay dold be.'

'Well, they're not a three-person job any more. Back to two.'

'How gum?'

'Because I'm having the third party watched by a couple of cash-in-hand blokes,' said Strike. 'They don't often play on the side of the angels, but they're experienced at surveillance – usually casing places to rob. It's costing me a fortune, but I want to prove Patterson's behind it. That fucker will rue the day he tried this on me.'

'Wadz hid problem wid you, anyway?'

'It pisses him off I'm better than him,' said Strike.

Dev laughed but stopped abruptly, wincing.

'I owe you a new phone,' said Strike. 'Give me the receipt and I'll reimburse you. You should get home and rest up. Send me that picture and I'll call Bigfoot's wife when I get back to the office.'

A sudden thought now occurred to Strike.

'How old's your wife?'

'Wad?' said Shah, looking up.

'I've been trying to track down a thirty-eight-year-old woman, for the UHC case,' said Strike. 'She's used at least three aliases that I know of. Where do women that age hang out online, d'you know?'

'Bubsned, probably,' said Shah.

'What?'

'Bub – fuggit – *Mumsnet*,' said Dev, enunciating with difficulty. 'Aisha'd alwayd on dere. Or Fadeboog.'

'Mumsnet and Facebook,' said Strike. 'Yeah, good thinking. I'll try them.'

He arrived back at the office half an hour later to find Pat there alone, restocking the fridge with milk, the radio playing hits of the sixties.

'Dev's just got punched in the face by Bigfoot,' said Strike, hanging up his coat.

'*What?*' croaked Pat, glaring at Strike as though he was personally responsible.

'He's fine,' Strike added, moving past her to the kettle. 'Going home to ice his nose. Who's next on the waiting list?'

'That weirdo with the mother.'

'They all have mothers, don't they?' said Strike, dropping a teabag into a mug.

'This one wants his mother watched,' said Pat. 'Thinks she's frittering away his inheritance on a toyboy.'

'Ah, right. If you pull the file for me, I'll give him a ring. Has Littlejohn showed his face in here today?'

'No,' said Pat, stiffening.

'Has he called?'

'No.'

'Let me know if he does either. I'll be through here. Don't worry about interrupting me, I'll just be trying to find a needle in a haystack on Facebook and Mumsnet.'

Once settled at his desk, Strike made his two phone calls. Bigfoot's wife was gratifyingly ecstatic to see concrete evidence of her wealthy husband's infidelity. The man who wanted his mother's movements watched, and who had an upper-class accent so pronounced Strike found it hard to believe he wasn't putting it on, was also delighted to hear from the detective.

'Ay was thinkin' of gettin' in touch with Patters'ns if I didn't hyar from yeh soon.'

'You don't want to use them, they're shit,' said Strike, and was rewarded with a surprised guffaw.

Having asked Pat to email the newest client a contract, Strike returned to his desk, opened the notebook in which he'd written every possible combination of the first names and surnames he knew Cherie Gittins had used in youth, logged into Facebook using a fake profile, and began his methodical search.

As he'd expected, the problem wasn't too few results, but too many. There were multiple results for every name he tried, not only in Britain, but also in Australia, New Zealand and America. Wishing he could hire people to do this donkey work for him, rather than pay two of Shanker's criminal mates to watch Littlejohn, he followed – or, in the case of private accounts, sent follower requests to – every woman whose photo might plausibly be that of a thirty-eight-year-old Cherie Gittins.

Two and a half hours, three mugs of tea and a sandwich later, Strike came across a Facebook account set to private with the name Carrie Curtis Woods. He'd included 'Carrie' in his search as a shortened version of 'Carine'. As the double surname was unhyphenated, he suspected the account owner would be American rather than English, but the photograph had caught his attention. The smiling woman had the same curly blonde hair and insipid prettiness of the first picture of Cherie he'd found. In the picture, she was cuddling two young girls Strike supposed were her daughters.

Strike had just sent a follow request to Curtis Woods when the music in the outer office ceased abruptly. He heard a male voice. After a moment or two, the phone on Strike's desk rang.

'What's up?'

'There's a Barry Saxon here to see you.'

'Never heard of him,' said Strike.

'He says he's met you. Says he knows an Abigail Glover.'

'Oh,' said Strike, closing Facebook, as the memory of a glowering, bearded man presented itself: Baz, of the Forester pub. 'OK. Give me a minute, then send him in.'

49

Nine in the third place means . . .
A goat butts against a hedge
And gets its horns entangled.

The I Ching or Book of Changes

Strike rose and went to the noticeboard on the wall, where he'd pinned various items relating to the UHC case, and folded the wooden wings to conceal the Polaroids of teenagers in pig masks and the photo of Kevin Pirbright's bedroom. He'd just sat down when the door opened, and Barry Saxon entered.

Strike judged him to be around forty. He had very small, deep-set hazel eyes with large pouches beneath them, and his hair and beard looked as though their owner spent a lot of time caring for them. He came to a halt before Strike, with his hands in his jeans pockets, feet planted wide apart.

'You weren' Terry, then,' he said, squinting at the detective.

'No,' said Strike. 'How did you find that out?'

'Ab told Patrick, an' 'e told me.'

With an effort, Strike recalled that Patrick was Abigail Glover's lodger.

'Does Abigail know you're here?'

'Not bloody likely,' said Saxon, with a slight snort.

'D'you want to sit down?'

474

Saxon cast a suspicious look at the chair where Robin usually sat, before taking his hands out of his pockets and doing as invited.

He and Saxon might only have been in direct contact for less than two minutes, but Strike thought he knew what kind of man was sitting opposite him. Saxon's attempt to scupper what he'd thought was Abigail's date with 'Terry', coupled with his present attitude of smouldering resentment, reminded Strike of an estranged husband who was one of the few clients he'd ever turned down. In that case, Strike had been convinced that if he located the man's ex-wife, who he claimed was unreasonably resisting all contact in spite of the fact that there were unspecified things that needed 'sorting out', he'd have been enabling an act of revenge, and possibly violence. While that particular man had worn a Savile Row suit as opposed to a tight red checked shirt with buttons that strained across his torso, Strike thought he recognised in Saxon the same barely veiled thirst for vengeance.

'How can I help?' asked Strike.

'I don' wan' help,' said Saxon. 'I've got fings to tell ya. You're investigatin' that church, incha? The one wiv Ab's farver?'

'I don't discuss open investigations, I'm afraid,' said Strike.

Saxon shifted irritably in the chair.

'She covered fings up when she talked to you. She didn't tell the troof. A man called Kevin somefing got shot, din' 'e?'

As this information was in the public domain, Strike saw no reason to deny it.

'An' 'e was tryna expose the church, wannee?'

'He was an ex-member,' said Strike non-committally.

'All righ', well – *Ab knows the church shot 'im*. She knows the church 'ad 'im killed. An' she killed someone 'erself, when she was in there! Never told you *that,* did she? An' she's freatened me. She's tole me I'm next!'

Strike wasn't quite as impressed by these dramatic statements as Saxon evidently wished him to be. Nevertheless, he drew his notebook towards him.

'Shall we start at the beginning?'

Saxon's expression became a degree less dissatisfied.

'What d'you do for a living, Barry?'

'Wha' d'you wanna know tha' for?'

'Standard question,' said Strike, 'but you don't have to answer if you don't want to.'

''M'a Tube driver. Same as Patrick,' he added, as though there were safety in numbers.

'How long have you known Abigail?'

'Two years, so I know a *lotta* stuff about 'er.'

'Met her through Patrick, did you?'

'Yeah, a bunch of us wen' ou' drinkin'. She's always go' men around 'er, I soon found that out.'

'And you and she went out together subsequently, alone?' asked Strike.

'Tol' you tha', did she?' said Saxon, and it was hard to tell whether he was more aggrieved or gratified.

'Yeah, after you came over to our table in the pub,' said Strike.

'Whaddid she say? 'Cause I bet she ain' told you the troof.'

'Just that you and she had been out for drinks together.'

'It was more'n drinks, a *lot* more. She's up for anyfing. Then I realised 'ow many other blokes she's got on the go. I'm lucky I never caugh' nuffing,' said Saxon, with a little upwards jerk of his chin.

Familiar with the commonplace male disdain for women who enjoyed an adventurous sex life that either excluded or no longer included them, Strike continued asking questions that were designed purely to assess how much credence should be given to any information Saxon had to offer. He had a feeling the answer might be zero.

'So you ended the relationship, did you?'

'Yeah, I ain' puttin' up wiv that,' said Saxon, with another little jerk of the chin, 'but then she gets pissy abou' me goin' up the gym an' the Forester's an' goin' round 'er flat to see Patrick. Accuses me of fuckin' stalkin' 'er. Don' flatter yourself, sweet'eart. I know a *lotta* stuff abou' 'er,' repeated Saxon. 'So she shouldn' be fuckin' freatenin' me!'

'You said she killed someone, while in the church,' said Strike, his pen poised.

'Yeah – well – good as,' said Saxon. 'Because, right, Patrick 'eard 'er 'aving a nightmare, an' she's yelling "Cut it up smaller, cut it up smaller!" An' 'e goes an' bangs on 'er door – he said she was makin' fuckin' 'orrible noises – this is after she met you. She told Patrick it brought stuff up for 'er, what you two talked about.'

Strike was rapidly coming to the conclusion that Abigail and her upbringing were a source of prurient interest for her lodger and his friend that amounted almost to an unhealthy hobby. Aloud, he said,

'How did she kill this person?'

'I'm tellin' ya. She told Patrick there was this kid at the farm 'oo was, you know,' Saxon tapped his temple, 'bit simple an' 'e'd done somefing wrong an' 'e was gonna be whipped. So she an' this ovver girl, they felt sorry for 'im, so they runs off an' 'gets the whip an' 'ides it.

'So then, when 'er stepmuvver can't find it, she tells a group of 'em to beat the shit out of the kid instead, an' Ab joined in, kickin' and punchin' 'im. An' after the stepmuvver decides the kid's 'ad enough, she says she's gonna search the farm for the whip an' 'ooever's taken it's gonna be in trouble. So Ab an' 'er friend goes runnin' off to the kitchen where they 'id it an' they was tryna cut it up wiv scissors when the stepmu-vver comes in an' finds 'em, an' then they was whipped wiv it themselves.'

There was a faint trace of salacious pleasure in Saxon's voice as he said this.

'An' the simple kid died,' he concluded.

'After the beating?'

'No,' said Saxon, 'few years later, after 'e left the farm. But it was 'er fault, 'er and the rest of 'em beating 'im up, 'cause she told Patrick 'e was never right after they all kicked the shit out of 'im, like maybe brain damage or somefing. An' she saw in the paper 'e'd died, an' she reckoned it was 'cause of what they'd done to 'im.'

'Why was his death in the paper?'

''Cause 'e got 'imself into a bad situation, which he wouldna done if 'e 'adn't 'ad brain damage, so she killed 'im, good as. She said it 'erself. Beatin' an' kickin' him. *She* did that.'

'She was forced to do it,' Strike corrected Saxon.

'Still GBH,' said Saxon. 'She still done it.'

'She was a child, or a teenager, in a very abusive envi—'

'Ah, righ', you fallen for the act as well, 'ave ya?' said Saxon with a sneer. 'Got you twisted round 'er little finger? You ain' never seen 'er pissed an' angry. Little church girl? She's got a scary fuckin' temper on 'er—'

'If that was a crime, I'd be inside myself,' said Strike. 'What did she say about Kevin Pirbright?'

'Well, this is when she freatened *me*,' said Saxon, rallying again.

'When was this?'

'Two days ago, in the Grosvenor—'

'What's that, a bar?'

'Pub. Yeah, so, she wen' off on one 'cause I was in there. It's a free fuckin' country. Not up to 'er where I drink. She was wiv some dick from the gym. All I done was give 'im a friendly warnin'—'

'Like the one you gave me?'

'Yeah,' said Saxon, with another little upwards jerk of the chin, ''cause men need to know wha' she's like. I come out the bog an' she's waitin' for me. She'd 'ad a few, she drinks like a fuckin' fish, an' she's tellin' me to stop followin' 'er round, an' I says, "You fink you're your fuckin' farver dontcha? Tellin' everyone where they're allowed to fuckin' go," an' she says, "You wanna bring my farver into this, I could 'ave you taken out, I'll tell 'im you go walkin' round slaggin' off the church, you don' know 'oo you're messin' wiv," an' I told 'er she was talkin' bollocks an' she started fuckin' jabbin' me on the shoul-der,' Saxon unconsciously raised his hand to touch the spot where Abigail had presumably hit him, 'an' she says, "They got guns—"'

'She said the church has got guns?'

'Yeah, an' she says, "They jus' killed a guy for talkin' shit about 'em, so you need to stop fuckin' pissin' me off", an' I says, "'ow's the fire service gonna like it when I go to the police abou' you freatenin' me?" I got a *lotta* dirt on 'er, if she wants to play that fuckin' game,' said Saxon, barely drawing breath, 'an' y'know wha' they do in tha' church, do ya? All fuckin' each other all the time? That's 'ow she was brung up, but if she di'nt like it, why's she still fuckin' a diff'rent guy every night? Two at a time, some—'

'Did she say she'd *seen* guns at Chapman Farm?'

'Yeah, so she's seen the fuckin' murder weapon, an' she's never reported—'

'She can't have seen the gun that killed Kevin Pirbright. He was killed by a model that didn't exist then.'

Temporarily stymied, Saxon said,

'She still freatened to 'ave me fuckin' shot!'

'Well, if you think that was a credible threat, by all means go to the police. Sounds to me like a woman trying to scare off a guy who can't take no for an answer, but maybe they'll see it differently.'

Strike thought he knew what was going on behind Saxon's tiny hazel eyes. Occasionally, when people in the grip of obsessive resentment were pouring out their ire and grievances, something in them, some small trace of self-awareness, heard themselves as others might, and was surprised to find they didn't sound quite as blameless, or even as rational, as they'd imagined themselves to be.

'Maybe I will go the fuckin' police,' said Saxon, heaving himself to his feet.

'Good luck with that,' said Strike, also getting up. 'In the meantime, I might ring Abigail and recommend she finds a lodger who doesn't tell his mate every time she screams in her sleep.'

Perhaps because Strike was six inches taller than him, Saxon contented himself with snarling,

'If that's your fuckin' attitude—'

'Thanks for coming in,' said Strike, moving to open the door onto the outer office.

Saxon strode out past Pat and slammed the glass door behind him.

'I never trust men with those piggy little eyes,' croaked the office manager.

'You'd be right not to trust him,' said Strike, 'but not because of his piggy little eyes.'

'What did 'e want?'

'Revenge,' said Strike succinctly.

He returned to the inner office, sat back down at the partners' desk and read the sparse notes he'd made while Saxon was talking.

Paul Draper brain damage? Death in newspaper? Guns at Chapman Farm?

With reluctance, but knowing it was the only sure way to get fast results, he picked up his mobile and pressed Ryan Murphy's number.

50

Six at the beginning means:
When there is hoarfrost underfoot,
Solid ice is not far off.

The I Ching or Book of Changes

Several things had happened lately at Chapman Farm to leave anxiety squirming in Robin's guts like a parasite.

It had been one thing to tell Strike in the safety of the office that she wasn't worried about being coerced into unprotected sex with male church members, quite another to sit through a two-hour lecture about spirit bonding in the farmhouse basement and watch all the women around her earnestly nodding as they were told 'flesh is unimportant, spirit is all-important' (Robin knew, now, where Penny Brown had got that line).

'What we stand against,' Taio said from the stage, 'is materialist possession. No human being owns another or should create any kind of framework to control or limit them. This is inevitable in carnal relationships – what we call CRs – which are based upon the possession instinct. CRs are inherently materialist. They venerate physical appearance and they inevitably stunt the natures of those in them, yet the bubble world exalts them, especially when they come draped in materialist trappings of property, weddings and the so-called nuclear family.

'There should be no shame attached to sexual desire. It is a natural, healthy need. We agree with the Hindus that one of the aims of a well-lived life is Kama, or sensual pleasure. Yet the purer the spirit, the less likely it is to crave what is superficially attractive over what is spiritually good and true. Where two spirits are in harmony – when each feels the divine vibration working in and through them – spirit bonding occurs naturally and beautifully. The body, which is subservient to the spirit, physically demonstrates and channels the spiritual connection felt by those who have transcended materialist ties.'

While she'd found it impossible to disagree that the outside world was full of cruelty and apathy while she was being bombarded with images of bombed and starving children, Robin had no difficulty whatsoever in disengaging from her environment this time and analysing Taio's argument as he spoke. If you cut through all the UHC jargon, she thought, he was arguing that spiritual purity meant agreeing to sex with anyone who wanted it, no matter how unattractive you might find them. Sleeping only with people you actually desired made you a shallow agent of the Adversary, whereas sex with Taio – and the very thought gave Robin an inner shudder – proved your innate goodness.

However, she seemed to be alone in this viewpoint, because all around her, men and women were nodding their agreement: yes, possessiveness and jealousy were bad, yes, it was wrong to control people, yes, there was nothing wrong with sex, it was pure and beautiful when done in the context of a spiritual relationship, and Robin wondered why they couldn't hear what she was hearing.

Robin wondered whether she was imagining Taio's lopsided blue eyes travelling to her more often than to any of the other listeners, or the slight smirk twisting his small mouth whenever he looked in her direction. Probably she was being paranoid, but she couldn't entirely convince herself she was imagining it. The spotlight didn't flatter Taio: his thick, greasy hair hung about his face like a wig, threw his long, pale, rat-like nose into sharp relief and emphasised his second chin.

Something in Taio's self-assured manner reminded Robin of her middle-aged rapist standing in court, neat in his suit and tie, giving a little laugh as he told the jury he'd been very surprised a young student like Robin had invited him into her hall of residence for sex. He'd explained that he was merely obliging her in strangling her, because she'd said she 'liked it rough'. His words had flowed easily; he was reasonable and rational, and she was the one, he intimated calmly, who'd regretted her unfettered carnality, and decided to put him through the dreadful ordeal of a court case to cover up her own shame. He'd had no problem looking at her in court; he'd glanced at her frequently while giving testimony, a slight smile playing on his lips.

At the end of the session, Taio treated them to an exhibition of the kind of power the pure spirit possessed: he turned his back on them and levitated inches off the stage. Robin saw it with her own eyes, saw his feet leave the floor, his arms rising heavenwards, and then, after ten seconds, saw him fall back to earth with a bang. There were gasps and applause, and Taio grinned at them all, his eyes flickering once more towards Robin.

She wanted to leave the basement as quickly as possible after that, but as she made her way towards the wooden stairs, Taio called her back by name.

'I was watching you,' he said, smirking again as he descended from the stage. 'You didn't like what I was saying.'

'No, I thought it was really interesting,' said Robin, trying to sound cheerful.

'You didn't agree,' said Taio. He was now standing so close to her that she could smell his pungent body odour. 'I think you're finding it hard to let go of the materialist framing of sex. You were engaged, weren't you? And your marriage was called off?'

'Yes,' said Robin.

'So until recently, materialist possession was very attractive to you.'

'I suppose so,' said Robin, 'but I do agree with what you said about control and limiting people—'

Taio now reached out and stroked her cheek. Robin had to resist the impulse to knock his hand away. Smiling, he said,

'I knew you were a Receptive the first time I saw you, in the Rupert Court Temple. "The Receptive is the most devoted of all things in the world." That's from the I Ching. Have you read it?'

'No,' said Robin.

'Some women – the Receptive is female, the Creative male – are constitutionally prone to devoting themselves to one man. That's their nature. Those women can be very valuable church members, but to become pure spirit, they must lose their attachment to material status or any notion of possession. It's not unacceptable to prefer only one man, as long as they're not trying to limit or control him. So there's a way forward for you, but you need to be aware of that tendency in yourself.'

'I will,' said Robin, trying to sound grateful for his input.

Another group of church members came down the stairs, ready for their lecture, and Robin was permitted to leave, but she'd seen the line between Taio's heavy brows deepen as she turned away, and feared her agreement had been insufficiently enthusiastic or, worse, that she ought to have responded physically to his caress.

Others, as she swiftly realised, had already begun to demonstrate their willingness to rise above the material and embrace the spiritual. Several times over the next few days Robin noticed young women, spiky-haired Vivienne included, dropping out of scheduled activities, then reappearing from the direction of the Retreat Rooms, sometimes in the company of a man. She was certain it was a matter of time before she, too, was pressured to join in.

The next destabilising occurrence was Robin's own fault: she went to the plastic rock a night early – at least, Robin thought she'd been a night early, but she had no means of knowing how many extra pebbles she'd picked up, forgetting that she'd already done so earlier in the day. She might, in fact, be as much as forty-eight hours out. Her disappointment at finding no letter from Strike and no chocolate had been severe. Someone from the agency would now have picked up her disappointingly news-less letter, but she didn't dare make another night-time trip before it was absolutely necessary, because of what happened the morning after her premature trip.

She'd been silently overjoyed to hear that her group would be going into Norwich for the first time to collect money for the UHC's many charitable enterprises. This would give her an opportunity to check the date on a newspaper and restart her pebble collecting again from the right day. However, shortly after breakfast, Robin was called aside by a stern-faced woman who'd never spoken to her before.

'Mazu wants you to stay at the farm today,' she said. 'You're to go up to the vegetable patch and help the workers there.'

'Oh,' said Robin, as Becca Pirbright led the rest of her group out of the dining hall, some of them looking curiously back at Robin. 'Er – all right. Should I go there now?'

'Yes,' said the woman curtly, and walked away.

Robin had been at Chapman Farm long enough to recognise the subtle signs that somebody was in disgrace. There were still a few people sitting along the breakfast table from her, and when she glanced towards them, all looked swiftly away. Feeling self-conscious, she got to her feet and carried her empty porridge bowl and glass over to a trolley by the wall.

As she left the dining hall and made her way towards the large vegetable patch, which she'd never worked on before, Robin wondered nervously what she'd done to be demoted from the high-level recruits. Was it her insufficiently enthusiastic response to the concept of spirit bonding? Had Taio been displeased with her reaction to their conversation and reported her to his mother? Or had one of the women in her dormitory reported seeing her leave it by night?

She found several adults planting carrot seeds on the vegetable patch, including the now very heavily pregnant Wan. A number of pre-school children were also there, in their miniature scarlet tracksuits. One of these was the white-headed Qing, who was easy to recognise because of her dandelion clock hair. Only when the man nearest Qing straightened up to his full height did Robin recognise Will Edensor.

'I've been told to come and help,' said Robin.

'Oh,' said Will. 'Right. Well, there are seeds here ...'

He showed her what to do then returned to his own planting.

Robin wondered whether the silence of the other adults was due to her presence. None of them were talking except to the children, who were more hindrance than help, more interested in scooping up the seeds and digging their fingers into the earth than in planting anything.

A strong smell wafted over the vegetable patch, which lay downwind of the pigsty. Robin had been working for a few minutes when Qing toddled over to her. The child had a crudely made toy spade of wood, which she banged on the earth.

'Qing, come here,' said Will. 'Come and help me plant.'

The child struggled away across the damp soil.

As Robin scattered seeds in their furrow, bent double and moving slowly, she watched Will Edensor out of the corner of her eye. This was the first chance she'd had of getting close to him, barring the night-time conversation between him and Lin he didn't know she'd overheard. Young though he was, his hair was already receding, heightening a look of fragility and illness. By speeding up her sowing, she managed, apparently naturally, to reach a spot beside Will as he worked an adjacent furrow with Qing.

'She's yours, isn't she?' she said to Will, smiling. 'She looks like you.'

He threw Robin an irritated glance and muttered,

'There's no "mine". That's materialist possession.'

'Oh, sorry, of course,' said Robin.

'You should've internalised that by now,' said Will sententiously. 'That's kind of basic.'

'Sorry,' said Robin again. 'I keep getting into trouble accidentally.'

'There's no "in trouble",' said Will, in the same critical tone. 'Spiritual demarcation is strengthening.'

'What's spiritual demarcation?' said Robin.

'*The Answer,* chapter fourteen, paragraph nine,' said Will. 'That's kind of basic, too.'

He wasn't bothering to keep his voice down. Robin could tell the other gardeners were listening. One young woman in glasses, who had long, dirty hair and a prominent mole on her chin, was wearing a faint smile.

'If you don't understand why spiritual demarcation's occurred,' Will said, unasked, 'you need to chant or medit— Qing, don't do that,' he said, because the little girl was now digging her wooden spade where he'd just patted down the earth over the seeds. 'Come and get more seeds,' said Will, standing up and leading Qing, hand in hand, towards the box where the packets were sitting.

Robin kept working, wondering at the difference in Will when church elders were present, when he looked hangdog and defeated, and Will here among the farmhands, where he seemed self-assured and dogmatic. She was also quietly reflecting on the young man's hypocrisy. Robin had seen clear signs that Will and Lin were trying to sustain a parental relationship with Qing in defiance of the church's teaching, and the conversation she'd overheard him having with Lin in the woods had proven he was trying to help her avoid spirit bonding with some other man. Robin wondered whether Will was oblivious to the fact that he was transgressing against the precepts of the UHC, or whether the lecturing tone was for the benefit of their listeners.

Almost as though the girl in glasses had read Robin's mind, she said with a strong Norfolk accent,

'You won't win agin Will on church doctrine. 'E knows it insoid out.'

'I wasn't trying to win anything,' said Robin mildly.

Will returned, Qing in tow. Determined to keep him talking, Robin said,

'This is a wonderful place for kids to grow up, isn't it?'

Will merely grunted.

'They'll know the right way from the start – unlike me.'

Will glanced at Robin again, then said,

'It's never too late. The Golden Prophet was seventy-two when she found The Way.'

'I know,' said Robin, 'that sort of gives me comfort. I'll get it if I keep working—'

'It isn't working, it's freeing yourself to discover,' Will corrected her. '*The Answer,* chapter three, paragraph six.'

Robin was starting to understand why Will's brother James found him infuriating.

'Well, that's what I'm trying—'

'You shouldn't be trying. It's a process of allowing.'

'I know, that's what I'm saying,' said Robin, as each of them scattered seeds and patted down the earth, Qing now poking idly at a weed. 'Your little – I mean, *that* little girl – is her name Qing?'

'Yes,' said Will.

'She won't make my mistakes, because she'll be taught to open herself up properly, won't she?'

Will looked up. Their eyes met, Robin's expression deliberately innocent, and Will's face turned slowly scarlet. Pretending she hadn't noticed, Robin returned to her work, saying,

'We had a really good lecture on spirit bonding the other—'

Will got up abruptly and walked back towards the seeds. For the rest of the two hours Robin spent on the vegetable patch, he came nowhere near her.

That night was the first at Chapman Farm in which Robin found it difficult to fall asleep. Recent events had forced her up against one incontrovertible fact: doing what she was in here to do – find out things to the church's discredit, and persuade Will Edensor to reconsider his allegiance – necessarily meant pushing at boundaries. The tactics that had seen her accepted as a full church member had to be abandoned: doglike obedience and apparent indoctrination wouldn't further her aims.

Yet she was scared. She doubted she'd ever be able to communicate to Strike – her touchstone, the person who was keeping her sane – just how intimidating the atmosphere was at Chapman Farm, how frightening it was to know you were surrounded by willing accomplices, or how unnerved she now felt at the prospect of the Retreat Rooms.

51

Nine at the top . . .
There is drinking of wine
In genuine confidence.
No blame.
But if one wets his head,
He loses it, in truth.

The I Ching or Book of Changes

Little though Strike wanted to meet Ryan Murphy for a drink, the Met's lack of action on the matter of the Franks' stalking had underlined the usefulness of personal contacts if you wanted swift action taken on a matter the overstretched police might not consider of immediate importance. As nobody on the force was likely to have a greater interest in establishing whether or not there were guns at Chapman Farm than Murphy, Strike had swallowed his increasing antipathy towards the man. A few days after first contacting him, Strike arrived at St Stephen's Tavern in Westminster to hear what the CID officer had managed to find out.

The last time Strike had entered this particular pub had been with Robin, and as Murphy hadn't yet arrived, he took his pint to the same corner table he and his detective partner had previously sat at, half-aware of a vaguely territorial instinct. The green leather benches echoed those in the House of Commons

491

a short distance away and Strike sat down beneath one of the etched mirrors, resisting the urge to read the menu, because his target weight remained unreached and pub food was one of the things he'd reluctantly decided to forgo.

If he wasn't particularly pleased to see the handsome Murphy, he was glad to see a folder under the man's arm, because this suggested he had research to share that Strike himself was unable to undertake.

'Evening,' said Murphy, having procured for himself a pint of what the eagle-eyed Strike noted with disappointment was alcohol-free beer. The policeman sat down opposite Strike, laid the folder on the table between them and said,

'Had to make quite a few phone calls to get hold of this lot.'

'Norfolk constabulary handled it, presumably?' said Strike, who was only too happy to dispense with personal chat.

'Initially, but Vice Squad got called in once they realised what they were dealing with. It was the biggest paedophile ring broken up in the UK at that point. There were men from up and down the country visiting.'

Murphy extracted a few pages of photocopied photos and handed them to Strike.

'As you can see there, they found plenty of nasty stuff: restraints, gags, sex toys, whips, paddles . . .'

These objects would all have been present, Strike thought, when he, Lucy and Leda had been at the farm, and against his will, a series of fragmented memories forced themselves upon him as he turned the pages: Leda, enthralled by firelight as Malcom Crowther talked of social revolution; the woods where the children ran free, sometimes with the portly Gerald chasing them, sweating and laughing, tickling them until they couldn't breathe if he caught them; and – oh fuck – that small girl curled up and sobbing in the long grass while other, older children asked her what was wrong, and she refused to say . . .

he'd been bored by her . . . he just wanted to leave the squalid, creepy place . . .

'. . . look at page five, though.'

Strike did as he was told and found himself looking at a picture of a black gun.

'Looks like it shoots out a banner saying "Bang".'

'It did,' said Murphy. 'It was in with a load of magic props one of the Crowther brothers had in his house.'

'That'll be Gerald,' said Strike. 'He worked as a kids' entertainer before committing full time to paedophilia.'

'Right. Well, they bagged up everything he had in his house to test it for kids' fingerprints, because he was claiming he'd never had children in there with him.'

'I don't think my source could've confused a prop for the real thing,' said Strike, looking down at the picture of the unconvincing plastic gun. 'She knew Gerald Crowther did magic tricks. What about Rust Andersen, did you get anything on him?'

'Yeah,' said Murphy, extracting another piece of paper from the file, 'he was pulled in and interviewed in '86, same as all the other adults. His house – I say house, but it was more like a glorified shed – was clean. No sex tapes or toys.'

'I don't think he was ever part of the Aylmerton Community proper,' said Strike, casting an eye down Rust Andersen's witness statement.

'That tallies with what's in here,' said Murphy, tapping the folder. 'None of the kids implicated him in the abuse and a couple of them didn't even know who he was.'

'Born in Michigan,' said Strike, skim-reading, 'drafted into the army at eighteen . . .'

'After he got out he went travelling in Europe and never returned to the States. But he can't have brought guns into the UK with the IRA active at the time and tight security at airports. 'Course, there's nothing to say someone at the farm didn't have a permit for a hunting rifle.'

'That occurred to me, too, although my information was "guns", plural.'

'Well, if they were there, they were bloody well hidden, because the Vice Squad virtually tore the place apart.'

'I knew it was a pretty thin thread to hang a raid on,' said Strike, handing Murphy back the papers. 'The mention of guns could've been said for threatening effect.'

Both men drank some beer. A definite air of constraint hung over the table.

'So how much longer d'you reckon you'll need her in there?' asked Murphy.

'Not down to me,' said Strike. 'She can come out whenever she likes, but at the moment, she wants to stay in. Says she's not coming out until she's got something on the church. You know Robin.'

Though not as well as I do.

'Yeah, she's dedicated,' said Murphy.

After a short pause he said,

'Funny, you two going after the UHC. First time I heard of them was five years ago.'

'Yeah?'

'Yeah. I was still in uniform. Bloke drove his car off the road, straight through the window of a Morrisons. Coked out of his head. Kept saying "D'you know who I am?" while I was arresting him. I didn't have a clue. Turned out he'd been a contestant on some reality show I'd never watched. Jacob Messenger, his name was.'

'Jacob?' repeated Strike, slipping his hand into his pocket for his notebook.

'Yeah. He was a real tit, all pecs and fake tan. He hit a woman shopping with her kid. The boy was OK, but the mother was a real mess. Messenger got a year, out in six months. Next I heard of him, he was in the paper because he'd joined the UHC. Trying to burnish up his reputation, you know. He'd seen the light and he was going to be a good boy from now on and here's a picture of me with some disabled kids.'

'Interesting,' said Strike, who'd written much of this down. 'Apparently there's a Jacob at Chapman Farm who's very ill. D'you know what this Messenger's doing now?'

'No idea,' said Murphy. 'So, what's she getting up to in there? She doesn't tell me a lot in her letters.'

'No, well, she won't have got time for duplicate reports, middle of the night in the woods,' said Strike, privately enjoying the fact that Murphy had to ask. He'd resisted looking at the notes Robin had scribbled for Ryan, but been pleased to see they seemed far shorter than his own. 'She's doing well. Seems to have kept her incognito going, no problem. She's already got us a couple of bits of decent information. Nothing we can credibly threaten the church with, though.'

'Tall order, waiting for something criminal to happen right in front of her.'

'If I know Robin,' *which I do, bloody well,* 'she won't just be sitting around for something to happen.'

Both men drank more beer. Strike had an idea Murphy had something he wanted to say and was preparing various robust pushbacks, whether against the suggestion Strike had acted recklessly in sending Robin undercover, or that he'd done so with the intent of messing up her relationship.

'Didn't know you were a mate of Wardle's,' said Murphy. 'He's not a big fan of mine.'

Strike settled for looking non-committal.

'I was a bit of an arsehole one night, in the pub. This is before I stopped drinking.'

Strike made an indeterminate noise somewhere between acknowledgement and agreement.

'My marriage was going tits-up at the time,' said Murphy.

Strike could tell Murphy wanted to know what Wardle had told him, and was enjoying being as inscrutable as possible.

'So what are you going to do now?' asked Murphy, when the continuing silence had told him plainly Strike wasn't going to disclose whatever he knew to Murphy's discredit. 'Tell Robin to go looking for guns?'

'I'll tell her to keep an eye out, certainly,' said Strike. 'Thanks for this, though. Very helpful.'

'Yeah, well, I've got a vested interest in my girlfriend not getting shot,' said Murphy.

Strike noted the nettled tone, smiled, checked his watch and announced that he'd better get going.

He might not have learned much about guns at Chapman Farm, but he felt it had been twenty minutes well spent, nonetheless.

PART FOUR

K'un/Oppression (Exhaustion)

There is no water in the lake:
The image of EXHAUSTION.
Thus the superior man stakes his life
On following his will.

> *The I Ching or Book of Changes*

52

Nine in the second place means . . .
There is some gossip.

The I Ching or Book of Changes

I'm so tired . . . you wouldn't believe how tired I am . . . I just want
to leave . . .

Robin was addressing her detective partner inside her head
while forking manure out of the Shire horses' stable. Five days
had passed since her demotion from the high-level group, but
her relegation to the lowest level of farm workers showed no
sign of being reversed, nor was she any the wiser about what
she'd done to merit punishment. Aside from very brief spells
of chanting in the temple, all of Robin's time was now devoted
to manual labour: looking after livestock, cleaning, or working
in the laundry and kitchens.

A new intake of prospective members had arrived for their
Week of Service, but Robin had nothing to do with them. She
saw them being moved around the farm, doing their different
tasks, but evidently she wasn't considered sufficiently trustworthy to shepherd them around, as Vivienne and Amandeep
were doing.

Those doing hard domestic and farm work received no
more food than those sitting in lectures and seminars, and
had less time to sleep, waking early to collect breakfast eggs

and cleaning dishes every night after dinner for a hundred people. Robin's exhaustion had reached such levels that her hands shook whenever they were free of tools or stacks of plates, shadows flickered regularly in her peripheral vision and every muscle in her body ached as though she were suffering from flu.

Resting for a moment on the handle of her pitchfork – the spring day wasn't particularly warm, but she was sweating nonetheless – Robin looked into the pigsty visible through the stable door, where a couple of very large sows were snoozing in the intermittent sunshine, both covered in mud and faeces, a sulphurous and ammoniac smell wafting over to Robin in the damp air. As she contemplated their naked snouts, tiny eyes and the coarse hair covering their bodies, she remembered that Abigail, Wace's daughter, had once been forced to sleep naked beside them, in all that filth, and felt repulsed.

She could hear voices over on the vegetable patch, where a few people were planting and hoeing. Robin knew for certain now that the scant number of vegetables produced on the patch by the pigsty were there merely to keep up the pretence that church members were living off the land, because she'd seen the cavernous pantry containing shelves of dehydrated noodles, own-brand tinned tomatoes and catering-sized tubs of powdered soup.

Robin had just returned to her mucking-out when a commotion over on the vegetable patch reached her ears. Moving back to the stable entrance, she saw Emily Pirbright and Jiang Wace shouting at each other while the other workers stared, aghast.

'You'll do as you're told!'

'I *won't*,' shouted Emily, who was scarlet in the face.

Jiang attempted to force a hoe into Emily's hands, so forcefully that she staggered back a few paces, yet stood her ground.

'I'm not fucking doing it!' she yelled at Jiang. 'I won't and you can't fucking make me!'

Jiang raised the hoe over Emily's head, advancing on her. A few of those watching shouted 'No!' and Robin, pitchfork in hand, dashed out of the stable.

'Leave her alone!'

'You get back to work!' Jiang shouted at Robin, but he seemed to think better of hitting Emily, instead grabbing her by the wrist and attempting to drag her onto the vegetable patch.

'Fuck off!' she yelled, beating him with her free hand. 'Fuck off, you fucking freak!'

Two of the young men in scarlet tracksuits now hurried to the struggling pair and in a few seconds had managed to persuade Jiang to release Emily, who immediately sprinted around the corner of the stable block and out of sight.

'You're in trouble now!' bellowed Jiang, who was sweating. 'Mama Mazu'll teach you!'

'What happened?' said a voice behind Robin, who turned and saw, with a sinking heart, the bespectacled young woman with the large mole on her chin whom Robin had first met on the vegetable patch. The girl's name was Shawna, and in the last few days Robin had seen far more of her than she'd have liked.

'Emily didn't want to work on the vegetable patch,' said Robin, who was still wondering what could have inspired Emily's act of resistance. However sullen she generally was, from Robin's observation she usually accepted her work stoically.

'She'll pay for that,' said Shawna, with great satisfaction. 'You're coming with me to the clarssrooms. We're taking Clarss One for an hour. Oi got to choose moi own 'elper,' she added proudly.

'What about mucking out the stables?' said Robin.

'One of them can do it,' said Shawna, waving grandly towards the workers on the vegetable patch. 'Come on.'

So Robin propped her pitchfork against the stable wall and followed Shawna out into the misty rain, still pondering Emily's behaviour, which she'd just connected with her refusal to eat vegetables at dinner.

'She's trouble, Emily,' Shawna informed Robin, as they passed the pigsty. 'Yew want to stay away from her.'

'Why's she trouble?' asked Robin.

'Ha ha, that's for me to know,' said Shawna, maddeningly smug.

Given Shawna's lowly status, Robin imagined the eighteen-year-old had very few opportunities to condescend to anyone at Chapman Farm, and she seemed to want to make the most of a rare opportunity. As Robin had found out in the last few days, Shawna's silence during Will Edensor's lecture on church doctrine had been far from representative of the girl's true nature. She was, in fact, an exhausting, non-stop talker.

Over the last few days Shawna had sought Robin out wherever possible, taking it upon herself to test Robin's understanding of various UHC terms, then rewording Robin's answers back to her, usually making definitions less precise or simply wrong. Their conversations had revealed Shawna's belief that the sun rotated around the earth, that the leader of the country was called the Pry Mister and that Papa J was in regular contact with extra-terrestrials, a claim Robin had heard nobody else at Chapman Farm make. Robin didn't think Shawna could read, because she shied away from written material, even instructions on the backs of seed packets.

Shawna had met Papa J through one of the UHC's projects for underprivileged children. Her conversion to believer and church member appeared to have been almost instantaneous, yet key parts of the UHC's teaching had failed to penetrate Shawna's otherwise highly permeable mind. She routinely forgot that nobody was supposed to name family relationships and, in spite of the UHC's insistence that fame and riches were meaningless attributes of the materialist world, evinced a breathless interest in the high-profile visitors to the farmhouse, even speculating on the cost and make of Noli Seymour's shoes.

'Yew hear about Jacob?' she asked Robin, as they passed the old barn where the latter had found the biscuit tin and the Polaroids.

'No,' said Robin, who was still wondering why Emily had such a strong aversion to vegetables.

'Papa J visited with him yesterday.'

'Oh, is he back?'

'He don' need to *come*. 'E can visit people in spirit.'

Shawna looked sideways at Robin through the dirty lenses of her glasses.

'Don'tchew believe me?'

'Of course I do,' said Robin, making an effort to sound convinced. 'I've seen amazing things in here. I saw the Drowned Prophet appear when Papa J summoned her.'

'It's not appearing,' said Shawna, at once. 'It's manny-fisting.'

'Oh, yes, of course,' said Robin.

'Papa J says it's toime for Jacob to pass. The soul's too diseased. 'E won't come roight now.'

'I thought Dr Zhou was helping him?' asked Robin.

''E's done way more'n they do outsoide for someone like Jacob,' said Shawna, echoing Penny Brown, 'but Papa J says there's no point goin' on any more.'

'What exactly's wrong with Jacob?'

''E's marked.'

'He's what?'

'Marked,' whispered Shawna, '*boi the devil.*'

'How can you tell someone's been marked by the devil?' asked Robin.

'Papa J can always tell. There's marked people everywhere. Their souls aren' normal. Some of 'em are in governments, so we gotta weed 'em out.'

'What d'you mean, "weed them out"?'

'Get rid of 'em,' said Shawna, with a shrug.

'How?'

''Owever we 'ave to, because thass one of the ways we'll git the Lotus Way farster. You know what the Lotus Way is, roight?'

Robin started saying that the Lotus Way was a term for the earthly paradise that would descend once the UHC won its battle against the materialist world, and which would segue smoothly into the afterlife, but Shawna interrupted.

'Thar she goes. BP, look.'

Becca Pirbright was crossing the yard ahead of them, her glossy hair shining in the sun. Robin had already overheard mutterings about Becca from the farmhands and kitchen workers. The consensus was that Becca was too young to have ascended so rapidly in the church, and had a very inflated opinion of herself.

'Know why we all call 'er "BP"?'

'Because her initials are the same as a bubble person?' Robin guessed.

'Yeah,' said Shawna, who seemed disappointed Robin had got the joke. 'Gawn,' she muttered scornfully, as Becca kneeled quickly at the fountain of the Drowned Prophet. 'She's always showin' off about 'ow she and Daiyu were mates, but she's lying. Sita told me. Yew know Sita?'

'Yes,' said Robin. She'd met the elderly Sita during her last session in the kitchens.

'She says BP an' Daiyu never loiked each other. Sita can remember all of that, what 'appened.'

'About Daiyu's drowning, you mean?' asked Robin, watching Becca disappear into the temple.

'Yeah, an' all the miracles BP says she saw 'er doin'. Sita dunt reckon BP saw all what she says she did. And Emily's BP's *sister*.'

'Yes, I—'

'We think that's why Papa J won't increase with BP, like she wants.'

'He won't what?' said Robin innocently.

'Increase with her,' said Shawna, as they stopped at Daiyu's pool to kneel and dab their foreheads with water. '*The Drowned Prophet will bless all 'oo worship 'er.* Yew don't know *nuffing,* do yew?' said Shawna, standing up again. 'Increase means 'ave a baby! Oi've 'ad two in 'ere,' said Shawna proudly.

'Two?' said Robin.

'Yeah, one right after I got 'ere, an' 'e went to Birmingham, an' one that's spirit born, so she's gonna be better than the firs' one. We all know BP wants to increase by Papa J, but 'e won't. She's got a disruptive sister and there's Jacob too.'

Thoroughly confused, Robin said,

'What's Jacob got to do with it?'

'Yew don't know *nuffing,* do yew?' said Shawna again, chuckling.

They passed under the archway to the area where the children's dormitory and classrooms were and entered a door numbered one.

The classroom was a ramshackle, shabby space with children's pictures pinned haphazardly on the walls. Twenty small children in scarlet tracksuits were already sitting at the tables, their ages, Robin guessed, between two and five. She was surprised that there weren't more of them, given that there were a hundred people at the farm having unprotected sex, but was primarily struck by their strange passivity. Their eyes wandered, their faces blank, and very few were fidgeting, the exception being little Qing, who was currently crouched under her desk pressing blobs of plasticine onto the floor, her mop of white hair contrasting with the rest of the class's buzz cuts.

On Robin and Shawna's appearance, the woman who'd been reading to them got to her feet with an appearance of relief.

'We're on page thirty-two,' she told Shawna, handing over the book. Shawna waited until the woman had closed the classroom door before throwing the book down on the teacher's desk and saying.

'Orlroight, less get 'em started on somefing.'

She took up a pile of colouring sheets.

'Yew can do us a nice picture of a prophet,' she informed the class, and she passed half the pile to Robin to hand out. 'Thass mine,' Shawna added carelessly, pointing to a colourless shrimp of a girl, before barking 'git back on yer chair!' at Qing, who started to wail. 'Ignore 'er,' Shawna advised Robin. 'She's gotta learn, that one.'

So Robin handed out colouring sheets, all of which featured a line drawing of a prophet of the UHC. The Stolen Prophet's noose, which Robin might have expected to be omitted from colouring pictures for such young children, hung proudly around his neck. When she passed Qing's desk she surreptitiously bent down, prised the plasticine off the floor and handed it back to the little girl, whose tears somewhat abated.

Moving among the children to offer encouragement and sharpen pencils, Robin found herself still more disturbed by their behaviour. Now that she paid them individual attention, they were unnervingly ready to be affectionate to her, even though she was a complete stranger. One little girl climbed into Robin's lap unasked; others played with her hair or cuddled her arm. Robin found their craving for the kind of loving closeness that was forbidden by the church pitiful and distressing.

'Stop that,' Shawna told Robin from the front of the class. 'Thass material possessiveness.'

So Robin gently disengaged herself from the clinging children and moved instead to examine some of the pictures pinned up on the wall, some of which had clearly been drawn by older students, as their subject matter was discernible. Most depicted daily life at Chapman Farm, and she recognised the tower like a giant chess piece which was visible on the horizon.

One picture caught Robin's attention. It was captioned *Aks Tre* and showed a large tree with what appeared to be a hatchet drawn on the base of its trunk. She was still looking at this picture, which had evidently been drawn recently given the freshness of the paper, when the classroom door opened behind her.

Turning, Robin saw Mazu, who was wearing long scarlet robes. Total silence fell inside the classroom. The children appeared frozen.

'I sent Vivienne to the stables to fetch Rowena,' said Mazu quietly, 'and I was told you'd removed her from the task I set her.'

'Oi was told I could choose moi own helper,' said Shawna, who looked suddenly terrified.

'From your *own group*,' said Mazu. Her calm voice belied the expression of her thin white face with its crooked near-black eyes. 'Not from any other group.'

'Oi'm sorry,' whispered Shawna. 'I thort—'

'You can't think, Shawna. You've proven that time and again. But you'll be made to think.'

Mazu's gaze ranged over the seated children, alighting on Qing.

'Cut her hair,' she told Shawna. 'I'm tired of seeing that mess. Rowena,' she said, now looking directly at Robin for the first time, 'come with me.'

53

A yang line develops below two yin lines and presses upward forcibly. This movement is so violent that it arouses terror . . .

The I Ching or Book of Changes

Light-headed with fear, Robin crossed the classroom and followed Mazu outside. She wanted to apologise, to tell Mazu she'd had no idea she was transgressing by agreeing to accompany Shawna to the classroom, but she feared unwittingly making her predicament worse.

Mazu paused, a few steps outside the classroom, and turned to look at Robin, who also halted. This was physically the closest the two women had ever been and Robin now realised that, like Taio, Mazu didn't seem to care much for washing. She could smell her body odour, which was poorly masked by a heavy incense perfume. Mazu said nothing, but simply looked at Robin with her dark, crookedly set eyes, and the latter felt obliged to break the silence.

'I – I'm really sorry. I didn't realise Shawna didn't have the authority to take me from the stables.'

Mazu continued to stare at her without speaking, and Robin again felt a strange, visceral fear tinged with revulsion that couldn't be entirely explained away by the power the woman held in the church. Niamh Doherty had described Mazu as a large spider; Robin herself had seen her as some malign, slimy thing lurking in a rockpool; yet neither quite captured her strangeness. Robin felt now as though she was staring into a yawning abyss of which the depths were unseeable.

She assumed Mazu expected something more than an apology, but Robin had no idea what it was. Then she heard a rustle of fabric. Glancing down, she saw that Mazu had raised the hem of her robe a few inches to reveal a dirty, sandalled foot. Robin looked back up into those strange, mismatched eyes. A hysterical impulse to laugh rose in her – Mazu couldn't, surely, be expecting Robin to kiss her foot, as the girls who'd let the toddler escape from the dormitory had done? – but it died at the look on Mazu's face.

For perhaps five seconds, Robin and Mazu stared at each other, and Robin knew this was a test, and that to ask aloud whether Mazu genuinely wanted this tribute would be as dangerous as revealing her disgust or her incredulity.

Just do it.

Robin knelt, bent quickly over the foot, with its black toenails, grazed it with her lips and then stood up again.

Mazu gave no sign that she'd even noticed the tribute, but dropped her robes and walked on as though nothing had happened.

Robin felt shaken and humiliated. She glanced around to see whether anyone had witnessed what had just happened. She tried to imagine what Strike would say, if he'd seen her, and felt another wave of embarrassment pass over her. How could she ever explain why she'd done it? He'd think she was mad.

At Daiyu's pool, Robin knelt and mumbled the usual observance. Beside her, Mazu said in a low voice,

'Bless me, my child, and may your righteous punishment fall upon all who stray from The Way.'

Mazu then got up, still without looking at or speaking to Robin, and headed towards the temple. With an upsurge of panic, Robin followed, with a presentiment of what was about to happen. Sure enough, on entering the temple, Robin saw all her former high-level associates, including Amandeep, Walter, Vivienne and Kyle, sitting in a circle on chairs set upon the shining black pentagon-shaped stage. All looked stern. With an increase of her awful foreboding, Robin saw that Taio Wace was also present.

'Rowena had taken it upon herself to do a different task to the one she was assigned, which is why you couldn't find her, Vivienne,' said Mazu, climbing the stairs to the stage and sitting down in a free seat, spreading out her glittering blood red robes as she did so. 'She has paid the tribute of humility, but we will now find out whether that was an empty gesture. Move your chair into the centre of the circle, please, Rowena. Welcome to Revelation.'

Robin picked up an empty chair and moved it to the centre of the black stage, beneath which lay the deep, dark baptismal pool. She sat down and tried to still her legs, which were shaking, by pressing down on them with palms that had become damp.

The temple lights began to dim, leaving only a spotlight on the stage. Robin couldn't remember the lights being lowered for any of the other Revelation sessions.

Get a grip, she told herself. She tried to picture Strike grinning at her, but it didn't work: the present was too real, closing in upon her, even as the faces and figures of those surrounding her grew indistinct in the dark, and her lips were tingling strangely, as though contact with Mazu's foot had left some acidic residue.

Mazu pointed a long, pale finger and the temple doors banged closed behind Robin, making her jump.

'A reminder,' said Mazu calmly, addressing those in the circle, 'Primal Response Therapy is a form of spiritual cleansing. In this safe, holy space, we use words from the materialist world to counter materialist ideas and behaviours. There will be a purging, not only of Rowena, but of ourselves, as we unearth and dispatch terms we no longer use, but which still linger in our subconsciousness.'

Robin saw the dark figures around her nodding. Her mouth was completely dry.

'So, Rowena,' said Mazu, whose face was so pale that Robin could still make it out, with those dark, crookedly set eyes shining. 'This is the moment for you to confess to things you may have done, or thought, about which you feel deep shame. What would you like to reveal first?'

For what felt like a long time, though was doubtless only seconds, Robin couldn't think of anything to say at all.

'Well,' she began at last, her voice sounding unnaturally loud in the silent temple, 'I used to work in PR and I suppose there was a lot of focus on appearances and what other people—'

The end of her sentence was drowned in an outbreak of jeering from the circle.

'False self!' barked Walter.

'Deflecting,' said a female voice.

'You can't blame your profession for *your* behaviour,' said Amandeep.

Robin's thought processes were sluggish after days of manual labour. She needed something that would satisfy her inquisitors, but her panicked mind was blank.

'Nothing to say?' said Mazu, and Robin could just make out her yellowish teeth in the gloom as she smiled. 'Well, let's see whether we can find a way in. Since entering our community, you felt entitled to criticise the colour of my hair, didn't you?'

There was an intake of breath all around the circle. Robin felt a wave of cold sweat pass over her. Was this why she'd been demoted to farm worker? Because she'd wondered to Penny Brown why Mazu's hair was still jet black in her forties?

'What,' said Mazu, speaking now to the rest of the circle, 'would you call somebody who judged another person's looks?'

'Spiteful,' said a voice out of the darkness.

'Shallow,' said a second.

'Bitch,' said a third.

'I'm sorry,' Robin said hoarsely, 'I honestly didn't mean to—'

'No, no, there's no need to apologise to *me*,' said Mazu softly. '*I* set no store on physical appearance. But it's an indication, isn't it, of what you think is important?'

'Judge people's looks a lot, do you?' asked a female voice from behind Robin.

'I – I suppose—'

'"Suppose" is obfuscatory,' snarled Kyle.

'You either do or you don't,' said Amandeep.

'Then – I did,' said Robin. 'When I worked in PR, there was a tendency—'

'Never mind tendencies,' boomed Walter. 'Never mind PR! What did *you* do? What did *you* say?'

'I remember saying a client looked too big for her dress,' invented Robin, 'and she heard me and I felt terrible about it.'

A storm of jeering broke over her. Taio, who was sitting beside his mother, was the only person remaining silent, but he was smiling as he watched Robin.

'*Did* you feel terrible, Rowena?' asked Mazu quietly. 'Or are you just giving us token examples, to avoid admitting to real shame?'

'I—'

'Why was your wedding called off, Rowena?'

'I – we were arguing a lot.'

'Whose fault was that?' demanded Vivienne.

'Mine,' said Robin desperately.

'What did you argue about?' asked Amandeep.

There shouldn't be any points of resemblance between your own life and Rowena's, Strike had said, but he wasn't here, stupefied by tiredness and fear, forced to come up with a story on the spot.

'I ... thought my fiancé was kind of ... he didn't have a proper job, wasn't earning much ...'

She was reversing the truth: it was Matthew who'd complained about her poor salary when she'd started working for Strike, Matthew who'd thought private detection a joke of a career.

The rest of the group began to call her names, their voices echoing off the dark walls, and Robin could make out only a few individual words: *mercenary fucking bitch, gold-digger, greedy slag*. Taio's smile was broadening.

'Tell us *specifically* what you said to your fiancé,' demanded Walter.

'That his boss was taking advantage of him—'

'The *exact* words.'

'"She's taking advantage of you", "she's only keeping you on because you're cheap"—'

While they jeered at and insulted her, she dredged her memory for the things Matthew had said about Strike during their marriage.

'—"she fancies you", "it's a matter of time before she makes a move"—'

Now the surrounding circle began to shout.

'Controlling cow!'

'Jealous, self-centred—'

'Stuckup, selfish bitch!'

'Go on,' Mazu said to Robin.

'—and he loved the job,' said Robin, her mouth now so dry her lips were sticking to her teeth, 'and I made it as hard as I could for him to continue with it—'

The shouts became louder, echoing off the temple walls. In the dim light she could see fingers pointing at her, flashes of teeth, and still Taio smiled. Robin knew she was supposed to cry, that mercy came only once the person in the middle of the circle had broken down, but even though she could now see little dots of light popping in front of her eyes, something stubborn in her resisted.

Now the circle demanded the excavation of intimate details and ugly scenes. Robin embellished scenes from her marriage, reversing her and Matthew's positions: now it was she who'd thought her partner was taking too many risks.

'What risks?' demanded Amandeep. 'What was his job?'

'He was kind of—'

But Robin couldn't think: what risky job could her imaginary partner have had?

'—I don't mean physical risks, it was more that he was sacrificing our financial security—'

'Money's very important to you, isn't it, Rowena?' called Mazu, over the continuing abuse of the circle.

'I suppose it was before I came here—'

The slurs became more derisory: the group didn't believe that she'd changed. Mazu let the insults roll over Robin for a full minute. Voices echoed off the dark walls, calling her worthless, pathetic, a craven snob, a narcissist, a materialist, contemptible—

Out of the corner of her eye, she saw something white and glowing high above her on the balcony running round the temple. Vivienne screamed and rose from her seat, pointing.

'Look! *Look!* Up there! A little girl, looking down at us! I *saw* her!'

'That will be Daiyu,' said Mazu calmly, glancing up at the now empty balcony. 'She manifests sometimes when psychic energy is particularly strong. Or she may have come as a warning.'

Silence fell. The group was unsettled. Some continued to stare up at the balcony, others glanced over their shoulders, as though they feared the spirit would come closer. Robin seemed to feel the dull thud of her heart in her throat.

'What finally made your fiancé end the relationship, Rowena?' asked Mazu.

Robin opened her mouth, then closed it. She couldn't, wouldn't, use Matthew as her model here. She refused to pretend she'd slept with someone else.

'Come on!' barked Walter. 'Out with it!'

'She's trying to invent something,' sneered Vivienne.

'Tell us the truth!' said Amandeep, his eyes shining through his glasses, 'Nothing but the truth!'

'I lied to him,' said Robin hoarsely. 'His mother died, and I lied about being able to get back in time to help with the funeral, because there was something I wanted to do at work.'

'You selfish, self-centred bitch,' spat Kyle.

'You piece of shit,' said Vivienne.

Hot tears burst from Robin's eyes. She doubled over, feigning nothing. Her shame was real: she really had lied to Matthew as she'd described, and she'd felt guilty about it for months afterwards. The cacophony of insults and taunts of the group continued until Robin heard, with a thrill of terror, a high-pitched childish voice joining in, louder than all of the others.

'You're *nasty*. You're a *nasty* person.'

The stage tilted. With a shriek, Robin fell sideways off her chair as it tipped over. The rest of the circle were also thrown off balance: they, too, fell off their lurching chairs, Walter crashing to the ground with a yell of pain. Kyle's chair leg caught Robin on the shoulder as she slid across the smooth surface of the tipping lid, preventing herself from falling into the sliver of black water revealed beneath only by throwing out her arm and pushing against the rim of the pool.

'Oh my God, oh my God,' whimpered Vivienne, scrambling to reach the foot-wide rim of the stage, where Mazu and Taio stood, untroubled.

Everyone was fighting to make their way off the slippery, tilted surface: all seemed to have a horror of slipping into the dark water, welcoming as it had seemed during their baptisms. Most of the group helped each other, but no hands were offered to Robin, who had to heave herself onto the ledge of the pool alone, her shoulder smarting where Kyle's chair had hit it. When everyone had got off the tilted stage, Mazu waved her hand. The lid covering the water moved gently back into place and the temple lights went up.

'Daiyu's very sensitive to certain kinds of wickedness,' said Mazu, her dark eyes on Robin, who stood tear stained and breathless. 'She had no funeral herself, and so she's particularly sensitive about the sanctity of rituals surrounding death.'

Though most of Robin's group mates looked merely frightened, and continued to peer around them for a further sign of Daiyu, a few were looking accusingly at Robin. She couldn't find her voice to say that she had, in fact, attended Matthew's mother's funeral. She was certain any attempt at self-defence would make things worse.

'We'll end Revelation here,' said Mazu. 'When Daiyu manifests in the temple, things can become dangerous. You may leave for lunch.'

Robin turned to leave, but before she'd taken a step towards the temple doors, a hand closed around her upper arm.

54

Six in the second place
Difficulties pile up . . .
He wants to woo when the time comes.
The maiden is chaste,
She does not pledge herself.

The I Ching or Book of Changes

'You're all right now,' said a low voice in Robin's ear, as Mazu swept past. 'It's over. You did well.'

Robin turned, realised it was Taio Wace who'd taken hold of her, and wrenched her arm free. His expression darkened.

'Sorry,' said Robin, mopping her tearstained face on her sleeve. 'I – thank you—'

'That's better.'

Taio replaced his hand around her upper arm, the knuckles pressing into her breast, and this time, Robin didn't resist.

'Revelation's always difficult, the first time you do it,' said Taio.

Robin permitted him to lead her out of the temple, trying to stem the streaming of her nose with her free forearm. Mazu had disappeared, but the rest of the group was now heading for Daiyu's pool. They threw furtive glances at Taio and Robin as they crossed the courtyard without stopping.

It wasn't until he led her down the passage between the

men's and women's dormitories, which was so familiar to her from her nocturnal journeys into the woods, that Robin realised where he was leading her. Sure enough, moments later they were pushing through the bushes that screened the Retreat Rooms. Robin had a split second to decide what to do: she was certain there'd be no going back if she pulled away from Taio, that her status would plummet to a point from which there'd be no recovery. She also knew Strike would advise freeing herself and leaving immediately; she could see her partner's expression now, hear his anger that she hadn't taken his warnings, and she remembered assuring him that the UHC only used emotional coercion, that there was no possibility of rape.

The glass door of the nearest Retreat Room slid open. Author Giles Harmon stood there, wearing a velvet jacket, his hand still on the flies he'd clearly just zipped up, his dandyish hair silver in the midday sunshine.

'Giles,' said Taio, sounding surprised and none too pleased.

'Ah, hello, Taio,' said Harmon, smiling.

There was a small movement in the cabin behind Harmon and to Robin's horror, Lin emerged, looking dishevelled and slightly sick. Without meeting anyone's eyes she walked quickly away.

'I didn't know you were here,' said Taio, maintaining his hold on Robin's upper arm.

'Arrived this morning,' said Harmon, who seemed untroubled by Taio's tone. 'I've spotted a marvellous opportunity. The British Association of Creatives is looking for sponsorship for their Ethics and Art project. If the UHC were minded to, I think we could broker a really fruitful partnership.'

'That'll need discussion by the Council,' said Taio.

'I've emailed Papa J,' said Harmon, 'but I know he's busy, so I thought I'd come down here and talk over the practicalities with you and Mazu. Thinking of staying a few days,' he said, theatrically breathing in the country air. 'Such a blissful change after London.'

'OK, well, we can talk in the farmhouse later,' said Taio.

'Oh, of course, of course,' said Harmon, with a small smile, and for the first time his eyes alighted briefly on Robin. 'See you there.'

Harmon walked away, humming to himself.

'Come on,' said Taio, and he tugged Robin into the cabin Harmon and Lin had just vacated.

The dingy, wood-walled interior was roughly fifteen feet square and dominated by a double bed covered with a much-stained and crumpled sheet. Two grubby pillows lay on the floor and a naked lightbulb hung from its flex over the bed. The shed-like smell of pine and dust mingled with a strong odour of unwashed human.

As Taio pulled a thin curtain over the sliding glass doors, Robin blurted,

'I can't.'

'Can't what?' said Taio, turning to face her. His scarlet tracksuit top stretched over his large belly, he smelled stale; his hair was greasy and his pointed nose and small mouth had never seemed more rat-like.

'You know what,' said Robin. 'I just can't.'

'This'll make you feel better,' said Taio, now advancing on her. 'Much better.'

He reached for her, but Robin threw out a hand, holding him at arm's length with as much force as she'd used to prevent herself falling into the baptismal pool. He tried to push past it, but when she continued to resist he took half a step backwards. Evidently some wariness of the law beyond Chapman Farm lingered in him, and Robin, still determined to remain at the centre if she could, said,

'It isn't right. I'm not worthy.'

'I'm a Principal. I decide who's worthy and who isn't.'

'I shouldn't be here!' said Robin, allowing herself to start crying again and adding a hysterical note to her voice. 'You heard me, in the temple. It's all true, all of it. I'm bad, I'm rotten, I'm impure—'

'Spirit bonding purifies,' said Taio, again trying to push past her resisting hands. 'You'll feel much better for this. Come—'

He attempted to take her in his arms.

'*No,*' gasped Robin, wriggling free of him to stand with her back to the glass doors. 'You can't want to be with me now you've heard what I'm like.'

'You need this,' said Taio insistently. 'Here.'

He sat down on the grubby bed and patted the space beside him. Robin exaggerated her distress, crying still more loudly, her wails echoing off the wooden walls, her nose running freely, taking deep gasps of air as though she might be on the verge of a panic attack.

'Control yourself!' commanded Taio.

'I don't know what I've done wrong, I'm being punished and I don't know why, I can't get any of it right, I've got to go—'

'*Come here,*' said Taio more insistently, again patting the bed.

'I wanted to do this, I really believed, but I'm not what you're looking for, I realise that now—'

'That's your false self talking!'

'It isn't, it's my honest self—'

'You're currently demonstrating high levels of egomotivity,' said Taio harshly. 'You think you know better than I do. *You don't.* This is why you drove away your fiancé, because you couldn't subsume your ego. You learned all this in lectures: there is no self, only fragments of the whole. You must surrender to the group, to union . . . *sit down,*' he added forcefully, but Robin remained standing.

'I want to leave. I want to go.'

She was gambling on the fact that Taio Wace wouldn't want to be responsible for her leaving. She was supposed to be rich and was definitely articulate and educated, which meant she might be taken seriously if she talked about her negative experiences of the church. Most importantly, she'd just witnessed a well-known writer leaving a Retreat Room with a girl who looked barely over-age.

The naked light falling from the overhead bulb highlighted Taio's rat-like nose and dirty hair. After a moment or two's silence he said coldly,

'You underwent spiritual demarcation because you've fallen behind the other recruits.'

'How?' said Robin, injecting a note of desperation into her voice and still failing to wipe her nose, because she wanted to repel Taio as much as possible. 'I've tried—'

'You make disruptive statements, like that comment about Mazu's hair. You haven't fully integrated, you've failed in simple duties to the church—'

'Like what?' said Robin in genuine anger, every inch of her body sore after long days of manual labour.

'Relinquishment of materialist values.'

'But I—'

'Step three to pure spirit: *divestment*.'

'I don't—'

'Everyone else who joined with you has made donations to the church.'

'I wanted to,' lied Robin, 'but I didn't know how!'

'Then you should have asked. Non-materialists offer freely, they don't wait for forms or invoices. *They offer.* Wipe your nose, for God's sake.'

Robin deliberately smeared the snot across her face with her sleeve and gave a loud, wet sniff.

'"I live to love and give",' quoted Taio. 'You were Typed as a Gift-Bearer, like the Golden Prophet, but you're hoarding your resources instead of sharing them.'

As he said it, his eyes rolled down her body to her breasts.

'And I know you've got no physical hang-ups about sex,' he added, with the ghost of a smirk. 'Apparently, you orgasm every time.'

'I think I should go to temple,' said Robin a little wildly. 'The Blessed Divinity's telling me to chant, I can feel it.'

She knew she'd angered and offended him, and that he didn't believe any divinity was speaking to her; but he was the one who'd conducted seminars in the basement room about opening the mind and heart to the divine force, and to contradict her was to undermine words he himself had spoken. Perhaps, too, his desire had been quenched by her deliberate smearing of snot over her face, because after a few seconds he got slowly to his feet.

'I think you'd do better to perform penance to the community,' he said. 'Fetch cleaning products from the kitchen, fresh sheets from the laundry and muck out these three Retreat Rooms.'

He ripped back the curtain, slid back the glass door and left.

Weak with immediate relief, yet full of dread of what harm she might have done in refusing him, Robin leaned for a moment against the wall, cleaned her face as best she could with her sweatshirt, then glanced around.

A tap was fixed to the wall in a corner, with a short length of hose attached and a drain hole beneath it. A slimy bottle of liquid soap and a dirty wet flannel stood beside the hole on a patch of mildewed floorboard. Presumably people washed themselves before having sex. Trying to dismiss a horrible mental image of Taio lathering his erection before joining her on the bed, Robin set off to find a bucket and mop. However, as she emerged from the bushes screening the Retreat Rooms from the courtyard, she stumbled to a halt.

Emily Pirbright was standing alone in front of the Drowned Prophet's fountain, on a wooden crate. Her head was bowed and she was holding a piece of cardboard on which words had been written.

Robin didn't want to approach the pool with Emily standing there, but she feared being punished if she was seen failing to make her tribute to Daiyu. Pretending she couldn't even see Emily, she advanced on the fountain, but almost against her will her eyes were drawn to the silent figure.

Emily's face and hair had been smeared with earth, as had her scarlet tracksuit. She was staring at the ground, as determinedly insensible of Robin's presence as the latter had meant to be of Emily's.

The words scrawled on the cardboard sign held between Emily's mud-stained hands read: *I AM A DIRTY PIG.*

55

Heaven and earth do not unite . . .
Thus the superior man falls back upon his inner worth
In order to escape the difficulties.

The I Ching or Book of Changes

. . . and Tao took me into one of the [illegible] rooms and wanted Spirit bonding but I managed to fend him off. Giles Harman had just been in there with Lin. She's barely of age, might be underage, I don't know.

Emily and [illegible] (can't remember if I told you about her, she's quite ~~yung~~ young) have been punished for disobedence. Emily had to stand on a crate with a sign saying she was a dirty pig but Shawna just [illegible] and came back 48 hours & looked terrible.

I found out why I've been [illegible] from top group. It's because I haven't given any money. I'll have to go to Mazu and offer a donation, but how do we [illegible] this, can you think of anything because it's the only way I'm going to be able to stay.

I was also in the little kids' classroom for the first time and they're not right, brainwashed and strange, it's horrible.

Shawna says Becca Pirbright is lying about her [illegible] with Daiyu. I'm going to try and find out more. Think that's everyting. Shawna also said [illegible] about Jacob being the

*reason Papa J won't have kids with Becca. She also says
Jacob's [illegible] by the devil.*

   R x

   *I forgot, there's a picture of a tree with axe in it on the
kid's [illegible], looks recent I'll try and find it if I can
but its hard to think up a reason to come into the woods by
daylight.*

Strike, who was sitting at the partners' desk in the office,
read Robin's letter through twice, noting the deterioration
of her handwriting and misspellings. This was the first of
her reports to contain concrete leads, not to mention information the church definitely wouldn't want made public,
but his expression betrayed no pleasure; on the contrary, he
was frowning as he re-read the line about spirit bonding.
Hearing footsteps he said, eyes still on the page,

'Bit worried about her.'

'Why?' asked Pat in her usual baritone, setting a mug down
beside Strike.

'Sorry, thought you were Midge,' said Strike. The subcontractor had just handed him the letter, which she'd retrieved
overnight.

'She had to go, she's on the Franks. What's wrong with
Robin?'

'Exhaustion and underfeeding, probably. Cheers,' he added,
picking up his tea.

'Ryan just called,' said Pat.

'Who? Oh, Murphy?'

'He wanted to know whether he's had a message from
Robin.'

'Yeah, he has,' said Strike, handing the folded paper over.
He'd resisted reading it, but had been glad to see through the
back of the paper that it looked as though it only comprised

two or three lines. 'Don't tell him I said I'm worried about Robin,' Strike added.

'Why would I?' said Pat, scowling. 'And you've had some voicemail messages. One at nine o'clock last night, from a man called Lucas Messenger. He says he's Jacob's brother.'

'Shit,' said Strike, who was now ignoring all office phone calls that diverted to his mobile in the evening, on the assumption they were from Charlotte. 'OK, I'll call him back.'

'And three more from the same woman,' said Pat, her expression austere, 'all early hours of the morning. She didn't give her name, but—'

'Delete them,' said Strike, reaching for his phone.

'I think you should listen to them.'

'Why?'

'She gets threatening.'

They looked at each other for a few seconds. Strike broke eye contact first.

'I'll call Messenger, then I'll listen to them.'

When Pat had closed the door to the outer office, Strike called Lucas Messenger. After a few rings, a male voice said,

'Yeah?'

'Cormoran Strike here. You left a message for me yesterday evening.'

'Oh—' A slight distortion on the line told Strike he'd been switched to speakerphone. 'You're the detective, yeah? What's Jacob done? Driven froo annuver window?'

Strike heard a few background sniggers and surmised that Lucas was sharing the conversation with workmates.

'I'm trying to find out where he is.'

'Why d'you wanna know? What's he done?'

'Did your brother join the Universal Humanitarian Church?'

The laughter on the other end of the line was louder this time.

'He did, yeah. Twat.'

'And where is he now?'

'Germany, I fink. We're not in touch. He's me half-brother. We don't get on.'

'When did he go to Germany, do you know?'

'Dunno, some time last year?'

'Was this a UHC thing? Was he sent to the centre in Munich?'

'Nah, I fink he met a girl. He's full of it, I don't listen to half what he tells me.'

'Would your parents know where Jacob is?'

'They're not talking to him neither. They had a row.'

'Can you think of anyone who might be in contact with Jacob?'

'No,' said Lucas. 'Like I say, we don't get on.'

This being the extent of Lucas' information, Strike hung up a minute later having written only the words *Jacob Messenger Germany?* on his notepad. Turning in his swivel chair, he looked up at the board on the wall onto which he'd pinned various pictures and notes concerning the UHC case.

In a column on the left-hand side were pictures of people Strike was still trying to locate. At the top were the pictures of the girl who'd variously called herself Carine, Cherie and Cherry, and a printout of the Facebook profile of Carrie Curtis Woods, who he hoped might prove to be the same person.

Beneath Cherie's pictures was a photo of dark-haired and tanned Jacob Messenger, who stood posing on a beach in his swimming shorts, tensing his abdominal muscles and beaming at the camera. Strike now knew Messenger's brief flicker of fame had peaked when he came third on a reality show, for which this was a publicity picture. Jacob's trial and imprisonment for driving under the influence had put his name back in the papers, and his last press appearance had featured photos of him at a UHC addiction services clinic, wearing a tight white T-shirt with the UHC's logo on it, and announcing how much he'd gained from joining the church. Since then, he'd disappeared from public view.

Strike got to his feet, tore out the page with *Jacob Messenger Germany?* written on it and pinned it beside the young man's photo, before picking up Robin's letter again and re-reading the lines about Jacob. *Shawna also said something about Jacob being the reason Papa J won't have kids with Becca. I didn't understand that, will try and find out more. She says Jacob's [illegible] by the devil.* Frowning slightly, Strike looked from the letter to the picture of beaming Jacob, with his tropical print swimming trunks and bright white teeth, wondering whether Messenger was indeed the Jacob lying ill at Chapman Farm, and if so, how this fact could possibly relate to Jonathan Wace's lack of interest in having children with Becca Pirbright.

His gaze moved to the next picture in the left-hand column: the faded photo of bespectacled Deirdre Doherty. In spite of Strike's best efforts, he still hadn't found any trace of Deirdre online or off.

The bottom picture on the left-hand side of the board was a drawing: Torment Town's strange depiction of a fair-haired woman in glasses floating in a dark pool. Strike was still trying to find the true identity of Torment Town, who'd finally responded to his online message.

To Strike's comment, *Amazing pictures. Do you draw from imagination?* the anonymous artist had written:

Thanks. Kind of.

Strike had replied:

You're really talented. You should do a comic book. Horror.

To which Torment Town had responded,

Nobody would want to read that lol

Strike had then said,

You really don't like the UHC, do you?

But to this, Torment Town had made no reply. Strike was afraid he'd come to the point too quickly and regretted, not for the first time, that he couldn't set Robin to work on extracting confidences out of whoever had drawn these pictures. Robin was good at building trust online, as she'd proven when she'd persuaded a teenager to give her vital information in one of their previous cases.

Strike closed Pinterest and opened Facebook instead. Carrie Curtis Woods still hadn't accepted his follower request.

With a sigh, he pushed himself reluctantly up from his chair, and carried his mug of tea and vape pen into the outer office, where Pat sat typing, e-cigarette clamped between her teeth as usual.

'All right,' Strike said, sitting down on the red sofa opposite Pat's desk, 'let's hear these threats.'

Pat pressed a button on her desk phone, and Charlotte's voice, slurred with drink as Strike had expected, filled the room.

''S me, pick up, you fucking coward. *Pick up . . .*'

A few moments' silence, then Charlotte's voice came almost in a shout.

'OK, then, I'll leave a fucking message for your precious fucking *Robin* to hear when she picks up your messages, before giving you your morning blow job. I was there when your leg got blown off, even though we were split up, I stayed with you an' I visit'd you ev'ry single day, an' I gave you a place to stay when your whole shitty family gave up on you, and ev'ryone around me saying, "You know he's on the make" an' "What're you doing, he's an abusive shit?" an' I wouldn't listen, even after *ev'rything you'd done to me,* I was there for you, an' now when I need a friend you can't even fucking meet me fr'a coffee when I've got fucking cancer, you fucking *leech*, you *user*, an' I'm still protecting you to the fucking press even though I could tell them things that'd fucking *finish* you, I could *finish you* if I told them, and why should I be fucking loyal wh—'

A loud beep cut the message off. Pat's expression was impassive. There was a click, then a second message began.

'Pick up. *Fucking pick up*, you cowardly bastard ... after *everything you did to me*, you expect me to defend you to the press. You walked out after I miscarried, you fucking *threw me across that fucking boat*, you fucked every girl that moved when we were together, does precious Robin know what she's letting hersel—'

This time there was no beep: Pat had slammed her hand onto a button on the phone, silencing voicemail. Littlejohn's silhouette had appeared outside the frosted glass in the door onto the stairwell. The door opened.

'Morning,' said Strike.

'Morning,' said Littlejohn, looking down at Strike through his heavy-lidded eyes. 'Need to file my report on Toy Boy.'

Strike watched in silence as Littlejohn retrieved the file from the drawer and added a couple of sheets of notes. Pat had begun typing again, e-cigarette waggling between her teeth, ignoring both men. When Littlejohn had replaced the file in the drawer, he turned to Strike and for the first time in their acquaintance, initiated conversation.

'Think you should know, I might be being followed.'

'Followed?' repeated Strike, eyebrows raised.

'Yeah. Pretty sure I've seen the same guy watching me, three days apart.'

'Any reason someone would be watching you?'

'No,' said Littlejohn, with a trace of defiance.

'Nothing you're not telling me?'

'Like what?' said Littlejohn.

'Wife not planning a divorce? Creditors trying to track you down?'

''Course not,' said Littlejohn. 'I thought it might be something to do with this place.'

'What, the agency?' said Strike.

'Yeah ... made a few enemies along the way, haven't you?'

'Yeah,' said Strike, after a sip of tea, 'but they're nearly all in jail.'

'You tangled with terrorists last year,' said Littlejohn.

'What did the person watching you look like?' asked Strike.

'Skinny black guy.'

'Probably not a neo-Nazi, then,' said Strike, making a mental note to tell Shanker the skinny black guy would need replacing.

'Could be press,' said Littlejohn. 'That *Private Eye* story about you.'

'Think they've mistaken you for me, do you?'

'No,' said Littlejohn.

'Well, if you want to hand in your notice because you're scared of—'

'I'm not scared,' said Littlejohn curtly. 'Just thought you ought to know.'

When Strike didn't respond, Littlejohn said,

'Maybe I made a mistake.'

'No, it's good you're keeping your eyes open,' said Strike insincerely. 'Let me know if you see the guy again.'

'Will do.'

Littlejohn left the office without another word, casting a sideways look at Pat as he passed her. The office manager continued to stare determinedly at her monitor. Once Littlejohn's footsteps had died away, Strike pointed at the phone.

'Is there much more of that?'

'She called again,' said Pat, 'but it's more of the same. Threatening to go to the press with all her made-up nonsense.'

'How d'you know it's made-up nonsense?' said Strike perversely.

'You never assaulted her, I know that.'

'You don't know anything of the bloody sort,' said Strike irritably, getting up from the sofa to fetch a banana from the kitchen area, instead of the chocolate biscuit he really fancied.

'You might be a grumpy sod,' said Pat, scowling, 'but I can't see you knocking a woman around.'

'Thanks for the vote of confidence,' said Strike. 'Be sure and tell the *Mail* that when they come calling – and delete those messages.'

Well aware that he was venting his anger on the office manager, he forced himself to say,

'You're right: I never threw her across a boat and I never did any of the other stuff she's shouting about, either.'

'She doesn't like Robin,' said Pat, looking up at him, her dark eyes shrewd behind the lenses of her reading glasses. 'Jealous.'

'There's nothing—'

'I know *that*,' said Pat. 'She's with Ryan, isn't she?'

Strike took a moody bite of banana.

'So what are you going to do?' asked Pat.

'Nothing,' said Strike, his mouth full. 'I don't negotiate with terrorists.'

'Hm,' said Pat. She took a deep drag on her e-cigarette then spoke through a cloud of vapour. 'You can't trust a drinker. Never know what they might do when the brakes are off.'

'I'm not going to be held over a barrel for the rest of my life,' said Strike. 'She had sixteen fucking years from me. That's enough.'

Throwing the banana skin into the bin, he headed back to the inner office.

Charlotte's swerve from kindliness to vehement recrimination and threats came as no surprise to Strike, who'd endured her mood swings for years. Clever, funny and often endearing, Charlotte was also capable of fathomless spite, not to mention a self-destructive recklessness that had led her to sever relationships on a whim or to take extreme physical risks. Various psychiatrists and therapists had had their say over the years, each trying to corral her unpredictability and unhappiness into some neat medical classification. She'd been prescribed drugs, ricocheted between counsellors and been admitted to therapeutic facilities, yet Strike knew something in Charlotte herself had stubbornly resisted help. She'd always insisted that nothing the medical or psychiatric profession offered would ever, or could ever, help her. Only Strike could do that, she'd insisted time and again: only Strike could save her from herself.

Without realising it, he'd sat down in Robin's chair instead of his own, facing the board on which he'd pinned the notes and pictures related to the UHC case, but thinking about Charlotte. He well remembered the night on the barge owned by one of her friends, the vicious row that had erupted after Charlotte had consumed a bottle and a half of wine, and the hasty departure of the rest of the intoxicated party, who'd left Strike alone to deal with a knife-wielding Charlotte who was threatening to stab herself. He'd disarmed her physically, and in the process she'd slipped over onto the floor. Ever afterwards, when she lost her temper, she'd claimed he'd thrown her. Doubtless if he'd listened to the third message he'd have been accused of other assaults, of infidelity and cruelty: in Charlotte's telling, whenever she was drunk or angry, he was a monster of unparalleled sadism.

Six years since the relationship had ended for good, Strike had come to see that the unfixable problem between them was that he and Charlotte could never agree what reality was. She disputed everything: times, dates and events, who'd said what, how rows started, whether they were together or had broken up when he'd had other relationships. He still didn't know whether the miscarriage she claimed she'd had shortly before they parted forever had been real: she'd never shown him proof of pregnancy, and the shifting dates might have suggested either that she wasn't sure who the father was, or that the whole thing was imaginary. Sitting here today, he asked himself how he, whose entire professional life was an endless quest for truth, could have endured it all for so long.

With a grimace, Strike got to his feet yet again, picked up his notebook and pen and approached the board on the wall, willing himself to focus, because the following morning he'd be heading up to HMP Bedford to interview Jordan Reaney. His eyes travelled back up the left-hand column to the picture of Cherie Gittins, whose spell at Chapman Farm had overlapped with that of Reaney. After a few moments' contemplation of her pictures, he called Pat through to the inner office.

'You've got a daughter, right?' he said.

'Yeah,' said Pat, frowning.

'How old is she?'

'The hell are you asking me that for?' said Pat, her simian face turning red. Strike, who'd never seen her blush before, had no idea what had engendered this strange reaction. Wondering whether she could possibly have imagined he had dishonourable designs on her daughter, whom he'd never met, he said,

'I'm trying to get access to this woman's Facebook profile. It's set to private and she hasn't accepted my follow request. I thought, if your daughter's already on Facebook, with an established history, she might have a better chance. Another mother might seem less—'

'My daughter's not on Facebook.'

'OK,' said Strike. 'Sorry,' he added, though he wasn't sure why he was apologising.

Strike had the impression Pat wanted to say something else, but after a few seconds, she returned to the outer office. The tapping of computer keys resumed shortly afterwards.

Still puzzled by her reaction, he turned back to the board, eyes now on the pictures in the right-hand column, which featured four people who'd lived at Chapman Farm and met unnatural deaths.

At the top was an old news clipping about the death of Paul Draper, which Strike had found a couple of days earlier. Headlined 'Couple Sentenced for Killing of "Modern Slave"', the article detailed how Draper had been sleeping rough when a couple offered him a bed for the night. Both of his putative rescuers had previous convictions for violence, and had set Draper to doing building work for them, forcing him to sleep in their shed. Draper's death six months later had occurred during a beating. His starved and partially burned body had been discovered on a nearby building site. The detective had had no success in tracing any living relative of Draper, whose picture showed a timid-looking, moon-faced youth of nineteen with short, wispy hair.

Strike's gaze now moved to the Polaroids Robin had sent from Chapman Farm, showing the naked foursome in pig masks. The hair of the male being sodomised by the tattooed man might possibly be Draper's, although given the age of the Polaroids, it was impossible to be certain.

Beneath Draper's picture was the only photo of Kevin Pirbright Strike had been able to find, again taken from the news report of his murder. It showed a pale, apologetic-looking young man whose skin was pitted with acne scars. Beside the picture of Kevin was that of the murder scene. For the umpteenth time, Strike stared at that bit of gouged-out wall, and the single word 'pigs' that remained.

The last two pictures on the board were the oldest: those of Jonathan Wace's first wife, Jennifer, and of Daiyu.

Jennifer Wace's teased and permed hairstyle reminded Strike of the girls he'd known during his school days in the mid-eighties, but she'd been a very attractive woman. Nothing Strike had found out so far contradicted her daughter's belief that her drowning had been a complete accident.

Lastly, he turned his attention to the picture of Daiyu. Rabbity-faced, with her overbite and her missing tooth, she beamed out of the blurry newsprint picture at the detective: dead at seven years old, on the same beach as Jennifer Wace.

He turned from the board and reached for his phone again. He'd already made multiple fruitless attempts to contact the Heatons, who'd witnessed Cherie running screaming up the beach after Daiyu's drowning. Nevertheless, more in hope than expectation, he called their number again.

To his amazement, the phone was answered after three rings.

'Hello?' said a female voice.

'Hi,' said Strike, 'is this Mrs Heaton?'

'No, iss me, Gillian,' said the woman, who had a strong Norfolk accent. 'Who's this?'

'I'm trying to contact Mr and Mrs Heaton,' said Strike. 'Have they sold their house?'

'No,' said Gillian, 'I'm jus' here waterin' the plants. They're still in Spain. Who's this?' she asked again.

'My name's Cormoran Strike. I'm a private detective, and I was wondering whether I could speak—'

'*Strike?*' said the woman on the end of the line. 'You're not him who got that strangler?'

'That's me. I was hoping to speak to Mr and Mrs Heaton

537

about the drowning of a little girl in 1995. They were witnesses at the inquest.'

'Blimey, yeah,' said Gillian. 'I remember that. We're old friends.'

'Are they likely to be back in the country soon? I'd rather speak to them in person, but if they can't—'

'Well, Leonard broke his leg, see,' said Gillian, 'so they stopped out in Fuengirola a bit longer. They've got a place out there. He's getting better, though. Shelley reckons they'll be back in a couple of weeks.'

'Would you mind asking if they'd be prepared to speak to me when they get home? I'm happy to come to Cromer,' added Strike, who wanted to take a look at the place where Jennifer and Daiyu had died.

'Oh,' said Gillian, who sounded quite excited. 'Right. I'm sure they'd be happy to help.'

Strike gave the woman his number, thanked her, hung up, then turned to face the board on the wall once more.

There was only one other item pinned to it: a few lines of a poem, which had been printed in a local Norfolk newspaper as part of a grieving widower's tribute to his dead wife.

Came up that cold sea at Cromer like a running grave
Beside her as she struck
Wildly towards the shore, but the blackcapped wave
Crossed her and swung her back . . .

The imagery was powerful, but it wasn't Wace's. Strike had had a feeling upon reading the lines that he'd heard something like them before, and sure enough, he'd traced them to poet George Barker's 'On a Friend's Escape from Drowning off the Norfolk Coast'. Wace had taken the opening lines of Barker's poem and switched the pronouns, for Barker's friend had been male.

It was a shameless piece of plagiarism and Strike was surprised that nobody at the newspaper had spotted it. He was interested not only in the brazenness of the theft, but in the egoism of the widower who'd wanted to figure as a man of poetic gifts in the immediate wake of his wife's drowning, not to mention the choice of a poem that described the way in which Jennifer must have died, rather than her qualities in life. Even though Abigail had painted her father as a grifter and a narcissist, she'd claimed Wace had been genuinely upset about her mother's death. The tawdry act of stealing Barker's poem to get himself into the local paper was not, in Strike's view, the act of a man truly grieving at all.

For another minute he stood contemplating the pictures of individuals who'd met unnatural deaths, two by drowning, one by beating, and one by a single gunshot to the head. His gaze moved again to the Polaroids of the four young people in pig masks. Then he sat back down at the desk, and scribbled a few more questions for Jordan Reaney.

Six at the beginning means ...
Even a lean pig has it in him to rage around.

                    The I Ching or Book of Changes

The following morning, Strike's bathroom scales informed him that he was now a mere eight pounds off his target weight. This boost to his morale enabled him to resist the temptation of stopping for a doughnut at the service station en route to HMP Bedford.

The prison was an ugly building of red and yellow brick. After queuing to present his visiting permit, he and the rest of the families and friends were shown into a visitors' hall that resembled a white and green gym, with square tables set at evenly spaced intervals. Strike recognised Reaney, who was already seated, from across the room.

The prisoner, who was wearing jeans and a grey sweatshirt, looked what he undoubtedly was: a dangerous man. Over six feet tall, thin but broad-shouldered, his head was shaven and his teeth a yellowish brown. Almost every visible inch of his skin was tattooed, including his throat, which was covered by a tiger's face, and part of his gaunt face, where an ace of spades adorned most of his left cheek.

As Strike sat down opposite him, Reaney glanced towards a large black prisoner watching him in silence from a table away, and in those few seconds Strike noticed a series of tattooed lines, three broken, three solid, on the back of Reaney's left hand, and also saw that the ace of spades tattoo was partially concealing what looked like an old facial scar.

'Thanks for agreeing to see me,' said Strike, as the prisoner turned to look at him.

Reaney grunted. He blinked, Strike noticed, in an exaggerated fashion, keeping his eyes closed a fraction longer than was usual. The effect was strange, as though his large, thick-lashed, bright blue eyes were surprised to find themselves in such a face.

'As I said on the phone,' said Strike, drawing out his note-book, 'I'm after information on the Universal Humanitarian Church.'

Reaney folded his arms across his chest, and placed both hands beneath his armpits.

'How old were you when you joined?' asked Strike.

'Seven'een.'

'What made you join?'

'Needed somewhere to kip.'

'Bit out of your way, Norfolk. You grew up in Tower Hamlets, right?'

Reaney looked unhappy that Strike knew this.

'I was on'y in Tower 'Amlets from when I was twelve.'

'Where were you before that?'

'Wiv me mum, in Norfolk.' Reaney swallowed, and his prominent Adam's apple caused the tiger tattooed on his throat to ripple. 'After she died I 'ad to go to London, live wiv me old man. Then I was in care, then I was 'omeless for a bit, then I went to Chapman Farm.'

'Born in Norfolk, then?'

'Yeah.'

This explained how a young man of Reaney's background

had ended up in deep countryside. Strike's experience of Reaney's type was that they rarely, if ever, broke free of the gravitational pull of the capital.

'Did you have family there?'

'Nah. Jus' fancied a change.'

'Police after you?'

'They usually were,' said Reaney, unsmiling.

'How did you hear about Chapman Farm?'

'Me an' anuvver kid was sleeping rough in Norwich an' we met a couple of girls collecting for the UHC. They got us into it.'

'Was the other kid Paul Draper?'

'Yeah,' said Reaney, again with displeasure that Strike knew so much.

'What d'you think made the girls from the UHC so keen to recruit two men sleeping rough?'

'Needed people to do the 'eavy stuff on the farm.'

'You had to join the church, as a condition of living there?'

'Yeah.'

'How long did you stay?'

'Free years.'

'Long time, at that age,' said Strike.

'I liked the animals,' said Reaney.

'But not the pigs, as we've already established.'

Reaney ran his tongue around the inside of his mouth, blinked hard, then said,

'No. They stink.'

'Thought they were supposed to be clean?'

'You fort wrong.'

'D'you often have bad dreams about things, because they stink?'

'I jus' don' like pigs.'

'Nothing to do with the pig "acting in the abysmal"?'

542

'Wha'?' said Reaney.

'I've been told the pig has a particular significance in the I Ching.'

'In the wha'?'

'The book where you got the hexagram tattooed on the back of your left hand. Can I have a look?'

Reaney complied, though unwillingly, pulling his hand out from under his armpit and extending it towards Strike.

'Which hexagram's that?' asked Strike.

Reaney looked as though he'd rather not answer, but finally said,

'Fifty-six.'

'What does it mean?'

Reaney blinked hard twice before muttering.

'The wanderer.'

'Why the wanderer?'

'"*'E 'oo 'as few friends: this is the wanderer.*" I was a kid when I done it,' he muttered, shoving his hand back under his armpit.

'Made a believer of you, did they?'

Reaney said nothing.

'No opinion on the UHC's religion?'

Reaney cast another glance towards the large prisoner at the next table, who wasn't talking to his visitor, but glaring at Reaney. With an irritable movement of his shoulders, Reaney muttered unwillingly,

'I seen fings.'

'Like what?'

'Jus' fings what they could do.'

'Who's "they"?'

'Them. That Jonafun an' . . . is she still alive?' asked Reaney. 'Mazu?'

'Why wouldn't she be?'

Reaney didn't answer.

'What things did you see the Waces do?'

'Jus' ... makin' stuff disappear. An' ... spirits an' stuff.'

'Spirits?'

'I seen 'er make a spirit appear.'

'What did the spirit look like?' asked Strike.

'Like a ghost,' said Reaney, his expression daring Strike to find this funny. 'In temple. I seen it. Like ... transparent.'

Reaney gave another hard blink, then said,

'You talked to anyone else 'oo was in there?'

'Did you believe the ghost was real?' Strike asked, ignoring Reaney's question.

'I dunno – yeah, maybe,' said Reaney. 'You weren' fuckin' there,' he added, with a slight show of temper, but after a glance over Strike's head at a hovering warder, he added, with effortful calmness, 'but maybe it was a trick. I dunno.'

'I heard Mazu forced you to whip yourself across the face,' said Strike, watching Reaney closely, and sure enough, a tremor passed over the prisoner's face. 'What had you done?'

'Smacked a bloke called Graves.'

'Alexander Graves?'

Reaney looked still more uncomfortable at this further evidence Strike had done his homework.

'Yeah.'

'Why did you smack him?'

''E was a tit.'

'In what way?'

'Fuckin' annoying. Talkin' fuckin' gibberish all the time. An' 'e got in me face a lot. It got on me wick so one night, yeah, I smacked 'im. But we weren' s'posed to get angry wiv each ovver in there. Bruvverly love,' said Reaney, 'an' all that shit.'

'You don't strike me as a man who'd agree to whip himself.'

Reaney said nothing.

'Is that scar on your face from the whipping?'

Still Reaney didn't speak.

'What was she threatening you with, to make you whip yourself?' asked Strike. 'The police? Did Mazu Wace know you had a criminal record?'

Again, those bright blue, thickly lashed eyes blinked, hard, but at last Reaney spoke.

'Yeah.'

'How did they know?'

'You 'ad to confess stuff. In front of the group.'

'And you told them you were on the run from the police?'

'Said I'd 'ad some trouble. You got ... sucked in,' said Reaney. The tiger rippled again. 'You can' unnerstand, unless you was part of it. 'Oo else you spoken to, 'oo was in there?'

'A few people,' said Strike.

''Oo?'

'Why d'you want to know?'

'Wondered, tha's all.'

'Who would you say you were closest to, at Chapman Farm?'

'Nobody.'

'Because "the wanderer has few friends"?'

Possibly because no other form of retaliation to this mild sarcasm was possible, Reaney freed his right hand to pick his nose. After examining his fingertip, then flicking the result of this operation away onto the floor, he reinserted his hand back under his armpit and glared at Strike.

'Me an' Dopey was mates.'

'*He* had a bad experience with some pigs, I heard. Let some out accidentally and got beaten for it.'

'Don' remember that.'

'Really? It was going to be a whipping, but two girls stole the whip, so church members were instructed to beat him up instead.'

'Don' remember that,' repeated Reaney.

'My information is, the beating was so severe it might've left Draper with brain damage.'

Reaney chewed the inside of his cheek for a few seconds, then repeated,

'You weren' fuckin' there.'

'I know,' said Strike, 'which is why I'm asking you what happened.'

'Dopey wasn't all there before 'e got beat up,' said Reaney, but he looked as though he regretted these words as soon as they'd escaped him and added forcefully, 'You can't pin Draper on me. There was a ton of people kicking and punching him. Wha're you after, anyway?'

'So you weren't friendly with anyone except Draper, at Chapman Farm?' asked Strike, ignoring Reaney's question.

'No,' said Reaney.

'Did you know Cherie Gittins?'

'Knew 'er a bit.'

Strike detected unease in Reaney's tone.

'Would you happen to know where she went, after she left Chapman Farm?'

'No idea.'

'What about Abigail Wace, did you know her?'

'A bit,' repeated Reaney, still looking uneasy.

'What about Kevin Pirbright?'

'No.'

'He'd have been a kid when you were there.'

'I didn't 'ave nuffing to do with the kids.'

'Has Kevin Pirbright contacted you lately?'

'No.'

'You sure?'

'Yeah, I'm fucking sure. I know 'oo's contacted me an' 'oo 'asn't.'

'He was writing a book about the UHC. I'd have expected him to try and find you. He remembered you.'

'So wha'? 'E never found me.'

'Pirbright was shot and killed in his flat, last August.'

'I was in 'ere last August. 'Ow'm I s'posed to 'ave fuckin' shot 'im?'

'There was a two-month period when Kevin was alive and writing his book, and you were still at liberty.'

'So?' said Reaney again, blinking furiously.

'Kevin's laptop was stolen by his killer.'

'I've just told you, I was in 'ere when 'e was shot, so 'ow'm I s'posed to 'ave nicked 'is fucking laptop?'

'I'm not suggesting you stole it. I'm telling you that whoever's got that laptop probably knows whether or not you spoke to Pirbright. It's not difficult to get a password out of someone, if you're pointing a gun at them.'

'I dunno what you're fuckin' talkin' about,' said Reaney. 'I never spoke to 'im.'

But there was sweat on Reaney's upper lip.

'Can you imagine the Waces killing in defence of the church?'

'No,' said Reaney automatically. Then, 'I dunno. 'Ow the fuck would I know?'

Strike turned a page in his notebook.

'Did you ever see guns when you were at Chapman Farm?'

'No.'

'You sure about that?'

'Yeah, 'course I'm fucking sure.'

'You didn't take guns there?'

'No I fucking didn't. 'Oo says I did?'

'Were livestock slaughtered at the farm?'

'Wha'?'

'Did church members personally wring chickens' necks? Slaughter pigs?'

'Chickens, yeah,' said Reaney. 'Not the pigs. They wen' to the abattoir.'

'Did you ever witness anyone killing an animal with a hatchet?'

'No.'

'Ever hide a hatchet in a tree in the woods?'

'The fuck you tryin' to pin on me?' snarled Reaney, now openly aggressive. 'Wha're you up to?'

'I'm trying to find out why there was a hatchet hidden in a tree.'

'I don' fuckin' know. Why would I know? Give a dog a bad name, is it? First guns and now you're tryna pin a fuckin' hatchet on me? I never killed nobody at Chapman Farm, if that's what you're fuckin'—'

Out of the corner of his eye, Strike saw the large black prisoner watching Reaney shift in his seat. Reaney appeared to sense the larger man's scrutiny, because he broke off again, though he found it harder to contain his agitation, fidgeting in his seat, blinking furiously.

'You seem upset,' said Strike, watching him.

'Fuckin' upset?' snarled Reaney. 'You come in 'ere sayin' I fuckin' killed—'

'I never mentioned killing anyone. I asked about livestock being slaughtered.'

'I never fuckin' – stuff at that farm – you weren' there. You don' fuckin' know what went on.'

'The point of this interview is to find out what went on.'

'What 'appened in there, what you were made to do, it plays on your fuckin' mind, that's why I still 'ave fuckin' nightmares, but I never killed nobody, all right? An' I don' know nuffin' about no fuckin' hatchet,' Reaney added, although he looked away from Strike as he said it, those hard-blinking eyes roaming over the visitors' room as though seeking safe haven.

'What d'you mean by "what you were made to do"?'

Reaney was chewing the inside of his cheek again. Finally he looked back at Strike and said forcefully,

'Ev'ryone 'ad to do stuff we didn' wanna do.'

'Like what?'

'Like all of it.'

'Give me examples.'

'Doin' stuff that – jus' to 'umiliate people. Shovellin' shit an' cleanin' up after them.'

'Who's "them"?'

'Them. The family, the Waces.'

'Any particular things you had to do that keep playing on your mind?'

'All of it,' said Reaney.

'What d'you mean by "cleaning up" after the Waces?'

'Jus' – you unnerstan' fuckin' English – cleanin' the bogs an' stuff.'

'Sure that's all it was?'

'Yeah, I'm fuckin' sure.'

'You were at the farm when Daiyu Wace drowned, weren't you?'

He saw the muscles in Reaney's jaw tighten.

'Why?'

'You were there, right?'

'I slept froo the ole fuckin' thing.'

'Were you supposed to be in the truck that morning? With Cherie?'

''Oo've you talked to?'

'Why does that matter?'

When Reaney merely blinked, Strike became more specific.

'Were you supposed to be on the vegetable run?'

'Yeah, bu' I overslept.'

'When did you wake up?'

'Why're you askin' abou' this?'

'I told you, I want information. When did you wake up?'

'I dunno. When ev'ryone was kickin' off because the little b—'

Reaney cut himself off.

'The little—?' prompted Strike. When Reaney didn't answer, he said,

'I take it you didn't like Daiyu?'

'Nobody fuckin' liked 'er. Fuckin' spoiled fuckin' rotten. Ask anyone 'oo was there.'

'So you woke up when everyone was kicking off because Daiyu had disappeared?'

'Yeah.'

'Did you hear the people on early duty telling the Waces they'd seen her leaving on the truck with Cherie?'

'Why the fuck d'you wanna know tha'?'

'Did you hear them saying she'd left in the truck?'

'I'm not gonna talk for them. Ask them what they seen.'

'I'm asking what *you* heard, when you woke up.'

Apparently deciding this answer couldn't incriminate him, Reaney finally muttered,

'Yeah ... they seen 'er leave.'

'Were Jonathan and Mazu both present at the farm when you woke up?'

'Yeah.'

'How soon did you find out Daiyu had drowned?'

'Can' remember.'

'Try.'

The tiger rippled yet again. The blue eyes blinked, over-hard.

'Later that mornin'. The police come. Wiv Cherie.'

'Was she distressed about Daiyu drowning?'

''Course she fuckin' was,' said Reaney.

'Cherie left the farm for good shortly before you did, right?'

'Can' remember.'

'I think you can.'

Reaney sucked in his hollow cheeks. Strike had a feeling this was a habitual expression prior to violence. He looked steadily back at Reaney, who blinked first, hard.

'Yeah, she wen' after the inquiry fing.'

'The inquest?'

'Yeah.'

'And she didn't tell you where she was going?'

'Didn't tell no one. She left in the middle of the night.'

'And what made *you* leave?'

'Jus' 'ad enough of the place.'

'Did Draper leave when you did?'

'Yeah.'

'Did you stay in touch?'

'No.'

'Did you keep in contact with anyone from the UHC?'

'No.'

'You like tattoos,' said Strike.

'Wha'?'

'Tattoos. You've got a lot of them.'

'So?'

'Anything on your upper right arm?' said Strike.

'Why?'

'Could I have a look?'

'No, you fuckin' can't,' snarled Reaney.

'I'll ask that again,' said Strike quietly, leaning forwards, 'this time reminding you what's likely to happen to you once this interview's over, when I inform my friend you weren't cooperative.'

Reaney slowly pushed up the sleeve of his sweatshirt. There was no skull on the bicep, but a large, jet black devil with red eyes.

'Is that covering anything up?'

'No,' said Reaney, tugging his sleeve back down.

'You sure?'

'Yeah, I'm sure.'

'I'm asking,' said Strike, now reaching into an inner pocket of his jacket, withdrawing a couple of the Polaroids Robin had found in the barn at Chapman Farm, 'because I thought you might once have had a skull where that devil is.'

He laid the two photos down on the table, facing Reaney. One showed the tall, skinny man with the skull tattoo penetrating the chubby, dark-haired girl, the other the same man sodomising the smaller man whose short, wispy hair might have been Paul Draper's.

Reaney's forehead had started shining in the harsh overhead light.

'That ain't me.'

'You sure?' said Strike. 'Because I thought this might explain the pig nightmares better than the smell of pig shit.'

Sweaty and pale, Reaney shoved the photos away from him so violently that one of them fell onto the floor. Strike retrieved it and replaced both in his pocket.

'This spirit you saw,' he said, 'what did it look like?'

Reaney didn't answer.

'Were you aware Daiyu re-materialises regularly now at Chapman Farm?' Strike asked. 'They call her the Drowned—'

Without warning, Reaney got to his feet. Had his plastic chair and the table not been fastened to the floor, Strike was prepared to bet the prisoner would have kicked them over.

'Oi!' said a nearby warder, but Reaney was walking fast towards the door into the main prison. A couple more warders caught up with him, and escorted him through the door out of the hall. Prisoners and visitors had turned to watch Reaney storm out, but swiftly turned back to their own conversations, afraid of wasting precious minutes.

Strike met the eyes of the large prisoner one table along, which were asking a silent question. Strike made a small, negative gesture. Further beatings wouldn't make Jordan Reaney any more cooperative, Strike was sure of that. He'd met terrified men before, men who feared something worse than physical pain. The question was, what exactly was putting Jordan Reaney into such a state of alarm that he was prepared to face the worst kind of prison justice rather than divulge it?

57

Nine at the beginning . . .
When you see evil people,
Guard yourself against mistakes.

The I Ching or Book of Changes

To Robin's relief, Strike's next letter offered a solution to the problem of giving money to the UHC.

I've spoken to Colin Edensor and he's prepared to make £1000 available for a donation. If you get their account details, we'll set up a bank transfer.

In consequence, Robin asked permission to visit Mazu in the farmhouse the following morning.

'I want to make a donation to the church,' she explained to the hard-faced woman who'd been supervising her stint in the kitchens.

'All right. Go now, before lunch,' said the woman, with the first smile Robin had received from her. Glad to escape the fug of boiling noodles and turmeric, Robin pulled off her apron and left.

The June day was overcast, but as Robin crossed the deserted courtyard the sun slid out from behind a cloud and turned Daiyu's fountain-dappled pool into a basin of diamonds. Thankfully, Emily was no longer standing on her crate. She'd remained there for a full forty-eight hours, ignored and unmentioned by all who passed, as though she'd always stood there and always would. Robin had pitied Emily doubly by the time urine stains had appeared on the inside of her tracksuit bottoms and track marks of tears had striped her muddy face, but she'd imitated all other church members and acted as though the woman was invisible.

The other absence currently improving life at Chapman Farm was that of Taio Wace, who was visiting the Glasgow centre. The removal of the ever-present fear that he'd try and take her into a Retreat Room again was such a relief that Robin even felt less tired than usual, although her regime of manual labour continued.

She knelt at Daiyu's pool, made the usual tribute, then approached the carved double doors of the farmhouse. As she reached them, Sita, a brown-skinned, elderly woman with a long rope of steel-grey hair opened it from the inside, carrying a bulging plastic sack. As they passed each other, Robin smelled a foul odour of faeces.

'Could you tell me where Mazu's office is?' she asked Sita.

'Straight through the house, at the back.'

So Robin walked past the staircase, along the red-carpeted corridor lined with Chinese masks and painted panels, right into the heart of the farmhouse. Walking past what she assumed to be the kitchen she smelled roasting lamb, which was in stark contrast to the depressing miasma of boiling tinned vegetables she'd just left.

At the very end of the corridor, facing her, was a closed black lacquer door. As she approached, she heard voices inside.

'... ethical question, surely?' said a man she was almost certain was Giles Harmon. Though he'd said he was staying only a few days, he'd now been at the farm a week, and Robin had spotted him leading other teenaged girls towards the Retreat Rooms. Harmon, who never wore the scarlet tracksuit of ordinary members, was usually attired in jeans and what looked like expensive shirts. His bedroom in the farmhouse overlooked the yard and he was often to be seen typing at the desk in front of the window.

Harmon's voice wasn't as carefully modulated as usual. In fact, Robin thought she heard a trace of panic.

'Everything we do here is ethical,' said a second male voice, which she recognised at once as that of Andy Zhou. 'This *is* the ethical course. Remember, he doesn't feel as we do. There is no soul there.'

'You approve?' Harmon asked someone.

'Absolutely,' said a voice Robin had no trouble identifying as Becca Pirbright's.

'Well, if *you* think so. After all, he's your—'

'There's no connection, Giles,' said Becca, almost angrily. 'No connection at all. I'm surprised you—'

'Sorry, sorry,' said Harmon placatingly. 'Materialist values – I'll meditate now. I'm sure whatever you all think is best. You've been dealing with the situation far longer than I have, of course.'

Robin thought he said it as though rehearsing a defence. She heard footsteps, and had seconds to dash back along the hall, making as little noise as possible on her trainered feet, so that when Harmon opened the office door, she appeared to be walking towards it from ten yards away.

'Is Mazu free?' Robin asked. 'I've been given permission to see her.'

'She will be, in a few minutes,' said Harmon. 'You should probably wait here.'

He passed her and headed upstairs. Seconds later, the study door opened for a second time and Dr Zhou and Becca emerged.

'What are you doing here, Rowena?' said Becca, and

Robin thought her bright smile was a little more forced than usual.

'I want to make a donation to the church,' said Robin. 'I was told I should see Mazu about it.'

'Oh, I see. Yes, carry on, she's in there,' said Becca, pointing towards the office. She and Zhou walked away, their voices too low for Robin to catch what they were saying.

Bracing herself slightly, Robin approached the office door and knocked.

'Come,' said Mazu, and Robin entered.

The office, which had been added to the rear of the building, was so cluttered and colourful, and smelled so strongly of incense, that Robin felt as though she'd stepped through a portal into a bazaar. A profusion of statuettes, deities and idols were crammed onto the shelves.

Daiyu's enlarged photograph sat in a golden frame on top of a Chinese cabinet, where joss paper was burning in a dish. Flowers and small offerings of food had been laid out in front of her. For a split second Robin felt a wholly unexpected spasm of compassion for Mazu, who sat facing her at an ebony desk that resembled Zhou's, wearing her long blood-red dress, her black waist-length hair falling either side of her white face, her mother-of-pearl fish pendant glimmering on her chest.

'Rowena,' she said, unsmiling, and Robin's moment of kindness vanished as though it had never been, as she seemed again to smell Mazu's dirty foot, revealed for her to kiss.

'Um – I'd like to make a donation to the church.'

Mazu surveyed her unsmilingly for a moment, then said, 'Sit down.'

Robin did as she was told. As she did so, she noticed an incongruous object on a shelf behind Mazu's head: a small, white plastic air freshener, which seemed entirely pointless in this room full of incense.

'So you've decided you want to give us money, have you?' said Mazu, scrutinising Robin with those dark, crooked eyes.

'Yes. Taio talked to me,' Robin said, certain that Mazu would know this, 'and I've been doing some hard thinking, and, well, I see he was right, I *am* still struggling with materialism, and it's time to put my money where my mouth is.'

A small smile appeared on the long, pale face.

'Yet you refused spirit bonding.'

'I felt so awful after Revelation, I didn't think I was worthy,' said Robin. 'But I want to eradicate the false self, I really do. I know I've got a lot of work to do.'

'How are you intending to donate? You didn't bring any credit cards with you.'

Robin registered this admission that her locker had been opened and searched.

'Theresa told me not to. Theresa's my sister, she – she didn't want me to come here at all. She said the UHC's a cult,' said Robin apologetically.

'And you listened to your sister.'

'No, but I really came here just to explore things. I didn't know I'd stay. If I'd known how I'd feel once I'd had my Week of Service I'd have brought my bank cards – but if you let me write to Theresa, I'll be able to arrange a bank transfer to the church's account. I'd like to donate a thousand pounds.'

She saw, by the slight widening of Mazu's eyes, that she hadn't expected so large a donation.

'Very well,' she said, opening a drawer in her desk and withdrawing a pen, writing paper and a blank envelope. She also pushed a template letter to copy and a card printed with the UHC's bank account details across the desk. 'You can do that now. Luckily,' said Mazu, taking a ring of keys from another drawer, 'your sister wrote to you just this morning. I was going to ask somebody to give you her letter at lunch.'

Mazu now headed towards the cabinet on which Daiyu's portrait stood and unlocked it. Robin caught a glimpse of piles of envelopes held together with elastic bands. Mazu extracted one of these, relocked the cabinet and said, still holding the letter,

'I'll be back in a moment.'

When the door had closed behind Mazu, Robin took a quick look around the office, her eye falling on a plug socket in the skirting board, into which nothing was plugged. With the camera she believed was hidden in the air freshener recording her every move she didn't dare examine it, but she suspected, having used such devices herself, that this innocent socket was also a covert recording device. Possibly Mazu had left the room to see what she'd do if left alone, so Robin didn't move from her chair, but set to work copying out the template letter.

Mazu returned a few minutes later.

'Here,' she said, holding out the letter addressed to Robin.

'Thank you,' said Robin, opening it. She was certain it had already been opened and read, judging by the suspiciously strong glue used to reseal it. 'Oh good,' said Robin, scanning the letter in Midge's handwriting, 'she's given me her new address, I didn't have it.'

She finished copying out the template letter, addressed the envelope and sealed it.

'I can get that posted for you,' said Mazu, holding out a hand.

'Thank you,' said Robin, getting to her feet. 'I feel much better for doing this.'

'You shouldn't be giving money to "feel better",' said Mazu.

They were the same height, but somehow, Robin still felt as though Mazu was the taller.

'Your personal bar to pure spirit is egomotivity, Rowena,' said Mazu. 'You continue to put the materialist self ahead of the collective.'

'Yes,' said Robin. 'I – I *am* trying.'

'Well, we'll see,' said Mazu, with a little waggle of the letter Robin had just handed her, and the latter surmised that not until the funds were safely in the UHC's bank account would she be deemed to have made spiritual progress.

Robin left the farmhouse holding her letter. Though it was lunchtime, and she was very hungry, she made a detour to the women's bathroom to examine the page in her hand more closely.

Robin noticed, tilting the paper beneath the overhead light in the toilet cubicle, there was an almost imperceptible line of strip Tippex: somebody had obliterated the date on which it had been sent. Flipping the envelope over she saw that the time and date of the postmark had also been blurred. So exhausted she could no longer estimate lengths of time with much accuracy, and having no recourse to any calendar, Robin couldn't remember exactly when she'd requested the fake letter from Theresa, but she doubted she'd ever have known it existed had Mazu not wanted her to have Theresa's address.

For the first time, it occurred to Robin that one reason for Will Edensor's lack of response to the letters informing him that his mother was dying might be that he'd never received them. Will was in possession of a large trust fund, and it was surely in the church's interests that he remain at the farm, meekly handing over money, rather than discover, on learning of his mother's death, that he couldn't see her as a flesh object, or treat her love as materialist possession.

58

Two daughters live together, but their minds are not directed to common concerns.

The I Ching or Book of Changes

Robin knew Colin Edensor's one thousand pounds must have reached the UHC's bank account because a few days after she'd given Mazu her letter ordering the bank transfer she was reunited with her original group of high-level recruits. Nobody mentioned her Revelation session, nor did anyone welcome her back; all behaved as though she'd never been away.

This mutually agreed silence extended to Kyle's unexplained absence from the group. Robin knew better than to ask how he'd transgressed, but she was certain he'd done something wrong because she soon spotted him doing the kind of hard manual work she'd just been allowed to give up. Robin also noticed that Vivienne now averted her eyes whenever her group and Kyle's passed each other.

Robin found out what Kyle's crime had been when she sat down opposite Shawna at dinner that night.

Following Shawna's ill-advised recruitment of Robin to help with the children's lessons, her head had been shaved. While she'd seemed cowed when she first appeared in her newly bald state, her fundamentally garrulous and indiscreet nature had now reasserted itself, and her first proud words to Robin were,

561

'Oi'm increasing again.'

She patted her lower belly.

'Oh,' said Robin. 'Congratulations.'

'Yew don't say that,' scoffed Shawna. 'Oi'm not doing it for *me*. Yew should be congratulating the church.'

'Right,' said Robin wearily. She'd deliberately sat with Shawna in the hopes of hearing more news about Jacob, because she had a hunch it was his fate she'd overheard Harmon, Zhou and Becca discussing in Mazu's office, but she'd forgotten how exasperating the girl could be.

'Did yew hear about *him*?' Shawna asked Robin in a gleeful whisper, as Kyle passed the end of the table.

'No,' said Robin.

'Hahaha,' said Shawna.

The people beside them were locked in their own intense conversation. Shawna glanced sideways to make sure she wouldn't be overheard before leaning in and whispering to Robin,

'He says he carn't spirit bond with, you know ... women. Said it right to Mazu's face.'

'Well,' said Robin cautiously, also whispering, 'I mean ... he's gay, isn't he? So—'

'Thass materialism,' said Shawna, louder than she'd intended, and one of the young men beside them glanced around and Shawna, greatly against Robin's wishes, said loudly to them,

'She thinks there's such a thing as "gay".'

Clearly deciding no good would come of responding to Shawna, the young man turned back to his conversation.

'Bodies don't matter,' Shawna told Robin firmly. 'On'y spirit matters.'

She leaned in again, once more talking in a conspiratorial whisper.

'Vivienne wanted to spirit bond with 'im and I 'eard 'e ran

out there, loike, *crying,* hahaha. Thass proper egomotability, thinking people aren' good enough to sleep with.'

Robin nodded silently, which appeared to satisfy Shawna. As they ate, Robin tried to lead Shawna onto the subject of Jacob, but other than Shawna's confident assertion that he was bound to pass soon, because Papa J had decreed it, found out no more information.

Robin's next letter to Strike was devoid of useful information. However, two days after placing it in the plastic rock, she and the rest of the high-level recruits, minus Kyle, were led to another crafting session by Becca Pirbright.

It was a hot, cloudless June day, and Becca was wearing a T-shirt emblazoned with the church's logo instead of a sweatshirt, although the ordinary members continued to wear their heavy tracksuits. Field poppies and daisies had bloomed along the path to the Portakabins, and Robin might have felt uplifted but for the fact that fine weather at Chapman Farm turned her thoughts to all the places she'd rather have been. Even central London, never the most comfortable place in a heatwave, had a halcyon quality to her these days. She could have put on a summer dress instead of this thick tracksuit, bought herself a bottle of water at will, walked anywhere, freely . . .

A startled mutter issued from the group as they approached the Portakabin where they usually made corn dollies. The tables had been moved outside, so that they wouldn't have to endure the stuffiness of the crafting room, but their surprise had nothing to do with the relocated tables.

Several church members were constructing a twelve-foot-high man of straw beside the Portakabin. It appeared to have a strong wire frame, and Robin now realised that the large straw sculpture she'd previously seen Wan working on had been the head.

'We make one of these every year, in celebration of the Manifestation of the Stolen Prophet,' the smiling Becca told the group, who were all contemplating the large straw man as they sat down at the crafting tables. 'The prophet was a gifted craftsman himself, so—'

Becca's voice faltered. Emily had just emerged from behind the straw sculpture, hands full of twine. Emily's head was freshly shaven; like Louise, she clearly hadn't been given permission to let her hair regrow yet. Emily threw Becca a cold, challenging look before returning to her work.

'—so we celebrate him by the means he chose to express himself,' Becca finished.

As the group reached automatically for their piles of hollow straws, Robin saw that her companions had now graduated to making Norfolk lanterns, which were more complex than those she'd previously made. As nobody seemed inclined to help her, she reached for the laminated instructions on the table to see what she had to do, the sun beating down upon her back.

Becca disappeared into the crafting room and returned with the leatherbound copy of *The Answer* from which Mazu had previously read while they worked. Removing a silk bookmark indicating where they'd last got to, Becca cleared her throat and began to read.

'"I come now to a part of my personal faith story that's as dreadful as it's miraculous, as heartrending as it's joyful.

'"Let me first state that to those who live in the bubble world, what I'm about to relate – or at least, my reaction to it, and my understanding of it – is likely to be baffling, even shocking. How, they'll ask, can the death of a child ever be miraculous or joyful?

'"I must begin by describing Daiyu. Materialists would call her my daughter, although I'd have loved her just the same had there been no fleshly bond.

"'From her earliest childhood, it was evident that Daiyu would never need awakening. She'd been born awake, and her metaphysical abilities were extraordinary. She could tame wild livestock with a glance and locate lost objects unerringly, no matter how far away they were. She showed no interest in childish games or toys, but turned instinctively towards scripture, able to read before being taught, and to speak truths it takes many people a lifetime to understand.'"

'And she could turn herself invisible,' said a cool voice from over beside the towering straw man.

Several of the group glanced at Emily, but Becca ignored the interruption.

"'As she grew, her powers became only more exceptional. The idea of a four- or five-year-old having her degree of spiritual calling would have seemed nonsensical to me had I not witnessed it. Every day she grew in wisdom and gave further proofs of her pure communication with the Blessed Divinity. Even as a child, she far surpassed me in understanding. I'd spent years struggling to understand and harness my own spiritual gifts. Daiyu simply accepted her abilities as natural, without inner conflict, without confusion.

"'I look back now and wonder how I didn't understand what her destiny was, although she spoke to me of it, a few short days before her earthly end.

"'"Papa, I must visit the Blessed Divinity soon, but don't worry, I'll come back.'

"'I imagined she was speaking of the state pure spirits attain when they see the face of the Divinity clearly, and which I have achieved myself, through chanting, fasting and meditation. I knew that Daiyu, like me, had already seen and spoken to the Divinity. The word 'visit' should have warned me, but I was blind where she saw plainly.

"'The Divinity's chosen instrument was a young woman

who took Daiyu to the dark sea while I slept. Daiyu walked joyfully towards the horizon before the sun had risen and disappeared from the material world, her fleshly body dissolving into the ocean. She was what the world calls dead.

"'My despair was unconfined. It was weeks before I understood that this is why she was sent to us. Hadn't she said to me, many times, 'Papa, I exist beyond mere matter'? She'd been sent to teach us all, but to teach me particularly, that the only truth, the only reality, is spirit. And when I fully understood as much, and after I'd humbly told the Blessed Divinity so, Daiyu returned.

"'Yes, she came back to me, I saw her as plainly—'"

Emily laughed scornfully. Becca slammed the book shut and got to her feet while the apprehensive corn dolly-makers pretended not to be watching.

'Come in here for a moment, Emily, please,' Becca told her sister.

Her expression defiant, Emily set down the straw she'd been binding to the torso of the gigantic statue and followed Becca into the cabin. Determined to know what was going on, Robin, who knew there was a small portable toilet to the rear of the crafting rooms, muttered, 'Loo,' and left the group.

All the windows of the Portakabin were open, doubtless in an effort to make it cool enough to work in. Robin moved round the building until she was out of sight of the other workers, then crept to stand beneath a window at the back, through which Becca and Emily's voices, though low, were just audible.

'. . . don't understand what the problem is, I was agreeing with you.'

'Why did you laugh?'

'Why d'you think? Don't you remember, when we recognised Lin—'

'Shut up. *Shut up now.*'

'Fine, I'll—'

'Come back. *Come back here*. Why did you say that, about invisibility?'

'Oh, I'm allowed to speak now, am I? Well, that's what you said happened. *You* were the one who told me what to say.'

'That's a lie. If you want to tell a different story now, go ahead, nobody's stopping you!'

Emily let out something between a gasp and a laugh.

'You filthy *hypocrite*.'

'Says the person who's back here because her EM's out of control!'

'*My* EM? Look at you!' said Emily, with contempt. 'There's more EM in this place than in any of the other centres.'

'Well, you'd know, you've been kicked out of enough of them. I'd have thought you'd realise you're hanging by a thread, Emily.'

'Says who?'

'Says Mazu. You're lucky you're not Mark Three, after Birmingham, but it could still happen.'

Robin heard footsteps and guessed Becca had chosen to leave on her threatening line, but Emily spoke again, now sounding desperate.

'You'd rather I went the same way as Kevin, wouldn't you? Just kill myself.'

'You *dare* talk about Kevin, to me?'

'Why shouldn't I talk about him?'

'*I know what you did, Emily.*'

'What did I do?'

'You spoke to Kevin, for his book.'

'What?' said Emily, now sounding blank. 'How?'

'The disgusting room where he shot himself was covered with writing, and he'd written *my name* on the wall, and something about a plot.'

'You think Kevin would have wanted contact with *me*, after we——?'

'*Shut up,* for God's sake, *shut up!* You don't care about anyone except yourself, do you? Not about Papa J or the mission——'

'If Kevin knew something about you and a plot, *I* didn't tell him. But he always agreed with me that you're full of shit.'

Robin didn't know what Becca did next, but Emily let out a gasp of what sounded like pain.

'You need to eat your vegetables,' said Becca, her menacing voice unrecognisable, compared to the bright tone in which she generally spoke. 'You hear me? And you'll work on the vegetable patch and you'll like it, or I'll tell the Council I know you cooperated with Kevin.'

'You won't,' said Emily, now sobbing, 'you won't, you bloody coward, because you know what I could tell them if I wanted!'

'If you're talking about Daiyu, go right ahead. I'll be informing Papa J and Mazu of this conversation, so——'

'No – no, Becca, don't——'

'It's my duty,' said Becca. 'You can tell them what you think you saw.'

'No, Becca, *please* don't tell them——'

'Could Daiyu become invisible, Emily?'

There was a short silence.

'Yes,' said Emily, her voice quaking, 'but——'

'Either she could or she couldn't. Which is it?'

'She . . . could.'

'Correct. So don't let me hear you saying anything different, *ever again,* you filthy little pig.'

Robin heard footsteps, and the door of the cabin slammed.

59

. . . to the thoughtful man such occurrences are grave omens that he does not neglect.

The I Ching or Book of Changes

The Frank brothers' purchase of rope while wearing dubious disguises had now been followed by the acquisition of a very old van. Considered alongside their continued surveillance of the actress's house and both brothers' previous court appearances for sex offences, Strike had been forced to the conclusion that the twosome might indeed be planning an abduction. He'd contacted the Met a second time, and given them his most recent information, which included pictures of both brothers lurking around the client's house, and warned Tasha Mayo to take all possible precautions.

'I'd strongly advise you to change your routine,' he told her over the phone. 'Vary the time you go to the gym and so on.'

'I like my routine,' she grumbled. 'Are you sure you aren't taking this a bit *too* seriously?'

'Well, the joke's on me if it turns out they're planning a camping trip, but they've definitely stepped up their surveillance of you lately.'

There was a slight pause.

'You're scaring me.'

'It'd be remiss not to give you my honest opinion. Is there

anyone who could come and stay with you for a bit? A friend, a family member?'

'Maybe,' she said gloomily. 'God. I thought they were just a bit weird and annoying, not actually *dangerous*.'

The following day found Strike sitting at a table in the Connaught Hotel's Jean-Georges restaurant, from which he could watch the antics of their most recently acquired client's wealthy mother, who was seventy-four and lunching with her forty-one-year-old male companion. Strike was wearing glasses he didn't need, but which had a minuscule camera hidden in the frame. He'd so far recorded a good deal of giggling from the woman, particularly after her dark-suited companion, who'd been solicitous in assisting her with her coat and making sure that she was comfortably seated, had been mistaken for a waiter by the diners at the next table.

Having watched the couple order food and wine, Strike asked for a chicken salad, took off his glasses, positioning them on the table so that they'd continue recording. As he did so, he caught the eye of a very good-looking dark-haired woman in a black dress, who was also dining alone. She smiled.

Strike looked away without returning the smile, picked up his phone to read the day's news, which was, inevitably, Brexit dominated. The referendum would be happening in a week's time and Strike was thoroughly bored of the febrile coverage it was generating.

Then he spotted a link to a story titled:

Viscountess Arrested for Assault on Billionaire Boyfriend

He clicked on the link. A dishevelled Charlotte appeared on the phone screen, flanked by a policewoman on a dark street.

Former nineties It-Girl Charlotte Campbell, 41, now Viscountess Ross, has been arrested on a charge of assault against billionaire American hotelier, Landon Dormer, 49.

Dormer's Mayfair neighbours called police in the early hours of June 14th, concerned about the noises coming from the residence. One, who asked not to be named, told *The Times*,

'We heard screams, shouting and breaking glass. We were really concerned, so we called 999. We weren't sure what was going on. We thought it might have been a break-in.'

Ross, whose marriage to the Viscount of Croy ended in divorce last year, is the mother of twins and has a well-documented history of substance abuse. Previously admitted to Symonds House, a psychiatric facility patronised by the wealthy and famous, the part-time model and journalist has been a staple of the gossip columns ever since running away from Cheltenham Ladies' College in her teens. With by-lines at *Harpers & Queen* and *Vogue*, she makes frequent appearances in the front row at both London and Paris fashion weeks, and was voted London's Most Eligible Singleton in 1995. She was previously in a long-term relationship with Cormoran Strike, private detective and son of rock star Jonny Rokeby.

Rumours of an imminent engagement to billionaire Dormer have circulated in gossip columns for months, but a source close to the hotelier told *The Times*, 'Landon wasn't intending to marry her even before this happened, but after this, believe me, they'll be finished. He isn't a man who likes drama or tantrums.'

Ross's sister, interior decorator Amelia Crichton, 42, told *The Times*,

'This is now a legal matter, so I'm afraid I can't say any more than that I'm confident that if this comes to court Charlotte will be fully exonerated.'

The Times approached both Charlotte Ross and Landon Dormer for comment.

There were multiple links below the article: Charlotte at the launch of a jewellery collection the previous year, Charlotte admitted to Symonds House the year before that, and Landon Dormer's acquisition of one of the oldest five-star hotels in London. Strike ignored these, instead scrolling back up the page to look again at the photograph at the top. Charlotte's make-up was smeared, her hair tousled, and she faced the camera defiantly as she was led away by the policewoman.

Strike glanced up at the table his glasses were filming. The elderly woman was feeding her companion something. As his chicken salad was deposited in front of him, his phone rang. Recognising the Spanish country code, he picked up.

'Cormoran Strike.'

'Leonard Heaton here,' said a jocular voice with a strong Norfolk accent. 'I hear you're ahter me.'

'After information, anyway,' said Strike. 'Thanks for calling me back, Mr Heaton.'

'I navver strangled anyone. I wus home all night with the wife.'

Evidently Mr Heaton considered himself something of a card. Somebody – Strike assumed his wife – was chortling in the background.

'Did your neighbour tell you what this is about, Mr Heaton?'

'Ah, the little gal that drowned,' said Heaton. 'Wut're you digging around in that fur?'

'A client of mine's interested in the Universal Humanitarian Church,' said Strike.

'Ah,' said Heaton. 'All right, we're game. We'll be home in a week, that suit you?'

After agreeing a time and date, Strike hung up and began to eat his salad, still letting his glasses do the surveillance for him, his mind unavoidably on Charlotte.

While she'd generally done most damage to herself when angry or distressed, Strike still bore a small scar over his eyebrow from the ashtray Charlotte had thrown at him as he walked out of her flat for the last time. She'd launched herself at him many times during rows, attempting to either claw his face or punch him, but this had been far easier to deal with than flying missiles, given that he was considerably larger than her and, as an ex-boxer, good at parrying attacks.

Nevertheless, at least four of their break-ups had come in the aftermath of her attempting to physically hurt him. He remembered the sobs afterwards, the desperate apologies, the vows made never to do it again, vows she sometimes kept for as much as a year.

Barely noticing what he was eating, Strike's eyes roamed over the chattering lunchers, the stained-glass windows and tasteful grey upholstery. Between Bijou and her QC lover, and Charlotte's alleged assault of a billionaire, his name was appearing a little too frequently in the press for his liking. He picked up the glasses concealing the hidden camera, and rammed them back on.

'Excuse me.'

He looked up. It was the woman in black, who'd stopped at his table on her way out.

'You aren't Corm—?'

'No, sorry, you must have me confused with someone,' he said, drowning out her voice, which was fairly loud. His target and her young friend seemed too immersed in their conversation to have noticed anything, but a couple of other heads had turned.

'I'm sorry, I thought I recognised—'

'You're mistaken.'

She was blocking his view of his target.

573

'Sorry,' she said again, smiling. 'But you do look awfully—'

'You're mistaken,' he repeated firmly.

She pressed her lips together, but her eyes looked amused as she passed out of the restaurant.

60

Six in the third place means:
Contemplation of my life
Decides the choice
Between advance and retreat.

The I Ching or Book of Changes

On Friday night Robin waited until the women around her had fallen asleep before slipping out of the dormitory yet again. Tonight she was more nervous and stressed than she'd been since the very first time she'd journeyed through the dark to the plastic rock in the woods, because she was twenty-four hours late in producing her letter, so felt an increased pressure to reassure the agency that she was all right. She climbed over the five-bar gate as usual, hurried across the dark field and entered the woods.

Inside the plastic rock she found two Yorkie bars and letters from Strike, Murphy and Shah. She read the three men's letters by the light of the pencil torch. Ryan's was essentially a thinly veiled request to know when she'd be leaving Chapman Farm. Strike's told her he'd soon be interviewing the Heatons, who'd met Cherie Gittins on the beach in the immediate aftermath of Daiyu's drowning.

Shah's note read:

> I checked the rock last night and I'm still in the
> vicinity. Strike says if there's nothing by midnight
> tomorrow he's driving up and he'll come in the front
> on Sunday.

'For God's sake, Strike,' muttered Robin, pulling the top
off the biro with her teeth. One day's delay didn't seem to
justify such extreme measures. Hungry as she was, she had far
more to write than usual, so she postponed eating the chocolate, instead taking out the paper and pen, putting the torch
between her teeth and setting to work.

Hi Cormoran,

*I'm sorry this is late, it was unavoidable, I'll explain why
below. A LOT has happened this week, so I hope this pen
doesn't run out.*

1. Row between the Pirbright sisters
*I overheard Emily accusing Becca of lying about Daiyu's
drowning. Emily seems really unhappy and I think if I can
get friendly with her she might talk. Becca also accused
Emily of collaborating with Kevin on his book, because of the
writing on Kevin Pirbright's walls — Becca's seen the photo
of his room.*
*NB: Apparently nobody's told Emily Kevin was murdered. She
thinks he committed suicide. Not sure whether Becca knows
the truth.*

2. Stolen Prophet's Manifestation
*This happened Weds night. Mazu led the service, telling
us all about Alexander Graves and how he went to live at
Chapman Farm because of his abusive family. A huge straw
man, bigger than life size, was standing in the middle on a
raised platform in a spotlight and*

Robin now stopped writing. She hadn't had time to fully process what had happened in the temple and with her fingers numb with cold she doubted she could convey to Strike just how frightening the Manifestation had been: the pitch darkness pierced by two spotlights, one trained on Mazu, in her blood red robes, the mother-of-pearl fish gleaming on its cord around her neck, the other on that towering straw figure. Mazu had commanded the straw figure to give proof that the Stolen Prophet lived on in the spirit world, and a hoarse shout had issued from the figure, echoing around the temple walls: *'Let me stay in the temple! Don't let them take me, don't let them hurt me again!'*

Robin resumed her letter.

when Mazu told it to, the figure spoke and lifted its arms. I saw it when they were building it: it was just a wire frame covered in straw, so how they made it move I don't know. Mazu said the Prophet died to show members how vulnerable pure spirits are when they're exposed to materialist wickedness again. Then a noose came snaking down from the ceiling

Robin saw it all again as she wrote: the thick rope snaking down out of the darkness, the noose falling around the figure's neck, then tightening.

and the rope lifted the figure up into the air and it started thrashing around and screaming and trying to chant, then went limp.

Maybe this doesn't sound as scary as it did when I was watching it, but it was terrif—

Robin second-guessed herself; she didn't want Strike to think she was cracking up. Crossing out the word, she wrote instead, *very creepy.*

1. <u>*Wan*</u>

   Right after we'd got back to the women's dormitory after the Manifestation, Wan went into labour. They've clearly got an established procedure for when women give birth because a group of the women, including Louise Pirbright and Sita (more on her below) snapped into action to help her. Becca ran out of the dormitory to tell Mazu, and then kept coming back every hour or so to see what was happening and to report back to the farmhouse.

   They had a medieval kind of kit in the bathroom, with a leather strap thing for Wan to bite on and rusty forceps. Wan wasn't supposed to make any noise. It was my night for coming to the plastic rock but I couldn't leave the dormitory because all the women were awake.

   Wan was in labour for thirty-six hours. It was absolutely awful and the closest I've come to wanting to reveal who I really am and telling them I'm going to the police. I don't know what's normal for a birth but she seemed to lose a huge amount of blood. I was present when the baby was actually born because one of the birthing team couldn't cope any more and I volunteered to take her place. The baby was breech and I was convinced she was going to be born dead. She looked blue at first, but Sita revived her. After all that, Wan wouldn't look at the baby. All she said was, 'Give it to Mazu.' I haven't seen the baby since. Wan's still in bed in the women's dormitory. Sita says she's going to be OK and I hope to God that's true but she looks terrible.

2. <u>*Sita*</u>

   The women who stayed up two nights with Wan were allowed to catch up on sleep today. I managed to get

*talking to Sita in the dormitory once we'd all woken up and
I sat beside her at din*

'Shit,' Robin muttered, shaking the ballpoint. As she'd feared, it seemed to be running out of ink.

Then Robin froze. In the absence of the scratching of pen on paper, she'd heard something else: footsteps and a female voice quietly and relentlessly chanting.

'*Lokah Samastah Sukhino Bhavantu ... Lokah Samastah Sukhino Bhav—*'

The chanting stopped. Robin extinguished the pencil torch she was holding in her mouth and flung herself flat among the nettles again, but too late: she knew the chanter had seen the light.

'Who's there? *Who's there?* I c-c-can see you!'

Robin slowly sat up, shoving the torch, pen and paper behind her as she did so.

'Lin,' said Robin. 'Hi.'

The girl was alone this time. A car swished past, and as the beam of its headlights slid over Lin Robin saw that her pale face was streaked with tears and her hands full of plants she'd tugged up by the roots. For what felt like a long time, though was really a few seconds, the two stared at each other.

'Wh-wh-why are you here?'

'I needed some fresh air,' said Robin, cringing inwardly at the inadequacy of the lie, 'and then – then I felt a bit dizzy, so I sat down. It's been an intense few days, hasn't it? With Wan and – and everything.'

By the faint moonlight, Robin saw the young girl glance up at the trees, in the direction of the closest security camera.

'What m-m-made you come *here*, though?'

'I got a bit lost,' Robin lied, 'but then I saw the light from the road and came here so I could get my bearings. What are you up to?'

'D-d-don't t-t-tell anyone you saw me,' said Lin. Her large eyes shone weirdly in the shadowed face. 'If you t-t-tell anyone, I'll say you were out of b-b-b-b-b—'

'I won't tell—'

'—*bed* and that I saw you and f-f-f-ollowed—'

'—I promise,' said Robin urgently. 'I won't tell.'

Lin turned and hurried away into the trees, still clutching her uprooted plants. Robin listened until Lin's footsteps died away completely, leaving a silence broken only by the usual nocturnal rustlings of the woods.

Waves of panic broke over Robin as she sat very still, contemplating the possible repercussions of this unexpected meeting. She turned her head to look at the wall behind her.

Shah was in the vicinity. Perhaps it would be better to climb onto the road now and wait for him to come back and check the rock? If Lin talked, if Lin told the church leaders she'd found Robin at the blind spot of the perimeter with a torch she definitely shouldn't possess ...

For several minutes, Robin sat very still, thinking, barely conscious of the cold earth beneath her and the breeze lifting the hair from her nettle-stung neck. Then, reaching a decision, she groped around to find her unfinished letter, pen and torch, re-read what she'd communicated so far, then continued writing.

She looks as though she's over 70 and has been here since the earliest days of the church. She came here at Wace's invitation to teach yoga and told me she soon realised Papa J was 'a very great swami', so she stayed.

I got her talking about Becca quite easily, because Sita doesn't like her (hardly anyone does). When I mentioned Becca knowing the Drowned Prophet, she told me Becca was really jealous of Daiyu when they were kids. She said all the little girls loved Cherie, and Becca was really envious of Daiyu getting special attention from her.

Robin stopped writing again, wondering whether to tell Strike about her encounter with Lin. She could imagine what he'd say: get out now, you're compromised, you can't trust a brainwashed teenager. However, after a further minute's deliberation, she signed the letter without mentioning Lin, took up a fresh piece of paper and turned instead to the task of explaining to Murphy why she still wasn't ready to leave Chapman Farm.

61

Nine in the third place.
All day long the superior man is creatively active.
At nightfall his mind is still beset with cares.

The I Ching or Book of Changes

Strike's primary emotion on receiving Robin's most recent dispatch from Chapman Farm was relief that the twenty-four-hour delay hadn't been due to injury or illness, although he found much food for thought in its contents, and re-read it several times at his desk, his notebook open beside him.

While he didn't doubt that the Manifestation of the Stolen Prophet had been disconcerting for those present, Strike still agreed with Abigail Glover: Mazu Wace had built on the lowly magic tricks Gerald Crowther had taught her, to the point that she was now able to perform large-scale illusions, using lighting, sound and misdirection.

Robin's account of Wan's labour, on the other hand, genuinely troubled him. He'd been concentrating so hard on deaths at Chapman Farm, with particular focus on proper record-keeping, that he'd overlooked possible wrong-doing with regard to births. Now he wondered what would have happened if the mother or baby had died, why Mazu, a woman with no medical background, had to see the baby the moment it was born, and why the baby hadn't been seen since.

The passages relating to Becca Pirbright also interested Strike, especially her accusation that her sister had passed information to Kevin for his book. Having re-read these paragraphs, he got up from his desk to re-examine the picture of Kevin Pirbright's room pinned to the board on the wall. Once again his gaze travelled over the writing that was legible on the walls, which included the name Becca.

An internet search enabled him to find pictures of the adult Becca onstage at UHC seminars. He remembered Robin describing her as being like a motivational speaker, and certainly this beaming, shiny-haired woman in her logo-embossed sweatshirt had a whiff of the corporate about her. He was particularly interested in the fact that Becca had been jealous of the attention Daiyu received from Cherie Gittins. Strike scribbled a few more notes for himself, relating to the questions he intended to ask the Heatons, who'd met the hysterical Cherie on Cromer beach after Daiyu's drowning.

The next week was busy, though unproductive in terms of advancing any of the cases on the agency's books. In addition to his various other general and personal preoccupations, Strike's mind kept flitting back to the dark woman at the Connaught, who claimed to have recognised him. It had been the very first time a stranger had done so, and it had worried him to the extent that he'd done something he'd never done before, and Googled himself. As he'd hoped and expected, there were very few pictures of him available online: the one used most often by the press had been taken back when he was still a military policeman and far younger and fitter. The rest showed him sporting the full beard that grew conveniently quickly when he needed it, and which he'd always worn when having to give evidence in court. He still found it strange that the woman had recognised him, clean-shaven and wearing glasses, and he couldn't escape the suspicion that she'd been trying to draw attention to him, thereby sabotaging his surveillance.

Having discounted the possibility that she was a journalist – the direct approach in the middle of the restaurant merely to confirm his identity, would be bizarre behaviour – he was left with three possible explanations.

First: he'd managed to acquire a stalker. He thought this highly unlikely. While he had plenty of supporting evidence to prove he was attractive to certain kinds of women, and his investigative career had taught him that even apparently successful and wealthy people could be harbouring strange impulses, Strike found it very hard to imagine a woman that good looking and well dressed would be following him around for kicks.

Second: she was something to do with the Universal Humanitarian Church. His chat with Fergus Robertson had made it clear to what extremes the church was prepared to go to protect its interests. Was it possible she was one of the church's wealthier and more influential members? If that was the explanation, the UHC evidently knew the agency was investigating them, which had serious implications not only for the case, but for Robin's safety. Indeed, it might imply that Robin had been identified at Chapman Farm.

The last, and, in his opinion, most likely possibility was that the woman was a second Patterson operative. In this case, her loud, public approach might have been done purely to draw attention to him and scupper his job. It was this possibility that made Strike text a description of the woman to Barclay, Shah and Midge, telling them to be on the lookout for her.

The evening before his trip to Cromer, Strike worked late in the otherwise empty office, dealing with tedious paperwork while eating a packaged quinoa salad. It was the day of the Brexit referendum, but Strike hadn't had time to vote: the

Franks had decided to split up that day and he'd been pinned down, watching for the younger brother in Bexleyheath.

A combination of tedium and hunger made him particularly irritated by the sound of the office phone ringing at nearly eleven at night. Certain it was Charlotte, he let it go to voice-mail. The phone rang again twenty minutes later, and at one minute to midnight rang for a third time.

Finally closing the various folders on the desk, he added his signature to a couple of documents and got up to file everything away.

Before leaving the office for his attic flat he paused at Pat's desk again and pressed a button on her phone. He didn't want anyone else to listen to Charlotte's tirades: once had been enough.

'Bluey, pick up. Seriously, Bluey, please, please pick up. I'm desp—'

Strike pressed delete, then played the next message. She sounded angry as well as pleading now.

'*I need to talk to you.* If you've got any humanity at a—'

He pressed delete, then play.

Now a malevolent whisper filled the room, and he could visualise Charlotte's expression, because he'd seen her like that at her most destructive, when there was no limit to her appetite to wound.

'You'll wish you'd picked up, you know. You will. And so will precious fucking *Robin,* when she hears what you really are. I know where she lives, you realise that? I'll be doing her a fav—'

Strike slammed his hand onto the phone, deleting the message.

He knew why Charlotte was taking things this far: she'd at long last admitted to herself that Strike wasn't ever coming back. For nearly six years she'd believed the craving she couldn't eradicate in herself lived on in him, too, and that her beauty, her vulnerability and their long, shared history would reunite them, no matter all that had gone before, no matter how determined he was not to return. Charlotte's flashes of insight and extraordinary ability to sniff out weak spots had always had something of the witch about them. She'd correctly intuited that he must be in love with his business partner, and this certainty was driving her to new heights of vindictiveness.

He'd have liked to comfort himself with the belief that Charlotte's threats were empty, but he couldn't: he knew her far too well. Possible scenarios ran through his head, each more damaging than the last: Charlotte turning up outside Robin's house, Charlotte tracking down Murphy, Charlotte making good on her threat, and speaking to the press.

He'd had a little malicious fun in the pub with Murphy, refusing to disclose what he might have heard from Wardle to Murphy's discredit. Now he looked back on what he felt might have been a dangerous bit of self-indulgence. Ryan Murphy would have no sense of loyalty to Strike, should Charlotte decide to spin him a line about what Strike was 'really like', or to pass on to Robin the vitriol Charlotte might choose to unleash in the press.

After what might have been one minute or ten, Strike became aware that he was still standing beside Pat's desk, every muscle in his arms and neck tense. The office looked strange, almost alien, in the overhead lights, with the darkness closing in against the windows. As he headed to the door with both partners' names engraved upon it, the only cold comfort he could draw from the situation was that Charlotte couldn't ambush Robin, as long as she was at Chapman Farm.

62

Strike learned in the car on the way to the Heatons' house in Cromer that Britain had voted to leave the EU. He switched off the radio after an hour of listening to commentators speculating on what this would mean for the country and listened instead to Tom Waits' *Swordfishtrombones*.

He might have chosen to pick up Robin's latest letter on the way back from Cromer, but he'd allotted the job to Midge. Having done it once already, he'd learned the hard way how difficult it was for a man with half his leg missing to get over the wall and barbed wire without injuring himself or falling into the nettle patch on the other side. However, he deliberately chose to drive past the entrance to Lion's Mouth and Chapman Farm, even though, under normal circumstances, it was the last place he'd have ventured near. Inevitably, more unpleasant memories assailed him, as he passed the electric gates, and saw on the horizon that curious tower that resembled a giant chess piece; he remembered being convinced, at the age of eleven, that it had something to do with the Crowther brothers, that it was a watchtower of some description, and even though he'd never known exactly what was going on in the cabins and tents, out of sight, his inner antenna for evil had imagined children locked up in there. The fact that Robin was momentarily so close, but unreachable, did nothing whatsoever to improve his spirits, and he drove away from Chapman Farm with his mood even lower than it had been over breakfast, when his thoughts had been dominated by Charlotte's threats of the previous night.

Cornishman that he was, proximity to the ocean generally cheered him up, but on entering Cromer he saw many old walls and buildings covered in rounded flints, which reminded him unpleasantly of the farmhouse into which Leda had periodically disappeared to discuss philosophy and politics, leaving her children unsupervised and unprotected.

He parked the BMW in a car park in the middle of town and got out beneath an overcast sky. The Heatons lived in Garden Street, which lay within walking distance, and narrowed into a pedestrian alley as it approached the seafront, the ocean framed between old houses as a small square of teal beneath a cloudy grey sky. Their house lay on the left side of the street: a solid-looking terraced residence with a dark green front door that opened directly onto the pavement. Strike imagined it would be a noisy place to live, with pedestrians tramping up and down from the beach to the shops and the Wellington pub.

When he rapped on the door using a knocker shaped like a horseshoe, a dog started yapping furiously from the interior. The door was opened by a woman in her early sixties, whose platinum hair was cut short and whose skin was the colour and texture of old leather. The dog, which was tiny, fluffy and white, was clutched to her sizeable bosom. For a split second, Strike thought he must have come to the wrong house, because gales of laughter issued from behind her, audible even over the still-yapping dog.

'Got friends over,' she said, beaming. 'They wanted to meet you. Everyone's excited.'

You have to be kidding me.

'I take it you're—?'

'Shelley Heaton,' she said, extending a hand, on which a heavy gold charm bracelet tinkled. 'Come on in. Len's through there with the rest of 'em. Do you *shet up*, Dilly.'

The dog's yapping subsided. Shelley led Strike down a dark hallway and left into a comfortable but not over-large sitting room, which seemed to be full of people. Hazy shadows of holiday-makers drifted to and fro behind the net curtains: as Strike had expected, the noise from the street was constant.

'Thass Len,' said Shelley, pointing at a large, ruddy-faced man with the most obvious comb-over Strike had seen in years. Leonard Heaton's right leg, which was encased in a surgical boot, was resting on a squat pouffe. The table beside him was crammed with framed photographs, many of them featuring the dog in Shelley's arms.

'Hare he is,' said Len Heaton loudly, offering a sweaty paw embellished with a large signet ring. 'Cameron Strike, I presume?'

'That's me,' said Strike, shaking hands.

'I'll juss make the tea,' said Shelley, looking hungrily at Strike. 'Don't go starting without me!'

She set down the small dog and left with a jangle of jewellery. The dog trotted after her.

'This is our friends George and Gillian Cox,' said Leonard Heaton, pointing at the sofa, where three plump people, also in their sixties, were tightly wedged, 'and thass Suzy, Shell's sister.'

Suzy's eager eyes looked like raisins in her doughy face. George, whose paunch rested almost on his knees, was entirely bald and wheezing slightly, even though he was stationary.

Gillian, who had curly grey hair and wore silver spectacles, said proudly,

'I'm the one you spoke to, on the phone.'

'Do you set down,' Heaton told Strike comfortably, pointing at the armchair with its back to the window, facing his own. 'Happy about the referendum?'

'Oh, yeah,' said Strike, who judged from Len Heaton's expression that this was the correct answer.

During the few minutes Heaton's wife moved in and out of the kitchen carrying tea, cups, plates and lemon drizzle cake, regularly crying 'Wait fur me, I wanna hear it all!', Strike had ample time to realise that the three blondes who'd cornered him at his godson's christening had been mere amateurs in nosiness. The sofa-dwellers bombarded him with questions, not only about all his most newsworthy cases, but also about his parentage, his missing half leg and even – here, his determined good nature nearly failed – his relationship with Charlotte Campbell.

'That was a long time ago,' he said as firmly as was compatible with politeness, before turning to Leonard Heaton. 'So you're just back from Spain?'

'Ah, thass right,' said Leonard, whose forehead was peeling. 'Got ourselves a little place in Fuengirola ahter I sowd my business. We're normally there November through to April, but—'

'He broke his bloody leg,' said Shelley, finally sitting down on a chair beside her husband, perching the tiny white dog on her knee and looking greedily at Strike.

'Liss of the "bloody", you,' said Leonard, smirking. He had the air of a joker used to commanding the room, but he didn't seem to resent Strike's temporary hogging of centre stage, perhaps because he and his wife were enjoying playing the role of impresarios who'd brought this impressive exhibit for their friends' amusement.

'Tell him what you was up to whan you broke it,' Shelley instructed her husband.

'Thass neither hare nor there,' said a smirking Leonard, clearly wanting to be prompted.

'Go on, Leonard, tell him,' said Gillian, giggling.

'I'll tell'm, then,' said Shelley. *'Minigolf.'*

'Really?' said Strike, smiling politely.

'Bloody *minigolf*!' said Shelley. 'I said to him, "How the hell d'you manage to break a leg doing *minigolf*?"'

'Tripped,' said Leonard.

'Pissed,' said Shelley, and the audience on the sofa chortled more loudly.

'Do you shet up, woman,' said Leonard, archly innocent. 'Tripped. Could've happened to anyone.'

'Funny how it olluz happens to *you*,' said Shelley.

'They're olluz like this!' the giggling Gillian told Strike, inviting him to enjoy the Heatons' madcap humour. 'They never stop!'

'We stayed out in Fuengirola till he could walk better,' said Shelley. 'He didn't fancy the plane and tryina manage the steps down the esplanade at home. We had to miss out on a couple of summer bookings, but thass the price you pay for marrying a man who breaks his leg tryina git a golf ball into a clown's mouth.'

The trio on the sofa roared with laughter, darting eager looks at Strike to see whether he was suitably entertained, and Strike continued to smile as sincerely as he could manage while drawing out his notebook and pen, at which a silence tingling with excitement fell over the room. Far from dampening anyone's spirits, the prospect of raking back over the accidental death of a child seemed to be having a stimulating effect on all present.

'Well, it's very good of you to agree to see me,' Strike told the Heatons. 'As I said, I'm really just after an eyewitness account of what happened that day on the beach. It's a long time ago now, I know, but—'

'Well, we were up right arly,' said Shelley eagerly.

'Ah, crack of dawn,' said Leonard.

'Before dawn,' Shelley corrected him. 'Still dark.'

'We were s'pposed to be driving up to Leicester—'

'Fur me auntie's funeral,' interjected Shelley.

'You can't leave a Maltese,' said Leonard. 'They do howl the place down if you leave 'em, so we needed t'ampty har before we got in the car. You're not s'posed to take dogs down on the beach in th'oliday season—'

'But Betty was like Dilly, she wus only tiny, and we always pick up,' said Shelley comfortably. After a split second's confusion, Strike realised she was referring to dog shit.

'So we took har along the beach, just out there,' said Leonard, pointing left. 'And the gal come a-runnin' out of the dark, screaming.'

'Give me a hell of a tann,' said Shelley.

'We thowt she'd had a sex attack or something,' said Leonard, not without a certain relish.

'Can you remember what she said?'

'"Hilp me, hilp me, she's gone under" sorta thing,' said Leonard.

'"I thenk she's drowned",' said Shelley.

'We thowt she meant a dog. Who goes swimming, five a.m. in the North Sea? She wus in her undies. Soaking wet,' said Leonard with a smirk and a waggle of his eyebrows. Shelley cuffed her husband with the back of her ringed hand.

'Behave yoursalf,' said Shelley, smirking at Strike, while the sofa-sitters snorted with renewed laughter.

'She wasn't in a swimsuit?'

'Undies,' repeated Leonard, smirking. 'Freezing cold.'

Shelley cuffed him again while the sofa-sitters laughed.

'I thowt at fust she'd stripped off to go in ahter the dog,' said Shelley. 'Navver dreamed she'd been swimming.'

'And she said, "Help me, she's gone under"?' asked Strike.

'Ah, something like that,' said Leonard. 'Than she says, "We wus over hare" and goes running off to—'

'No, she navver,' said Shelley. 'She asked us to git the coast-guard fust.'

'No, she navver,' said Leonard. 'She showed us the stuff fust.'

'No, she navver,' said Shelley, 'she said, "Git the coastguard, git the coastguard."'

''Ow come I seen the stuff, then?'

'You seen the stuff ahter you come back, you dozy foal,' said Shelley, to further chuckles from the sofa.

'What stuff was this?' Strike asked.

'Towels and clothes – the little gal's driss and shoes,' said Shelley. 'She took me over to tham, and whan I seen the shoes, I realised it was a kid. Orful,' she said, but her tone was matter-of-fact. Strike could tell that the drowning had receded into the distant past for the Heatons. Such shock as it might have caused them two decades ago had long since subsided.

'I come along with yarsalves,' said Leonard stubbornly. 'I warn't gonna call up the coastguard fur a dog. I wus there, I seen the shoes—'

'All right, Leonard, you wus with us, ha'it your own way,' said Shelley, rolling her eyes.

'So *then* I go to phone the coastguard,' said Leonard, satisfied.

'And you stayed with Cherie, Mrs Heaton?'

'Ah, and I said to har, "The hell was you doing in the water, this hour of the morning?"'

'And what did she say?' asked Strike.

'Said the little gal wanted a paddle.'

'I said to Shelley ahter,' interjected Leonard, '"thass what the word "no"'s for. We see kids like that hare avery summer, spoiled as hell. We navver had any ourselves—'

'How'm I supposed to manage kids? I've got my hands full with you, breaking your bloody legs playing minigolf,' said Shelley, drawing more giggles from the sofa. 'I should tell *you* no more often.'

'You tell me no plenny, thass why we ha'n't got kids,' said Leonard, which provoked shrieks of laughter from George, Gillian and Suzy and another cuff from his smirking wife.

'Did Cherie tell you what had happened in the sea?' Strike asked Shelley patiently.

'Ah, she said the little gal went too deep and went under, said she tried to reach har and couldn't, so she swum back to shore. Than she seen us and come a-running.'

'And how did Cherie seem to you? Upset?'

'More scared'n upset, I thowt,' said Shelley.

'Shell din't like har,' said Leonard.

'*He* liked har, 'cause he was gitting an arly morning eyeful,' said Shelley, while the chorus on the sofa chuckled. 'She said to me, "I nearly drowned mysalf, the current's right strong." Looking fur sympathy for harsalf, and thar's a kid dead.'

'You've olluz been hard on—'

'*I* weren't the one with the hard on, Len,' said Shelley.

The trio on the sofa shrieked with scandalised laughter, and both Heatons threw a triumphant glance at Strike, as if to say they doubted he'd ever been entertained like this during an investigation. The detective's jaw was starting to ache with all the fake smiling he was having to do.

'An' she giggled and all,' Shelley told Strike, over the others' laughter. 'I said to har, put your clothes back on, no point standing there like that. "Oh yeah," she said, an' she giggled.'

'Narves,' said Leonard. 'Shock.'

'You warn't there whan that happened,' said Shelley. 'You wus phoning.'

'You didn't think she was genuinely upset Daiyu had drowned, Mrs Heaton?' Strike asked.

'Well, she wus crying a bit, but if it'd been me—'

'You took agin har,' Leonard told Shelley.

'She bent down to Betty and fussed har,' said Shelley. 'Whass she doing playing with a dog whan there's a little gal drowning?'

'Shock,' said Leonard staunchly.

'How long were you away, Mr Heaton?' asked Strike.

'Twenny minutes? Haaf hour?'

'And how quickly did the coastguard get out?'

'They wus out there not long ahter I got back to the beach,' said Leonard. 'We seen the boat going out, seen the lights, and the police wus on the beach not long ahter that.'

'She was bloody scared whan the police got there,' said Shelley.

'Natural,' said Leonard.

'She run awff,' said Shelley.

'She navver,' scoffed Leonard.

'She did,' said Shelley. '"Whass that over there?" She went tanking off to see something along the beach. Pebbles or weed or something. Sun wus just coming up by then. It wus an excuse,' said Shelley. 'She wanted to look busy whan they arrived, poking around in the weed.'

'Thass not running awff,' said Leonard.

'Lump of seaweed, a seven-year-old gal? She wus playing up fur the police. "Look at me trying averything t'find har." No, I din't like har,' Shelley told Strike unnecessarily. 'Irresponsible, warn't she? It wus har fault.'

'What happened when the police arrived, can you remember?' asked Strike.

'They asked how she and the little gal got there, 'cause she warn't local,' said Shelley.

'She took us up to the scrappy owd truck with dirt and straw all over it, in the car park,' said Leonard. 'Said they wus from that farm, that church place full of weirdos, up Aylmerton way.'

'You already knew about the Universal Humanitarian Church, did you?' asked Strike.

'Friends of aars in Felbrigg, they'd towd us about the place,' said Shelley.

'Weirdos,' repeated Leonard. 'So we're standing in the car park and the police wants us all to go t'station, to make statements. I says, "We've got a funeral to git to." The gal was crying. Then owd Muriel come out the café, to see whass going on.'

'This is Muriel Carter, who saw Cherie take Daiyu down to the beach?'

'Know your stuff, don'tchew?' said Shelley, as impressed by Strike's thoroughness as Jordan Reaney had been disconcerted. 'Ah, thass her. Used to own a café down by that bit of beach.'

'Did you know her?'

'We'd navver spoken to har before all this happened,' said Shelley, 'but we knew her ahter that. She told the police she'd seen Cherie carrying the little gal out the truck and off down the beach. She thowt it was stupid, that time in the morning, seeing Cherie with towels and that.'

'Muriel was in her café very early,' commented Strike. 'This must have all been – what, five in the morning?'

'Coffee machine wus on the blink,' said Leonard. 'She'n har husband wus in there tryina fix it before opening time.'

'Ah, right,' said Strike, making a note.

'Muriel said the kid wus sleepy,' said Shelley. 'I said to Leonard ahter, "So she warn't pestering har for a paddle, then, thass just an excuse." I thenk it wus Cherie who wanted to go swimming, not the little gal.'

'Do you give it a rest, woman,' said Leonard before saying to Strike, 'Th'only reason Muriel thowt the kid wus sleepy wus 'cause Cherie was carrying har. Kids like being carried, that don't mean nothen.'

'Wut about wut come out at the inquest?' Shelley asked Leonard sharply. 'About har swimming? Tell'm.' But before Leonard could do so, Shelley said,

'Cherie wus a champion swimmer. She said it at the inquest, in the dock.'

'Champion,' said Leonard, with an eye roll, 'she warn't a *champion*, she wus juss good at it whan she wus a kid.'

'She wus on a team,' said Shelley, still speaking to Strike. 'She'd won medals.'

'So?' said Leonard. 'Thass not a bloody crime.'

'If *I* wus a bloody champion swimmer I'd've stayed out thar to halp the little gal, not gawn back to the beach,' said Shelley firmly, to a murmur of agreement from the sofa.

'Don't matter how many medals you've got, a rip tide's a rip tide,' said Leonard, now looking disgruntled.

'This is interesting,' said Strike, and Shelley looked excited. 'How did the subject of Cherie's swimming come up at the inquest, can you remember?'

'Ah, I can,' said Shelley, 'because she wus tryin' to make out it wusn't irresponsible, takin' the little gal into the sea, because she wus a strong swimmer harself. I said to Len after, "Medals make you see in the dark, do they?" "Medals make it ollright to take a little gal who can't swim into the North Sea, do they?"'

'So it was established at the inquest that Daiyu couldn't swim, was it?'

'Ah,' said Leonard. 'Har mother said she'd navver larned.'

'I didn't take to that mother,' said Shelley. 'Looked like a witch.'

'Wearin' robes, Shell, warn't she?' piped up Suzy from the sofa.

'Long black robes,' said Shelley, nodding. 'You'd thenk, ef you were going to court, you'd put on proper clothes. Juss respectful.'

'Iss their religion,' said Leonard, forgetting that he'd just described the church members as weirdos. 'You carn't stop people following thar religion.'

'Ef you ask me, *Cherie* wus the one who wanted the swim,' Shelley told Strike, disregarding her husband's interjection. 'The kid was sleepy, *she* warn't asking to go. It was Cherie's idea.'

'You don't know that,' said Leonard.

'Navver said I knew it,' said Shelley loftily. '*Suspected*.'

'Can you remember any details Cherie gave about her swimming career?' asked Strike. 'The name of a club? Where she trained? I'm trying to trace Cherie and if I could find old teammates, or a coach—'

'Hang on,' said Leonard, perking up.

'What?' said Shelley.

'I might be able to 'elp thar.'

''Ow?' said Shelley sceptically.

''Cause after court, I spoke to har. She wus crying outside. One of the little gal's family had just been talking to har – havin' a go, probably. He walked off quick enough when I gone over to har,' said Leonard, with a slight swelling of the chest. 'I felt sorry fur har, an' I towd her, "I know you done averything you could, love." You warn't thar, you wus in the bog,' said Leonard, forestalling Shelley. 'She said to me, crying, like, "But I could've stopped it", and—'

'Hang on,' said Strike. 'She said, "But I could've stopped it"?'

'Ah,' said Leonard.

'Those exact words? "I could've stopped it", not "I could have saved her"?'

Leonard hesitated, absent-mindedly smoothing down the few strands of greying hair doing such a poor job of disguising his baldness.

'Ah, it wus "I could've stopped it",' he said.

'You can't remember th'exact words, not after all this time,' said Shelley scornfully.

'Do you shet up, woman,' said Leonard, for the second time, no longer smiling. 'I can, an' I'll tell you why, because I said back to her: "Nothing on earth'll stop a rip tide." Thass wut I said. An' then she said, "I'll navvar go swimming again" or sumthing, an' I said, "Thass juss silly, after all tham medals," an' she kinda laughed—'

'Laughed!' said Shelley indignantly. 'Laughed, an' there's a kid dead!'

'—an' she started telling me a bit about what she'd won, an' then you come outta the bog,' Leonard told Shelley, 'an' said we needed to get back to Betty, so off we went. But I know whar she practised wus open air, 'cause—'

''Cause you started picturing har in har undies again, probably,' said Shelley, eyes on her audience, but nobody sniggered: they were all now interested in Leonard's story.

'—cause she said she trained at a lido. I remember that. You've olluz been hard on that gal,' he said, looking sideways at his wife. 'She warn't as bad as you make out.'

'It wus her fault,' said Shelley implacably, with a supporting murmur from the two women on the sofa. 'Bloody stupid thing to do, take a kid who can't swim to the beach, that time in the morning. I spoke to the little gal's aunt in the bathroom,' she added, possibly to even up the score between herself and Leonard, who'd just excited so much interest from Strike, 'an' she agreed the blame wus what it belonged an' she thanked me an' Leonard fur whut we'd done, gettin' the coastguard an' oll that, an' she said it wus a relief it wus oll over. Posh woman,' Shelley added judiciously, 'but very nice.'

'Nearly there, just a few more questions,' said Strike, casting an eye over his notes to check he hadn't missed anything. 'Did either of you see anyone else on the beach, before the police got there?'

'No, there warn't—' began Shelley, but Leonard spoke over her.

'There wus. There wus tha' jogger.'

'Oh, yeah, there wus him,' said Shelley grudgingly. 'But *he* warn't nothing to do with it.'

'When did you see him?' asked Strike.

'He run past us,' said Leonard. 'Not long after we got on the beach.'

'Running towards the place where you met Cherie, or away from it?' asked Strike.

'Away,' said Leonard.

'Can you remember what he looked like?'

'Big guy, I thenk,' said Leonard, 'but it wus dark.'

'And he was on his own? Jogging, not carrying anything?'

'No, he warn't carrying nothing,' said Leonard.

'Given the timings, would he have passed Cherie and Daiyu when they were still on the beach, do you think? Or after they entered the water?'

The Heatons looked at each other.

'Ahter,' said Leonard. 'Can't've been more'n five minutes after we seen him, she come out the sea, screaming.'

Strike made a note, then asked,

'Did you see or hear any boats in the area – before the coastguard went out, I mean?'

Both Heatons shook their heads.

'And the van was empty when you got there?'

'Ah, empty and locked up,' said Leonard.

'And how long did the coastguard look for the body, d'you know?'

'Ah, they give it a good few days,' said Leonard.

'They said at the inquest she must've got dragged down and got stuck somewhar,' said Shelley. ''S'orful, really,' she said, fondling her tiny dog's ears. 'Whan you thenk about it ... poor little gal.'

'One last thing,' said Strike, 'would you happen to remember another drowning off the beach, back in 1988? A woman had a seizure in the water, not far from the shore.'

''Ang on a mo,' piped up the wheezy George from the sofa. ''Eighty-eight? I remember that. I was *thar*!'

His companions all looked round at him, surprised.

'Ah,' said George excitedly, 'if iss the one I'm thenking of, she wus with a little gal, too!'

'That sounds right,' said Strike. 'The drowned woman was there with her husband and daughter. Did you see what happened?'

'I seen a bloke with long har a-running into the sea and then him an' another bloke dragging her up along the beach. The little gal wus crying and screaming. Tarrible business. The firs' man gev har mouth to mouth until the ambulance came, but I hard after it was no good, she died. It wus in the paper. Epileptic. Tarrible business.'

'Wut's that got to do with our little gal?' asked a curious Shelley.

'The man whose wife died of the seizure in the water was Daiyu's stepfather,' said Strike.

'*No!*' said Shelley and Suzy together.

'Yes,' said Strike, closing his notebook.

'*Thass* a funny coincidence,' said the wide-eyed Shelley.

'It is, isn't it?' said Strike. 'Well, I think that's everything. You've been very helpful, thank you. I wonder whether you could give me directions to the bit of beach where you met Cherie?'

'Straight down th'end of our road, turn left,' said Leonard, pointing. 'You can't miss it, the old café and car park's still thar.'

'And where——?' began Strike, turning to George, but the latter anticipated the question.

'Same place,' he said, and the three women gasped. 'Exact same place.'

63

The heart thinks constantly. This cannot be
changed, but the movements of the heart— that is,
a man's thoughts— should restrict themselves to the
immediate situation. All thinking that goes beyond
this only makes the heart sore.

The I Ching or Book of Changes

It took Strike a further twenty minutes to extricate himself from the Heatons and their friends, but he did so as tactfully and pleasantly as he could manage, in case he needed to speak to them again. Once outside, he relaxed his facial muscles with relief, walked to the end of Garden Street and onto the esplanade.

The sky was a flat grey, with one silvered patch where the sun was attempting to break through. As Strike walked along the high promenade, he pulled his vape pen out of his pocket. Even after losing so much weight over the last year, the end of his stump was sore and the muscles in his right thigh tight. At last he spotted a short stretch of cabins selling coffees, burgers and beach toys, beside which was a small car park.

This, then, was the place where, twenty years previously, Cherie Gittins had parked the old farm truck and carried Daiyu down to the sea.

A salty breeze stung Strike's tired eyes as he leaned on the railings, and squinted down onto the beach. In spite of the unpropitious weather, there were still people walking over the patches of dun-coloured sand that were strewn with rounded flints, like those that adorned the town's older walls. A number of roosting seagulls appeared between the sea-worn stones like larger rocks. Strike could see neither seaweed nor shells, nor were there any danger flags flying; the sea looked fairly placid, and its briny smell, coupled with the familiar sound of the rhythmic rush and retreat of the waves, intensified an underlying melancholy he was doing his hardest to keep at bay.

Focus.

Two drownings had happened here, seven years apart, to two individuals connected to Jonathan Wace. What had the sobbing Cherie said to Leonard Heaton? 'I could have stopped it.' Not 'I could have stopped *her*,' but 'I could have stopped *it*.' What was 'it'? A plot, as Kevin Pirbright had written on his bedroom wall? And if so, whose?

It hadn't escaped Strike's notice that while three witnesses had seen Cherie and Daiyu driving away from Chapman Farm, and a further witness had seen Cherie carrying Daiyu down onto the beach, there were no witnesses at all for what had actually happened once they reached the sea. Neither the Heatons nor the jogger who'd passed them (who appeared in no press reports) had anything to say about that. For the critical stretch of time in which Daiyu had disappeared forever, the world had only the uncorroborated word of Cherie Gittins, and the myths that had been spun around the Drowned Prophet.

It had still been night when they reached the beach, Strike thought, looking down at the flint-strewn beach. Could Cherie have been meeting somebody secretly here, by arrangement? She'd been a very strong swimmer: had that been part of the plan? Had Cherie plunged into the black water, Daiyu perhaps clinging to her shoulders, so that Daiyu could be taken to a boat moored offshore, where somebody was waiting? Had that person spirited Daiyu away, perhaps killed her and buried her elsewhere, leaving Cherie to swim back to the shore and enact the tragedy of the accidental drowning? Or was it possible that Daiyu was still alive somewhere, living under a different name? After all, some abducted children weren't killed, but kept captive, or raised by families unconnected to them by blood.

Or had Cherie perhaps carried Daiyu down to the beach because the child had been doped at some point during the journey? She must have been alive and alert on leaving Chapman Farm, given that she'd waved at the people who'd watched the van pass. Could Cherie have given Daiyu a drugged drink en route ('There was a night when all the kids were given drinks that I now think must have been drugged,' Kevin Pirbright had written), so that Daiyu drowned, not because she'd waded unwisely into the deeper water, but because she was barely conscious while Cherie held her down beneath the surface? In which case, had Cherie's swimming prowess been required to drag the body out into deep water, in the hope that it would be forever lost, so that nobody could ever perform a post mortem?

Or did the truth lie between these two theories? A body dragged to a boat, where it could be tied to weights, and disposed of in a patch of water the coastguard wouldn't think to search, because the tides should have taken Daiyu in an entirely different direction? Yet if a boat had been moored off the dark beach, it would have been exceptionally lucky to escape the notice of the coastguard: the time margins were too slim for anything but a large, powerful vessel to escape the area in time, in which case the Heatons would surely have heard the motor across the sea in the stillness of the dawn.

There was, of course, one other possibility: that this was a case of two genuine accidents, happening in the same place, seven years apart.

Came up that cold sea at Cromer like a running grave . . .

Strike gazed out at the measureless mass of water, wondering whether what remained of Daiyu was somewhere out there, her bones long since picked clean, entangled in a broken fishing net, perhaps, her skull rolling gently on the sea bed as the waves tumbled far above. In which case, 'I could have stopped it' meant 'I could have stopped her demanding to go to the sea' or 'I could have stopped doing everything she told me to do'.

Come off it.

All right, he argued with himself, *where's the evidence it wasn't a coincidence?*

The common denominator. Jonathan Wace.

That's not evidence. That's part of the coincidence.

After all, if Wace had planned his stepdaughter's murder to get his hands on the quarter of a million pounds Daiyu was worth dead, why instruct Cherie to take her to precisely the same spot where his first wife had lost her life?

Because murderers tended to be creatures of habit? Because, having successfully murdered once, they stuck to the same modus operandi ever after? Might Wace have been planning a brazen double bluff to the police? 'If I was going to drown her, why would I do it *there*?' Could Wace have been hubristic enough to believe he could charm everyone into believing it was all a ghastly twist of fate?

Except that there was a problem with this theory, too: the death of the first Mrs Wace really had been an accident. George's testimony corroborated Abigail's: Wace hadn't been in the water when his wife drowned, and had tried his utmost to save her. Unless . . . watching the waves break on the flints below, Strike wondered whether it was possible to induce an epileptic fit in somebody. He tugged his notebook out of his pocket and wrote a reminder to himself to look into this. He then looked back out to sea, postponing the moment when he'd have to walk again, and thinking about Cherie Gittins.

The girl who'd so foolishly driven her larcenous, knife-toting boyfriend to the pharmacy by daylight a few short years later, and who'd been loose-lipped enough to blurt out 'I could have stopped it' to Leonard Heaton outside the coroner's court, was no mastermind. No, if Daiyu's disappearance had been planned, Strike was certain Cherie had been a tool, rather than the architect of the plot.

His stomach rumbled loudly. He was tired, hungry and his leg was still aching. The last thing he felt like doing was driving back to London this evening. Turning reluctantly away from the sea, he retraced his steps, registering the presence of an enormous and fairly ugly redbrick hotel facing the pier as he turned back into Garden Street. The temptation of checking in was increased by the sight of the King's Head pub, which had a paved beer garden, tucked up the High Street to his left. The rear entrance to the redbrick Hotel de Paris (why Paris?) lay directly opposite the beer garden, beckoning invitingly.

Fuck it.

He'd explain the overnight stay to the agency's pernickety accountant by claiming to have been detained by his investigation. Inside the King's Head, he glanced at a menu on the bar before ordering a pint of Doom Bar and a burger and chips, justifying the latter by the seven preceding days of good dietary behaviour.

The damp beer garden was deserted, which suited Strike, because he wanted to concentrate. Once settled at a table with his vape pen, he took out his mobile and got back to work. Having looked up lidos in the vicinity of Cherie's childhood home, he found one in Herne Hill. Not forgetting that her youthful swimming career would have happened under her birth name of Carine Makepeace, Strike kept Googling, and at last, on page four of his search results, he found what he was looking for: an old photo of a swimming team comprising both boys and girls, posted to the Facebook page of a woman called Sarah-Jane Barnett.

There in the middle of the picture was a girl of eleven or twelve, in whose plump face Strike recognised the simpering smile of the teenager later known as Cherie Gittins. Beneath the picture, Sarah-Jane had written:

Happy memories of the old Brockwell Lido! Oh, to be that fit again, but it was easier when I was 12! L-R John Curtis (who we all fancied!!!), Tamzin Couch, Stuart Whitely, Carrie Makepeace, yours truly, Kellie Powers and Reece Summers.

Strike now pulled up the Facebook page of Carrie Curtis Woods, who still hadn't accepted his follower request. However, he now knew that Cherie had once gone by Carrie too, and better even than that, he had a reason she might have chosen the pseudonym 'Curtis': in tribute to a childhood crush.

Having finished his burger, chips and pint, Strike returned to the car park to pick up a small rucksack containing tooth-brush, toothpaste, clean underwear and a recharging lead for his phone, which he kept in the boot of his car for unforeseen overnight stays, then walked back to the Hotel de Paris.

He could have predicted the interior from the exterior: there was grandeur in the high archways, crystal chandeliers and sweeping staircase of the lobby, but a whiff of the youth hostel about the cork noticeboard on which a laminated history of the hotel had been printed. Incapable as ever of leaving a question unanswered, Strike cast an eye over this, and learned that the hotel had been established by a man whose family had fled France during the revolution.

As he'd hoped, he was able to secure a single room, and as he supposed was inevitable in the summer season, it didn't have a sea view, but looked out over the rooftops of Cromer. Consciously looking for the good, he noted that the room was clean and the bed seemed comfortable, but now that he was shut inside it, surrounded by the same soft yellow and red colour scheme as the lobby, he felt claustrophobic, which he knew to be entirely irrational. Between his childhood and the army, he'd slept in cars, tents pitched on hard ground, squats, that bloody awful barn at Chapman Farm and a multi-storey car park in Angola: he had no reason to complain of a perfectly adequate hotel room.

But as he hung up his jacket and glanced around to determine how many balancing aids were available between the bed and the ensuite bathroom, which he'd need to navigate one-legged next morning, the depression he'd been fighting off all day sagged down upon him. Letting himself drop down onto the bed, he passed a hand over his face, unable to distract himself any longer from the twin causes of his low mood: Charlotte and Robin.

Strike despised self-pity. He'd witnessed serious poverty, trauma and hardship, both in the military and during his detective career, and he believed in counting your blessings. Nevertheless, Charlotte's midnight threats were gnawing at him. If she followed through on them, the consequences wouldn't be pretty. He'd had enough press interest to know how severe a threat it posed to his business, and he was already dealing with an attempt at sabotage from Patterson. He'd hoped never to have to decamp from his office again, or to lose clients who needed an anonymous sleuth, not an unwilling celebrity, least of all one tarred with the suspicion of violence against a woman.

He took out his phone again and Googled his name and Charlotte's.

There were a few hits, mostly old newspaper articles in which their relationship had been mentioned in passing, including the recent one about her assault on Landon Dormer. So she hadn't talked, yet. Doubtless he'd know about it immediately if she did: helpful friends would text him their outrage, as people always did on reading bad news, thinking this would help.

He yawned, plugged the mobile in to charge and, even though it was still early, went to shower before turning in. He'd hoped the hot water would improve his mood, but as he soaped himself, he found his thoughts drifting towards Robin, which brought no consolation. He'd been with her on his last two visits to seaside towns, both taken in the course of other cases: he'd eaten chips with her in Skegness, and stayed overnight in neighbouring rooms in Whitstable.

He remembered particularly the hotel dinner they'd shared that evening, shortly after he'd just broken up with his last girl-friend, and before Robin had gone on her first date with Ryan Murphy. Robin, he remembered, had been wearing a blue shirt. They'd drunk Rioja and laughed together, and waiting upstairs had been those two bedrooms, side by side on the top floor. Everything, he thought, had been propitious: wine, sea view, both of them single, nobody else around to interrupt, and what had he done? Nothing. Even telling her that his relationship – short, unsatisfactory and undertaken purely to distract himself from inconvenient desire for his partner – was over might have precipitated a conversation that would have drawn out Robin's own feelings, but instead he'd maintained his habitual reserve, determined not to mess up their friendship and business partnership, but afraid, too, of rejection. His one, admittedly aborted, drunken move to kiss Robin, outside the Ritz Hotel on her thirtieth, had been met with such a look of horror that it remained branded on his memory.

Naked, he returned to the bedroom to take off his prosthesis. As it parted unwillingly with the gel pad at the end of his stump, he listened to the seagulls wheeling overhead in the sunset and wished to God he'd said something that night in Whitstable, because if he had, he might not currently be feeling so bloody miserable, and resting all his hopes on Ryan Murphy succumbing to one more alcoholic drink.

64

Nine in the third place . . .
Darkening of the light during the hunt in the south . . .
One must not expect perseverance too soon.

The I Ching or Book of Changes

Strike woke next morning to a moment of confusion as to where he was. He'd been dreaming that he was sitting beside Robin in her old Land Rover and exchanging anecdotes about drowning, which in the dream both had experienced several times.

Bleary eyed, he reached across to his mobile to silence the alarm and immediately saw that seven texts had come in over the last half an hour: from Pat, Lucy, Prudence, Shanker, Ilsa, Dave Polworth and journalist Fergus Robertson. With a lurch of dread, he opened Pat's message.

Her sister's just called. I said you weren't here. Hope you're all right.

Strike opened Lucy's next.

Stick, I'm so sorry, I've just seen. It's awful. I don't know what else to say. Hope you're ok xxx

Now with a real sense of foreboding, Strike hitched himself up in bed and opened the text from Fergus Robertson.

I've got the news desk asking if you've got a comment. Might be wise to give them something, get everyone off your back. Don't know if you're aware, but there's a rumour she left a note.

His heart now beating uncomfortably fast, Strike opened his phone browser and typed in Charlotte's name.

Death of an It-Girl: Charlotte Campbell Found Dead

Former Wild Child Charlotte Campbell Found Dead by Cleaner

Charlotte Campbell Dead in Wake of Assault Charge

He stared at the headlines, unable to take in what he was seeing. Then he pressed the link to the last story.

Charlotte Campbell, model and socialite, has died by suicide at the age of 41, her family's lawyer confirmed on Friday evening. In a statement issued to The Times, *Campbell's mother and sister said,*

'Our beloved Charlotte took her own life on Thursday night. Charlotte was under considerable stress following a baseless accusation of assault and subsequent harassment by the press. We request privacy at this very difficult time, particularly for Charlotte's adored young children.'

'We've lost the funniest, cleverest, most original woman any of us knew,' said Campbell's half-brother, actor Sacha

Legard, in a separate statement. 'I'm just one of the heartbroken people who loved her, struggling to comprehend the fact that we'll never hear her laugh again. Death lies on her like an untimely frost Upon the sweetest flower of all the field.'

The younger daughter of broadcaster Sir Anthony Campbell and model Tara Clairmont, Campbell married Jago Ross, Viscount of Croy, in 2011. The couple had twins before divorcing last year. Prior to her marriage she was the long-term girlfriend of private detective Cormoran Strike, eldest son of rock star Jonny Rokeby. More recently Campbell dated Landon Dormer, American billionaire scion of the Dormer hotel empire, but the relationship ended ten days ago with Campbell's arrest for assault. Friends of Dormer assert that he required stitches to his face after an altercation at Dormer's Fitzrovia apartment.

Campbell, who first made news when she ran away from Cheltenham Ladies' College aged 14, gained a degree in Classics at Oxford before becoming a regular fixture on the London social scene. Described as 'mercurial and mesmerising' by Vogue, *she worked intermittently as a model and fashion writer, and spent several spells in rehab during the 90s and 00s. In 2014 she was admitted to the controversial Symonds House, a private psychiatric and addiction clinic, from which she was hospitalised after what was later described as an accidental overdose.*

Campbell's body is believed to have been discovered by a cleaner yesterday morning at her Mayfair flat.

Blood thudded in Strike's ears. He scrolled slowly back up the article.

Two pictures accompanied the piece: the first showed Charlotte in academic gown alongside her parents on her graduation day at Oxford in the nineties. Strike remembered seeing the picture in the press while stationed in Germany with the military police. Unbeknownst to Sir Anthony and his wife, Tara, both of whom had loathed Strike, he and Charlotte had already resumed their affair at long distance.

The second picture showed Charlotte smiling into the camera, wearing a heavy, emerald-studded choker. This was a publicity still for a jewellery collection, and the irrelevant thought flashed through his numb brain that the designer, whom he'd briefly dated, would surely be glad it had been used.

'Fuck,' he muttered, pushing himself up on his pillows. '*Fuck.*'

Shock was battling a heavy sense of absolute inevitability. The final hand had been played and Charlotte had been wiped out, with nothing more to bet and nowhere to find credit. She must have done it right after calling him. Had one of the voicemail messages he'd deleted made her intentions explicit? After threatening to go to Robin and tell her what Strike really was, had Charlotte broken down and pleaded with him to contact her once more? Had she threatened (as she'd done so many times before) to kill herself if he didn't give her what she wanted?

Mechanically, Strike opened the other texts he'd been sent. He could have predicted all of them except Dave Polworth's. Dave had always loathed Charlotte, and had often told Strike he was a fool to keep taking her back.

Bit of a fucker this, Diddy.

These were the exact words Polworth had spoken on first visiting Strike in Selly Oak Military Hospital, following Strike's loss of half a leg.

Strike set down his phone without answering any of the

texts, swung his one and a half legs out of the bed and hopped off towards the bathroom, using the wall and the door jamb to balance. Amidst the many emotions now assailing him was a terrible echo of the day he'd found out his mother had died. Grief stricken though he'd been, the burden of worry and dread he'd carried with him like a dead weight through-out Leda's second marriage to a violent, volatile, drug-using younger man had become redundant: he'd never again need to fear hearing terrible news, because the news had come. A similar, shameful trace of relief was twisted in among his conflicting emotions now: the worst had happened, so he need never again fear the worst.

Having emptied his bladder and cleaned his teeth, he dressed and put on his prosthesis, entirely forgetting breakfast. He checked out of the hotel, so distracted that he couldn't have said with any certainty what sex the receptionist was.

Could he have stopped it happening? Yes, probably, but at what cost? Ongoing contact, escalating demands and pleas to reunite with a woman who lived half addicted to her own pain. He'd long since abandoned the hope of any possibility of real change in Charlotte, because of her adamantine resistance to any succour but drink, drugs and Cormoran Strike.

He drove out of rainswept Cromer thinking about Charlotte's messy, fractured family, which was littered with step-parents and half-siblings and riven with feuds and addiction. *Our beloved Charlotte . . .*

Strike was passing Chapman Farm. He glanced left, and spotted that odd tower on the horizon again. On a whim, he took the next left turn. He was going to find out what that tower actually was.

Why on earth this, now? said Charlotte's angry voice in his head. *What does it matter?*

It matters to me, Strike replied silently.

His one unfailing refuge and distraction in times of trouble, ever since he could remember, had been to detangle and unravel, to try and impose order on the chaotic world, to resolve mysteries, to scratch his persistent itch for truth. Finding out what that tower really was had nothing to do with Charlotte, yet had everything to do with Charlotte. He wasn't a little boy any more, vaguely threatened by the watching tower, even though there were far more things to worry about closer at hand, with his mother out of sight in the woods and predators all around him. Nor was he the nineteen-year-old who'd fallen in love with Oxford's most beautiful student, too dazzled and disarmed that she seemed to love him back to see her clearly. If he did nothing else today, he'd demystify the tower that had lurked in his memory as a symbol of one of the worst times of his life.

It took him only a few minutes to reach the hilltop in the BMW, and there it was: a church, as he should have known it would be: a very old Norfolk church, faced with flint rubble like so many of the buildings he'd passed in Cromer.

He got out of the car. A sign at the entrance to the small graveyard told him this was St John the Baptist Church. Driven by impulses he didn't fully understand he passed through the gate, and found himself trying the door of the church. He'd expected it to be locked, but it opened.

The interior was small, white-walled, and empty. Strike's footsteps echoed as he walked up the aisle, eyes fixed on a plain gold cross on the altar. Then he sat down on one of the hard wooden pews.

He didn't believe in God, but some of the people he'd loved and admired did. His Aunt Joan had had an unshowy faith, and her belief in certain forms and structures had provided a jarring contrast to his mother's disdain for boundaries and every form of small-town respectability. Joan had made Strike and Lucy go to Sunday school during their spells in St Mawes, and these sessions had bored and oppressed him as a child, yet the memory of those lessons was strangely pleasing as he sat on the hard pew: how much sweeter had the dash to the beach been, afterwards? How much more satisfying the games of imagination he and Lucy had played, once released from the tiresome activities they were forced to do while Ted and Joan were taking communion? Perhaps, he thought vaguely, a bit of boredom was no bad thing for kids.

Footsteps behind Strike made him look round.

'Good morning,' said the newcomer, a man in late middle age with a long, pale face and mild eyes, like a sheep. His trousers were fastened with bicycle clips, which Strike hadn't seen for years.

'Morning,' said the detective.

'Everything ollright?'

Strike wondered whether the man was the rector. He wore no dog collar, but then, of course, it wasn't Sunday. *How can you think about that now, why do you care about his dog collar, why this mania for working things out?*

'Someone I know's just died.'

'I'm very sorry to hear that,' said the man, with such obvious sincerity that Strike said, as though to console the stranger,

'She'd been unwell for a long time.'

'Ah,' said the man. 'Still.'

'Yeah,' said Strike.

'I'll leave you,' said the other, his voice now hushed, and he proceeded down the aisle and out of sight, into what Strike assumed was the vestry, probably removing himself so that Strike could pray in peace. He did in fact close his eyes, though not to speak to God. He knew what Charlotte would have said to him now, if she were here.

I'm out of your hair now, Bluey. You should be glad.

I didn't want you dead, he answered, inside his head.

But you knew you were the only one who could save me. I warned you, Bluey.

You can't hold onto someone by threatening to top yourself if they leave. It isn't right. You had kids. You should have stayed alive for them.

Ah, OK. He could visualise her cold smile. *Well, if that's how you want to frame this. I'm dead. I can't argue.*

Don't play that game with me. His anger was rising as though she were really here in this silent church. *I gave you everything I had to give. I put up with shit I'll never put up with again.*

Robin's a saint, is she? How boring, said Charlotte, now smirking at him. *You used to like a challenge.*

She's not a saint any more than I am, but she's a good person.

And now, to his anger, he felt tears coming.

I want a good person for a change, Charlotte. I'm sick of filth and mess and scenes. I want something different.

Would Robin kill herself over you?

Of course she wouldn't. She's got more bloody sense.

Everything we had, everything we shared, and you want someone sensible? The Cormoran I knew would have laughed at the idea of wanting someone sensible. Don't you remember? 'Suns rise and set, but for us there's one brief day then one perpetual night. So kiss me a thousand times . . .'

I was a messed-up fucking kid when I quoted that at you. That's not who I am any more. But I'd still rather you'd lived, and been happy.

I was never happy, said the Charlotte who was sometimes brutally honest, when nothing else had worked, and another vicious scene had left both of them exhausted. *Amused, sometimes. Never happy.*

Yeah, I know.

And he echoed the kindly man in the bicycle clips.

Still.

He opened his damp eyes again to stare at the cross on the altar. He might not believe, but the cross meant something to him, nonetheless. It stood for Ted and Joan, for order and stability, but also for the unknowable and unresolvable, for the human craving for meaning in chaos, and for the hope of something beyond the world of pain and endless striving. Some mysteries were eternal and unresolvable by man, and there was relief in accepting that, in admitting it. Death, love, the endless complexity of human beings: only a fool would claim to fully understand any of them.

And as he sat in this humble old church, with the round tower that lost its sinister aspect when seen up close, he looked back on the teenager who'd left Leda and her dangerous naivety only to fall for Charlotte, and her equally dangerous sophistication, and knew definitively, for the first time, that he was no longer the person who'd craved either of them. He forgave the teenager who'd pursued a destructive force because he thought he could tame it, and thereby right the universe, and make all comprehensible and safe. He wasn't so different from Lucy, after all. They'd both set out to refashion their worlds, they'd just done it in very different ways. If he was lucky, he had half his life to live again, and it was time to give up things far more harmful than smoking and chips, time to admit to himself he should seek something new, as opposed to what was damaging but familiar.

The kindly sheep-faced man had reappeared. As he made his way back down the aisle, he paused uncertainly beside Strike.

'I hope you've found what you needed.'

'I have,' said Strike. 'Thank you.'

PART FIVE

K'uei/Opposition

Above, fire; below, the lake:
The image of OPPOSITION.
Thus amid all fellowship
The superior man retains his individuality.

The I Ching or Book of Changes

65

*The line is yielding and stands between two strong
lines; it can be compared to a woman who has lost her
veil and is consequently exposed to attack.*

The I Ching or Book of Changes

As Strike saw no reason to inform Robin either of Charlotte's
suicide or his detour to St John the Baptist in his next letter, she
only knew that he'd been to Cromer to interview the Heatons.
Learning that her partner passed within a mile of Chapman
Farm on his way to the coast made Robin feel even lonelier.
She, too, thought back to the two seaside towns they'd visited
together in the course of previous investigations, especially the
dinner in Whitstable: the white coral on the mantelpieces set
against slate-coloured walls, and the sight of Strike laughing
opposite her, framed against a window through which she
watched the sea turning indigo in the fading light. Luckily,
Robin's tiredness curtailed a tendency to dwell on or analyse
the feelings these memories evoked.

She read his account of his interview with the Heatons
three times by torchlight, wanting to be absolutely sure she
remembered all of it before tearing it up. Now even more
determined to find out as much as she could about Daiyu's
death, Robin resolved to renew her efforts to befriend Emily
Pirbright, a task far easier planned than accomplished. Over

the next few days, she tried and failed to place herself within Emily's vicinity until, a week after receiving Strike's last letter, an unexpected opportunity arose.

Robin was approached at breakfast by the young man with short dreadlocks, who informed her she'd be joining a group going into Norwich that morning to collect money for the church.

'Tidy yourself up,' he told her. 'There'll be a clean tracksuit on your bed. The minibus leaves in half an hour.'

Robin had become used to casual mention of lengths of time that were impossible to measure for ordinary church members, and had learned it was safest to assume the instruction meant 'do it as quickly as possible'. In consequence, she gulped down the rest of her porridge rather than trying, as she usually did, to make it last.

When she entered the dormitory she saw fresh tracksuits laid out on their beds, which were no longer scarlet but white. From this, Robin deduced that the church had now moved into the season of the Drowned Prophet. Then she spotted Emily, who was pulling off her red top.

'Oh, you're coming too, Emily?' said Vivienne in surprise, when she entered the dormitory a couple of minutes after Robin. Emily threw Vivienne an unfriendly look as she turned away, tugging on a clean sweatshirt.

Robin deliberately left the dormitory alongside the silent Emily, hoping to sit beside her on the minibus, but they'd gone only a few yards when Robin heard a male voice calling, 'Rowena!'

Robin turned and her spirits plummeted: Taio had returned to the farm. He, too, was wearing a clean white tracksuit, and appeared to have washed his hair for once.

'Hello,' Robin said, trying to look happy to see him, as Emily walked on, head down, arms folded.

'I chose you to come out with the fundraising group today,' Taio said, beckoning her to walk with him across the courtyard, 'because I've been thinking about you while I was away, thinking you should be given a few more opportunities to demonstrate a change in thinking. I hear you donated to the church, incidentally. Very generous.'

'No,' said Robin, who wasn't going to fall into the kind of trap the church elders regularly set for the unwary, 'it wasn't generous. You were right, I should have done it earlier.'

'Good girl,' said Taio, reaching out and massaging the back of her neck, causing gooseflesh to rise on Robin's back and arms again. 'On the other matter,' he said in a lower voice, his hand still resting on her neck, 'I'm going to wait for you to come to me, and ask for spirit bonding. That will show a real change of attitude, a real abandonment of egomotivity.'

'OK,' said Robin, unable to look at him. She saw Emily glance back at the pair of them, her face expressionless.

Boxes of UHC merchandise and collecting boxes bearing the UHC's heart-shaped logo were already being loaded onto the minibus by Jiang and a couple of other men. When Robin got on the bus she found Emily already sitting beside Amandeep, so chose to sit next to Walter, with Emily directly across the aisle.

It was still very early and the sky overhead had a pearlescent glow. As the minibus drove down the drive and out through the electric gates, Robin felt a surge of elation: she was as excited about seeing the outside world again as she'd have been boarding a plane to a fabulous holiday. Emily's right leg, she noticed, was jumping nervously up and down.

'Right,' said Taio, speaking from the front of the bus, which his brother Jiang was driving. 'A word for those of you who haven't yet fundraised for us. Some of you will be manning the stall selling merchandise, and the rest will be using the collecting boxes. Any interest in the church, give them a pamphlet. Today's take will be divided between our young people's drop-in centre in Norwich and our climate change awareness programme. We've got posters, but be ready to answer questions.

'Remember, every single contact with a BP is an opportunity to save a soul, so I want to see lots of positivity. All interactions with the public are a chance to show how passionate we are about our mission to change the world.'

'Hear, hear,' said Walter loudly; he was far thinner than he'd been on joining the church and his skin now had a slightly grey tinge. He seemed neither as confident nor as talkative as he'd been on arrival at Chapman Farm, and his hands had a slight tremor.

Almost an hour after it had left the farm, the minibus passed over the River Wensum and entered the city of Norwich. Robin, who'd only ever seen the city while travelling to Chapman Farm, noticed more flint-covered walls and many church spires on the horizon. The colourful shopfronts, billboards and restaurants brought a double sense of familiarity and strangeness. How odd, to see people in normal clothing going about their business, all in possession of their own money, their own phones, their own door keys.

Now, for the first time, Robin truly appreciated the bravery it must have taken for Kevin Pirbright, who'd lived at the farm since the age of three, to break free and walk out into what must have seemed to him a strange and overwhelming world of which he didn't know the rules, with hardly any money, no job, and only the tracksuit he was wearing. How had he managed to get himself a rented room, small and shabby though it had been? How challenging had it been to find out how to claim benefits, to get himself a laptop, to set about writing his book? Glancing at Emily, Robin saw the woman transfixed by all she was seeing through the window, and wondered when was the last time Emily had been permitted to set foot outside one of the UHC centres.

Once Jiang had parked the minibus, the merchandise was unloaded and three of the younger men shouldered the heavy components of the stall they were about to set up. The rest, including Robin, carried the boxes of plush turtles, corn dollies, posters and pamphlets. Taio carried nothing, but walked ahead, occasionally exhorting the rest of the struggling group to keep up, the metal poles of the stall clanking in an army kit bag.

Once they'd reached the junction of three pedestrianised streets, which would be a busy thoroughfare once the surrounding shops opened, the experienced younger men set up the stall in surprisingly quick time. Robin helped set out the merchandise and pin glossy posters of UHC projects to the front of the stall.

She'd hoped to be given a collecting box, because that would give her most freedom; she might even be able to slip into a shop and check a newspaper. However, Taio told her to man the stall with Vivienne. He then informed those departing to collect money so that members 'averaged' a hundred pounds a day. While he didn't say so explicitly, Robin could tell that the collectors got the message that they shouldn't come back without that amount, and she watched in frustration as Emily and Jiang, who'd been put in a pair together, walked out of sight.

Once the surrounding shops had opened, the numbers of people passing the stall increased steadily. Taio hung around for the first hour, watching Robin and Vivienne interact with customers and critiquing them between sales. The cuddly turtles, which were popular with children, were the biggest draw. Taio told Robin and Vivienne that if people decided not to buy a turtle or a corn dolly, they should still be offered the collecting box for a donation to the church's projects, a strategy that was surprisingly effective: most of those they asked donated a few coins or even a note to escape the awkwardness of not having bought anything.

At last, to Robin's relief, Taio left to check how those with collecting boxes were getting on. As soon as he was out of earshot, Vivienne turned to Robin and said, in her usual would-be working-class voice that lapsed when she forgot herself,

'I can't believe 'e let Emily come.'

'Why?' asked Robin.

'Don't you know abou' what happened in Birmingham?'

'No, what?'

Vivienne glanced around, then said in a lower voice,

'She got into a CR with a guy up there.'

This, Robin knew, meant a relationship anybody outside the church would consider unexceptional: a monogamous partnership beginning in mutual sexual attraction, which the UHC considered an unhealthy extension of the possession instinct.

'Oh, wow,' said Robin. 'I didn't know.'

'Yeah, but that's not all,' said Vivienne. 'She told the guy a ton of lies that made 'im question his faith, and he ended up talking to a church elder about it, which is why she got relocated to Chapman Farm.'

'Wow,' said Robin again. 'What kind of lies?'

Again, Vivienne glanced around before speaking.

'OK, don't spread this around, but you know 'ow she and Becca knew the Drowned Prophet?'

'Yes, I've heard that,' said Robin.

'Well, it was stuff about Daiyu, apparently. Just utter shit.'

'What did she tell him?'

'I don't know,' said Vivienne, 'but it was so bad, this guy nearly left the church.'

'How d'you know all this?' asked Robin, careful to sound admiring of Vivienne's superior knowledge.

'I got talking to one of the other girls who got relocated. She told me Emily and this guy were, like, sneaking off together and refusing spirit bonding with anyone else. It was pure materialism. The girl thinks Emily was actually trying to make him go DV with her.'

'That's terrible,' said Robin.

'I know,' said Vivienne. 'Apparently, they had to drag her onto the minibus. She was shouting "I love you" at the guy.' Vivienne's expression was disgusted. 'Can you imagine? But thank God he just walked away.'

'Yeah,' said Robin. 'Thank God.'

Vivienne turned away to serve a mother whose small child had dragged her over to look at the plush turtles. When they'd departed, the little boy clutching his new turtle, Vivienne turned back to Robin.

'You know Papa J's been in LA?' Her voice softened as she said 'Papa J'; clearly, Robin's companion was now as thoroughly smitten with the church's founder as most of the women at Chapman Farm, and indeed some of the men. 'Well, he's coming back next week.'

'Really?' said Robin.

'Yeah. He always comes back for the Manifestation of the Drowned Prophet . . . Have you spirit bonded with him?'

'No,' said Robin. 'Have you?'

'No,' sighed Vivienne, her longing quite evident.

Taio came back several times over the next couple of hours to check how much money was in the strongbox underneath the table. On one of these occasions, he arrived chewing, and brushed flakes of what looked like pastry from around his mouth. He neither suggested that the other two eat anything, nor brought them any food.

Hours passed, and Robin started to feel light-headed by what she knew, from the position of the sun, must be mid-afternoon. Inured though she was to hunger and tiredness at the farm, it was a new challenge to stand on one spot for so long, having to smile, make cheerful conversation and proselytise for the church while the sun beat down on you, and without even the usual meal of sloppy noodles and overcooked vegetables to sustain her.

'Robin!'

'Yes?'

She turned automatically towards the person who'd spoken her name, and one second of icy horror later, realised what she'd done. A little boy who was holding a plush, red-breasted bird in one hand, and introducing it to the turtle his father had just bought him. Vivienne was looking at Robin strangely.

'It's my nickname,' Robin told Vivienne, forcing a laugh, as the father and son walked away. 'It's what my sis— I mean, one of my flesh objects calls me, sometimes.'

'Oh,' said Vivienne. 'Why's she call you Robin?'

'She had a book about Robin Hood,' Robin invented wildly. 'It was her favourite, before I was born. She wanted my parents to call me Rob—'

She broke off. Taio was running down the street towards them, red-faced and sweaty: heads turned as he galumphed past shoppers in his white tracksuit, his face both angry and panicked.

'Problem,' he panted, on arriving at the stall. 'Emily's gone.'

'What?' gasped Vivienne.

'*Fucking* Jiang,' said Taio. 'Give me the strongbox and pack up the merchandise. We've got to find her.'

66

DECREASE combined with sincerity . . .
It furthers one to undertake something.
How is this to be carried out?
One may use two small bowls for the sacrifice.

The I Ching or Book of Changes

When Taio had run off clutching the strongbox, Robin and Vivienne stripped the stall, leaving the metal frame standing.

'Just leave all that,' said Vivienne in panic, as Robin stuffed the last of the turtles and corn dollies back into their boxes. 'Oh my God. What if she's gone DV?'

The collecting box rattled in Robin's hands as she and Vivienne set off at a jog up Castle Street. Robin wondered at Vivienne's total, unquestioning acceptance of the fact that a grown woman choosing to break away from the group was dangerous. Did nothing about Vivienne's own panic make her ask why such strict control was necessary? Apparently not: Vivienne was darting into every shop they passed, as alarmed as a mother might be on finding out her toddler had gone missing. In their matching white tracksuits, with the noisy collecting box clutched to Robin's chest, the pair drew more startled looks from passers-by.

'Is that her?' gasped Vivienne.

Robin saw the flash of white Vivienne had spotted, but it turned out to be a shaven-headed youth in an England football strip.

'Wait,' panted Robin, jogging to a halt. 'Vivienne, wait! We should split up, we'll cover more ground. You check down there –' Robin pointed at Davey Place '– and I'll keep going this way. We'll meet back at the stall if we haven't found her in an hour, OK?'

'How will we know—?'

'Just ask someone the time!'

'All right,' said Vivienne, although she looked scared at being left on her own, 'I suppose that makes sense.'

Fearing that Vivienne might change her mind if given time to think about it, Robin set off at a run again and, glancing over her shoulder, was relieved to see Vivienne disappear into Davey Place.

Robin immediately turned left up a side road, emerging onto a wide street, which ran past a huge grassy mound on top of which stood Norwich Castle, an enormous and imposing crenellated cube of stone.

Robin leaned back against the wall of a shop to catch her breath. Aftershocks at having been so foolish as to respond to her real name were still ricocheting through her. Had her explanation been good enough? Might Vivienne forget the lapse, in the shock of hearing that Emily had disappeared? Looking up at the imposing façade of the castle, she heard Strike's voice in her head:

You're compromised. You've put your real identity within grasping distance of anyone who gets suspicious of you. Get out now. One more mistake and you're toast.

And that, Robin thought guiltily, was without Strike knowing that Lin had caught her with the torch in the woods. She could just imagine what he'd say to that, too.

Just because she hasn't talked yet doesn't mean she won't. All it needs is a few people to share their suspicions.

Robin imagined going to a telephone box now, just as Niamh Doherty's father had done so many years ago, and making a reverse charge call to the office to tell Pat she needed to come out. The thought of hearing Pat's gruff voice, of knowing she'd never have to return to Chapman Farm, of being safe forever against the threat of Taio and spirit bonding, was incredibly tempting.

But against all of that was the job still undone. She'd discovered nothing sufficiently damaging about the church to force a meeting between Will Edensor and his family. While she had a few titbits that might be compromising, such as Giles Harmon's liaison with the possibly underage Lin, Robin doubted her word would stand up against the might of the UHC's lawyers, especially as Lin, born and raised in the UHC, was highly unlikely to give evidence against a Principal of the church.

I've got to stay, she told the Strike in her head, *and I know you would, too, if you were me.*

Robin closed her eyes for a moment or two, exhausted and hungry, and among the disconnected thoughts sliding through her mind was, *and there's Ryan.*

Ryan, whom she thought about far less than Strike these days . . . but that, surely, was because she was so focused on the job . . . it was natural, inevitable . . .

Robin took a deep breath and set off again, scanning the street for Emily, though she was certain the woman was long gone. She might have hitched a lift, or made a reverse charge call of her own to some relative who might be able to come and collect her. With luck, though, the agency would be able to trace Emily on the outside . . .

'*What?*' Robin exclaimed, coming to an abrupt halt, her

eyes on a folded copy of *The Times* in a rack at the entrance to a newsagents. Evidently, Britain had voted to leave the EU.

She'd just lifted the paper out of the rack to read the story, when she saw a white-clad figure in the distance. Jiang was approaching from the opposite direction, his expression furious. Robin stuffed the paper hastily back into its slot, wheeled around and hurried back the way she'd come: she didn't think Jiang had spotted her, and had no desire to meet him. Having hurried down a narrow, pedestrianised side street, she entered a covered arcade she hadn't previously seen. Glancing behind her, she saw Jiang pass in front of the castle and disappear from view.

The arcade in which Robin now stood was old and rather beautiful, with a high vaulted glass ceiling, Art Nouveau tiles above the shopfronts and pendant lights like giant harebells. Desperate for further tidings of the outside world, Robin walked on, looking for a newsagents until, out of the corner of her eye, she saw a patch of white.

Through a gap between the colourful puppets displayed in a toy shop's window she saw the bald Emily gazing blankly at shelves of toys as though hypnotised, her collecting box cradled to her chest.

After one astonished moment, Robin doubled back to enter the shop. Moving quietly in her trainers, she rounded the end of a row of shelves.

'Emily?'

Emily jumped and stared at Robin as though she'd never seen her before.

'Um ... people are looking for you. Are you ... what are you doing?'

The resentment bordering on occasional anger that Emily displayed at Chapman Farm had gone. She was chalk white and shaking.

'It's OK,' said Robin, speaking as she might have spoken to somebody disorientated who'd just suffered a physical accident.

'Is Taio angry?' Emily whispered.

'He's worried,' said Robin, not entirely untruthfully.

If she hadn't known better, she'd have thought Emily had taken some kind of stimulant. Her pupils were dilated and a muscle in her cheek was flickering.

'I did that thing to him – you know – in the Retreat Room – that thing where you suck their—?'

'Yes,' said Robin, very aware of children's voices on the other side of the shelves.

'—so he'd let me come to Norwich.'

'Right,' said Robin. Various courses of action were running through her mind. She could call Strike and see whether he'd pick Emily up, advise Emily to call a relative, if she had any outside the church, or tell Emily to turn herself in to the police, but all of these options would necessarily reveal Robin's lack of allegiance to the UHC, and if Emily refused, Robin would have placed her own security in the hands of the woman now quivering uncontrollably in front of the shelves of Sylvanian Families.

'Why did you want to come to Norwich so much?' Robin asked quietly, certain of the answer, but wanting to hear Emily say it.

'I was going to . . . but I can't. I'll only kill myself. That's why they warn us. You can't survive out here, once you reach step eight. I suppose I must be nearer pure spirit than I thought,' said Emily, with an attempt at a laugh.

'I didn't know that,' said Robin, moving closer to Emily. 'About step eight.'

'*I am master of my soul*,' said Emily, and Robin recognised the mantra of the Stolen Prophet. 'Once your spirit's really evolved, you can't take rejoining the materialist world. It'll kill you.'

Emily's gaze shifted back to the shelves of Sylvanian Families: little model animals dressed as humans, packaged as parents and babies, with their houses and furniture ranged beside them.

'Look,' she said to Robin, pointing at the animals. 'It's all materialist possession. Tiny little flesh objects and their houses . . . all in boxes . . . *I'll* have to go in the box, now,' said Emily, with another laugh that turned into a sob.

'What box?'

'It's for when you've been bad,' whispered Emily. '*Really* bad . . .'

Robin's mind was working rapidly.

'Listen,' she said. 'We'll tell them you needed the bathroom, but you came over faint, OK? You nearly passed out, and a woman came to help you and wouldn't let you leave until you got your colour back. I'll back you up – I'll say when I came into the bathroom, the woman was threatening to get an ambulance. If we both tell the same story, you won't be punished, OK? I'll back you up,' she repeated. 'It'll be all right.'

'Why would you help me?' asked Emily incredulously.

'Because I want to.'

Emily held up her collecting box pathetically.

'I didn't get enough.'

'I can help with that. I'll bump you up a bit. Wait there.'

Robin had no qualms about leaving Emily, because she could tell the latter was too paralysed with fear to move. The girl at the cash register, who was chatting to a young man, handed over a pair of scissors from behind the desk almost absent-mindedly. Robin rejoined Emily and used the point of the scissors to prise open the collecting box.

'I'll have to keep something, because Vivienne saw money going in,' said Robin, emptying out most of the cash inside and shoving it into Emily's box instead. 'There you go.'

'Why are you doing this?' Emily whispered, watching Robin stuff the last five pound note through the slot.

'I told you, I want to. Stay there, I've got to give the scissors back.'

She found Emily standing exactly where she'd left her when she returned.

'OK, shall we——?'

'My brother killed himself and it was all our fault,' said Emily jerkily. 'Mine and Becca's.'

'You can't be sure of that.'

'I can. It was us, we did it to him. He shot himself. You can get guns really easily in the materialist world,' said Emily with a nervous glance at the shoppers passing the toy shop window, as though she feared they might be armed.

'It might've been an accident,' said Robin.

'No, it wasn't, it definitely wasn't. Becca made me sign a thing . . . she told me I'd suppressed what he did to us. She's always done that,' said Emily, her breathing rapid and shallow, 'told me what happened, and what didn't happen.'

Despite her genuine concern for Emily and the urgent need to get back to the group, this was an opening Robin couldn't ignore.

'What does Becca say didn't happen?'

'I can't tell you,' said Emily, shifting her gaze back on to the rows of happily paired animals smiling out of their neat cellophane-wrapped boxes. 'Look,' she said, pointing at a family of four pigs. 'Pig demons . . . that's a sign,' she said, breathing rapidly.

'A sign of what?' said Robin.

'That I need to shut up.'

'Emily, they're just toys,' said Robin. 'They aren't super-natural, they're not signs. You can tell me anything, I won't give you away.'

'The last person who said that to me was in Birmingham and he didn't – he didn't mean it – he—'

Emily began to cry. She shook her head as Robin laid a consoling hand on her arm.

'Don't, don't – you'll be in trouble, being nice to me – you shouldn't be helping me, Becca will make sure you're punished for it—'

'I'm not scared of Becca,' said Robin.

'Well, you should be,' said Emily, drawing deep breaths in an effort to control herself. 'She'll ... do *anything* to protect the mission. *Anything*. I ... I should know.'

'How could you threaten the mission?' asked Robin.

'Because,' said Emily, staring at a pair of small pandas in pink and blue nappies, 'I know things ... Becca says I was too young to remember ...' Then, in a rush of words, Emily said, 'But I *wasn't* really small, I was nine, and I know, because they moved me out of the kids' dormitory after it happened.'

'After what happened?' said Robin.

'After Daiyu became "invisible",' said Emily, her tone putting quotation marks around the word. 'I *knew* Becca was lying, even then, only I went along with it, because,' fresh tears gushed forth, 'I loved ... *loved* ...'

'You loved Becca?'

'No ... not ... it doesn't matter, it doesn't matter ... I shouldn't be ... talking about any of this ... forget it, please ...'

'I will,' lied Robin.

'It's just Becca,' said Emily, struggling to regain control of herself again, wiping her face, 'telling me I'm *lying* all the time ... she's not ... since she went away ... I feel like she's not who she was before ...'

'When did she go away?' asked Robin.

'Ages ago ... they sent her to Birmingham ... they split up flesh objects ... they must have thought we were too close ...

and when she came back . . . she wasn't . . . she was really one of them, she wouldn't hear a word against any of them, even Mazu . . . Sometimes,' said Emily, 'I want to *scream* the truth, but . . . that's egomotivity . . .'

'It isn't egomotivity to tell the truth,' said Robin.

'You shouldn't talk like that,' said Emily, on a hiccup. 'That's how I got relocated.'

'I joined the church to find truth,' said Robin. 'If it's just another place where you can't tell it, I don't want to stay.'

'"A single event, a thousand different recollections. Only the Blessed Divinity knows the truth,"' said Emily, quoting from *The Answer*.

'But there is truth,' said Robin firmly. 'It's not all opinions or memories. There *is* truth.'

Emily looked at Robin with what seemed to be frightened fascination.

'D'you believe in her?'

'In who? Becca?'

'No. In the Drowned Prophet.'

'I . . . yes, I suppose so.'

'Well, you shouldn't,' whispered Emily. 'She wasn't what they say she was.'

'What d'you mean?'

Emily glanced through the window of the toy shop, then said, 'She was always up to secret stuff at the farm. *Forbidden* things.'

'What kind of things?'

'Stuff in the barn and the woods. Becca saw it, too. She says I'm making it up, but she knows what happened. I *know* she remembers,' said Emily desperately.

'What did you see Daiyu doing in the barn and the woods?'

'I can't tell you,' said Emily. 'But I *know* she didn't die. I *know* that.'

'What?' said Robin blankly.

'She's not dead. She's out there, somewhere, grown up. She never drow—'

Emily gave a little gasp. Robin turned: a woman in a white top and trousers had come around the corner of the shelves, holding the hands of two boisterous little boys, and Robin knew Emily had momentarily mistaken the mother for another UHC member. The two little boys began clamouring for Thomas the Tank Engine models.

'I want Percy. There's Percy! I want Percy!'

'You'll really say I felt faint?' Emily whispered to Robin. 'In the bathroom, and all that?'

'Yes, of course,' said Robin, afraid to push Emily further right now, but hopeful that she'd now established a rapport that would survive, back at the farm. 'Are you OK to go now?'

Emily nodded, still sniffing, and followed Robin out of the shop.They'd walked just a few steps along the arcade when Emily grabbed Robin by the arm.

'Taio wants you to spirit bond with him, doesn't he?'

Robin nodded.

'Well, if you don't want to,' said Emily in a low voice, 'you need to go with Papa J when he comes back. None of the other men are allowed to touch Papa J's spirit wives. Becca's a spirit wife, that's why she never has to go in the Retreat Rooms with anyone else.'

'I didn't know that,' said Robin.

'Just go with Papa J,' said Emily, 'and you'll be OK.'

'Thanks, Emily,' said Robin, who valued the helpful intention behind the words, if not the advice itself. 'Come on, we'd better hurry.'

67

It is not I who seek the young fool;
The young fool seeks me.

The I Ching or Book of Changes

Strike took Robin's next letter with him to reread while on overnight surveillance on the Franks on Monday evening, because he found much in there to interest him.

Wan, Robin wrote, had been moved on from Chapman Farm, though Robin didn't know where she'd gone. She'd left her baby behind with Mazu, who'd named the little girl Yixin, and was now carrying her around and speaking as though she were the biological mother. Robin also described her trip into Norwich, but as she'd omitted to mention her accidental response to her own real name, Strike was unencumbered by fresh worries about Robin's safety as he pondered Emily's assertion that Daiyu hadn't really drowned.

Even without supporting evidence, Emily's opinion interested the detective, because it took him back to his musings on the esplanade in Cromer, when he'd mulled over the possibility that Daiyu had been carried down onto the beach, not to die, but to be handed to someone else. Sitting in his dark car, casting regular glances up at the windows of the Franks' flat which, atypically at this hour, were lit up, he asked himself

641

how likely it was that Daiyu had survived the trip to the beach, without reaching any conclusions.

The Waces had had a clear motive for Daiyu's disappearance: to prevent the Graves family from obtaining DNA evidence and regaining control of that quarter of a million pounds in blue chip shares. Death hadn't been necessary to achieve that objective: merely putting Daiyu beyond the Graves' reach would have done it. But if Daiyu hadn't died, where was she? Were there relatives of either Mazu or Jonathan he didn't know about, who might have agreed to take the girl in?

Daiyu would be twenty-eight if she were still alive. Would she be content to remain silent, knowing that a cult had grown up around her supposedly drowned seven-year-old self?

In the penultimate line of her letter, Robin answered the question Strike had posed in his last: did she have any reason to believe her cover might have been blown at Chapman Farm, given that an unknown woman had approached Strike, apparently to disrupt his surveillance?

I don't know whether that woman you mentioned has got anything to do with the church but I don't think anyone here knows or suspects who I really am.

Movement at the door of the Franks' block made Strike look up. The two brothers were walking, bow-legged, towards their dilapidated van, laden with heavy boxes and what looked like bags of groceries. As the younger Frank reached the vehicle he stumbled and several large bottles of mineral water tipped out of a box and rolled away. Strike, who by this time was filming them, watched as the older brother berated the younger, setting down his own box to help chase down the bottles. Strike zoomed in, and saw what looked like a coil of rope protruding from the older brother's box.

Strike gave the van a head start, then followed them. After a short drive, they came to a halt outside a large lock-up facility in Croydon. Here, the detective watched as they unloaded the boxes and groceries and disappeared into the building.

It wasn't, of course, a crime to buy rope or a van, or to hire a storage unit and put food and water in there, but Strike considered this activity highly ominous. Try as he might, he could think of no plausible explanation for these activities other than that the brothers were indeed planning the abduction and imprisonment of the actress whom they seemed determined to punish for being insufficiently accommodating of their demands for her attention. As far as he knew, the police hadn't yet paid a call on the Franks to warn them off. He couldn't help suspecting that the matter was being deprioritised because Mayo could afford a private detective agency to keep a watch on her stalkers.

He sat watching the entrance to the facility for twenty minutes, but the brothers didn't emerge. After a while, knowing he'd hear the van starting up again, he did something he'd so far resisted doing, and Googled 'Charlotte Campbell funeral' on his phone.

Since the newspaper-reading public had learned of Charlotte's death, further details of her suicide had leaked into the papers. Thus Strike knew that Charlotte had taken a cocktail of drink and anti-depressants before slitting her wrists and bleeding out in a bath. The cleaner had found the bathroom door locked at nine o'clock in the morning and, having pounded on it and shouted to no avail, called the police, who'd broken into the room. Much as he'd have preferred it not to, Strike's imagination insisted on showing him a vivid picture of Charlotte submerged in her own blood, her black hair floating on the clotted surface.

He'd wondered where the family would choose as

Charlotte's final resting place. Her late father's family had been Scottish, whereas her mother, Tara, had been born and lived in London. When Strike learned from *The Times* that Charlotte would be buried in Brompton Cemetery, one of the smartest in the capital, he knew Tara must have been given the casting vote. The choice of Brompton also ensured publicity, for which Tara had always had a weakness. Thus Strike was able to scan through photographs of the mourners on the *Daily Mail* website as he sat in the dark.

Many of the black-clad people who'd left Charlotte's funeral earlier that day were familiar to him: Viscount Jago Ross, Charlotte's ex-husband, looking as ever like a dissolute arctic fox; her floppy-haired stepbrother, Valentine Longcaster; Sacha Legard, her handsome half-brother, who was an actor; Madeline Courson-Miles, the jewellery designer Strike had previously dated; Izzy Chiswell, one of Charlotte's old schoolfriends; Ciara Porter, a model with whom Strike had once had a one-night stand; and even Henry Worthington-Fields, the skinny red-headed man who'd worked at Charlotte's favourite antiques shop. Unsurprisingly, Landon Dormer was conspicuous by his absence.

Strike hadn't received an invitation to the funeral, not that this bothered him: as far as he was concerned, he'd said his farewells in the small Norfolk church overlooking Chapman Farm. In any case, given his personal history with some of the people who'd have been his fellow mourners, the funeral would undoubtedly have been one of the most uncomfortable occasions of his life.

The last photograph in the *Mail* article featured Tara. From what Strike could see through the thick black veil on her hat, her once-beautiful features had been severely distorted by what looked like overuse of cosmetic fillers. She was flanked on one side by her fourth husband and on the other by Charlotte's only full sibling, Amelia, who was two years older than his ex-fiancée. This was the sister who'd called Strike's office on the morning after Charlotte's suicide had been announced to the press and who, on learning from Pat that Strike was unavailable, had simply hung up. Amelia had made no contact with Strike since, nor had he tried to contact her. If the rumour that Charlotte had left a suicide note was true, he was happy to remain in ignorance of what it said.

The noise of a slamming car door made him look up. The Frank brothers had emerged from the facility and were now attempting to make their cold van start. On the fourth attempt, it sputtered into life, and Strike tailed them back to their block of flats. The lights in their flat went out after twenty more minutes and Strike turned back to the news on his phone, to kill time until Shah arrived to take over from him at eight.

The Brexit referendum might be over, but the subject continued to dominate the headlines. Strike scrolled down past these articles without opening them, vaping, until, with misgivings, he saw another familiar face: that of Bijou Watkins.

The picture, which had been taken as she left her flat, showed Bijou wearing a tight peacock blue dress that emphasised her figure. Her dark hair was freshly styled, she was expertly made up as usual and carried a glossy briefcase in her hand. Beside Bijou's picture was another, of a stout, bare-faced and frizzy-haired woman in an unflattering evening dress of pink satin, who was named as Lady Matilda Honbold in the caption. Above the two photos was the headline: *Andrew 'Honey Badger' Honbold to Divorce.*

Strike skim-read the article below, and in paragraph four found what he'd feared: his own name.

> *A committed Catholic, high-profile donor to the Conservative party and patron of both The Campaign for Ethical Journalism and Catholic Aid to Africa, Honbold's alleged*

infidelity was first reported in Private Eye. *The magazine
alleged that Honbold's unnamed mistress had also enjoyed a
dalliance with well-known private detective Cormoran Strike,
stories that were denied by Honbold, Watkins and Strike,
with Honbold threatening legal action against the magazine.*

'Shit,' muttered Strike.

He'd thought the rumour of his involvement with Bijou
had been successfully quashed. The last thing he needed was
a signpost in *The Times* telling Patterson and Littlejohn exactly
where to mine for dirt.

Promptly at eight o'clock, Shah arrived to take over surveillance on the Franks.

'Morning,' he said, getting into the passenger seat of the
BMW. Before Strike could tell him what had happened overnight, Shah held out his own phone and said,

'This your woman from the Connaught? I got a few.'

Strike swiped through the pictures. All showed different
angles of the same dark woman, who was wearing a beanie
hat and baggy jeans, and standing on the corner of Denmark
Street nearest the office.

'Yeah,' he said, 'looks like her. When did you take these?'

'Yesterday evening. She was there when I came out of the
office.'

'Was she working for Patterson Inc when you were there?'

'Definitely not. She'd have stuck in my mind.'

'OK, do me a favour and forward these to Midge and
Barclay.'

'What d'you reckon she's after?'

'If she's another Patterson operative, she could be checking
out what clients we've got, to try and scare them off. Or she
might be trying to identify people working for the agency, to
see if she can get anything on them.'

'I'll hold off on starting that heroin habit, then.'

By the time Strike had briefed Shah, then driven back into central London, he was both tired and irritable, and his mood wasn't improved when, waiting at some traffic lights, he spotted a gigantic poster he'd ordinarily have overlooked. It showed Jonathan Wace against a deep blue, star-flecked background, dressed in white robes, his arms outstretched, a smile on the handsome face that was tilted heavenwards. The legend read: *'SUPERSERVICE 2016! Interested in the Universal Humanitarian Church? Meet PAPA J at Olympia on Friday 12th August, 2016!'*

'Charlotte Ross's sister's called again,' were Pat's first, unwelcome words when an unshaven Strike appeared at half past nine, clutching a bacon roll he'd purchased on his way to the office: diet be damned.

'Yeah? Any message?' asked Strike.

'She said she's going to the country for a month, but she'd like to meet you when she gets back.'

'Is she expecting an answer?' asked Strike.

'No, that's all she said.'

Strike grunted and headed for the kettle.

'And you've had a call from a Jacob Messenger.'

'What?' said Strike, surprised.

'He says his half-brother told you were after him. Says you can call him any time this morning.'

'Do me a favour,' said Strike, stirring sweetener into his coffee, 'and ring him back and ask him if he's happy to FaceTime. I want to make sure it's really him.'

Strike headed into the inner office, still thinking about the beautiful woman who was apparently keeping the office under surveillance. If he could only clear up the Patterson mess his life would be considerably less complicated, not to mention less expensive.

'He's fine to FaceTime,' Pat announced five minutes later, entering Strike's office carrying a Post-it note with Messenger's number on it. Once she'd gone, Strike opened FaceTime on his computer and tapped in Jacob Messenger's number.

The call was answered almost immediately by the same very tanned young man who beamed out of the picture on Strike's noticeboard. With his white-toothed smile, slicked dark hair and overplucked eyebrows, he looked excited to be speaking to Strike, whereas the detective's primary emotion was frustration. Whoever was critically ill or dying at Chapman Farm, it clearly wasn't Jacob Messenger.

A couple of minutes later, Strike had learned that Messenger's interest in the church had been ignited when his agent received a request for Jacob to attend one of the UHC's charity projects, continued through a photoshoot in which Jacob had worn a UHC sweatshirt, lingered through a short press interview in which he spoke of his new interest in spirituality and charity work, only to wither away when invited on a week-long retreat at a farm, with no media presence.

'I wan't gonna go to no bloody farm,' said Jacob, blindingly white teeth fully on display as he laughed. 'What would I wanna do that for?'

'Right,' said Strike. 'Well, this has been very—'

'Listen, though,' said Jacob, ''ave you ever fort of doing a show?'

'Have I what?'

'Like, fly on the wall, follow you investigating stuff. I looked you up. Seriously, I reckon my agent would be interested. I was finking, if you and me teamed up, and you could be, like, showing me the ropes and stuff, wiv a camera crew—'

'I don't—'

'Could be good publicity for ya,' said Messenger, while a blonde in a mini-dress drifted across the screen behind him, looking vague. 'It'd raise your profile. I in't boasting or nuffing but I'd def'nitely get us an audience—'

'Yeah, that wouldn't work,' said Strike firmly. 'Goodbye.'

He hung up while Messenger was still talking.

'Stupid tit,' Strike muttered, getting to his feet again to tug Messenger's picture off the UHC noticeboard, rip it in half and put it in the bin. He then scribbled 'WHO'S JACOB?' on a piece of paper and pinned it where Messenger's photo had been.

Taking a few steps backwards, Strike contemplated yet again the various photos of the dead, untraced and unknown people connected to the church. Other than the note about Jacob, the only other recent change to the board was another piece of paper, which he'd pinned up after his trip to Cromer. It read 'JOGGER ON BEACH?' and it, too, was in the 'still to be found/identified' column.

Frowning, Strike looked from picture to picture, coming to rest on that of Jennifer Wace, with her big hair and her frosted lipstick, frozen forever in the 1980s. Since his trip to Cromer, Strike had tried to find out all he could about the ways in which somebody might induce a seizure in an epileptic and as far as he could see, the only plausible possibility would be withdrawing medication or, perhaps, substituting genuine medication with some ineffective substance. But supposing Wace had indeed tampered with his first wife's pills, how could he have known a seizure would occur at that specific moment, while Jennifer was in the water? As a murder method it was ludicrously chancy, though admittedly no less risky than taking a child swimming, and hoping the sea would hide her body forever.

Stroking his unshaven chin, the detective wondered whether he wasn't becoming fixated on what might turn out to be a dead end. Maybe he was joining the ranks of conspiracy theorists, who saw hidden plots and stratagems where other, saner folk said, like Shelley Heaton, '*That's* a funny coincidence,' and moved on with their lives? Was it arrogant, he asked himself, to think he'd manage to trace a connection where nobody else had succeeded in doing so? Possibly – but then, he'd been called arrogant before, most often by the woman who now lay freshly interred in Brompton Cemetery, and it had never yet deterred him from doing precisely what he'd set out to do.

68

Nine in the second place means:
The abyss is dangerous.
One should strive to attain small things only.

The I Ching or Book of Changes

A strange mood seemed to have infected Chapman Farm ever since members' tracksuits had changed to white. There was a jitteriness in the air, a sense of strain. Robin noticed an increased tendency on the part of church members to be even more performatively considerate in their treatment of each other, as though some hidden entity were constantly watching and judging.

This generalised anxiety heightened Robin's own. While she hadn't precisely lied in her last letter to Strike, she hadn't told the whole truth, either.

When she and Emily had returned to the abandoned stall in Norwich and told their story of Emily coming over faint in a bathroom, Taio had seemed to accept their account at face value. Relieved as he was to get Emily back, most of his ire was directed at Jiang for losing sight of her and putting her at the mercy of the bubble people, and he spent much of the journey back to Chapman Farm muttering what looked like insults and imprecations at the back of his brother's head. Jiang didn't respond, but remained hunched and silent over the steering wheel.

However, over the next couple of days Robin had detected a shift in Taio's attitude. Doubtless the large amount of money Emily was supposed to have collected on her own, coupled with the very small amount left in the collecting box from the stall, had raised his suspicions. Several times, Robin caught Taio staring at her in no friendly manner, and she also noticed sidelong glances from others who'd been in Norwich. When Robin saw Amandeep hastily hushing Vivienne and Walter as she approached them in the courtyard, she knew she'd been the subject under discussion. Robin wondered whether Vivienne had told anyone about her answering to her real name and if so, how far the information had spread.

Robin knew she'd reached the absolute limit of allowable mistakes, and as she wasn't prepared to have sex with either Taio or Jonathan Wace, she was now on borrowed time at Chapman Farm. Exactly how she was going to leave, she wasn't yet sure. It would take a certain amount of courage to tell Taio and Mazu she wanted to go, and perhaps it would be easier to struggle over the barbed wire at the perimeter by night. However, her immediate concern, given that her time was now definitely running out, was to identify priorities and achieve them as quickly as possible.

Firstly, she wanted to capitalise on the secret understanding she'd brokered with Emily to get as much information out of her as possible. Secondly, she was determined to try and engineer a one-on-one conversation with Will Edensor, so as to be able to give Sir Colin up-to-date information on his son. Lastly, she thought she might try and find the hatchet hidden in a tree in the woods.

She knew that even this limited agenda would be tricky. Whether deliberately or not (and Robin suspected the former), ever since they'd returned from Norwich she and Emily had been given tasks that kept them as far apart as possible. She noticed that Emily was always flanked by the same people in the dining hall, as though an order had been given to keep her under watch at all times. Emily had twice made an attempt to sit beside Robin in the dining hall, before being blocked by one of the people who seemed to be constantly shadowing her. Robin and Emily's eyes had also met several times in the dormitory and on one of these occasions, Emily had offered a fleeting smile before turning quickly away as Becca entered.

Catching Will Edensor alone was also difficult, because Robin's contact with him had always been negligible, and since their joint stint on the vegetable patch she'd rarely been assigned a task with him. His status at Chapman Farm remained that of manual labourer, in spite of his clear intelligence and his trust fund, and such joint work as they did together was always supervised and therefore afforded no opportunities for conversation.

As for the hatchet supposedly hidden in the woods, she knew it would be unwise to use the torch to look for it by night, in case the beam was spotted by someone looking out of the dormitory windows. Unfortunately, searching the woods by daylight would be almost as difficult. Other than its use as an occasional adventure playground for children, the patch of uncultivated land was barely used, and barring Will and Lin, who'd been there illicitly, and the young man who'd searched it on the night Bo had gone missing, Robin had never seen an adult enter it. How she was to slip away from her tasks, or justify her presence in the woods if found there, she currently had no idea.

Since her excursion to Norwich, Robin seemed to have been given a new hybrid status: part manual worker, part high-level recruit. She wasn't invited back into the city to fundraise, although she continued to study church doctrine with her group. Robin had a feeling her thousand pound donation had made her too valuable to relegate entirely to the status of a skivvy, but that she was on a kind of unspoken probation. Vivienne, who was always a good barometer of who was in favour and who wasn't, was pointedly ignoring her.

Robin's next letter to Strike was short and, as she was well aware, disappointingly short of information, but the morning after she'd deposited it in the plastic rock, a significant event happened at Chapman Farm: the return of Jonathan Wace.

Everyone turned out to watch Papa J's silver Mercedes come up the drive with a convoy of lesser cars behind it, and before the procession had even drawn to a halt, all members began to cheer and applaud, Robin included. When Wace stepped out of the car, the crowd became almost hysterical.

He looked tanned, rested and as handsome as ever. His eyes grew wet again as he looked around at the cheering throng, pressing his hand over his heart and making one of his self-deprecating little bows. When he walked to Mazu, who was holding baby Yixin in her arms, he embraced her and delightedly examined the baby, as though it was his own – which, Robin suddenly realised, she might well be. The screams of the crowd became deafening, and Robin made sure to clap so enthusiastically her hands hurt.

From the car behind Wace's, five young people emerged, all of them strangers, and Robin thought, mainly because of their perfect teeth, they were American. Two preppy young men and three noticeably beautiful young women, all dressed in white UHC tracksuits, stood beaming at the British church members, and Robin guessed that they'd been brought over to Chapman Farm from the San Francisco centre. She watched as Jonathan introduced them one by one to Mazu, who received them graciously.

That evening, there was another feast in the dining hall, which had once again been decorated with scarlet and gold paper lanterns. They were served real meat for the first time in weeks, and Wace gave a long, impassioned speech about the wars in Syria and Afghanistan, and lambasted the campaign speeches of presidential candidate Donald Trump. The American visitors, Robin noticed, nodded vehemently as Wace painted a vivid picture of the fascist terror that would be unleashed should Trump win the election.

Once Wace had described the horrors of the materialist world, he moved on to describe the UHC's continuing success, and explain how the church alone could turn back the forces of evil now rallying across the planet. He praised the American visitors for their fundraising efforts and described the imminent creation of a new UHC centre in New York, then summoned various individuals onto the stage to praise them for their individual efforts. Evidently Mazu had been keeping Wace informed about happenings at Chapman Farm, because Amandeep was one of those called to the stage. He sobbed and shook his head as he approached Wace, who embraced him before announcing that Amandeep had now equalled the record for funds raised in a single day for the church. The five Americans who'd just arrived stood up to applaud and whoop, their fists pumping in the air.

When Wace's speech ended, music broke out, just as it had at the end of the last feast, and people began to dance. Robin got up, too: she was determined to show willing whenever possible, and hoped to find a way, in the crush, to speak to either Will or Emily. However, this proved impossible. She found herself instead dancing opposite Kyle, who'd once been a high-level recruit, but whose inability or refusal to have sex with Vivienne had seen him relegated to one of the lowliest farm workers. Blank-faced, he moved jerkily in front of Robin, never meeting her gaze, and she wondered where he was imagining himself, until she noticed that his mouth was constantly, silently moving in a chant unrelated to the music.

69

In dealing with persons as intractable and as difficult to influence as a pig or a fish ... one must first rid oneself of all prejudice and, so to speak, let the psyche of the other person act ...

The I Ching or Book of Changes

Breakfast at Chapman Farm was usually the quietest meal of the day, given that it happened at half past five in morning. During Jonathan Wace's previous stay at the farm his appearances at communal meals had been limited to two dinners, so when Wace and Mazu entered the hall at six o'clock the morning following his arrival, Robin gathered from the looks of surprise from all around her that this was highly unusual. There was an outbreak of uncertain applause: heads turned, and total silence fell as Wace clambered back onto the stage, already wearing his microphone. Mazu stood behind him, unsmiling, her face shadowed by her long wings of black hair.

'My friends,' said Wace, with a sad smile, 'my beloved wife has suffered a loss. Some of you may have noticed, she wears a special pendant – a mother-of-pearl fish. It once belonged to Daiyu, the Drowned Prophet. The fish was found in Daiyu's bed on the morning of her ascension.'

A little gasp ran through the hall.

'My wife realised two days ago that the cord had broken

657

and the fish is lost. She's looked, but hasn't found it. You understand, I'm sure, that I'm not asking you to search for a meaningless, materialist token. This is an artefact of the church. We – Mazu and I – will be deeply grateful to whoever manages to retrieve this precious item. I'm asking you all to set aside your usual tasks and help us find it.'

Robin scented opportunity. Only once before, on the night little Bo had gone missing from the children's dormitory, had the rigid group structure at the farm dissolved. If everyone was going their separate ways, spreading out over the church grounds, she might be able to accomplish something. Taking a quick survey of the hall, she spotted Becca approaching the table where Emily was sitting and issuing instructions. Robin was certain the group had been told to stick together during the search.

Will Edensor, by contrast, was already leaving the hall, alone. Grabbing her porridge bowl, Robin hastened to put it on one of the trolleys before following.

It was warm, but a light summer drizzle was falling. Will was heading for the courtyard, his head bowed as he scanned the ground. Pretending to look for the lost pendant herself, Robin proceeded slowly past the barns and laundry, keeping a covert eye on Will, who soon reached the courtyard and started searching it. Robin was peering around the base of the Healer Prophet's tomb, the rain sliding down the back of her neck, when a loud voice said:

'Oi've already looked thar.'

'Hi Shawna,' said Robin, her heart sinking.

'Will!' called Shawna, whose pregnancy was now becoming evident, 'Oi've looked thar, too!'

Will gave no answer, but turned and traipsed off in the direction of the farmhouse. To Robin's disappointment, two other men joined him, and Robin guessed by their gestures they were suggesting a systematic joint search of the garden behind it.

'I heard someone saying it might have fallen off in the children's classroom,' Robin lied to Shawna, determined to throw the girl off if she could. 'Apparently Mazu was in there a couple of days ago.'

'Come on, then,' said Shawna.

'I can't,' said Robin regretfully. 'They told me to do the kitchen after the courtyard, but I can't see why it would be there. I bet whoever finds it's going to be a bit of a hero.'

'Ah,' said Shawna. 'They will. Oi'm gonna do the clarsrooms.'

She bustled off. Immediately Shawna was out of sight, Robin headed, not for the laundry but for the passage between the men's and women's dormitories, eyes on the ground, still pretending to be looking for the fallen fish. She knew she'd be taking a risk in crossing the field by daylight to enter the woods, but as Emily and Will were currently beyond reach, she was determined to fulfil one of her objectives.

Robin kept to the edge of the field rather than taking a straight line across it, glancing back frequently and wishing she could be wearing any other colour than white, which would stand out against the hedgerow should anyone look over the gate. At last she reached the sanctuary of the trees and began her search for any trunk that seemed old enough to contain the hollow and hatchet described by Niamh Doherty.

It was strange to be in the woods by daylight, and even stranger not to be taking her usual route to the plastic rock. The woods were overgrown, untended and perhaps even dangerous for the children who played there, given the number of fallen boughs. Ducking under hanging branches, lifting her feet high over roots and nettles, feeling around trunks to check for hollows, Robin knew she'd be exceptionally lucky to find the right tree in the time she could remain there safely.

The light rain pitter-pattered on the leaves as Robin moved past a thick oak whose trunk was disappointingly solid. She soon found herself on the edge of the small clearing she'd entered once before by night, where a circle of thick posts had been driven into the ground. These had mostly rotted away to stumps, though a couple showed evidence of having been hacked at with an axe.

Robin stepped carefully into the ring, once again noting its ritualistic appearance. The ground underfoot was uneven and slippery with rotting leaves. Somebody had definitely cut down the posts, and now Robin asked herself whether this was the reason a hatchet had been taken to the woods: to try and destroy the ring. Possibly the axe had then been hidden because of the difficulty of smuggling it back up to the main farm? Better, surely, to let suspicion of theft hang over everyone, than be caught with it?

She bent down to examine something black she thought might be a lump of coal, but it wasn't; after a few seconds, Robin decided it was a knot of charred rope. Instead of picking it up, she took a tiny pebble from the ground, which would serve as today's marker, and was just slipping it into her bra when the unmistakeable crack of a twig breaking under a human foot made her whirl round. Jiang was standing between two trees on the edge of the clearing.

'Jiang,' said Robin, forcing herself to laugh, though sweat had broken out on her neck and chest, 'you really made me jump.'

'What're you doing?' he asked suspiciously.

'Looking for Mazu's pendant,' said Robin. At least she'd been found bending over, staring at the ground.

'Why would it be in here?' said Jiang. His right eye had begun to flicker. He rubbed it to disguise the tic.

'I just had a funny feeling it might be,' said Robin, her

voice high and unnatural in her own ears, 'so I thought I'd check.'

'You playing at being Daiyu?' said Jiang with a sneer, and Robin remembered that one of the Drowned Prophet's supposed gifts was that she could find lost objects, no matter how far away they were.

'No,' said Robin. 'No, I don't know why, but I just felt this pull to the woods. I thought maybe one of the children could have picked up the fish and brought it in here, then dropped it.'

The story sounded extremely thin, even to Robin.

'This place is odd, isn't it?' she added, gesturing at the stumps of posts in their circle. 'What d'you think this ring was for? It looks like a miniature Stonehenge.'

'Like what?' said Jiang irritably.

'It's a prehistoric monument,' said Robin. 'In Wiltshire.'

'*I* know what you're up to,' said Jiang, advancing on her.

'What?' said Robin.

'You were gonna meet Emily here.'

'Wh—no, I wasn't. Why would—?'

'*Friends,* aren't you?'

'I barely know her.'

'When we were up on the vegetable patch, you came interfering—'

'I know. I thought you were going to hit her, with the hoe.'

Jiang advanced a few steps, dragging his feet through the overgrown weeds. The dense canopy overhead made dappled shadows move across his face. His eye was winking frantically. He raised his hand to hide it again.

'Emily sneaks off, to fuck,' he said.

It was the first time Robin had heard sex described as anything other than spirit bonding in the church.

'I . . . don't know anything about that.'

'Were you a *lesbian*, outside?'

'No,' said Robin.

'So how come you knew where Emily was, in Norwich?'

'I didn't,' said Robin. 'I just checked all the bathrooms I could find, and she was in one of them.'

'Were you *doing it* with her, in that bathroom?'

'No,' said Robin.

'Why's she looking at you so much since Norwich, then?'

'I haven't noticed her looking at me,' lied Robin.

She couldn't tell whether Jiang's grubby accusation was made to shock and offend, or because he really believed it: he'd never given her the impression of much intelligence, although he'd certainly just proved himself to be surprisingly observant. As though he'd read her thoughts, Jiang said,

'I see more than the rest of 'em with my eyes shut.'

'Can I ask you something?' Robin said. She needed to placate him: he was potentially violent, and her interference on the vegetable patch, and her association with Emily, whose disappearance had caused him to be harangued by his brother on the way back from Norwich, had clearly left him with considerable animus towards her.

'What?'

'You're obviously very high up in the church.'

She knew this wasn't true; Jiang had no real position of authority, though he displayed a definite liking for exerting power within the limited scope he was given. He now lowered the hand concealing his flickering eye and said,

'Yeah.'

'Well,' said Robin, 'how come you seem to work harder than anyone else in . . .' She deliberately let the words 'your family' hang in the air before finishing, '*you* know – in your position?'

'I ain't got no false self,' said Jiang. 'Don't need any of that other crap.'

As she'd hoped, he seemed subtly flattered by her question, and she sensed a slight diminution of aggression.

'I just noticed you kind of . . . *live* what we're all supposed to do. You don't just preach it.'

She was momentarily afraid she'd overdone it, but Jiang squared his shoulders, with the beginnings of a smirk on his grubby face.

'That why you won't fuck Taio? 'Cause he don't live it?'

'I didn't mean Taio doesn't—'

''Cause you're right,' said Jiang, aggressive again. 'He's full of fucking EM, him and that Becca. Both of 'em. I work harder than anyone.'

'I know,' said Robin. 'I've seen it. You never stop. You're out in all weathers, helping run the farm, and it's not like you don't know doctrine. What you told me about the kids, and materialist possession – you know, that day Will was fussing over that little blonde girl? – that really stuck with me. It actually opened my eyes to how weird and abusive the materialist parent-child thing is.'

'That's good,' said Jiang. He gave the bottoms of his track-suit an unnecessary tug upwards. His tic had subsided and he was almost smiling. 'That's good you remembered that.'

'You've got a way of putting things really clearly. Don't get me wrong,' Robin added, careful to sound nervous, 'Taio and Becca are good at it, too, but they . . .'

'Taio wanted to fuck her,' said Jiang, smirking, reverting to what seemed to be his favourite subject. 'Did you know that?'

'No,' said Robin.

'But then Papa J went with her, so Taio wasn't allowed any more.'

'*Oh,*' said Robin, eyebrows raised, and she lied, 'I *thought* I kind of sensed something between Becca and Taio . . .'

'Got your eyes open too, then, haven't you?'

Perhaps because he was so rarely praised or appreciated, Jiang now seemed almost friendly.

'Know what I was always good at, better'n Taio when we were kids?' he asked Robin.

'No,' said Robin, 'what?'

'There's a game, with cards, and you've got to make pairs, and remember where the pictures are,' said Jiang, with a pathetic pride. 'I remember stuff,' he said, tapping his temple with a filthy fingernail. 'And I *see* stuff. More'n they do.'

'I can tell,' said Robin, her sole objective now to get out of the woods while Jiang was in this friendlier state of mind. 'So ... d'you think I should keep looking for the fish in here, or d'you think it's pointless?'

Jiang looked pleased to be asked for his opinion.

'Nobody's gonna find it here,' he said, surveying the many fallen leaves and branches, twisted roots and patches of nettles.

'No, you're right,' said Robin. 'This is my first time in the woods. I didn't realise they were so overgrown.'

She took a step towards Jiang and to her immense relief, he simply turned to walk with her, back the way he'd come.

'There's a tree over there,' said Jiang, pointing to an aged ash, visible through the younger growth, 'with a hollow in it and there's an axe hidden in it.'

'Wow,' said Robin, taking careful note of the tree's position.

'I found it in here, when I was a kid. Nobody else knows,' said Jiang complacently.

'Wonder what an axe is doing in a tree?'

'Ha,' said Jiang, smirking again, ''cause Daiyu hid it in there. But don't go telling anyone that.'

'Seriously?' said Robin. 'The Drowned Prophet hid it?'

'Yeah,' said Jiang.

'How d'you know?'

'I just do,' said Jiang, with precisely the kind of smugness

Shawna always displayed when given the chance. 'I know stuff. I told you. I keep my eyes open.'

They emerged from the woods and began to cross the field, Robin careful to pause every now and then and poke at bits of grass, pretending she was still searching for Mazu's mother-of-pearl fish, but also trying to think of a way of leading the conversation back to Daiyu without raising Jiang's suspicions. The rain had gone off; the grass sparkled, buttercups and clover shining enamel bright in the watery sunshine.

'Wanna know something else?' Jiang said, halfway back to the five-bar gate.

'Yes,' said Robin, with complete sincerity.

'There's somebody here, right now, who was here a long time ago. They've come back again – and I'm the only one who realises.'

He cast a sly sidelong look at Robin out of his dark, narrow eyes.

'Really?' said Robin. 'Who is it?'

'Ha. I'm not telling,' said Jiang. 'I'm just keeping an eye on them.'

'Can't you even tell me, male or female?' said Robin.

'Nosy, aren't you?' said Jiang, his grin widening. 'Nah, that's for me to know. Funny how Taio and Becca are so clever and they haven't realised. I'm gonna go to Papa J, when I've finished my investigations,' he added importantly.

They climbed over the five-bar gate, Robin now burning with curiosity.

The curtains of the nearest Retreat Room were closed, meaning it was in use. Robin anticipated a ribald comment from Jiang, but his good humour seemed to fade somewhat as they passed the cabin.

'Know why I'm not allowed in them?' he asked her, pointing a dirty thumb behind him.

'No,' said Robin. It was welcome news that Jiang wasn't permitted to spirit bond; she'd been worried her flattery of him might be taken as a sexual overture.

'Nobody's told you?' said Jiang, suspicious again. 'Not Taio?'

'No,' said Robin. 'Nobody's said anything.'

'It's 'cause of Jacob,' said Jiang sourly. 'But that wasn't my fault, it was Louise's, Dr Zhou says so. It won't happen again.'

'How *is* Jacob?' Robin asked, hoping once and for all to resolve this mystery.

'I dunno, I never see him,' said Jiang. 'It wasn't my bloody fault.'

The courtyard was still full of people, all of them combing the ground for some sign of Mazu's fallen fish, and to Robin's relief, her reappearance with Jiang occasioned neither look nor comment.

'Need the loo,' Robin told Jiang, smiling at him to prove she wasn't trying to get away from him, which she had no intention of doing, because he was proving an unexpected source of interesting possible leads. 'Then we can look more.'

'Yeah, all right,' said Jiang, pleased.

Once inside the dormitory, which was deserted, Robin hurried to her bed to deposit the latest pebble beneath the mattress, marking yet another day at Chapman Farm. On kneeling down, however, she saw that several of the tiny pebbles she'd already deposited there this week had been dislodged and lay scattered on the floor.

Disconcerted, she ran her hand beneath the mattress, finding only one pebble still in place. Then her fingers touched something small, flat, loose and smooth. She pulled it out and saw a pearly bright, intricately carved fish.

Robin hastily scooped all the dislodged pebbles up, thrust them all inside her bra, leapt to her feet and ran to the bathroom. Here she clambered up onto the sink, opened the high window, checked that the coast was clear, and threw the fish outside. It landed in a clump of tall grass.

Robin jumped back down onto the floor, wiped her foot-prints off the sink and turned on a tap, just in time: she heard a group of women enter the dormitory.

'Hi,' said Robin, emerging from the bathroom and hoping that she didn't look too red in the face. Vivienne, who was among the women, ignored her, instead saying to the group,

'Check *everywhere,* OK? Even under the mattresses.'

'How could the pendant have got under a mattress?' Robin asked Vivienne, her heart still thumping rapidly from the shock of her discovery.

'I don't know, it's just what Becca wants,' said Vivienne irritably.

'Oh, right,' said Robin.

'Aren't you going to help?' said Vivienne, as Robin made to leave.

'Sorry,' said Robin, 'Jiang wants me to help him.'

As she walked outside to rejoin Jiang, she noticed Becca talking to Dr Zhou on the other side of Drowned Prophet's fountain.

'Where should we look?' Robin asked Jiang. She had no intention whatsoever of pursuing the fish into its clump of grass: let somebody else find it.

'Craft rooms,' suggested Jiang, who was clearly enjoying Robin looking to him for orders.

'Great,' said Robin.

As they walked away, Robin glanced back at Becca, and was unsurprised to find her eyes following them.

70

Strike was having an extremely trying day.

At shortly after ten, as he was following Toy Boy and the client's mother into Selfridges, Shanker called. Hoping for confirmation that Littlejohn was working undercover for Patterson Inc, Strike answered quickly, placing a finger in his free ear to block out the sound of canned music and talkative shoppers.

'Hi,' said Strike, 'what've you got?'

'Reaney's tried to top 'imself. Fort you'd wanna know.'

'He's *what?*'

'Yeah,' said Shanker. 'Overdose. Me mate in Bedford jus' called an' told me.'

'When was this?'

'Few days back. Silly cunt. Bought up and nicked all the pills 'e could get 'is 'ands on and took the lot.'

'Shit. He's still alive, though?'

'Just abaht. In 'ospital. Me mate said 'e was yellow an' covered in puke when the screws found 'im.'

'Anyone know why he did it?'

'Yeah, 'e got a phone call from 'is wife, a week ago. After

668

that 'e started buying up everyfing anyone could give 'im and dahned the lot.'

'OK,' said Strike. 'Cheers for letting me know.'

'No bovver. Lot of it goin' abaht, in't there?'

'What? Oh,' said Strike, realising Shanker was talking about Charlotte. 'Yeah, I s'pose. Listen, can you give those boys of yours a kick up the arse? I need something on Littlejohn, fast.'

Strike hung up and set off in pursuit of Toy Boy and his companion, thinking of Reaney as he'd last seen him, shoving away those Polaroids of naked youths in pig masks, then standing up, pale and sweaty, after mention of the Drowned Prophet.

He spent the next four and a half hours trailing around Selfridges after his targets.

'He's got a couple of suits and a watch out of her so far,' Strike informed Barclay at three o'clock, when the latter arrived to take over.

'Starting tae think I'm in the wrong line o' work,' said Barclay. 'I could use a Rolex.'

'If you can look that woman straight in the eye and tell her she's beautiful, you deserve one.'

Strike left the store and walked off along Oxford Street, craving a kebab. He was crossing the road when his mobile rang again, this time from an unfamiliar number.

'Strike.'

'It's me,' said a woman's voice.

'Who's "me"?' asked Strike irritably.

'Bijou. *Don't be angry.* I had to ask Ilsa for your number again. *This is serious, please don't hang up.*'

'What d'you want?'

'I can't say it on the phone. Can I meet you?'

As Strike hesitated, a youth on a skateboard cuffed him in passing, making Strike yearn to slap the inconsiderate little fucker into the gutter.

'I'm in Oxford Street. I can give you twenty minutes in the Flying Horse if you hurry.'

'Fine,' she said, and hung up.

It took Strike a quarter of an hour to reach the pub and he found Bijou already there, sitting at the tall table at the back beneath the glass cupola, wrapped in a black coat and nursing what looked like water. Strike bought himself a pint he felt he'd more than earned, and joined her at the high table.

'Go on,' he said, omitting a greeting.

Bijou glanced around before saying in a low voice,

'Somebody's bugged Andrew's office. He thinks it was you.'

'Oh, for fuck's sake,' said Strike, who felt he'd reached his full monthly capacity for unsought problems and obstacles. 'It'll be some bloody tabloid. Or his wife.'

'I *told* him that,' said Bijou, her bright blue eyes moist, 'but he doesn't believe me!'

'Well, what d'you expect me to do about it?'

'Talk to him,' she whimpered. *'Please.'*

'If he doesn't believe you, why the hell would he believe me?'

'Please, Cormoran! I'm – I'm pregnant!'

For a split second, he felt as though dry ice had slid down through his guts, and evidently his horror had shown on his face, because she said quickly,

'Don't worry, it's not *yours*! I only just found out – it's Andy's, but—'

Bijou's face crumpled and she buried her face in her beautifully manicured hands. Strike surmised that Andrew Honbold QC hadn't evinced joy at the fact that an embryo of his own creation was currently nestling inside the cosmetically enhanced body of a mistress he now believed had had his office bugged.

'Has Honbold had anyone new in his office lately? Taken meetings with anyone he hasn't met before?'

'*I* don't know,' said Bijou, raising a tearstained face. '*I* think it's bloody Matilda. Will you talk to him? *Please*?'

'I'll think about it,' said Strike, not because he felt any sympathy for Bijou, but because an idea had occurred to him that was as unpleasant as it was plausible. Bijou now reached a hand across the table, but Strike withdrew his own hand, unpleasantly reminded of Charlotte.

'I was only going to thank you,' she said, with the hint of a pout.

'Don't. I'm not promising to do anything.'

She slid off the bar stool and stood for a moment, looking at him, and even now, he sensed her wish for some sign that he still desired her, and he was again reminded of Charlotte.

'Cormoran—'

'I said I'll think about it.'

She swept up her handbag and left.

Strike, who had paperwork waiting for him at the office, sipped his pint and tried to tell himself he didn't want a burger and chips. There was a burning sensation behind his eyes, born of tiredness. His stomach growled. The myriad problems of the day seemed to buzz around him like mosquitos. Andrew Honbold, Bijou, Patterson: did he not have enough to worry about, without all these extraneous difficulties?

Caving in, he went to the bar to order food. Once back at the table beneath the cupola, Strike took out his phone and, in masochistic spirit, checked the Facebook account of Carrie Curtis Woods, who naturally hadn't responded to his follower request, and Torment Town's Pinterest page, on which no new comments had been posted since his own. Tired of the stalemate, he typed out another question for Torment Town, determined to force something out of whoever ran the account.

671

Did you ever know a woman called Deirdre Doherty?

He pressed send. If the drawing of the fair-haired woman in glasses floating in the dark pool was indeed supposed to be Deirdre, that, surely, would get a reaction.

He next looked up the phone number of Reaney's wife's nail salon, Kuti-cles. After asking for Ava there was a wait of a few seconds, then he heard her approaching the phone while talking loudly to someone in the background.

'—keep 'em in there and don't touch 'em. Hello?'

'Hi, Mrs Reaney, it's Cormoran Strike again. The private detective.'

'Oh,' said Ava, sounding displeased. 'You.'

'I've just heard some news about Jord—'

'Yeah, I know he's overdosed.'

'I hear you called him a week before he did it. Was that about your divorce?'

'I never called 'im. Why would I? 'E's known abou' the divorce for monfs.'

'So you didn't phone him a week ago?'

'I 'aven't called him in ages. I've changed my numbers to stop him pestering me. It'll have been one of his girlfriends, pretending to be me to make sure 'e took the call. He'll put his dick in anything, Jordan will. First 'e shags you, then 'e slaps you around. She's welcome to 'im, whoever she is.'

'Right,' said Strike, thinking fast. 'Seems an extreme reaction to the call, if it was just a girlfriend. Has he ever attempted suicide before?'

'No, more's the pity. Listen,' she added, in a lower voice, 'if you want the truth, I'd sooner 'e died. I won't be looking over me shoulder for the rest of me life. Got it?'

'Got it,' said Strike. 'Thanks for your time.'

He sat for another minute, thinking. Of course, the phone

call from an unknown woman posing as Reaney's wife might have had nothing whatsoever to do with Reaney's suicide attempt; the connection might just be an assumption of Shanker's mate's.

His mobile rang again: the office number.

'Hi Pat.'

'Hi,' she said. 'Will you be coming back to the office this afternoon?'

'In a bit. I'm having a late lunch at the Flying Horse. Why?'

'I wanted a word with you.'

'What kind of word?' said Strike, frowning as he rubbed his sore eyes.

'Well,' said Pat, 'I don't think you're going to like it.'

'*What is it?*' said Strike, now on the verge of losing his temper.

'I just need to tell you something.'

'Can you tell me what it is now?' said Strike, whose neck was rigid with tension.

'I'd rather say it face to face.'

What on earth the office manager needed to communicate in person Strike couldn't imagine. However, he had a dim idea that if he employed a human resources person they'd advise him to accede to the request, and possibly not swear at Pat.

'Fine, come up to the pub, I'm waiting for a burger,' he said.

'All right. I'll see you in five minutes.'

The office manager and Strike's burger arrived at exactly the same time. Pat took the seat Bijou had just vacated and Strike's unease increased, because the expression on Pat's monkeyish face was frightened, and she was clutching her handbag tightly on her lap, as though in self-protection.

'Want a drink?' he asked.

'No,' said Pat.

Much as he wanted his chips, Strike felt he ought to hear Pat out before eating.

'Go on,' he said. 'What's up?'

Pat swallowed.

'I'm sixty-seven.'

'You're what?'

'Sixty-seven. Years old,' she added.

Strike merely looked at her.

'I lied,' croaked Pat. 'On my CV.'

'Yeah,' said Strike. 'You did.'

'Well, I had to. Nobody wants anyone my age.'

Strike suspected he might know the reason Pat had suddenly come clean.

'I'm fired, aren't I?' she said.

'Oh Christ, don't cry,' said Strike, seeing her lip tremble: one bawling woman a day was enough. 'Littlejohn knows this, I take it?'

'How did you know that?' gasped Pat.

'Has he been blackmailing you?'

'Not until just now,' said Pat, retrieving a handkerchief from her handbag and pressing it against her eyes. 'He told me he knew, right after he started with us. I couldn't tell you without admitting how old I am, could I?

'But I was in the loo just now and when I went in the office he was there, and he had the Edensor file and I think he was going to take photos of it, because he had his phone out. I said to him, "What the hell d'you think you're doing?" and he closed the file and said, "You didn't see that, and I'll forget you're a pensioner, all right?"'

'You don't think he got pictures?'

'No, I heard him pass the loo. He wouldn't have had time.'

Strike picked up a couple of chips and ate them, while Pat watched him. When Strike didn't speak, she repeated,

'I'm fired, aren't I?'

'You should've told me.'

'You wouldn't have hired me if I'd told the truth,' said Pat, tears now falling faster than she could wipe them away.

'I'm not talking about then, I'm talking about now. Stop bloody crying, you're not fired. Where'm I going to get another manager like you?'

'*Oh,*' said Pat, and, pressing the handkerchief to her face, she began to cry in earnest.

Strike got to his feet and went to the bar, buying a glass of port, which was Pat's preferred drink, and returning to set it down in front of her.

'Why the hell d'you want to keep working at sixty-seven?'

''Cause I like working,' gulped Pat, frantically wiping her face. 'I get bored, sitting at home.'

'Me too,' said Strike, who'd been making certain deductions while at the bar. 'So how old's your daughter?'

'Just turned fifty,' muttered Pat. 'I had her young.'

'That's why you bit my head off when I asked?'

Pat nodded.

'Is she on Facebook?'

'Never off it,' said Pat, reaching for her port with an unsteady hand.

'Then—'

'Yeah. I'll ask Rhoda. She'll like helping,' said Pat, taking a shaky sip of port.

'Where's Littlejohn now?'

'He left. I made sure he'd really gone before I called you. He got in a taxi at the end of the road. He wasn't happy I caught him. He's off for a week now,' said Pat, blowing her nose. 'They're going to Greece on holiday.'

'By the time I've finished with him he'll wish he'd bloody stayed there.'

He started on his burger. When Pat had finished her drink, she said,

'Better get back, I was halfway through next week's rota ... thanks, Cormoran.'

'You're welcome,' said Strike, through a mouthful of burger. Pat left.

Strike knew full well he was guilty of an inconsistency. He'd damned Littlejohn on the principle that where there was one lie, there were more, but he was confident that Pat's lie hadn't been born of a fundamental lack of honesty. Quite the reverse: she was often far too honest for his liking. In the early days of her employment he'd have jumped at the chance to fire her, but time had brought about a complete revolution in his feelings: now, he'd have been extremely loath to lose her. Nevertheless, he thought, as he reached absently for more chips, he might delay the pay rise he'd been planning to give her. Forgiveness was one thing, but it was a poor management strategy to reward employees for coming clean only when they were forced to do so.

For the next ten minutes, Strike was left alone to enjoy his burger. When at last he'd finished eating, he reached for his mobile and called Shanker back.

'I want to trace the call Reaney got, before he overdosed. D'you know any bent screws up in Bedford?'

'There's always bent screws, Bunsen,' said Shanker, cynical as ever.

'Five hundred for you and five hundred for them, if they can give me any solid information about that call,' said Strike recklessly, 'particularly the number it was made from.'

71

In spite of Robin's gentle probing, Jiang had revealed nothing more about Daiyu or Jacob during their search for Mazu's mother-of-pearl fish, nor had he told Robin which person had allegedly reappeared at Chapman Farm after a long absence. All she'd learned for certain was that Jiang's inner life was dominated by two preoccupations: a sense of injury that his brother had gone so far in the church while he was relegated to the status of farmhand and chauffeur, and a prurient interest in the sex lives of other church members, which appeared to spring from the frustration he felt at his own exclusion from the Retreat Rooms. However, their meeting in the woods had definitely left Jiang feeling more kindly towards Robin than hitherto, and this was some comfort, because Robin felt she needed all the allies she could get.

She had no doubt that Becca had hidden Mazu's fish beneath her mattress. Robin had seen Becca's expression of confusion and anger when the fish was found in the long grass by a triumphant Walter, and her immediate, accusatory glance at Robin.

Exactly what had provoked Becca to try and incriminate her, Robin didn't know, but her best guess was that Becca, like Taio, suspected some kind of alliance had been forged between Emily and Robin in Norwich, and that she was consequently determined to see Robin disgraced, punished, or even moved on from Chapman Farm.

Becca was a formidable enemy to have made. Robin worried that it might not take much to break the silence of Lin, Jiang or Vivienne if Becca pressed them for any incriminating information they might have on Robin. Unauthorised trips to the woods, possession of a torch, the fact that she'd answered to her real name: Robin had enough respect for Becca's intelligence to know it wouldn't take her long to guess that 'Rowena' was an undercover investigator. While Robin had told Strike about the pendant in her last letter, she'd again omitted mention of Lin discovering her in the woods, and her foolish slip in front of Vivienne.

As if this wasn't enough to fret about, Robin was also aware that for every day she failed to seek Taio out and offer him sex, her status at Chapman Farm was worsening. Taio glowered at her from afar as she moved round the farm, and she was starting to fear an outright demand for spirit bonding which, if refused, would certainly produce some kind of crisis. Yet hour to hour, day to day, Robin clung on, in the hope she might yet get more information out of Emily or Jiang, or find an opportunity to talk to Will Edensor.

Meanwhile, Noli Seymour, Dr Zhou and the rest of the church Principals had all descended on the farm. Robin understood from overheard conversations that the Manifestation of the Drowned Prophet, which was fast approaching, usually drew the entire council to the church's birthplace. While Dr Zhou remained cloistered in his luxurious office and Giles Harmon continued to spend most of each day typing in his bedroom, visible to everyone who crossed the courtyard, Noli and a couple of the men donned white tracksuits like the ordinary members. While they didn't lower themselves to sleeping in the dormitories, all three could be seen moving around the farm working at various tasks, each with an air of conscious virtue and often with an ineptitude that would have drawn fierce criticism down upon any other church member.

Robin, who was still existing in a strange limbo somewhere between high-level recruit and manual worker, was sent to help cook dinner one evening, after a long session on church doctrine led by Mazu. She entered the kitchen to see Will Edensor chopping a mound of onions. Having donned an apron, she headed to help him without waiting to be given orders.

'Thanks,' he muttered, when she joined him.

'No problem,' said Robin.

'It always does this to me,' said Will, mopping his watery, pink-rimmed eyes on his sleeve.

'It's easier if you freeze them first,' said Robin.

'Seriously?'

'Yes, but it's a bit late for us to try that now. I s'pose we'll just have to work fast.'

Will smiled. For a brief moment he looked much younger than he usually did.

The noise in the kitchen was relentless, what with the clanging of the enormous pans, the hissing of the vector fan over the industrial ovens and the bubbling and spitting of the usual slop of tinned vegetables, cooking on multiple gas rings.

'How long have you been in the church, Will?' Robin asked.

'Um ... four years or something, now.'

'So that's how long I'll have to be here, to know doctrine as well as you do?'

She'd thought the question would either flatter him or provoke him into a lecture, either of which would provide an opening to push him on his allegiance to the UHC.

'You just have to study,' he said dully.

Wondering whether he was being less opinionated because his eyes were bothering him, or for some deeper reason, she said,

'So you've been here for four Manifestations of the Drowned Prophet?'

Will nodded, then said,

'But I can't talk about it. You've got to experience it, to really understand.'

'I feel as though I got a kind of preview,' said Robin, 'during my Revelation session. Daiyu came to the temple. She made the stage tip up.'

'Yeah, I heard about that,' said Will.

'I know I deserved it,' said Robin, 'so I suppose I should be glad it happened. It's like you said to me on the vegetable patch, there's no "in trouble", is there? It's all strengthening.'

For a moment or two Will was silent. Then he said,

'Have you been in the library yet?'

'I searched it for Mazu's fish,' said Robin. 'I haven't used it properly.'

Though beautifully appointed, with mahogany tables and brass reading lights, the library contained few books, and half of them had been written by Jonathan Wace. The rest of the stock comprised holy texts of all major religions. While Robin would have welcomed a quiet hour in the library, she doubted she'd be able to concentrate long on the Guru Granth Sahib or the Torah without falling asleep.

'Have you read the Bible?' asked Will.

'Um . . . bits,' said Robin cautiously.

'I was reading it yesterday. John, chapter one, verse 4:1:

"Beloved, do not believe every spirit, but test the spirits to see whether they are from God, for many false prophets have gone out into the world.'"

Robin glanced at him. She might be mistaken, given his reddened, puffy eyes, but she thought he looked worried.

'Oh *Lord,* I'm going to need help,' said a loud female voice. Robin and Will looked round. Noli Seymour had just entered the kitchen wearing a pristine white tracksuit, and was making a comical expression, hands pressed against her face. 'I'm an *awful* cook!' she said, looking round. 'Some of you experts are going to have to help me!'

If Noli had imagined a stampede to assist her, or that the kitchen workers would be charmed by her admission of helplessness, she'd miscalculated. Tired and sweaty, none of them smiled, although Sita handed her an apron. Robin had a presentiment about what was about to happen, and sure enough, one of the older women pointed Noli to the pile of onions Robin and Will were tackling, doubtless thinking that this was where she could do least harm. Noli was enough of an actress to fake enthusiasm.

'Great . . . um . . . have you got gloves?'

'No,' said the woman, returning to the large vat containing a gallon of tinned tomatoes bubbling on the stove.

'Hi, I'm Noli,' said the actress to Will and Robin. 'Have you got—? Oh, thanks,' she said, as Robin passed her a knife. 'So what are your names?'

They told her.

'Rowena, wow, that's so funny, I played Rowena in *Ivanhoe* at drama school,' said Noli, looking sideways at the way Robin was slicing her onion, and trying to copy her. 'It was kind of a challenge, actually. I much prefer playing characters with *substance,* you know? And Rowena's basically just, you know, beautiful and kind and noble,' Noli rolled her eyes, 'and I'm like, "Um, wouldn't it be easier to use a mannequin or something?" Oh, God, I hope you aren't named after Lady Rowena!' Noli added, with a peal of laughter. 'Were your parents fans, or something?'

Before Robin could answer, Will, whose streaming eyes were still fixed on the onion he was chopping, muttered:

'Materialist possession.'

'What?' said Noli.

'"Parents",' said Will, still not looking at Noli.

'Oh – yeah, right,' said Noli. 'You know what I mean, though.'

'No, I wasn't named after Lady Rowena,' said Robin.

'I just get typecast, you know?' said Noli, who was doing her best to touch the onion she was chopping as little as possible, holding it steady with her fingertips. 'I'm *constantly* saying to my agent, "Just once, can you get me a character *with character*?" I've been feeling that *so much more* since joining the church,' she added earnestly.

The threesome chopped in silence for a little while until Will, after wiping his irritated eyes on the sleeve of his sweat-shirt again, glanced at Noli and said,

'Are you really going to make a film about the Drowned Prophet?'

The actress looked up at him, startled.

'How on *earth* did you know about that?'

'Are you?' said Will, his reddened eyes fixed on his work again.

'Well, not just about – nothing's definite. I've been talking to Papa J about maybe doing a film about *him*. How on earth did you know that?' she added, with another little laugh.

'I was the one serving you your potatoes when you were talking about it to Papa J,' said Will. 'In the farmhouse.'

The kitchen workers in their immediate vicinity were now

listening to the conversation. Some had deliberately slowed down in their tasks, so as to make less noise.

'Oh, of *course* you were, yes,' said Noli, but Robin could tell Noli had no memory of Will at all. 'Well, it's just something I think could be really interesting. We could make sure a big cut of the profits go to the UHC, obviously. I think it would be an incredible way to bring awareness of the church to a wider audience. Of course, *he* doesn't think anyone would watch a movie about him,' she said, with a giggle. 'That's the funny thing about him, he doesn't realise *what he is,* does he? He's so modest, it's one of the things I really admire about him, it makes a really nice change from the people I meet in *my* business, I can tell you.'

'Would you be Daiyu, in the film?' said Will.

'No, of course not, I'm too old,' said Noli. 'I'd *quite* like to play his first wife, because he's told me a bit about her, and she sounds like a – well, she was no Lady Rowena, put it that way.'

'D'you think it's strange,' said Will, still dicing onions, 'that Papa J married twice and nobody in the church is supposed to marry?'

'What?' said Noli. Her knife slipped off the onion she was mangling.

'Will!'

One of the older women had spoken, her tone a definite warning. The kitchen workers around the onion choppers seemed to have come back to life: there was a resumption of the usual clanging and clattering as they moved away.

'Of course it's not strange,' said Noli. 'His first marriage was before he even – anyway, it's a Higher-Level Truth, isn't it?'

'What is?' said Will, still looking at the onion he was chopping.

'Papa J and Mama Mazu, you can't – it's not the same. They're, like, our parents – all of our parents.'

'Materialist possession,' muttered Will again.

'Oh, come—'

'Have you read the Bhagavad Gita?'

'Yes, of course,' said Noli, clearly lying.

'Lord Krishna talks about people of demonic nature. *"Self-conceited, stubborn, intoxicated by pride in wealth, they perform sacrifice in name only, with ostentation."'*

'Ohmigod, there are *so many* people in acting like that,' said Noli. 'The last show I did—'

But her voice was drowned out by another. Somebody outside the kitchen was screaming.

72

The kitchen door banged open to reveal Penny, whose once-green hair was now straggly and brown, and the front of whose sweatshirt was stained with what looked like blood.

'It's Lin,' she wailed. 'In the women's bathroom. She's – oh my God—'

Robin and Will were the first to move. Robin followed the younger man at a sprint, her apron slightly impeding the motion of her knees, and behind her she could hear some of the older women also running. They dashed down the pathway into the courtyard, but at the dormitory door, Will checked. Men weren't supposed to enter the women's dormitory. Robin pushed him aside, ran through the empty dormitory and through the bathroom door.

'Oh Jesus,' she said aloud.

There was a puddle of blood seeping from under one of the toilet cubicle doors. She could see Lin's bloodstained legs, which weren't moving.

'Lin,' Robin yelled, pounding on the locked door, but there was no answer. Robin dashed into the neighbouring cubicle, jumped up onto the toilet seat, seized hold of the top of the partition and pulled herself over it.

'Shit,' said Robin, landing and slipping in the blood surrounding the teenager, who sat slumped against the toilet.

She'd expected suicide, but saw at once that the blood, of which there seemed a terrifying amount, seemed to be issuing from Lin's vagina. Her tracksuit bottoms were sodden and she was wheezing, while her neck, face and hands were covered in an angry red rash.

'Lin,' said Robin, 'what's happened?'

'Leave m-m-me,' whispered Lin. 'J-j-just leave m-m-me.'

Robin heard footsteps outside the cubicle and hastily unlocked the door to reveal the worried faces of Penny and assorted female kitchen workers.

'I'll get Dr Zhou,' said Sita, who disappeared.

'N-no,' gasped Lin. 'N-n-not Zhou, n-not Zhou . . .'

'You need a doctor, Lin,' said Robin. 'You've got to see a doctor.'

'N-n-not him . . . I d-d-don't want him . . . I'm fine . . . it's fine . . .'

Robin reached for Lin's hand, which was hot, and held it.

'It's going to be OK,' she said.

'N-n-no it won't,' said Lin faintly, now gasping for breath. 'N-n-not if she g-g-gets Zhou . . . p-p-please . . .'

Robin could hear men talking outside the dormitory and a few minutes later, loudest of all, she heard Dr Zhou.

'Get out of the way!' he shouted as he entered the bathroom, and the women surrounding the cubicle scattered. Robin remained exactly where she was, and felt Lin's fingers tighten on hers as Zhou appeared in the open doorway.

'What the bloody hell have you done to yourself?' he shouted, looking down at Lin, and Robin read panic in his face.

'Nothing . . . nothing . . .' wheezed Lin.

'I think,' said Robin, feeling terribly guilty about betraying Lin, but afraid of the consequences if she didn't speak, 'she might have eaten some plants.'

'What plants?' shouted Zhou, his voice echoing off the tiled walls.

'Lin, tell him,' said Robin, 'please tell him. Think of Qing,' she whispered.

'M-m-mug . . . wort,' said Lin, now gasping for breath.

'Get up,' snarled Zhou.

'Are you mad?' said Robin, looking up at him. 'She can't stand!'

'Get two of the men in here!' Zhou bellowed at the women who'd retreated back into the dormitory.

'What are you going to do?' Robin demanded.

'You, move!' Zhou barked at Robin, who remained exactly where she was, still gripping Lin's hand.

Now Will and Taio appeared at the cubicle door. Taio looked disgusted, Will, simply horrified.

'Wrap a towel around her,' said Zhou, 'we don't want mess everywhere. Then carry her to the farmhouse.'

'N-n-no,' said Lin, starting feebly to resist as Taio began to roughly bundle a bath towel around her.

'I'll do it,' said Robin, batting Taio's hand away.

Lin was hoisted to her feet, the towel wrapped around her, then carried away by Will and Taio.

'Clean that mess up,' were Zhou's parting words to Robin, and as he left the bathroom, she heard him bark at somebody else, 'You, go and help her.'

Robin's tracksuit bottoms were soaked in the warm red liquid. She got slowly to her feet, her nostrils full of the ferrous smell of Lin's blood, as Penny came creeping back into the bathroom, her eyes wide.

'What happened to her?' she whispered.

'I think she tried to give herself a miscarriage,' said Robin, who felt nauseated.

'*Oh,*' said Penny. 'I didn't know what to do. I just saw the blood under the door ...'

The ramifications of what had just happened were hitting Robin. She wondered whether Lin was going to die, whether Zhou was competent to deal with the emergency. She also knew she'd reacted to the crisis as Robin Ellacott, not as Rowena Ellis, shouting at Zhou and ignoring his orders, pushing Taio away, siding with the girl who'd tried to abort her baby. Then there was her admission she knew Lin had eaten plants ...

'Dr Zhou told me to help you clean up,' said Penny timidly.

'It's fine,' said Robin, who very much wanted to be left alone. 'I can do it.'

'No,' said Penny, who looked queasy but determined, 'he told me to ... you really yelled at him,' she added nervously.

'I was just shocked,' said Robin.

'I know ... but he *is* the doctor.'

Robin said nothing, but went to get one of the stiff, rough towels the women used after showers, spread it over the blood and began to mop it up, all the while wondering how on earth she was going to explain that she knew Lin had had those plants, without admitting she'd been in the woods where they grew, at night.

Imitating Robin, Penny too fetched a towel to soak up the blood. When most of it was mopped up, Robin dropped the stained towel into the laundry basket, went to get a fresh one and ran it under the cold water tap. As she did so, she glanced up at the high windows over the sinks again. Her heart hammered almost painfully as she imagined leaving immediately. She'd just heard the first indication that Will Edensor might be having doubts about the church, but she had no idea how to talk her way out of the trouble she'd now surely landed herself in. If only she could get rid of Penny, she might be able to climb out of one of those windows and drop down on the other side of the building, out of sight of the courtyard; then she could run for the woods while the higher-ups were distracted by Lin, raise the alarm and get an ambulance to the farm. That, surely, was the right thing to do. Her time was up.

She returned to the mess on the floor with her wet towel and began wiping up the last traces of blood.

'Go to dinner,' she told Penny. 'I'll finish up here, it's nearly done.'

'OK,' said Penny, getting to her feet. 'I hope you don't get in trouble.'

'Thanks,' said Robin.

She waited until Penny's footsteps had died away, then got up, threw the wet towel into the laundry basket too, and had taken two strides towards the sink when a white figure appeared in the doorway.

'Papa J wants to see you,' said Louise Pirbright.

73

We find ourselves close to the commander of darkness . . .

The I Ching or Book of Changes

'I haven't finished,' said Robin stupidly, pointing at the floor, which was still faintly pink.

'I'll send someone else to do it,' said Louise. She was holding her hands in front of her, nervously interlocking her swollen-jointed fingers. 'You'd better come.'

It took a moment for Robin to make her trembling legs behave. She followed Louise out of the bathroom and through the deserted dormitory. For a brief moment, she contemplated breaking away, sprinting down the passage between the dormitories and climbing over the five-bar gate, but she had no confidence that she'd make the woods without being caught: there were too many people in the courtyard, some of them grouped around Daiyu's pool to make the usual obeisance, others heading for the dining hall.

Louise and Robin, too, paused at the pool. When Robin said, 'The Drowned Prophet will bless all who worship her,' she felt her tongue sticking to the roof of her mouth. Having daubed her forehead with water, she followed Louise towards the dragon-carved doors of the farmhouse.

Inside, they passed the scarlet-carpeted staircase, then

stopped at a shiny black door on the left-hand side of the hall. Louise knocked.

'Come,' said Jonathan Wace's voice.

Louise opened the door, indicated that Robin should walk inside and then closed the door behind her.

The room Robin entered was large and very beautiful. Unlike Mazu's study, there was no clutter here. The walls were covered in peacock blue fabric, against which figures of ivory and silver, most of them Chinese, stood in graceful, modern shelving cabinets, in pools of carefully directed light. A fire burned beneath a modern surround of white marble. In front of this, on a black leather couch, sat Jonathan Wace, alone, eating off a low black lacquer table that was laden with various dishes.

'Aha,' said Wace, smiling as he set down his knife and fork and got to his feet. 'Rowena.'

He was wearing an upmarket version of the white track-suits nearly everyone at the farm wore, which appeared to be made of raw silk. On his feet he wore very expensive-looking leather slides. Robin felt the colour leave her face as he walked towards her.

Wace pulled her into a hug. Robin could still feel herself shaking, and knew he could feel it too, because he was holding her so tightly her breasts were squashed against his chest. He smelled of sandalwood cologne and held her far too long for her comfort. She tried to relax, but every muscle was tense. At last Wace loosened his grip, though still holding her in his arms, so he could look down at her, smiling.

'You're quite wonderful, aren't you?'

Robin didn't know whether he was being sarcastic. He looked sincere. At last, he released her.

'Come,' he said again, and returned to the sofa, beckoning her to a black leather chair that sat at right angles to the fire.

'I've heard how you helped deliver Mazu's baby, Rowena,' said Wace. 'Thank you, very sincerely, for your service.'

Momentarily confused, Robin realised he was talking about Wan's daughter.

'Oh,' she said. Her mouth was still so dry it was hard to get out the words. 'Yes.'

'And tonight you offered poor little Lin solace,' said Wace, still smiling as he added ragout to his plate. 'You are forgiven,' he added, 'for speaking intemperately to Dr Zhou.'

'I . . . oh good . . . I mean, thank you,' said Robin.

She felt certain Wace was playing some kind of game. The smell of rich food, coming as it did immediately after the smell of blood, was making her stomach churn. *Breathe*, she told herself. *Talk*.

'Is Lin going to be all right?' she asked.

'"The way of yang goes to and fro, up and down,"' quoted Wace, still smiling. 'She's been foolish, as you've probably realised. Why didn't you tell anyone she was consuming mugwort?' he asked, apparently idly, as he picked up his knife and fork again.

'I didn't know,' said Robin, as sweat broke out over her scalp again. 'I guessed. I saw her with some plants a while ago.'

'When was this?'

'I can't remember, I just saw her holding them one day. When I saw that rash she's got tonight, I thought it looked like an allergy.'

'There are no allergies,' said Wace smoothly. 'The rash was her flesh revolting at what her false self made her do.'

'Will Dr Zhou be able to help her?'

'Of course. He understands spirit work better than anyone now alive.'

'Has he taken her to a hospital?'

'He's treating her now, and Taio's about to remove her to a

place of recuperation, so you needn't distress yourself about Lin,' said Wace. 'I want to talk about *you*. I hear ... conflicting reports.'

He smiled at her, chewing, then, widening his eyes, he swallowed and said,

'But this is shocking of me ... you're missing dinner.'

He pressed a small bell sitting among the various dishes on the table. Moments later, bald Shawna appeared, beaming.

'Shawna, another plate, glass, knife and fork for Rowena, please,' said Wace.

'Yes, Papa J,' said Shawna importantly, bowing before leaving the room again.

'Thank you,' said Robin, trying to act the part of an innocent woman and church member, one who desperately wanted Jonathan Wace's approval. 'Sorry, but ... what conflicting reports are there about me?'

'Well,' said Wace, 'I'm told you're a very hard worker. You never complain of tiredness. You show resourcefulness and courage – the labour was long, I hear, and you forwent sleep to help. You also found our Emily in Norwich when she was taken ill, didn't you? And I believe you previously rushed to her defence when Jiang was giving her instructions. Then, tonight, you were the first to go to Lin's aid. I think I'll have to call you Artemis. You know who Artemis is?'

'Um ... the Greek goddess of hunting?'

'Hunting,' repeated Jonathan. 'Interesting you speak of hunting, first.'

'Only because I've seen statues of her with a bow and arrow,' said Robin, who was pressing her hands between her knees to stop them shaking. 'I don't really know much else about her.'

The door opened and Shawna reappeared with everything Wace had asked for. She laid out a plate, knife, fork and glass in front of Robin, bowed again to Wace, beaming, and disappeared, closing the door behind her.

'Eat,' Wace ordered Robin, filling her water glass himself. 'There are many contradictions in Artemis, as in so many human representations of the divine. She's a huntress, but also protector of the hunted, of girls up to marriageable age, the goddess of childbirth and ... strangely ... of chastity.'

He glanced at her before turning his attention back to his food. Robin took a gulp of water, trying to ease the dryness of her mouth.

'Personally,' Wace continued, 'I don't disdain the teachings of those whom conventional religious people would see as pagans. I don't believe the Christian conception of God is any more valid than the ancient Greeks'. All subjective attempts to draw a complete picture of the Blessed Divinity are necessarily partial and flawed.'

Except yours, thought Robin. She'd served herself ragout and polenta, and now took a mouthful. It was one of the best things she'd ever eaten, or perhaps it was simply that she'd been deprived of real food for so long.

'And you've been generous to the church, Artemis,' said Wace. 'A thousand pounds! Thank you,' he said, making his familiar expression of humility and gratitude, as he pressed one hand to his heart.

'I should have made that sooner,' said Robin.

'Why d'you say that?' Wace asked, eyebrows raised.

'Because I know other people donated before me. I should have—'

'There is no "should have",' said Wace. 'All that counts is what is *done*. The journey to pure spirit is essentially a process of becoming ever more active. Prayer, meditation, study: these are actions. Regret is inactive and useful only in so far as it propels us onwards, to *more* action. So, all of this is very good, but,' said Wace, his smile now fading, 'your journal is ... a little disappointing.'

Robin's heart beat faster. When it came to her journal, she'd taken a line from what Niamh Doherty had told her: one thing enjoyed, one thing learned, every day.

'No questions,' said Wace. 'No doubts. Certainly no indication of Rowena's inner life.'

'I was trying not to show egomotivity,' said Robin.

Wace let out a bark of laughter that made her jump.

'That's exactly what I expected you to say, Artemis.'

Robin disliked the repetition of the new nickname. She knew it was meant both to flatter and destabilise her.

'And I hear you're the same way in doctrinal lectures. You never seek discussion or clarification. You're studious, but silent. No curiosity.'

'I thought—'

'—that would show egomotivity? Not at all. It's a maxim of mine that I'd rather face an honest sceptic than a hundred who believe they know God but are really in thrall to their own piety. But it interests me, this lack of curiosity and argument, because you're not a submissive, are you? Not really. You've shown that repeatedly.'

As Robin struggled for an answer, she heard movement outside the room, a scuffling and then the sound of Lin's voice.

'I d–d–don't want to g–g–go – no! N–n–n–no!'

'Music,' said Wace, setting down his knife and fork with a clatter, getting to his feet and moving calmly to a discreet panel on the wall. With the press of a button, classical music filled the room. Robin heard the front doors of the farmhouse slam. She had time to remember that Lin was almost certainly Wace's own daughter before he moved back to the sofa and said, as though nothing had happened,

'So I'm puzzled by you, Artemis. On the one hand, passivity, unquestioning obedience, an uncomplaining work ethic, a journal that asks no questions, a large donation to the church.

'But on the other hand, a strong and dynamic individuality. Outside of doctrinal seminars, you challenge authority and resist deeper engagement with the church's precepts. You demonstrate a strong materialist adherence to the importance of the body, over the requirements of the spirit. Why these contradictions, Artemis?'

Robin, who felt slightly stronger for the ingestion of food and water, said,

'I'm trying to learn and change. I was argumentative before I joined the church. That's why my fiancé broke up with me. I suppose . . . my false self is still there, still clinging on.'

'A very nice, neat, pat answer,' said Wace, smiling again.

'I'm trying to be honest,' said Robin. She wondered whether crying would help convince Wace of her sincerity. It wouldn't take much for the tears to flow, after the shocks of the last hour.

'I hear,' said Wace, 'the only time you seemed to show any interest in challenging church doctrine was with young Will, up at the vegetable patch.'

'I wasn't challenging him,' said Robin, careful not to sound defensive. 'I made a mistake and he corrected me. Several times, actually.'

'Ah, well . . . Will's better at memorising doctrine than living it,' said Wace, smiling again. 'He's a clever young man, but hasn't yet made pure spirit because he falters, constantly, at step six. You know what step six is?'

'"The pure spirit knows acceptance is more important than understanding,"' quoted Robin.

'Very good,' said Wace. 'The materialist seeks understanding, where the pure spirit seeks truth. Where the materialist sees contradictions, the pure spirit grasps that disparate notions and ideas are all part of the whole, which only the Divinity can comprehend. Will cannot rid himself of adherence to a materialist conception of knowledge. He tries, he seems to succeed, but then he falls back again.'

Wace scanned Robin's face, but she said nothing, certain that showing a particular interest in Will would be dangerous. When it became clear that she wasn't going to speak, Wace went on,

'And you challenged Jiang when he was instructing Emily, also on the vegetable patch.'

'Yes,' said Robin, 'I reacted instinctively, I was—'

'"Instinctively",' repeated Wace, 'is an interesting choice of word, and a great favourite of materialists. Only when mankind has rid itself of the base emotions we call "instinct" are we likely to win our battle against evil. But your – to use your word – "instinct" seems to be particularly engaged by Disruptives, Artemis.'

'I don't know what you mean,' said Robin.

'Will. Emily. Even quiet little Lin has her Disruptive tendencies,' said Wace.

'I barely know any of them,' said Robin.

Wace said nothing for a few moments. He cleaned his plate then dabbed at his mouth with a linen napkin before saying,

'Your Revelation was difficult, I hear. Daiyu manifested.'

'Yes,' said Robin.

'She does that,' said Wace, 'when she feels the church is under threat.'

He looked at Robin, no longer smiling, and she forced herself to look back at him, to school her features into a look of confusion rather than panic. His large, dark blue eyes were opaque.

'You ... can't think I'm a threat to the church?'

The words came out as a whisper, which wasn't feigned. Robin's throat felt constricted.

'Well, let's see,' said Wace, without smiling. 'Stand up for me.'

Robin let her knife and fork fall to her plate and stood up.

'Here,' said Wace, moving away from the sofa to a patch of clear carpet in the middle of the room.

Now they faced each other. Robin didn't know what was coming: sometimes Becca or Mazu led them in simple yoga movements as part of their meditations, and Wace stood as though about to give physical instructions.

After staring at her dispassionately for ten seconds, he reached out and placed his hands on her breasts, his eyes boring into hers. Robin stood stock still, feeling nothing but shock. She seemed to be watching from outside her own body, barely feeling Wace caressing her.

'Spirit is all that matters,' said Wace. 'The body is immaterial. Do you agree?'

Robin said 'yes' automatically, or tried to do so, but no sound issued from her mouth.

Wace removed his right hand from her breast, placed it between her legs and began to rub.

At the exact moment Robin jumped backwards, the door behind her opened. She and Wace both turned, his hand falling from her breast. Becca and Mazu entered the room, the former in her white tracksuit, the latter wearing long white robes, a witch bride with her long black hair. With the door open, baby Yixin could be heard crying from upstairs.

It would have been hard to say which woman looked more furious and outraged. Neither Mazu nor Becca seemed to have learned the lesson of materialist possession: both, it was clear, were incensed to find Wace's hands upon Robin. After a few frozen moments of silence, Becca said in a high, cold voice:

'Giles has a query.'

'Then send him in. You may go, Artemis,' said Wace, entirely relaxed and now smiling again.

'Thank you,' said Robin.

She smelled Mazu's particular odour of grime and incense as she passed the two furious women. Down the hall Robin hurried, the baby wailing overhead, her mind a hum of panic, her body burning where Wace had touched her, as though he'd branded her through her clothes.

Run, now.

But they'll see me on the cameras.

Robin pushed through the dragon-carved doors. The sun was sinking bloodily in the sky. People were criss-crossing the courtyard, busy about their after-dinner tasks. Robin headed automatically for Daiyu's pool, its dimpled surface glittering like rubies in the sunset, the constant patter of the fountain in her ears.

'The Drowned Prophet will bless—'

But Robin couldn't get the words out. Knowing she was going to vomit and not caring whether she drew curious eyes, she set off at a run towards the dormitory where she just made one of the toilets, where she threw up the small amount of ragout and polenta she'd swallowed with Jonathan Wace, then fell to her knees to dry-heave, her flesh clammy with revulsion.

74

Nine at the top means . . .
Perseverance brings the woman into danger.
The moon is nearly full.

The I Ching or Book of Changes

Two days passed, during which fear was with Robin constantly, to a degree she'd never felt before. There was no refuge, no place of safety: she knew an order must have gone out to keep her under close, constant watch, because one or other of the female church members was constantly at her side throughout her waking hours, even when she went to the bathroom. The only positive in her environment was that Taio, who'd taken Lin to some unknown location, still hadn't returned to the farm.

It took more courage than ever before for Robin to leave her bed on Thursday night to write to Strike. She waited far longer than usual to set off, determined to make sure everyone was fast asleep, in no danger of dozing off herself because her adrenalin level was so high. Having slipped out of the dormitory, she sped across the field towards the woods, convinced that she'd hear a shout behind her at any moment.

When she reached the perimeter wall she found two letters in the rock. Murphy's told her he was off to San Sebastian for two weeks, and while he'd written affectionately, she'd noted the undertone of displeasure that she wouldn't be going with him. Strike's note detailed the attempted suicide of Jordan Reaney.

After writing her two responses, Robin remained sitting on the cold ground, paralysed with indecision. Should she leave, now, while she had the chance? Clamber over the barbed wire and wait for whoever was going to collect her letters to pick her up? It was too late to get an ambulance for Lin, but the intensity of the surveillance she was currently under made her wonder whether she'd be able to achieve anything more if she stayed. She was losing hope that she'd ever be able to talk to Emily Pirbright again, given that both of them were constantly surrounded by other church members.

Yet there was Will, who'd shown definite signs of doubting the church during his conversation with Noli in the kitchen. Now she'd learned that this was no anomaly, that Will kept faltering at step six to pure spirit, she understood at last why a clever, educated young man with a large trust fund was being kept at Chapman Farm instead of being fast-tracked to conducting seminars and travelling the world with Jonathan Wace. If she could only engineer one last conversation with Will, it would be worth staying.

So Robin folded her letters and placed them in the plastic rock, ripped up Strike's and Ryan's notes and threw them into the road, spent another two minutes devouring the Double Decker the agency had left her, then set off back through the woods.

She'd only gone ten yards when she heard a car slow behind her and darted behind a tree. By the car's interior light, she saw Barclay, and watched as he got out of his Mazda, climbed carefully over the barbed wire fence and extracted Robin's messages from the plastic rock. Still hidden, peering through the branches, Robin considered calling out to him, but couldn't bring herself to do it. Separated from her colleague by only ten yards, she felt like a ghost who had no business conversing with the living. She watched Barclay climb back over the wall, get into the car and drive away, then turned slowly away, fighting the urge to weep.

She crossed the chilly field and finally regained her dormitory bed without detection. Partly because of the sugar in her system, but also because the panic engendered by her journey was so slow to subside, Robin remained awake for the rest of the night, and was almost relieved when the bell rang to wake everyone else up.

75

*Thus the superior man controls his anger
And restrains his instincts.*

The I Ching or Book of Changes

'What d'ye think?'

Strike, who'd just finished reading Robin's latest missive from Chapman Farm, looked up at Barclay, who'd brought the letter back from Norfolk twenty minutes previously and now stood in the doorway of the inner office, holding a mug of coffee Pat had made him.

'It's time for her to come out,' said Strike. 'We might have enough here for a police investigation, if they haven't taken this Lin girl to hospital.'

'Aye,' said Barclay, 'and that's before ye get tae the sexual assault.'

Strike said nothing, dropping his eyes again to the last few lines of Robin's letter.

and Wace groped me. He didn't get far, because Mazu and Becca came in.

I know you'll say I should come out, but I've got to find out whether Will could be persuaded to leave. I can't come out now, I'm too close. One more week might do it.

Please, if you can, check and see whether Lin was admitted to the local hospital, I'm worried sick about her.

Robin x

'Yeah, she definitely needs to come out,' said Strike. 'Next letter, I'll tell her to wait by the rock and we'll pick her up. Enough's enough.'

He was worried, not only by what Robin termed Wace's grope – what exactly did that mean? – but by the fact she'd witnessed something that was highly incriminating of the church. This, of course, was exactly what she'd gone to Chapman Farm to do, but Strike hadn't anticipated Robin hanging around afterwards, a dangerous witness to serious wrongdoing. While he understood why she'd admitted seeing Lin with those plants, she'd seriously compromised herself by doing so, and ought to have got out immediately that had happened. There was a board on the wall behind him showing how many people had died or disappeared in the vicinity of Papa J.

'What?' he said, under the impression that Barclay had just spoken to him.

'I said, what're ye up tae this morning?'

'Oh,' said Strike. 'Sacking Littlejohn.'

He brought up a photograph on his phone, then handed it to Barclay.

'First thing he did when he got back from Greece was go and see Patterson. About bloody time I got something for all the money I've been shelling out.'

'Great,' said Barclay. 'Can we replace him wi' whoever took this picture?'

'Not unless you want this office stripped of everything sellable by Tuesday.'

'Where ye gonnae do it?'

'Here. He's on his way.'

'Can I stay an' watch? Might be my one and only chance tae hear his voice.'

'Thought you were on Frank Two?'

'I am, aye,' sighed Barclay. 'Which means I'll be watchin' him watchin' Mayo for hours. If they're gonnae make a move, I wish they'd fuckin' hurry up.'

'Keen to see our client kidnapped, are you?'

'Ye know what I mean. This could go on for months.'

'I've got a feeling it's going to hot up pretty soon.'

Barclay left. Strike heard him pass Littlejohn in the doorway with pleasure: he was looking forward to this.

'Morning,' said Littlejohn, appearing in the doorway Barclay had just vacated, his short salt-and-pepper hair as neat as ever, his world-weary eyes fixed on Strike. 'Can I get a coffee before—?'

'No,' said Strike. 'Come in, sit down and close the door.'

Littlejohn blinked, but did as he was bid. Now looking wary, he crossed to Robin's chair at the partners' desk and sat down.

'Care to explain that?' asked Strike, pushing his phone across the desk, face up, displaying a photograph taken the previous day of Littlejohn and Patterson outside the latter's office in Marylebone.

The silence that ensued lasted nearly two minutes. Strike, who was inwardly debating whether Littlejohn was about to say 'I just bumped into him' or 'OK, fair cop,' allowed the silence to spool through the room undisturbed. At last, the subcontractor made a noise somewhere between a grunt and a gasp. Then, which Strike hadn't anticipated, he began to cry.

If Strike had been asked to rank everyone he'd witnessed crying recently according to how much sympathy he felt for their distress, he'd have given Bijou last place without hesitation. Now, however, he realised there was a category of weeper he despised even more than a woman who'd played a duplicitous game that had blown up in her face: a man who'd done his best to take down another person's business, destroy that person's reputation, undermine an investigation into men stalking a woman, and cause that woman additional fear and alarm, all of which he'd presumably done for money, but who now seemed to expect pity for being found out.

While tempted to give the man what Strike would have considered a proper reason for crying, he judged that there might be capital to be made out of what he supposed was Littlejohn's attempt to show contrition. Strike therefore made no comment as Littlejohn sobbed, but waited to see what came next.

'I'm in a lot of debt,' Littlejohn finally blurted out. 'I got myself in trouble. Online gambling. Blackjack. I've got a problem.'

I'll show you fucking problems. You wait.

'How's that relevant?'

'I'm up to my ears,' sobbed Littlejohn. 'The wife doesn't know how bad it is. Mitch,' said Littlejohn, brandishing the phone showing Patterson's picture, 'gave me a loan to get the worst people off my back. Interest-free.'

'In exchange for which, you agreed to take me down.'

'I never—'

'You posted a snake through Tasha Mayo's door. You tried to gain entry to this office when there shouldn't have been anyone here, presumably to bug it. You were caught by Pat trying to take pictures of the Edensor—'

'She's lied to you, that Pat.'

'If you're about to tell me she's sixty-seven, I already know. Big fucking deal.'

Littlejohn's disappointment that this titbit was of no use was palpable, but Strike was pleased to learn that ratting other people out was Littlejohn's preferred strategy for getting out of messes. Much could be done with such a man.

'Why's Patterson doing this?' asked Strike.

'He's got a real fucking thing about you,' said Littlejohn, trying to stem the stream of snot from his nose. 'He's an old mate of Roy Carver's. He blames you for Carver getting forced out and it pisses him off you get all the publicity, and clients want you, not him. He says you're taking all his business. He was really fucked off about Colin Edensor sacking us and coming here instead.'

Tears were still dripping from Littlejohn's world-weary eyes.

'I prefer working for you, though. I'd rather stay here. I could be useful to you.'

With immense difficulty, Strike refrained from asking what use he could possibly have for a treacherous, weak-willed man who had neither the morals to refuse to terrorise a woman who was already scared, nor the brains to stop himself being rumbled as a saboteur. Strike could only assume it was this mixture of delusion and wishful thinking that had led Littlejohn to lose a fortune at blackjack.

'Well, if you want to be useful,' said Strike, 'you can start now. Give me my phone.'

He brought up the picture of the black-haired woman who'd been skulking on the corner of Denmark Street.

'Who's she?'

Littlejohn looked at the picture, swallowed, then said,

'Yeah, she's one of Mitch's. I told him I thought you were having me watched. He put Farah on you as a back-up.'

'What's her full name?' said Strike, opening his notebook.

'Farah Navabi,' muttered Littlejohn.

'And what would you know about bugs in Andrew Honbold's office?'

'Nothing,' said Littlejohn, too fast.

'Listen,' said Strike quietly, leaning forwards. 'Honbold's not going to let just anyone in there. His wife's got him bang to rights already, she doesn't need to bug him to take him to the cleaners. Somebody thought it was worth their while to put an illegal bug in Honbold's office, and my name and Honbold's have been in the press lately. So when I go and see Honbold and show him Patterson's picture, *your* picture, Farah's—'

'It was Farah,' muttered Littlejohn.

'Thought it might be,' said Strike, sitting back in his chair. 'Well, I think we're done here. You'll understand why, under the circumstances, I won't be asking Pat to give you the salary you're owed.'

'No, listen,' said Littlejohn, in what looked like panic: evidently he could see his employment with Patterson Inc terminating soon as well. 'I've got more stuff for you.'

'Like what?'

Littlejohn pulled his own phone out of his pocket, tapped something into it, then shoved it across the desk. Strike found himself looking down at a photograph of Midge and Tasha Mayo laughing together outside Mayo's Notting Hill house, both holding bags of Waitrose shopping.

'Scroll right,' said Littlejohn.

Strike did so and saw a picture of Midge leaving Mayo's house by evening.

'The second one was last night,' said Littlejohn. 'I was going to give it to Mitch.'

'I'm sure there's an innocent explanation,' said Strike, who was sure of nothing of the sort. 'If that's your best shot—'

'It's not – I've got stuff on Patterson.'

'I'll get it myself if I want it.'

'No, listen,' said Littlejohn again, 'I can get you something for that church case. Mitch has got a recording. He didn't hand it over when Edensor sacked him.'

'What recording would this be?' asked the sceptical Strike.

'Of that Kevin whatever he was called, who got out of the church – Kevin Purvis?'

'Pirbright,' said Strike.

'Yeah, exactly. Mitch got an undercover recording of him.'

'Why would Patterson covertly record Pirbright, when Pirbright had already told Colin Edensor everything he knew?'

'They fell out, Pirbright and Edensor,' said Littlejohn. 'Didn't they? Before Pirbright got shot? They weren't talking to each other.'

Strike's interest level rose slightly, because it was true Sir Colin and Kevin Pirbright had argued, then had little contact, in the interval between Kevin heckling Giles Harmon at his book reading, and Pirbright's murder.

'There was an email, I think it was an email, Pirbright sent to Edensor,' Littlejohn went on, his expression pleading, 'where Pirbright said he was piecing things together he'd repressed or something, right? Mitch was getting nowhere on the case, so he sent Farah to chat up Pirbright and see what new stuff she could get out of him. Pirbright wasn't right mentally, see, so Mitch was worried if they interviewed him over the counter, Pirbright might blab on his blog. He was getting too mouthy.'

'Why didn't Patterson hand over this recording to Edensor?'

'Because it's shit quality. You can't hear much. Farah fucked up, but she told Mitch afterwards Pirbright didn't have anything useful to say anyway.'

'And this is the valuable bit of evidence you think will persuade me to keep you in employment? A recording you can't hear, of a conversation containing nothing useful?'

'Yeah, but it's you, isn't it?' said Littlejohn, desperate. '*You* can do something with it.'

If there was one thing that truly added insult to injury, in Strike's opinion, it was attempts to flatter in the aftermath of proven treachery. Once again, it cost him some effort to suppress a straightforward 'go fuck yourself'.

'If it's useless, why didn't Patterson chuck it?'

'He did – well, he chucked it in the safe and forgot about it. I saw it in there last time I opened it.'

'All right,' said Strike slowly, 'bring me that recording and we can have another talk about your employment prospects.'

A very short fucking talk.

'Thank you,' said Littlejohn effusively. 'Thank you, Cormoran, I can't thank you enough. I really need this job, you don't understand what it's been like for me, the strain of everything, but as long as I've got regular work I can work something out, get a loan or something – you won't regret this. I'm a loyal man,' said Littlejohn shamelessly, 'I don't forget a good turn. You won't have anyone more dedicated to this agency—'

'You can save all that. You haven't brought back the recording yet.'

Once Littlejohn was safely out of the office, Strike called Midge.

'Wotcha,' she said, answering after a couple of rings.

'Want to tell me why you're going shopping with our client?'

'What?' said Midge, startled.

'You. Tasha Mayo. Waitrose,' said Strike, barely keeping a lid on his temper.

'I weren't *shopping* with her,' said Midge, sounding incredulous. 'One of them split, that's all.'

'One of what split?'

'One of her bags, what d'you think? I just helped her pick it all up.'

'And how's that keeping undercover, helping her pick up all her shopping?'

'Fook's sake, Strike,' said Midge, now sounding annoyed, 'what were I s'posed to do, stand there and watch her chasing tins all over the road? I'd've looked more suspicious if I hadn't helped her. It's what women do, help each other out.'

'Why were you leaving her house last night?'

'It weren't bloody night, it was barely nine o'clock – and how d'you—?'

'Answer the bloody question.'

'She called me,' said Midge, now sounding nettled. 'She heard noises outside the back door. Her brother's gone back up north and she's jumpy being there alone, after you put the fear of God into her about the Franks.'

'What was the noise?'

'A cat knocked off a dustbin lid.'

'How long were you inside her house?'

'Dunno, 'bout an hour?'

'The fuck were you doing in there for an hour?'

'I told you, she's jumpy! How d'you even—?'

'You were photographed. Littlejohn's just shown me the pictures.'

'That fookin' arsehole,' gasped Midge.

'What happened while you were inside the house?'

'The fook are you insinuating?' said Midge hotly.

'I'm asking you a straightforward question.'

'We had a coffee, all right?'

'And how the bloody hell did you not notice Littlejohn was watching the house?'

'He weren't there. It must've been someone else.'

'I'm taking you off the Mayo case,' said Strike. 'You can stick with Toy Boy going forwards.'

'I've done nothing wrong!' said Midge. 'Ask Tasha!'

'It's what it'll look like to the papers,' said Strike.

'Did you think of that when you shagged that lawyer with the fake tits?'

'I'm going to pretend I didn't hear that,' said Strike, through clenched teeth. 'I've told you how it's going to be. *Stay away from Mayo.*'

He hung up, seething.

76

Here every step, forward or backward, leads into danger.
Escape is out of the question.

The I Ching or Book of Changes

The Manifestation of the Drowned Prophet was now imminent, and Robin was instructed to join the group decorating the outside of the temple with long white banners on which stylised, dark blue waves had been printed. This entailed climbing high ladders, and while struggling to affix one of the banners to just beneath the temple roof, Robin thought how easy it would be for somebody below to kick the ladder out from under her: a tragic accident, they'd doubtless call it. However, no such attempt on her life was made, and she returned safely to the ground, castigating herself for her paranoia.

'Looks cool, doesn't it?' said one of the good-looking American youths Wace had brought back from LA, who'd also helped decorate the temple. The banners were fluttering in the breeze, so that the printed waves seemed to be falling down its sides.

'Yes, it looks great,' said Robin. 'D'you know when the Manifestation is?'

She was dreading Daiyu's reappearance in the temple almost as much as she feared the possibility of being summoned back into the farmhouse to see Jonathan Wace.

713

'Week's time,' said the American. 'Man, I can't wait. I've heard so much about it. You guys are blessed, living here, where the church started.'

He looked down at Robin, smiling.

'Hey, wanna spirit bond?'

'She can't.'

It was Shawna who'd spoken. She, too, had been helping decorate the temple, cheerily climbing ladders even though her pregnancy had now given her a definite bump.

'Huh?' said the American.

'Spirit wife,' said Shawna, smiling broadly before walking away to help Walter, who was struggling to collapse one of the ladders.

'Oh, man, I didn't realise,' the American told Robin, looking scared.

'It's fine,' said Robin, but the young man escaped swiftly from her presence, as though now frightened to be seen talking to her.

Robin was confused and alarmed by what Shawna had said. Surely women didn't become spirit wives just because Jonathan Wace had sexually assaulted them? She assisted in the carrying of the ladders back to a barn, consumed by fresh fears.

Over the next few days, Robin sensed an undercurrent of gossip swirling around her. It was in the sidelong glances of the women and even some of the men, and especially in the antagonistic looks of Vivienne. Since Shawna had announced it outside the temple, the rumour that Robin was Papa J's new spirit wife had evidently travelled widely.

As nobody, even the people making sure she went nowhere unaccompanied, had posed a direct question, Robin was in no position to contradict the report; indeed, she wasn't entirely sure of the facts herself. Perhaps Wace's mere laying-on of hands was sufficient to create a spirit wife? However, if, as

Robin suspected, Shawna had leapt to a false conclusion, Robin was afraid she might be accused of starting the canard herself. In fact, she had a nasty feeling this unsought dilemma might be the thing to finally break her cover, that the little eruption of envy caused by Shawna would lead all who had suspicion of her to pool their knowledge. Robin found herself constantly fantasising about making a break for it and running for the woods, even though there was no doubt an aborted escape attempt would make her situation far worse. The sensible thing to do, she knew, was to leave via the perimeter blind spot on Thursday night, when somebody from the agency would be in the vicinity to pick her up. As long as she left then, she'd miss the Manifestation of the Drowned Prophet, which she'd now learned would take place on Friday evening. It was an experience Robin was perfectly happy to forgo, after what had happened during her Revelation session.

Taio had returned to the farm, without Lin. Robin, who'd seen him only from a distance, studiously avoided eye contact. All her efforts now were concentrated on securing a one-to-one conversation with Will Edensor. Finding out how deep his doubts about the church ran would justify everything she'd been through, and she'd leave knowing she'd truly made an advance in the case.

On Tuesday afternoon, Robin was sent to work in the laundry, a utilitarian, concrete-floored building of brick, housing rows of industrial-sized washing machines and drying racks on pulleys, which could be hoisted up to the ceiling. The women who'd escorted Robin to the door left after seeing her inside, clearly feeling there were enough people loading and unloading clothes and sheets to keep an eye on her.

The steady chug and hum of the washing machines necessitated the raising of voices if the workers wanted to make themselves heard. Having received a sack of dirty clothing and instructions as to the correct machine settings, Robin rounded a corner into the second row of washing machines and with a jolt of excitement saw Will kneeling in front of one of them, dragging a mound of wet clothing into a basket. Beside him, entering settings on a second machine, was Marion Huxley, who'd been so obviously infatuated with Jonathan Wace when she'd arrived at the farm, and with whom Robin hadn't interacted in weeks.

The punishing work regime and commensurate weight loss had had an extremely ageing effect on Marion, whose gaunt face now sagged as it certainly hadn't when she'd boarded the minibus in London. Her dyed red hair had now grown out to show two inches of silver roots.

Neither Will nor Marion heard Robin's approach, and only when she'd chosen the washing machine next to Will's did he glance up at her.

'Hi,' said Robin.

'Hi,' mumbled Will.

Having unloaded the tangled mass of wet clothes, he picked up the heavy basket and walked away.

Robin began to load her own washing machine. The surrounding noise was such that only when a voice said loudly in her ear, '*Oi!*' did she realise Marion had been trying to speak to her.

'Hi,' said Robin, smiling before she registered that Marion looked livid.

'I don't know how you've got the gall to be walking around, smirking!'

'Sorry?' said Robin, taken aback.

'You should be! *Lying* about Papa J.'

'I haven't said a word about—'

'You claimed he spirit bonded with you.'

'No, I—'

'And we *all know* you're lying. You're no spirit wife!'

'I never said—'

'And you know what?' said Marion. '*The Drowned Prophet will sort you out.*'

'I don't know what you—'

'She's been seen, already,' said Marion. 'In the woods. She comes, around her Manifestation time. She comes to defend Papa J.'

Robin knew she was looking into the authentic face of fanaticism. Something rigid and alien lived beneath the skin of the human being facing her, something that couldn't be argued with. Nevertheless, she heard herself say pleadingly 'Marion', without any idea of what she was going to tell the woman, but before she could find any words, Marion had spat in her face.

Robin felt the saliva hit her, just beneath her left eye, and something broke inside her, some last vestige of restraint. *They're all mad. They're fucking mad.* Robin pushed Marion roughly aside and strode away, to where Will Edensor was draping wet tracksuits and socks onto a drying rack.

'Will,' she said loudly, over the noise of the machines. 'D'you want to spirit bond?'

'What?'

'Do you want to spirit bond?' Robin repeated, enunciating clearly.

'Oh,' said Will. He looked as though she'd just offered him coffee: he showed little interest, but no embarrassment or surprise, and she wondered how many times he'd been to the Retreat Rooms in the last four years. 'Yeah, OK.'

They walked together towards the door, Robin consumed with rage at Marion, at the church, at the hypocrisy and insanity. She couldn't pretend any more. She was done with all of it.

'Where—?' said an older woman near the door, looking suspicious.

'Spirit bonding,' said Robin firmly.

'*Oh,*' said the woman. She looked confused and panicked, probably because she didn't know what should take priority: Robin being kept under surveillance, or an act of submission and compliance that appeared to demonstrate true allegiance to the UHC. 'I – all right . . .'

Robin and Will walked together down the path towards the courtyard in silence, Robin trying to formulate a plan of action. The warning ripples of anxiety barely registered in her rage and determination to force something useful out of Will in her final hours at the farm.

When they reached the Retreat Room, Robin pulled open the glass door and stood back to let Will walk inside first. She then jerked the curtain across the glass windows, so that the only light came from the single light bulb dangling from the ceiling.

In silence, Will sat down on the bed to remove his socks and trainers.

'Will,' said Robin, 'there's no need for that, I really just wanted to talk to you.'

He glanced up at her.

'That's not allowed. We spirit bond, or we leave.'

He stood up and peeled off his tracksuit top to reveal a pale, hairless torso, every rib visible in the harsh overhead light. As he turned to throw his clothes into a corner, Robin saw on his back the same strange marks she'd noted on the black girl who'd let Bo escape from the children's dormitory, as though his spine had been rubbed raw.

'What's happened to you?' she asked. 'What are those marks on your back?'

'I was in the box,' muttered Will.

'Why?'

Will ignored the question, instead pulling off his greying

Y-fronts and tracksuit bottoms. Now he stood completely naked in front of her, his penis flaccid.

'Will, I just wanted to—'

'Get undressed,' said Will, walking to the corner of the cabin, where the short length of hose pipe was attached to the tap. Picking the slimy soap off the floor, he began to wash his genitalia.

'That thing you said to Noli, in the kitchen,' said Robin, raising her voice over the splattering of water on the wooden floor, 'it made me th—'

'Forget that!' said Will, looking over his shoulder at her. 'That's why I had to go in the box. I shouldn't have said it. If you're going to talk about that, I'm leaving.'

He towelled himself off with a mouldy-looking towel, sat back down on the grubby bed and began to masturbate in an effort to achieve an erection.

'Will, stop,' said Robin, looking away from him. 'Please stop.'

He did so, but not because of Robin. Something that sounded like a lawnmower had roared into life just outside the cabin. Robin crossed to the gap in the curtains and saw Amandeep mowing out there, an expression of grim determination on his face.

'Who is it?' said Will, from behind her.

'Amandeep,' said Robin. 'Mowing the grass.'

'That's because you're on a Mark Three,' said Will. 'He's making sure you stay in here. Get undressed.' He'd recommenced masturbating. 'Take your clothes off, we're supposed to be done in twenty minutes.'

'Please stop doing that,' Robin implored him. 'Please. I just wanted to talk to you.'

'Get undressed,' he repeated, his hand still working furiously.

719

'Will, that thing you said—'

'Forget what I said,' he retorted angrily, still struggling to achieve an erection. 'It was false self, I didn't mean it!'

'Why did you say it at all, then?'

'I was . . . I don't like Seymour, that's all. She shouldn't be a Principal. She's a BP. She doesn't understand doctrine.'

'But what you said makes sense,' said Robin, 'there *is* a contradiction between—'

'"Human knowledge is finite,"' said Will, '"divine truth is infinite." *The Answer,* chapter eleven.'

'D'you believe everything the church says? All of it?' asked Robin, forcing herself to turn and face him, his semi-erect penis in his hand.

'"Persistent refusal to merge the self with the collective reveals ongoing egomotivity." *The Answer,* chapter five.'

The motor of the lawnmower continued to roar right beside the glass doors.

'For God's sake,' said Robin, trapped between Amandeep and the masturbating Will, 'you're really intelligent, why are you afraid of *thinking,* why d'you just keep quoting?'

'"Materialist thought patterns are entrenched at a young age. Breaking those patterns requires, in the first instance, the focusing of the mind on essential truths through repetition and meditation." *The Answer,* chap—'

'So you've voluntarily brainwashed yourself?'

'Get undressed!'

Will stood up, towering over her, his hand still working to maintain his erection. 'It's a sin to come in here for anything other than spirit bonding!'

'If you force me to have sex with you,' said Robin in a low voice, 'it'll be rape, and how will the UHC like being hit with a lawsuit?'

The lawnmower outside banged against the far wall of the

cabin. Will's hand stopped moving. He stood in front of her, painfully thin, still holding his penis.

'Where have they taken Lin?' Robin asked, determined to break through to him.

'Somewhere safe,' he said, before adding angrily, 'but that's nothing to do with you.'

'So I'm to merge myself with the collective by not thinking, and having sex with anyone who wants it, but I'm not allowed to be worried about a fellow church member, is that what you're saying?'

'You need to shut up,' said Will furiously, 'because I know things about you. You were in the woods at night, with a torch.'

'No, I wasn't,' said Robin automatically.

'Yeah, you were. I didn't say anything, to protect Lin, but it can't hurt her now.'

'Why did you want to protect Lin? That's materialist possession, caring about one person more than everyone else. Is it because she's the mother of your child? Because Qing belongs to everyone in the church, not just—'

'Shut up,' said Will, and he raised his hand threateningly. *'Shut the fuck up.'*

'No quotations for any of that?' asked Robin, still angrier than she was scared. 'You haven't told anyone I had a torch in all the days since Lin's been gone. Why didn't you report me?'

'Because they'll say I should have done it sooner!'

'Or did you secretly like thinking someone was wandering around with a torch at night?'

'Why would I?'

'You could have refused to come with me to the Retreat R—'

'No, I couldn't, you've got to go when you're asked—'

'I think you're having doubts about the church.'

Will's eyes narrowed. He let go of his penis and backed away several steps.

'Did my father send you here?'

'Why would you think that?'

'He's done it before. He sent a man to spy on me.'

'I'm not a spy.'

Will snatched his pants and tracksuit bottoms off the floor and began to pull them on. Certain he was going to walk out and immediately reveal the conversation, Robin, now planning to make a break for the woods the moment she left the cabin, said,

'What if I told you your family sent me?'

Will was now jumping on the spot as he pulled up his tracksuit bottoms.

'I'm going to Papa J, right now,' he said furiously. 'I'm going to tell him—'

'Will, your family loves you—'

'They hate me,' he spat at her. '*Especially* my father.'

'That isn't true!'

Will bent to grab his sweatshirt, his face suffused with angry colour.

'My moth—Sally loves me. He doesn't. He writes me lies, trying to force me to abandon the church.'

'What lies does he write you?'

'He pretended Mu—Sally was ill. I didn't care, particularly,' Will added savagely, pulling his top back on. 'She's no more to me now than you are. I'm not her flesh object. Anyway, she always sticks up for my—for Colin. But M—Sally wasn't ill. She's fine.'

'How do you know that?' said Robin.

'I just know.'

'Will,' said Robin, 'your mother's dead. She died in January.'

Will froze. Outside, the lawnmower whined as Amandeep cut the power. Evidently he was counting down their twenty minutes. After what felt like a very long pause, Will said quietly,

'You're lying.'

'I really wish I was,' whispered Robin, 'but I'm n—'

A rush of wild movement, the thump of bare feet on wood: Robin flung up her arms too late, and Will's punch hit her squarely on the side of her face and with a scream of pain and shock she fell sideways, hitting the wall before landing hard on the floor.

Through a haze of pain she heard the glass door slide open and the curtains being tugged back.

'What happened?' said Amandeep.

Will said something Robin didn't catch through the ringing in her ears. Her panic was nothing compared to the sharp, pulsing pain in her jaw, which was such that she wondered if it was fractured.

Hands hoisted her roughly up onto the bed.

'. . . tripped?'

'Yeah, and hit her face on the wall. Didn't you?' Will barked at Robin.

'Yes,' she said, unable to tell whether she was speaking too loudly. Black spots were popping in front of her eyes.

'Had you finished?' asked Amandeep.

'Yeah, of course. Why d'you think she's dressed?'

'Where were you both, before bonding?'

'Laundry,' said Will.

'I'll go back now,' said Robin.

She got shakily to her feet, careful not to look at Will. She'd run for it the second she could: off to the five-bar gate and across the field to the perimeter.

'I'll take you both back to the laundry,' said Amandeep.

Robin's head was swimming with pain and panic. She massaged her jaw, which she could feel swelling rapidly.

'We can go on our own,' she said.

'No,' said Amandeep, taking a firm hold of Robin's wrist. 'You've both been judged to need more spiritual support.'

77

Six at the top . . .
Bound with cords and ropes,
Shut in between thorn-hedged prison walls . . .
Misfortune.

The I Ching or Book of Changes

After a further three hours in the laundry, during which nobody commented on her increasingly swollen face, Robin was escorted to temple for a meditation session led by Becca. Looking over her shoulder, she saw Will peel away from the rest of the group and march towards the farmhouse, omitting even to kneel at Daiyu's fountain. Panic-stricken, Robin knelt obediently on the hard temple floor, her lips forming the words of the chant, her mind fixed solely on escape. Perhaps, she thought, she could slip away into some shadowy recess of the temple at the end of the session, lurk until the others had left, then make a break for the blind spot at the perimeter. She'd run across country, find a call box – anything but spend another night at Chapman Farm.

However, at the end of the chanting session, Becca, who'd been leading the meditation from the raised pentagonal stage that hid the baptismal pool, descended before Robin had any chance of implementing this risky plan and walked directly up to her, while everyone else filed out of the temple for the dining hall.

'Have you had an accident, Rowena?'

'Yes,' said Robin. It hurt to talk; the pain from her jaw radiated up into her temple. 'I slipped and fell.'

'Where did that happen?'

'In the Retreat Room.'

'Who were you in the Retreat Room with?' demanded Becca.

'Will Edensor,' said Robin.

'Did Will suggest spirit bonding, or did you?'

'I did,' said Robin, because she knew laundry workers had witnessed her approaching Will.

'I see,' said Becca. Before she could ask anything else, a figure appeared silhouetted in the temple doorway and Robin, her heart rate now tripling, saw Jonathan Wace in his silk pyjamas. The subtle spotlights in the temple ceiling illuminated him as he walked towards them, smiling.

'I thank you for your service, Becca,' he said, pressing his hands together and bowing.

'And I for yours,' said Becca, now wearing a transported smile as she, too, bowed.

'Good evening, Artemis the chaste ... but what's happened here?' said Wace, placing a finger underneath Robin's chin and tilting it to the light. 'Have you had an accident?'

With no more idea whether he was playing a game with her than she'd had in the farmhouse, Robin said through clenched teeth,

'Yes. I slipped over.'

'In the Retreat Room,' said Becca, whose smile had vanished at the words 'Artemis the chaste'.

'Really?' said Wace, running his finger lightly over the bruised swelling. 'Well, this represents a turning point, doesn't it, Artemis? And who did you choose to bond with?'

'Will Edensor,' said Becca, before Robin could answer.

'Goodness,' said Wace quietly. 'That's an interesting choice, after what I told you about him during our last encounter.'

Robin wasn't sure she could have spoken, even if she'd wanted to. Her mouth had become very dry again, and Wace was still tilting her face backwards, which was causing her pain.

'Well, run along to dinner,' said Wace, releasing her after another searching look. 'I've got things to discuss with Becca.'

Robin forced herself to say, 'Thank you.'

'Thank you, *Papa J,*' said Becca.

'Thank you, Papa J,' mumbled Robin.

She walked away as fast as she could. On reaching the temple steps she saw two of her usual escorts waiting for her, so was forced to walk with them to the dining hall.

Tonight, she told herself, *you go tonight.*

That, of course, was assuming she wasn't about to be summoned back to the farmhouse to account for herself. Every second, as she ate her noodles, Robin expected a tap on the shoulder, but none came. Her now swollen and bruised face was attracting a few glances, but nobody asked what had happened to her, which was a relief, because talking hurt and she preferred to be left in peace.

When dinner ended, Robin walked with the rest of the women towards the dormitory. As they entered the courtyard, some of those ahead of her uttered exclamations of surprise.

Sixteen teenaged girls, all dressed in long white robes and holding flaming torches, were ascending the temple steps in the twilight. As the onlookers paused to watch, the girls positioned themselves in pairs on the eight stone steps leading to the temple doors, turned to face the courtyard, then stood in silence, their faces illuminated by the fire. Each girl's eyes had been painted with dark shadow to mimic running make-up, which gave them a very eerie appearance.

'Countdown to the Manifestation,' Robin heard a woman behind her say.

'How long do they stand there?' said a voice Robin recognised as Penny's.

'Just tonight. It's the boys' turn tomorrow. Then the Principals.'

Robin walked into the dormitory, appalled. If church members would be keeping watch on the temple steps for the following three nights, she'd have no chance whatsoever of slipping out of the dormitory unseen. Grabbing her pyjamas, Robin headed for the bathroom, locked herself in the same cubicle where she'd found Lin bleeding, sat down on the toilet lid and fought the urge to break down and cry. The uncertainty of what was going to happen next was terrifying her.

The bathroom door outside her cubicle banged open and Robin heard the sounds of teeth-cleaning and running taps. Knowing the stall would be needed by somebody else, Robin got up, unlocked the door, went through to the dormitory and began changing into her pyjamas.

'Oh my God, look!'

The cry came from the other side of the dormitory: a group of women had hurried to the window. Some were gasping, others clapping hands to their mouths.

'What is it?' said Marion Huxley, rushing to look. 'Is it her?'

'Yes – yes – *look!*'

Robin climbed up onto her bed, so she could see over their heads.

A small, luminous figure was standing motionless in the middle of the field Robin had so often crossed by night, wearing a limp white dress. She shone brightly for a few more seconds, then vanished.

The women at the window turned away, talking in

frightened, awestruck whispers. Some looked scared, others enthralled. Marion Huxley headed back across the dormitory smiling, and on reaching her bed, threw Robin a look of malicious triumph.

PART SIX

K'an/The Abysmal

Forward and backward, abyss on abyss.
In danger like this, pause at first and wait,
Otherwise you will fall into a pit in the abyss.
Do not act in this way.

The I Ching or Book of Changes

78

In the life of man ... acting on the spur of every
caprice is wrong and if continued leads to humiliation.

The I Ching or Book of Changes

Had Strike known what had happened to his detective partner over the previous twenty-four hours, he'd have been driving full speed towards Norfolk. However, as he remained in ignorance of developments at Chapman Farm, he rose on Wednesday morning buoyed by the idea that he'd be picking Robin up the following evening, having informed his subcontractors he wanted to do this job himself.

His bathroom scales showed an unwelcome regain of five pounds, doubtless due to the recent reappearance of burgers, chips and bacon rolls in his diet. Strike therefore breakfasted on porridge made with water, resolving to be strict again. While eating, he checked Pinterest on his phone, to see whether Torment Town had yet answered his question about Deirdre Doherty. To his dismay, he found the entire page deleted. The many grotesque drawings, including the eyeless Daiyu and the fair-haired woman floating in the five-sided pool, were gone, leaving Strike none the wiser as to who'd drawn them, but with the strong suspicion that his question had triggered the deletion, which suggested the blonde in the pool had, indeed, represented Deirdre.

At the precise moment he'd muttered *'Fuck'*, the mobile in his hand rang and he saw, with foreboding, Lucy's number.

'What's happened?' he said. Lucy wouldn't call at half past six in the morning for no good reason.

'Stick, I'm sorry it's so early,' said Lucy, whose voice was thick with tears, 'but I've just had Ted's neighbour on the phone. They noticed his front door was wide open, they went over there and he's gone, he's not there.'

An icy fog seemed to descend on Strike.

'They've called the police,' said Lucy, 'and I don't know what to do, whether to go down there—'

'Stay put for now. If they haven't found him in a couple of hours, we'll both go down.'

'Can you get away?'

'Of course,' said Strike.

'I feel so guilty,' said Lucy, breaking into sobs. 'We knew he was bad . . .'

'If – when they find him,' said Strike, 'we'll talk about what we're going to do next. We'll make a plan.'

He, too, felt inordinately guilty at the thought of his confused uncle setting off at dawn for some destination unknown. Remembering Ted's old sailing boat, the *Jowanet,* and the sea into which Joan's ashes had disappeared, Strike hoped to God he was being fanciful in thinking that was where the old man had gone.

His first appointment of the day wasn't calculated to take his mind off his personal troubles and he resented having to do it at all. After several days of procrastination, Bijou's lover, Andrew Honbold QC, had sent Strike a curt email inviting him to his flat to discuss 'the matter under advisement'. Strike had agreed to this meeting because he wanted to shut down forever the complications in which his ill-considered liaison with Bijou had involved him, but he was in no very conciliatory mood as he approached Honbold's duplex shortly before nine o'clock, his mind still on his uncle in Cornwall.

After ringing the bell of the barrister's presumably recently rented residence, which lay a mere two minutes' walk from Lavington Court Chambers, Strike had time to estimate that the place was probably costing Honbold upwards of ten thousand pounds a month. Bijou had had many lucrative reasons to be careless with her birth control.

The door was opened by a tall, supercilious-looking man with bloodhound-like jowls, a broken-veined complexion, a substantial paunch and pure white hair which had receded to show an age-spotted pate. Honbold led Strike into an open-plan living area decorated in expensive but bland taste which didn't suit its occupant, whose Hogarthian appearance cried out for a backdrop of velvet drapes and polished mahogany.

'So,' said Honbold loudly, when the two men had sat down opposite each other, with the glass coffee table between them, 'you have information for me.'

'I do, yeah,' said Strike, perfectly happy to dispense with the niceties. Taking out his phone, he laid it on the table with the photograph of Farah Navabi in Denmark Street displayed. 'Recognise her?'

Honbold retrieved his gold-rimmed reading glasses from his shirt pocket, then picked up the phone and held it at various distances from his eyes, as though the picture might transform into a different woman if he found the right number of inches from which to view it.

'Yes,' he said finally, 'although she certainly wasn't dressed like that when I met her. Her name's Aisha Khan and she works for Tate and Brannigan, the reputation management people. Jeremy Tate phoned me to ask if I'd see her.'

'Did you call him back?'

'Did I what?' boomed Honbold, throwing his voice as though trying to reach the back of a courtroom.

'Did you call Tate and Brannigan back, to check it was genuinely Jeremy Tate who'd rung you?'

'No,' said Honbold, 'but I looked her up. I don't usually see people ad hoc like that, without the client. She was on their website. She'd just joined them.'

'Was there a picture of her on the website?'

'No,' said Honbold, now looking uneasy.

'Her real name,' said Strike, 'is Farah Navabi. She's an undercover detective working for Patterson Inc.'

There was a second's silence.

'*Bitch!*' Honbold exploded. 'Working for some tabloid, is she? Or is it my bloody wife?'

'Could be either,' said Strike, 'but Patterson had someone planted at my agency for the last few months. The aim could've been getting me in the dock for bugging you. Was Navabi alone in your office at any point?'

'Yes,' groaned Honbold, running a hand through his thinning hair. 'I showed her in, but I needed a pee. She had a few minutes in there, alone. *Shit,*' he exploded again. 'She was bloody convincing!'

'Acting's clearly her strong suit, because she's not much cop at undercover surveillance.'

'Mitchell fucking Patterson . . . how he got off, after all the fucking phone hacking he did – I'll have him banged up for this if it's the last bloody thing I—'

Strike's mobile rang.

'Excuse me,' he said, picking it up from the table. 'Luce?'

'They've found him.'

'Oh, thank Christ,' said Strike, feeling the relief wash over him like warm bath water. 'Where was he?'

'Down on the beach. They say he's very confused. Stick,

I'm going to go straight down there now and persuade him to come back with me, just for a visit, so we can talk to him about what he wants. He can't go on like this.'

'OK. D'you want me to—?'

'No, I can manage alone, but will you come over to ours once I've got him here, to help me talk to him? Tomorrow night?'

'I will, yeah, of course,' said Strike, his spirits sinking slightly. Somebody else would have to pick up Robin from Chapman Farm.

He returned to the sitting room to find Honbold holding a coffee pot.

'Want some?' he barked at Strike.

'That'd be great,' said Strike, sitting down again.

Once both men were sitting again, a slightly awkward silence fell. Given that both of them had been having sex with the same woman over roughly the same time period, and that Bijou was now pregnant, Strike supposed this was inevitable, but he wasn't going to be the one to bring up the subject.

'Bijou told me you two had a couple of drinks,' boomed the barrister. 'Nothing more.'

'That's right,' lied Strike.

'Met at a christening, I understand? Isla Herbert's child.'

'Ilsa,' Strike corrected him. 'Yeah, Ilsa and her husband are old friends of mine.'

'So Bijou didn't—?'

'She never mentioned you. I don't discuss work outside the office and she never asked about it.'

This, at least, was true. Bijou had talked about nothing but herself. Honbold was now eyeing Strike thoughtfully. Having sipped his coffee, he said,

'You're very good at what you do, arentcha? I've heard glowing reports from clients.'

'Nice to know,' said Strike.

'Wouldn't fancy helping me get something on my wife, would you?'

'Our client list's full, I'm afraid,' said Strike. He hadn't extricated himself from the Bijou-Honbold mess to plunge straight back into it.

'Pity. Matilda's out for revenge. *Revenge*,' boomed Honbold, and Strike could picture him in his barrister's wig, throwing the word at a jury. Honbold began to enumerate the many outrageous ways in which his wife was currently behaving, one of which was refusing to give him access to his wine cellar.

Strike let the man talk, desirous only of defusing Honbold's animosity to himself once and for all. Though the accent, the grievances and the objects of their ire might be very different, he was reminded of Barry Saxon as he listened to Honbold. Just like the Tube driver, the QC seemed perplexed and outraged that a woman he'd wronged might want to make things unpleasant for him in turn.

'Well, thanks for the coffee,' said Strike, when a convenient pause arose, getting to his feet. 'I'll look forward to seeing Patterson in court.'

'"So you shall,"' quoted Honbold, also rising, and raising his already loud voice he declaimed, *"And where the offence is let the great axe fall."'

79

Six in the third place means:
One is enriched through unfortunate events.

The I Ching or Book of Changes

Relieved to have one problem crossed off his list, Strike returned to the office, eating and despising the carob bar he'd picked up en route in tribute to his renewed commitment to weight loss. He half hoped Littlejohn would have reneged on his promise to provide the Pirbright recording today, thereby giving Strike an opportunity to vent his tetchiness on a deserving target.

'Littlejohn dropped this off,' were Pat's first words when he entered the office.

She indicated a plain brown envelope lying beside her, inside which was a small oblong object. Strike grunted, heading for the kettle.

'And Midge has just been in,' Pat continued. 'She's in a right mood. She says you insulted her.'

'If she thinks her boss asking legitimate questions about her working practices is an insult, she's led a very sheltered life,' said Strike irritably, now adding an additional teabag to his mug, feeling he needed all the caffeine he could get.

In truth, his anger at Midge had abated somewhat during the last few days. Little though he wanted to admit it, he knew he'd overreacted about her getting caught on camera at Tasha Mayo's house, because of his own anxiety about the fallout from Honbold's divorce. He'd been toying with the idea of telling Midge she could go back on the Frank case as long as there was no more fraternising with the client, but the news that she'd been complaining to Pat aggravated him.

'I knew another lesbian, once,' said Pat.

'Yeah?' said Strike, as the kettle lid began to rattle. 'Did she bitch behind her boss's back, as well?'

'No,' said Pat. 'She *was* the boss. Nice woman. People took her for hard as nails, but she was soft underneath. Very kind when I had my divorce.'

'Is this a thinly veiled suggestion I should grovel for hurting Midge's feelings?'

'Nobody said anything about grovelling.'

'Just as well, because that's not going to happen,' said Strike.

'No need to be snappy,' said Pat. 'Anyway, Rhoda's done what you asked.'

It took Strike a couple of seconds to remember that this was Pat's daughter.

'You're kidding?' he said, turning back towards her.

'No,' said Pat. 'She's got into that Carrie Curtis Woods' Facebook page.'

'Best news I've had all day,' said Strike. 'Want a cuppa?'

Once both had tea, Pat logged onto Facebook with her daughter's details, and navigated to the account of the woman Strike hoped had been Cherie Gittins twenty-one years previously. Turning the monitor so Strike could view it, Pat puffed on her e-cigarette, watching him peruse the page.

Strike scrolled slowly downwards, carefully examining the many pictures of Carrie Curtis Woods' two little blonde girls. The pictures of Carrie herself showed a woman who was heavier than in her profile picture. There was no indication of her having a job, though plenty of mention of her volunteering at her daughters' school. Then—

'It's her,' Strike said.

The picture, which had been posted to mark Carrie Curtis Woods' anniversary, showed her wedding day, when she'd been at least two dress sizes smaller. There, unmistakeably, was the blonde with the simpering smile who'd once been an inmate of Chapman Farm: older, wearing less eyeliner, cinched into a tight lace dress, her curly blonde hair pulled up into a bun, beside a thickset man with heavy eyebrows. A little further down the page was a phone number: Carrie Curtis Woods was offering swimming lessons to toddlers.

'Pat, you've played a blinder.'

'It was Rhoda, not me,' said Pat gruffly.

'What does she drink?'

'Gin.'

'I'll get her a bottle or two.'

A further five minutes' scrolling helped Strike identify Carrie Curtis Woods' husband, Nathan Woods, who was an electrician, and her home town.

'Where the hell's Thornbury?' he muttered, switching to Google maps.

'Gloucestershire,' said Pat, who was now washing up mugs in the sink. 'My Dennis' cousin lives over that way.'

'Shit,' said Strike, now reading Carrie Curtis Woods' most recent posts. 'They're off to Andalusia on Saturday.'

Having checked the weekly rota, Strike called Shah to ask him to pick up Robin from Chapman Farm the following night.

'I think,' said Strike, having hung up, 'I'll go down to Thornbury on Friday. Catch Carrie before she goes on holiday. Robin'll be knackered, she's not going to be up for a trip to Gloucestershire right after getting out.'

Privately, he was thinking that if he could manage the trip in a day, he'd have an excuse to go over to Robin's that evening for a full debrief, a very cheering thought, given that he knew Murphy was still in Spain. Feeling slightly happier, Strike logged out of Facebook, picked up his tea and headed into his own office carrying the brown envelope left by Littlejohn.

Inside was a tiny Dictaphone tape, wrapped in a sheet of paper with a scrawled date on it. The recording had been made nearly a month after Sir Colin and Kevin had fallen out over the latter's heckling at Giles Harmon's book reading and five days before Kevin's murder. Strike took a Dictaphone out of his desk drawer, inserted the tape and pressed play.

He understood at once why Patterson hadn't handed over the tape to Sir Colin Edensor: because it would have been hard to imagine a poorer advertisement for his agency's surveillance skills. For a start, there were far better devices for this kind of work than a Dictaphone, which had to be concealed. The recording was of extremely poor quality: whichever pub Farah had taken Kevin to had been crowded and noisy, a rookie error for which Strike would have severely reprimanded any of his own subcontractors. It was, he thought, the kind of thing his now departed, unlamented hireling Nutley would have done.

Farah's voice came over more clearly than Kevin's, presumably because the Dictaphone had lain closer to her. From what Strike could make out, she'd suggested twice they leave for somewhere quieter in the first five minutes, but Kevin, pathetically, said they should stay, because he knew it was her favourite bar. Apparently Kevin had been thoroughly convinced the good-looking Navabi was interested in him sexually.

Strike turned the volume up to maximum and listened closely, trying to make out what was being said. Farah kept asking Kevin to speak up or repeat things, and Strike was forced to rewind and relisten multiple times, pen in hand, trying to transcribe anything that was audible.

Initially, as far as Strike could make out, their chat had nothing to do with the UHC. For ten minutes, Farah talked indistinctly about her supposed job as an air stewardess. At last, the church was mentioned.

Farah: ... ways been interested in the UH ...
Kevin: ... on't do it ... isters ... still in b ... aybe leave
        one d ...

Somewhere close to where Farah and Kevin were sitting, a rowdy song broke out which, typically, was as clear as a bell.

And we were singing hymns and arias,
'Land of my Fathers', 'Ar hyd y nos'.

'Fuck's sake,' muttered Strike. The group of what Strike assumed were elderly Welshmen, because he wasn't sure who else would be singing a Max Boyce song, struggled for the next ten minutes to remember all the lyrics, breaking out intermittently into fragments of verses that petered out again, rendering Kevin and Farah's conversation completely inaudible. At last, the Welshmen reverted to merely talking loudly, and Strike was able to pick up the faint thread of what Farah and Kevin were saying again.

Kevin: ... vil people. Evil.
Farah: How were they ev ... ?
Kevin: ... ean, cruel ... hypocr ... 'm writing a b ...
Farah: Oh wow that's gr ...

One of the Welshmen broke into song again.

> *But Will is very happy though his money all has gone:*
> *He swapped five photos of his wife for one of Barry John.*

Cheers greeted these remembered lines and when the yelling had subsided, Strike heard Kevin again: '. . . orry, need a . . .'

From the lack of chat from Farah, Strike surmised that Kevin had gone to the bathroom.

The next fifty minutes of recording were worthless. Not only had the noise in the pub become ever louder, but Kevin's voice grew progressively more indistinct. Strike could have told Farah that offering unlimited drink to a young man who'd grown up never touching alcohol was a mistake, and soon Kevin was slurring and rambling, Farah trying very hard to keep track of what he was saying.

Kevin: . . . 'n she drown . . . said sh'drowned . . .

Farah: (loudly) . . . talking about Dai . . . ?

Kevin: . . . unny thing zappenin . . . ings I keep . . . emembrin . . . or of 'em . . .

Farah: (loudly) Four? Did you say f . . . ?

Kevin: . . . more 'n jus' Shree . . . nice to kids, an' she . . . Bec made Em l . . . visible . . . ullshit . . .

Farah: (loudly) . . . ecca made Em lie, did you s . . . ?

Kevin: . . . drugged . . . sh'wuz allowed out . . . sh'could get things . . . smuggle it'n . . . let her 'way with stu . . . didn' care 'bout 'er real . . . sh'ad chocolate once n'I stole some . . . bully though . . .

Farah: (loudly) . . . oo wa . . . ully?

Kevin: . . . ake 'lowances . . . gonna talk t'er . . . z'gonna meet m . . .

Farah: (very loudly) Is someone from the church going
            meet you, Kev . . . ?

Kevin: . . . 'n'answer f'r it . . .

Strike slammed his hand onto pause, rewound and listened again.

Kevin: . . . gonna talk t'er . . . z'gonna meet m . . .

Farah: (very loudly) Is someone from the church going
            meet you, Kev . . . ?

Kevin: . . . 'n'answer f'r it . . . opey . . . part'f . . .

Farah: (insistent) Are you going to meet someone
            from . . . ?

Kevin: . . . sh'ad 'ard ti . . . 'n th'pigs . . .

Farah: (exasperated) Forget the pigs . . .

'Let him talk about the fucking pigs,' growled Strike at the recorder.

Kevin: . . . e liked pigs . . . ew what t'd . . . 'cos why . . . 'n
            I wuz in th'woo . . . 'n Bec . . . old me off cuz . . .
            ace's daught . . . m'sn't snitch . . .

Farah: . . . Daiyu in the woods?

Kevin: . . . unno . . . was sh . . . . . ink there was a plot . . .
            in it t'gether . . . alwuz t'geth . . . f'I'm right . . .
            bution . . . 'n woods . . . wasn't a . . . gale blow-
            ing on . . . ire but too wet . . . weird'n I . . .
            eatened me . . . an out'f the . . . ought it was for
            pun'shmen . . . ecca tole me . . . sorry, gotta . . .

Strike heard a loud clunk, as though a chair had fallen. He had a feeling Kevin might have set off clumsily for the bathroom, possibly to vomit. He kept listening, but nothing whatsoever happened for a further twenty-five minutes except that the Welshmen became ever more rambunctious. At last he heard Farah say,

'Excuse me ... f you're going ... n the loo? He's wearing a blue ...'

Five minutes later, a loud Welsh voice said,

''E's in an 'orrible state, love. You might 'ave to carry 'im 'ome.'

'Oh, for God's s ... anks for checking, any ...'

There was a rustle, the sound of breathing, and the recording ended.

80

External conditions hinder the advance, just as loss of the wheel spokes stops the progress of a wagon.

The I Ching or Book of Changes

Shah departed for Norfolk at midday on Thursday, bearing a letter from Strike instructing Robin to stay beside the plastic rock after reading it, because Shah would be waiting in the vicinity with his car lights off and cutters at the ready to ensure safe passage through the barbed wire. Strike set off for dinner at Lucy's that evening feeling surprisingly cheerful given that he'd be up at six the following morning to drive to Gloucestershire, and wasn't looking forward to the evening ahead.

Although Ted was pleased to see his nephew, it was immediately clear to Strike that his uncle had deteriorated even in the few weeks since he'd last seen him. There was a vagueness, a sense of disconnection, that hadn't been there before. Ted smiled and nodded, but Strike wasn't convinced he was following the conversation. His uncle watched Lucy's three sons bustle in and out of the kitchen with an air of bemusement and treated them with a formal courtesy that suggested he wasn't sure who they were.

Strike and Lucy's attempts to draw Ted out about where and how he wanted to live went nowhere, because Ted tended to agree with every proposition put to him, even if they were contradictory. He agreed that he wanted to stay in Cornwall, that it might be better to move to London, that he needed a bit more help, then, with a sudden flicker of the old Ted, stated spontaneously that he was managing just fine and nobody ought to be worrying about him. All through dinner, Strike sensed tension between his sister and brother-in-law, and sure enough, once Ted was settled in the sitting room in front of the television with a cup of decaffeinated coffee, there was an uncomfortable three-way conversation in which Greg made plain his sense of ill-usage.

'She wants him to live with us,' he told Strike, scowling.

'I said, if we sell the house in Cornwall, we could build an extension on the back,' Lucy told her brother.

'And lose half the garden,' said Greg.

'I don't want him going into a home,' said Lucy tearfully. 'Joan would've *hated* the idea of him in a home.'

'What're you going to do, give up work?' Greg demanded of his wife. 'Because he's going to be a full-time job if he gets much worse.'

'I think,' said Strike, 'we need to get him a full medical assessment before we decide anything.'

'That's just kicking the can down the road,' said Greg, whose irritation was undoubtedly informed by the fact that Strike was unlikely to be discommoded by any change in Ted's living arrangements.

'There are homes and homes,' Strike told Lucy, ignoring Greg. 'If we got him into somewhere decent in London, we could make sure we're seeing him regularly. Take him for days out—'

'Then Lucy'll be running round after him like he's living here,' said Greg, his clear implication that Strike wouldn't be doing any running round at all. 'He wants to stay in Cornwall, he's just said so.'

'He doesn't know what he wants,' said Lucy shrilly. 'What happened on Tuesday was a warning. He isn't safe to live alone any more, anything could have happened to him – what if he'd tried to take his boat out?'

'That's what I was worried about,' admitted Strike.

'So sell the boat,' said Greg angrily.

The conversation ended, as Strike could have predicted from the first, with no decision in place other than getting Ted seen by a specialist in London. As Ted was exhausted after his unexpected journey to London he turned in at nine, and Strike left shortly afterwards, hoping to maximise his sleep before getting up to drive to Thornbury.

He'd decided against giving Cherie, or Carrie, as she was now, prior notice of his arrival, due to her well-established pattern of flight and reinvention: he had a feeling that if he called her first, she'd make sure she was unavailable. Strike doubted the woman who posted endless pictures on Facebook of her family's outings to Longleat and Paultons Park, of her contributions to school bake sales and of the fancy dress costumes she'd made her little girls was going to enjoy being reminded of her unsavoury past.

Strike had been travelling along the motorway for two hours when he received a phone call from Tasha Mayo, asking why Midge wasn't looking after her any more, and requesting that Midge be reassigned to her case. The phrase 'looking after' did nothing to allay Strike's faint suspicion that Midge had become over-friendly with the actress, and he didn't much appreciate their client dictating to him which personnel they wanted assigned to them.

'It's just more natural for me to be seen walking around with another woman,' Mayo told him.

'If what my agency provided was private securit[...] wanted to keep it discreet, I'd agree,' said Stri[...]

shouldn't be any walking around together, given that what we're providing is surveillance—'

To his consternation, he then realised Tasha was crying. His heart sank: he seemed to have had to deal with an endless train of crying people lately.

'Look,' she sobbed, 'I can't afford you *and* private security, and I *like* her, she makes me feel safe, and I'd rather have some-one around I can have a laugh with—'

'All right, all right,' said Strike. 'I'll put Midge back on the job.'

Little though Strike liked what he thought of as mission creep, he couldn't pretend it was unreasonable of Mayo to want a bodyguard.

'Take care of yourself,' he finished lamely, and Tasha rang off.

Having contacted a frosty Midge to give her the news, Strike continued driving.

Twenty minutes later, Shah called.

'Have you got her?' said Strike, smiling in anticipation of hearing Robin's voice.

'No,' said Shah. 'She didn't turn up and the rock's gone.'

For the second time in two weeks, Strike felt as though dry ice had slid down through his guts.

'What?'

'The plastic rock's gone. No sign of it.'

'Fuck. Stay there. I'm on the M4. I'll be with you as soon as I can.'

81

The upper trigram K'an stands for the Abysmal, the
dangerous. Its motion is downward ...

The I Ching or Book of Changes

Three nights of vigil had now been held on the temple steps, making it impossible for Robin to leave her bed. On Wednesday, teenaged boys in long white robes had replaced the girls, and on Thursday night, the church Principals took up their positions at the temple entrance, the flickering flames of their torches illuminating the painted faces of Jonathan and Mazu Wace, Becca Pirbright, Taio Wace, Giles Harmon, Noli Seymour and others, all of them wearing black smeared around their eyes. Daiyu had appeared twice more by night, her luminous figure visible from afar from the rear windows of the dormitories.

The ghost, the watchful figures on the temple steps, the constant dread, the impossibility of escaping or calling for help: all made Robin feel as though she was inhabiting a nightmare from which she couldn't wake. Nobody had confronted her about her real identity, nobody had spoken to her about what had happened in the Retreat Room with Will or challenged her explanation of why her face was swollen and bruised, and she found all of this ominous rather than reassuring. She felt certain that a reckoning was coming at a time of the church's choosing, and afraid that the Manifestation would be the moment it happened. *The Drowned Prophet will sort you out.*

She saw Will from a distance, moving blank-faced about his daily tasks, and occasionally she saw his lips moving silently, and knew he was chanting. Once, she spotted him sitting on his haunches to talk to little Qing, before hurrying away as Mazu swept through the courtyard, cradling baby Yixin in her arms. Robin was still being accompanied everywhere she went.

The day of the Manifestation was marked by a fast for all church members, who were once again served hot water with lemon for breakfast. The church Principals, who were presumably catching up on their sleep in the farmhouse after their overnight vigil, remained out of sight. Exhausted, hungry and scared, Robin fed chickens, cleaned the dormitories and spent a few hours in the craft room, stuffing more plush turtles for sale in Norwich. She kept remembering her blithe request of an extra day's grace from Strike, should she be late putting a letter in the plastic rock. Had she not overruled him, someone from the agency would be coming to get her the following day, although she now knew enough about Chapman Farm to be certain anyone who tried to gain entry at the front gate would be turned away.

If I get through the Manifestation, she thought, *I'll get out tomorrow night.* Then she tried to mock herself for thinking she might *not* get through the Manifestation. *What d'you think's going to happen, ritual sacrifice?*

After an evening meal of more hot water with lemon, all church members over the age of thirteen were instructed to return to their dormitories and put on the outfits laid out for them on their beds. These proved to be long white robes made of worn and much-washed cotton that might once have been old bed sheets. The loss of her tracksuit made Robin feel still more vulnerable. The now-robed women talked in hushed voices, waiting to be summoned to the temple. Robin spoke to nobody, wishing she could somehow psychically summon those who cared about her in the outside world.

When the sun had at last fallen, Becca Pirbright reappeared in the women's dormitory, also wearing robes, though hers, like Mazu's, were made of silk, and beaded.

'Everyone, take off your shoes,' Becca instructed the waiting women. 'You'll walk barefoot, as the Prophet walked into the sea, in pairs across the courtyard, in silence. The temple will be dark. Assistants will guide you to your places.'

They lined up obediently. Robin found herself walking next to Penny Brown, whose once-round face was now hollow and anxious. They crossed the courtyard beneath a clear, starry sky, chilly in their thin cotton robes and bare feet, and two by two entered the temple, which was indeed pitch black.

Robin felt a hand take her by the arm and was led, she assumed, past the pentagonal stage, then pushed down into a kneeling position on the floor. She no longer knew who was beside her, although she could hear rustling and breathing, nor did she know how those assisting people to their places were able to see what they were doing.

After a while, the temple doors closed with a bang. Then Jonathan Wace's voice spoke through the darkness.

'Together: *Lokah Samastah Sukhino Bhavantu . . . Lokah Samastah Sukhino Bhavantu . . .*'

The members took up the chant. The darkness seemed to intensify the rumble and rhythm of the words, but Robin, who'd once felt relief in dissolving her voice into the mass, experienced neither euphoria nor relief; fear continued to burn like a coal lodged beneath her diaphragm.

'. . . and finish,' called Wace.

Silence fell again. Then Wace spoke:

'Daiyu, beloved Prophet, speaker of truths, bringer of

justice, come to us now in holiness. Bless us with your presence. Light the way for us, that we may see clearly into the next world.'

There was another silence in which nobody stirred. Then, clearly and loudly, came a small girl's giggle.

'Hello, Papa.'

Robin, who'd been kneeling with her eyes tight shut, opened them. All was dark: there was no sign of Daiyu.

'Will you manifest for us, my child?' said Wace's voice.

Another pause. Then –

'Papa, I'm afraid.'

'*You're* afraid, my child?' said Wace. '*You?* The bravest of us, and the best?'

'Things are *wrong,* Papa. Bad people have come.'

'We know there is wickedness in the world, little one. That's why we fight.'

'Inside and outside,' said the child's voice. 'Fight inside and outside.'

'What does that mean, Daiyu?'

'Clever Papa knows.'

Another silence.

'Daiyu, do you speak of malign influences within our church?'

There was no answer.

'Daiyu, help me. What does it mean, to fight inside and out?'

The childish voice began to wail in distress, its cries and sobs echoing off the temple walls.

'Daiyu! Daiyu, Blessed One, don't cry!' said Wace, with the familiar catch in his voice. 'Little one, I will fight for you!'

The sobs quietened. Silence fell again.

'Come to us, Daiyu,' said Wace, pleading now. 'Show us you live. Help us root out evil, inside and out.'

For a few seconds, nothing happened. Then a very faint glow appeared a few feet off the floor in front of Robin, and she realised she was kneeling in the front row of the crowd surrounding the pentagonal baptismal pool, from which the greenish light was emanating.

Now the glowing water rose upwards in the smooth shape of a bell jar, and revolving slowly inside it was the figure of a limp, eyeless child in a white dress.

There were several screams: Robin heard a girl shout, 'No, no, no!'

The water was sinking again, and with it, the dreadful figure, and after a few seconds the greenish water was flat again, though glowing brighter still, so that the figures of Jonathan and Mazu, who were standing on the edge of the pool in their long white robes, were illuminated from beneath.

Now Mazu spoke.

'I, who birthed the Drowned Prophet, have dedicated my life to honouring her sacrifice. When she left this world to join the Blessed Divinity, she conferred gifts upon those of us destined to carry on the fight against evil on earth. I have been granted the gift of divine sight by the grace of my daughter, and her Manifestation confirms me in my duty. There are those among us whom Daiyu will test tonight. They have nothing to fear if their hearts, like hers, are pure . . .

'I call to the pool Rowena Ellis.'

Gasps and whispers issued from among the kneeling crowd. Robin had known it was going to happen, but nevertheless, her legs could barely support her weight as she got to her feet and walked forwards.

'You entered the pool once before, Rowena,' said Mazu, looking down at her. 'Tonight, you join Daiyu in these holy waters. May she give you her blessing.'

Robin climbed up the steps to stand on the edge of the

illuminated pool. Looking down, she could see nothing in it except the dark bottom. Knowing that resistance or refusal would be taken as infallible signs of guilt, she stepped over the edge and allowed herself to drop down under the surface of the cold water.

The light in the water dimmed. Robin expected her feet to touch the bottom, but they met no resistance: the bottom of the pool had disappeared. She tried to swim for the surface but then, to her terror, felt something like smooth cord twist around her ankles. In panic she fought, trying to kick herself free, but whatever had hold of her dragged her downwards. In darkness she flailed and kicked, trying to rise, but whatever was holding her back was more powerful, and she saw splinters of memories – her parents, her childhood home, Strike in the Land Rover – and the cold water seemed to be crushing her, pressing on her very brain, it was impossible to breathe, she opened her mouth in a silent scream and sucked in water . . .

82

The trigrams Li, clarity, and Chên, shock, terror,
give the prerequisites for a clearing of the atmosphere
by the thunderstorm of a criminal trial.

The I Ching or Book of Changes

Hands were pressing hard on her ribcage. Robin vomited.

She was lying in the pitch black on the cold temple floor. A nightmarish face loomed over her wearing something like skiing goggles. Gasping for air, Robin tried to get up and was forced flat again by the one who'd just been pressing on her chest. She could hear frightened voices in the darkness, and see shadowy figures moving around by the greenish light in the pool.

'Taio, remove Rowena from the temple,' said Mazu calmly.

Shivering, soaked to her skin, Robin was dragged to her feet. She retched again, then vomited more water and fell back to her knees. Taio, who she now realised was wearing night vision goggles, pulled her roughly upright again, then marched her through the dark temple, Robin's legs almost giving way at each step. The doors opened automatically and she saw the starlit courtyard, and felt the freezing night air against her soaking skin. Taio led her roughly past the dragon-carved doors of the farmhouse and then to the side entrance which opened onto the stairs to the basement.

They proceeded through the deserted underground lecture theatre in silence. Taio unlocked the second door leading off the screen room, through which Robin had never gone before. The room beyond was empty except for a small table at which stood two metal-legged plastic chairs.

'Sit there,' said Taio, pointing at one of the chairs, 'and wait.'

Robin sat. Taio walked out, locking the door behind him.

Terrified, Robin fought with herself not to cry, but lost. Leaning forwards on the table, she hid her bruised face in her arms and sobbed. Why hadn't she left with Barclay a week ago? Why had she stayed?

She didn't know how long she cried before pulling herself together, attempting to breathe slowly and deeply. The horror of her near drowning was now eclipsed by terror of what would come next. She stood up and tried the door, even though she knew it was locked, then turned to look at the room to see nothing but blank walls: no air vent, no window, no hatch, but one very small round black camera in a corner of the ceiling.

Robin knew she must think, to prepare for whatever was coming, but she felt so weak after the twenty-four-hour fast she couldn't make her brain work. The minutes dragged by, Robin shivering in her wet robe, and she wondered what was taking so long. Perhaps other people were being subjected to near drowning in the pool? Doubtless other misdemeanours had been committed at Chapman Farm, by people to whom she'd never spoken.

At long last, the key turned in the lock, and four robed people entered the room: Jonathan, Mazu, Taio and Becca. Wace took the chair opposite Robin. The other three lined up against the wall, watching.

'Why d'you think Daiyu's so angry with you, Rowena?' asked Wace quietly and reasonably, like a disappointed headmaster.

'I don't know,' whispered Robin.

She'd have given anything to be able to look inside Wace's mind and see what he already knew.

'I think you do,' said Wace gently.

There was a minute's silence. At last, Robin said,

'I've been thinking . . . of leaving.'

'But *that* wouldn't make Daiyu angry,' said Wace, with a little laugh. 'Church members are free to leave. We compel nobody. You know that, surely?'

Robin thought he was playing to the camera in the corner, which presumably also picked up sound.

'Yes,' she said, 'I suppose so.'

'All we ask is that church members don't try and manipulate others, or act cruelly towards them,' said Wace.

'I don't think I've done that,' said Robin.

'No?' said Wace. 'What about Will Edensor?'

'I don't understand what you mean,' lied Robin.

'After his trip to the Retreat Room with you,' said Wace, 'he asked for writing materials, to contact the person he used to call his mother.'

It took everything Robin had to feign perplexity.

'Why?' she said.

'That's what we want you to—' began Taio harshly, but his father raised a hand to silence him.

'Taio . . . let her answer.'

'*Oh,*' said Robin slowly, as though she'd just remembered something. 'I did tell him . . . oh God,' she said, playing for time. 'I told him I thought . . . you're going to be angry,' she said, allowing herself to cry again.

'I'm only angered by injustice, Rowena,' said Wace quietly. 'If you've been unjust – to us, or to Will – there will be a sanction, but it will fit the transgression. As the I Ching tells us, penalties must not be imposed unfairly. They should be restricted to an objective guarding against unjustified excesses.'

'I told Will,' said Robin, 'that I wondered whether all our letters were being passed on.'

Mazu let out a soft hiss. Becca was shaking her head.

'Were you aware that Will has signed a non-contact declaration regarding his family?' asked Wace.

'No,' said Robin.

'Some church members, like Will, voluntarily sign a declaration that they no longer wish to receive letters from former flesh objects. Step five: renunciation. In such cases, the church carefully preserves the correspondence, which can be viewed at any time, should the member ever wish to see it. Will has never made such a request, and so his letters are kept safely filed away.'

'I didn't know that,' said Robin.

'So why should he suddenly wish to write to his mother, after almost four years without contact?'

'I don't know,' said Robin.

She was shivering, very aware of the wet robe's transparency. Was it possible that Will had kept most of their conversation secret? He'd certainly had reason to suppress Robin's possession of a torch, because of potential punishment for not having revealed it sooner. Perhaps he'd also omitted mention of her testing of his faith?

'Are you sure you didn't say anything to Will in the Retreat Room that would make him anxious about the woman he used to call mother?'

'Why would I talk about his mother?' asked Robin desperately. 'I – I told him I didn't think the letter from my sister had been passed on as soon as it arrived. I'm sorry,' said Robin, allowing herself to cry again, 'I didn't know about non-contact declarations. That explains why there were so many letters in Mazu's cabinet. I'm sorry, I really am.'

'That injury to your face,' said Wace. 'How did it *really* happen?'

'Will pushed past me,' said Robin. 'And I fell over.'

'That sounds as though Will was angry. Why should he be angry with you?'

'He didn't like me talking about the letters,' said Robin. 'He seemed to take it really personally.'

There was a short silence in which Jonathan's eyes met Mazu's. Robin didn't dare look at the latter. She felt as though she'd read her ultimate fate in Mazu's crooked eyes.

Jonathan turned back to Robin.

'Did you, at any time, mention the death of family members?'

'Not death,' lied Robin. 'I might've said, "What if something happened to one of them?"'

'So you continue to see relationships in materialist terms?' said Wace.

'I'm trying not to,' said Robin, 'but it's hard.'

'Did Emily really earn all the money that was in her collection box at the end of your trip to Norwich?' asked Wace.

'No,' said Robin, after a pause of several seconds. 'I gave her some from the stall box.'

'Why?'

'I felt sorry for her, because she hadn't got much on her own. She wasn't very well,' Robin said desperately.

'So you lied to Taio? You misrepresented what had really happened?'

'I didn't ... I suppose so, yes,' said Robin hopelessly.

'How are we supposed to believe anything you say, now we know you're prepared to lie to church Principals?'

'I'm sorry,' said Robin, again allowing herself to cry. 'I didn't see it as being a bad thing, helping her out ... I'm sorry ...'

'Small evils mount up, Rowena,' said Wace. 'You may say to yourself, "What does it matter, a little lie here, a little lie there?" But the pure spirit knows there can be no lies, big or small. To promulgate falsehoods is to embrace evil.'

'I'm sorry,' said Robin again.

Wace contemplated Robin for a moment, then said,

'Becca, fill in a PA form and bring it back to me, with a blank.'

'Yes, Papa J,' said Becca, and she strode out of the room. When the door had closed, Jonathan leaned forwards and said quietly,

'Do you want to leave us, Rowena? Because, if so, you're completely free to do so.'

Robin looked into those opaque dark blue eyes and remembered the stories of Kevin Pirbright and Niamh Doherty, of Sheila Kennett and Flora Brewster, all of which had taught her that if there were any safe, easy route out of Chapman Farm, it wouldn't have taken bereavement, mental collapse or night-time escapes through barbed wire to free them. She no longer believed the Waces would stop short of murder to protect themselves or their lucrative fiefdom. Wace's offer was for the camera, to prove Robin had been given a free choice that was, in reality, no choice at all.

'No,' Robin said. 'I want to stay. I want to learn, I want to do better.'

'That will mean performing penance,' said Wace. 'You understand that?'

'Yes,' said Robin, 'I do.'

'And do you agree that any penance should be proportionate to your own self-confessed behaviour?'

She nodded.

'Say it,' said Wace.

'Yes,' said Robin. 'I agree.'

The door behind Wace opened. Becca had returned holding two pieces of paper and a pen. She was also holding a razor and a can of shaving foam.

'I want you to read what Becca's written for you,' said Wace, as Becca laid the two forms and the pen before Robin on the table, 'and, if you agree, copy the words out onto the blank form, then sign it.'

Robin read what had been written in Becca's neat, rounded handwriting.

I have been duplicitous.

I have spoken falsehoods.

I have manipulated a fellow church member and undermined his trust in the church.

I have manipulated and encouraged a fellow church member to lie.

I have acted and spoken in direct contravention of the church's teachings on kindness and fellowship.

By my own thought, word and deed, I have damaged the bond of trust between myself and the church.

I accept a proportionate punishment as penance for my behaviour.

Robin picked up the pen and her four accusers watched as she copied out the words, then signed as Rowena Ellis.

'Becca's going to shave your head now,' said Wace, 'as a mark—'

Taio made a slight movement. His father looked up at him for a moment, then smiled.

'Very well, we'll forgo the shaving. Taio, go with Becca and fetch the box.'

The pair left the room, leaving Wace and Mazu to watch Robin in silence. Robin heard scuffing footsteps, and then the door opened once more to reveal Taio and Becca carrying a heavy wooden box, the size of a large travel trunk, with an envelope-sized rectangular hole at one end and a hinged, lockable lid.

'I'm going to leave you now, Artemis,' said Wace, getting to his feet, and his eyes were wet again. 'Even where the sin has been great, I hate the necessity for punishment. I wish,' he pressed his hand to his heart, 'it weren't necessary. Be well, Rowena, I'll see you on the other side, purified, I hope, by suffering. Don't think I don't recognise your gifts of intelligence and generosity. I'm very happy,' he said, making her a little bow, 'in spite of everything, that you chose to stay with us. Eight hours,' he added to Taio.

He left the room.

Taio now threw back the lid of the box.

'You face this way,' he told Robin, pointing at the rectangular hole. You kneel and bend over in an attitude of penance. Then we close the lid.'

Shaking uncontrollably, Robin stood up. She climbed into the box, facing the rectangular hole, then knelt down and curled up. The floor of the box hadn't been sanded: she felt the splintered surface digging into her knees through the thin, wet robe. Then the lid banged down on her spine.

She watched through the rectangular hole as Mazu, Taio and Becca left the room, only the hems of their robes and their feet visible. Mazu, the last to leave, turned out the light, closed the door of the room and locked it.

83

Nine in the fifth place . . .
In the midst of the greatest obstructions,
Friends come.

The I Ching or Book of Changes

Strike, who'd arrived in Lion's Mouth at one o'clock that afternoon, was now sitting in the dark in his BMW at the blind spot in Chapman Farm's perimeter with the car's head-lights off. Shah had given Strike the night vision binoculars and wire cutters, and he was using the former to stare at the woods for any sign of a human figure. He'd sent Shah back to London: there was no point in two of them sitting here in the dark for hours.

It was nearly midnight, and raining heavily, when Strike's mobile rang.

'Any sign of her?' said Midge anxiously.

'No,' said Strike.

'She *did* miss a Thursday once before,' said Midge.

'I know,' said Strike, peering through the rain-flecked window at the dark trees, 'but why the fuck's the rock gone?'

'Could she have moved it herself?'

'Possibly,' said Strike, 'but I can't see why.'

'You sure you don't want company?'

'No, I'm fine on my own,' said Strike.

'What if she doesn't turn up tonight?'

'We agreed I wouldn't do anything until Sunday,' said Strike, 'so she's got another night, assuming she doesn't turn up in the next few hours.'

'God, I hope she's all right.'

'Me too,' said Strike. With the aim of maintaining these friendlier relations with Midge, even in the midst of his larger worries, he asked,

'Tasha all right?'

'Yeah, I think so,' said Midge. 'Barclay's outside her house.'

'Good,' said Strike. 'I might've overreacted about the photos. Didn't want to give Patterson another stick to beat us with.'

'I know,' said Midge. 'And I'm sorry for what I said about her with the fake tits.'

'Apology accepted.'

When Midge had hung up, Strike continued to stare through the night vision binoculars at the woods.

Six hours later, Robin still hadn't appeared.

84

Six in the fifth place . . .
Persistently ill, and still does not die.

The I Ching or Book of Changes

Every attempt to relieve pressure or numbness in either of Robin's smarting legs resulted in more pain. The rough lid of the box scraped her back as she tried to make minor readjustments of her position. Folded down upon herself in the pitch dark, too scared and in too much pain to escape the present by sleeping, she imagined dying, locked inside the box inside the locked room. She knew nobody would hear even if she screamed, but she cried intermittently. After what she thought must be two or three hours, she was forced to urinate inside the box. Her legs were burning with the weight they were supporting. She had nothing to hold on to except that Wace had said 'eight hours'. There would be a release. It would come. She had to hold on to that.

And, at long last, it came. She heard the key turn in the lock of the door. The light was switched on. A pair of trainer-clad feet approached the box, and the lid was opened.

'Out,' said a female voice.

Robin initially found it almost impossible to unfold herself, but by pushing herself upwards with her hands, she forced herself into a standing position, her legs numb and weak.

The now dry robe was sticking to her knees, which had bled during the night.

Hattie, the black woman with long braids who'd checked in her possessions when she'd arrived, pointed her silently back to a seat at the table, then left the room to pick up a tray, which she set down in front of Robin. There was a serving of porridge and a glass of water on it.

'When you've eaten, I'll escort you to the dormitory. You're permitted to shower before starting your daily tasks.'

'Thank you,' said Robin weakly. Her gratitude for being released was unbounded; she wanted the stony-faced woman to like her, to see she'd changed.

Nobody looked at Robin as she and her companion crossed the courtyard, pausing as usual at Daiyu's fountain. Robin noticed that everyone was now wearing blue tracksuits. Evidently the season of the Drowned Prophet had ended: the season of the Healer Prophet had begun.

Her escort stayed outside the shower cubicle while Robin was washing herself with the thin liquid soap provided. Her knees were scraped and raw, as was a patch of her spine. She wrapped herself in a towel and followed her companion back into the empty dormitory, where Robin found a fresh blue tracksuit and underwear laid out on her bed. When she'd changed, watched by the other woman, the latter said,

'You're going to be looking after Jacob today.'

'OK,' said Robin.

She yearned to lie down upon the bed and sleep, because she was almost delirious with tiredness, but she followed Hattie meekly out of the dormitory. Nothing mattered to her now except the approval of the church Principals. Terror of the box would be with her forever; all she wanted was not to be punished. She was now scared of somebody from the agency arriving to get her out, because if they did so, Robin might be shut up in the box again and hidden away. She wanted to be left where she was; she dreaded the agency endangering her safety further. Perhaps some time in the future, when she'd recovered her nerve and round-the-clock surveillance had been lifted from her she might find a way to break free, but she couldn't think that far ahead today. She must comply. Compliance was the only safety.

Hattie led Robin back to the farmhouse, through the dragon-carved doors and up the scarlet-carpeted stairs. They walked along a corridor with more shiny black doors and then up a second staircase, this one narrow and uncarpeted, which led to a corridor with a sloping roof. At the end of this was a plain wooden door, which her companion opened.

Robin was hit by an unpleasant smell of human urine and faeces as she entered the small attic room. Louise was sitting beside a cot. There were various cardboard boxes sitting higgledy-piggledy on the floor, which was covered in sheets of old newspaper, along with a black bin liner that was partially full.

'Tell Rowena what to do, Louise,' said the woman who'd escorted Robin, 'then you can go and sleep.'

She left.

Robin stared at the occupant of the cot, horrified. Jacob was perhaps three feet long, but even though he was naked except for a nappy, he didn't look like a toddler. His face was sunken, the fine skin stretched over the bones and torso; his arms and legs were atrophied and Robin could see bruises and what she assumed to be pressure sores on his very white skin. He appeared to be sleeping, his breathing guttural. Robin didn't know whether illness, disability or persistent neglect had placed Jacob in this pitiable state.

'What's wrong with him?' she whispered.

To Robin's horror, the only answer from Louise was a strange keening noise.

'Louise?' said Robin, alarmed by the sound.

Louise doubled over, her bald head in her hands, and the noise became an animal screech.

'Louise, don't!' said Robin frantically. 'Please don't!'

She grabbed Louise by the shoulders.

'We'll both be punished again,' Robin said frantically, certain that screaming from the attic would be investigated by those downstairs, that their only safety was silence and obedience. 'Stop it! *Stop*!'

The noise subsided. Louise merely rocked backwards and forwards on her chair, her face still hidden.

'They'll be expecting you to leave. Just tell me what to do for him,' said Robin, her hands still on the older woman's shoulders. 'Tell me.'

Louise raised her head, her eyes bloodshot, her looks ruined, her bald head cut in a couple of places where, doubtless, she'd shaved it while exhausted, with her arthritic hands. Had she broken down at any other time, Robin would have felt more compassion than impatience, but all she cared about at this moment was to avoid any more scrutiny or punishment, and least of all did she want to be accused, again, of causing distress in another church member.

'Tell me what to do,' she repeated fiercely.

'There are nappies in there,' whispered Louise, tears still leaking out of her eyes as she pointed at one of the cardboard boxes, 'and wipes over there. He won't need food ... give him water in a sippy cup.' She pointed to one on the window sill. 'Leave the newspaper down ... he sometimes vomits. He has ... he has fits sometimes, as well. Try and stop him banging himself on the bars. And there's a bathroom opposite if you need it.'

Louise dragged herself to her feet and stood for a moment, looking down at the dying child. To Robin's surprise, she pressed her fingers to her mouth, kissed them, then placed them gently on Jacob's forehead. Then, in silence, she left the room.

Robin moved slowly towards the hard wooden chair Louise had vacated, her eyes on Jacob, and sat down.

The boy was clearly on the brink of death. This was the most monstrous thing she'd yet seen at Chapman Farm, and she didn't understand why today, of all days, she'd been sent to care for him. Why order somebody in here who'd lied and broken church rules, and who'd admitted questioning their allegiance to the church?

Exhausted though she was, Robin thought she knew the answer. She was being made complicit in Jacob's fate. Perhaps the Waces knew, in some long-repressed part of themselves, that hiding this child away, starving him and giving him no access to medical care except the 'spirit work' provided by Zhou would be considered criminal in the outside world. Those sent to watch over his steady decline, and who didn't seek help for him, would surely be considered guilty by the authorities beyond Chapman Farm, if they ever found out what had happened. Robin was being further enfolded in self-silencing, damned by virtue of being in this room, and not seeking help for the child. He might die while she was watching over him, in which case the Waces would have something over her, forever. They'd say it was her fault, no matter the truth.

Quietly and completely unconsciously, Robin began to whisper.

'*Lokah Samastah Sukhino Bhavantu ... Lokah Samastah Sukhino Bhavantu ...*'

With an effort, she stopped herself.

I mustn't go mad. I mustn't go mad.

85

Patience in the highest sense means putting brakes on strength.

The I Ching or Book of Changes

Knowing he couldn't remain in the vicinity of Chapman Farm by daylight without getting his car caught on camera, and certain Robin wouldn't be able to reach the perimeter until night fell again, Strike had checked himself into one of the guest cabins of nearby Felbrigg Lodge, the only hotel for miles around. He'd intended to catch a few hours' sleep, yet he, who was usually able to nap on any surface, including floors, found himself far too tightly wound to relax even when lying on the four-poster bed. It felt too incongruous to be lying in a comfortable, genteel room with leaf-patterned cream wallpaper, tartan curtains, a plethora of cushions and a ceramic stag head over the mantelpiece, when his thoughts were this agitated.

He'd talked blithely of 'coming in the front' if Robin was out of contact this long, but the absence of the plastic rock made him fear that she'd been identified as a private detective and had now been taken hostage. Taking out his phone, he looked up satellite pictures of Chapman Farm. There were a lot of buildings there, and Strike thought it odds on that some of them had basements or hidden rooms.

He could, of course, contact the police, but Robin had

voluntarily entered the church and he might have to jump through a lot of procedural hoops to persuade them it was worth getting a warrant. Strike hadn't forgotten that there were also UHC centres in Birmingham and Glasgow to which his partner might have been relocated. What if she became the new Deirdre Doherty, of whom no trace could be found, even though the church claimed she'd left thirteen years previously?

Strike's mobile rang: Barclay.

'What's happening?'

'She didn't show up last night, either.'

'Fuck,' said Barclay. 'What's the plan?'

'I'll give it tonight, but if she doesn't show, I'll call the police.'

'Aye,' said Barclay, 'ye'd better.'

When Barclay had hung up, Strike lay for a while, still telling himself he should sleep while he could, but after twenty minutes he gave up. Having made himself a cup of tea with the kettle provided, he stood for a few minutes looking out of one of the windows, through which he could see a wooden hot tub belonging to his cabin.

His mobile rang again: Shanker.

'What's up?'

'You owe me a monkey.'

'You've got intel on Reaney's phone call?'

'Yeah. It was made from a number wiv area code 01263. Woman contacted the prison, said she was 'is wife and it was urgent—'

'It was definitely a woman?' said Strike, scribbling down the number.

'Screw says it sounded like one. They agreed a time for 'er to call 'im. Claimed she wasn't at 'ome and didn't want 'im 'aving 'er friend's number. 'S'all I could get.'

'All right, the monkey's yours. Cheers.'

Shanker rang off. Glad to have something to do for a few minutes other than agonise about what had happened to Robin, Strike looked up the area code in question. It covered a large area including Cromer, Lion's Mouth, Aylmerton, and even the lodge he was currently sitting in.

Having removed a few cushions, Strike sat down on the sofa, vaping, drinking tea and willing the hours to pass quickly, so he could return to Chapman Farm.

86

Six in the fourth place means:
Waiting in blood.
Get out of the pit.

The I Ching or Book of Changes

Robin had been sitting with Jacob all day. He had, indeed, had a fit: she'd tried to stop him hurting himself against the cot bars, and finally he'd grown limp and she'd laid him gently back down. She'd changed his nappy three times, putting the soiled ones into the black bin bag sitting there for that purpose, and tried to give him water, but he seemed unable to swallow.

At midday she'd been brought food by one of the teenage girls who'd stood vigil outside the temple four nights previously. The girl said nothing to her, and kept her eyes averted from Jacob. Barring this one interruption, Robin was left entirely alone. She could hear people moving around in the farmhouse below, and knew she was only allowed this solitude because it would be impossible for her to creep back down the farmhouse stairs without being apprehended. Her fatigue kept threatening to overwhelm her; several times, she nodded off in the hard wooden chair and jerked awake as she slid sideways.

As the hours wore on, she took to reading pages of the newspaper spread over the floor in an attempt to stay awake.

Thus she learned that the Prime Minister, David Cameron, had resigned after the country had voted to leave the EU, that Theresa May had now taken his place and that the Chilcot Inquiry had found that the UK had entered the Iraq War before peaceful options for disarmament had been exhausted.

The information Robin had been denied for so long, information unfiltered by Jonathan Wace's interpretation, had a peculiar effect on her. It felt as though it came from a different galaxy, making her feel her isolation even more acutely, yet at the same time, it pulled her mentally back towards the outer world, the place where nobody knew what 'flesh objects' were, or dictated what you wore and ate, or attempted to regulate the language in which you thought and spoke.

Now two contradictory impulses battled inside her. The first was allied to her exhaustion; it urged caution and compliance and urged her to chant to drive everything else from her mind. It recalled the dreadful hours in the box and whispered that the Waces were capable of worse than that, if she broke any more rules. But the second asked her how she could return to her daily tasks knowing that a small boy was being slowly starved to death behind the farmhouse walls. It reminded her that she'd managed to slip out of the dormitory by night many times without being caught. It urged her to take the risk one more time, and escape.

She was brought a second bowl of noodles and a glass of water at dinner time, this time by a boy who also kept his gaze carefully averted from Jacob and looked repulsed by the smell in the room, to which Robin had become acclimatised.

Dusk arrived, and Robin had now read almost all of the newspapers lying on the floor. Not wanting to put on the electric light in case it disturbed the child in the cot, she got up and moved to the small dormer window to continue reading an article about Labour leader Jeremy Corbyn. Having finished this, she turned the page over and saw the headline SOCIALITE DIED IN BATH, INQUEST TOLD, before realising that the picture below was of Charlotte Ross.

Robin's gasp was so loud Jacob stirred in his sleep. With one hand pressed over her mouth, Robin read the article, the paper held inches from her eyes in the dying light. She'd just read how much alcohol and how many sleeping pills Charlotte had taken before slitting her wrists in the bath, when there was a soft knock on the attic door.

Robin threw the report about Charlotte back onto the floor and hastened back to her chair as the door opened to reveal Emily, whose head, like her mother's, was freshly shaven.

Emily closed the door quietly. From what Robin could see of her through the rapidly darkening room, she looked apprehensive, almost tearful.

'Rowena – I'm so sorry, I'm really, *really* sorry.'

'What about?'

'I told them you gave me money in Norwich. I didn't want to, but they were threatening me with the box.'

'Oh, that . . . it's OK, I admitted it, too. It was stupid to expect them not to notice.'

'You can go. Jiang's waiting downstairs to escort you to the dormitory.'

Robin stood up and had taken a couple of steps towards the door when something strange happened.

She suddenly knew – didn't guess, or hope, but *knew* – that Strike had just arrived beside the blind spot at the perimeter fence. The conviction was so strong that it stopped her in her tracks. Then she turned slowly to face Emily again.

'Who are Jacob's parents?'

'I don't – we don't . . . you shouldn't ask stuff like that.'

'Tell me,' said Robin.

Robin could just make out the whites of Emily's eyes by

the fading light from the window. After a few seconds Emily whispered,

'Louise and Jiang.'

'Lou—seriously?'

'Yeah . . . Jiang isn't allowed to go with the younger women. He's an NIM.'

'What does that mean?'

'Non-Increasing Male. Some of the men aren't allowed to go with fertile women. I don't think anyone thought Louise could still get pregnant, but . . . then Jacob came.'

'What did you mean, when you told me Daiyu did forbidden things at the farm?'

'Nothing,' whispered Emily, now sounding panicky. 'Forget I—'

'Listen,' said Robin (she knew Strike was there, she was certain of it), *'you owe me.'*

After a couple of seconds' silence, Emily whispered,

'Daiyu used to sneak off instead of doing lessons, that's all.'

'What was she doing, when she sneaked off?'

'She went into the woods, and into barns. I asked her and she said she was doing magic with other people who were pure spirit. Sometimes she had sweets and little toys. She wouldn't tell us where she'd got them, but she'd show us. She wasn't what they say she was. She was spoiled. Mean. Becca saw it all, too. She pretends she didn't—'

'Why did you tell me Daiyu didn't drown?'

'I can't—'

'Tell me.'

'You've got to go,' whispered Emily frantically. 'Jiang's waiting for you.'

'Then talk quickly,' said Robin. *'What made you say Daiyu didn't drown?'*

'Because . . . it was just . . . Daiyu told me she was going to go away with this older girl and live with her.' Emily's voice was full of a strange longing.

'D'you mean Cherie Gittins?'

'How—?'

'Was it Cherie?'

'Yes . . . I was so jealous. We all really loved Cherie, she was like . . . like a real . . . like what they'd call a mother.'

'Where does invisibility come in?'

'How did you—?'

'Tell me.'

'It was the night before they went to the beach. Cherie gave us all special drinks, but I didn't like the taste. I poured mine down the sink. When everyone else was asleep, I saw Cherie helping Daiyu out of the dormitory window. I knew she didn't want anyone to see what she'd done, so I pretended to be asleep, and she went back to bed.'

'She pushed Daiyu out of the window and then went back to bed herself?'

'Yes, but she'll just have been helping Daiyu do whatever she wanted to do. Daiyu could get people in trouble with Papa J and Mazu, if they didn't do what she wanted.'

From downstairs came a shout:

'Rowena?'

'I'm in the bathroom,' Robin shouted. Turning back to Emily, whom she could no longer see in the dark, she said,

'Quickly – did you ever tell Kevin what you saw? Tell me, *please*.'

'Yes,' said Emily. 'Later. Ages later. When I told Becca I'd seen Cherie helping Daiyu out of the window, she said, "You didn't see that, you can't have done. If you couldn't see Daiyu in her bed, it was because she can turn invisible." Becca loved Cherie too. Becca would've done anything for her. When Cherie left, I cried for days. It was like losing – oh God,' said Emily, panicked.

Footsteps were coming along the corridor. The door opened and the light was slapped on. Jiang stood revealed in the doorway, wearing a blue tracksuit. Jacob's eyes opened and he began to whimper. Scowling, Jiang averted his gaze from his son.

'Sorry,' Robin said to Jiang. 'I needed the loo and then I had to tell Emily when I last gave him a drink and changed his—'

'I don't need the details,' snapped Jiang. 'Come on.'

87

Nine in the fourth place means:
Then the companion comes,
And him you can trust.

The I Ching or Book of Changes

As Jiang and Robin walked together down the stairs he said, 'Stinks, that room.'

His eye was flickering worse than ever.

Robin said nothing. Perhaps it was her advanced state of exhaustion, but she seemed to have become a mass of nerves and hypersensitivities: just as surely as she'd known Strike had arrived at the perimeter, she had a sense that the longer she remained in the farmhouse, the worse it would be for her.

As they walked down the last flight of scarlet-carpeted stairs into the hall, Robin heard a gust of laughter, and Wace appeared from a side room, holding a glass of what looked like wine. He was now wearing a silk version of the blue tracksuit worn by ordinary members, his expensive leather slides on his feet.

'Artemis!' he said, smiling as though the previous night hadn't happened, as though he didn't know he'd ordered her to be locked in a box, or that she was now into her thirty-sixth hour without sleep. 'Are we friends again?'

'Yes, Papa J,' said Robin, with what she hoped was adequate humility.

'Good girl,' said Wace. 'One moment. Wait there.'

Oh God, no.

Robin and Jiang waited while Wace entered the study with the peacock blue walls. Robin heard more loud laughter.

'Here we are,' said the smiling Wace, reappearing with Taio. 'Before you rest, Artemis, it would be a very beautiful act of contrition to reaffirm your commitment to our church by spirit bonding with one who has much to teach you.'

Robin's heart began pumping so fast she thought she might pass out. There didn't seem to be enough air in the hall for her lungs to inflate.

'Yes,' she heard herself say. 'All right.'

'Papa J!' came a merry voice, and Noli Seymour came lurching out of the sitting room, flushed, no longer wearing a tracksuit but leather trousers and a tight white T-shirt. 'Oh Lord, sorry,' she giggled, seeing the group.

'There's nothing to apologise for,' said Wace, extending an arm and drawing Noli to his side. 'We're merely arranging a beautiful spirit bonding.'

'Oooh, lucky you, you get Taio, Rowena?' said Noli to Robin. 'If I weren't spirit married . . .'

Noli and Wace laughed. Taio allowed his lips to curl in a smirk. Jiang merely looked sulky.

'Shall we, then?' said Taio to Robin, taking her firmly by the hand. His was hot and damp.

'Jiang,' said Wace, 'go with them, wait outside and escort Artemis to her dormitory afterwards.'

As Robin and the two Wace brothers walked towards the front door, Robin heard Noli say,

'Why d'you call her Artemis?'

She missed Wace's answer in another outburst of laughter from the sitting room.

The night was cool and cloudless, with many stars overhead

and a thin, fingernail moon. Taio led Robin towards the pool of the Drowned Prophet and she knelt down between Daiyu's two brothers.

'The Drowned Prophet will bless all who worship her.'

'I need the bathroom,' Robin said, as she stood up again.

'No you don't,' said Taio, pulling her on.

'I do,' said Robin. 'I just want to pee.'

She was terrified Jiang was going to say 'You were just in the bathroom.' Instead, he said, scowling at his brother,

'Let her bloody pee.'

'Fine,' said Taio. 'Be quick.'

Robin hurried into the dormitory. Most of the women were getting ready for bed.

Robin pushed her way into the bathroom. Marion Huxley was bent over the sink, cleaning her teeth.

In one fluid movement, Robin had stepped up onto the sink beside Marion, and before Marion could shout in surprise, had forced the window open, heaved herself up on the high sill, swung one leg over and then, as Marion screamed, '*What are you doing?*' let herself fall, hitting the ground on the other side so hard she fell over.

But she was up in an instant and running – her only advantage over the Wace brothers, given her present hunger and exhaustion, was how well she knew her way to the blind spot in the dark. Through the pounding in her ears she heard distant shouts. She was over the five-bar gate, and now she was sprinting across the wet field, her breath coming fast and ragged – she was wearing blue now, far harder to see in the dark than white – there was a stitch like a sword wound in her chest but she sped up – and now she could hear Taio and Jiang behind her.

'*Get her – GET HER!*'

She crashed her way into the wood, following the familiar path, leaping over nettles and roots, passing familiar trees –

And in the BMW, Strike saw her coming. Throwing aside the night vision goggles and picking up the foot-long wire cutters, he left the car at a run. He'd got through three strands of barbed wire when Robin screamed,

'They're coming, they're coming, help me—'

He reached over the wall and dragged her with him; her tracksuit bottoms tore on the remaining wire, but she was out onto the road.

Strike could hear the sound of running men.

'How many?

'Two – let's go, please—'

'Get in,' he said, pushing her away, 'just get in the car – GO!' he bellowed, as Taio Wace came bursting through a thicket of trees and ran for the figure silhouetted ahead.

As Taio launched himself at the detective, Strike swung back the heavy metal wire cutters and smashed them into the side of Taio's head. Taio crumpled and the figure behind him skidded to a halt. Before either man could return the attack, Strike was heading for the car. Robin had already started the engine; she saw Taio rise again, but Strike was inside the car; he slammed his foot on the accelerator, and in an exhilarating burst of speed they were driving away, Strike having found a glorious release for his days of anxiety, Robin shaking and sobbing in relief.

88

'Drive, drive, drive,' said Robin frantically. 'They'll see the number plates on the cameras—'

'Doesn't matter if they do, they're fake,' said Strike.

He glanced at her and even in the dim light was appalled at what he saw. She looked a good couple of stone lighter and her swollen face was covered either in dirt or bruises.

'We've got to call the police,' said Robin, 'there's a child dying in there – Jacob, that's who Jacob is, and they've stopped feeding him. I've been with him all day. *We've got to get the police.*'

'We'll call them when we stop. We'll be there in five minutes.'

'Where?' said Robin, alarmed.

She'd imagined travelling straight to London; she wanted to put as many miles as possible between herself and Chapman Farm, wanted to get back to London, to sanity and safety.

'I've got a room in a hotel up the road,' said Strike. 'It'll be the local force we need, if you want police.'

'What if they come after us?' said Robin, looking over her shoulder. 'What if they come looking?'

'Let them come,' growled Strike. 'Nothing would give me greater fucking pleasure than to belt some more of them.'

But when he glanced at her again, he saw naked fear.

'They're not going to come,' he said in his normal voice. 'They've got no authority outside the farm. They can't take you back.'

'No,' she said, more to herself than to him. 'No, I ... I s'pose not ...'

Her sudden re-emergence into freedom was too massive for Robin to absorb in a few seconds. Waves of panic kept hitting her: she was imagining what was happening back at Chapman Farm, wondering how soon Jonathan Wace would know she'd gone. She found it almost impossible to grasp that his jurisdiction didn't extend to this dark, narrow road bordered with trees, or even to the interior of the car. Strike was beside her, large and solid and real, and only now did it occur to her what would have become of her had he not been there, in spite of her absolute certainty that he was waiting.

'This is it,' said Strike five minutes later, as he pulled up in a dark car park.

As Strike turned off the engine, Robin undid her seat belt, half rose from her seat, threw her arms around him, buried her face in his shoulder and burst into tears.

'*Thank you.*'

''S all right,' said Strike, putting his arms around her and speaking into her hair. 'My job, innit ... you're out,' he added quietly, 'you're OK now ...'

'I know,' sobbed Robin. 'Sorry ... sorry ...'

Both were in very inconvenient positions in which to hug, especially as Strike still had his seat belt on, but neither let go for several long minutes. Strike gently rubbed Robin's back, and she held him in a tight grip, occasionally apologising while his shirt collar grew wet. Instead of recoiling when he pressed his lips to the top of her head, she tightened her hold on him.

'It's all right,' he kept saying. 'It's OK.'

'You don't know,' sobbed Robin, 'you don't know . . .'

'You can tell me later,' said Strike. 'There's plenty of time.'

He didn't want to let her go, but he'd dealt with enough traumatised people in the army – had indeed been one of those people himself, after the car in which he'd been travelling had been blown up, taking half his leg with it – to know that being asked to re-live calamity in its immediate aftermath, when what was really needed was physical comfort and kindness, meant a debrief ought to wait.

They walked together across the lawn towards the low guest house, one of three in a row, Strike's arm around Robin's shoulders. When he unlocked the door and stood back to let her in, she passed across the threshold in a state of disbelief, her eyes roving from the four-poster to the multitude of cushions Strike had found excessive, from the kettle standing on a chest of drawers to the television in the corner. The room seemed unimaginably luxurious: to be able to make yourself a hot drink, to have access to news, to have control of your own light switch . . .

She turned to look at her partner as he closed the door.

'Strike,' she said, with a shaky laugh, 'you're so *thin*.'

'*I'm* fucking thin?'

'D'you think I could eat something?' she said timidly, as though asking for something unreasonable.

'Yeah, of course,' said Strike, moving to the phone. 'What d'you want?'

'Anything,' said Robin. 'A sandwich . . . anything . . .'

She moved restlessly around the room as he dialled the number of the main hotel, trying to convince herself she was genuinely here, touching surfaces, gazing around at the leaf-strewn wallpaper and the ceramic deer head. Then, out of one of the windows, she spotted the hot tub, the water looking black by night and reflecting the trees behind it, and she seemed to see the eyeless child rising again from the depths of the baptismal pool. Strike, who was watching her, saw her flinch and turn away.

'Food's on its way,' he told her, having hung up. 'There are biscuits by the kettle.'

He closed the curtains as she picked up two plastic-wrapped biscuits and ripped them open. Having devoured them in a few mouthfuls, she said,

'I should phone the police.'

The call, as Strike could have predicted, wasn't straightforward. While Robin sat on the edge of the bed, explaining to the emergency operator why she was calling and describing the condition and location of the boy called Jacob, Strike scribbled 'We're here: Felbrigg Lodge, Bramble guest house' onto a bit of paper and passed it to her. Robin duly read out this address when asked for her location. While she was still talking, Strike texted Midge, Barclay, Shah and Pat.

Got her. She's OK.

He wasn't convinced the second sentence was true, except in the very broadest sense of lacking a disabling physical injury.

'They're going to send someone out to talk to me,' Robin told Strike at last, having hung up. 'They said it might be an hour.'

'Gives you time to eat,' said Strike. 'I've just been telling the others you're out. They've been crapping themselves about you.'

Robin started crying again.

'Sorry,' she gasped, for what felt like the hundredth time.

'Who hit you?' he asked, looking at the yellowish purple marks on the left side of her face.

'What?' she said, trying to stem the flood of tears. 'Oh . . . Will Edensor . . .'

'Wh—?'

'I told him his mother was dead,' said Robin wretchedly. 'It was a mistake . . . or . . . I don't know if it was a mistake . . . I was trying to get through to him . . . that was a couple of days ago . . . it was that or have sex with him . . . sorry,' she said again, 'so much has happened these last few days . . . it's been—'

She gasped.

'Strike, I'm so sorry about Charlotte.'

'How the hell did you know about that?' he said, amazed.

'I saw it in an old newspaper this afternoon . . . it's awful . . .'

'It's what it is,' he said, far less interested in Charlotte at this moment than in Robin. His mobile buzzed.

'That's Barclay,' he said, reading the text. 'He says "thank fuck."'

'Oh, Sam,' sobbed Robin, 'I saw him a week ago . . . was it a week ago? I watched him, in the woods . . . I should've gone then, but I didn't think I had enough to leave . . . sorry, I don't know why I keep c-crying . . .'

Strike sat down next to her on the bed and put his arm around her again.

'Sorry,' she said, sobbing as she leaned into him, 'I'm really sorry—'

'Stop apologising.'

'It's just . . . relief . . . they locked me up in a b-box . . . and Jacob . . . and the Manifestation was—' Robin gasped again, 'Lin, what about Lin, did you find her?'

'She's not in any of the hospitals Pat called,' said Strike, 'unless she was admitted under another name, but—'

His mobile buzzed again.

'That's Midge,' he said, and he read the text aloud. '"Thank fuck for that."'

The phone buzzed a third time.

'Shah. "Thank fuck." What d'you say we get them all thesauruses for Christmas?'

Robin started to laugh, and found she couldn't stop, though tears were still dribbling out of her eyes.

'Hang on,' said Strike, as his phone buzzed yet again. 'We've got an outlier. Pat says, "Is she really OK?"'

'Oh . . . I love Pat,' said Robin, her laughter turning immediately to sobs again.

'She's sixty-seven,' said Strike.

'Sixty-seven what?'

'That's exactly what I said when she told me. Sixty-seven years old.'

'S-seriously?' said Robin.

'Yeah. I haven't sacked her, though. Thought you'd be pissed off at me.'

There was a knock on the door, and Robin jumped as violently as if she'd heard gunshots.

'It's only your brandy,' said Strike, getting to his feet.

When he'd taken the glass from the helpful woman from the hotel, handed it to his partner and sat back down on the bed beside her, Strike said,

'In other news: Littlejohn was a plant. From Patterson Inc.'

'Oh my God!' said Robin, who'd just gulped down some brandy.

'Yeah. But the good news is, he'd rather work for us, and he assures me he's very trustworthy and loyal.'

Robin laughed harder, though she didn't seem able to stop her eyes streaming. Strike, who was deliberately talking about life outside Chapman Farm rather than interrogating her on what had happened inside it, laughed too, but he'd silently registered everything Robin had so far told him about her last few days: *they locked me in a box. It was that or have sex with him. And the Manifestation was . . .*

'And Midge has been fucked off at me because I thought she and Tasha Mayo might be getting overfamiliar.'

'*Strike!*'

'Don't bother, Pat's already told me off. She knew another lesbian once, so it's very much her area of expertise.'

There might be an edge of hysteria to Robin's laughter, but Strike, who knew the value of humour in the wake of horror, and the necessity of emphasising that Robin had rejoined the outside world, continued to fill her in on what had been happening with the agency while she'd been away, until the woman from the hotel knocked on the door again, this time carrying soup and sandwiches.

Robin drank a few mouthfuls of soup as though she hadn't seen food for days, but after a couple of minutes she laid down her spoon and pushed the bowl onto the bedside table.

'Is it all right if I just . . . ?'

Drawing her legs up onto the bed, she fell sideways onto the pillow and was instantly asleep.

Strike got carefully off the bed so as not to wake her and moved to an armchair, no longer grinning. He was worried: Robin seemed far more fragile than any of her letters had suggested and through the ripped portion of her tracksuit trousers he could see raw skin on her right knee, which looked as though she'd been walking on it. He supposed he should have anticipated the dramatic weight loss and the profound exhaustion, but the hysteria, the unbridled fear, the strange reaction to the view of the hot tub, the ominous fragments of information, all added up to something more serious than he'd expected. What the fuck was 'the box' she'd been locked in?

And why did she say the only alternative to getting punched in the face had been coerced sex with their client's son? He knew his partner to be physically brave; indeed, there'd been more than one occasion on which he'd have called her recklessly so. Had he not had confidence in her, he'd never have let her go undercover at Chapman Farm, but now he felt he should have put one of the men in there instead, should have overruled Robin's request to do the job.

The sound of a car made Strike get to his feet and peer through the curtains.

'Robin,' he said quietly, moving back to the bed, 'the police are here.'

She remained asleep, so he tentatively shook her shoulder, at which she woke with a start and looked wildly at him, as though he was a stranger.

'Police,' he said.

'Oh,' she said, 'right ... OK ...'

She struggled back into a sitting position. Strike went to open the door.

89

Six in the fourth place means:
Grace or simplicity?
A white horse comes as if on wings.
He is not a robber,
He will woo at the right time.

The I Ching or Book of Changes

The two Norfolk officers were both male: one older, balding and stolid, the other young, skinny and watchful, and they spent a full eighty minutes taking Robin's statement. Strike couldn't blame them for wanting as full an account as possible of what Robin was alleging, given that pursuing an investigation would mean securing a warrant to gain entry to a compound owned by a wealthy, highly litigious organisation. Nevertheless, and even though he himself would have acted similarly under the circumstances, he was irritated by the slow, methodical questioning and the painstaking clarification of every minute detail.

'Yes, on the top floor,' said Robin, for the third time. 'End of the corridor.'

'And what's Jacob's surname?'

'It should be either Wace or Birpright ... Pirbright, sorry,' said Robin, who was struggling to remain alert. 'I don't know which – but those are his parents' surnames.'

Strike could see the men's eyes travelling from her ripped tracksuit with its UHC logo to the bruising on her face. Doubtless her story seemed very strange to them: she'd admitted being punched in the jaw, but said she didn't want to press charges, had brushed off enquiries about the injury to her knee, kept insisting that she simply wanted them to rescue the child who was dying in an upstairs room, behind double doors carved with dragons. They'd cast suspicious looks in Strike's direction: was the large man watching the interview in silence responsible for the bruising? Robin's explanation that she was a private detective from the Strike and Ellacott agency in London had been treated, if not with overt suspicion, then with a certain reserve: the impression given was that this would all need verifying, and that what might be accepted without question in the capital would by no means be taken at face value in Norfolk.

At last, the officers appeared to feel there was no more to be gleaned tonight, and took their leave. Having seen them out into the car park, Strike returned to the room to find Robin eating the sandwich she'd temporarily abandoned.

'Listen,' said Strike, 'this was the only free room. You can have the bed, I'll put two chairs together or something.'

'Don't be stupid,' said Robin. 'I'm with Ryan, you're with ... whassername? ... Bougie ...'

'True,' said Strike, after a slight hesitation.

'So we can share the bed,' said Robin.

'Murphy's in Spain,' said Strike, slightly resentful he had to mention the man.

'I know,' said Robin. 'He said in his last l ... ' She yawned '... letter.'

After finishing her sandwich, she said,

'You haven't got anything I can sleep in, have you?'

'Got a T-shirt,' said Strike, pulling it out of his kit bag.

'Thanks ... I really want a shower.'

Robin got to her feet and headed into the bathroom, taking Strike's T-shirt with her.

He sat back down in the armchair in which he'd listened to Robin's police interview, prey to a number of conflicting emotions. Robin seemed less disorientated for having eaten, had a cat nap and spoken to the police, which was a relief, though he couldn't help wondering whether a dispassionate observer would still think he was taking advantage of the situation if he did, indeed, share a bed with Robin. He couldn't imagine Murphy being happy about it – not that keeping Murphy happy was any concern of his.

The sound of the shower now running in the bathroom gave rise to thoughts he knew he oughtn't to be thinking. Getting to his feet again, he cleared away Robin's used crockery and cutlery, noisily clinking both together as he placed them back on their tray, which he placed outside the door for collection. He then did some wholly unnecessary rearranging of his personal effects, put his phone on to charge and hung up his jacket, taking care to clatter the hangers together as he did so: nobody could accuse him of sitting in a chair, listening to the shower and picturing his business partner naked.

Robin, meanwhile, was soaping her scraped knees, breathing in the smell of the unfamiliar shower gel, and beginning to grasp that she really wasn't in Chapman Farm any more. Onerous as the police interview had been, it had somehow grounded her. Standing under the hot water, grateful for the privacy, the lockable door and the thought of Strike outside, she reflected that there were worse things than what she'd been through: there was being a child who wasn't strong enough to run, who had no friends to rescue him and was therefore utterly at the mercy of the regime at Chapman Farm. In spite of her bodily fatigue, she now felt nervily awake again.

Having towelled herself dry, she took a squeeze of Strike's toothpaste, cleaned her teeth as best she could with the corner of a flannel and put on Strike's T-shirt, which was the length of a mini dress on her. Then, wishing she could burn them immediately, she took the folded UHC tracksuit and trainers back into the bedroom, put them down on an armchair and, without noticing that Strike was avoiding looking at her, got into bed. The glass of brandy he'd ordered was still sitting on the bedside table. She reached for it and took another large gulp: it contrasted unpleasantly with the taste of toothpaste, but she liked the way it burned her throat.

'You all right?' said Strike.

'Yes,' said Robin, sitting back on the pillows. 'God, it's so . . . so *good* to be out.'

'Glad to hear it,' said Strike heartily, still avoiding looking at her.

'They're evil,' said Robin, after taking another swig of brandy, '*evil*. I thought I knew what that was . . . we've seen stuff, you and me . . . but the UHC is something else.'

Strike sensed her need to talk, but he was worried about tipping her back into the state of distress she'd been in before talking to the police.

'You don't have to tell me now,' he said, 'but I'm taking it this last week was bad?'

'Bad,' said Robin, whose colour had come back after a few gulps of brandy, 'is'n understatement.'

Strike sat back down in the armchair, and Robin began to relate the events of the last ten days. She didn't dwell on how scared she'd been, and she omitted certain details – Strike didn't need to know she'd peed herself in the box, didn't have to hear that mere hours ago she'd been convinced she was about to face rape, for the second time in her life, didn't need to know exactly where Jonathan Wace had put his hands, the night they'd been alone together, in the peacock blue study – but the bald facts were sufficient to confirm some of her partner's worst fears.

'Fuck,' was his first word, when she'd finished talking. 'Robin, if I'd—'

'It had to be me,' she said, correctly anticipating what he was about to say. 'If you'd put Barclay in there, or Shah, they'd never have got as much. You'd have to be a woman to see everything I did.'

'That box – that's a fucking torture technique.'

'It's a good one,' said Robin, with a small laugh, now flushed from the brandy.

'If—'

'I chose to go in. This isn't on you. I wanted it.'

'But—'

'At least we know, now.'

'Know what?'

'The lengths they're prepared to go to. I can imagine Wace crying as he pressed the trigger of a gun. "I wish I didn't have to do this."'

'You think they killed Kevin Pirbright?'

'I do, yes.'

Strike decided not to debate the point, tempting though it was. Letting Robin vent was one thing, theorising about murder was a step too far at nearly midnight, when she was pink-cheeked from alcohol but hollow-eyed with exhaustion.

'You're sure about sharing the—?'

'Yez, no problem,' said Robin, now slurring slightly.

So Strike repaired to the bathroom himself, emerging ten minutes later in boxer shorts and the T-shirt he'd worn all day. Robin appeared to have fallen asleep where she sat.

Strike turned off all the lights and eased himself into bed, trying not to wake her, but when he'd finally settled his full weight onto the mattress, Robin stirred, and groped in the darkness for his hand. Finding it, she squeezed.

'I knew you were there,' she murmured drowsily, half-asleep. 'I *knew* you were there.'

Strike said nothing, but continued to hold her hand until, five minutes later, she gave a long sigh, released him, and rolled over onto her side.

PART SEVEN

Fu/Return (The Turning Point)

Going out and coming in without error.
Friends come without blame.
To and fro goes the way.
On the seventh day comes return.
It furthers one to have somewhere to go.

The I Ching or Book of Changes

90

Now it is the time of struggle.
The transition must be completed.

The I Ching or Book of Changes

Five days after Robin had left Chapman Farm, Strike set out from the office at midday to meet Sir Colin Edensor for a full update on the UHC case. Over Robin's protestations, Strike had insisted she take a full week off work, because he remained concerned about both her mental and physical health, and was glad to hear that her parents had come down from Yorkshire to stay with her.

Sir Colin, who'd only just returned from a week's holiday with his eldest son's family, naturally wanted a full update on Robin's discoveries without delay. As he was coming into central London for a charity board meeting, he offered Strike lunch at Rules restaurant in Covent Garden. While Strike feared the comfortable glamour of the old restaurant would provide an incongruous backdrop for revelations that were certain to dismay the retired civil servant, he had no objection to being offered a full cooked lunch and therefore accepted. However, he resolved to resist pudding, and chose to walk to Covent Garden from the office, in tribute to his continued commitment to weight loss.

He'd been en route for five minutes, enjoying the sunshine, when his mobile rang and he saw Lucy's number.

'Hey,' he said, answering, 'what's up?'

'I've just got back from the specialist, with Ted.'

'Oh Christ, sorry,' said Strike, with a familiar gut-twist of guilt. 'I should've called you. It's been a very busy week. What's the news?'

'Well, the specialist was very nice and very thorough,' said Lucy, 'but he definitely doesn't think Ted's fit to live alone any more.'

'OK,' said Strike. 'Good to know going back to the old house isn't an option. What was Ted's reaction? Did he take it all in?'

'He sort of nodded along while we were there, but he's literally just told me he thinks he ought to be getting home. I've found him packing twice in the last few days, although if you distract him he's completely happy to come downstairs and watch TV or have something to eat. I just don't know what to do next.'

'Is Greg agitating to get him out of the spare room?'

'Not *agitating*,' said Lucy defensively, 'but we've talked it through and I suppose it *would* be hard having Ted to live with us while we're both working. Ted would still be alone for most of the day.'

'Luce, I think it's got to be a care home in London.'

He expected his sister to start crying, and wasn't disappointed.

'But Joan would've *hated*—'

'What she'd have hated,' said Strike firmly, 'would be for Ted to break his neck trying to get down those stairs, or for him to wander off and get lost again because nobody's keeping an eye on him. If we sell the house in Cornwall, we'll be able to get him into a good place up here where both of us can visit.'

'But his *roots* – Cornwall's all he's ever—'

'It's not all he's ever known,' said Strike. 'He was a Red Cap for seven years, he went all over the bloody place. I want to know he's being fed properly, and that someone's keeping an eye on his health. If he moves up here, we can see him regularly and take him out. It's a bloody nightmare, him being five and a half hours away, every time something goes wrong. And before you say he'll miss all his friends, half of them are dead, Luce.'

'I know, I just . . .'

'This is the answer. You know it is.'

He could tell that somewhere beneath Lucy's distress was relief that he was taking charge, that the decision wasn't hers alone. After some more reassurance and encouragement, she bade him farewell, sniffing but sounding calmer. This left Strike with a few minutes in which to relegate his own family problems to the back of his mind, and focus on those of the Edensors.

Rules, which Strike had never visited before, lay in Maiden Lane and had an impressive old-world frontage. Upon telling the maître d' who he was meeting, Strike was shown through the restaurant, of which the walls were bestrewn with antlers, Victorian prints and antique clocks, to a red velvet booth in which Sir Colin, kindly faced as ever, was sitting.

'Very good of you to meet at my convenience,' said Sir Colin as they shook hands. He was scanning Strike's face rather anxiously for some intimation of what he was about to hear.

'Very grateful for the lunch,' said Strike, easing himself into the booth. 'Did you have a good holiday?'

'Oh, yes, it was wonderful spending some time with the grandchildren,' said Sir Colin. 'Constantly thinking how much Sally would have . . . but anyway . . .'

A waiter arrived to offer menus and drinks. Both men declined the latter.

'So, your partner's out of Chapman Farm?' said Sir Colin.

'She is, yes,' said Strike, 'and she's got us a lot of good information. Firstly,' said Strike, who could see no way of cushioning the worst blow and thought it was best delivered immediately, 'Will had no idea your wife's died.'

Sir Colin's hand went to his mouth.

'I'm sorry,' said Strike. 'I know that must be hard to hear.'

'But we wrote,' said Sir Colin shakily, lowering his hand. 'We wrote *multiple times*.'

'Robin found out that church members are pressured to sign a declaration that they don't want to be given letters from the outside. This seems to be something the church does with people who've progressed up a certain number of levels to what they call pure spirit – in other words, people they think they've really got their hooks into, and whose isolation they want to cement. From the moment the declaration's signed, the church withholds all correspondence. It's supposedly viewable upon request, but from what Robin's told me, asking to read letters would put a church member in line for immediate demotion to manual labour and possibly punishment.'

Strike fell silent while four rotund men in expensive suits passed the booth, then went on,

'Someone at the church – probably Mazu Wace, who Robin says is in charge of correspondence – informed Will that you'd written to say his mother was ill. Robin thinks this was probably to cover themselves, in case of legal action from you. She thinks Mazu will have encouraged Will to see this as a ruse to manipulate him, and asked whether he wanted further news. If he'd said "yes", Robin believes he'd have been punished, possibly severely. In any case, we know no further information about your wife was passed on. When Robin told Will his mother was dead, he was very distressed and went immediately to the church superiors to ask to write to you. I presume you haven't received any such letter?'

'No,' said Sir Colin faintly. 'Nothing at all.'

'Well, that's the last contact with Will Robin had before she escaped, but—'

'What d'you mean, "escaped"?'

'She found herself in a dangerous situation and had to run for it, by night.'

A waiter now appeared to take their food order. Strike waited until the man was out of earshot before saying,

'In slightly better news, Will's definitely having doubts about the church. Robin witnessed Will challenging a Principal on church doctrine, and Jonathan Wace personally informed Robin that Will keeps getting stuck on step six to pure spirit, which means accepting the church's teaching, rather than understanding it.'

'That's the Will I know,' said Sir Colin, looking slightly more encouraged.

'Yeah, that's obviously good,' said Strike, wishing he didn't have to immediately dash any faint hopes he'd raised, 'but, ah, there's something else Robin found out, which explains why Will hasn't followed through on these doubts, and left. I wouldn't tell you this if we didn't have very strong reasons for believing it, but he appears to have fathered a child at Chapman Farm.'

'Oh God,' said Sir Colin, aghast.

'Obviously, without a DNA test we can't be absolutely sure,' said Strike, 'but Robin says the little girl looks like Will, and from observing his behaviour with the child and from conversations she overheard in there, she's certain he's the father.'

'Who's the mother?'

Wishing he had almost any other answer Strike said,

'She's called Lin.'

'Lin . . . not the one Kevin wrote about? With the stammer?'

'That's the one, yes,' said Strike.

Neither man spoke aloud what Strike was sure was upper-most in Sir Colin's mind: that Lin was the product of Jonathan Wace's rape of Deirdre Doherty. Strike now dropped his voice. Little though he wanted to alarm Edensor further, he felt it would be unethical to withhold the next bit of information.

'I'm afraid it's likely Lin was underage when she gave birth to Will's daughter. According to Robin, Lin doesn't look much older than fifteen or sixteen now, and as far as she could judge, the daughter's around two years old.'

Strike couldn't entirely blame Sir Colin for burying his face in his hands. He then took a deep breath, let his hands fall, straightened up in his seat and said quietly,

'Well, I'm glad James isn't here.'

Remembering Sir Colin's eldest son's rage at Will during their only previous meeting, Strike silently concurred.

'I think it's important to remember that it's a punishable offence at Chapman Farm to refuse to "spirit bond" – in other words, to refuse sex. Will and Lin's relationship has to be seen in that context. They'd both been groomed to believe spirit bonding wasn't just acceptable, but righteous.'

'Even so—'

'The church doesn't celebrate birthdays. Lin herself might not know how old she is. Will might have believed she was of age when it happened.'

'Nevertheless—'

'I don't think Lin would want to press charges,' said Strike, again lowering his voice as a portly middle-aged couple were led past their table. 'Robin says Lin's fond of Will and she loves the daughter they had together. Will seems to feel warmly towards Lin, too. Robin thinks that as Will's doubts about the church have grown, his awareness of what's considered immoral in the outside world has begun to reassert itself, because he's now refusing to have sex with her.'

The waiter now arrived with their food. Strike glanced with some envy at Sir Colin's steak and kidney pudding; he'd ordered sea bass, and he was becoming increasingly bored of fish.

Sir Colin ate a single mouthful, then put down his knife and fork again, looking queasy. Keen to cheer up a client for whom he felt a great deal more empathy than others who'd hired the agency, Strike said,

'Robin's got us a few solid leads, though, and I'm hopeful at least one of them will lead to building a case against the church. Firstly, there's a small boy called Jacob.'

He outlined Jacob's precarious state of health, the neglect and lack of medical treatment he was enduring, then described Robin's interview with the police, hours after leaving the church compound.

'If the authorities manage to gain entry to the farm and examine the boy, which they may already have done, we'll have something very significant against the UHC. Robin's expecting to hear back from the police any time now.'

'Well, that's certainly – not good news, not for the poor child,' said Sir Colin, 'but if we can only put the Waces on the back foot for a change—'

'Exactly,' said Strike. 'And Jacob's only one of the leads Robin got. The next is Lin herself. She was removed from the farm after having an adverse reaction to some plants she was eating in an attempt to give herself a miscarriage – this wasn't Will's child,' Strike added. 'As I told you, he's been refusing to sleep with her now.'

'What d'you mean by "removed"?'

'She didn't want to leave, doubtless because of her daughter, but they took her forcibly off the premises. We haven't been able to trace her yet. No hospital's admitting to having her. Of course, she might be at one of the other UHC centres, but I've done a bit of research and my hunch is that she's at a residential clinic run by Dr Zhou in Borehamwood.'

'I know about that place,' said Sir Colin. 'Pattersons got one of their people in there to have a look around, but it didn't turn up anything of value. It seems to be a glorified spa, no obvious wrongdoing and nobody tried to recruit their detective to the UHC.'

'Even so, it seems the most likely place for them to have hidden Lin. As I say, she was in need of urgent medical care and I don't think they'd want her anywhere she couldn't be watched over by a senior member of the church, because she's a definite flight risk – Robin overheard her suggesting to Will that they do "what Kevin did".'

'If we can trace Lin and get her out of their clutches, we'd have a very valuable witness. Robin thinks Lin would value getting custody of her daughter over her loyalty to the church, and if we can get the child out, Will might well follow. But I want to tread very carefully in trying to locate Lin, because we don't want to spook the UHC into hiding her somewhere unreachable. If you're happy to bear the expense, I'd like to get one of our own people into that clinic – not Robin, obviously, but possibly our other female detective.'

'Yes, of course. I have a duty of care to the girl. She's the mother of my granddaughter, after . . .'

His eyes brimmed with tears.

'I *do* apologise . . . every time we meet I seem to . . .'

Their waiter now returned to the table to ask Sir Colin whether there was something wrong with his steak and kidney pudding.

'No,' said Sir Colin weakly, 'it's very good. Just not particularly hungry . . . *so* sorry,' he added to Strike, wiping his eyes as the waiter retreated again. 'Sally really craved a granddaughter, you know. We run to boys a lot in both our families . . . but for it to happen under these circumstances . . .'

Strike waited for Sir Colin to compose himself before continuing.

'Robin got a third possible lead: one of Kevin Pirbright's sisters.'

Strike now told the story of Emily's aborted escape attempt in Norwich.

'It would mean more costs, I'm afraid,' Strike said, 'but I suggest putting one of our people in Norwich, to attempt a direct approach to Emily the next time she goes out collecting money for the church. Robin's given us a good physical description. She and Emily struck up a rapport in there and I think, if one of our operatives mentions Robin, Emily might be persuaded to leave with them.'

'Yes, I'd be happy for you to try that,' said Sir Colin, whose virtually untouched pie was growing cold in front of him. 'I'd feel as though I were doing something for Kevin, if I helped his sister get out . . . well,' said Sir Colin, who was clearly shaken but trying to focus on the positive, 'your partner's done an astounding job. She's achieved more in four months than Pattersons managed in eighteen.'

'I'll tell her you said that. It'll mean a lot to her.'

'She couldn't come to lunch?' asked Sir Colin.

'No,' said Strike. 'I want her to take some time off. She went through a lot in there.'

'But you wouldn't want her to testify,' said Sir Colin, with no hint of a question in his voice. It was a relief to Strike to have an intelligent client, for a change.

'Not as things stand. The church's lawyers would have a field day with Robin's lack of impartiality, given that she was paid to go in there and gather dirt on them. The culture of fear in the church is such that I think they'd close ranks and terrify anyone at Chapman Farm who could back up her account. If she starts talking about supernatural events and torture techniques without corroboration—'

'Torture techniques?'

'She was shut up in a box for eight hours, unable to move out of a bent kneeling position.'

As far as Strike could tell in the flattering, diffused lighting, Sir Colin now turned rather pale.

'Kevin told me he was tied to trees at night and so on, but he never mentioned being locked in a box.'

'I think it's reserved for the very worst transgressions,' said Strike, choosing not to tell Sir Colin that his son, too, had been subjected to the punishment.

He now hesitated, considering how best to frame what he wanted to say next. He was loath to ruin the very slight sense of hope he'd induced in his client, and only too aware that Sir Colin had already committed to tripling the fees he was paying the agency.

'Robin's leads have definitely put us in a far better position than we were in,' he said. 'If we're lucky, and we get Lin and Emily out, and they're prepared to talk, and if there's a police investigation into Jacob, we'll definitely land a few heavy punches on the church.'

'But those are significant "ifs",' said Sir Colin.

'Right,' said Strike. 'We've got to be realistic. The Waces are adept at batting off critics. They could choose a few scapegoats to take the blame for everything Robin, Lin and Emily allege – and that's assuming the other two are prepared to testify. They might not be up to taking the stand against a church that's intimidated and coerced them for most of their lives.'

'No,' said Edensor, 'I can see we'd better not count our chickens yet.'

'I keep going back to something Wace's eldest daughter said to me,' said Strike. 'Words to the effect of "It's like cancer. You've got to cut the whole thing out, or you'll be back where you started."'

'But how do you cut out something that's metastasised across continents?'

'Well,' said Strike, 'there might be a way. Did Kevin ever talk to you in any depth about Daiyu?'

'Daiyu?' said Sir Colin, looking puzzled. 'Oh, you mean the Drowned Prophet? No more than he put in the blog and emails I gave you. Why?'

'Because the one sure-fire way of bringing down the church would be to dismantle the myth of the Drowned Prophet. If we could smash the central pillar of their whole belief system—'

'That's surely rather ambitious?' said Sir Colin. As Strike had feared, he now looked slightly mistrustful.

'I've been looking into what actually happened on that beach in Cromer and I've got a lot of questions. I've now tracked down the key witness: Cherie Gittins, the woman who took Daiyu to the beach where she drowned. I'm hoping to interview her shortly. And then we've got Kevin's murder.'

At that moment, the waiter came to collect their plates and offer the pudding menu. Both men declined, but asked for coffee.

'What about Kevin's murder?' said Sir Colin, when the waiter had gone.

'I'm afraid,' said Strike, 'I think it far more likely that the UHC had Kevin killed, than that he was dealing drugs.'

'But—'

'Initially, I was of your opinion. I couldn't see why they'd need to shoot him. They've got excellent lawyers and he was undoubtedly unstable and easy to discredit. But the longer the investigation's gone on, the less I've bought the drug-dealing theory.'

'Why? What have you found out?'

'Most recently, I've heard an unsubstantiated allegation that there have been guns at Chapman Farm. The source was second-hand,' Strike admitted, 'and not particularly trustworthy, so I'll have to try and confirm his account, but the fact remains I think it would be unwise to underestimate the kinds of contacts the UHC have made over the last thirty years. There were no guns found in the raid on the farm in eighty-six, but since then they've had at least one violent criminal living at the farm. All they needed was a recruit who knew where to lay hands on guns illegally – assuming Wace didn't already have that knowledge.'

'You really think they murdered Kevin because of his book?' said Sir Colin, sounding sceptical.

'I don't think the book, in and of itself, was a problem, because a journalist I interviewed called Fergus Robertson had already accused the UHC of pretty much everything Kevin was alleging: physical assault, sexual abuse and supernatural mind games. The church went after Robertson hard with lawyers, but he's still alive.'

Their coffees arrived.

'So what was the motive, if not the book?' said Sir Colin.

'Kevin told you he was piecing things together during the last weeks of his life, didn't he? Things he thought he'd suppressed?'

'Yes – as I told you, he was becoming increasingly erratic and troubled. I deeply regret that I didn't offer more support—'

'I don't think any amount of support could have stopped him being shot. I think Kevin pieced together something about Daiyu's drowning. The church would've been able to bully a publisher into deleting unsubstantiated allegations, but they'd lost the power to bully Kevin into silence in his daily life. What if he blabbed his suspicions to the wrong person?'

'But, as you say, this is guesswork.'

'Were you aware Patterson didn't hand over all their evidence when you fired them?'

'No,' said Sir Colin. 'I wasn't.'

'Well, I've got hold of a taped interview with Kevin they'd recorded covertly, five days before he was shot. It's a botched job: most of what he said isn't audible, which is why they didn't bother giving it to you. In that tape, Kevin told Patterson's operative he was intending to meet somebody from the church to "answer for it". What "it" is, I don't know, but he was talking a lot about Daiyu during the conversation. And you never visited Kevin's bedsit, did you?'

'No – I wish I had.'

'Well, he'd scribbled all over the walls – and somebody had gouged a few words out of the plaster. It might've been Kevin himself, of course, but there's a possibility his killer did it.

'Robin got some strange information about Daiyu's movements the night before she supposedly drowned, from Kevin's sister Emily. What Emily said tallied with something Kevin had written on his bedsit wall, about a plot. As a matter of fact,' said Strike, picking up his coffee cup, 'Emily doesn't believe Daiyu's dead.'

'But,' said Sir Colin, still frowning, 'that's incredibly unlikely, surely?'

'Unlikely,' said Strike, 'but not impossible. As it happens, alive or dead, Daiyu was worth a lot of money. She was the sole beneficiary of her biological father's will, and he had a lot to leave. Where there's no body, there's got to be a doubt – which is why I want to talk to Cherie Gittins.'

'With respect,' said Sir Colin, with the polite but firm air Strike imagined he'd once brought to discussions of hare-brained political projects during his professional life, 'I'm more hopeful that your partner's leads will achieve my immediate aim – that of getting Will out of Chapman Farm – than that anyone can bring the entire religion down.'

'But you don't object to me interviewing Cherie Gittins?'

'No,' said Sir Colin slowly, 'but I wouldn't want this investigation to devolve into a probe into Daiyu Wace's death. After all, it was ruled an accident, and you've no proof it wasn't, have you?'

Strike, who couldn't blame his client for this scepticism, reassured Sir Colin that the agency's aim remained extracting his son from the UHC. The lunch concluded amicably, with Strike promising to pass on any new developments promptly, particularly as regarded the police investigation into the mistreatment of Jacob.

Nevertheless, it was the deaths of Daiyu Wace and Kevin Pirbright about which Strike was thinking as he set off back to Denmark Street. Sir Colin Edensor was correct in saying that Strike still had no concrete evidence to support his suspicions. It might indeed be overambitious to think that he'd be able to destroy the myth of the Drowned Prophet, which had survived uncontested for twenty-one years. But after all, thought the detective, still hungry after his meagre meal of fish, yet noticing how much more easily he was walking without the several stone he'd already shed, it was sometimes surprising what concerted effort in pursuit of a worthwhile goal could achieve.

91

Nine in the fourth place means:
Joyousness that is weighed is not at peace.

The I Ching or Book of Changes

While Strike was having coffee with Sir Colin Edensor, Robin was drinking a mug of tea at the table in her sitting room, her laptop and notebook open in front of her, hard at work and savouring the temporary peace. The man upstairs, whose music was usually audible, was at work, and she'd managed to get her parents out of the flat by asking them to do some food shopping.

Robin's adjustment from life at Chapman Farm to her flat in London was proving far more difficult than she'd anticipated. She felt agitated, disorientated and overwhelmed, not only by her freedom, but also by her mother's constant vigilance which, while kindly meant, was aggravating Robin, because it reminded her of the unrelenting surveillance she'd just escaped. She realised now, when it was too late, that what she'd really needed on returning to London was silence, space and solitude in which to reground herself in the outside world, and to concentrate on the long report for Strike in which she was tabulating everything she hadn't yet told him about life at Chapman Farm. Guilt about her parents' four months of anxiety on her behalf had made her agree to their visit but, much as she loved them, all she wanted now was their return to Yorkshire. Unfortunately, they were threatening to stay another week, 'to keep you company' and 'to look after you'.

With a sinking heart, she now heard the lift doors out on the landing. As she got up to let her parents back in, the mobile on the table behind her started to ring.

'Sorry,' she said to her mother, who was laden with heavy Waitrose bags, 'I need to get that, it might be Strike.'

'You're supposed to be taking time off!' said Linda, a comment Robin ignored. Sure enough, on returning to her phone she saw her partner's number, and answered.

'Hi,' said Robin, as Linda said, deliberately loudly,

'Don't be long, we've bought cakes. You should be eating and putting your feet up.'

'Bad time?' said Strike.

'No,' said Robin, 'but could you give me two minutes? I'll ring you back.'

She hung up and headed to the doorway of the cramped kitchen, where her parents were putting the shopping away.

'I'm just going to nip out and get some fresh air,' said Robin.

'What aren't we allowed to hear?' said Linda.

'Nothing, he's just giving me an update I asked for,' said Robin, keeping her tone light with some difficulty. 'I'll be back in ten minutes.'

She hurried out of the flat, keys in hand. Having reached Blackhorse Road, which offered exhaust fumes rather than clean air, she called Strike back.

'Everything OK?'

'It's fine, I'm fine,' said Robin feverishly. 'My mother's just driving me up the wall.'

'Ah,' said Strike.

'I've told her about a *hundred times* it was my choice to go Chapman Farm, and my choice to stay in that long, but—'

Robin bit back the end of the sentence, but Strike knew perfectly well what she'd been about to say.

'She thinks it's all on me?'

'Well,' said Robin, who hadn't wanted to say it, but was yearning to unburden herself, 'yes. I've *told* her I had to argue you into letting me do the job, and that you wanted me to come out earlier, I've even told her she should be bloody grateful you were there when I ran for it, but she ... *God,* she's infuriating.'

'You can't blame her,' said Strike reasonably, remembering how appalled he'd been at Robin's appearance when he'd first seen her. 'It's your parents, of course they're going to be worried. How much have you told them?'

'That's the joke! I haven't told them a *tenth* of it! I had to say I didn't get enough food, because that's obvious, and they know I'm not sleeping very well –' Robin wasn't about to admit she'd woken herself up the previous evening by yelping loudly in her sleep '– but given what I *could* have said – and I think Ryan's been winding them up, telling them how worried he was, all the time I was in there. He's trying to get an earlier flight home from Spain, but honestly, the last thing I need is for him and my mother to get together ... oh, and they've put up a huge poster of Jonathan Wace on the side of a building just up the road.'

'Advertising his Super Service at Olympia? Yeah, it's everywhere.'

'I feel like I can't get *away* from ... sorry, I know I'm ranting,' said Robin, exhaling as she leaned up against a convenient wall and watched the passing traffic. At least she couldn't see Wace's face from here. 'Tell me about Colin Edensor. How did he take it all?'

'About as well as could be expected,' said Strike. 'Full of praise for you and all the leads you got. He's approved funds to try and find Lin and get Emily out, but he's far less enthused by the idea of debunking Daiyu's myth. Can't say that was a surprise. I know full well it's a long shot.'

'The police still haven't got back to me about Jacob.'

'Well, getting warrants take time,' said Strike, 'although I'd have thought they'd have been in touch by now, given it's a dying child.'

'Well, exactly. Listen, Strike, I really think I could—'

'You're taking this week off,' said Strike. 'You need to catch up on sleep and get some food into you. A doctor would probably say it should be longer.'

'Listen, you know how Jiang said he'd recognised someone who'd been at Chapman Farm a long time ago? Did I tell you that, I can't remember?'

'You did,' said Strike, who considered it a bad sign that Robin's conversation was jumping around so much, 'yes.'

'OK, so I've been trying to find out who that could be, and I think—'

'Robin—'

'—it must be either Marion Huxley or Walter Fernsby. Jiang made it sound like they'd *just* come back, and they were the only ones of the recent intake who're old enough to have been there years ago. So I've been trying to trace—'

'This can wait,' said Strike loudly, talking over her. 'This can all wait.'

'For God's sake, you sound like my mother! She keeps interrupting me when I'm trying to look things up, like I'm some – some geriatric convalescent.'

'I don't think you're a geriatric convalescent,' said Strike patiently, 'I just think you need a break. If either Walter or Marion were there before, we can look into it when you're—'

'Don't say "better", I'm not ill. Strike, I want to get that bloody church, I want to find something on them, I want—'

'I know what you want, and I want the same thing, but I don't want my partner having a breakdown.'

'I'm not—'

'Get some rest, eat some food and calm the fuck down. Listen,' he added, before she could respond. 'I'm going to drive to Thornbury on Monday to try and interview Cherie Gittins – or Carrie Curtis Woods, as she is now. She'll be back from her holidays, her husband should be at work, and I think she'll be home with her kids, because there's no indication of her having a job on her Facebook page. D'you fancy coming with me to interview her?'

'Oh God, yes,' said Robin fervently. 'That'll give me an excuse to get rid of my parents, telling them I'm going back to work. Much more of this will tip me over the edge. What are you up to for the rest of the day?'

'On the Franks this evening,' said Strike. 'Everything's in place for them to make their big move and they still haven't bloody done it. Wish they'd hurry up.'

'You *want* them to try and abduct Tasha Mayo?'

'Honestly, yes. Then we can get the bastards arrested. Did I tell you one of them's been done for stalking and the other one for flashing? And that they're using a different surname to the one they used to have? A good reminder to all of us that oddballs aren't necessarily harmless.'

'I've been thinking about that constantly since I got out of Chapman Farm,' said Robin. 'Thinking about how the church has got so big, and how they've got away with it, all this time. People have just let them get on with it . . . a bit weird, but harmless . . .'

'If you'd met my mother,' said Strike, who was now waiting to cross Charing Cross Road, 'you'd have seen the purest example of that mindset I've ever come across. It was a point of pride with her to like anyone who was a bit off. In fact, the more off, the better, which is how I ended up with Shanker as a stepbrother – speaking of whom, he rang me last night to say Jordan Reaney's back in the nick, but they're keeping him on suicide watch.'

'Are you thinking of interviewing him again?'

'Don't think there's any point. I think he'll keep shtum even if Shanker's mates beat the shit out of him again. That's a very frightened man.'

'Frightened of the Drowned Prophet?' said Robin, to whom Strike had related the story of his encounter with Reaney on their drive back to London from Felbrigg Lodge.

'There wasn't a Drowned Prophet when Reaney was in the church, Daiyu was still alive for most of his time there. No, the more I think about it, the more I think what's scaring Reaney is a gate arrest.'

'Meaning . . . ?'

'That he's done something he's worried he could be nicked for the moment he leaves jail.'

'But he can't have had anything to do with Daiyu's drowning. You told me he overslept.'

'I know, but he could have done any number of dodgy things that had nothing to do with Daiyu. He might be worried he'll be done for what was going on in those Polaroids.'

'You think he was one of them?'

'Dunno. He could be the guy with the skull tattoo. He's got a devil on his upper arm now, which could be covering up an old marking. Skull Tattoo was sodomising a man we know had a low IQ and possibly brain damage, so Reaney might be scared he's going to be done for rape.'

'Oh God,' said Robin quietly, 'it's terrible, all of it.'

'Of course, if it *was* him, Reaney could argue in court he was forced to do it,' said Strike. 'If the church really has got guns, someone could've had one trained on those kids in the pig masks and forced them to perform. I can understand why Reaney wouldn't want the episode publicised, though. Rapists and paedos are bottom of the food chain, even among hardened cons.

'Anyway,' said Strike, remembering a little late that he wasn't supposed to be encouraging his partner to focus on violence and depravity, but encouraging her to keep her mind on pleasanter matters, 'go and eat cake and watch a film with your mother or something. That should keep her happy.'

'She's probably hidden my laptop while I've been talking to you. I'll let you know if the police get back to me about Jacob.'

'Do,' said Strike, 'but in the meantime—'

'Doughnuts and romcoms,' sighed Robin. 'Yes, all right.'

92

The power of the inferior people is growing.
The danger draws close to one's person; already there
are clear indications . . .

The I Ching or Book of Changes

Relieved by the prospect of getting back to the investigation on Monday, Robin took the lift back upstairs to her flat. In the sitting room she quietly closed her laptop, with the intention of resuming work once her parents were safely tucked into the sofa bed that evening, then accepted a fresh mug of tea and a chocolate éclair from her mother.

'What did he want?' Linda said, sitting herself down on the sofa.

'To tell me to take it easy and eat cake, so he'd be happy about this,' she added, indicating the éclair.

'So Ryan's coming home on—?'

'Next Sunday, unless he gets an earlier flight,' said Robin.

'We do like Ryan,' said Linda.

'I'm glad,' said Robin, pretending she hadn't heard the unspoken *but not Strike.*

'He's been very good about keeping us updated,' added Linda, again with a silent addendum: *unlike Strike.* 'D'you think he'd like children?'

Oh, for God's sake.

'No idea,' lied Robin. Ryan had in fact made it perfectly clear he'd like children.

'He always asks after Annabel,' said Linda warmly, referring to Robin's niece. 'Actually – we've got news. Jenny's pregnant again.'

'Fantastic!' said Robin, who liked her sister-in-law, but wondered why this information had so far been withheld from her.

'And,' said Linda, taking a deep breath. '*Martin's* girlfriend's pregnant, too.'

'I didn't even know he had a girlfriend,' said Robin. Martin, who came immediately after her in birth order, was the only son who still lived with their parents, and had a patchy job history.

'They've only been together three months,' said Linda.

'What's she like?'

Linda and Michael looked at each other.

'*Well,*' said Linda, and the monosyllable rang with disapproval.

'She likes a drink,' said Michael.

'She's called Carmen,' said Linda.

'Is Martin pleased?'

'We don't really know,' said Linda.

'Might be the making of him,' said Robin, who wasn't convinced, but felt it was best to be optimistic in front of her parents.

'That's what I said,' said Michael. 'He's talking about getting his HGV licence. Long-distance lorry driving, you know.'

'Well, he's always liked driving,' said Robin, choosing not to mention the many near misses Martin had had, full of drink and bravado.

'Like you,' said her father, 'with that advanced driving qualification.'

Robin had taken her advanced driving course in the months after the rape that had finished her university career, when command of a vehicle had given her back a sense of safety and control. Relieved to be offered a conversational topic that was neither children nor her career, Robin began to talk about the old Land Rover, and whether it would pass its next MOT.

The afternoon passed relatively peacefully because Robin found a documentary on TV which fortunately caught both her parents' interest. Itching to return to her laptop but afraid of disturbing the precarious calm, Robin watched mindlessly until, with evening drawing in, she suggested a takeaway, and ordered a Deliveroo.

The pizzas had only just been delivered when the buzzer beside the flat door sounded.

'Robin Ellacott?' said a tinny male voice, when Robin pressed the intercom.

'Yes?'

'This is PC Blair Harding. Could we come in?'

'Oh, yes, of course,' said Robin, pressing the button to let them through the outer door downstairs.

'What do the police want with you?' said Linda, looking alarmed.

'It's OK,' said Robin soothingly. 'I've been waiting for this – I gave a statement about something I witnessed at Chapman Farm.'

'What thing?'

'Mum, it's fine,' said Robin, 'it's to do with someone who wasn't getting proper medical attention. The police said they'd get back to me.'

Rather than be drawn into further explanations, Robin stepped out onto the landing to wait for the police to arrive, wondering how strange the police might think her if she asked for the update on Jacob downstairs, in their car.

The lift doors opened a couple of minutes later to reveal a white male officer and a far shorter Asian policewoman, whose black hair was pulled back into a bun. Both looked serious, and Robin felt suddenly anxious: was Jacob dead?

'Hi,' she said apprehensively.

'Robin Ellacott?'

'Yes – is this about Jacob?'

'That's right,' said the policewoman, glancing at the open door to Robin's flat. 'Is that where you live?'

'Yes,' said Robin, disconcerted by the sternness of the officers' expressions.

'Can we go in?' said the female officer.

'Yes, of course,' said Robin.

Linda and Michael, who'd both got to their feet, looked worried to see the two officers entering the flat after their daughter.

'These are my parents,' said Robin.

'Hi,' said the male officer. 'I'm PC Harding and this is PC Khan.'

'Hello,' said Linda uncertainly.

'You obviously know what this is about,' said PC Khan, looking at Robin.

'Yes. Jacob. What's happened?'

'We're here to invite you down to the station, Mizz Ellacott,' said PC Harding.

Robin, who was experiencing a slow-motion lift-drop of the stomach without knowing exactly why, said,

'Can't you just tell me what's happened here?'

'We're inviting you to an interview under caution,' said PC Khan.

'I don't understand,' said Robin. 'Are you saying I'm under arrest?'

'No,' said PC Harding. 'This would be a voluntary interview.'

825

'What about?' said Linda, before Robin could get the words out.

'We've had an accusation of child abuse,' said PC Harding.

'Against – against *me*?' said Robin.

'That's right,' said PC Harding.

'*What?*' exploded Linda.

'It's a voluntary interview,' said PC Harding again.

Robin was vaguely aware that Linda was talking, but couldn't take in what she was saying.

'Fine,' said Robin calmly. 'Let me get my coat.'

However, the first thing she did was to go back to the table, pick up a pen and scribble down Strike's mobile number, the only one she knew by heart other than her own.

'Phone Strike,' she told her father, pressing the number into his hands.

'Where are you taking her?' Linda demanded of the officers. 'We want to come!'

PC Khan gave the name of the police station.

'We'll find it, Linda,' said Michael, because it was obvious to everyone that Linda intended either to force her way into the police car or ride bumper-to-bumper after it.

'It'll be fine,' Robin reassured her parents, pulling on her coat. 'I'll sort this out. *Phone Strike,*' she added firmly to her father, before picking up her keys and following the police out of the flat.

93

*The seeds are the first imperceptible beginning
of movement, the first trace of good fortune (or
misfortune) that shows itself. The superior man
perceives the seeds . . .*

The I Ching or Book of Changes

At the precise moment Robin was getting into a police car on Blackhorse Road, Strike was sitting in his BMW in Bexleyheath watching the Frank brothers climbing into their old van, which was parked a short distance from their block of flats. Having let the van set off, Strike set off in pursuit, then called Midge.

'Wotcha.'

'Where's Mayo?'

'With me. Well, not *with* me – I'm waiting for her to come out of her gym.'

'I told her to vary her bloody routine.'

'It's the only evening she's got off from the theatre, and it's less crowded this—'

'I think tonight might be the night. They've just got in the van with what look like balaclavas in their hands.'

'Oh, fook,' said Midge.

'Listen, if Mayo's up for it – and only if she is – I say proceed as normal. Let this happen. I'll pull Barclay off Toy Boy

827

to make sure we've got enough manpower and we'll get the fuckers in the attempt.'

'She'll be up for it,' said Midge, who sounded excited. 'She just wants this over.'

'Good. Keep me posted on your location. I've got eyes on them now and I'll let you know if anything changes. Gonna ring Barclay.'

Strike hung up, but before he could contact Barclay, an unknown number called him. Strike refused the call and pressed Barclay's number instead.

'Where are you?'

'Outside Mrs Moneybags' house. She was gettin' pretty fuckin' frisky wi' Toy Boy on the way up the street.'

'Well, I need you in Notting Hill, pronto. Looks like the Franks are planning their big move. Balaclavas, both of them in the van—'

'Great, I fancy punchin' someone. The mother-in-law's staying. See ye there.'

No sooner had Barclay cut the call, Strike's phone rang again. He jabbed at the dashboard with his finger, his eyes still on the van now separated from his BMW by a Peugeot 108.

'Who's been pissing off the UHC, then?' said an amused voice.

'Who's this?'

'Fergus Robertson.'

'Oh,' said Strike, surprised to hear from the journalist, 'you. Why're you asking?'

'Because your Wikipedia page just tripled in length,' said the journalist, who sounded as though he'd had a couple of drinks. 'I recognise the house style. Beating girlfriends, fucking clients, drink problem, daddy issues – what've you got on them?'

'Nothing I can tell you yet,' said Strike, 'but that doesn't mean I won't have something eventually.'

Whichever Frank brother was driving had either realised he

was being followed, or was inept: he'd just earned several blasts of the horn from the Peugeot for indicating late. Robertson's news, though deeply unwelcome to Strike, would have to be processed later.

'Just thought I'd let you know,' said the journalist. 'We had an agreement, though, right? I get the story if—'

'Yeah, fine,' said Strike. 'I've got to go.'

He hung up.

The Franks definitely seemed to be heading for Notting Hill, Strike thought, as they entered the Blackwall Tunnel. The same unknown number as before called again. He ignored it because the Franks had just sped up, and while this might mean they were worried about missing Tasha on her way back from the gym, Strike remained concerned that they'd realised he was following them.

His phone rang yet again: Prudence, his sister.

'Fuck's sake,' Strike growled at the speaker, 'I'm busy.'

He let the call go to voicemail, but Prudence called back. Again, Strike ignored the call, although vaguely perturbed; Prudence had never done this before. When she called back a third time, Strike picked up.

'I'm kind of in the middle of something,' he told her. 'Could I call you back later?'

'This will be short,' said Prudence. To his surprise, she sounded angry.

'OK, what's up?'

'I asked you *very clearly* to stay away from my client who was in the UHC!'

'What are you talking about? I haven't been near them.'

'Oh, really,' said Prudence coldly. 'She's just told me somebody approached her online, probing her for information. She's absolutely distraught. Whoever it was threatened her with the name of a woman she knew in the church.'

'I don't know who your client is,' said Strike, eyes on the van ahead, 'and I haven't been threatening anyone online.'

'Who else would have tracked her down and told her he knew she'd met this woman? *Corm?*' she added, when he didn't answer immediately.

'If,' said Strike, who'd just done some rapid mental deduction, 'she had a Pinterest page—'

'So it *was* you?'

'I didn't know she was your client,' Strike said, now aggravated. The unknown number that kept calling was trying to get through again. 'I saw her drawings and left a couple of comments, that's all. I had no idea who was behind the acc— I've got to go,' he said, cutting the call, as the Franks sped through a red light, leaving Strike stuck behind a Hyundai with a large dent in its rear.

'FUCK,' bellowed Strike, watching impotently as the Franks sped out of sight.

The unknown number called yet again.

'Fuck off,' said Strike, refusing the call and instead ringing Midge, who answered immediately. 'Where are you?'

'Tasha's showering.'

'OK, well, don't let her leave the gym until you hear from me. Barclay's on his way, but the fuckers just ran a red light and I've lost them. They might've known I was tailing them. Stay where you are until I give the word.'

The Hyundai moved off and Strike, now choosing his own route to Notting Hill, called Barclay.

'I'm nearly there,' said the Scot.

'I'm not, I lost the bastards. They might've spotted me.'

'You sure? They're bloody thick.'

'Even morons get it right occasionally.'

'Think they'll abort?'

'Possibly, but we should assume it's happening. Midge and

Mayo are waiting in the gym until I tell them to go. Call me if you spot the van.'

Mercifully, the unknown number that kept pestering Strike appeared to have given up. He drove as fast as he could without incurring a speeding ticket in the direction of Notting Hill, trying to guess where the Franks might attempt to grab Tasha Mayo, and was ten minutes from her house, the sun now setting in earnest, when Barclay called.

'They're here,' he said. 'Parked in that cul-de-sac two blocks away from the gym. They've got their fuckin' balaclavas on.'

'Where are you?'

'Opposite pavement, fifty yards down.'

'All right, I'm going to call Midge and get back to you.'

'What's happening?' said Midge, answering on the first ring.

'They're parked two blocks from the gym in that cul-de-sac on the left as you head towards her house. Are you with Mayo?'

'Yes,' said Midge.

'Put her on.'

He heard Midge say something to the actress, then Tasha's nervous voice.

'Hello?'

'You know what's happening?'

'Yes.'

'You've got a choice. I can pick you up from the gym and take you straight home, but if we do that, they're going to try it another day, or—'

'I want it to end tonight,' said Tasha, but he could hear the tension in her voice.

'I swear you won't be in any danger. They're idiots and we'll be ready for them.'

'What d'you want me to do?'

'When I give the word, you'll leave the gym alone. I want to get them on film trying to get you into that van. We won't let it happen, but I can't guarantee you won't have an unpleasant few seconds and possibly a bruise or two.'

'I'm an actress,' said Tasha, with a shaky little laugh. 'I'll just pretend someone's going to yell "cut".'

'That would be me,' said Strike. 'All right, hand me back to Midge.'

When Tasha had done so, Strike said,

'I want you to leave the gym now, alone, walk straight up the cul-de-sac and take up a good vantage point behind their van, but somewhere where they can't see you until things hot up. I want this on camera in case it doesn't get picked up on CCTV.'

'Could Barclay not do that and I'll—?'

'What did I just say?'

'Fine,' said Midge huffily, and rang off.

Strike turned into the road where Tasha's gym was, parked, then called Barclay.

'Move so you'll be walking towards Tasha when they come at her. I'll be behind her. I'll let you know when she's on her way.'

'Righto,' said Barclay.

Strike watched Midge leaving the gym in the gathering darkness. He could just make out Barclay, ambling along on the other side of the road. He waited until both had vanished from view, then got out of the BMW and phoned Tasha.

'Head for the door but don't come out until I tell you. You'll have me right behind you, and Barclay ahead. Pretend to be texting. Midge is already behind their van. They've chosen a place where they shouldn't see either of us coming.'

'OK,' said Tasha nervously.

'Right,' said Strike, now fifteen yards from the gym entrance, 'go.'

Tasha emerged from the gym, a bag over her shoulder, head bowed over her phone. Strike followed, keeping a short distance between himself and the actress. His mobile rang again: he pulled it out, refused the call and shoved it back into his pocket.

Tasha was approaching the cul-de-sac. As she passed beneath a street light, Strike heard the van doors open.

The balaclavaed men were running, the foremost with a large mallet in his gloved hand. As he broke into a run, Strike heard Barclay bellow 'OI!' and Tasha's scream.

Barclay's shout had caused the mallet-holder to check – Strike's hands closed on Tasha's shoulders – as he pushed her sideways, the unwieldy weapon missed her by three feet; Strike, too, dodged it, his left hand already in a fist, which hit the wool-covered jaw so hard his victim let out a high-pitched squeak and fell backwards onto the pavement, where he lay momentarily stunned, his arms outstretched like Christ.

'Stay *down*,' snarled Strike, smacking his own victim again as he attempted to scramble to his feet. Barclay's man was gripping the Scot round the waist in a fruitless attempt to evade the former's punches, but as Strike watched, Frank Two's legs gave way.

'Search the van,' Strike called to Midge, who'd come running out of her hiding place, her mobile still held up, recording, 'see if there are restraints – *stay fucking down*,' he added, hitting the first brother in the head again.

'AND YOU,' yelled Barclay, whose own Frank had just attempted to punch him in the balls and who'd got a boot in the diaphragm in return.

'Oh my God,' muttered Tasha, who'd picked up the mallet. She looked from Barclay's groaning victim, who was lying in the foetal position, to Strike's motionless one. 'Is he – have you knocked him out?'

'No,' said Strike, because he'd just seen the balaclavaed man readjust his position slightly. 'He's faking, silly bastard. It's called reasonable force, arsehole,' he added to the prone figure, as Midge came running back with several black plastic security restraints.

'Might not need tae call the police ourselves,' said Barclay, glancing across the road at a dogwalker with a cocker spaniel, who stood immobile, transfixed by the scene.

'All the better,' said Strike, who was forcing his struggling Frank's wrists together, the man having stopped pretending to be unconscious. This done, Strike pulled off the balaclava to see the familiar high forehead, squint and thinning hair.

'Well,' said Strike, '*that* didn't go the way you thought it would, did it?'

In an unexpectedly high voice, the man said,

'I want my social worker!' which surprised Strike into a loud guffaw.

'There ye go, dickhead,' said Barclay, who'd successfully restrained his own man and unmasked him, at which point the younger brother started to cry.

'I didn't do nothing. I don't understand.'

'Get tae fuck,' said Barclay, and looking over at Strike he added, 'Nice footwork. 'Specially fur a bloke who's only got one o' them.'

'Cheers,' said Strike. 'Let's—' His mobile started to ring again, '*for fuck's sake*. Somebody keeps – *what?*' he said angrily, answering the unknown number.

Barclay, Midge and Tasha watched as Strike's face became blank.

'Where?' he said. 'All right ... I'm on my way now.'

'What's happened?' said Midge, as Strike hung up.

'That was Robin's father. She's been taken in for questioning.'

'*What?*'

'Can you handle these two without me, until the police get here?'

'Yeah, of course. We've got a mallet,' said Midge, pulling it out of Tasha's hands.

'Fair point,' said Strike. 'I'll let you know what's going on once I find out.'

He turned and set off as fast as his now throbbing right knee would allow.

94

There are secret forces at work, leading together those who belong together. We must yield to this attraction; then we make no mistakes.

The I Ching or Book of Changes

It took Strike an hour to reach the police station to which Robin had been taken. As he slowed down, looking for a place to park, he passed three figures who appeared to be arguing outside the square stone building. Once he'd found a parking space and walked back towards the station, he recognised the threesome as Robin and her parents.

'Strike,' said Robin in relief, when she spotted him.

'Hello,' said Strike, holding out his hand to Michael Ellacott, a tall man in horn-rimmed glasses. 'Sorry I didn't pick up sooner. I was in the middle of something I couldn't drop.'

'What's happened?' said Robin.

'The Franks made their move. What's going—?'

'We're about to take Robin home,' said Linda. 'She's been through—'

'For God's sake, Mum,' said Robin, shrugging off the hand Linda had laid on her arm, 'I need to tell Cormoran what's just happened.'

'He can come back to the flat,' said Linda, as though this was a favour Strike didn't deserve.

'I know he can come back to *my* flat,' said Robin, who was rapidly reaching breaking point with her mother, 'but that's not what's going to happen. He and I are going for a drink. Take my keys.'

She thrust them into her father's hands.

'You can grab a taxi, and Cormoran can drop me off later. Look – there's a cab now.'

Robin raised her hand, and the black taxi slowed.

'I'd rather—' began Linda.

'*I'm going for a drink with Cormoran. I know* you're worried, Mum, but there's nothing you can do about this. *I've* got to sort it out.'

'You can't blame your mum for being worried,' said Strike, but judging by Linda's frigid expression, this effort to ingratiate himself was unsuccessful. Once her parents had been successfully bundled into the cab, Robin waited until the vehicle had drawn away before letting out a huge sigh of relief.

'Un-bloody-believable.'

'In fairness—'

'I really, *really* need a drink.'

'There's a pub up there, I just passed it,' said Strike.

'Are you limping?' said Robin, as they set off.

'It's fine, I twisted my knee a bit when I punched Frank One.'

'Oh God, did—?'

'It's all good, police will have got them by now, Mayo's safe – tell me what happened at the station.'

'I'm going to need alcohol first,' said Robin.

The pub was crowded, but a small corner table became available a minute after their entrance. Strike's bulk, always useful in such situations, ensured that other would-be sitters were blocked from taking it before Robin could.

'What d'you want?' he asked Robin, as she sank onto a banquette.

'Something strong – and could you get me some crisps? I was about to eat a pizza when the police arrived. I haven't had anything since mid-afternoon.'

Strike returned to the table five minutes later with a neat double whisky, half a pint of lager for himself and six packets of salt and vinegar crisps.

'Thank you,' said Robin fervently, reaching for her glass.

'Right, tell me what happened,' said Strike, lowering himself onto an uncomfortable stool, but Robin had thrown back half the neat whisky so fast she got some in her windpipe and had to cough for a minute before she could talk again.

'Sorry,' she gasped, her eyes watering. 'Well, the Norfolk police have been to the farm. Jonathan and Mazu were completely bemused as to why the police wanted to search the top floor of the farmhouse, but led them up there—'

'And there was no Jacob,' guessed Strike.

'Correct. There was nothing in the end room but some old suitcases. They searched the whole top floor but he wasn't there, but when the police asked where Jacob was, Jonathan said, oh, you want *Jacob,* and took them to him . . . except it wasn't Jacob.'

'They showed them a different child?'

'Exactly. He answered to Jacob and told them a nasty lady called Robin—'

'He used your real name?'

'Yes,' said Robin hopelessly. 'Vivienne must have talked. I answered accidentally to "Robin" one day – I passed it off as a nickname and I'm sure she believed me at the time, but I s'pose – anyway, the fake Jacob told the police I'd taken him into a bathroom and . . . and done things to him.'

'What things?'

'Asked him to pull his pants down and show me my willy. He claims that when he wouldn't do it, I hit him round the head.'

'Shit,' Strike muttered.

'That's not all. They've got two adult witnesses saying I was rough with the children at the farm and kept trying to take them off on my own. The police wouldn't tell me who they are, but I said, if it was Taio or Becca, they had good reason to want me incriminated on a child abuse charge. I explained I was there to investigate the church. I had the feeling Harding – that's the man – thought I was cocky or something, coming from our agency.'

'There's a bit of that about,' said Strike. 'Patterson's an old mate of Carver's, as I found out from Littlejohn. Were the police recording the interview?'

'Yes.'

'How did it end?'

'They told me they've got no further questions at the moment,' said Robin. 'I think the female officer believed me, but I'm not sure about Harding. He kept going back over the same ground, trying to make me change my story, and he got quite forceful at one point. I asked them whether anyone was going to go back to the farm and find the real Jacob, but obviously, as I'm now a person of suspicion, they weren't going to tell me that. What the *hell* have the Waces done with that boy? What if—?'

'You've already done as much for Jacob as you can,' said Strike. 'With luck, you've worried the police enough to make them do another search. Eat your crisps.'

Robin ripped open one of the packets and did as she was told.

'I already knew the church must've identified us,' said Strike. 'Fergus Robertson just called me. Apparently my Wikipedia page has been given a UHC makeover.'

'Oh no,' said Robin.

'It was inevitable. Someone found that plastic rock, and Taio got a good look at me at the perimeter fence before I hit him. Now we've just got to try and limit the damage.'

'Have you read the Wikipedia stuff about you?'

'Not yet, I haven't had time, but Robertson gave me a good idea of what's on there. I might need a legal letter to get it taken down. Matter of fact, I know just the bloke I can ask for advice.'

'Who?'

'Andrew Honbold. He's a QC. Bijou's partner.'

'I thought you and Bijou were—?'

'Christ, no, she's a fucking nutter,' said Strike, forgetting he'd pretended he was still seeing Bijou when he and Robin had been at Felbrigg Lodge. 'Honbold's fairly well disposed to me at the moment and as defamation's his speciality—'

'He's well disposed to you?' said Robin, thoroughly confused. 'Even though—?'

'He thinks Bijou and I had nothing more than a couple of drinks and she's not going to tell him different, not when she's pregnant with his kid.'

'Right,' said Robin, who was finding this onslaught of information dizzying.

'Murphy booked an early flight yet?' said Strike, who hoped not.

'No, he hasn't managed to get one,' said Robin. 'So it'll be Sunday.'

'And he'll be all right with you heading to Thornbury on Monday, will he?'

'Yes, of course,' said Robin, ripping open a second pack of crisps. 'He's back at work himself Monday morning. Mind you, he might ditch me once he finds out I'm facing child abuse charges.'

'You're not going to be charged,' said Strike firmly.

Easy for you to say, thought the shaken Robin, but aloud she said,

'Well, I hope not, because I found out this afternoon I'm soon going to have another two nieces or nephews. I'd rather not be barred from ever seeing them ...'

95

The undertaking requires caution . . . the dark nature
of the present line suggests that it knows how to
silence those who would raise the warning.

The I Ching or Book of Changes

To Robin's enormous relief, her parents left for Yorkshire at midday on Sunday. This enabled her to finally complete the report about Chapman Farm she'd prepared for Strike. He'd now sent her a similar document, giving her all the information he'd found out while she'd been away. Robin was still reading this when Murphy arrived, straight from the airport.

She'd forgotten not only how good looking he was, but how kind. Though Robin had attempted to push her considerable worries aside in an effort to make the reunion a happy one, Ryan's questions, which were mercifully posed without her mother's hectoring undertone of accusation and outrage, elicited far more information than Linda had received about her daughter's long stay at Chapman Farm. Robin also told Murphy what had happened when she was interviewed by PCs Khan and Harding.

'I'll find out what's going on there,' said Murphy. 'Don't worry about that.'

Slightly tipsy – alcohol was affecting her far more strongly after her long period of abstinence and her weight loss – Robin entered the bedroom. She'd bought condoms prior to Ryan's arrival, having had an enforced break from the contraceptive pill over the last four months. Sex, which at Chapman Farm had been an almost constant danger rather than a pleasure, was as welcome a release as the wine, and temporarily obliterated her anxiety. As she lay in Murphy's arms afterwards, her brain slightly fuzzy from alcohol and the tiredness she'd felt ever since she'd returned to London, he lowered his mouth to her ear and murmured,

'I realised something while you were away. I love you.'

'I love you, too.'

Caught off guard, she'd said the words automatically, as she'd done hundreds of times in the years she'd spent with Matthew. She'd said them even when she'd no longer meant them, because that was what you did when there was a wedding ring on your finger and you were trying to make a marriage work, even though the pieces were falling apart in your hands, and you didn't know how to put them back together. Unease stirred in her alcohol-blunted brain. Had she just lied, or was she overthinking?

Murphy held her even closer, murmuring endearments, and Robin hugged him back and responded in kind. Even though Robin was dazed with wine and tiredness, she remained awake for half an hour after Murphy fell asleep. Did she love him? Would she have said it unprompted? She'd been truly happy to see him, they'd just had great sex and she was immensely grateful for his sensitivity and tact in the conversation about Chapman Farm, even if she'd left out some of the worst bits. But was what she felt love? Perhaps it was. Still ruminating, she sank into dreams of Chapman Farm, waking with a gasp at five in the morning, believing herself to be back in the box.

Murphy, who hadn't meant to stay the night because he

was due back at work the next day, had to leave the flat at six to return home and change. Robin, who'd arranged to pick Strike up in the Land Rover for their long drive to Thornbury, was dismayed by how relieved she felt not to have much time to talk to her boyfriend.

When she pulled up outside Wembley station, where she'd agreed to meet Strike at eight, she saw him already there, vaping while waiting.

'Morning,' he said, getting into the car. 'How're you feeling?'

'Fine,' said Robin.

While she looked slightly better rested than she had a week previously, she was still pale and drawn.

'Murphy get back all right?'

'Well, his plane didn't crash, if that's what you mean,' said Robin, who really didn't want to talk about Murphy at the moment.

Though surprised by this slightly caustic response, Strike was perversely encouraged: perhaps Robin and Murphy's mutual attraction had petered out during four months of enforced separation? With the aim of emphasising that while Murphy might not appreciate her, he certainly did, he said,

'So, I've read your report. Bloody good job. Good work on Fernsby and Huxley, as well.'

Robin's online research, completed in the interval between her parents leaving and Ryan arriving, had enabled her to send Strike a long list of universities at which Walter had worked, the names of his ex-wife and two children, and the titles of his two out-of-print books.

As for Marion, Robin had discovered that she'd been raised as a Quaker and had been very active in the church until abandoning it for the UHC. Robin had also found the names and addresses of her two daughters.

'Fernsby seems a restless kind of bloke,' said Strike.

'I know,' said Robin. 'Academics don't usually move around that much, do they? But there were no start and finish dates, so it's hard to know whether there was a period in between jobs he could have spent at the farm.'

'And Marion deserted the family undertakers,' said Strike.

'Yes,' said Robin. 'She's a bit pathetic. Utterly besotted with Jonathan Wace, but relegated to the laundry and the kitchen most of the time. I think her dream would be to become a spirit wife, but I don't think there's much chance. Bodies aren't supposed to matter in there, but trust me, Wace isn't sleeping with any women his own age. Not widows of undertakers, anyway – maybe if another Golden Prophet came along, he would.'

Strike wound down the window so he could continue vaping.

'I don't know whether you saw,' he said, reluctant to introduce the subject but feeling it necessary, 'but the UHC have been putting in more hours on Wikipedia. You've, ah, got your own page now.'

'I know,' said Robin. She'd found it the previous afternoon. It alleged she went to bed with any man from whom she wanted to elicit information, and that her husband had divorced her on account of these multiple infidelities. She hadn't mentioned the existence of the Wikipedia page to Murphy. It might be irrational, but the baseless allegations had still made Robin feel grubby.

'But I'm on it,' said Strike. 'Honbold's been very helpful. He put me in touch with a lawyer who's going to fire off some letters. I checked again this morning and Wikipedia's already flagged both pages as unreliable. Just as well, because the UHC keeps adding more. Did you see the bit that went live last night, saying we team up with grifters and fantasists who're after pay-offs?'

'No,' said Robin. This had evidently been added after Murphy arrived at her flat.

'There are links to a couple of websites listing all the scumbags who're helping to attack noble charitable enterprises. Kevin Pirbright, the Graves family, Sheila Kennett and all three Doherty siblings are listed. They say the Graves family neglected and mistreated Alexander, Sheila bullied her husband and that the Dohertys are drunks and layabouts. They also say Kevin Pirbright sexually abused his sisters.'

'Why would they attack Kevin, now?'

'Must be worried we talked to him before he died. They haven't bothered smearing Jordan Reaney; s'pose he's done a good enough job himself, and they haven't gone after Abigail Glover, either. Presumably Wace would rather not draw the press's attention to the fact his own daughter ran away from the church at sixteen – but the odds of press interest in all these ex-members just got a lot higher, so I thought I'd better call and warn them.'

'How did they take it?'

'Sheila was upset and I think Niamh's regretting talking to us now.'

'Oh, no,' said Robin sadly.

'She's worried about the effect on her brother and sister. Colonel Graves told me he wanted to "let the damned UHC have it with both barrels", but I told him retaliating through the press will just draw more attention to the online bullshit and that I'm on it, legally. He's pleased we're about to interview Cherie-slash-Carrie. And I don't know how Abigail's feeling, because she didn't pick up.'

Strike's mobile now rang. Pulling it out of his pocket, he saw an unknown number.

'Hello?'

'Nicholas Delaunay here,' said a cool, upper-class voice.

'Hi,' said Strike, switching to speakerphone and mouthing 'Graves' son-in-law' at Robin. 'Apologies for the noise, we're—'

'On your way to interview Cherie Gittins,' said Delaunay. 'Yes. M'father-in-law told me. Evidently you didn't listen to a damn word my wife said, at the Hall.'

'I listened to all your wife's words.'

'But you're still determined to wreak havoc?'

'No, just determined to do my job.'

'And bugger the consequences, is that it?'

'As I can't predict the consequences—'

'The consequences, which were *entirely* predictable, are already on the bloody internet! You think I want my children to see what's been written about their mother's family, *their* family—?'

'Do your children regularly Google my agency, or the UHC?'

'You've already *admitted* that, entirely due to you, the press are likely to be on the prowl—'

'It's a possibility, not a likelihood.'

'Every moment those defamatory bloody lies are up, there's a risk journalists will see them!'

'Mr Delaunay—'

'*It's Lieutenant-Colonel Delaunay!*'

'Ah, my apologies, Lieutenant-Colonel, but your parents-in-law—'

'*They* might've bloody well agreed to all this, but Phillipa and I didn't!'

'I'm surprised I have to say this to a man of your rank, but you don't actually feature in this chain of command, Lieutenant-Colonel.'

'I'm involved, my family's involved, and I have a right—'

'I answer to my client, and my client wants the truth.'

'Whose truth? *Whose truth?*'

'Is there more than one?' said Strike. 'Better update my library of philosophy.'

'You jumped-up bloody monkey,' shouted Delaunay, and he hung up. Grinning, Strike returned his phone to his pocket.

'Why did he call you a monkey?' said Robin, laughing.

'Slang for military police,' said Strike. 'Still better than what we called the navy.'

'What was that?'

'Cunts,' said Strike.

He glanced into the back seat and saw a carrier bag.

'No biscuits,' said Robin, 'because you said you're still dieting.'

Strike sighed as he hoisted the bag into the front to take out the flask of coffee.

'Is Delaunay really this angry just because of his children?' asked Robin.

'No idea. Maybe. Can't see why he and his wife haven't just told them what happened. Lies like that always come back to bite you on the arse.'

They drove on in silence for a couple of minutes, until Robin said,

'Have you talked to Midge yet, about going undercover in Zhou's clinic?'

'No,' said Strike, who was now pouring himself coffee. 'I wanted to discuss that with you, in the light of this Wikipedia stuff. I think we've got to assume the church will be trying to identify all our operatives, and have you looked at Zhou's clinic's website? Seen how much even a three-day stay costs?'

'Yes,' said Robin.

'Well, even if they haven't yet identified Midge as one of ours, I'm not sure she'd blend in that well. She doesn't come across as the kind of woman who's prepared to waste money on crackpot treatments.'

'Which particular treatments are you calling crackpot?'

'Reiki,' said Strike. 'Know what that is?'

'Yes,' said Robin, smiling, because she knew her partner's aversion to anything that smacked of mysticism. 'The practitioner puts their hands on you, to heal your energy.'

'Heal your energy,' scoffed Strike.

'An old schoolfriend of mine had it done. She said she could feel heat moving all over her body wherever the hands went and felt a real sense of peace afterwards.'

'Tell her if she slings me five hundred quid, I'll fill her a hot water bottle and pour her some gin.'

Robin laughed.

'You'll be telling me I'm not a Gift-Bearer-Warrior next.'

'Not a what?'

'That's what Zhou told me I was,' said Robin. 'You had to fill in a questionnaire and you got typed according to your answers. The categories aligned with the prophets.'

'Christ's sake,' muttered Strike. 'No, what we need is someone who looks the part, designer clothes and the right moneyed attitude ... Prudence would've been ideal, come to think of it, but as she's seriously pissed off at me just now ...'

'Why's she pissed off?' said Robin, concerned.

'Didn't I—? Shit, I forgot to put Torment Town into your update.'

'Torment – what?'

'Torment Town. It's – or it was – an anonymous account on Pinterest. I was looking for pictures of the Drowned Prophet and found a cache of horror-style drawings, all UHC-themed. A picture of Daiyu caught my eye, because it genuinely looked like her. I complimented the artist, who thanked me, then I said, "You aren't keen on the UHC, are you?" or words to that effect, and they went quiet.

'But there was this one picture Torment Town had drawn, of a woman floating in a dark pool, with Daiyu hovering over her. The woman was blonde, wearing glasses and looked a lot like that old picture of Deirdre Doherty we got from Niamh. Having had no response to my UHC question for days, I thought, fuck it, and asked the artist if they'd ever known a woman called Deirdre Doherty, at which point the whole account disappeared.

'Fast-forward to the night you were taken in for questioning: I get a phone call from Prudence, accusing me of tracking down her client and threatening her.'

To Strike's surprise, Robin said nothing at all. Glancing at her, he thought she looked even paler than she had on getting into the car.

'You all right?'

'What shape was the pool?' said Robin.

'What?'

'The pool in Torment Town's drawing. What shape?'

'Er . . . a pentagon.'

'Strike,' said Robin, whose ears were ringing, 'I think I know what happened to Deirdre Doherty.'

'D'you want to pull over?' Strike asked, because Robin had turned white.

'No, I – actually,' said Robin, who was feeling light-headed, 'yes.'

Robin indicated and pulled over onto the hard shoulder. Once they were stationary, she turned a stricken face to Strike and said,

'Deirdre drowned in the temple, during the Manifestation of the Drowned Prophet. The pool in the Chapman Farm temple's five-sided. Deirdre had a weak heart. They must've wanted to punish her for what she'd written about Wace raping her, but it went too far. She either drowned, or had a heart attack.'

Strike sat in silence for a moment, considering the probabilities, but could find no flaw in Robin's reasoning.

'Shit.'

Robin's head was swimming. She knew exactly what Deirdre Doherty's last moments on earth must have felt like, because she'd been through exactly the same thing, in the very same pool. Deirdre, too, would have seen fragments of her life flicker before her – her children, the husband who'd abandoned her, perhaps snapshots of a long-gone childhood – and then the water would have crushed the air from her lungs, and she'd have drunk in fatal quantities, and suffocated in darkness ...

'What?' she said numbly, because Strike was talking and she hadn't heard a word.

'I said: so we've got a witness to the church committing manslaughter, and possibly even murder, and they're on the outside?'

'Yes,' said Robin, 'but we don't know who they are, do we?'

'That's where you're wrong. I know exactly who they are – well,' Strike corrected himself, 'I'd be prepared to bet a grand on it, anyway.'

'How on earth can you know that?'

'Worked it out. For starters, Prudence doesn't come cheap. She's very well regarded in her field and she's written successful books. You've seen the house they live in – she sees clients in a consulting room opposite the sitting room. She's very discreet and never names names, but I know perfectly well her client list's full of fucked-up A-listers and wealthy people who've had breakdowns, so whoever Torment Town is, they or their family must have money. They're also likely to be living in or close to London. Prudence let slip that the client's female, and we know Torment Town must have been at Chapman Farm at the same time as Deirdre Doherty.'

'So . . .'

'It's Flora Brewster, the housing heiress. She was listed as living at Chapman Farm on the 2001 census. Flora's friend Henry told me she stayed in the church for five years and Deirdre disappeared in 2003.

'According to Fergus Robertson, his contact's family shunted her off to New Zealand after her suicide attempt, but Henry Worthington-Fields says Flora's back in the country now, though still in poor mental health. He begged me not to go near her, but I know where she's living, because I looked her up: Strawberry Hill, a five-minute walk from Prudence and Declan's.'

'*Oh,*' said Robin. 'But we can't approach her, can we? Not if she's that fragile.'

Strike said nothing.

'Strike, we can't,' said Robin.

'You don't want justice for Deirdre Doherty?'

'Of course I do, but—'

'If Brewster wanted to keep what she witnessed private, why draw it and post it on a public forum?'

'I don't know,' said Robin distractedly. 'People process things differently. Maybe, for her, that was a way of letting it all out.'

'She'd have done better to let it out to the bloody police, instead of doing drawings and moaning about how miserable she feels to Prudence.'

'That's not fair,' said Robin heatedly. 'Speaking as someone who's experienced what goes on at Chapman Farm—'

'I don't see you sitting on your arse feeling sorry for

yourself, or deciding you'll just draw pictures of everything you witnessed—'

'I was only in for four months, Flora was there five years! You told me she was gay and forced to go with men – that's five years of corrective rape. You realise that as far as we know, Flora might have had kids in there that she was forced to leave when they chucked her out?'

'Why didn't she go back for them?'

'If she had the full-on mental breakdown Henry described to you, she might have believed they were in the safest place: somewhere they'd grow up with the approval of the Drowned Prophet! *Everyone* comes out of that place altered, even the ones who seem all right on the surface. D'you think Niamh would have ended up married to a man old enough to be her dad if her family hadn't been smashed up by the church? She went for safety and a father figure!'

'But you're happy for Niamh to never to know what happened to her mother?'

'Of course I'm not *happy*,' said Robin angrily, 'but I don't want it on my conscience if we tip Flora Brewster into a second suicide attempt!'

Now regretting his tone, Strike said,

'Look, I didn't mean to—'

'*Don't* say you didn't mean to upset me,' said Robin through gritted teeth. 'That's what men *always* say when – I'm *angry*, not sad. You don't get it. You don't know what that place does to people. I do, and—'

Strike's mobile rang again.

'Shit,' he said. 'Abigail Glover. Better take this.'

Robin looked away at the passing traffic, arms folded. Strike answered the call and switched it to speakerphone, so Robin could listen.

'Hi.'

"I,' said Abigail. 'I got your message, about press.'

'Right,' said Strike. 'Sorry to be the bearer of bad tidings, but as I said, I don't think there's any immediate—'

'I wanna ask you somefing,' said Abigail, cutting across him.

'Go on.'

'Did Baz Saxon come an' see you?'

'Er – yeah,' said Strike, deciding honesty was the best policy.

'That *fucker*!'

'Did he tell you himself or . . .?'

'Fuckin' Patrick told me! Me lodger. I've 'ad enough. I've told Patrick to get the *fuck* out of my flat. It's all a fuckin' *game* to them, pair of bastards,' she added, and Strike could hear distress as well as anger now. 'I'm sick an' fuckin' tired of bein' their fuckin' reality show!'

'I think a new lodger's a good move.'

'So what did Baz tell you? 'Ow I'll fuck anyfing that moves except 'im, was it?'

'He certainly struck me as a man with a grievance,' said Strike. 'But since you're on the line, I wondered whether you could answer a couple more questions?'

'You don'—'

Her voice was momentarily drowned out, as two articulated lorries roared past the stationary Land Rover.

'Sorry,' said Strike, his voice raised. 'I'm on the A40, I missed most of that.'

'I *said*,' she shouted, 'you don' wanna believe anyfing that bastard says abou' me – except that I freatened 'im. I *did* freaten 'im. I'd 'ad a coupla drinks, an' 'e was buttin' in on me an' Darryl, this guy from my gym, an' I lost it.'

'Understandable,' said Strike, 'but when you told Saxon the church had guns, was that to frighten him, or true?'

'To frighten 'im,' said Abigail. After a slight hesitation she added, 'but I migh' – they migh' not've been real. I dunno. I couldn't swear to it in court tha's wha' I saw.'

'So you *did* see a gun, or guns?'

'Yeah. Well – that's what they looked like.'

Robin now turned her head to look at the phone in Strike's hand.

'Where were these guns?' Strike asked.

'Mazu 'ad 'em. I wen' in 'er study one day to tell 'er sumfing an' I saw the safe open an' she slammed the door. It looked like two guns. She's weird about Chapman Farm, I toldja. It's 'er private kingdom. She usedta talk about when the police come, when the Crowthers were there. When I saw them guns, I fort, she's not gonna be caught out again – but I dunno, they might not 'ave been real, I on'y saw 'em for a second.'

'No, I appreciate that,' said Strike. 'While I've got you, I also wanted to ask—'

'Did Baz tell you about my nightmare?' asked Abigail, in a deadened voice.

Strike hesitated.

'Yes, but that isn't what I was going to ask about, and let me emphasise, as far as I'm concerned, the fact that you and your friend tried to prevent a whipping says far more—'

'Don' do that,' said Abigail. 'Don't fuckin' – don't try an' make – *bastards*. I'm not even allowed to 'ave private fuckin' nightmares.'

'I appreciate—'

'Oh, fuck off,' said Abigail. 'Just fuck off. You don't "appreciate". You don't know nuffing.'

Strike could tell she was now crying. Between the small noises coming out of the phone and his partner's stony stare from the seat beside him, he didn't feel particularly good about himself.

'Sorry,' he said, though not very sure what he was apologising for, unless it was letting Barry Saxon into his office. 'I wasn't going to mention any of that. I was going to ask you about Alex Graves' sister, Phillipa.'

'What about 'er?' said Abigail, in a thickened voice.

'You told me your father had her eating out of his hand, when we met.'

''E did,' said Abigail.

'She hung around the farm a bit, then, did she?'

'Coming to see 'er bruvver, yeah,' said Abigail, who was clearly trying to sound natural. 'Wha're you doing on the A40?'

'Going to Thornbury.'

'Never 'eard of it. OK, well – I'll let you go.'

And before Strike could say anything else, she hung up.

Strike looked around at Robin.

'What d'you think?'

'I think she's right,' said Robin. 'We should go.'

She turned the engine on and, having waited for a break in the traffic, pulled back out onto the road.

They drove on for five minutes without talking to each other. Keen to foster a more congenial atmosphere, Strike finally said,

'I wasn't going to bring up her nightmare. I feel bad about that.'

'And where's this sensitivity when it comes to Flora Brewster?' said Robin coldly.

'Fine,' said Strike, now nettled, 'I won't go near bloody Brewster, but as you're the one who's experienced the full bloody horror of Chapman—'

'I never called it "horror", I'm not saying I went through *war crimes* or anything—'

'Fuck's sake, I'm not saying you're exaggerating how bad

it was, I'm saying, if there's a witness to them actually *killing* someone, I'd have thought—'

'The fact is,' said Robin angrily, 'Abigail Glover's more your kind of person than Flora Brewster is, so you feel bad for making her choke up, whereas—'

'What's that mean, "more my kind of—"?'

'Pulls herself up by her bootstraps, joins the fire service, pretends none of it ever hap—'

'If it makes you feel any better, she's got a borderline drink problem and seems recklessly promiscuous.'

'Of *course* it doesn't make me feel better,' said Robin furiously, 'but you're chippy about rich people! You're judging Flora because she can afford to see Prudence and she's "sitting on her arse", whereas—'

'No, it's about Brewster doing art instead of—'

'What if she was so mentally ill she wasn't sure what was real or not? You didn't press Abigail on what these supposed guns looked like, did you?'

'She's not bloody drawing them and posting them online with UHC logos attached! I note Brewster's not so fucking ill she didn't go to ground the moment I mentioned Deirdre Doherty, thinking, "Shit, that got a bit more attention than I wanted!"'

Robin made no response to this, but stared steely-eyed at the road ahead.

The frosty atmosphere inside the car persisted onto the motorway, each partner consumed by their own uncomfortable thoughts. Strike had had the always unpleasant experience of having his own prejudices exposed. Whatever he might have claimed to Robin, he *had* formed an unflattering mental picture of the young woman who'd drawn the corpse of Deirdre Doherty, and if he was absolutely honest (which he had no intention of being out loud), he *had* classed her with the women enjoying reiki sessions at Dr Zhou's palatial clinic, not to mention those of his father's children who lived off family wealth, with expensive therapists and private doctors on hand should they need them, cushioned from the harsh realities of working life by their trust funds. Doubtless the Brewster girl had had a bad time of it, but she'd also had years in the Kiwi sunshine to reflect upon what she'd seen at Chapman Farm, and instead of seeking justice for the woman who'd drowned and closure for the children now bereft of a mother, she'd sat in her comfortable Strawberry Hill flat and indulged in a spot of art.

Robin's inner reverie was disturbing in a different way. While she stood by what she'd just said to her partner, she was uncomfortably aware (not that she intended to admit this) that she'd subconsciously wanted to force an argument. A small part of her had sought to disrupt the pleasure and ease she'd felt on finding herself back in the Land Rover with Strike, because she'd just told Murphy she loved him, and shouldn't be feeling unalloyed pleasure at the prospect of hours on the road with somebody else. Nor should she be thinking about the man she supposedly loved with guilt and discomfort . . .

The silence in the car lasted a full half an hour, until Robin, resenting the fact that she was the one to have to break the ice, but ashamed of the hidden motive that had led her to become so heated, said,

'Look, I'm sorry I got shirty. I'm just – I'm probably more on Flora's side than you are because—'

'I get it,' said Strike, relieved that she'd spoken. 'No, I don't mean – I know I haven't been in the Retreat Rooms.'

'No, I can't see Taio wanting to spirit bond with you,' said Robin, but the mental image of Taio trying to lead Strike, who was considerably larger, towards one of the wooden cabins made her laugh.

'No need to be offensive,' said Strike, reaching for the coffee again. 'We might've had a beautiful thing together if I hadn't brained him with those wire cutters.'

96

Punishment is never an end in itself but serves merely to restore order.

The I Ching or Book of Changes

'Shit,' said Strike.

A little over two hours after he and Robin had resolved their argument, they'd arrived in Oakleaze Road, Thornbury, to find Carrie Curtis Woods' residence empty. The modest but well-maintained semi-detached house, which shared a patch of unfenced lawn with its Siamese twin, was almost indistinguishable from every other house within view, except for slight variations in the style of front door.

'And no car,' said Strike, looking at the empty drive. 'But they're definitely back from holiday, I checked her Facebook page before I left this morning. She documents virtually every movement the family makes.'

'Maybe she's gone grocery shopping, if they're just back from abroad?'

'Maybe,' said Strike, 'but I think we might make ourselves a bit conspicuous if we hang around here for too long. Bit open plan. You won't get away with much in a place like this.'

There were windows everywhere he looked, and the flat lawns in front of all the houses offered no hint of cover. The ancient Land Rover also looked conspicuous, among all the family cars.

'What d'you say we go and get something to eat and come back in an hour or so?'

So they returned to the car and set off again.

The town was small, and they reached the High Street in minutes. There was less uniformity here, with shops and pubs of varying sizes, some of them painted in pastel colours or bearing old-fashioned awnings. Robin finally parked outside the Malthouse pub. The interior proved to be roomy, modern and white-walled, with grey checked carpet and chairs.

'Too early for lunch,' said Strike gloomily, returning from the bar with two packets of peanuts, a zero-alcohol beer for himself and a tomato juice for Robin, who was sitting in a bay window overlooking the high street.

'Never mind,' she said, 'check your phone. Barclay's just texted us.'

Strike sat down and took out his mobile. Their subcontractor had sent everyone at the agency a one-word message: **SHAFTED**, with a link to a news story, which Strike opened.

Robin started laughing again as she saw her partner's expression change to one of pure glee. The news story, which was brief, was headed: BREAKING: TABLOID'S FAVOURITE PRIVATE EYE ARRESTED.

Mitchell Patterson, who was cleared of wrongdoing in the News International phone hacking scandal of 2011, has been arrested on a charge of illegally bugging the office of a prominent barrister.

Strike let out a laugh so loud that heads turned.

'Fucking excellent,' he said. 'Now I can sack Littlejohn.'

'Not in here,' said Robin.

'No,' agreed Strike, glancing around, 'not very discreet. There's a beer garden, let's do it there.'

'Is my presence necessary?' said Robin, smiling, but she was already gathering up her glass, peanuts and bag.

'Killjoy,' said Strike, as they set off through the pub. 'Barclay would've paid good money to hear this.'

Once seated on benches at a brown painted table, Strike called Littlejohn and switched his mobile to speakerphone again.

'Hi, boss,' said Littlejohn, on answering. He'd taken to calling Strike 'boss' ever since Strike had revealed he knew Littlejohn was a plant. The jauntiness of Littlejohn's tone suggested his duplicitous subcontractor didn't yet realise Patterson had been arrested, and Strike's pleasurable anticipation increased.

'Where are you right now?' asked Strike.

'Following Toy Boy,' said Littlejohn. 'We're on Pall Mall.'

'Heard from Mitch this morning?'

'No,' said Littlejohn. 'Why?'

'He's been arrested,' said Strike.

No sound of human speech issued from Strike's phone, though this time they could hear the background rumble of London traffic.

'Still there?' said Strike, a malicious smile on his face.

'Yeah,' said Littlejohn hoarsely.

'So, you're fired.'

'You – what? You can't – you said you'd keep me on—'

'I said I'd think about it,' said Strike. 'I did, and I've decided you can fuck off.'

'You cunt,' said Littlejohn. 'You fucking—'

'I'm doing you a favour, when you think about it,' said Strike. 'You're going to need a lot more time on your hands, what with the police wanting you to help them with their enquiries.'

'You fucking – you bastard – I was going to – I had stuff for you on that church case – *new stuff*—'

862

'Sure you did,' said Strike. 'Bye, Littlejohn.'

He hung up, reached for his beer, took a long draught, wishing it wasn't alcohol-free, then set down his glass. Robin was laughing, but shaking her head.

'What?' said Strike, grinning.

'It's lucky we haven't got an HR department.'

'He's a subcontractor, all I owe him is cash – not that he's getting any cash.'

'He could sue you for it.'

'And I could tell the court he posted a snake through Tasha Mayo's door.'

They ate their peanuts and drank their drinks beneath hanging baskets and a bright August sun.

'You don't think he *really* had something for us, on the UHC?' said Robin after a while.

'Nah, he's bullshitting,' said Strike, setting down his empty glass.

'What if he goes to the office while we're away and—?'

'Tries to photograph case files again? Don't worry about that. I've taken precautions, I had Pat do it last week. If the fucker tries using a skeleton key again, he'll get his comeuppance – which reminds me,' said Strike, pulling a new set of office keys out of his pocket. 'You'll need those ... Right, let's go and see whether Cherie/Carrie's home yet.'

97

> *K'an represents the pig slaughtered in the small*
> *sacrifice.*
>
> *The I Ching or Book of Changes*

They'd been sitting in the Land Rover, which was parked a few doors down from Carrie Curtis Woods' still empty house, for forty minutes when a silver Kia Picanto passed them.

'Strike,' said Robin, having caught a glimpse of a blonde female driver.

The car turned into the Woods family's drive. The driver got out. She had short, blonde, curly hair, and was wearing a pair of unflatteringly tight jeans, which caused a roll of fat under her white T-shirt to spill over the waistband. She was tanned, wore a lot of spiky mascara, and her eyebrows were thinner than was currently fashionable, giving her a surprised look. A polyester shopper was slung over her shoulder.

'Let's go,' said Strike.

Carrie Curtis Woods was halfway to her front door when she heard the footsteps behind her and turned, keys in hand.

'Afternoon,' said Strike. 'My name's Cormoran Strike and this is Robin Ellacott. We're private detectives. We believe you lived at Chapman Farm in the mid-nineties, under the name Cherie Gittins? We'd like to ask you some questions, if that's all right.'

Twice before, while working at the agency, Robin had
thought a female interviewee might faint. Carrie's face lost all
healthy colour, leaving the surface tan patchy and yellow and
her lips pale. Robin braced, ready to run forwards and break
the woman's fall onto hard concrete.

'We just want to hear your side of the story, Carrie,' said
Strike.

The woman's eyes darted to the opposite neighbour's windows, and back to Strike. He was interested in the fact that
she wasn't asking them to repeat their names, as people often
did, whether out of confusion, or to play for time. He had the
feeling their appearance wasn't entirely a surprise, that she'd
been dreading something of this kind. Perhaps the UHC had
a Facebook page, and she'd seen attacks on him and Robin
there, or perhaps she'd been dreading this reckoning for years.

The seconds ticked past and Carrie remained frozen, and
it was already too late to credibly deny that she didn't know
what they were talking about, or that she'd ever been Cherie
Gittins.

'All righ',' she said at last, her voice barely audible.

She turned and walked towards the front door. Strike and
Robin followed.

The interior of the small house smelled of Pledge. The only
thing out of place in the hall was a small, pink doll's pushchair,
which Carrie moved aside so that Strike and Robin could enter
the combination sitting and dining room, which had pale blue
wallpaper and a blue three-piece suite bearing stripy mauve
cushions, all of which were balanced on their points.

Enlarged family photographs in pewter-coloured frames
covered the wall behind the sofa. Carrie Curtis Woods' two
little girls, familiar to Strike from his perusal of her Facebook
page, were pictured over and over again, sometimes with
one or other of their parents. Both daughters were blonde,

dimpled and always beaming. The younger child had several missing teeth.

'Your daughters are lovely,' said Robin, turning to smile at Carrie. 'They're not here?'

'No,' said Carrie, in a croak.

'Play date?' asked Robin, who was trying to quieten the woman's nerves.

'No. I jus' took them over to their nana's. They wan'ed to give her the presents they got her, in Spain. We've been on holiday.'

There was barely a trace of London in her voice now: she spoke with a Bristol drawl, the vowels elongated, consonants at the end of words cut off. She dropped into an armchair, setting her shopper onto the floor beside her feet.

'You can siddown,' she said weakly. Strike and Robin did so, on the sofa.

'How long have you lived in Thornbury, Carrie?' Robin asked.

'Ten – 'leven years?'

'What made you move here?'

'I met my husband,' she said. 'Nate.'

'Right,' said Robin, smiling.

'He wuz on a stag weekend. I wuz workin' in the pub when they all come in.'

'Ah.'

'So I moved, 'cause he lived here.'

Further small talk revealed that Carrie had moved to Thornbury a mere two weeks after meeting Nathan in Manchester. She'd got herself a waitressing job in Thornbury, she and Nate had found themselves a rented flat, and married just ten months later.

The speed with which she'd relocated to be with a man she'd only just met and her chameleon-like transformation into what might have been a Thornbury native made Strike think Carrie was of a type he'd met before. Such people clung to more dominant personalities, training themselves like mistletoe on a tree, absorbing their opinions, their mannerisms and mirroring their style. Carrie, who'd once ringed her eyes in black liner before driving her knife-toting boyfriend to rob a pharmacy and stab an innocent bystander, was now telling Robin in her adopted accent that the local schools were very good and talked with something like reverence about her husband: what long hours he worked, and how he had no truck with people who didn't, because he was like that, he'd always been a grafter. Her nerves seemed to dissipate slightly during the banal conversation. She seemed glad of the opportunity to set out the little stall of her life for the detectives' consideration. Whatever she'd once been, she was blameless now.

'So,' said Strike, when a convenient pause presented itself, 'we'd like to ask you a few questions, if that's all right. We've been hired to look into the Universal Humanitarian Church and we're particularly interested in what happened to Daiyu Wace.'

Carrie gave a little twitch, as though some invisible entity had tugged her strings.

'We hoped you might be able to fill in a few details about her,' said Strike.

'All righ',' said Carrie.

'Is it all right if I take notes?'

'Yeah,' said Carrie, watching Strike draw out his pen.

'You confirm you're the woman who was living at Chapman Farm in 1995, under the name Cherie Gittins?'

Carrie nodded.

'When did you first join the church?' asked Robin.

'Ninety ... three,' she said. 'I think. Yeah, ninety-three.'

'What made you join?'

'I wen' along to a meetin'. In London.'

'What attracted you to the UHC?' asked Strike.

'Nothin',' said Carrie baldly. 'The buildin' wuz warm, tha's all. I'd run off ... run away from home. I wuz sleepin' in a hostel ... I didn't get on with my mum. She drank. She had a new boyfriend and ... yeah.'

'How soon after that meeting did you go to Chapman Farm?' asked Strike.

'I wen' right after the meetin' finished ... they had a mini-bus outside.'

Her hands were clutching each other, the knuckles white. There was a henna tattoo drawn onto the back of one of them, doubtless done in Spain. Perhaps, Robin thought, her small daughters had also had flowers and curlicues drawn onto their hands.

'What did you think of Chapman Farm, when you got there?' asked Strike.

There was a long pause.

'Well, it wuz ... weird, wuzn' it?'

'Weird?'

'Yeah ... I liked some of it though. I liked bein' with the kids.'

'They liked you, too,' said Robin. 'I've heard some very nice things about you from a woman called Emily. She'd have been around seven or eight when you knew her. D'you remember her? Emily Pirbright?'

'Emily?' said Carrie distractedly. 'Um – maybe. I'm not sure.'

'She had a sister, Becca.'

'Oh ... yeah,' said Carrie. 'Have you – where's Becca, now?'

'Still in the church,' said Robin. 'Both sisters are. Emily told me she really loved you – that both of them did. She said all the kids felt that way about you.'

Carrie's mouth made a tragi-comic downwards arc and she began to cry, noisily.

'I didn't mean to upset you,' said Robin hastily, as Carrie bent down to the shopper at her feet and extracted a packet of tissues from its interior. She mopped her eyes and blew her nose, saying through her sobs,

'Sorry, sorry . . .'

'No problem,' said Strike. 'We understand this must be difficult.'

'Can I get you anything, Carrie?' said Robin. 'A glass of water?'

'Y—y—yes please,' wept Carrie.

Robin left the room for the kitchen, which lay off the dining area. Strike let Carrie cry without offering words of comfort. He judged her distress to be genuine, but it would set a bad precedent to make her think tears were the way to soften up her interviewers.

Robin, who was filling a glass with tap water in the small but spotless kitchen, noticed Carrie's daughters' paintings on the fridge door, all of which were signed either Poppy or Daisy. One was captioned *Me and Mummy* and showed two blonde figures hand in hand, both wearing princess dresses and crowns.

'Thank you,' whispered Carrie when Robin returned to the sitting room and handed her the glass. She took a sip, then looked up at Strike again.

'OK to continue?' he asked formally. Carrie nodded, her eyes now reddened and swollen, the mascara washed away onto her cheeks, leaving them grey. Strike thought she looked like a piglet, but Robin was reminded of the teenaged girls keeping vigil before the Manifestation of the Drowned Prophet.

'So you met Daiyu for the first time at the farm?' asked Strike.

Carrie nodded.

'What did you think of her?'

'Thought she wuz lovely,' said Carrie.

'Really? Because a few people have told us she was spoiled.'

'Well . . . maybe a bit. She wuz still sweet.'

'We've heard you spent a lot of time with her.'

'Yeah,' said Carrie, after another brief pause, 'I s'pose I did.'

'Emily told me,' said Robin, 'that Daiyu used to boast you and she were going to go away and set up house together. Is that true?'

'No!' said Carrie, sounding shocked.

'Daiyu made that up, did she?' said Strike.

'If – if she said it, yeah.'

'Why d'you think she'd claim she was going to leave to live with you?'

'I dunno.'

'Maybe to make the other children jealous?' suggested Robin.

'Maybe,' agreed Carrie, 'yeah.'

'How did you like the Waces?' asked Strike.

'I . . . thought the same as everyone else.'

'What d'you mean by that?'

'Well, they wuz . . . they could be strict,' said Carrie, 'but it wuz for a good cause, I s'pose.'

'You thought that, did you?' said Strike. 'That the church's cause was good?'

'It did good things. *Some* good things.'

'Did you have any particular friends at Chapman Farm?'

'No,' said Carrie. 'You weren' supposed to have special friends.'

She was holding her water tightly. Its surface was shivering.

'All right, let's talk about the morning you took Daiyu to Cromer,' said Strike. 'How did that come about?'

Carrie cleared her throat.

'She jus' wan'ed to go with me to the beach.'

'Had you ever taken any other children to the beach?'

'No.'

'But you said yes to Daiyu?'

'Yeah.'

'Why?'

'Well – 'cause she wan'ed to go, and – she kept goin' on about it – so I agreed.'

'Weren't you worried about what her parents would say?' asked Robin.

'A bit,' said Carrie, 'but I thought we'd get back before they wuz awake.'

'Walk us through what happened,' said Strike. 'How did you wake yourself up so early? There aren't clocks at Chapman Farm, are there?'

Cherie looked unhappy that he knew this, and he was reminded of Jordan Reaney's clear displeasure that Strike had so much information.

'If you wuz on the vegetable run, they gave you a little clock to wake yourself.'

'You were sleeping in the children's dormitory the night before the trip to the beach, right?'

'Yeah,' she said uneasily, 'I wuz on child duty.'

'And who was going to be looking after the kids, once you'd left on the vegetable run?'

After yet another pause, Carrie said,

'Well ... there'd still be someone there, after I'd gone. There wuz always two grown-ups or teenagers in with the children overnight.'

'Who was the other person on duty that night?'

'I ... can' remember.'

'Are you sure someone else was there, Carrie?' asked Robin.

'Emily told me that there were usually two adults in the room, but that that night it was only you.'

'She's wrong,' said Carrie. 'There wuz always two.'

'But you can't remember who the other person was?' said Strike.

Carrie shook her head.

'So you were woken up by your alarm clock. Then what happened?'

'Well, I – I woke Daiyu up, di'n' I?'

'Had Jordan Reaney been given an alarm clock, too?'

'Wha'?'

'He was supposed to be on the vegetable run, too, wasn't he?'

Another pause.

'He overslept.'

'You wouldn't have had room for Daiyu if he hadn't over-slept, would you?'

'I can' remember all the details now. I jus' know I woke up Daiyu and we got dressed and went to the van.'

'Did you have to load vegetables onto the truck?' asked Strike.

'No. Everythin' was already in it. From the night before.'

'So you and Daiyu got in, taking towels for your swim?'

'Yeah.'

'Can I ask something?' said Robin. 'Why was Daiyu wear-ing a dress, instead of a tracksuit, Carrie? Or didn't church members wear tracksuits, in the nineties?'

'No, we wore 'em ... but she wan'ed to wear her dress.'

'Were the other children allowed normal clothes?' asked Strike.

'No.'

'Did Daiyu get special treatment, because she was the Waces' child?'

'I s'pose – a bit,' said Carrie.

'So you drove out of the farm. Did you pass anyone?'

'Yeah,' said Carrie. 'The people on early duty.'

'Can you remember who they were?'

'Yeah ... what's-his-name Kennett. And a bloke called Paul, and a girl called Abigail.'

'Where did you go, after you'd left the farm?'

'To the two grocers.'

'What grocers?'

'There wuz one in Aylmerton and one in Cromer we used to sell to.'

'Did Daiyu get out of the van at either of the grocers?'

'No.'

'Why not?'

'Well – why would she?' said Carrie, and for the very first time, Strike heard a trace of defiance. 'People came out from the shops to unload the boxes. I on'y got out to make sure they took what they'd ordered. She stayed in the van.'

'Then what happened?'

'We wen' to the beach,' said Carrie, her voice noticeably stronger now.

'How did you get down to the beach?'

'What d'you mean?'

'Did you walk, run—?'

'We walked. I carried Daiyu.'

'Why?'

'She wan'ed me to.'

'Did anyone see this?'

'Yeah ... an old woman in the café.'

'Did you see her watching you at the time?'

'Yeah.'

'Were you parked very near her café?'

'No. We wuz a bit along.'

Strangely, Strike thought, she seemed more confident now they were discussing the events that were presumably among the most traumatic of her memories than she'd seemed talking about Chapman Farm.

'What happened when you got to the beach?'

'We got undressed.'

'So you were intending to swim, rather than to paddle?'

'No, jus' to paddle.'

'So why take off all your outer clothing?'

'I didn' want Daiyu gettin' her dress soakin' wet. I told her she'd be uncomfortable on the way back. Daiyu said she wouldn' take off her dress if I didn' take off my tracksuit, so I did.'

'Then what happened?'

'We wen' into the sea,' said Carrie. 'We paddled a bit and she wanted to go deeper. I knew she would. She wuz like that.'

'Like what?'

'Brave,' said Carrie. 'Adventurous.'

These were exactly the words she'd used at the inquest, Strike remembered.

'So she went in deeper?'

'Yeah. An' I wen' after her. An' then she sort of – launched herself forwards, like she wuz goin' to swim, but I knew she couldn'. I called to her to come back. She wuz laughin'. Her feet could still touch the bottom. She wuz wadin' out, tryin' to get me to chase her. And then – she wuz gone. She just went under.'

'And what did you do?'

'Swam out to try an' get her, obviously,' said Carrie.

'You're a strong swimmer, right?' said Strike. 'You give lessons, don't you?'

'Yeah,' said Carrie.

'Did you hit the rip current as well?'

'Yeah,' she said. 'I got pulled into it, but I knew what to do. I got out, but I couldn' get to Daiyu, an' I couldn' see 'er any more, so I wen' back to the beach, to get the coastguard.'

'Which is when you met the Heatons, walking their dog?'

'Yeah, exactly,' said Carrie.

'And the coastguard went out, and the police came?'

'Yeah,' said Carrie. Robin had the sense she relaxed slightly as she said it, as though she'd come to the end of an ordeal. Strike turned a page in the notebook in which he'd been writing.

'Mrs Heaton says you ran off up the beach when the police came, and started poking at some seaweed.'

'No, I didn',' said Carrie quickly.

'She remembered that quite clearly.'

'It didn' happen,' said Carrie, the defiance now pronounced.

'So the police arrived,' said Strike, 'and walked you back up to the van, right?'

'Yeah,' said Carrie.

'Then what happened?'

'I can' remember exactly,' said Carrie, but she immediately contradicted herself. 'They took me to the station and I told them what had happened and then they took me back to the farm.'

'And informed Daiyu's parents what had happened?'

'On'y Mazu, because Papa J wuzn' – no, he *wuz* there,' she corrected herself, 'he wuzn' supposed to be, but he wuz. I saw Mazu first, but Papa J called me to see him after a bit, to talk to me.'

'Jonathan Wace wasn't supposed to be at the farm that morning?' said Strike.

'No. I mean, yeah, he wuz. I can' remember. I thought he wuz goin' away that mornin', but he didn' go. And I didn' see him the moment I got back, so I thought he'd gone, but he wuz there. It's a long time ago, now,' she said. 'It all gets jumbled up.'

'Where was Wace supposed to be that morning?'

'I don' know, I can' remember,' said Carrie, a little desperately. 'I made a mistake: he wuz there when I got back, I just didn' see him. He wuz there,' she repeated.

'Were you punished, for taking Daiyu to the beach without permission?' said Robin.

'Yeah,' said Carrie.

'What punishment were you given?' asked Robin.

'I don' wanna talk about that,' said Carrie, her voice strained. 'They wuz angry. They had every right to be. If somebody had taken one of my little—'

Carrie emitted something between a gasp and a cough and began to cry again. She rocked backwards and forwards, sobbing into her hands for a couple of minutes. When Robin silently mimed to Strike an offer of comfort to Carrie, Strike shook his head. Doubtless he'd be accused of heartlessness again on the return journey, but he wanted to hear Carrie's own words, not her response to somebody else's sympathy or ire.

'I've regretted it all my life, *all my life*,' Carrie sobbed, raising her swollen-eyed face, tears still coursing down her cheeks. 'I felt like I didn' deserve Poppy and Daisy, when I had 'em! I shouldn' of agreed ... why did I do it? *Why?* I've asked myself that over 'n' over, but I swear I never wan'ed – I wuz young, I knew it wuz wrong, I never wan'ed it to happen, oh God, and then she wuz dead and it wuz *real,* it wuz *real* ...'

'What d'you mean by that?' said Strike. 'What d'you mean by "it was real"?'

'It wuzn' a joke, it wuzn' pretend – when you're young, you don' think stuff like that *happens* – but it wuz real, she wuzn' comin' back ...'

'The inquest must have been difficult for you,' said Strike.

'Of course it wuz,' said Carrie, her face wet, her breathing still laboured, but with a trace of anger.

'Mr Heaton says you spoke to him outside, after it was over.'

'I can' remember that.'

'He remembers. He particularly remembers you saying to him, "I could have stopped it."'

'I never said that.'

'You're denying saying "I could have stopped it" to Mr Heaton?'

'Yeah. No. I don'... maybe I said somethin' like, "I could've stopped her goin' in so deep." That's wha' I meant.'

'So you remember saying it now?'

'No, but if I said it . . . that's what I meant.'

'It's just a strange form of words,' said Strike. '"I could have stopped *it*", rather than, "I could have stopped *her*." Were you aware there was a custody battle going on for Daiyu, at the time you took her to the beach?'

'No.'

'You hadn't heard any talk about the Graves family wanting Daiyu to go and live with them?'

'I heard . . . I heard somethin' about how there wuz people who wanted to take Daiyu off her mum.'

'That's the Graveses,' said Strike.

'Oh. I thought it wuz social workers,' said Carrie, and she said a little wildly, 'they have too much power.'

'What makes you say that?'

'A friend of mine's fosterin'. She has a terrible time with the social workers. Power mad, some of them.'

'Can we go back to the night before you and Daiyu went swimming?' said Strike.

'I've already told you everythin'. I've said it all.'

'We've heard you gave the children special drinks that night.'

'No, I didn'!' said Carrie, now turning pink.

'The Pirbright children remember differently.'

'Well, they're wrong! Maybe someone else gave 'em drinks and they're confusin' it with that night. *I* never gave them any.'

'So you didn't give the younger children anything that might have made them fall asleep more quickly?'

'Of course not!'

'Were there any medicines like that at the farm? Any sleeping pills or liquids?'

'No, never. Stuff like tha' wuzn' allowed.'

'Emily says she didn't like her drink, and poured it away,' said Robin. 'And she told me that after everyone else was asleep, you helped Daiyu out of the dormitory window.'

'That didn' happen. That never happened. That's a lie,' said Carrie. 'I never, *never* put her out of a window.'

She seemed far more distressed about this allegation than she'd been while discussing the drowning.

'So Emily's making that up?'

'Or she dreamed it. She could of dreamed it.'

'Emily says Daiyu did quite a bit of sneaking around at the farm,' said Robin. 'She claimed to be doing magic with older children in the woods and the barns.'

'Well, *I* never saw her sneakin' around.'

'Emily also told me Daiyu sometimes had forbidden food and small toys, things the other children weren't allowed. Did you get those for her?'

'No, of course not! I couldn've done, even if I'd wan'ed. You weren' allowed money. I never went to the shops. Nobody did. It wuzn' allowed.'

A short silence followed these words. Carrie watched Strike taking his mobile out of his pocket. Colour was coming and going in her face, and the hand with the henna tattoo was now frantically twisting her wedding and engagement rings.

Strike had deliberately left the Polaroids of the naked youths in pig masks at the office today. Since Reaney had knocked them to the floor during his interview, Strike had rethought the advisability of handing these original pieces of evidence to angry or frightened interviewees.

'I'd like you to look at these photos,' he told Carrie. 'There are six of them. You can swipe right to see the others.'

He stood up to hand his mobile to Carrie. She began to visibly shake again as she looked down at the screen.

'We know the blonde is you,' said Strike.

Carrie opened her mouth, but no sound came out at first. Then she whispered,

'It's not me.'

'I'm afraid I don't believe you,' said Strike. 'I think that's you, and the man with the skull tattoo is Jordan Reaney—'

'It's not.'

'Who is he, then?'

There was a long pause. Then Carrie whispered,

'Joe.'

'What's his surname?'

'I can' remember.'

'Was Joe still at the farm when you left it?'

She nodded.

'And who's the smaller man?' (who in the second photograph was penetrating the blonde from behind).

'Paul,' whispered Carrie.

'Paul Draper?'

She nodded again.

'And the girl with the long hair?'

Another long pause.

'Rose.'

'What's her surname?'

'I can' remember.'

'What happened to her?'

'I dunno.'

'Who's taking the pictures?'

Again, Carrie opened her mouth and closed it again.

'Who's taking the pictures?' Strike repeated.

'I dunno,' she whispered again.

'How can you not know?'

Carrie didn't answer.

'Was this a punishment?' Strike asked.

Carrie's head jerked again.

'Is that a yes? Somebody forced you to do this?'

She nodded.

'Carrie,' said Robin, 'was the person taking the pictures masked too?'

Carrie raised her head to stare at Robin. It looked as though the woman had vacated her body: Robin had never seen anybody who so resembled a somnambulist, every muscle in her face slack, her eyes blank.

Then, making both Carrie and Robin jump, a song began to play from inside the shopper at Carrie's feet.

> I like to party, mm-mm, everybody does
> Make love and listen to the music
> You've got to let yourself go-go, go-go, oh-oh . . .

Carrie bent down automatically, rummaged in the shopper, pulled out her mobile and answered it, cutting the song off.

'Hi Nate,' she whispered. 'Yeah . . . no, I took them over to your mum's . . . yeah . . . no, I'm fine. Can I call you back? . . . no, I'm fine. I'm fine. I'll call you back.'

Having hung up, Carrie looked from Robin to Strike, then said, in a flat voice,

'You need to go now. You need to go.'

'All right,' said Strike, who could tell there was no point trying to press her further. He pulled one of his business cards out of his wallet. 'If there's anything else you'd like to tell us, Mrs Woods—'

'You need to go.'

'If you wanted to tell us anything else about Daiyu's death—'

'You need to go,' Carrie said, yet again.

'I realise this is very difficult,' said Strike, 'but if you were made to do anything you now regret—'

'*GO!*' shouted Carrie Curtis Woods.

98

K'an means something deeply mysterious . . .

The I Ching or Book of Changes

Strike and Robin returned to the Land Rover in silence.

'Want some lunch?' said Strike, as he put on his seat belt.

'Seriously, that's your first—?'

'I'm hungry.'

'OK, but let's not go back to the Malthouse. It'll be crowded by now.'

'You don't want to discuss Mrs Woods' dark past somewhere her neighbours might hear?'

'No,' said Robin, 'not really. This is a small place.'

'Felt sorry for her, did you?'

Robin glanced back at Carrie Curtis Woods' house, then said,

'I just don't feel comfortable hanging around here. Shall we buy some food and eat in the car? We can pull over once we're out of Thornbury.'

'OK, as long as there's plenty of food.'

'Ah, yes,' said Robin, switching on the engine, 'I remember your theory that nothing eaten on a car journey contains calories.'

'Exactly. Got to make the most of these opportunities.'

So they purchased food on the High Street, got back into the Land Rover and headed out of Thornbury. After five minutes, Strike said,

'This'll do. Pull in by that church.'

Robin turned up Greenhill Road and parked beside the graveyard.

'You got pork pies?' said Robin, looking into the bag.

'Problem?'

'Not at all. Just wishing I'd brought biscuits in the first place.'

Strike took a few satisfying bites of his first pie before saying,

'So: Carrie.'

'Well,' said Robin, who was eating a cheese sandwich, 'there's something off, isn't there? *Very* off.'

'Where d'you want to start?'

'The dormitory,' said Robin. 'She was very worried talking about all of that: Daiyu going out of the window, the fact that there should have been two adults in the room, the special drinks. Whereas when she got to the drowning—'

'Yeah, that all came out very fluently. 'Course, she's told that story multiple times; practice makes perfect ...'

The pair sat in silence for a moment or two, before Strike said,

'"The night before".'

'What?'

'Kevin Pirbright wrote it on his bedroom wall: *the night before.*'

'Oh ... well, yes. Why *did* all this stuff happen, the night before?'

'And you know what else needs explaining? Reaney oversleeping. There's something very fishy there. How did Carrie know he wasn't going to turn up?'

'Maybe she gave him a special drink, too? Or special food?'

'Very good point,' said Strike, reaching for his notebook.

'But where did she get stuff in enough quantities to drug all these people, when she never went shopping and didn't have access to cash?'

'*Someone* must've been going out shopping, unless the church farms its own bog rolls and washing powder,' Strike pointed out. 'Delivery services weren't nearly as common in ninety-five.'

'True, but – oh, hang on,' said Robin, struck by a sudden idea. 'She might not have needed to buy drugs. What if whatever she used was grown there?'

'Herbs, you mean?'

'Valerian's a sleep aid, isn't it?'

'You'd need a bit of expertise if you're messing around with plants.'

'True,' said Robin, remembering the blood in the bathroom, and Lin's rash.

There was another brief silence, both of them thinking.

'Carrie was defensive about Daiyu not getting out of the van at those two different grocers, as well,' said Strike.

'Daiyu might not have wanted to get out. There's no reason she should have.'

'What if Carrie gave Daiyu a "special drink" somewhere between waving goodbye to the early duty lot and carrying her down to the sea? Maybe Daiyu was too sleepy to get out of the van, even if she'd wanted to.'

'So you think Carrie killed her?'

'Don't you?'

Robin ate more sandwich before answering.

'I can't see it,' she said at last. 'I can't imagine her doing it.'

She waited for Strike's agreement, but none came.

'D'you *honestly* think the woman we just met could hold that child underwater until she was dead?' Robin asked him. 'Or drag her out into the deep, knowing she couldn't swim?'

'I think,' said Strike, 'the proportion of people who could be persuaded to commit terrible acts, given the right circumstances, is higher than most of us would like to think. You know the Milgram experiment?'

'Yes,' said Robin. 'Participants were instructed to administer increasingly strong electric shocks to another person, every time that person answered a question wrongly. And sixty-five per cent continued turning up the dial until they were administering what they thought was a dangerously high level of electricity.'

'Exactly,' said Strike. 'Sixty-five per cent.'

'All the participants in that experiment were male.'

'You don't think women would have complied?'

'Just pointing it out,' said Robin.

'Because if you don't think young women are capable of committing atrocities, I'd refer you to Patricia Krenwinkel, Susan Atkins and – whatever the others were called.'

'Who?' said Robin, perplexed.

'I'm talking about the Manson Family, which differed from the UHC only in laying slightly more emphasis on murder and a lot less on generating revenue, although by all accounts Charles Manson would've been happy to get cash as well. They committed nine murders in all, one of them of a pregnant actress, and those young women were right in the thick of the action, ignoring the victims' pleas for mercy, dipping their fingers in the victims' blood to scrawl – Jesus,' said Strike, with a startled laugh, as he remembered a detail he'd forgotten, '*they* wrote "pigs" on the wall as well. In blood.'

'You're kidding?'

'Yeah. "Death to pigs".'

Having finished two pork pies, Strike rummaged in the bag for a Yorkie bar, and the apple he'd bought as an afterthought.

'How're we feeling about "Joe" and "Rose"?' he asked, as he unwrapped the chocolate.

'You sound sceptical.'

'Can't help thinking "Rose" might've been a name she thought of on the spur of the moment, given that she named her kids Poppy and Daisy.'

'If she was going to lie, wouldn't she deny her own involvement?'

'It would've been too late. Her reaction when she saw the pictures gave her away.'

'We know Paul Draper was real, though.'

'Yeah, but he's dead, isn't he? He can't testify.'

'But . . . in a way, he still can.'

'You about to whip out a Ouija board?'

'Ha ha. No. I'm saying, if Carrie knows Paul's dead, she must also know *how* he died: kept as a slave and beaten to death.'

'So?'

'What happened to Draper at Chapman Farm makes those Polaroids *more* incriminating, not less. He'd been groomed to accept abuse in the church, and that made him vulnerable to that pair of sociopaths who killed him.'

'Not sure Carrie's bright enough to think that through,' said Strike.

Both sat for a minute, eating and following their own trains of thought, until Strike said,

'You didn't see any pig masks while you were in there, did you?'

'No.'

'Hmm,' said Strike. 'Maybe they got bored of them once they discovered the virtues of the box. Or maybe what's on those Polaroids was a secret, even from most people inside the church. Somebody was enjoying their fetish in private, knowing full well it couldn't be given any kind of spiritual interpretation.'

'And that person had the authority to compel the teenagers to do what they were told, and keep quiet about it afterwards.'

'Pigs seem to have been Mazu's particular preoccupation. Can you imagine Mazu telling teenagers to strip and abuse each other?'

Robin considered the question before saying slowly,

'If you'd asked me before I went in there whether a woman could make kids do that, I'd have said it was impossible, but she's not normal. I think she's a true sadist.'

'And Jonathan Wace?'

Robin felt as though Wace's hands touched her again when Strike spoke his name. Gooseflesh rose once more over her torso.

'I don't know. Possibly.'

Strike pulled out his phone and brought up the photographs of the Polaroids again. Robin, who felt she'd looked at them quite enough, turned to look out of the window at the graveyard.

'Well, we know one thing about Rose, if that's her real name,' said Strike, eyes on the chubby girl with the long black hair. 'She hadn't been at Chapman Farm very long before this happened. She's too well nourished. All the others are very skinny. I could've sworn,' said Strike, his gaze moving to the youth with the skull tattoo, 'that guy was Reaney. His reaction when I showed him the – oh, shit. Hang on. *Joe*.'

Robin looked round again.

'Henry Worthington-Fields,' said Strike, 'told me a man called Joe recruited him into the church, in a gay bar.'

'Oh . . .'

'So if that really is Joe, "Rose" looks much more credible as the name of the dark girl. Of course,' said Strike thoughtfully, 'there's *one* person who's got more to fear from these pictures than anyone in them.'

'Yes,' said Robin. 'The photographer.'

'Precisely. Judges don't tend to look very kindly on people who photograph other people being raped.'

'The photographer and the abuser must have been one and the same, surely?'

'I wonder,' said Strike.

'What d'you mean?'

'Maybe the price of not having to whip himself across the face again was for Reaney to take dirty pictures? What if he was forced to take them, by the ringmaster?'

'Well, it'd explain Carrie's insistence she didn't know who the photographer was,' said Robin. 'I doubt many people would welcome Jordan Reaney having a grudge against them or their families.'

'Too true.'

Having eaten the last of the Yorkie bar, Strike picked up his pen again and began making a 'to do' list.

'OK, so we need to try and trace Joe and Rose. I'd also like to clarify whether Wace was absent from the farm that morning, because Carrie tied herself up in knots there, didn't she?'

'How're we supposed to find that out, after all this time?'

'Christ knows, but can't hurt to try,' said Strike.

He started unenthusiastically on his apple. Robin had just finished her sandwich when her phone rang.

'Hi,' said Murphy. 'How's it going in Thornbury?'

Strike, who thought he recognised Murphy's voice, feigned interest in the passenger side of the road.

'Good,' said Robin. 'Well – interesting.'

'If you fancy coming over this evening, I've got something you'll also find interesting.'

'What?' asked Robin.

'The interview tapes of the people who're accusing you of child abuse.'

'Oh my God.'

'Needless to say, I shouldn't have them. Called in a favour.'

The idea of seeing anyone from Chapman Farm again, even on film, gave Robin goosebumps for the second time in ten minutes.

'OK,' she said, checking her watch, 'what time will you be home?'

'Eightish, probably. I've got a lot to catch up on here.'

'OK, great, I'll see you then.'

She hung up. Strike, who gathered from what he'd just overheard that Robin and Murphy's relationship had not, in fact, fallen apart during the separation, said,

'Everything OK?'

'Fine,' said Robin. 'Ryan's managed to get hold of the interview tapes of the people saying I abused Jacob.'

'Ah,' said Strike. 'Right.'

He not only resented Murphy being able to access information he couldn't, he resented Murphy being in a position to inform or assist Robin, when he couldn't.

Robin was now staring ahead through the windscreen. Her pulse was racing: the child abuse accusation, which she'd tried to relegate to the back of her mind, now seemed to loom over her, blocking out the August sun.

Strike, who suspected what was going through Robin's mind, said,

'They're not going to go through with it. They'll have to drop it.'

And how can you be so sure? thought Robin, but, well aware that her predicament wasn't Strike's fault, she merely said,

'Well, I hope so.'

'Any other thoughts on Carrie Curtis Woods?' said Strike, hoping to distract her.

'Um ...' said Robin, forcing herself to concentrate, 'yes, actually. Carrie asking what had happened to Becca was odd. She didn't seem to remember any of the other kids.'

Strike, who hadn't particularly registered this point at the time, said,

'Yeah, now you mention it – remind me how old was Becca, when Daiyu died?'

'Eleven,' said Robin. 'So she wouldn't have been in the kids' dormitory that night. Too old. And then we've got "It wasn't a joke, it wasn't pretend", haven't we?'

Yet again, both sat in silence, but this time, their thoughts were running on parallel tracks.

'I think Carrie knows or believes Daiyu's dead,' said Robin. 'I don't know ... maybe it really *was* an accidental drowning?'

'Two drownings, in exactly the same place? No body? Possibly drugged drinks? An escape through a window?'

Strike pulled his seat belt back across himself.

'No,' he said, 'Daiyu was either murdered, or she's still alive.'

'Which are *very* different possibilities,' said Robin.

'I know, but if we can prove it either way, the Drowned Prophet – pun intended – is dead in the water.'

99

This line is the representative of the evil that is to be rooted out.

The I Ching or Book of Changes

Robin arrived at Murphy's flat in Wanstead at ten past eight that evening. Like her own, Murphy's dwelling was cheap, one-bedroomed and came with unsatisfactory neighbours, in his case below, rather than above. It lay in an older and smaller block than Robin's, with stairs rather than a lift.

Robin climbed the familiar two flights, carrying her over-night bag and a bottle of wine she thought she might need, given that the centrepiece of the night's entertainment was to be watching videoed interviews accusing her of child abuse. She very much hoped the smell of curry was coming from Murphy's flat, because she was craving hot food after a day eating sandwiches and peanuts.

'Oh, wonderful,' she sighed, when Murphy opened the door and she saw the takeaway cartons laid out on the table.

'Me or the food?' asked Murphy, bending to kiss her.

'You, for getting the food.'

When they'd first started going out together, Robin had found the interior of Murphy's flat frankly depressing, because except for the fact that there were no cardboard boxes and his clothes were hung up in the wardrobe, it looked as though

891

he'd just moved in. Of course, Strike's flat was the same, in that there were no decorative objects there at all, except for the school photo of his nephews Lucy never failed to send him, which was updated yearly. However, the fact that Strike lived under the eaves gave his flat a certain character, which was entirely lacking in Murphy's identikit dwelling. It had taken a couple of visits to Robin's own flat for Murphy to comment aloud, with an air of faint surprise, that pictures and plants made a surprising difference to a space, which had made Robin laugh. However, she hadn't made the slightest attempt to change Murphy's flat: no gifted cushions or posters, no helpful suggestions. She knew such things might be interpreted as a proprietorial statement of intent, and with all its drawbacks, her own flat was dear to her for the independence it gave her.

However, the sitting room was looking less barren than usual tonight. Not only were Robin's three houseplants, which she'd asked Murphy to keep alive while she was at Chapman Farm, standing on a side table, there was also a single framed print on the wall, and lit candles on the table among the foil trays of food.

'You've decorated,' she said.

'D'you like it?' he said.

'It's a map,' said Robin, moving to look at the picture.

'An antique map.'

'Of London.'

'But it's antique. Which makes it classy.'

Robin laughed and turned to look at her plants.

'And you've kept these *really*—'

'I'm not gonna lie. Two of them died. I bought replacements. That one –' he pointed at the philodendron which Strike had bought Robin as a housewarming present '– must be bloody hard to kill. It's the sole survivor.'

'Well, I appreciate the replacements,' said Robin, 'and thank you for saving Phyllis.'

'Did they all have names?'

'Yes,' said Robin, though this wasn't actually true. 'But I won't be calling the new ones after dead ones. Too morbid.'

She now noticed Murphy's laptop sitting on the table, beside the curry and plates.

'Are the videos on there?'

'Yeah,' said Murphy.

'Have you watched them?'

'Yeah. D'you want to wait until after we've had dinner to—?'

'No,' said Robin. 'I'd rather get it over with. We can watch while we're eating.'

So they sat down together at the table. As Murphy poured her a glass of wine and Robin heaped her plate with chicken and rice, he said,

'Listen, before we watch – what they're saying is clearly bullshit.'

'Weirdly, I already know that,' said Robin, trying to sound light-hearted.

'No, I mean, it's *clearly* bullshit,' said Murphy. 'They aren't convincing – there's only one who sounds like she might be for real, but then she goes off on a bloody weird tangent.'

'Who?'

'Becca some—'

'Pirbright,' said Robin. Her pulse had started racing again. 'Yes, I'm sure Becca's convincing.'

'She just speaks more naturally than the others. If she didn't go off into the batshit stuff at the end, you'd think she was credible. You'll see what I mean when we watch it.'

'Who else gave statements?'

'An older woman called Louise and a younger one called Vivienne.'

'*Louise* gave evidence against me?' said Robin furiously.

'I'd have expected it of Vivienne, she's desperate to be a spirit wife, but *Louise*?'

'Look, with both of them, it's like they're working off a script. I couldn't get footage of the kid accusing you, my contact wouldn't hand it over. Can't really blame him – it's a seven-year-old. I shouldn't even have these. But I'm told the kid behaved as though he'd been coached.'

'OK,' said Robin, taking a large swig of wine. 'Show me Becca.'

Murphy clicked on a folder, then on one of the video files inside, and Robin saw a police interview room, viewed from above. The camera was fixed in a corner near the ceiling. A large, solid-looking policeman was visible, back to the camera, so that his tonsure-like bald patch caught the light.

'I think that's one of the guys who interviewed me at Felbrigg Lodge,' said Robin.

Murphy pressed play. A female officer led Becca into the room and gestured her towards an empty chair. Becca's dark hair was as shiny as ever, her creamy skin unblemished, her smile diffident and humble. In her clean blue tracksuit and very white trainers, she might have been a youth leader at some harmless summer camp.

The male officer told Becca the interview was being recorded and she nodded. He asked for her full name, and then how long she'd lived at Chapman Farm.

'Since I was eight,' said Becca.

'And you look after the children?'

'I'm not often involved *directly* in childcare, but I oversee our home-schooling programme,' said Becca.

'Oh, please,' Robin said to the onscreen Becca. '*What* home-schooling programme? "The pure spirit knows acceptance is more important than understanding".'

'. . . involve?' said the female officer.

'Making sure we're complying with all Ofsted—'

'Total shit,' Robin said loudly. 'When do materialist inspectors get into Chapman Farm?'

Murphy paused the video.

'What?' said Robin.

'If you keep talking over her,' said Murphy mildly, 'you're not going to hear it.'

'Sorry,' said Robin in frustration. 'I just – it's hard, hearing their crap again. Those kids aren't being educated, they're being brainwashed. Sorry. Go on. I'll keep quiet.'

She took a large mouthful of curry and Murphy restarted the video.

'—requirements. Members with particular skill sets take classes, after being background checked, obviously. We've got a couple of fully qualified primary school teachers, but we've also got a professor who's introducing the children to basic philosophical concepts, and a very talented sculptor who leads them in art projects.' Becca gave a deprecating little laugh. 'They're probably getting the best primary-age education in the country! We've been *so* lucky with the people who join us. I remember, last year, I was worried our maths teaching might be a little behind, and then we had a maths postgrad arrive at the farm and he looked over the children's work and told me he'd seen worse scores at A-Level!'

Robin remembered the Portakabin where those closed-down children sat with their shaven heads, mindlessly colouring pictures of the Stolen Prophet with his noose around his neck. She remembered the dearth of books in the classroom and the spelling on the picture captioned 'Aks tre'.

Yet Becca's manner was indeed convincing. She came across as an enthusiastic and diligent educator, a little nervous about speaking to the police, of course, but with nothing at all to hide, and determined to do her duty.

'It's just incredibly troubling,' she said earnestly. 'We've never had anything like this happen before. Actually, we aren't even certain her name was really Rowena Ellis.'

Robin now saw the real Becca peeping out from behind the careful, innocent façade: her dark eyes were watchful, trying to wheedle information out of the police. From the datestamp on the video, she knew this interview had taken place late on the afternoon following her escape from Chapman Farm: at that point, the church must have been scrambling for information on who Robin had really been.

'What makes you think she was using a fake name?' asked the female officer.

'One of our members heard her answering to "Robin",' said Becca, watching the officers for any reaction. 'Not that that's necessarily indicative – I mean, we had another woman at the farm once, who used a fake name, but she couldn't have been more—'

'Let's go back to the beginning,' said the male officer. 'Where were you when the incident took place?'

'In the kitchens,' said Becca, 'helping prepare dinner.'

Robin, who'd never once seen Becca help prepare dinner or do any of the more menial tasks around the farm, bit back another scathing comment. Doubtless this activity had been selected to present a hard-working, down-to-earth persona.

'When did you first become aware that something had happened?'

'Well, Vivienne came into the kitchen, looking for Jacob—'

'*How could Jacob have been walking?*' said Robin angrily. 'He was *dying!* Sorry,' she added quickly, as Murphy's hand moved towards the mouse. She took a gulp of wine.

'—and Louise had been supervising some of the children on the vegetable patch, and Jacob hurt himself with a trowel. Apparently Rowena offered to take him into the kitchens to wash the cut and put a sticking plaster on it – we keep a first aid kit in there.

'When they didn't come back, Vivienne went to look for them, but of course, they hadn't come into the kitchen at all. I thought it was strange, but I wasn't worried at that point. I told Vivienne to return to the other children, and I'd go and look for Rowena and Jacob, which I did. I thought perhaps Jacob had needed the bathroom, so that's where I looked first. I opened the door and—'

Becca shook her head and closed her dark eyes: a woman shocked and scandalised.

'I didn't understand what I was seeing,' she said quietly, opening her eyes again. 'Rowena and Jacob were there, he had his pants and trousers down, crying – they weren't in a cubicle, they were in the sink area. When he saw me, he ran to me and said, *"Becca, Becca, she hurt me!"'*

'And what did Rowena do?'

'Well, she just pushed past me without saying anything. I was obviously much more concerned about Jacob, at the time. I said I was sure Rowena hadn't hurt him on purpose, but then he told me about how she'd pulled his trousers and pants down and exposed his genitalia, and then she was trying to take a picture—'

'How?' exploded Robin. 'What was I taking a picture with? I wasn't allowed a bloody phone or a – sorry, don't pause, don't pause,' she added hastily to Murphy.

'—and hit him round the head, when he wouldn't stand still,' Becca said. 'And, I mean, we take child safeguarding *incredibly* seriously within the church—'

'Sure you do,' said Robin furiously, unable to control herself, 'toddlers wandering around in nappies at night—'

'—never had *any* instances of sexual abuse at Chapman Farm—'

'Strange words,' shouted Robin, to the onscreen Becca, 'from a woman who said her brother sexually abused her there!'

Murphy paused the video again.

'You all right?' he said gently, putting a hand on Robin's shoulder.

'Yes – no – well, *obviously,* I'm not,' said Robin, standing up and running her hands through her hair. 'It's bullshit, it's all bullshit, and *she*—'

She pointed at the onscreen Becca, who was frozen with her mouth open, but Robin couldn't find words to adequately express her contempt.

'Shall we watch the rest after—?' Murphy began.

'No,' said Robin, dropping back down into her seat, 'sorry, I'm just *so* bloody angry. *The boy she's talking about isn't Jacob!* Where's the real one? Is he dead? Is he starving away in the b-base—?'

Robin began to cry.

'Shit,' said Murphy, moving his chair so he could put his arms around her. 'Robin, I shouldn't've shown you this crap, I should've just told you they're speaking a load of bollocks and you've got nothing to worry about.'

'It's fine, it's fine,' Robin said, pulling herself together. 'I want to watch it ... she might say something useful ... the woman with the fake name ...'

'Cherie?' said Murphy.

Robin pulled free of his hug.

'She names her?'

'Yeah, towards the end. That's where it all goes a bit ...'

Robin got up and strode to her bag to fetch her notebook and pen.

'Cherie's the woman Strike and I interviewed today.'

'OK,' said Murphy uncertainly. 'Let's fast-forward, watch the Cherie bit and forget the rest of it.'

'Fine,' said Robin, sitting back down with her notebook. 'Sorry,' she added, wiping her eyes again, 'I don't know what's wrong with me.'

'Yeah, it's like you've just escaped from a cult or something.'

But Robin couldn't adequately explain to Murphy how it felt to listen to these naked lies covering up terrible neglect, or the fabricated story of sexual abuse, when all she'd done was to care for and try to save a dying child; the gulf between what the UHC pretended to be, and what it really was, had never been more starkly apparent to her, and a small part of her would have liked to scream and throw Murphy's laptop across the room, but instead she pressed out the nib of her pen, and waited.

Murphy fast-forwarded, and together they watched Becca gesticulating, shaking her head and nodding at double time.

'Too far,' muttered Murphy, 'she brushed her hair off her face before . . .'

He rewound and finally pressed play.

'. . . other woman with a false name?' said the female police officer.

'Oh,' said Becca, sweeping her shining hair off her face, 'yes. I mention her because *she* was an actual instrument of the divine.'

Robin could almost feel the two police officers resisting the urge to look at each other. The male policeman cleared his throat.

'What d'you mean by that?'

'Cherie was a messenger of the Blessed Divinity, sent to take Daiyu, our prophet, to the sea. Cherie confided her purpose to me—'

Robin began scribbling in her notebook.

'—and I trusted her, and I was right to. What *seemed* wrong was right, you see? Papa J will confirm everything I'm saying,'

Becca continued, in exactly the same earnest and reasonable a tone as she'd used throughout the interview. 'I'm pure spirit, which means I understand that what might seem devilish may be divine, and vice—'

'See what I m——?' began Murphy.

'Shh,' said Robin urgently, listening.

'Cherie came, attained her purpose, and then she left us.'

'Died, you mean?' said the male officer.

'There *is* no death, in the sense the material world means when it uses the word,' said Becca, smiling. 'No, she left the farm. I believe she'll come back to us one day, and bring her little girls, too.' Becca gave a small laugh. 'I can tell this sounds strange to you, but that's all right. Papa J always says—'

'"I'd rather face an honest sceptic than a hundred who believe they know God, but are really in thrall to their own piety,"' said Robin, repeating the words along with Becca.

'I'm trying to explain,' continued Becca, onscreen, 'that my personal connection to the Drowned Prophet, and my relationship with the divine vessel, who suffered and was blameless, means I was very ready to hear Rowena's explanation of what had happened. I would have extended understanding and compassion . . . but she didn't stay to explain,' said Becca, her smile fading. 'She ran, and a man was waiting for her on the outskirts of the farm, in a car. He picked her up, and they drove away. So it's hard not to think that she and this man were plotting something together, isn't it? Were they hoping to abduct a child? Has she been trying to get pictures of naked children, to send to this man?'

'The rest is just her crapping on about how fishy it was you ran for it,' said Murphy, shutting down the video. 'You all right?'

'Yes,' said Robin quietly, reaching for her wine. She drank half the glass before saying. 'I suppose it's just a shock.'

'Of course it is, being accused—'

'No, not that . . . I suppose I've just realised . . . she believes. She believes in the whole thing and – she *genuinely* thinks she's a good person.'

'Well,' said Murphy, 'I s'pose that's a cult for you.'

He closed the laptop.

'Eat your curry.'

But Robin looked down at her notes.

'I will. I just need to call Strike.'

100

Nine in the second place means:
Dragon appearing in the field.

The I Ching or Book of Changes

Strike was walking slowly back up Charing Cross Road from Chinatown, where he'd eaten a solitary evening meal in a restaurant on Wardour Street. Looking down into the darkening street while eating his Singapore noodles, he'd watched a couple of people in blue tracksuits passing at a slow walk, deep in conversation, before turning into Rupert Court. He couldn't make out their faces, but was ill-natured enough to hope they were fretting about the private detective who'd been undercover at their precious farm for four months.

A familiar faint depression settled over him as he made his way back to the office. The knowledge that Robin was currently at Murphy's flat watching those interview tapes had formed a dispiriting backdrop to his meal. Vaping morosely as the traffic passed him, he acknowledged to himself that he'd thought Robin might call him after watching the interviews. Of course, Murphy was on hand to offer succour and support now . . .

His mobile rang. He pulled it out of his pocket, saw Robin's number and answered.

'Can you talk?' she said.

'Yeah, I've been doing it for years.'

'Very funny. Are you busy?'

'No. Go on.'

'I've just watched the police interview with Becca Pirbright and she said some odd things about Cherie. Carrie, I mean.'

'How the hell did Carrie come up?'

'As an example of how the devilish may sometimes be divine.'

'I'm going to need footnotes.'

'She was explaining how she'd have been happy to hear my explanation of what I did to Jacob, because she once knew a divine vessel who did something that *seemed* awful but was actually – you get the gist. Then she said Carrie "confided her purpose" to her.'

'Very interesting,' said Strike.

'And she knows Carrie's got daughters. She said, "I believe she'll come back to us one day, and bring her little girls, too."'

Strike, who was crossing the road, pondered this for a few moments.

'Are you still there?'

'Yeah,' said Strike.

'What d'you think?'

'I think that's even more interesting than her "confiding her purpose" to an eleven-year-old.'

As he turned into Denmark Street he said,

'So the church kept tabs on Cherie after she left? It'll have taken them a fair bit of work, as I know. I told you Jordan Reaney got a mysterious phone call from Norfolk before trying to top himself, didn't I?'

'Yes – why's that relev—? *Oh* . . . you mean the church kept tabs on him, too?'

'Exactly,' said Strike. 'So do they do this to everyone who leaves, or only to people they know are particularly dangerous to them?'

'They managed to trace Kevin to his rented flat, as well . . . you *know* they killed Kevin,' Robin added, when Strike didn't say anything.

'We don't know it,' he said, as he unlocked the main door to the office. 'Not yet. But I'll accept it as a working hypothesis.'

'And what about those letters Ralph Doherty kept tearing up after he and the kids left the farm, even after they'd moved to a different town and changed their surname?'

Strike started climbing the stairs.

'So, what have all those people got in common, other than having been members of the UHC?'

'They're all connected to the drownings of Deirdre and Daiyu,' said Robin.

'Reaney's connection's tenuous,' said Strike. 'He overslept; that's it. Kevin's connection's shaky, too. He was, what – six, when Daiyu died? And I doubt the church knows what Emily said to him about her suspicions. Was he old enough to attend the Manifestation where we think Deirdre drowned?'

'Yes,' said Robin, doing some rapid mental calculations. 'He'd have been thirteen or fourteen when it happened.'

'Which is strange,' said Strike, 'because he seemed to buy the line about her taking off of her own accord.'

'OK,' said Robin, who could hear Strike's footsteps on the metal stairs, 'well, I'll see you tomorrow, anyway. I just wanted to tell you about Cherie.'

'Yeah, thanks. Definitely something to think about.'

Robin rang off. Strike continued to climb until he reached the office door. He'd gone directly to Chinatown after Robin had dropped him off, which meant this was his first opportunity to examine the lock since Littlejohn had been fired. Strike turned on his phone torch and bent down.

'I thought so, you fucker,' he murmured.

The expensive new lock, which was skeleton-key resistant,

had gained new scratches since that morning. A tiny fleck of paint had also been chipped away beside it. Somebody, Strike surmised, had made strenuous efforts to force the door.

He now looked up at the second precaution he'd taken against Patterson's revenge. The tiny camera sat in a dark corner near the ceiling, almost invisible unless you knew what you were looking for.

Strike unlocked the door, turned on the lights and went to sit at Pat's desk, where he'd be able to view the day's camera footage. He opened the software, then fast-forwarded past the arrivals of Pat, the postman and Shah, then Pat visiting the bathroom on the landing, Shah departing . . .

Strike slapped his hand down on pause. A tall, stocky balaclavaed figure was creeping up the stairs, dressed all in black and looking both up and down as it came, checking the coast was clear. As Strike watched, the figure reached the landing, moved to the office door, withdrew a set of skeleton keys and began trying to unlock it. Strike glanced at the timestamp, which showed the footage had been taken shortly after sunset. This suggested the intruder didn't know Strike lived in the attic – something of which Littlejohn was well aware.

For nearly ten minutes, the black-clad figure continued to try and open the office door, without success. Finally giving up, they backed off, contemplating the glass panel, which Strike had made sure was reinforced when he had it put in. They seemed to be trying to decide whether it was worth attempting to smash the panel when they turned to look at the stairs behind them. Evidently, they knew themselves to be no longer alone.

'Fuck,' said Strike quietly, as the figure pulled a gun from somewhere inside their black clothing. They backed very slowly away from the landing, and retreated slowly up the flight that led to Strike's flat.

A delivery man appeared, holding a pizza. He knocked on the office door and waited. After a minute or two, he made a phone call, presumably learned he was at the wrong address, and left.

Another couple of minutes passed, long enough for the hidden intruder to hear the street door close. Then they crept out of their hiding place to stand contemplating the office door for a full minute, before turning the gun in their hands and trying, with their full force, to shatter the glass with the butt. The glass remained intact.

The balaclavaed figure slid the gun back inside their jacket, descended the stairs and disappeared from sight.

Strike rewound the footage to get stills he could study, poring over every second of film. It was impossible to tell whether or not the gun was real, given the poor lighting on the landing and the fact it hadn't been fired, but even so, the detective knew he'd have to take this to the police. As he rewatched the recording, Strike found the way the figure had behaved ominous, over and above the fact of an attempted break-in. The careful scrutiny of the stairs ahead and behind them, the stealthy movements, the unflustered retreat when threatened with discovery: all suggested someone who wasn't a novice.

His mobile rang. He picked it up and answered, eyes still on the screen.

'Hello?'

'Are you Cormoran Strike?' said a deep, breathless male voice.

'Yes. Who's this?'

'Wha' did you do to my wife?'

Strike looked away from the computer screen, frowning.

'Who's this?'

'WHA' DID YOU DO TO MY WIFE?' bellowed the man, so loudly Strike had to remove the phone from his ear. In the background, at the other end of the line, Strike now heard a female voice saying, 'Mr Woods – Mr Woods, calm down—' and what sounded like the wails of crying children.

'I don't know what you're talking about,' said Strike, but some part of his brain did, and a worse sensation than that which had followed Bijou's announcement that she was pregnant now petrified his guts.

'MY WIFE – MY WIFE—'

The man was crying as he yelled.

'Mr Woods,' said the female voice, louder now, 'give me the phone. We can take care of this, Mr Woods. Give me the phone. Your daughters need you, Mr Woods.'

Strike heard the sounds of a phone being passed over. A Bristolian female voice now spoke in his ear; he could tell the woman was walking.

'This is PC Heather Waters, Mr Strike. We believe you might have visited a Mrs Carrie Woods today? We found your card here.'

'I did,' said Strike. 'Yeah.'

'Can I ask what that was in relation to?'

'What's happened?' said Strike.

'Can I ask what you were talking to Mrs Woods about, Mr—?'

'What's happened?'

He heard a door close. The background noise disappeared.

'Mrs Woods has hanged herself,' said the voice. 'Her husband found her body in the garage this evening, when he came home from work.'

PART EIGHT

Kuai/Break-through

One must resolutely make the matter known
At the court of the king.
It must be announced truthfully.
Danger.

The I Ching or Book of Changes

101

Nine in the third place means . . .
Awareness of danger,
With perseverance, furthers.
Practice chariot driving and armed defence daily.

                          The I Ching or Book of Changes

Robin took the news of Carrie's death, which Strike relayed by phone, very hard. The two detectives were questioned separately by the police the following day. Strike, who'd also shown the footage of the balaclavaed man to the police, had his own police interview later that afternoon.

Over the ensuing twenty-four hours, Strike and Robin saw very little of each other. Strike had given his partner the task of contacting Walter Fernsby's and Marion Huxley's children to see whether they'd be happy to talk about their respective parents' involvement with the UHC, and to interview any who agreed. He'd done this because he knew Robin needed to keep busy, but had insisted she did it from home, because he didn't want her running into any church members in the vicinity of the office. He, meanwhile, was taking care of their new client, who'd replaced the Franks: yet another wife who suspected her wealthy husband of infidelity.

Strike held a full team meeting, minus Shah, who was in Norwich keeping an eye out for Emily Pirbright, on Thursday.

They met, not in the office, but in the red-carpeted basement room of the Flying Horse where they'd previously retired to evade Littlejohn, and which Strike had hired for a couple of hours. While careful observation of Denmark Street hadn't revealed anyone who seemed to be keeping the office under surveillance, a locksmith who Strike wanted to disturb as little as possible was fitting a skeleton-key-proof lock on the street door, with the agreement of the landlord and second floor tenant. Neither knew what had occasioned Strike's desire for more security, but as Strike was offering to pay for it, both were amenable.

The first part of the meeting was taken up by the subcontractors interrogating Robin, who they hadn't seen since her return. They were mainly interested in the supposedly supernatural aspects of what she'd witnessed at Chapman Farm, and discussion ensued of how each illusion had been achieved, with only Pat remaining silent. Shortly after Barclay had suggested that Wace's conjuring of Daiyu in the basement must have been a variation on the Victorian illusion called Pepper's ghost, Strike said,

'All right, enough, we've got work to do.'

He was afraid that Robin's surface good humour might soon crack. She had purplish shadows under her eyes, and her smile was becoming increasingly strained.

'I know we've seen no evidence of it yet,' said Strike, 'but I want eyes peeled at all times for anyone who seems to be watching the office, and get pictures if you can. I've got a feeling the UHC will be on the prowl.'

'Any word on our gun-toting visitor?' asked Barclay.

'No,' said Strike, 'but the police have got the footage. With the street door secured, they'll have a job getting back inside, whoever they were.'

'What were they after?' asked Midge.

'UHC case file,' suggested Barclay.

'Probably,' said Strike. 'Anyway: I've got good news. Heard from the police this morning: both Franks are going to be charged with stalking and attempted kidnap.'

The others applauded, Robin joining in a little late, trying to appear as cheerful as the rest.

'Excellent,' said Barclay.

'They'd better get bloody jail time this time,' said Midge fiercely. 'And not wriggle out of it again because,' she affected a high-pitched squeak, '"I won't be able to see my social worker!"'

Barclay and Strike laughed. Robin forced a smile.

'I think they're definitely going down this time,' said Strike. 'They had some nasty stuff in that lock-up where they were planning to keep her.'

'Like wh—?' began Barclay, but Strike, concerned about what his partner's feelings might be on hearing about sex toys and ball-gags, said,

'Moving on: Toy Boy update. Client told me yesterday he wants us to concentrate on the bloke's background.'

'We've *looked*,' said Midge in frustration. 'He's clean!'

'Well, we're being paid to look again and find dirt,' said Strike, 'so it's time to start milking family, friends and neighbours. You two,' he said to Barclay and Midge, 'put your heads together and come up with some workable covers, run them past me or Robin, and we'll work out the rota accordingly.'

Strike ticked Toy Boy off the list in front of him and moved to the next item.

'New client: her husband took a detour to Hampstead Heath last night, after dark.'

'I'm guessing he wasn't there for the views,' said Midge.

As Hampstead Heath was a well-known gay cruising area, Strike tended to agree.

'He didn't meet anyone. Probably got the wind up: there was a gang of kids wandering around near where he got out of the car. Only stayed ten minutes – but if that's his game, I doubt it'll be long before we get the wife what she wants.'

'Good,' piped up Pat, 'because I had that cricketer on the phone this morning, asking when we're going to get to him.'

'Let him go to McCabes,' said Strike indifferently. 'He's an arsehole. Anyway, until we've got a replacement for Littlejohn, we haven't got the manpower.'

He ticked 'Hampstead' off the list.

'Which brings us to Patterson Inc.'

'Or, as they're now known, Royally Fucked Inc,' said Barclay. 'Patterson's been charged, did ye see that?'

'Yeah,' said Strike. 'Turns out, if you're going to illegally bug an office, best not to do it to a leading barrister. Hope Patterson enjoys prison food. Anyway, I've now had three job applications from people struggling to get off the sinking Patterson ship. I'll check with Shah and see if any of them are worth an interview. I'm happy to forgo the pleasure of working with Navabi, given how shit she is at surveillance. However, her pitch for the job was that she'd be the ideal person to get into Zhou's clinic.'

'The fuck does she know we're trying to get in there?' asked Barclay.

'Because she was in there herself, while Patterson Inc were still doing the UHC case, and that explains Littlejohn's insistence he had something else for me – presumably she told him what she saw in there.'

'You're not going to get anything out of Littlejohn now,' said Midge.

'I know,' said Strike, crossing 'Patterson' off the list, 'but this makes me even keener than I was to get a woman into that bloody clinic – it's got to be a woman, Navabi said it was ninety per cent women there. I just don't think you fit the profile, Midge,' Strike added, as the subcontractor opened her mouth, 'we need someone—'

'I wasn't gonna suggest me,' said Midge, 'I was gonna say, we've got the ideal person.'

'Robin can't do it, she—'

'I know that, Strike, I'm not fookin' stupid. *Tasha.*'

'Tasha,' repeated Strike.

'Tasha. She's the type, isn't she? Actress, got a bit of money. Her play's finished as well. She'd do it for us, no problem. She's dead grateful for—'

'Still in touch with her, are you?' said Strike.

Barclay and Robin both reached for their coffees and drank in perfect synchronicity.

'Yeah,' said Midge. 'She's not a client any more. Not a problem, is it?'

Strike caught Pat's eye.

'No,' he said. 'Not a problem.'

102

Inquire of the oracle once again
Whether you possess sublimity, constancy, and
perseverance;
Then there is no blame.

The I Ching or Book of Changes

The meeting had concluded. Pat returned to the office with Barclay, who had receipts to file, and Midge left to ask Tasha Mayo whether she'd be prepared to enjoy a week at the exclusive clinic of Dr Andy Zhou, expenses paid by the agency.

'Want a coffee?' Strike asked Robin.

'OK,' said Robin, even though she'd just had two.

They walked together to Frith Street and Bar Italia, which lay across the road from Ronnie Scott's jazz club, and which Strike preferred to Starbucks. While he was buying their drinks, Robin sat at one of the round metal tables, watching the passers-by and wishing she was any one of them.

'You all right?' Strike said, once he'd set the drinks on the table and sat down. He knew perfectly well what the answer was, but was unable to think of any other opening. Robin took a sip of her cappuccino before saying,

'I just keep thinking about her daughters.'

'Yeah,' said Strike. 'I know.'

Both watched the cars pass for a moment or two, before Strike said,

'Look—'

'Don't tell me we didn't make it happen.'

'Well, I *am* going to tell you that, because we didn't.'

'Strike—'

'*She* did it. She chose to do it.'

'Yes – because of us.'

'We asked questions. That's the job.'

'That's exactly what Ryan said. "That's the job."'

'Well, he's not wrong,' said Strike. 'Do I feel good about what happened? No. But we didn't put the rope round her neck. She did that herself.'

Robin, who'd done a lot of crying when not at work in the last two days, had no tears left to shed. The terrible burden of guilt she'd carried with her ever since Strike had told her that the mother of two had been found hanged in the family's garage wasn't eased by his words. She kept visualising the picture stuck to Carrie Curtis Woods' fridge door, of two figures hand in hand in princess dresses: *Me and Mummy*.

'We went to interview her,' said Strike, 'because a seven-year-old child who was in her care vanished off the face of the earth. D'you think Carrie should've been able to walk away from that and never answer any questions, ever again?'

'She'd already answered questions from the police and at the inquest. It was over, it was behind her, she had a happy life and a family, and we went raking it all up again . . . I feel as though they've made me one of them,' Robin added quietly.

'What are you talking about?'

'I've become an agent of infection for the church. I carried the virus back to Carrie and this time she didn't survive it.'

'With respect,' said Strike, 'that's complete bollocks. We're just going to ignore the neon elephant in the room, are we?

If Carrie was going to kill herself because of what the church did to her, it'd have happened in the last two decades. This wasn't about the church. There was something she didn't want to face, something she couldn't stand people knowing, and that's not our fault.'

'But—'

'What I want to know,' said Strike, 'is who called her that morning, before we arrived. Did the police ask you about that mobile number her husband didn't recognise?'

'Yes,' said Robin dully. 'It could have been anyone. Wrong number.'

'Except that she called it back, after we left.'

'Oh,' said Robin. 'They didn't tell me that.'

'They didn't tell me, either. I read it upside down on the notes of the guy who was interviewing me. Reaney got a call shortly after I interviewed him, and he then started amassing sleeping pills. I never checked whether he'd had one before I met him, but it looks like the church is warning people we're on the prowl, and demanding to be told what was said, afterwards.'

'That implies the church knew we were going to Cherie's that day.'

'They could've seen she was back from holiday, from Facebook, and wanted to tell her to take the meeting when we turned up. I had the feeling when we introduced ourselves she wasn't completely surprised to see us. Panicked, yeah. Not entirely surprised.'

Robin made no answer. Strike watched her take another sip of coffee. She'd tied back her hair; the expensive haircut she'd had before going to the Rupert Court Temple had long since grown out, and it hadn't yet occurred to Robin to visit a hairdresser.

'What d'you want to do?' said Strike, watching her.

'What d'you mean?' she said.

'D'you want to take another few days off?'

'No,' said Robin. More time to spend dwelling on her guilt about Carrie and her anxiety about the child abuse charges was the very last thing she wanted.

'D'you feel up to talking about the case?'

'Yes, of course.'

'Get anything on Walter Fernsby's and Marion Huxley's kids?'

'Not much,' said Robin, forcing herself to focus. 'I spoke to Marion's elder daughter and, bottom line, it definitely can't be Marion who's gone back to the farm after years away. While her husband was alive, she hardly ever left Barnsley. After Marion disappeared, the family checked the PC she used at work, and she'd been watching Wace videos non-stop. They think she must have attended a meeting. Now they're getting letters from Marion that don't sound like her, telling them she wants to sell the undertakers and give all the profits to the UHC.'

'And Walter?'

'The only child I've been able to contact is his son, Rufus. He works for the Institution of Civil Engineers. The moment I mentioned Walter, he hung up.'

'Maybe he's been getting the same "sell everything, I want to give it to the church" letters as Marion's daughter?'

'Maybe.'

'Well, I found something last night, too, after Hampstead Heath went home.'

Strike pulled out his phone, typed in a couple of words, then handed it to Robin, who found herself looking at a picture of a tall man with a long jaw and steel-grey hair, who was pictured mid-speech on stage, his arms stretched wide. Robin didn't immediately understand why she was being shown the picture until she saw the caption: *Joe Jackson of the UHC, speaking at the Climate Change Conference, 2015.*

'*Oh,*' she said. 'Joe, from the Polaroids?'

'Could well be. He's based at the San Francisco centre these days. He's the right kind of age. He might not look much like the type to have a skull tattoo *now,* but there are plenty of people wandering around with tattoos they wish they hadn't got when they were younger. Schoolmate of mine in Cornwall got his first girlfriend's name tattooed on his neck. She dumped him as soon as she saw it.'

Robin didn't smile. Instead she said quietly, her eyes on Ronnie Scott's,

'I feel as though we're up against something we can't fight. They've got it stitched up, and it's genius, really. No wonder people either self-destruct or never talk once they get out. They've either had sex with underage teens, or participated in abuse, or watched people die in agony. People who stay are either too frightened or ground down to think of escaping, or they're like Becca and *him* –' she gestured towards Strike's phone, '– true believers. They rationalise the abuse, even if they've suffered from it. I'll bet you anything, if we went to Joe Jackson and asked him whether he'd ever been made to put on a pig mask and sodomise a man with a low IQ, he'd deny it, and not even because he's frightened. He must have got quite high up in the hierarchy, if he's giving speeches like that. He'll have shut down part of his brain. Watching Becca on that tape … she *knew* she was lying and she didn't flinch. It was all justified, all necessary. In her mind, she's a heroine, helping the whole world towards the Lotus Way.'

'So we give up, do we?' said Strike. 'We let Will Edensor rot in there?'

'I'm not saying that, but—'

Strike's mobile rang.

'Hi Pat, what's up?'

Robin could hear Pat's gravelly voice, though she couldn't make out the words.

'Righto, we're coming straight back. Five minutes.'

Strike hung up with an odd expression on his face.

'Well, I'm glad you don't think we should let Will Edensor rot,' he told Robin.

'Why?'

'Because,' said Strike, 'he's just turned up at the office.'

103

*In this hexagram we are reminded of youth and
folly . . . When the spring gushes forth, it does not
know at first where it will go. But its steady flow fills
up the deep place blocking its progress . . .*

The I Ching or Book of Changes

Robin entered the office first, with Strike just behind her. Will Edensor was sitting on the sofa by Pat's desk, wearing his blue tracksuit, which was not only filthy, but torn at the knees. He looked even thinner than when Robin had last seen him, although perhaps she'd simply become re-habituated to people who looked decently fed. At Will's feet sat an old plastic bag that appeared to contain some large, solid object, and on his lap sat little Qing, who was also wearing a blue tracksuit, and eating a chocolate biscuit with an expression of ecstasy on her face.

Will turned scarlet when he saw Robin.

'Hi Will,' she said.

Will looked down at the floor. Even his ears were red.

'That child needs some proper food,' said Pat, sounding as though this was Strike and Robin's fault. 'We've only got biscuits.'

'Good thinking,' said Strike, pulling out his wallet, 'could you get us all some pizza, Pat?'

Pat took the notes Strike had handed her, pulled on her coat and left the office. Robin wheeled Pat's computer chair out from behind the desk to sit down at a short distance from Will and Qing. Strike, conscious of looming over everyone, went to the cupboard to take out one of the folding plastic chairs. Will sat hunchbacked, holding his daughter, blushing furiously, staring at the carpet. Qing, who was munching her biscuit, was easily the most at ease person in the room.

'It's great to see you, Will,' said Robin. 'Hello, Qing,' she added, smiling.

'More!' said the toddler, stretching out her hands towards the biscuit tin on Pat's desk.

Robin took out two chocolate fingers and gave them to her. Will remained hunched over, as though in pain, holding Qing around her middle. Strike, who had no idea that the last time Will had seen Robin he'd been naked and masturbating – Robin's account had left her partner assuming both had been fully clothed when Will had thrown his punch – assumed his embarrassment stemmed from having hit her.

'How did you get out?' Robin asked Will, while Qing munched joyfully.

She hadn't forgotten what Will had done to her in the Retreat Room, but at the moment that was of far less importance to her than the extraordinary fact that he'd left Chapman Farm.

'Climbed over the wall at the blind spot,' he muttered. 'Same as you.'

'By night?'

'No, because I had to bring Qing.'

He forced himself to look up at Robin, but was unable to hold her gaze long, and instead addressed the leg of Pat's desk.

'I've got to find out where Lin is,' he said, a little desperately.

'We're looking for her,' Robin assured him.

'Why?'

'Because,' said Robin, before Strike could say anything tactless about Lin's potential usefulness in discrediting the church, 'we care about her. I was there, remember, when she was miscarrying?'

'Oh, yeah,' said Will. 'I forgot ... they've got centres in Birmingham and Glasgow, you know,' he added.

'Yes, we know,' said Robin. 'But we think she might be in Dr Zhou's clinic, just outside London.'

'Has he got a clinic?' said Will naively. 'I thought he was just the church's doctor?'

'No, he's a doctor on the outside, too,' said Robin.

'Lin doesn't like him. She won't like being in his clinic,' muttered Will.

He glanced up at Robin and back at his own feet.

'My father hired you, didn't he?'

Strike and Robin looked at each other. The former, happy for Robin to take the lead, gave a slight shrug.

'Yes,' said Robin.

'*You can't tell him I'm out*,' said Will, with a mixture of desperation and ferocity, looking up at Robin from beneath his eyebrows. 'All right? If you're going to tell my father, I'll leave now. I only came here because I've got to find Lin, before I go to jail.'

'Why d'you say you're going to jail?' asked Robin.

'Because of all the things I've done. I don't want to talk about it. As long as Lin and Qing are OK, I don't mind, I deserve it. But you *can't tell my father*. He'll have to know once I've been arrested, but I won't have to talk to him then, because I'll be in custody. Anyway, once I start talking, the Drowned Prophet will probably come for me, so it won't matter. But Lin'll be able to get a council flat or something, won't she? If she's got a kid? Because I haven't got any money,' he added pathetically.

'I'm sure something will be worked out,' said Robin.

The glass door opened and Pat re-entered, carrying four boxes of pizza.

'That was quick,' said Strike.

'It's only up the road, isn't it?' said Pat, setting the pizzas down on the desk, 'and I've just rung my granddaughter. She's got clothes you can have, for the little one,' she told Will. 'Her youngest's just turned three. She'll bring them over.'

'Hang on,' said Strike, momentarily distracted. 'You're a—?'

'Great-grandmother, yeah,' said Pat, unemotionally. 'We have 'em young in my family. Best way, when you've still got the energy.'

She hung up her bag and coat and went to fetch plates out of the kitchen area. Little Qing, who appeared to be having a fine time, now looked curiously towards the pizza boxes, from which an appetising smell was emanating, but Will's lips had begun silently moving in what Robin recognised as the familiar chant, '*Lokah Samastah Sukhino Bhavantu.*'

'I just need to have a quick word with Robin,' Strike said to Will, disconcerted by his silent chanting. 'You OK here with Pat for a bit?'

Will nodded, his lips still moving. Strike and Robin got up and, with a jerk of his head, Strike indicated to his partner that the landing would be the safest place to talk.

'He and the kid should stay here,' said Strike, having closed the glass door behind him. 'They can have my place, and I'll put up a camp bed in the office. I don't think we can put them in a local hotel, it's too close to Rupert Court, and I think he needs someone with him, in case he starts hallucinating the Drowned Prophet.'

'OK,' said Robin quietly, 'but *don't* tell him we've got to let Sir Colin know.'

'Edensor's the client. We've got to tell him.'

'*I* know that,' said Robin, 'but Will doesn't have to.'

'Don't you think, if we tell him his dad already knows about the kid—?'

'I don't think he's scared of his father knowing about Qing. I think he's worried Sir Colin will try and stop him going to prison.'

Strike looked down at her, nonplussed.

'He's obviously feeling really guilty about whatever he's done in there, and prison's just another Chapman Farm, isn't it?' said Robin. 'Far less scary to him than the outside world.'

'What are all these things, plural, he's done, that are criminal?' said Strike.

'It might just be sleeping with Lin when she was underage,' said Robin uncertainly. 'I'm worried about pressing him for details, though, especially with Qing there. He might get upset, or kick off.'

'You realise this is all down to you, him leaving?'

'I don't think so,' said Robin. 'It's Lin disappearing that made him do it. He was already having doubts when I turned up.'

'You pushed his doubts to breaking point. He's probably left early enough for his daughter not to be completely screwed up, as well. I think you might've saved two lives.'

Robin looked up at him.

'I know why you're saying this, Stri—'

'It's the truth. This is the job, as well as the other thing.'

But Robin drew little comfort from his words. It would take more than the unexpected escape of Will Edensor to erase her mental image of Carrie's two little girls crying for their mother.

They returned to the office. Both Will and Qing were devouring slices of pizza, Will ravenously, Qing looking as though she was experiencing nirvana.

'So how did you do it, Will?' Robin asked, sitting down again. 'How did you get out?'

Will swallowed a large mouthful of pizza and said,

'Stole twenty pounds from Mazu's office. Went to the classroom when Shawna was in charge. Said Qing had to see Dr Zhou. Shawna believed me. Ran across the field. Climbed out at the blind spot, like you did. Flagged down a car. Woman took us to Norwich.'

Robin, who fully appreciated how difficult every single part of this plan would have been to execute, said,

'That's incredible. And then you hitched to London?'

'Yeah,' said Will.

'But how on earth did you find our office?'

Will pushed the plastic bag at his feet towards Robin with his toe, rather than dislodge the child on his lap. Robin bent to pick it up and extracted the plastic rock.

'Oh,' she said. 'It was *you* who moved it . . . but it was empty. There weren't any letters in it.'

'I know,' said Will, his mouth full of pizza, 'but I worked it out. After what – after the Retreat Room –' he dropped his gaze to the floor again – 'I sneaked out at night to see if there was anything on the edge of the woods, because Lin had seen you with the torch, and I thought you must be an investigator. I found the rock and looked inside, and there were imprints on the paper, from what you'd written on the sheets on top, so I could tell I was right, and you'd been writing about what was going on at Chapman Farm. After you left, Vivienne was telling everyone you'd answered to "Robin" in Norwich, and Taio said there was a big guy waiting for you at the blind spot when you escaped. So I looked up "Robin" and "detective" in a library in Norwich – got a lift to London – and—'

'Bloody hell,' said Strike, 'we've been told you're bright, but this is impressive.'

Will neither looked at Strike nor acknowledged his words, except by a slight frown. Robin suspected this was because Will knew it must have been Sir Colin who'd told the two detectives his son was clever.

'Water,' said Pat, as Qing began to cough, because she'd stuffed so much pizza into her mouth.

Robin joined Pat at the sink to help her fill glasses.

'Could you distract Qing,' Robin whispered to the office manager, the sound of running water drowning her voice, 'while Strike and I talk to Will in our office? He might not want to talk openly in front of her.'

'No problem,' said Pat, in the growl that was her whisper. 'Say the name again?'

'Qing.'

'Kind of name's that?'

'Chinese.'

'Huh . . . mind you, my great-granddaughter's called Tanisha. Sanskrit,' said Pat, with a slight eye roll.

When Pat and Robin had handed out glasses of water, Pat said gruffly,

'Qing, look at these.'

She'd taken a block of bright orange Post-it notes out of her desk.

'They come off, look,' said Pat. 'And they stick to things.'

Fascinated, the little girl slid off Will's lap, but still clung to his knee. Having seen the other children at Chapman Farm, Robin was glad of this sign that Qing knew her father was a place of safety.

'You can play with them, if you want,' said Pat.

The little girl toddled uncertainly towards Pat, who held out the block to her, and rummaged for some pens. Strike and Robin's eyes met again, and Strike stood up, holding his pizza.

'Fancy coming through here a moment, Will?' he asked.

928

They left the connecting door between the offices open, so that Qing could see where her father was. Strike brought his plastic chair with him.

Robin had forgotten that all the pictures relating to the UHC case were on the board on the inner office wall. Will stopped dead, staring at them.

'Why have you got all these?' he said, in an accusatory voice, and to Robin's dismay, he backed away. 'That's the Drowned Prophet,' he said, pointing at the Torment Town pictures, sounding panicked now. 'Why have you drawn her like that?'

'We didn't draw her,' said Strike, moving quickly to close the flaps of the board, but Will said suddenly,

'*That's Kevin!*'

'Yes,' said Strike. Changing his mind about closing up the board, he stepped away from it, allowing Will a clear view. 'Did you know Kevin?'

'Only for a few ... he left, not long after I ... why ... ?'

Will took a few steps closer to the board. Kevin's picture, which Strike had taken from the newspaper archive, still had the caption attached: *'Murder of Kevin Pirbright was drug-related, say police.'*

'Kevin killed himself,' said Will slowly. 'Why're they saying ... ?'

'He was shot by someone else,' said Strike.

'No, he killed himself,' said Will, with some of the dogmatism he'd displayed the first time Robin had ever heard him talk, on the vegetable patch. 'He committed suicide, because he was pure spirit, and couldn't cope with the materialist world.'

'There was no gun found at the scene,' said Strike. 'Somebody else shot him.'

'No ... they can't have done ...'

'They did,' said Strike.

Will was frowning. Then –

'Pig demons!' he said suddenly, pointing at the Polaroids.

Strike and Robin looked at each other.

'Kevin told me they appear, if there are too many impure spirits at the farm.'

'Those aren't demons,' said Strike.

'No,' said Will, with a trace of impatience. 'I know *that*. They're wearing masks. But that's how Kevin described them to me. Naked, with pig heads.'

'Where did he see them, Will, did he say?' asked Robin.

'In the barn,' said Will. 'He and his sister saw them, through a gap in the wood. I don't want her looking at me,' he added in a febrile voice, and Robin, who knew he meant the Drowned Prophet, strode to the board and covered it over.

'Why don't you sit down?' said Strike.

Will did so, but he looked very wary as the other two also sat. They could hear Qing chattering to Pat in the outer office.

'Will, you said you've done things that are criminal,' said Strike.

'I'll tell the police all about that, once we've found Lin.'

'OK,' said Strike, 'but as we're—'

'I'm not talking about it,' said Will, turning red again. 'You're not the police, you can't make me.'

'Nobody's going to make you do anything,' said Robin, with a warning look at her partner, whose demeanour, even when trying to be sympathetic, was often more threatening than he realised. 'We only want what you want, Will: to find Lin and make sure Qing's OK.'

'You're doing more than that,' said Will, with a nervous jab of the finger towards the covered board. 'You're trying to take the UHC on, aren't you? That won't work. It won't, it definitely won't. You're messing with stuff you don't understand. I know, if I tell the police everything, she'll come for me. That's a chance I'll have to take. I don't care if I die, as long as Lin and Qing are OK.'

'You're talking about the Drowned Prophet?' Robin asked.

'Yeah,' said Will. 'You don't want her after you, as well. She protects the church.'

'We won't need to take on the UHC now,' lied Robin. 'All that stuff on the board – we were just trying to find ways to put pressure on the Waces, so your family could see you.'

'But I don't want to see them!'

'No, I know,' said Robin. 'I'm just saying, there's no point us going on with that part of the investigation –' she pointed at the board '– now you're out.'

'But you'll find Lin?'

'Yes, of course.'

'What if she's dead?' Will burst out suddenly. 'There was all that blood—'

'I'm sure we'll find her,' said Robin.

'It'll be punishment on me, if she's dead,' said Will, 'for what I did to my m-mum.'

He burst into tears.

Robin wheeled her chair out from behind the desk and drew nearer to Will, although she didn't touch him. She guessed he'd seen his mother's obituary online, in the internet café in Norwich. She said nothing, but waited for Will's sobs to subside.

'Will,' she said, when at last she thought he was in a condition to take in what she was saying, 'we're only asking what you've done that might be criminal, because we need to know whether the church has got something on you that they could publish, before you've got a chance to talk to the police. If they do that, you could be arrested before we can find Lin, d'you see? And that would mean Qing being taken into care.'

931

Full of admiration for how Robin was handling this interview, Strike had to suppress a wholly inappropriate grin.

'*Oh,*' said Will, raising a grubby, tear-stained face. 'Right. Well ... they can't publish it, without making themselves look really bad. It was either stuff we all had to do, or that I should've gone to the police about. They're doing something *really* terrible in there. I didn't realise how bad it was, 'til I had Qing.'

'But you haven't personally hurt anyone, have you?'

'Yes, I have,' he said miserably. 'Lin. And – I'll tell the police all of it, not you. Once we've got Lin, I'll tell the police.'

Pat's mobile rang and they heard her say,

'Stay on the corner, I'll come and get 'em off you.' She appeared in the doorway. 'Someone'll have to look after Qing. That's Kayleigh, with the clothes for her.'

'That was—' began Strike, but before he could say 'quick' for the second time that morning, Pat had disappeared. Qing now tottered into the inner office, in search of her father, demanding to go to the bathroom. By the time Will and Qing had returned from the landing, Pat had reappeared holding two bulging bags of second-hand children's clothes, looking cross.

'Bloody nosy, the lot of 'em,' she complained, setting the bags on her desk.

'Who?' asked Robin, as Pat took out a small pair of dungarees, got awkwardly down on her knees and sized them up against a fascinated Qing.

'My family,' said Pat. 'Always trying to find out what sort of office I work in. That was my granddaughter. Met her on the corner. No need for her to know what we do.'

'You haven't told any of them you work here?'

'Signed an NDA, didn't I?'

'How did Kayleigh—?'

'Her boyfriend brought 'em into town. She works up the road in TK Maxx. Told her it was urgent. Right, missus,' she told Qing, 'let's get you into this clean stuff. You wanna do it,' she asked Will, squinting up at him, 'or shall I?'

'I can do it,' said Will, taking the dungarees, though looking slightly at a loss as to how they worked.

'Robin can help you,' said Pat. 'Can I have a word?' she added to Strike.

'Can't it—?'

'No,' she said.

So Strike followed Pat back into the room they'd just left, and Pat closed the door on Will, Qing and Robin.

'Where're they gonna stay?' Pat demanded of Strike.

'Here,' said Strike, 'I've just worked that out with Robin. They can go upstairs.'

'That's no good. They want looking after. They should come and stay with me.'

'We can't impose—'

'It's not imposing, I'm offering. We've got room, my Dennis won't mind, and Dennis can be with them, while I'm at work. There's a garden for the little girl and I can get her some toys off my granddaughters. *They want looking after,*' repeated Pat, with a gimlet look that told Strike she didn't consider him qualified for the job. 'There's no harm in that boy,' said Pat, as though Strike had been arguing the contrary. 'Just did a bloody silly thing. I'll take care of them, 'til he's ready to see his dad.'

104

There are dangers lurking . . . pay especial attention
to small and insignificant things.

The I Ching or Book of Changes

'It's *really* good of Pat,' said Robin the following afternoon, as she and Strike headed out of London in the latter's BMW to meet Sir Colin Edensor at his home in Thames Ditton. 'We should give her that pay rise, you know.'

'Yeah, fine,' sighed Strike, winding down the window so he could vape.

'How did Sir Colin take it, when you told him Will's out?'

'Er – "stunned" sums it up, I think,' said Strike, who'd rung their client the night before with the news, 'but then I had to tell him Will doesn't want to see him, so that poured a few gallons of cold water on the celebrations. I didn't tell him Will's determined to go to jail, or that he's convinced the Drowned Prophet'll come for him, once he's interviewed by the police. Thought all that might be best discussed in person.'

'Probably wise,' said Robin. 'Listen, while I'm thinking about it, I've swapped my evening surveillance on Hampstead Heath with Midge, if that's OK. I've got something I need to do this evening.'

'No problem,' said Strike. As Robin didn't elaborate on the 'something' she needed to do, he assumed it had to do with

934

Murphy. Home-cooked dinner, or something even worse, like viewing a house together?

Robin, who was glad not to be questioned about her evening plans, because she doubted Strike would like them, went on,

'I've got some case news, too – although now Will's out, it might not matter.'

'Go on.'

'I ordered copies of Walter Fernsby's out-of-print books, and one of them arrived yesterday while I was at work.'

'Any good?'

'Couldn't tell you. I didn't get further than the dedication: *To Rosie.*'

'*Ah,*' said Strike.

'I already knew his daughter's name was Rosalind, but I didn't twig,' said Robin. 'Then I remembered something else. When we were all being told to write and tell our families we were staying at Chapman Farm, we were asked which people would object most. Walter said his son wouldn't like it, but his daughter would be understanding.'

'Really?'

'So I went back online to look for Rosalind Fernsby. She's listed as living with her father in West Clandon between 2010 and 2013, but I can't find any trace of her after that – no death certificate,' she added. 'I checked.'

'Where's West Clandon?'

'Just outside Guildford,' said Robin. 'But the house has been sold now.'

'You said you contacted her brother and he hung up on you?'

'Immediately I mentioned his father, yes. I've tried the mother's landline, but she's not answering. But it doesn't matter now, does it? Sir Colin probably won't want to pay for any more of this.'

'The case isn't closed yet. He still wants us to find Lin. Speaking of which, did you get the email about Tasha Mayo?'

'I did, yes,' said Robin. 'Fantastic news.'

Tasha Mayo had not only agreed to go undercover at Zhou's clinic for a week, she'd evinced real gusto for the job and unless something unexpected had happened, might already have arrived in Borehamwood. Her email enquiry had led within half an hour to a call from Dr Zhou in person, who'd taken a long history of her imaginary ailments over the phone, diagnosed her as in need of immediate treatment, and told her she'd need to stay a week and possibly longer.

'You wouldn't think she was that gutsy, looking at her,' said Robin.

'Appearances are definitely deceptive there,' said Strike. 'You should've seen her braving the Franks ... can't say I'm over-happy about her and Midge, though.'

'You think they're—?'

'Yeah, I think they're *definitely*,' said Strike, 'and it's not a good idea to sleep with clients.'

'But she's not a client any more.'

A brief silence fell. As far as Strike was aware, Robin had no idea how seriously his entanglement with Bijou Watkins had threatened to compromise the agency and he hoped to keep it that way. Little did he know that Robin had had the whole story from Ilsa the previous evening, by phone. Their mutual friend, who'd been cross at learning that Robin was out of Chapman Farm and that nobody had told her, had regaled Robin with everything she knew about the saga of Strike and Bijou. Robin therefore had a fairly shrewd idea as to why Strike would currently be sensitive about any subcontractor sleeping with people who might expose them to gossip.

'Anyway,' said Strike, keen to usher in a fresh topic of

conversation, 'Edensor's got a second motive to keep digging for dirt on the church, unless he hasn't realised yet.'

'Which is?'

'His Wikipedia page has undergone a lot of overnight modifications, too.'

'Shit, really?'

'Exactly the same m.o. as they used on the Graves family. Brutal abuse towards Will by his father, family dysfunction, etc.'

'Edensor might think lawyers are a better way of dealing with that, than us trying to take down the church.'

'He might,' said Strike, 'but I've got counter-arguments.'

'Which are?'

'For one: does he really want Will hallucinating the Drowned Prophet and killing himself?'

'He might argue psychotherapy would sort that out better than us trying to solve the mystery of Daiyu's death. I mean, it's not really even a mystery to anyone except us, is it?'

'That's because everyone else is a bloody idiot.'

'The police, the coastguard, the witnesses and the coroner? They're *all* bloody idiots?' said Robin, amused.

'You're the one who said the UHC have got away with it because everyone thought them a "bit weird, but harmless". Too many people, even intelligent ones – no, *especially* intelligent ones – presume innocence when they meet weirdness. "Bit odd, but I mustn't let my prejudices cloud my judgement." Then they over-correct, and what d'you get? A kid disappears off the face of the earth, and the whole story's bloody odd, but the robes and the mystic bullshit get in the way, and nobody wants to look like a bigot, so they say, "Strange, going paddling in the North Sea at five in the morning, but I s'pose that's the kind of thing people like that do. Probably something to do with moon phases."'

Robin made no response to this speech, partly because she didn't want to express aloud her real opinion, which was that her partner, too, was prejudiced: prejudiced in the opposite direction to the one he was describing, prejudiced against alternative lifestyles, because large parts of his own difficult and disrupted childhood had been spent in squats and communes. The other reason Robin didn't respond was because she'd noticed something vaguely disquieting. After a full minute of silence, Strike noticed her regular glances into the mirror.

'Something up?'

'I'm . . . probably being paranoid.'

'About what?'

'Don't look back,' said Robin, 'but we might be being followed.'

'Who?' said Strike, now watching the wing mirror.

'The red Vauxhall Corsa behind the Mazda . . . but it might not be the same one.'

'What d'you mean?'

'There was a red Corsa right behind us as we drove away from the garage in London. *That* one,' said Robin, glancing in the rear-view mirror again, 'has been keeping a car between us and it for the last few miles. Can you see the number plate?'

'No,' said Strike, squinting into the wing mirror. The driver was a fat man in sunglasses.

'Weird.'

'What?'

'There's another adult in there but they're in the back seat . . . try speeding up. Overtake this Polo.'

Robin did so. Strike watched the Corsa in the wing mirror. It pulled out, overtook the Mazda, then settled back in behind the Polo.

'Coincidence?' said Robin.

'Time will tell,' said Strike, his eyes on the pursuant car.

105

Conflict within weakens the power to conquer danger without.

The I Ching or Book of Changes

'I was being paranoid,' said Robin.

She'd just taken the turning onto the A309 leading to Thames Ditton, but the red Vauxhall Corsa had continued along the A307 and vanished.

'I'm not so sure,' said Strike, checking the pictures he'd taken covertly of the Corsa in the wing mirror. 'They might just've wanted confirmation we're visiting the Edensors.'

'Which we've just given them, by turning off,' said Robin anxiously. 'Maybe they think Will and Qing are staying with Sir Colin?'

'They might,' agreed Strike. 'We'd better warn him to keep a lookout for that car.'

The house in which Sir Colin and Lady Edensor had raised their three sons lay on the banks of the Thames, on the edge of a suburban village. Though its street face was unpretentious, its considerable size became apparent when Sir Colin led the two detectives through the house to the rear. A succession of airy rooms full of comfortable furniture culminated in a modern kitchen-cum-dining area, with walls composed largely of glass, revealing a long lawn running at a gentle slope down to the river.

Will's older brothers were waiting silently in the kitchen: James, dark and scowling, was standing beside an expensive-looking coffee machine, while the younger and fairer son, Ed, was sitting at a large dining table, his walking stick propped against the wall behind him. Robin sensed tension in the room. Neither brother looked as though they'd been rejoicing that Will had, at last, left the UHC, nor did they make any noise or sign of welcome. The strained atmosphere suggested that hot words had been exchanged, prior to their arrival. With unconvincing cheeriness, Sir Colin said,

'James and Ed wanted to be here, for the full update. Please, sit down,' he said, gesturing towards the table where Ed was already sitting. 'Coffee?'

'That'd be great,' said Strike.

Once five coffees had been made, Sir Colin had joined them at the table, although James remained standing.

'So, Will's staying with your office manager,' said Sir Colin.

'Pat, yes,' said Strike. 'I think it's a good arrangement. Keeps him out of the vicinity of Rupert Court.'

'I must give her some money for his food and board, until he . . . while he's there.'

'Very good of you,' said Strike. 'I'll pass that on.'

'Could I send over some of his clothes?'

'I'd advise against,' said Strike. 'As I said to you on the phone, he's threatened to take off again, if we tell you he's out.'

'Then perhaps, if I give you some extra money, you could pass that on, too, so he can buy some clothing, without saying where the money came from? I hate to think of him wandering around in that UHC tracksuit.'

'Fine,' said Strike.

'You said you had more to tell me, in person.'

'That's right,' said Strike.

He proceeded to give the Edensors full details of their

interview the previous day with Will. When Strike had finished, there was a short silence. Then Ed said,

'So basically, he wants you to find this Lin girl, then turn himself in to the police?'

'Exactly,' said Strike.

'But you don't know what he's done, to warrant arrest?'

'It could just be sleeping with Lin when she was underage,' said Robin.

'Well, I've spoken to my lawyers,' said Sir Colin, 'and their view is that if Will's worried about the statutory rape charge – and we've currently got no reason to suppose he's done worse than that – immunity from prosecution could be arranged, if he's prepared to give evidence against the church, and Lin doesn't want to press charges. Extenuating circumstances, coercion and so on – Rentons think he'd have a good chance of immunity.'

'It's not quite as simple as that,' Robin said. 'As Cormoran's said, Will believes the Drowned Prophet will come for him if he—'

'But he's *prepared* to talk, right?' said Ed, 'Once this girl Lin's found?'

'Yes, but only because—'

'Then we get him some psychotherapy, explain to him clearly that there's no need for him to go to jail if immunity's arranged—'

Robin, who'd liked Ed on their first meeting, found herself frustrated and angered by the slight trace of patronage in his voice. He seemed to think she was making difficulties about matters that, to him, were completely straightforward. While Robin had no intention of pressing charges against Will for assaulting her, the memory of him advancing on her, naked, penis in hand, in the Retreat Room was among the memories of Chapman Farm that would take a long time to fade.

The Edensors were not only operating in ignorance of what Will had endured, they were also failing to comprehend the full scope of what he'd done to others; compassionate though Robin felt towards Will, she remained most worried about Lin.

'The problem is,' she said, 'Will *wants* to go to jail. He's institutionalised and riddled with guilt. If you offer him psychotherapy, he'll refuse.'

'That's quite a presumption,' said Ed, raising his eyebrows. 'It hasn't been offered yet. And you're contradicting yourself: you just said he's scared of the Drowned Prophet coming for him, if he talks. How's he going to serve a prison term, if he's – what does the Drowned Prophet do, exactly? Put curses on people? Kill them?'

'You're asking Robin to explain the irrational,' said Strike, who allowed all the impatience into his voice that his partner was carefully repressing. 'Will's on a kind of kamikaze mission. Make sure Qing's safely with her mother, then 'fess up to everything he's done wrong, and either get sent down, or let the Prophet take him out.'

'And you're suggesting we allow him to implement this plan?'

'Not at all,' said Robin, before Strike could speak. 'We're simply saying Will needs very careful handling right now. He's got to feel safe, and that he's in control, and if he knows we've told his family he's out, he might take off again. If we can just find Lin—'

'What d'you mean, "if"?' said James, from over beside the coffee machine. 'Dad told us you know where she is.'

'We *think* she's at Zhou's Borehamwood clinic,' said Strike, 'and we've just put someone in there undercover – but we can't *know* she's there until we're inside.'

'So we're going to mollycoddle Will, and let him have it all his own way as usual, are we?' said James. 'If I were you,' he said to the back of his father's head, 'I'd go straight over to this Pat woman's house and tell him he's caused enough bloody trouble and it's time he got a grip.'

He now turned the coffee machine back on. Raising his voice over the loud grinding noise, Strike said,

'If your father did that, the risk to Will might be bigger than you realise, and I'm not just talking about his mental health. On Monday, a masked figure holding a gun tried to break into our office, possibly to get their hands on the UHC case file,' said Strike. Shock now registered on all three Edensors' faces. 'The church now knows they've had a private investigator undercover with them for sixteen weeks. Will had direct, one-on-one contact with Robin before he escaped, which means the UHC might assume he's now told her everything he's feeling so guilty about.

'Will's also taken off with Wace's granddaughter. Wace doesn't seem particularly attached to either Lin or Qing, but he values his own bloodline enough to keep all the children related to him at the farm, so I doubt he's going to be happy Qing's disappeared. Meanwhile, if we can get word to Lin that Qing's out, it makes it very likely she'll want to leave. Lin grew up in the church and is likely to know a damn sight more than Will does about what goes on in there.

'In short, Will's got his finger in the ring pull of a large can of worms which, incidentally, also incriminates a well-known novelist, who appears to be going to Chapman Farm to sleep with young girls, and an actress who's been pouring money into a dangerous and abusive organisation. As far as we know, the church has no idea yet where Will is, but if family members start visiting him, or if he starts visiting family lawyers, that could change. We think we were followed here this morning—'

'We aren't *sure*,' said Robin, in response to the increasing alarm on Sir Colin's face.

'—by a red Vauxhall Corsa,' said Strike, as though there'd been no interruption. 'I'd advise you to keep an eye out for it. It's possible the UHC is keeping tabs on us, and on you.'

There was a brief, appalled silence.

'You've been to the police about this masked intruder?' said Sir Colin.

'Naturally,' said Strike, 'but they've got nothing so far. Whoever it was was well disguised, right down to a balaclava, and dressed all in black – and that description tallies with the only sighting of Kevin Pirbright's shooter.'

'Dear God,' muttered Ed.

James, who'd refilled his own mug without offering coffee to anyone else, now advanced on the table.

'So, Will's potentially put all of us in danger? My wife? My kids?'

'I wouldn't go that far,' said Strike.

'Oh, *wouldn't* you?'

'They've never yet gone after the families of ex-members, except—'

'Online,' said Sir Colin. 'Yes, I've seen my new Wikipedia page. Not that I care—'

'*You* might not,' said James loudly, 'but I bloody well do! So what's *your* solution to this mess?' James threw at Strike. 'Keep Will in hiding for a decade, while my father single-handedly funds an investigation into the whole fucking church?'

Strike deduced from this comment that Sir Colin had confided his doubts about the Daiyu line of enquiry to his elder son.

'No,' he began, but before he could elaborate on any course of action, Ed piped up.

'It seems to me—'

'Will you *piss off* with the bloody psychotherapy?' spat James. 'If they're following and shooting people—'

'I was going to say,' said Ed, 'that if this girl Lin's prepared to give evidence against the church—'

'She's Wace's daughter, she's not going to—'

'How the hell do you know?'

'I know enough to know I don't want to be beholden to her—'

'We've got a duty of care—' began Sir Colin.

'*No, we bloody don't*,' shouted James. 'Neither she, nor her bloody misbegotten child, are of *any* interest to me. That stupid little shit's dragging Jonathan Wace's people into our lives in place of our mother, who *wouldn't be bloody dead but for the UHC*, and as far as I'm concerned, Will, this Lin and their bloody kid can go drown themselves—'

James swung his coffee mug towards the distant river, so that an arc of near-boiling black liquid hit Robin across the chest.

'—and join his fucking prophet!'

Robin let out a shriek of pain; Strike yelled 'Oi!' and stood up; Ed also attempted to stand, but his weak leg gave way; Sir Colin said, *'James!'* and while Robin was pulling scalding fabric away from her skin and looking frantically around for something to wash herself off with, Ed pushed himself back up on a second attempt and shouted at his elder brother, leaning on the table with both hands:

'You've got this *fucking* narrative in your head – it was inoperable by the time they found it, it had been there since before Will joined the fucking church! You want to blame someone, blame *me* – she didn't get herself checked because she was sitting next to *me* in hospital for five bloody months!'

With the two brothers yelling at each other so loudly nobody else could hear themselves speak, Robin left the table to grab some kitchen roll, which she ran under the cold tap then pressed beneath her shirt to relieve the burning on her skin.

'Be quiet – BE QUIET!' shouted Sir Colin, getting to his feet. 'Miss Ellacott, I'm so sorry – are you . . . ?'

'I'm fine, I'm fine,' said Robin, who, preferring not to mop hot coffee off her breasts with four men watching, turned her back on them.

James, who didn't seem to have realised he was responsible for the large black stain across Robin's cream shirt, began again.

'As far as *I'm* concerned—'

'Not going to apologise, then?' snarled Strike.

'It's not *your* bloody place to tell me—'

'You've just thrown boiling coffee all over my partner!'

'What?'

'I'm fine,' lied Robin.

Having bathed the smarting area with cold kitchen roll, she put the wad into the bin and returned to the table, her wet shirt clinging to her. Taking her jacket off the back of her chair, she pulled it back on, silently reflecting that she'd now been injured by two Edensor sons; perhaps Ed would make it a hat trick before she left the house, and smash her round the head with his walking stick.

'I'm sorry,' said James, taken aback. 'I genuinely – I didn't mean to do that . . .'

'Will didn't mean to do what he's done, either,' said Robin, feeling that if she had to get scalded, the least she was owed was to be able to capitalise on it. 'He did a really stupid, careless thing, and he knows it, but he never meant to hurt anyone.'

'I want this girl Lin found,' said Sir Colin in a low voice, before James could respond. 'I don't want to hear another word about it, James. I want her found. And after that . . .'

He looked at Strike.

'I'm prepared to fund another three months of investigation into Daiyu Wace's death. If you can prove it was suspicious,

946

that she's not the deity they've turned her into, that might help Will – but if you haven't found out anything after three months, we'll drop it. In the meantime, please thank your office manager for looking after Will, and ... we'll keep our eyes open for that Vauxhall Corsa.'

106

It is true that there are still dividing walls on which we stand confronting one another. But the difficulties are too great. We get into straits, and this brings us to our senses. We cannot fight, and therein lies our good fortune.

The I Ching or Book of Changes

'Well, that's that,' said Robin. 'No Corsa.'

She'd been checking her rear-view mirror far more often than usual all the way back to London, and was certain they hadn't been followed.

'Maybe you should ring the Edensors and say it was a false alarm?' she suggested.

'Whoever was in that Corsa might've realised we'd seen them,' Strike replied. 'I still think the Edensors need to keep their eyes peeled ... You can charge the dry-cleaning on that shirt to the agency,' he added. He hadn't liked to mention it, but the BMW now smelled strongly of coffee.

'No dry-cleaner on earth's going to get this out,' said Robin, 'and the accountant wouldn't let me charge it, anyway.'

'Then charge it to the busi—'

'It's old, and it was cheap when it was new. I don't care.'

'I do,' said Strike. 'Careless arsehole.'

Robin might have reminded Strike he'd once almost broken

her nose when she'd tried to stop him punching a suspect, but decided against.

They parted at the garage where Strike kept his BMW. As Robin hadn't said anything more about what she was up to that evening, Strike was confirmed in his view that it had something to do with Murphy, and set off back to the office in an irritable mood he chose to attribute to James Edensor's barely veiled accusation that the agency was financially exploiting his father. Robin, meanwhile, headed straight to Oxford Street, where she bought a cheap new shirt, changed in a department store bathroom, then sprayed herself liberally with a perfume tester to get rid of the coffee smell, because she had no time to go home and change before she met Prudence.

She'd called the therapist the previous evening, and Prudence, who had a dental appointment, had suggested they meet in an Italian restaurant close by the surgery. Robin found herself hyper-alert as she travelled to Kensington High Street by Tube. She'd been followed before, doing this job, and Strike's refusal to be reassured by the Corsa's non-appearance on their return journey to London had put her slightly on edge. At one point, she thought a large man with heavy eyebrows might be following her, but on moving aside to let him pass, he merely strode past her, muttering under his breath.

On arriving at Il Portico, Robin was pleased to find it smaller and cosier than she'd imagined, given its upmarket location; her workday clothes were entirely appropriate, even if Prudence, who was already seated, looked far more elegant in her dark blue dress.

'I'm still numb,' Prudence said, pointing at her left cheek as she stood to kiss Robin on both cheeks. 'I'm a bit scared of drinking, in case it all dribbles out ... you've lost a *lot* of weight, Robin,' she added, as she sat back down.

'Yes, well, they don't feed you a lot in the UHC,' said

Robin, taking the opposite seat. 'Did you have to have anything awful done at the dentist?'

'It was supposed to be replacing an old filling, but then he found another one that needed doing,' said Prudence, fingering the side of her face. 'Have you ever been here before?'

'Never.'

'Best pasta in London,' said Prudence, passing Robin the menu. 'What d'you want to drink?'

'Well, I'm not driving,' said Robin, 'so I'll have a glass of Prosecco.'

Prudence asked for this while Robin perused the menu, well aware that Prudence's good mood might be about to change. When each had given their order, she said,

'You were probably surprised to hear from me.'

'Well,' said Prudence, smiling, 'not entirely. I've had a sort of impression, from what Corm's told me, that you're the emotionally intelligent side of the partnership.'

'Right,' said Robin cautiously. 'So ... did you think I wanted to meet to try and make things right between you and Strike?'

'Didn't you?'

'Afraid not,' said Robin. 'I'm here to talk about Flora Brewster.'

The smile slid off Prudence's face. As Robin had anticipated, she looked not only dismayed, but angry.

'So he's sent you—?'

'He hasn't sent me. I'm here entirely on my own account. He might well be furious, once he finds out what I've done.'

'But he's clearly worked out who—'

'Yes,' said Robin. 'He knows Torment Town's Flora. We had an argument about it, actually. He thinks Flora ought to be testifying against the UHC, not drawing pictures of what she witnessed in there, but I told him, maybe the Pinterest stuff was her way of processing it all. I said she probably went through appalling things in there. In the end, Strike agreed not to go after her, not to pursue her, as a lead.'

'I see,' said Prudence slowly. 'Well, thank you for—'

'But I've changed my mind.'

'What?'

'I've changed my mind,' repeated Robin. 'That's why I asked you to meet me. I want to talk to Flora.'

Prudence, as Robin had expected, now looked openly angry.

'You can't do this, Robin. You can't. Do you realise what kind of position this puts me in? The only way Corm could have worked out who she was—'

'He already knew Flora had been in the church. He had dates, knew when she left – everything. That's how, when you rang him and accused him of badgering your client, he was able to work out who Torment Town was.'

'It's immaterial what you knew, *before*. With respect, Robin—'

'With equal respect, Prudence, you had a choice whether or not to tell us you had a client who'd escaped the UHC, and you told us. You also had a choice as to whether or not to call Strike and accuse him of badgering your client. *You* were the one who enabled him to work out her identity. You can't blame him for doing his job.'

The waiter now arrived with Robin's Prosecco and she took a large swig.

'I'm here because the person we were hired to extract from the UHC got out yesterday, but they're very messed up, and probably in danger. Not just of suicide,' she added, when Prudence made to speak. 'We think the church might take a more active role in their death, if given the chance.'

'Which proves,' said Prudence, in a heated whisper, 'that

you two don't understand what you're meddling with. People who get out of the UHC are often delusional. They think the church, or the Drowned Prophet, is stalking them, watching them, maybe going to kill them, but it's all paran—'

'A masked gunman tried to break into our office on Monday. They were caught on camera. An ex-member of the church was shot through the head last year. We know for a fact they kept tabs on a mother of two, who hanged herself this week after getting a call from an anonymous number.'

For the second time that day, Robin watched the effect of this kind of information on somebody who'd never had to face the threat of violence in their daily lives.

The waiter now set down antipasti on the table between the two women. Robin, who was extremely hungry, reached for some Parma ham.

'I'm not going to do *anything* that will endanger the well-being of my client,' Prudence told Robin in a low voice. 'So if you've come here wanting – I don't know – an introduction, or confidential information on her—'

'Maybe, subconsciously, you want her to testify,' said Robin, and she watched the colour mount in Prudence's face. 'That's why you said too much.'

'And maybe, *subconsciously,* you only talked Corm out of meeting me himself, so you could—'

'Make myself a heroine in his eyes? If we're taking cheap shots, I might say your secondary motive for telling us you had a client who was just out of the UHC was because you wanted to increase intimacy with your new brother.'

Before Prudence could articulate the undoubtedly furious speech germinating behind her brown eyes, Robin continued,

'There's a child at Chapman Farm. He's called Jacob. I don't know his surname – it should be Wace or Pirbright, but they probably never registered his birth ...'

Robin told the story of her ten hours looking after Jacob. She described the boy's convulsions, his laboured breathing, his attenuated limbs, his pitiful fight to remain alive in spite of starvation and neglect.

'Somebody's got to hold them accountable,' Robin said. '*Credible* people – and more than one. I can't do it alone, I'm too compromised by the job I went in to do. But if two or three intelligent people were to take the stand, and say what goes on in there, what happened to them and what they witnessed happening to others, I'm certain others would come forward. It would snowball.'

'So you want me to ask Flora to back up your client's relative?'

'And he'd back *her* up,' said Robin. 'There's also a chance of two more witnesses, if we can get them out. They both want to leave.'

Prudence took a large gulp of red wine, but half of it dribbled out of the side of her mouth.

'*Shit.*'

She dabbed at the stain with her napkin. Robin watched, unmoved. Prudence could afford the dry-cleaning, and indeed a new dress, if she wanted it.

'Look,' said Prudence, chucking down her wine-stained napkin and lowering her voice again, 'you don't realise: Flora's deeply troubled.'

'Maybe it would help her to testify.'

'That's an *incredibly* glib thing to say.'

'I'm speaking from personal experience,' said Robin. 'I became agoraphobic and clinically depressed after I was raped, strangled and left for dead when I was nineteen. Testifying was important in my recovery. I'm not saying it was easy, and I'm not saying it was the only thing that helped, but it *did* help.'

'I'm sorry,' said Prudence, startled, 'I didn't know—'

'Well, I'd rather you still didn't know,' said Robin bluntly. 'I don't really enjoy talking about it, and people have a tendency to think you're using it, when you bring it up in discussions like this.'

'I'm not saying you're—'

'I know you're not, but most people would rather not hear it, because it makes them uncomfortable, and some people think it's indecent to mention it at all. I'm trying to tell you that I can very much sympathise with Flora not wanting the worst time in her life to define her forever – but the fact is, it's *already* defining her.

'I got back a sense of power and self-worth from getting that rapist sent down. I'm not claiming it was easy, because it was horrible – it was hard, and to be honest, I frequently felt like I didn't want to live any more, but it still helped, not while I was going through it, but afterwards, because I knew I'd helped stop him doing it to anyone else.'

Prudence now looked deeply conflicted.

'Look, Robin,' she said, 'obviously I sympathise with you wanting to take the church to court, but I can't say what I'd like to say, because I've got a duty of confidentiality – which,' she added, 'as you've already pointed out, it might be argued I've broken merely by telling you and Corm I've got a client who's ex-UHC.'

'I never said you'd broken—'

'Fine, maybe that's my guilty conscience talking!' said Prudence, with sudden heat. 'Maybe I felt bad, after you and Corm left, that I'd said that much! Maybe I *did* wonder whether I hadn't said it for *exactly* the reason you've just suggested: to bind myself closer to him, to be part of the investigation, somehow.'

'Wow,' said Robin. 'You must be a *really* good therapist.'

'What?' said Prudence, disconcerted.

'To be that honest,' said Robin. 'I've had therapy. To be totally honest, I only liked one of them. Sometimes there's a . . . a *smugness.*'

She drank more Prosecco, then said,

'You're wrong about me wanting to be a heroine in Corm's eyes. I'm here because I thought he'd mess it up if he did it, and he might get personal.'

'What does *that* mean?' said Prudence, looking tense.

'You'll have noticed he's got a massive chip on his shoulder about people with unearned wealth. He's down on Flora for not working, for – as he sees it – sitting at home doing drawings of what she experienced, rather than reporting it. I was worried, if you pushed back at him the way you're pushing back now, he'd start having a go at you for – oh, you know.'

'For taking our father's money?'

'Whether you do or you don't is none of my business,' said Robin. 'But I didn't want you two to fall out any worse than you have already, because I meant what I said to you before. I think you might be *exactly* what he needs.'

The waiter now reappeared to clear away the antipasti, of which only Robin had partaken. Prudence's expression had softened somewhat, and Robin decided to press her advantage.

'Let me tell you, from my experience of Chapman Farm, what factors I think might make Flora afraid of testifying. Firstly,' she said, counting on her fingers, 'the sex stuff. I empathise. I've already told Strike she'll have been effectively raped for five years.

'Secondly, all sex is unprotected, so there's a possibility she had children in there.'

She saw the tiniest flicker of Prudence's left eye, but pretended she hadn't noticed.

'Thirdly, she might have done things in there that are criminal, and be terrified of prosecution. It's well-nigh impossible not to end up coerced into criminal behaviour at Chapman Farm, as I know.'

This time, Prudence's hand rose, apparently unconsciously, to obscure her face, as she brushed her hair unnecessarily out of her face.

'Lastly,' said Robin, wondering whether she was about to ruin the interview entirely, but certain she ought to say it, 'you, as her therapist, might have urged caution about testifying or going to the police, because you're worried she's not mentally strong enough to cope with the fallout, especially as a lone witness.'

'Well,' said Prudence, 'let me repay the compliment. You're clearly very good at *your* job, too.'

The waiter now brought their main courses. Too hungry to resist, Robin took one mouthful of her tagliatelle with ragu and let out a moan of pleasure.

'Oh my God, you weren't wrong.'

Prudence still looked tense and anxious. She started on her own spaghetti and ate in silence for a while. Finally, having cleared half her plate, Robin said,

'Prudence, I swear to you I wouldn't say this if it weren't true. We believe Flora witnessed something very serious inside the church. *Very* serious.'

'What?'

'If she hasn't told you, I don't think I should.'

Prudence now put down her spoon and fork. Judging it best to let Prudence speak in her own time, Robin continued to eat.

At last, the therapist said quietly,

'There's something she won't tell me. She skirts around it. She comes close, then backs off. It's to do with the Drowned Prophet.'

'Yes,' said Robin, 'it would be.'

'Robin . . .'

Prudence appeared to have reached a decision. In a whisper, she said,

'Flora's morbidly obese. She self-harms. She's got a drink problem. She's on so many anti-depressants she barely knows what day it is.'

'She's trying to block out something terrible,' said Robin. 'She witnessed something most of us will never witness. At best, it was gross negligence manslaughter. At worst, it was murder.'

'*What?*'

'All I wanted to say to you tonight,' said Robin, 'all I wanted to ask, is that you bear in mind how much good she could do, if she testified. We're certain immunity from prosecution could be arranged. Flora and our client's relative were both young and vulnerable, and I can testify as to what the church does to enforce silence and obedience.

'The thing is,' said Robin, 'I was a nice intelligent middle-class girl with a steady boyfriend when I was raped. The only two other girls who survived him – they weren't like that. It shouldn't matter, but it did. One of the girls fell apart completely under questioning. They made out the other one was so promiscuous, she'd almost certainly had sex with him consensually – all because she'd once worn a pair of fluffy handcuffs to have sex with a man she met in a club.

'Flora's well educated and wealthy. Nobody can paint her as some chancer who's after a pay-out.'

'There'd be other ways to discredit her, Robin.'

'But if our client's relative testifies, she'd have back-up. The trouble is, our other two potential witnesses have been in the church pretty much all their lives. One of them's sixteen at most. They're going to struggle to reorientate themselves, even if we get them out. No clocks, no calendars, no normal frames of reference – I can see the church's lawyers making mincemeat out of them, unless they're given cover by people with more credibility.

'Think about it, Prudence, please,' Robin said. 'Flora's got the power to set thousands of people free. I wouldn't ask, if I didn't know lives are depending on it.'

107

Nine at the beginning means:
Waiting in the meadow.
It furthers one to abide in what endures.
No blame.

The I Ching or Book of Changes

While Robin was in Kensington, Strike was back in the Denmark Street office, eating his second Chinese meal in two weeks, this time a takeaway. He was finding the last stone to go before hitting his target weight very hard to shift, and while he supposed a nutritionist might tell him the reappearance of takeaways and pub food in his diet might have something to do with that, the lure of sweet and sour chicken and fried rice had proved too strong for him this evening.

He was eating in the office rather than at his flat, because he wanted to look through the CVs of two detectives he thought might be worth interviewing. He also wanted to review the UHC case file within view of the board now covered in pictures and notes relating to the church. He was staring at the board while eating, willing his subconscious to make one of those unexpected leaps that explained everything, when his mobile rang.

'Hi,' said Midge. 'Tasha's just called. She's checked in, and she's already been given a cold green tea enema.'

Strike hastily swallowed a mouthful of sweet and sour chicken.

'Jesus, there was no need for her to—'

'She had to, Dr Zhou ordered it. She says it wasn't bad. Apparently—'

'No details. I'm eating. What's the place like, other than the tube up her arse?'

'Like the lair of a Bond villain, apparently,' said Midge. 'All black and smoked glass – but get this. She thinks she might know where they're keeping your girl.'

'Already?' said Strike, pushing away his plate and reaching for a pen.

'Yeah. There's an annexe with a "staff only" notice on it. A woman who's been there before was surprised, because she told Tasha she had a room in the annexe six months ago, so it used to be for guests. Tasha's already seen a member of the staff taking a tray of food in. Bit of a weird thing to do, unless a masseuse is ill, I suppose.'

'This sounds promising,' said Strike.

'Tasha says she doesn't want to nose around too much, seeing as she's only just arrived. She's gonna do a full day's treatments tomorrow and then, in the evening, take a walk round the annexe and see whether she can get a peek through any of the windows.'

'OK, but remind her to be *very* discreet. If there's the slightest chance of discovery, she's to back right off. We don't want—'

'You said all this in that forty-odd page email you sent her,' said Midge. *'She knows.'*

'She'd better, because it's not just her who'll pay if she slips up.'

When Midge had hung up, Strike returned to his take-away, his slight irritability increased, because it was highly

unsatisfactory to be relying on a non-employee in these circumstances. Having finished his food, he got up and peered
down through the Venetian blind at the street below.

A tall, fit-looking black man was standing in a doorway on
the opposite side of the road. He had short dreadlocks, wore
jeans and a padded jacket, but his most distinctive feature, as
Strike had noticed when they'd passed each other in Denmark
Street earlier, were his pale green eyes.

Having taken a couple of photographs of the man on his
phone, Strike let the blinds fall back into place, cleared away
the takeaway things, washed his plate and cutlery, then sat back
down to look at the CVs of the two ex-Patterson potential
hires. Across that of Dan Jarvis, Shah had scrawled '*Worked
with him, he's an arsehole.*' Having faith in Shah's character
judgement, Strike tore the CV in half, put it in the bin, and
picked up that of Kim Cochran.

His phone rang for a second time. Seeing it was Robin, he
answered immediately.

'Thought you had evening plans?'

'I did, that's what I'm calling about. I've just had dinner with
Prudence. Your sister, Prudence,' Robin added, when Strike
didn't say anything.

'What did she want?' asked Strike suspiciously. 'Trying to
send messages through you, was she? Warning me not to go
near Brewster?'

'No, the exact opposite. Dinner was my idea – *not* to try and
get you two to make up or anything, I'm not meddling in your
private life – I wanted to talk to her about Flora. Prudence says
she knows Flora's hiding something she witnessed at Chapman
Farm, something connected to the Drowned Prophet. Apparently
she keeps sidling up to it in therapy, then backing off again. So,
anyway—'

Robin found it hard to judge whether Strike's silence was

ominous, because she was walking along Kensington High Street with a finger in her free ear, to block out the noise of traffic.

'—I made a hard pitch for Prudence not standing in the way of Flora going to the police, or agreeing to testify against the church in court. I told her I thought immunity could be arranged. I said it might be good for Flora to let it all out.

'I also asked whether Prudence would be prepared to help somebody who's just got out of the church, seeing as she's got experience of what the UHC does to people. It's probably safer if Will doesn't visit her house, in case the church is trying to find him, but they could FaceTime or something. If he knows Prudence is your sister, and completely unconnected to his own family, he might agree to speak to her. And if we managed to get Flora and Will talking to each other, they might, I don't know, find it therapeutic. It might even make them braver, don't you think?'

Silence was Strike's only response.

'Can you hear me?' said Robin, raising her voice over the rumble of a passing double-decker.

'What happened,' said Strike, 'to me being a chippy, brutal bastard who needs to back right off Brewster, and let her keep drawing pictures for Pinterest?'

'What happened,' said Robin, 'is that I heard Will saying he's convinced the Drowned Prophet's going to come and get him. And I can't get Jacob out of my head. We've *got* to find witnesses who'll testify against the church. I suppose I've come round to your way of thinking. This is the job.'

She was almost at the station. When Strike didn't speak, she drew aside and leaned up against the wall, phone still pressed to her ear.

'You're pissed off I went to Prudence behind your back, aren't you? I just thought it was easier if she ended up hating me instead of you. I *did* tell her I was there on my own account. She knows you didn't ask me to do it.'

'I'm not pissed off,' said Strike. 'If you get results, bloody hell, that'll be the first ray of light we've had in a long time. With Brewster as a witness to what happened to Deirdre Doherty, we might have enough to get police in there, even if Will's still determined to let the Drowned Prophet get him. Where are you?'

'Kensington,' said Robin, who was immensely relieved Strike wasn't angry.

'Any red Corsas about?'

'None,' she said. 'I did think a big guy was following me earl—'

'What?'

'Calm down, he wasn't, it was just my imagination. I moved aside and he walked right past me, muttering.'

Now scowling, Strike got to his feet and peered down into Denmark Street again. The green-eyed man was still there, now talking on his phone.

'Might've realised you were wise to him. There's been a bloke with dreadlocks hanging around outside for about – oh, hang on, he's off,' said Strike, watching as the man ended his call and walked away towards Charing Cross Road.

'You think he was watching the office?'

'I did, yeah, but he was doing it bloody badly if the aim was to keep undercover. Mind you,' said Strike, once again letting the Venetian blinds fall, 'the aim might be to let us know we're being watched. Little bit of intimidation. What did this large bloke following you look like?'

'Balding, fifties – I honestly don't think he was following me, not really. I'm just jumpy. But listen: something weird happened just now, while I was having coffee with Prudence. I got a call from Rufus Fernsby, Walter's son. The one who slammed the phone down on me, two days ago.'

'What did he want?'

'For me to go and visit him at his office tomorrow.'

'Why?'

'No idea. He sounded quite tense, and just said, if I wanted to talk to him about his father, I could meet him at the office at a quarter to one and he'd speak to me ... why aren't you saying anything?'

'It's just odd,' said Strike. 'What's happened to make him change his mind?'

'No idea.'

There was another pause, in which Robin had time to reflect upon how tired she felt, and the fact that she still had an hour-long journey home. Since leaving Chapman Farm, she'd both craved and dreaded sleep, because it came punctuated with nightmares.

'I thought you'd be angry about Prudence and pleased about Rufus,' she told Strike.

'I might yet be pleased about both of them,' said Strike. 'I just find the volte face strange. OK, I'll rejig the rota so you can go and interview him at lunchtime. You heading home now?'

'Yes,' said Robin.

'Well, keep your eyes peeled for muttering men, or for a tall black guy with green eyes.'

Robin promised to do so, and rang off.

Strike pulled out his vape pen, inhaled deeply, then picked up Kim Cochran's CV again. Like Midge, Cochran was ex-police, and had only worked for Patterson for six months before the bugging scandal had sunk the business. Strike was just thinking that she might be worth an interview, when the landline rang in the outer office.

Charlotte, he thought at once – and then, with a strange chill, he remembered that Charlotte was dead.

Getting to his feet, he walked through to Pat's desk, and answered.

'Cormoran Strike.'

'Oh,' said a female voice. 'I was going to leave a message, I didn't expect anyone to—'

'Who's this?'

'Amelia Crichton,' said Charlotte's sister.

'Ah,' said Strike, bitterly regretting that he hadn't let the call go to voicemail. 'Amelia.'

He was momentarily stymied for appropriate words. They hadn't seen each other in years, and hadn't liked each other, then.

'Very sorry about . . . I'm sorry,' said Strike.

'Thank you,' she said. 'I was just calling to say, I'm back in town next week and I'd like to see you, if that's possible.'

Possible, he thought, *just not desirable.*

'To tell you the truth, I'm very busy at the moment. Would it be all right if I call you when I know I've got a couple of free hours?'

'Yes,' she said coldly, 'all right.'

She gave him her mobile number and rang off, leaving Strike irked and unsettled. If he knew Charlotte, she'd left some kind of dirty bomb behind her, which her sister felt honour bound to pass on: a message, or a note, or some legacy in her will designed to haunt and oppress him, to be one last, and lasting, 'fuck you'.

Strike returned to the inner office only to pick up the UHC file and Kim Cochran's CV, then left through the glass door, which he locked. He felt as though Amelia's call had temporarily polluted his workspace, leaving a wraith of Charlotte peering at him vengefully from the shadows, defying him to return callously to work when he'd just (as she'd undoubtedly see it) turned his back on her, one more time.

108

. . . one must move warily, like an old fox walking
over ice . . . deliberation and caution are the
prerequisites of success.

The I Ching or Book of Changes

When she arrived at 1 Great George Street the following day at half past twelve, Robin discovered that she'd been quite wrong in vaguely imagining the Institution of Civil Engineers would be based in a brutalist building where function had been prioritised over elegance. Rufus Fernsby's place of work was a gigantic Edwardian building of considerable grandeur.

When she gave the name of the man she'd come to see, Robin was sent up a crimson-carpeted staircase which, coupled with the white walls, reminded her faintly of the farmhouse at Chapman Farm. She passed oil paintings of eminent engineers, and a stained-glass window with a coat of arms supported by a crane and a beaver bearing the motto *Scientia et Ingenio,* and finally reached a long open-plan room with rows of desks, where two men stood having what looked like a heated discussion while the other workers kept their heads down.

With one of those strange intuitions that admit of no explanation, Robin guessed immediately that the taller, angrier and odder looking of the two men was Rufus Fernsby. Perhaps he looked like the kind of man who'd slam down a phone on someone who mentioned his unsatisfactory father. His argument with the shorter man seemed to centre on whether somebody called Bannerman should, or shouldn't, have forwarded an email.

'Nobody's claiming Grierson shouldn't have been *copied in*,' he was saying heatedly, 'that's not the point. What I'm raising here is a pattern of persistent—'

The shorter man, becoming aware of Robin, and possibly looking for a route of escape, said,

'Can I help you?'

'—failure to follow an established procedure, which increases the risk of miscommunications, because *I* might not have realised—'

'I'm here to meet Rufus Fernsby.'

As she'd feared, the taller man broke off mid-sentence to say angrily,

'I'm Fernsby.'

'I'm Robin Ellacott. We spoke—'

'What are you doing here? You should have waited in the atrium.'

'The man on the desk sent me up.'

'Right, well, that's unhelpful,' said Rufus.

Dark, lean and wearing a Lycra T-shirt with his work trousers, he had the weather-beaten, sinewy look common to dedicated runners and cyclists, and was sporting what Robin thought was the oddest of all facial hair variations: a chin curtain beard with no moustache.

'Good luck,' murmured the second man to Robin as he walked away.

'I was going to meet you in the café,' said Rufus irritably, as though Robin should have known this, and perhaps already ordered his food. He checked his watch. Robin suspected he'd have liked to find she'd arrived too early, but as she was exactly on time he said,

'Come on then – *no, wait!*' he added explosively, and Robin came to a halt, wondering what she'd done wrong now, but Rufus had merely realised he was still clutching papers in his hand. Having stalked off to put them back on his desk, he rejoined her, walking out of the room so fast she had to almost jog to keep up.

'This is a very beautiful building,' she said, hoping to ingratiate herself. Rufus appeared to consider the comment beneath his notice.

The café on the ground floor was infinitely more upmarket than any that had graced the offices where Robin had once worked as a temporary secretary; there were booths of black leather banquettes, sleek light fittings and expressionist prints on the walls. As they headed for the queue at the counter, and in what she feared would be another doomed attempt to conciliate herself, Robin said,

'I'm starting to think I should have done engineering, if these are the perks.'

'What d'you mean?' said Rufus suspiciously.

'It's a nice café,' said Robin.

'Oh.'

Rufus looked around as though he'd never before considered whether it was pleasant or not.

'Yes. I suppose so,' he said grudgingly. She had the impression he'd rather have found fault with the place.

From the moment Rufus had agreed to meet her, Robin had known that her main objective, that of finding out whether Rosalind Fernsby was the naked girl in the pig mask, would have to be approached tactfully. She didn't like to imagine how any of her own brothers would react, if shown such a photograph featuring Robin. Having now met Rufus, she was afraid there might be a truly volcanic explosion when she showed him the pictures on her phone. She therefore decided that her secondary objective – that of finding out whether Walter was the person Jiang had recognised as someone who'd come back after many years – would form her first line of questioning.

Having purchased sandwiches, they sat down at a corner table.

'Well, thanks very much for meeting me, Rufus,' Robin began.

'I only called you back because I want to know what exactly's going on,' said Rufus severely. 'I had a call from a policewoman – well, she *said* she was a policewoman – a week ago. She was asking for contact details for my sister.'

'Did you give them to her?'

'I haven't got any. We don't talk, haven't for years. Nothing in common.'

He said it with a kind of pugnacious pride.

'Then she told me two individuals called Robin Ellacott and Cormorant Strike might make contact with me, because they were trying to dig up dirt on my family. Naturally, I asked for further details, but she said she couldn't give them, as it was an open investigation. She gave me a number to call if you contacted me. So, when you called – well, you know what happened,' said Rufus unapologetically. 'I phoned the number I'd been given and asked for PC Curtis. The man who answered laughed. He passed me to this woman. I was suspicious. I asked for her badge number and jurisdiction. There was a silence. Then she hung up.'

'Pretty sharp of you to check,' commented Robin.

'Well, of course I checked,' said Rufus, with a whiff of gratified vanity. 'There's more at stake for engineers than getting a bad review in some joke social sciences journal, if we don't check.'

'D'you mind if I take notes?' she asked, reaching into her bag.

'Why should I mind?' he said irritably.

Robin, who knew from online records that Fernsby was married, offered up a silent vote of sympathy for his wife as she reached for her pen.

'Did PC Curtis – so-called – give you a landline number, or mobile?'

'Mobile.'

'Have you still got it?'

'Yes.'

'Could I have it?'

'I'll need to think about that,' he said, confirming Robin's impression that this was a man who believed information was very definitely power. 'I decided to call you back because you, at least, were telling the truth about who you are. I checked you out online,' he added, 'though you don't look much like your pictures.'

His tone left Robin in no doubt that he thought she looked worse in person. Feeling sorrier for his wife by the minute, she said,

'I've lost some weight recently. Well, my partner and I—'

'This is Cormorant Strike?'

'Cormoran Strike,' said Robin, who didn't see why Fernsby should corner the market in pedantry.

'Not the bird?'

'Not the bird,' said Robin patiently. 'We're investigating the Universal Humanitarian Church.'

'Why?'

'We've been hired to do so.'

'By a newspaper?'

'No,' said Robin.

'I'm not sure I want to talk to you, unless I know who's paying you.'

'Our client has a relative inside the church,' said Robin, deciding it was simpler, given Rufus's clearly nit-picking nature, not to say that the relative had in fact left.

'And how's my father relevant to the situation?'

'Are you aware he's currently—?'

'At Chapman Farm? Yes. He wrote me a stupid letter saying he'd gone back.'

'What d'you mean by "gone back"?' asked Robin, her pulse rate accelerating.

'I mean he's been there before, obviously.'

'Really? When?'

'In 1995, for ten days,' said Rufus, with pernickety though useful precision, 'and 2007, for ... possibly a week.'

'Why such short stays? My client's interested in what makes people join, and what makes them leave, you see,' she added mendaciously.

'He left the first time because my mother took legal action against him. Second time, my sister Rosie was ill.'

Disguising her keen interest in these answers, Robin asked, 'What made him want to join in '95, do you know?'

'That man who started it, Wace, gave a talk at the University of Sussex, where my father was working. He went along in a spirit of supposed academic enquiry,' said Rufus, with a slight sneer, 'and fell for it. He resigned his post, and decided he was going to devote himself to the spiritual life.'

'So he just took off?'

'What d'you mean by "took off"?'

'I mean, this was unexpected?'

'Well,' said Rufus, frowning slightly, 'that's hard to answer. My parents were in the middle of their divorce. I suppose you could argue my father was having what's known as a mid-life crisis. He'd been passed over for promotion at work and was feeling unappreciated. He's actually a very difficult personality. He's never got on with colleagues, anywhere he worked. Argumentative. Obsessed with rank and titles. It's rather pathetic.'

'Really,' said Robin. 'And your mother took legal action against him, to make him leave?'

'Not to make *him* leave,' said Rufus. 'He'd taken me and Rosie, to the farm.'

'How old were you?' asked Robin, her pulse speeding up further.

'Fifteen. We're twins. It was the school summer holidays. My father lied to us, said it was going to be a week's holiday in the country. We didn't want to hurt his feelings, so we agreed to go.

'At the end of that week, he sent a letter to my mother full of church jargon saying the three of us had joined the UHC and wouldn't be coming back. My mother got an emergency court order and threatened him with the police. We ended up sneaking out in the middle of the night, because my father had got himself into some ludicrous agreement with Wace and was scared of telling him it wouldn't be happening.'

'What kind of agreement?'

'He wanted to sell the family home and give all the money to the church.'

'I see,' said Robin, who'd barely eaten any of her sandwich, she was making so many notes. 'I'd imagine you and your sister were happy to leave?'

'I was, but my sister was furious.'

'Really?'

'Yes,' said Rufus, with another sneer, 'because she was smitten with Jonathan Wace. He was s'posed to be taking her up to the Birmingham centre the next day.'

'She was being transferred?' asked Robin. 'After a week?'

'No, no,' said Rufus impatiently, as though Robin were a

particularly slow pupil. 'It was a pretext. Get her off on her own. She was quite pretty and well developed, for fifteen. Bit chubby, actually,' he added, straightening up to display his abs. 'Most of the girls in there were after Wace. One girl clawed Rosie's face over him – but that got hushed up, because Wace liked to think everyone was living in harmony. Rosie's still got a scar under her left eye.'

Far from sounding sorry, Rufus seemed rather pleased about this.

'Would you happen to remember the date you left?' asked Robin.

'Twenty-eighth of July.'

'How can you be so precise?' asked Robin.

As she'd expected, Rufus didn't seem offended, but further gratified at a chance to show his deductive powers.

'Because it was the night before a child at the farm drowned. We read about it, in the papers.'

'How exactly did you leave?' asked Robin.

'In my father's car. He'd managed to get the keys back, pretending he wanted to check the battery hadn't gone flat.'

'Did you see anything unusual as you were leaving the farm?'

'Like what?'

'People awake when they shouldn't have been? Or,' said Robin, thinking of Jordan Reaney, 'someone sleeping more deeply than perhaps they should have been?'

'I can't see how I'd have known that,' said Rufus. 'No, we saw nothing unusual.'

'And did either you or your sister ever return to Chapman Farm?'

'I certainly didn't. As far as I'm aware, Rosie didn't, either.'

'You said your father returned to Chapman Farm in 2007?'

'Correct,' said Rufus, now speaking as though Robin was at

last showing some intellectual promise in remembering this fact from a couple of minutes previously. 'He'd moved university, but he was bickering with his colleagues again and feeling hard done by, so he resigned again and went back into the UHC.'

Robin, who was doing some rapid mental calculation, deduced that Jiang would have been in his mid-teens on Walter's second appearance at Chapman Farm and therefore, surely, old enough to remember him.

'Why did he leave so quickly that time?'

'Rosie got meningitis.'

'Oh, I'm so sorry,' said Robin.

'She survived,' said Rufus, 'but my mother had to track him down all over again, to let him know.'

'This is all very helpful,' said Robin.

'I don't see why,' said Rufus. 'Surely plenty of people have joined and left that place by now? I dare say our story's quite common.'

Deciding not to argue the point, Robin said,

'Would you have any idea where Rosie is now? Even a town? Is she going under a married name?'

'She's never married,' said Rufus, 'but she goes by Bhakta Dasa now.'

'She – what, sorry?'

'Converted to Hinduism. She's probably in India,' said Rufus, sneering again. 'She's like my father: silly crazes. Bikram yoga. Incense.'

'Would your mother know where she is?' said Robin.

'Possibly,' said Rufus, 'but she's currently in Canada, visiting her sister.'

'Ah,' said Robin. This explained why Mrs Fernsby never picked up her phone.

'Well,' said Rufus, looking at his watch, 'that's really all I can tell you, and as I've got a lot of work on—'

'Just one last question, if you don't mind,' said Robin, her heart beginning to race again as she took her mobile out of her bag. 'Can you remember anyone at the farm having a Polaroid camera?'

'No. You weren't supposed to take anything like that in there. Luckily, I left my Nintendo in my father's car,' Rufus said, with a satisfied smirk. 'Rosie tried to take hers in with her and it was confiscated. Probably still there.'

'This might seem an odd question,' said Robin, 'but was Rosie ever punished at the farm?'

'Punished? Not that I'm aware of,' said Rufus.

'And she definitely seemed distressed at leaving? Not glad to go?'

'Yes, I've told you that.'

'And – this is an even weirder question, I know – did she ever mention wearing a pig mask?'

'A *pig* mask?' repeated Rufus Fernsby, frowning. 'No.'

'I want to show you a picture,' said Robin, thinking, even as she said it, how untrue the statement was. 'It's – distressing, especially for a relative, but I wondered whether you could tell me if the dark girl in this picture is Rosie.'

She brought up one of the pig mask pictures, in which the dark-haired girl sat alone, naked, with her legs wide open, and passed it across the table.

Fernsby's reaction was instantaneous.

'How—? You – *this is disgusting!*' he said, so loudly heads in the now crowded café turned. 'That is definitely *not* my sister!'

'Mr Fernsby, I—'

'I'll be contacting lawyers about you!' he thundered, scrambling to his feet. '*Lawyers!*'

109

. . . there are annoying arguments like those of a
married couple. Naturally this is not a favourable
state of things . . .

The I Ching or Book of Changes

'And then he stormed out,' concluded Robin forty minutes later. She was now sitting beside Strike in his parked BMW, from which he was observing the office of the man they'd nicknamed Hampstead.

'Hmm,' said Strike, who was holding one of the takeaway coffees Robin had bought en route. 'So did he go apeshit because it *is* his sister, or because he was afraid we're going to claim it is?'

'From his reaction, it could have been either, but if it *wasn't* Rosie—'

'Why did somebody posing as a policewoman try and warn him off speaking to us?'

'Well, exactly,' said Robin.

She'd called Strike immediately after leaving the Institution of Civil Engineers, and he'd asked her to meet him in Dorset Street, a short Tube journey away. Strike had been sitting in his parked car all morning, watching the entrance of Hampstead's office: an exercise he'd guessed would be fruitless, as Hampstead's only suspicious activity had so far been conducted by night.

Strike sipped his coffee, then said,

'I don't like this.'

'Sorry, I got what you—'

'Not the coffee. I mean these mysterious phone calls to everyone we interview. I don't like that Corsa following us, or the bloke watching the office last night, or that guy stalking you on the Tube.'

'I told you, he *wasn't* stalking me. I'm just jumpy.'

'Yeah, well, I wasn't being jumpy when an armed intruder tried to smash their way through our office door with a gun, although Kevin Pirbright might well have been when he realised he was about to get shot through the head.'

Strike now pulled his mobile out of his pocket and handed it to Robin. Looking down, she saw the same flattering picture of Jonathan Wace that was on the enormous poster on the side of a building near her flat. It was captioned:

Interested in the Universal Humanitarian Church? Join us at

7pm Friday 12th August

SUPERSERVICE 2016

PAPA J AT OLYMPIA

'Doubt there'll be anyone at Olympia tonight who's more interested in the Universal Humanitarian Church than I am,' said Strike.

'You can't go!'

Though instantly ashamed of her own panic, and worried that Strike would think her foolish, the very idea of entering a space where Papa J was in charge brought back memories Robin had been trying to suppress every day since she'd left Chapman Farm, but which resurfaced almost nightly in her dreams.

Strike understood Robin's disproportionate reaction better than she realised. For a long time after half his leg had been ripped off in that exploding car in Afghanistan, certain experiences, certain noises, even certain faces, had evoked a primal response over which it had taken him years to gain mastery. A particular brand of rough humour, shared with those who understood, had got him through some of his bleakest moments, which was why he said,

'Typical materialist reaction. Personally, I think I'll go pure spirit very fast.'

'You can't,' said Robin, trying to sound reasonable, and not as though she was trying to dispel a vivid recollection of Jonathan Wace advancing on her in that peacock blue room, calling her Artemis. 'You'll be recognised!'

'Bloody well hope so. That's the whole point.'

'What?'

'They know we're investigating them, we know they know, they know we know they know. It's time to stop playing this dumb game and actually look Wace in the eye.'

'Strike, if you tell him any of the things people told me at Chapman Farm, those people will be in deep, deep trouble!'

'You mean Emily?'

'And Lin, who's still inside, really, and Shawna, and even Jiang, not that I like him much. You're messing—'

'With forces I don't understand?'

'This isn't funny!'

'I don't think it's remotely funny,' said Strike, unsmiling. 'As I've just said, I don't like the way this is going, nor have I forgotten that at the current tally, we've got one definite murder, one suspected murder, two coerced suicides and two missing kids – but whatever else Wace is, he's not stupid. He can fuck around with Wikipedia pages all he likes, but it'd be a massive strategic error to shoot me through the head at Olympia. If they realise I'm there, I'll lay you odds Wace'll want to talk to me. He'll want to know what we know.'

'You won't get anything out of interviewing him! He'll just lie and—'

'You're presuming I want information.'

'What's the point in interviewing him, if you don't want information?'

'Has it occurred to you,' said Strike, 'that I was in two minds whether to let you go and see Rufus Fernsby on your own today, in case something happened to you? Do you realise how easy it would be to make your killing look like suicide? "She threw herself off the bridge – or stepped into moving traffic, or hanged herself, or slit her wrists – because she couldn't face the child abuse charge." You wouldn't be much of a match for the guy who was watching our office last night, not if he decided to drag you into a car. I let you interview Fernsby because his office is in central London and it'd be pure insanity to risk a kidnapping there, but that doesn't mean I don't think it's a risk – so going forwards, I want you to stick to taxis, no public transport, and I'd rather you weren't out on jobs on your own.'

'Strike—'

'You can't have it both bloody ways! You can't tell me they're evil and dangerous, and then prance around London—'

'You know what,' said Robin furiously, 'I'd *really* appreciate it if, every time we have a discussion like this, you don't use words like "prance" for how I get around.'

'Fine, you don't prance,' said the exasperated Strike. 'Fuck's sake, how complicated is this? We're dealing with a bunch of people we believe are capable of murder, and the two people who are most dangerous to them right now are you and Rosie Fernsby, and if anything happens to either of you, it'll be on me.'

'What are you talking about? How's it on you?'

'I was the one who put you into Chapman Farm.'

'Again,' said Robin, infuriated, 'you didn't *put me* anywhere. I'm not a bloody pot plant, I wanted the job, I volunteered for the job, and I seem to remember getting there by minibus, not being carried there by *you*.'

'All right, great: if you end up dead in a ditch it won't be my fault. Cheers. Unfortunately, the same can't be said for Rosie, or Bhakta, or whoever the fuck she is now.'

'How on *earth* could that be your fault?'

'Because I fucked up, didn't I? Think! Why's the church so interested in the whereabouts of a girl who was only at Chapman Farm for ten days, twenty-one years ago?'

'Because of the Polaroids.'

'Yeah, but how does the church know we've got the Polaroids? Because,' said Strike, answering his own question, 'I showed them to the wrong fucking person, who reported back. I strongly suspect that person of being Jordan Reaney. He told whoever it was who phoned him after our interview, posing as his wife.

'From Reaney's reaction, he knew *exactly* who was behind those pig masks. I'm not interested right now in whether he was present when they were taken. The point is that the person on the other end of the phone found out I had evidence that could see the church buried in a tsunami of filth. Pig masks, teenagers sodomising each other? That's the front page of every tabloid guaranteed, and all the old Aylmerton Community stuff'll be dragged up again. They'll want to close the mouths of everyone who was in those pictures, because if one of the subjects testifies, the church is properly fucked. I've put Rosie Fernsby in danger, and *that's* why I want to meet Jonathan Wace.'

110

Nine in the fifth place means:
Flying dragon in the heavens.
It furthers one to see the great man.

The I Ching or Book of Changes

Strike had known before arriving at Olympia late on Friday afternoon that the Universal Humanitarian Church had spread internationally and that the church had tens of thousands of members. He was also well aware, having watched a couple of YouTube videos of Jonathan Wace preaching, that the man was possessed of undeniable charisma. Nevertheless, he found himself taken aback by the sheer numbers of people heading for the Victorian façade of the enormous events centre. All ages were represented in the crowd, including families with children.

About a fifth of the crowd were already wearing UHC tracksuits of royal blue. These church members were wholesome-looking people in the main, though noticeably thinner than those who wore civilian clothes. They wore no jewellery, didn't dye their hair and had no visible tattoos, nor were there any family groups among the tracksuit-wearers. If they were grouped at all, it was by age, and as he drew nearer to the entrance, he found himself following in the wake of a bunch of twenty-somethings talking excitedly in German, a language

981

of which Strike knew just enough (having been stationed in Germany during his military career) to understand that one of their number had never yet heard Papa J speak in person.

Around twenty young men in UHC tracksuits, all of whom appeared to have been selected for size, strength or both, were standing just outside the doors, their eyes swivelling constantly as they scanned the crowd. Remembering that Patterson's operative had been turned away from the Rupert Court Temple on sight, Strike assumed they were looking out for known troublemakers. He therefore made sure to stand up a little straighter, separating himself as far as was possible from the German group, and deliberately caught the crooked eye of a short, heavy-set man with fuzzy hair, who recalled Robin's description of Jiang Wace. Borne on by the crowd, he didn't have time to see any reaction.

The venue's security men were searching bags just inside the doors. Strike was funnelled towards the pre-bought ticket queue rather than the row of pretty young UHC women selling tickets to the less organised. He made sure to smile broadly at the young woman who checked his own ticket. She had short, spiky black hair, and he didn't think he imagined the sudden widening of her eyes.

As he walked onwards, Strike heard the strains of a rock song he didn't recognise, which grew steadily louder as he approached the Great Hall.

> ... *another dissident,*
> *Take back your evidence* ...

As he'd needed only one seat, Strike had managed to buy one in the second row of what was a rapidly filling hall. Edging with apologies past a line of young people in tracksuits, he finally reached the seat and sat down between a young blonde in a blue tracksuit, and an elderly woman chewing stoically on a toffee.

Seconds after he'd sat down, the girl on his right, who he guessed to be twenty at most, said, revealing herself to be American,

'Hi, I'm Sanchia.'

'Cormoran Strike.'

'First time at a service?'

'Yes, it is.'

'Wow. You've chosen a really auspicious day to come. You wait.'

'Sounds promising,' said Strike.

'What made you interested in the UHC, Cormoran?'

'I'm a private detective,' said Strike. 'I've been hired to look into the church, particularly with regard to sexual abuse and suspicious deaths.'

It was as though he'd spat in her face. Mouth open, she stared at him unblinkingly for a few seconds, then looked quickly away.

The rock song was still playing loudly over speakers.

> *. . . sometimes it's hard to breathe, Lord*
> *at the bottom of the sea, yeah yeah . . .*

In the centre of the floor, beneath a high curved ceiling of white-painted iron and glass, was a shining, black pentagonal stage. Above this were five enormous screens that would doubtless enable even those in the furthest seats to see Jonathan Wace close up. Higher still were five bright blue banners bearing the UHC's heart-shaped logo.

After a bit of whispering to her companions, Sanchia vacated her seat.

The excitement in the hall mounted as it filled. Strike

estimated that there were at least five thousand people here. A different song now began to play: REM's 'It's The End of the World as We Know It'. With five minutes to go until the official start of the service, and almost every seat filled, the lights began to dim, and a premature wave of applause broke out, along with several screams of excitement. These re-erupted when the screens over the pentagonal stage came to life, so that everybody in the hall could watch a short procession of robed people walking in spotlights down an aisle, towards the front seats on the opposite side of the hall. Strike recognised Giles Harmon, who was comporting himself with the dignity and gravity appropriate to a man about to receive an honorary degree; Noli Seymour, whose robes had a discreet amount of glitter and looked as though they'd been tailored for her; the tall, handsome and scarred Dr Andy Zhou; a glossy-haired, wholesome-looking young woman with perfect teeth Strike recognised from the church website as Becca Pirbright, and several others, among them a frog-eyed MP whose name Strike wouldn't have known, had Robin not put it in a letter from Chapman Farm, and a packaging multimillionaire, who was waving at the cheering crowds in a manner Strike would have categorised as gormless. These, he knew, were the church Principals, and he took a photograph on his phone, noting the absence of Mazu Wace, and also of the overweight, rat-faced Taio, who he'd smashed over the head with the wire-cutters at the perimeter of Chapman Farm.

Right behind Dr Zhou, and captured in the edge of the spotlight onscreen as the doctor sat down, was a middle-aged blonde whose hair was tied back in a velvet bow. As Strike was staring at this woman, the screen changed to black, projecting a written request to turn off all mobile phones. As Strike obeyed, his American neighbour came back down the row, retook her seat and bent away from him to whisper to some of her companions.

The lights dimmed still further, heightening the crowd's anticipation. Now they began to clap rhythmically. Calls of 'Papa J!' filled the air and at last, as the opening bars of 'Heroes' began to play, the hall went black, and with screams echoing off the high metal ceiling, five thousand people (with the exception of Cormoran Strike) scrambled to their feet, whistling and applauding.

Jonathan Wace appeared in a spotlight, already standing on the stage. Wace, whose face now filled the screens, waved to every corner of the stadium, pausing every now and then to wipe his eyes; he shook his head while pressing his hand to his heart; he bowed and bowed again, his hands pressed together, namaste-style. Nothing was overdone: the humility and self-deprecation seemed entirely authentic, and Strike, who as far as he could see was the only person in the hall not clapping, found himself impressed by the man's acting abilities. Handsome and fit, with his thick, dark, barely silvered hair and square jaw, had he been wearing a tuxedo rather than long, royal blue robes, he'd have fitted in on any red carpet in the world.

The ovation lasted five minutes and died away only after Wace had made a calming, dampening gesture with his hands. Even then, when a near silence had fallen, a woman screamed,

'I love you, Papa J!'

'And I love you!' said a smiling Wace, at which there was a further eruption of screams and applause.

At last, the crowd retook their seats, and Wace, who was wearing a headset microphone, began to walk slowly clockwise around the pentagonal stage, looking out into the crowd.

'Thank you ... thank you for that welcome,' he said. 'You know ... before every super service, I ask myself ... am I a worthy vehicle? No!' he said seriously, because there were further screams of adoration. 'I ask, because it's no light matter, to put yourself forward as the Blessed Divinity's vessel! Many men before me have proclaimed to the world that they're conduits of light and love, have perhaps even believed it, but have been wrong ...

'How arrogant of any human to call themselves a holy man! Don't you think so?' He looked around, smiling, as a hail of 'no's rained down upon him.

'You ARE a holy man!' bellowed a man somewhere up in the higher seats, and the crowd laughed, as did Wace.

'Thank you, my friend!' he called back. 'But this is the question that confronts every honest man when he ascends a stage like this. It's a question certain members of the press –' a storm of boos broke out '– ask of me often. No!' he said, smiling and shaking his head, 'don't boo! They're right to ask the question! In a world full of charlatans and conmen – although some of us might wish they'd focus a little more on our politicians and our captains of capitalism –' a deafening round of applause '– it is perfectly fair to ask by what right I stand before you, saying that I have seen Divine Truth, and that I seek nothing more than to share it with all who are receptive.

'So all I ask of you this evening – to those who've already joined the Universal Humanitarian Church, and to those who haven't, to the sceptics and the non-believers – yes, perhaps especially to them,' he said with a little laugh, which the crowd obligingly echoed 'is to make one simple statement, if you feel you can. It commits you to nothing. It requires nothing but an open mind.

'Do you think it possible that I've seen God, that I know God as well as I know my closest companions, and that I have proof of everlasting life? Is that *possible*? I ask no more than this – no belief, no blind acceptance. If you think you can say it, then I ask you to say the following to me now . . .'

The screens changed to black, with four words written on them in white.

'Together!' said Jonathan Wace, and the crowd roared the four words back at him:

  'I admit the possibility!'

Cormoran Strike, who was sitting with his arms folded and a look of profound boredom on his face, admitted nothing whatsoever.

III

. . . the second place may be that of the woman, active within the house, while the fifth place is that of the husband, active in the world without.

The I Ching or Book of Changes

Robin was in the Denmark Street office. Pat had already left, and Robin had half a mind to stay until Strike returned from Wace's meeting, because Murphy was working tonight.

Her anxiety made it hard to concentrate on anything. Wace's meeting would be well underway by now. Robin was worried about Strike, picturing things she knew to be unlikely if not irrational: Strike being met by police, who'd been informed of some false charge against him, concocted by the church; Strike being dragged onto a UHC minibus, just as he'd suggested she might be kidnapped off the street, a few days ago.

You're being completely ridiculous, she told herself, yet her nerves remained.

Even though there were two top-grade, skeleton-key-proof locks between her and the street, she felt far more frightened than at any time since she'd left Chapman Farm. Right now, she understood how those who'd been truly indoctrinated remained consumed by dread of the Drowned Prophet even after they'd recognised that the church's other beliefs were fallacies. A nonsensical notion had her in its grip: that, merely by inserting himself boldly into the same physical space as Jonathan Wace, Strike would reap some kind of supernatural penalty. Intellectually, she knew Wace to be a crook and a conman, but her fear of his influence couldn't be dismantled by her intellect alone.

Moreover, in her solitude, it was impossible to stop those memories she kept trying to suppress intruding into her thoughts. She seemed to feel Jonathan Wace's hand between her legs again. She saw Will Edensor, penis in hand, advancing on her, and felt the punch. She remembered – and it was almost as shameful a recollection as the others – kneeling to kiss Mazu's foot. Then she remembered Jacob, wasting away, untreated, in that filthy attic room, and that the police remained entirely silent about whether she was going to be charged for child sex abuse. *Stop thinking about it all,* she told herself firmly, heading for the kettle.

Having made herself what was probably her eighth or ninth coffee of the day, Robin took the mug through to the inner office, to stand in front of the noticeboard. Determined to do something productive rather than brood, she scrutinised the six Polaroids of naked teenagers she'd found in the biscuit tin at Chapman Farm far more closely than she'd done before. This was far easier to do without Strike present.

The dark, naked, chubby girl – Rosalind Fernsby, assuming their identification was correct – was the only person in the pictures who featured alone. Had it been the only photo, Robin might almost have believed Rosie had posed willingly, except for the deliberate degradation of the pig mask. Robin, of course, had a particular aversion to animal masks. Her rapist had worn a latex gorilla's face to commit his serial crimes.

The next photo showed Carrie being penetrated from behind by Paul Draper, recognisable by his wispy hair.

In the third picture, Draper was being sodomised by Joe Jackson, assuming this identification, too, was correct. Jackson was dragging Draper's head back by his hair, and the sinews were rigid in Draper's neck, and Robin could almost see the grimace of pain on the moon face of the teenager pictured, looking timid, in the old newspaper article, at the top right of the board. The camera flash had illuminated the edge of something that looked like a vehicle in this picture. The UHC's lawyers, of course, would probably argue that many vehicles were stored in many barns up and down the country.

The fourth Polaroid showed the dark girl being penetrated by Skull Tattoo from the front, her legs splayed, and now Robin noticed a deep graze on her left knee that hadn't been there in the first picture. Either these Polaroids came from more than one photographic session, or she'd sustained the injury during it.

In the fifth picture, blonde Carrie had pushed up her mask far enough to give Draper oral sex while Skull Tattoo entered her from behind. The flash had illuminated the edge of something that looked like a wine bottle. Having read Strike's notes on his interview with Henry Worthington-Fields, Robin knew Joe Jackson had later recruited Henry in a bar, in spite of the church's prohibition on alcohol.

In the sixth and last picture, the dark girl was giving Skull Tattoo oral sex, and Draper was penetrating her vaginally. Now Robin noticed something she hadn't seen before. What she'd thought was a shadow wasn't: Skull Tattoo appeared to be wearing a black condom.

Self-disgust seized Robin, and she turned away from the pictures. They weren't, after all, mere puzzle pieces. Joe Jackson, towards whom she could muster no pity, might now be flourishing in the church, but Carrie and Paul were both dead in dreadful circumstances and Rosie, though she almost certainly didn't know it yet, was being hunted, all because she'd once been naive enough to trust whoever had lured her into the barn.

Robin sat back down in Strike's chair, picturing the teenage Rosie creeping out of the farm with her father and brother, mere hours before the vegetable truck left Chapman Farm with Daiyu on board . . .

An idea came to Robin so suddenly she sat up straight in her chair as though called to attention. There should have been a second person in the children's dormitory that night . . . could it have been Rosie? Had the girl performed the old trick of hiding pillows under her blankets, to convince Carrie she was present, before sneaking out of the farm forever? That would explain why Emily hadn't seen a second supervisor, and it might also explain why Carrie had been curiously averse, before she saw the Polaroids and knew there was no hiding what had happened in the barn, to identifying the other person who ought to have been on duty, because if found, she might talk, not only about child duty, but pig masks and sodomy.

Robin returned to the outer office, unlocked the filing cabinet and took out the UHC case file. Back at the partners' desk, she ran her eye back over the notes she'd made during her interview with Rufus, then checked the printouts of the housing records for the Fernsby family again. Walter no longer owned property. Rosie's mother lived in Richmond, whereas Rufus and his wife lived in Enfield.

In spite of diligently searching all available records, Robin had found no evidence that Rosie had ever owned property in the UK under either of her known names. She'd never married and had no children. She was now nearing forty. *Converted to Hinduism. Possibly in India. Silly crazes. Bikram yoga. Incense.*

A vague picture was forming in Robin's mind of a woman who saw herself as a free spirit, but who might, perhaps, have suffered emotional or financial reverses (would many solvent thirty-year-olds voluntarily go and live with their father, as Rosie had done before her name change, unless they had no alternative?). Perhaps Rosie was in India, as her brother had suggested? Or was Rosie one of those chaotic people who left little trace of themselves in records, flitting, perhaps, between sub-lets and squats, rather as Leda Strike had done?

The ringing of her mobile made Robin jump.

'Hello?'

'Hi,' said Prudence's voice. 'How are you?'

'Fine,' said Robin. 'You?'

'Not bad ... so, um ... I had a session with Flora this afternoon.'

'Oh,' said Robin, bracing herself.

'I've told her – I had to – who the person was, who'd contacted her about her Pinterest pictures. I apologised, I said it was my fault Corm worked it out, even though I didn't name her.'

'Right,' said Robin.

'Anyway ... we talked about your investigation, and I told her somebody else has managed to get out of Chapman Farm, and that you helped them do it, and ... long story short ... she'd like to meet that person.'

'Really?' said Robin, who realised she'd been holding her breath.

'She's not committing to anything beyond that, at the moment, OK? But if you and Cormoran are agreeable, she says she's prepared to meet your ex-UHC person, with me present – and for the other individual to have someone there for support, too.'

'That's fantastic,' said Robin. 'That's wonderful, Prudence, thank you. We'll talk to our client's son, and see whether he'd like to meet Flora. I'm sure he'd find it helpful.'

After Prudence had rung off, Robin checked the rota, then texted Pat.

Sorry to disturb you after working hours Pat, but would it be ok for Strike and me to come over to your house tomorrow morning at 10am to talk to Will?

Pat, as was her invariable habit, called Robin back five minutes later, rather than texting.

'You want to come and see him?' she asked, in her usual baritone. 'Yeah, that's fine.'

'How is he?'

'Still chanting a bit. I tell him, "Stop doing that and give me a hand with the washing up," and he does. I got him more clothes. He's seemed happier, being out of that tracksuit. He's playing chess with Dennis just now. I've just put Qing to bed. Right little chatterbox, all of a sudden. I read her the Hungry Caterpillar. She wanted it five times in a row.'

'Pat, we really can't thank you enough for this.'

'No trouble. He's well brought up, you can tell. He'll be a nice enough boy, once he's got all their rubbish out of his system.'

'Has he mentioned the Drowned Prophet at all?' asked Robin.

'Yeah, last night,' said Pat unemotionally. 'Dennis said to him, "You don't believe in ghosts, intelligent bloke like you?" Will said Dennis would, if he'd seen what Will's seen. Said he'd seen people levitate. Dennis said, "How high did they go?" Few inches, said Will. So Dennis showed him how they fake it. Silly sod nearly fell over onto our gas fire.'

'How does Dennis know how to fake levitation?' asked Robin, diverted.

'Mate of his, when he was young, used to do stuff like that

to impress girls,' said Pat laconically. 'Some girls are bloody silly, let's face it. When does anyone need a man who can rise two inches into the air?'

Robin laughed, thanked Pat again, and wished her a good evening. Having hung up, she found herself in a considerably improved state of mind. She now had both a new theory and a potentially crucial meeting to tell Strike about when he returned. She checked her watch. Strike would now have been in Wace's meeting for over an hour, but Robin knew Papa J: he'd probably just be getting started. Perhaps she'd order some food, to be delivered to the office while reviewing the UHC file.

She got to her feet, mobile in hand, and moved to the window, wondering what kind of pizza she fancied. The sun was falling and Denmark Street was now in shadow. The shops were closed, many of their windows covered in metal blinds.

Robin had just decided she wanted something with capers on it, when she spotted somebody tall, bulky and dressed all in black walking along the street. Bizarrely, for a mild evening in August, they had their hood up. Robin raised her phone and switched it to camera mode, recording the figure as it walked down the steps in front of the music shop opposite, disappearing into the basement area below.

Perhaps they knew the shop owner? Maybe they'd been instructed to go to the door beneath street level?

Robin pressed pause on the camera and watched the few seconds of footage back. Then, with a return of her earlier feeling of foreboding, she returned to the UHC file and withdrew the still photographs of the masked intruder with the gun Strike had printed off from the camera footage.

It might be the same person, but equally, it might not. They were wearing similar black jackets, but the photographs from

994

the dimly lit landing were too blurry to make an identification certain.

Should she call the police? But what would she say? That someone in a black jacket had their hood up in the vicinity of the office, and had walked down some steps? It was hardly criminal behaviour.

The person with the gun had waited until nightfall, and the extinguishment of all lights in the building, to act, Robin reminded herself. She now wondered whether a pizza delivery was such a good idea. She'd have to open the ground-floor door to let them in; what if the lurker in the black jacket forced entry, along with the delivery man, a gun pressed to their back? Or was she being absurdly paranoid?

No, said Strike's voice in her head. *You're being smart. Keep an eye on them. Don't leave the office until you're certain they've gone.*

Aware that her silhouette might be visible even through the Venetian blinds, Robin went to turn out the office lights. She then drew Strike's chair to the window, the UHC file on her lap, glancing regularly down into the street. The black-clad figure remained out of sight.

112

Nine in the fourth place means:
He treads on the tail of the tiger.

The I Ching or Book of Changes

Jonathan Wace had already explained how the UHC found commonality in all faiths, uniting and fusing them into a single, all-encompassing belief system. He'd quoted Jesus Christ, the Buddha, the Talmud and, mostly, himself. He'd called Giles Harmon and Noli Seymour separately onto the stage, where each had paid heartfelt tributes to the inspirational genius of Papa J, Harmon with an intellectual gravitas that earned a round of applause, Seymour with an effusive girlishness that the crowd appreciated even more.

The sky visible through the glass panes in the vaulted ceiling deepened gradually to dark blue, and Strike's one and a half legs, cramped in the second row of seats, had developed pins and needles. Wace had moved on to denouncing world leaders, while the screens above him showed images of war, famine and environmental devastation. The crowd was punctuating his shorter sentences with whoops and cheers, greeting his oratorical flourishes with applause, and roaring their approval of every castigation and accusation he flung at the elites and the warmongers. Surely, Strike thought, checking his watch, they were nearly done? But another twenty minutes passed, and

Strike, who now needed a piss, was becoming uncomfortable as well as bored.

'So which of you will help us?' shouted Wace at long last, his voice cracking with emotion as he stood alone in the spotlight, all else in shadow. 'Who will join? Who'll stand with me, to transform this broken world?'

As he spoke, the pentagonal stage began to transform, to further screams and applause. Five panels lifted like rigid petals to reveal a pentagonal baptismal pool, their undersides ridged in steps that would afford easy access to the water. Wace was left standing on a small circular platform in the middle. He now invited all those who felt they'd like to be received into the UHC to join him, and be reborn into the church.

The lights came up and some of the audience began to make their way towards the exits, including the elderly toffee-chewer to Strike's left. She'd seemed impressed by Wace's charisma and stirred by his righteous anger, but evidently felt a dip in the baptismal pool would be taking things too far. Some of the other departing audience members were carrying sleepy children; others were stretching stiff limbs after the long period of enforced sitting. No doubt many would enrich the UHC further, by purchasing a copy of *The Answer* or a hat, T-shirt or keyring before leaving the building.

Meanwhile, trickles of people were descending down the aisle to be baptised by Papa J. The cheers of existing members continued to ring off the metal supports of the Great Hall as one by one the new members were submerged, then rose, gasping and usually laughing, to be wrapped in towels by a couple of pretty girls on the other side of the pool.

Strike watched the baptisms, until the sky was black and his right leg had gone to sleep. At last, there were no more volunteers for baptism. Jonathan Wace pressed his hand to his heart, bowed, and the stage area went dark to a final burst of applause.

'Excuse me?' said a soft voice in Strike's ear. He turned to see a young redhead in a UHC tracksuit. 'Are you Cormoran Strike?'

'That's me,' he said.

To his right, American Sanchia hastily averted her face.

'Papa J would be so pleased if you felt like coming backstage.'

'Not as pleased as I am,' said Strike.

He pushed himself carefully into a standing position, stretching his numb stump until the feeling returned, and followed her through the mass of departing people. Cheery young people in UHC tracksuits were rattling collecting buckets on either side of the exit. Most who passed dropped in a handful of change, or even a note, doubtless convinced that the church did wonderful charitable work, perhaps even trying to appease a vague sense of guilt because they were leaving in dry clothes, unbaptised.

Once they'd left the main hall, Strike's companion led him off along a corridor into which she was allowed admission, by virtue of the badge on a lanyard around her neck.

'How did you enjoy the service?' she asked Strike brightly.

'Very interesting,' said Strike. 'What happens to the people who've just joined? Straight onto a bus to Chapman Farm?'

'Only if they'd like to come,' she said, smiling. 'We aren't tyrants, you know.'

'No,' said Strike, also smiling. 'I didn't know.'

She sped up, walking slightly ahead of him, so that she didn't see Strike taking out his mobile, setting it to record, and replacing it in his pocket.

As they neared what Strike assumed would be the green room, they came across two of the burly young men in UHC tracksuits who'd been standing outside earlier. A tall, rangy-looking, long-jawed man was admonishing them.

'. . . shouldn't even have gotten *near* Papa J.'

'She didn't, we told her there was no—'

'But the fact she even got as far as this corrid—'

'Mr Jackson!' said Strike, coming to a halt. 'I thought you were based in San Francisco these days?'

Joe Jackson turned, frowning, tall enough to look straight into Strike's eyes.

'Do we know each other?'

His voice was a strange compound of Midlands, overlain with west coast American. His eyes were a light grey.

'No,' said Strike. 'I recognised you from your pictures.'

'Please,' said the disconcerted redhead, 'come, if you'd like to speak to Papa J.'

Judging that his odds of getting a truthful answer from Joe Jackson to the question 'Got any tattoos?' were minimal under these circumstances, Strike walked on.

They arrived at last at a closed door, from beyond which came a buzz of talk. The girl knocked, opened the door and stood back to allow Strike to enter.

There were at least twenty people inside, all of them wearing blue. Jonathan Wace was sitting in a chair in the middle of the group, a glass of clear liquid in his hand, a crumpled towel in his lap, with a cluster of young people in tracksuits around him. Most of the robed church Principals were also present.

Silence crept over the room like a rapidly moving frost as those nearest the door became aware that Strike had arrived. It reached Giles Harmon last. He was talking to a couple of young women in a distant corner.

'. . . said to him, "What you fail to appreciate is the heterodox—"'

Apparently realising his voice was ringing alone through the room, Harmon broke off mid-sentence.

'Evening,' said Strike, moving further into the room.

If Jonathan Wace had meant to intimidate Strike by

receiving him amid a crowd, he'd greatly mistaken his opponent. Strike found it positively stimulating to come face to face with the kind of people he most despised: fanatics and hypocrites, as he mentally dubbed all of them, each of them undoubtedly convinced of their own critical importance to Wace's grandiose mission, blind to their own motives and indifferent to the sometimes irreversible damage done by the man to whom they'd sworn allegiance.

Wace rose, let the towel in his lap fall onto the arm of his chair and walked towards Strike, glass in hand. His smile was as charming and self-deprecating as it had been when he'd first mounted the pentagonal stage.

'I'm glad – genuinely glad – you're here.'

He held out his hand, and Strike shook it, looking down at him.

'Don't stand behind Mr Strike,' said Wace, to the ordinary members who'd moved to surround the pair. 'It's bad manners. Or,' he looked back at Strike, 'may I call you Cormoran?'

'Call me whatever you like,' said Strike.

'I think we're a little crowded,' said Wace, and Strike had to give him this much credit: he'd intuited in a few seconds that the detective was indifferent to the numbers in the room. 'Principals, remain please. The rest of you, I know you won't mind leaving us ... Lindsey, if Joe's still outside, tell him to join us.'

Most of the attractive young women filed out of the room.

'Got a bathroom?' asked Strike. 'I could do with a pee.'

'Certainly, certainly,' said Wace. He pointed to a white door. 'Over there.'

Strike was mildly amused to find, on washing his hands, that Wace appeared to have brought his own toiletries with him, because he doubted very much that Olympia routinely provided soaps from Hermès or bathrobes from Armani. Strike slipped his hand into the pockets of the latter, but they were empty.

'Please, sit down,' Wace invited Strike, when he emerged. Somebody had pulled up a chair to face the church leader's. As Strike did as he was bid, Joe Jackson entered the room and crossed to join the other Principals, who were either standing or sitting behind the church leader.

'She's gone,' Jackson informed Wace. 'She wanted you to have this note.'

'I'll read it later,' said Wace lightly. 'It's Cormoran I'm interested in now. Would you mind,' Wace asked the detective, 'if my wife listened in to our talk? I know she'd love to hear from you.'

'Not at all,' said Strike.

'Becca,' said Wace, indicating a smart-looking laptop lying on a chair nearby, 'could you get Mazu on FaceTime for me? Bless you. Water?' Wace asked Strike.

'That'd be great,' said Strike.

Noli Seymour was glaring at Strike as though he'd just told her his hotel hadn't received her booking. Becca Pirbright was busy with the laptop and not looking at Strike. The rest of the Principals were variously looking uneasy, contemptuous, studiously uninterested or, in the case of Joe Jackson, definitely tense.

'How's your partner?' said Wace earnestly, settling back in his chair as Becca handed Strike a cold bottle of water.

'Robin? A lot better for being outside the box,' said Strike.

'Box?' said Wace. 'What box?'

'Do you remember the box you locked my partner in, Miss Pirbright?' Strike asked.

Becca gave no sign she'd heard him.

'Is Miss Ellacott a business partner, or something more, by the way?' asked Wace.

'Your sons not here?' said Strike, looking around. 'I saw the one who looks like Piltdown Man outside.'

'Papa J,' said Becca quietly, 'Mazu.'

She adjusted the laptop so that Mazu could see her husband, and for the first time in thirty years, Strike looked into the face of the girl who'd led his sister away from the football game at Forgeman Farm, and shut her in with a paedophile. She was sitting in front of shelves cluttered with Chinese statuettes. Her long black hair fell in two wings over her face, emphasising the pale, pointed nose. Her eyes were in shadow.

'It's Cormoran Strike, my love,' said Wace, to the face on the screen. 'Our Miss Ellacott's detective partner.'

Mazu said nothing.

'Well, Cormoran,' said Wace, smiling, 'shall we speak plainly?'

'I wasn't intending to speak any other way, but go on.'

Wace laughed.

'Very well: you aren't the first, and won't be the last, to investigate the Universal Humanitarian Church. Many have tried to uncover scandals and plots and wrongdoing, but none have succeeded, for the simple reason that we are exactly who we profess to be: people of faith, living as we believe the Blessed Divinity requires us to live, pursuing the ends They wish to see achieved, fighting against evil wherever we find it. That necessarily brings us into conflict with both the ignorant, who fear what they don't understand, and the malevolent, who understand our purpose and wish to thwart us. Are you familiar with the work of Dr K. Sri Dhammananda? No? "Struggle must exist, for all life is a struggle of some kind. But make certain that you do not struggle in the interest of self against truth and justice."'

'I see we've got different definitions of "speaking plainly",' said Strike. 'Tell me: is the boy Robin saw dying in the attic of the farmhouse still alive?'

A tiny noise, somewhere between a grunt and a gulp, escaped Giles Harmon.

'Wind?' enquired Strike of the novelist. 'Or have you got something to say?'

'Jonathan,' said Harmon, ignoring the detective, 'I should be going. I'm on a flight to Paris at eleven tomorrow. Need to pack.'

Wace rose to embrace Harmon.

'You were marvellous tonight,' he told the writer, releasing Harmon but holding him by the upper arms. 'I believe we owe at least half the new recruits to you. I'll call you later.'

Harmon stalked out past Strike without looking at him, giving the latter time to reflect on what a mistake it was for short men to wear robes.

Wace sat back down.

'Your partner,' he said quietly, 'has invented a story to cover up the incriminating position she found herself in with Jacob, in the bathroom. She panicked, and she lied. We are all of us frail and subject to temptations, but I want to reassure you: in spite of appearances, I don't really believe Miss Ellacott meant to assault little Jacob. Possibly she was trying to get information out of him. Much as I deplore trying to force falsehoods out of children, we'd be prepared to drop charges, subject to an apology and a donation to the church.'

Strike laughed as he stretched out his right leg, which was still sore. Wace's earnest expression didn't flicker.

'Has it occurred to you,' Wace said, 'that your partner invented dying children and other such dramatic incidents, because she observed nothing of any note during our time with us, but had to justify the fees you charge your clients?'

'You know,' said Strike, 'I always think it's a mistake to diversify too far away from the core brand. I'm sure Dr Zhou would agree,' he added, looking over at the doctor. 'Just because a man knows how to market enemas to idiots, doesn't mean he knows shit about pig farming – to take a random example.'

'I'm sure there's meaning in that cryptic statement,' said Wace, looking entertained, 'but I must confess, I can't find it.'

'Well, let's say a failed car salesman finds out he's supremely good at flogging liquid bullshit to the masses. Would he be smart to try parcelling up solid chunks for the likes of me?'

'Ah, you're cleverer than everyone else in this room, are you?' said Wace. Though still smiling, it was as though his large blue eyes had become a little more opaque.

'On the contrary. I'm just like you, Jonathan,' said Strike. 'Every day, I get up, look myself in the mirror and ask, "Cormoran, are you a righteous vessel for truth and justice?"'

'*You're disgusting!*' burst out Noli Seymour.

'Noli,' said Wace, making a small version of the gesture with which he'd quelled the crowd's applause. 'Remember the Buddha.'

'"Conquer anger with non-anger"?' asked Strike. 'Always thought that'd make a pretty substandard fortune cookie, personally.'

Becca was now looking at him with a little smile, as though she'd seen many like him before. A muscle flickered at the scarred corner of Zhou's mouth. Joe Jackson had folded his long arms, looking down at Strike with a slight frown. Mazu was so motionless, the screen might have frozen.

'Now, I'm the first to admit, I wouldn't be any good at what you do, Jonathan,' said Strike. 'But you seem to think you've got a flair for my game.'

'What does that mean?' said Wace, with a puzzled smile.

'Surveillance of our office. Tailing us by car.'

'Cormoran,' said Wace slowly, 'I can't tell whether you know you're inventing things, or not.'

'As I say,' said Strike, 'it's all about diversifying from the core brand. You're top notch at picking out people who're happy to be sucked dry of all their worldly goods, or slave on the farm for no wages, but less good, if you don't mind me saying, at picking people to stake out premises, or follow targets discreetly. Bright red Vauxhall Corsas aren't discreet. Unless you meant to let us know what you're up to, I'm here to tell you: this isn't your forte. You can't just pick some random guy who's fucked up this year's carrot crop to stand opposite my office, staring up at the windows.'

'Cormoran, we're not watching you,' said Wace, smiling. 'If these things have indeed happened, you must have offended someone who takes a less tolerant view of your activities than we do. We choose – like the Buddha—'

'The bullet through Kevin Pirbright's brain was shot in non-anger, was it?'

'I'm afraid I have no idea what emotions Kevin was feeling when he shot himself.'

'Any interest in who murdered your brother?' Strike said, turning to Becca.

'What you don't perhaps realise, Mr Strike, is that Kevin had a guilty conscience,' said Becca sweetly. 'I forgive him for what he did to me, but apparently he couldn't forgive himself.'

'How d'you choose the people making the phone calls?' Strike said, looking back at Wace. 'Obviously, a woman had to pretend to be Reaney's wife to persuade the authorities to let the call through, but who spoke to him once he'd picked up? You?'

'I have *literally* no idea who or what you're talking about, Cormoran,' said Wace.

'Jordan Reaney. Overslept the morning he was supposed to be on the vegetable run, conveniently leaving room for Daiyu in the front of the truck.' Out of the corner of his eye, Strike saw the smile vanish from Becca's face. 'Currently in jail. Got a call after I interviewed him, which appears to have precipitated a suicide attempt.'

'This all sounds very upsetting and unfortunate and more than a little strange,' said Wace, 'but I promise you, I don't have the slightest knowledge about any phone calls to any prison.'

'You remember Cherie Gittins, of course?'

'I'm hardly likely to forget her,' said Wace quietly.

'Why were you so careful to keep track of her, after she left?'

'We did no such thing.'

Strike turned again to Becca, and he gained some satisfaction from her sudden look of panic.

'Miss Pirbright here knows Cherie had daughters. She told the police so. Volunteered the information, for some reason. Went right off script, talking about how what seems devilish may, in fact, be divine.'

Some women blush becomingly, but Becca wasn't one of them. She turned a purplish red. In the short silence that followed, both Noli Seymour and Joe Jackson turned their heads to look at Becca.

'How many important religious figures would you say end up hanged?' asked Strike. 'Offhand, I can only think of Judas.'

'Cherie wasn't hanged,' said Becca. Her eyes flickered towards Wace as she said it.

'Do you mean that in a metaphysical sense?' asked Strike. 'Same as Daiyu didn't really drown, but dissolved into pure spirit?'

'Papa J,' said Jackson unexpectedly, pushing himself off the wall, 'I wonder whether there's much point—?'

'Thank you, Joe,' said Wace quietly, and Jackson fell immediately back into line.

'Now, *that's* what I like to see,' said Strike approvingly.

'Military-level discipline. Shame it doesn't extend to the foot soldiers.'

The door behind Strike opened. He glanced round. Taio entered the room, large, greasy-haired, rat-faced and dressed in a UHC tracksuit that strained across his belly. On seeing Strike, he stopped dead.

'Cormoran's here at my invitation, Taio,' said Wace, smiling. 'Join us.'

'How's the head?' said Strike, as Taio took up a standing position beside Jackson. 'Need stitches at all?'

'We were talking about Cherie,' said Wace, again addressing Strike. 'As a matter of fact – I know this may be hard for you to understand – Becca's perfectly right in what she said: Cherie played a divine role, a necessarily difficult role, in the ascension of Daiyu as a prophet. If she has indeed hanged herself, that, too, may have been ordained.'

'You'll be hanging up a second thrashing straw figure in temple to celebrate, will you?'

'I see you're one of those who prides themselves on disrespecting rites, mysteries, and religious observance,' said Wace, smiling again. 'I shall pray for you, Cormoran. I mean that sincerely.'

'I'll tell you one book I've read, that's right up your street,' said Strike. 'Came across it in a Christian mission where I was spending a night, just outside Nairobi. This was when I was still in the army. I'd drunk too much coffee, and there were only two books in the room, and it was late, and I didn't think I'd be able to make much of a dent in the Bible, so I went for *Who Moved the Stone?* by Frank Morison. Have you read it?'

'I've heard of it,' said Wace, sitting back in his chair, still smiling. 'We recognise Jesus Christ as an important emissary of the Blessed Divinity, though, of course, he's not the only one.'

'Oh, he had nothing on you, obviously,' said Strike. 'Anyway, Morison was a non-believer who set out to prove the resurrection never happened. He did an in-depth investigation into the events surrounding Jesus' death, drawing on as many historical sources as he could find, and as a direct result, was converted to Christianity. You see what I'm driving at?'

'I'm afraid not,' said Wace.

'What questions d'you think Morison would've wanted answered, if he set out to disprove the legend of the Drowned Prophet?'

Three people reacted: Taio, who let out a low growl, Noli Seymour, who gasped, and Mazu, who, for the first time, spoke.

'Jonathan.'

'My love?' said Wace, turning to look at the face on screen.

'The sage casts out all that is inferior and degrading,' said Mazu.

'Well said.'

It was Dr Zhou who'd spoken. He'd drawn himself up to his full height, and unlike the absent Harmon, he looked undeniably impressive in his robes.

'Is that from the I Ching?' asked Strike, looking from Zhou to Mazu. 'Funnily enough, I've got a few questions on the subject of degradation, if you'd rather hear those? No?' he said, when nobody answered. 'Back to what I was saying, then. Let's suppose I fancy writing the new *Who Moved the Stone?* – working title, "Why Paddle in the North Sea at Five a.m.?" As a sceptical investigator of the miraculous ascension into heaven of Daiyu, I think I'd start with how Cherie knew Jordan Reaney would oversleep that morning. Then I'd be finding out why Daiyu was wearing a dress that made her as visible as possible in the dark, why she drowned off exactly the same stretch of beach as your first wife and – parallels with *Who Moved the Stone?* here – I'd want to know where the body went. But unlike Morison, I might include a chapter on Birmingham.'

'Birmingham?' repeated Wace. Unlike everyone else in the room, he was still smiling.

'Yeah,' said Strike. 'I've noticed there's a lot of going to Birmingham round about the time Daiyu disappeared.'

'Once again, I have literally no—'

'*You* were supposed to be in Birmingham that morning, but you called it off, right? You sent your daughter Abigail up to Birmingham, shortly after Daiyu died. And I think *you* were banished to Birmingham, too, weren't you, Miss Pirbright? For three years, is that correct?'

Before Becca could answer, Wace had leaned forwards, hands clasped between his knees, and said quietly,

'If the mention of my eldest daughter is supposed to worry me, you're shooting wide of the mark, Cormoran. The most of which I can be reproached regarding Abigail is that I spoiled her, after the – after the dreadful death of her mother.'

Incredibly, at least to Strike, who found it difficult to cry in extremity, let alone on cue, Wace's eyes now welled with tears.

'Do I regret that Abigail left the church?' he said. 'Of course – but for her sake, not mine. If you are indeed in contact with her,' said Wace, now placing a hand over his heart, 'tell her, from me, "Popsicle misses you". It's what she used to call me.'

'Touching,' said Strike indifferently. 'Moving on: you remember Rosie Fernsby, I presume? Well-developed fifteen-year-old you were going to take up to Birmingham, on the morning Daiyu died?'

Wace, who was wiping his eyes on the crumpled towel, didn't answer.

'You were going to "show her something",' Strike went on. 'What kinds of things does he show young girls in

1009

Birmingham?' he asked Becca. 'You must have seen some of them, if you were there three years?'

'Jonathan,' said Mazu again, more insistently. Her husband ignored her.

'You talk about "spoiling",' said Strike, looking back at Wace. 'There's a word with a double meaning, if ever there was one ... which brings us to pig masks.'

'Cormoran,' said Wace, his tone world-weary, 'I think I've heard enough to realise that you're determined to write some lurid exposé, full of innuendo, short on facts and embellished with whatever fictional details you and Miss Ellacott can dream up together. I regret to say we'll have to proceed with our action against Miss Ellacott for child abuse. It would be best if you communicate henceforth through my lawyers.'

'That's a shame. We were getting on so well. To return to the pig masks—'

'I've made my position clear, Mr Strike.'

Wace's charm and ease of manner, his smile, his warmth, had vanished. Once before, Strike had faced a killer whose eyes, under the stress and excitement of hearing their crimes described, had become as black and blank as those of a shark, and now he saw the phenomenon again: Wace's eyes might have turned into empty boreholes.

'Abigail and others were made to wear pig masks and crawl through the dirt to do their chores, at the command of your charming wife,' said Strike.

'That never happened,' said Mazu contemptuously. 'Never. *Jonathan*—'

'Unfortunately for you, Mrs Wace, I have concrete evidence of those masks being worn at Chapman Farm,' said Strike, 'although it'd be in your own interests to deny you knew all the ways in which they were used. Perhaps Mr Jackson could enlighten you?'

Jackson glanced at Wace, then said, in his strange hybrid drawl,

'You're off on some kinda fantastical kick, Mr Strike.'

'Then let me do a bit more plain speaking before I go. The police don't like too many coincidences. Twice in the last couple of months, phone calls from unknown numbers had been followed by suicide attempts, one of them successful. I don't think anyone but my agency has connected them yet, but that can soon change.

'Late last year, Kevin Pirbright was caught on tape saying he had an appointment with someone from the church. Five days later, he was murdered. That's two unnatural deaths and one close shave for three of the people who were at Chapman Farm when Daiyu drowned – assuming, of course, she ever drowned at all.'

Becca's mouth fell open. Mazu began to shout, but unfortunately for her, so did both Taio and Noli Seymour who, both being in the room, easily obliterated the oaths now pouring from Mazu's thin lips.

'You bastard—'

'You vile, evil, *disgusting* man, how *dare* you say these things about a dead child, have you no *conscience*—'

Strike raised his voice over the tumult.

'There are witnesses to the fact that Rosie Fernsby was at Chapman Farm when certain Polaroids were taken. Rosie was identified by Cherie Gittins as one of the subjects of those photos. I know you're trying to find her, so I'm warning you,' he said, pointing directly into the face of Jonathan Wace, 'if she's found dead, whether by her own hand, or by accident, or by murder, rest assured, I'll be showing those Polaroids to the police, drawing their attention to the fact that we've now got four unnatural deaths of ex-UHC members within a ten-month period, urging them to recheck certain phone records and making sure my journalistic contact makes as much of a noise about it all as possible.

'To tell you the truth, I'm not as humble as you are, Jonathan,' said Strike, getting to his feet. 'I don't need to ask myself whether I'm up to the job, because I know I'm fucking great at it, so be warned: if you do anything to hurt either my partner or Rosie Fernsby, *I will burn your church to the fucking ground.*'

113

*. . . one may spend a full cycle of time with a friend
of kindred spirit without fear of making a mistake.*

The I Ching or Book of Changes

Spending the night curled up on what she'd previously
found a fairly comfortable sofa, which revealed unexpected
crevices and hard edges when asked to double as a bed, was
bad enough. Insult was added to injury when, having finally
achieved a couple of hours of deep sleep, Robin was woken
rudely by a loud exclamation of 'What the——?' from a man
in her immediate vicinity. For a fraction of a second she had
no idea where she was: her flat, the dormitory at Chapman
Farm, Ryan's bedroom, all of which had doors in different
relative positions. She sat up fast, disorientated; her coat slid off
her onto the floor, and then she realised she was in the office,
looking blearily up at Strike.

'Jesus Christ,' he said. 'I wasn't expecting to find a body.'

'You nearly gave me a heart——'

'What are you doing here?'

'I think our gunman came back last night,' Robin said,
bending down to retrieve her coat.

'*What?*'

'Black jacket, hood up – they lurked in those basement steps
opposite for a bit and when the street was clear, they crossed

1013

the street and tried to get in through our front door, but this time, they couldn't.'

'Did you call the police?'

'It happened too fast. They must have realised the lock had changed, because they left. I watched them to the end of Denmark Street, but I was afraid they might be waiting for me on Charing Cross Road. I didn't fancy risking it, so I slept here.'

At this moment, the alarm on Robin's mobile went off, making her jump again.

'Good thinking,' said Strike. 'Very good thinking. Were the lights on when they arrived?'

'Until I spotted the black jacket and the hood on the opposite pavement, then I turned them off. It's possible they didn't notice, and thought the office was empty, but they might have known someone was here and been determined to get in anyway. Don't look like that,' said Robin, 'the lock worked, and I didn't take any chances, did I?'

'No. That's good. Don't suppose you got any pictures?'

'I did,' said Robin, bringing them up on her mobile and handing it to Strike. 'It was a tricky angle, because they were directly beneath me, obviously, when they were trying to get in.'

'Yeah, that looks like the same person … same jacket, anyway … face carefully hidden … I'll pass these to the police, too. With luck, they took down their hood and were caught on CCTV once they were out of here.'

'Did you get my text about Will, Flora and Prudence?' said Robin, trying to detangle her hair with her fingers, without much success. 'Pat's fine with us going over there this morning, which is good of her, given it's Saturday.'

'I did, yeah,' said Strike, moving to the kettle. 'Excellent work that, Ellacott. Want a coffee? We've got time. I only came in here to put my notes in the file, from last night.'

'Oh God, of course!' said Robin, who in her exhaustion had briefly forgotten where Strike had been. 'What happened?'

Strike gave Robin a full account of the UHC meeting and his subsequent interview with Wace while they drank their coffees. When he'd finished, Robin said,

'You told him you'd "burn his church to the fucking ground"?'

'Might've got a bit carried away there,' admitted Strike. 'I was on a roll.'

'Don't you think that's a bit ... declaration of all-out war?'

'Not really. Come on, they already knew we're investigating them. Why else does everyone we want to talk to get warning phone calls?'

'We don't know for sure the church is behind those calls.'

'We don't know for sure the people in pig masks lived at Chapman Farm, either, but I think it's safe to hazard a guess. I'd've liked to say a damn sight more than I did, but Deirdre Doherty drowning drags in Flora Brewster, Daiyu going out of the window incriminates Emily Pirbright, and if I'd told Harmon I knew he was fucking underage girls, it would've put Lin in the firing line. No, the only new information they got from me last night was that we think Daiyu's death is fishy, and I said that deliberately, to see the reactions.'

'And?'

'Shock, outrage; exactly what you'd expect. But I warned them what's going to happen if Rosie Fernsby turns up dead, which was the main point of the exercise, and I've told them we know they're keeping tabs on us, however ineptly, so as far as I'm concerned, job done. Er ... if you want a shower or anything, you can go upstairs.'

'That'd be great, thanks,' said Robin. 'I'll be quick.'

Her reflection in Strike's bathroom mirror looked just as bad as Robin felt: a large crease had been pressed into the side of her face and her eyes were puffy. Trying not to visualise Strike standing naked in exactly the same spot she was now occupying in the tiny bathroom, Robin showered, pinched some of his deodorant, put yesterday's clothes back on, brushed her hair, applied lipstick to make herself look less washed out, wiped it off because she thought it made her look worse, and returned downstairs.

Robin usually drove when the two of them were out together, but today, in deference to her tiredness, Strike volunteered. The BMW, being automatic, wasn't nearly as hard for a man with a prosthetic to drive as the Land Rover would have been. Robin waited until they were on their way to Kilburn before saying,

'I actually had a couple of thoughts myself last night, going through the UHC file.'

Robin outlined her theory that Rosie Fernsby had been the other teenager in the dormitory, the night before Daiyu had drowned. Strike drove for a minute, thinking.

'I quite like it—'

'Only quite?'

'I can't see Cherie not checking Rosie's bed, not if she wanted to be sure everyone was out for the count before she gave all the kids their special drinks, then shunted Daiyu out of the window.'

'Maybe she *did* check, and it suited her that Rosie wasn't there?'

'But how would she know Rosie wouldn't come back later? The pillows could've been there so Rosie could, I dunno, have an assignation in a Retreat Room or go into the woods to smoke a joint.'

'If you'd been at Chapman Farm, you'd know the only permissible reason for alone time is going to the bathroom. If Rosie was supposed to be on child duty, that's exactly where she should have been ... What if Rosie told Cherie she and her father and brother were leaving that night?'

'She'd only been at Chapman Farm a week or so. She'd've been putting a hell of a lot of trust in Cherie, telling her they were escaping.'

'Maybe Rosie and Cherie had been through something together that would have bonded them quite quickly?'

'Ah,' said Strike, remembering the Polaroids. 'Yeah. There's that, of course ... and yet Rosie was sorry to leave the farm, according to her brother.'

'Teenage girls can be weird,' said Robin quietly. 'They rationalise things ... tell themselves it wasn't as bad as they know, deep down, it was ... She had a big crush on Jonathan Wace, remember. Maybe she walked willingly into the barn, not knowing what was about to happen. Afterwards, if Wace is telling her how wonderful she is, how beautiful and brave and free spirited ... telling her she's proved herself somehow ... But I know it's all speculation until we find her, which is the other thing I was going to tell you. There's a chance – only a chance, don't get too excited – that I *have* found her.'

'You're kidding me?'

'I had an idea in the early hours of the morning. Well, two ideas, actually, but this one first. I've drawn a total blank on property records, but then I thought, *dating apps*. I had to join about half a dozen to get access. Anyway, on mingleguru. co.uk—'

'Mingle Guru?'

'Yes, Mingle Guru – is one Bhakta Dasha, age thirty-six, so the right age for Rosie, and very much *not* Asian, unlike everyone else on the site.'

As Strike pulled up at a red light, she held up a profile picture for him to see.

'Fuck's sake,' said Strike.

The woman was pretty, round-faced and dimpled, wearing a stuck-on bindi and with very orange skin. As the lights changed and they moved off again, Strike said,

'That should be brought to the attention of the Advertising Standards Authority.'

'She's a practising Hindu,' said Robin, reading Bhakta's details, 'who loves India, has travelled extensively there, would very much like to meet someone who shares her outlook and religion, and gives her current location as London. I wondered whether—'

'Dev,' said Strike.

'Exactly, unless he's getting tired of being the resident good-looking man we always send to sweet talk women.'

'There are worse problems to have,' said Strike. 'Starting to think you should sleep on the sofa more often. It seems to bring something out in you.'

'You haven't heard my second idea yet. I was trying to get to sleep and thinking about Cherie, and then I thought, *Isaac Mills*.'

'Who?'

'Isaac Mills. Her boyfriend after Chapman Farm. The one who robbed the pharmacy.'

'Oh, yeah. The junkie with the teeth.'

'I thought, what if she told Isaac what had happened at Chapman Farm?' said Robin. 'What if she confided in him? It was all very recent when she met him.'

'That,' said Strike, 'is a very sound bit of reasoning and I'm pissed off I didn't think of it myself.'

'So you think it's worth looking for him?' said Robin, pleased that this theory, at least, wasn't getting short shrift.

'Definitely. Just hope he's still alive. He didn't have the look of a man who gets a lot of fresh air and vitamins – shit, I forgot to tell you something else, from last night.'

'What?'

'I might be wrong,' said Strike, 'but I could've sworn I saw Phillipa Delaunay in the audience at Wace's meeting. Daiyu's aunt – brother of the Stolen Prophet.'

'Why on earth would she be there?'

'Good question. Mind you, as I say, I could be wrong. Hearty blondes in pearls all blur into one to me. Dunno how their husbands tell them apart.'

'Pheromones?' suggested Robin.

'Maybe. Or some kind of special call. Like penguins.'

Robin laughed.

114

What has been spoiled through man's fault can be made good again through man's work.

The I Ching or Book of Changes

As they admitted to each other afterwards, for the first hour Strike and Robin spent talking to Will in Pat's house in Kilburn, each privately thought their mission was doomed. He was implacably opposed to meeting Flora Brewster and insisted he didn't want immunity from prosecution, because he deserved jail. All he wanted was for Lin to be found, so she could look after Qing once he'd handed himself over to the police.

Pat had taken Will's daughter to the shops to allow them to talk in peace. The room in which they were sitting was small, neat, smelled strongly of stale Superkings and was cluttered with family photographs, although Pat also had an unsuspected weakness for crystal animal figurines. Will was wearing a new green sweater which, though it hung loosely on his still very thin frame, both suited and fitted him better than his filthy UHC tracksuit. His colour had improved, the shadows under his eyes had gone, and for a full sixty minutes, he made no mention of the Drowned Prophet.

However, when Strike, starting to lose patience, pushed Will on why he didn't want to at least talk to another ex-member with a view to joining forces and freeing as many people as possible from the church, Will said,

'You can't free them all. She wants to keep them. She'll let some go, like me, who aren't any good—'

'Who's "she"?' said Strike.

'You know who,' muttered Will.

They heard the front door open. Strike and Robin assumed Pat and Qing had returned, but instead a pudgy, bespectacled, fair-haired man of around seventy appeared. He was wearing a Queens Park Rangers football strip, brown trousers of the kind Strike was used to seeing on Ted, and had a copy of the *Daily Mail* under his arm.

'Ah. You'll be the detectives.'

'That's us,' said Strike, standing up to shake hands.

'Dennis Chauncey. Everyone all right for tea? I'm having some, it's no trouble.'

Dennis disappeared into the kitchen. Robin noticed that he was limping slightly, possibly due to the fall he'd suffered while demonstrating levitation.

'Look, Will—' Strike began.

'If I talk to Flora before the police, I'll never *get* to the police,' said Will, 'because she'll come for me before I can—'

'Who'll come for you?' Dennis, who evidently had sharp hearing, had reappeared at the door of the sitting room, munching on a chocolate bourbon. 'Drowned Prophet, is it?'

Will looked sheepish.

'I've told you, son.' Dennis tapped his temple. 'It's in your head. It's all in your head.'

'I've seen—'

'You've seen tricks,' said Dennis, not unkindly. 'That's all you've seen. *Tricks*. They've done a right number on you, but it's *tricks*, that's all.'

He disappeared again. Before Strike could say anything

else, they heard the front door open for a second time. Shortly afterwards, Pat entered the room.

'Walked her around and she fell asleep,' she said in the growl that passed for her whisper. 'I've left her in the hall.'

She wriggled out of her jacket, pulled a pack of Superkings out of its pocket, lit one, sat down in the armchair and said,

'What's going on?'

By the time Robin had explained about Flora Brewster's wish to meet Will, Dennis had returned with a fresh pot of tea.

'Sounds like a good idea,' said Pat, peering beadily at Will. She took a long drag on her cigarette. 'If you want the police to take you seriously,' she said, exhaling, so that her face was momentarily obscured by a cloud of blue smoke, 'you need corroboration.'

'Exactly,' said Strike. 'Thank you, Pat.'

'Mr Chauncey, you sit here,' said Robin, getting up, as there were no other chairs.

'No, you're all right love, gotta do the pigeons,' said Dennis. He poured himself a mug of tea, added three sugars and left again.

'Racing pigeons,' said Pat. 'He keeps them out the back. Just don't get him onto Fergus McLeod. I've had nothing else, morning, noon and night, for a month.'

'Who's Fergus McLeod?' asked Robin.

'He cheated,' said Will unexpectedly. 'With a microchip. The bird never left his loft. Dennis told me all about it.'

'It's been a bloody relief, having someone else around to listen to him bang on about it,' said Pat, rolling her eyes.

Strike's mobile now rang: Midge.

''S'cuse me,' he said.

Not wanting to risk waking Qing, who was fast asleep in a pushchair just inside the front door, he moved through to the kitchen and let himself carefully into the small garden. Half of it was given over to the pigeons, and Dennis was visible at the window of the coop, apparently cleaning out cages.

'Midge?'

'Lin's at the clinic,' said Midge excitedly. 'Tasha just called me. Zhou wasn't around last night, so Tasha went creeping around that annexe. The doors were locked, but blinds have been down over one of the windows all the time she's been there. She was trying to peer through a gap when, get this – a skinny blonde girl lifted it up and peered right back out at her. Tash says they were nearly nose to nose. She nearly fell over backwards onto her arse. Then Tasha thinks the girl realised she wasn't in a staff uniform and she mouths "help me". Tasha mimed at her to push up the window, but it's bolted. Then Tash could hear someone coming, so she had to leg it, but she mouthed at Lin that she was going to come back.'

'Excellent,' said Strike, his mind now working rapidly as he watched Dennis talking to the pigeon in his hand. 'All right, listen: I want you to head down to Borehamwood. Tasha might need back-up. You can check in to a B&B in the vicinity or something. If Tasha can get back to that window tonight, get her to tap on it and hold up a note to tell Lin Will's out, he's got Qing and they're both safe.'

'Will do,' said Midge, who sounded delighted. 'How about I—?'

'For now, just stay within hailing distance of the clinic, in case they try and move Lin by night. Don't try any rescue attempts, and tell Tasha not to take any more risks than she has to, OK?'

'OK,' said Midge.

'With any luck,' said Strike, 'this news will put a stick of dynamite under Will Edensor, because Christ knows what else'll do it.'

115

'It took another hour and a half to persuade him,' Robin told Murphy later, at her flat. He'd wanted to take her out to dinner, but Robin, who was exhausted, had told him she'd rather eat in, so Murphy had picked up a Chinese takeaway. Robin was avoiding the noodles; she never wanted to eat another noodle in her life.

'We went round and round in circles,' Robin went on, 'but Pat clinched it. She told Will that Lin probably won't be in a fit state to have sole charge of Qing the moment she gets out – if we can get her out, obviously – and said the best thing Will can do is to keep himself out of jail, so he can help. Anyway, it's all arranged: we're going to take Will over to Prudence's on Monday evening.'

'Great,' said Murphy.

He hadn't been particularly talkative since arriving, and didn't smile as he said this. Robin had assumed he, too, was tired, but now she detected a certain constraint.

'You OK?'

'Yeah,' said Murphy, 'fine.'

He tipped more chow mein onto his plate, then said,

'How come you didn't call me last night, when the guy in black was trying to get into the building?'

'You were working,' said Robin, surprised. 'What could you have done about it?'

'Right,' said Murphy. 'So you'd only call me if I could be useful?'

A familiar mixture of unease and frustration, one she'd felt all too many times in her marriage, rose inside Robin.

'Of course not,' she said. 'But we've changed the locks. The guy didn't get in. I wasn't in any danger.'

'But you still spent the night there.'

'As a precaution,' said Robin.

She now knew exactly what was bothering Murphy: the same thing that had bothered Matthew, both before and after they'd got married.

'Ryan—'

'How come Strike didn't realise you were still in the office, when he got back from this religious meeting?'

'Because the lights were out,' said Robin.

'So you heard him go upstairs, but you didn't go out and ask him what had happened with Wace? You waited until this morning.'

'I didn't hear him going upstairs,' said Robin truthfully. 'You can't, in the inner office, which is where I was.'

'And you hadn't texted him, to say you were staying the night?'

'No,' said Robin, trying not to become openly angry, because she was too tired to want a row, 'because I didn't decide to stay the night until one in the morning. It was too late to take the Tube and I was still worried the person in the black jacket would be hanging around.'

'You just told me you weren't in any danger.'

'I wasn't, not inside the building.'

'You could've got a taxi.'

'I know I could, but I was really tired, so I decided to stay.'

'Weren't you worried about where Strike had got to?'

Now on the brink of losing the fight with her anger, Robin said,

'I'm not his wife and he can handle himself. Anyway, I told you: I was busy joining dating sites to try and find this woman we need to interview.'

'And he didn't call you after he left the meeting?'

'No. It was late and he probably assumed I'd be in bed.'

'Right,' said Murphy, with precisely the edge in his voice Matthew had once had, whenever they discussed Strike.

'For God's sake, just ask,' said Robin, losing her temper. 'Ask me whether I slept upstairs.'

'If you say you slept in the office—'

'That *is* what I say, because that's the truth, and you can keep giving me the third degree, but the story won't change, because *I'm telling you what actually happened.*'

'Fine,' said Murphy, and the monosyllable had so much of Matthew in it, that Robin said,

'Listen, I've done this shit before, and I'm not going to do it again.'

'Meaning?'

'Meaning you're not the first man who thinks I can't be in partnership with Strike without screwing him. If you don't trust me—'

'It's not a question of trust.'

'*How can it not be a question of trust?* You've just been trying to catch me out in a lie!'

'You might've wanted to spare my feelings. Slept upstairs, and maybe nothing happened, but you didn't want to admit you'd been there.'

'That *isn't – what – happened*. Strike and I are *friends* – and he happens to be dating a lawyer.'

The lie fell easily and instinctively out of Robin's mouth, and when she saw Murphy's expression clear, she knew it had served its purpose.

'You never told me that.'

'I had no idea you were so interested in Strike's love life. I'll keep you briefed in future.'

Murphy laughed.

'I'm sorry, Robin,' he said, reaching for her hand. 'I am, seriously. Shit ... I didn't mean to ... Lizzie went off with a supposed "friend", in the end.'

'I know that, but what you're failing to factor in here is, *I'm not Lizzie.*'

'I know. I'm sorry, seriously. How long's Strike been with this lawyer?'

'I don't know – months. I don't keep notes,' said Robin.

The rest of the evening passed amicably enough. Tired, still annoyed but wanting to keep the peace, Robin told herself she'd worry later about what might happen if Nick, Ilsa, or Strike himself revealed that his affair with Bijou was over.

116

Nine at the beginning means:
Hidden dragon.
Do not act.

The I Ching or Book of Changes

Robin spent a good deal of the next three days asking herself unanswerable questions about the state of her own feelings, and in speculation about the likely future trajectory of Murphy's newly revealed jealousy. Would this relationship go the same way as her marriage, through increasing levels of suspicion to a destructive explosion, or was she projecting old resentments onto Murphy, much as he'd done to her?

Though she'd accepted the truce, and did her best to act as though all was forgiven and forgotten, Robin remained annoyed that, yet again, she'd been forced to justify and dissemble on matters relating to Cormoran Strike. Those fatal four words, 'I love you, too', had brought about a shift in Murphy. It would be going too far to call his new attitude possessiveness, but there was a certain assurance that had been lacking before.

In her more honest moments, Robin asked herself why she *hadn't* called him when worried a gunman might be lurking out of sight round the corner. The only answers she could come up with were confused, and some opened doors onto further questions she didn't want to answer. At the admissible end of the scale was her fear that Murphy would have over-reacted. She hadn't wanted to hand her boyfriend a justification for dictating what risks she took, because she'd had quite enough of that already, from her mother. Yet, whispered her conscience, she'd let Strike tell her to be more careful, hadn't she? She'd also done as he'd suggested, with regard to taxis and taking on no jobs on her own. What was the difference?

The answer (so Robin told herself) was that she and Strike were in business together, which gave him certain rights – but here, her self-analysis stopped, because it might be argued that Murphy, too, had rights; it was simply that she found them less admissible. Such musings came dangerously close to forcing her to confront something she was determinedly avoiding. Ruminations on Strike's true feelings, as she knew from past experience, led only to confusion and pain.

Strike, meanwhile, had personal worries of his own. On Saturday afternoon, Lucy called him with the news that Ted, who was still staying at her house, had had a 'funny turn'. Guilt-stricken that he hadn't so much as visited Ted in the last couple of weeks, Strike abandoned surveillance of the husband they'd nicknamed Hampstead to drive straight to Lucy's house in Bromley, where he'd found Ted even more disorientated than usual. Lucy had already made a doctor's appointment for their uncle, and had promised to get back to Strike with news as soon as she had it.

He spent most of Monday on surveillance of Toy Boy, handing over to Barclay in the late afternoon, then heading back to the office at four o'clock. Robin had been there all day, trying to sublimate in work the anxiety she felt about moving Will out of the safe haven of Pat's house to visit Prudence that evening.

'I still think Will and Flora could have FaceTimed,' Robin

said to Strike, when he joined her at the partners' desk, coffee in hand.

'Yeah, well, Prudence is a therapist, isn't she? Wants the in-person touch.'

He glanced at Robin, who looked both tired and tense. Assuming this was due to her continuing fear of the church, he said,

'They'd be stupider than I think they are to try and tail us after what I said to Wace on Friday, but if we spot anyone, we'll pull over and confront them.'

Strike chose not to mention that if, as he half-suspected, Wace was playing mind games rather than genuinely attempting covert surveillance, the church leader might equally decide to ramp up harassment in retribution for their face-to-face chat at Olympia.

'I'm afraid I've got some bad news,' Robin said. 'I can't be a hundred per cent certain, but I think Isaac Mills might be dead. Look: I found it an hour ago.'

She passed the printout of a small news item in the *Telegraph* dated January 2011 across the desk. It described an incident in which Isaac Mills, 38, had died in a head-on collision with a van which, unlike Mills, had been driving on the correct side of the road.

'Right age,' said Robin, 'and wrong side of the road sounds like he was drunk or stoned.'

'Shit,' said Strike.

'I'll keep looking,' said Robin, taking back the clipping, 'because there are other Isaac Millses out there, but I've got a horrible feeling that was our man. Did you talk to Dev about taking Rosie Fernsby out for dinner, by the way?'

'Did, yeah, he's going to make a profile on Mingle Guru tonight. I had another thought about Rosie, actually. If that profile *is* hers, and she really *has* been travelling around India for the last few years, it makes sense that she hasn't got a permanent base here. I wondered whether she might be house-sitting while her mother's in Canada.'

'Nobody's answered the landline in all the time I've tried. It just goes straight to voicemail.'

'Even so, it wouldn't be far out of our way, going through Richmond on the way back from Strawberry Hill. We could just knock on the door in Cedar Terrace and see what happens.'

Strike's mobile rang. Expecting Lucy, he instead saw Midge's number.

'Everything all right?'

'No,' said Midge.

With a sense of foreboding, Strike switched the mobile to speakerphone and laid it down on the desk between him and Robin.

'It's not Tash's fault,' said Midge defensively, 'OK? She hasn't been able to get back to the annexe for the last couple of nights, so she seized a chance when she was coming back from a massage an hour ago.'

'She was spotted?' said Strike sharply.

'Yeah,' said Midge. 'Some bloke who works there saw her tapping on the window.'

Strike's and Robin's eyes met. The latter, who feared Strike was about to explode, made a grimace intended to prevent any unhelpful outburst.

'Obviously, Tash walked straight off,' said Midge, 'but the bad thing is—'

'*That's* not the bad thing?' said Strike ominously.

'Look, she's done us a favour, Strike, and at least she's found out Lin's there!'

'Midge, what else happened?' said Robin, before Strike could retort.

'Well, she had the note in the pocket of her robe, the one

to show Lin, saying Will and Qing are out, and ... and now she can't find it. She thinks she might've taken the wrong robe when she left the massage room. Or, maybe, she's dropped it.'

'OK,' said Robin, gesturing to Strike to withhold the stream of recriminations she knew he was bursting to deliver, 'Midge, if she can pretend she's lost a ring or something—'

'She's already gone back to the massage room to look, but she called me first because, obviously—'

'Yeah,' said Strike. '*Obviously.*'

'Let us know what happens,' said Robin. 'Call us.'

'Will do,' said Midge. She rang off.

'Fuck's *sake!*' said Strike, seething. 'What did I tell Tasha? Take *no* risks, be *ultra*-cautious, then she goes to that fucking window by daylight—'

'I know,' said Robin, 'I know.'

'We should never have put an amateur in there!'

'It was the only way,' said Robin. 'We had to use someone they'd never realise had a connection to us. Now we've just got to hope she gets that note back.'

Strike got to his feet and began to pace.

'If they've found that note, Zhou's probably scrambling to pull another Jacob – hide Lin and come up with an alternative blonde, fast. Fuck – this isn't good ... I'm going to call Wardle.'

Strike did so. Robin listened as her partner laid out the problem to his best police contact. As she could have predicted, Wardle needed quite a lot of explanation and repetition before he fully grasped what Strike was telling him.

'If Wardle finds it hard to believe, I can just imagine how regular officers are going to react,' said Strike bitterly, having hung up. 'I don't think they'll see it as a top priority, rescuing a girl who's living at a luxury spa. What's the time?'

'Time to go,' said Robin, shutting down her computer.

'Are we giving Pat a lift home?'

'No, she's meeting her granddaughter. Dennis is going to look after Qing while Will's with us.'

So Strike and Robin walked together towards the garage where Strike kept his BMW. It was a warm evening; a pleasant change from the intermittent drizzle of the last few days. They'd just reached the garage when Strike's mobile rang again: Lucy.

'Hi, what did the GP say?' he asked.

'He thinks Ted's had a mini-stroke.'

'Oh, shit,' said Strike, unlocking the car with his free hand.

'They want to scan him. The earliest they can do is Friday.'

'Right,' said Strike, getting into the passenger's seat while Robin took the wheel. 'Well, if you like, I'll go with him. You're picking up all the slack here.'

'Thanks, Stick,' said Lucy. 'I appreciate that.'

'Thank Christ he was with you when it happened. Imagine if he'd been alone in St Mawes.'

'I know,' said Lucy.

'I'll take him for the scan, and afterwards we'll talk plans, OK?'

'Yes,' said Lucy, sounding defeated. 'OK. How are things with you?'

'Busy,' said Strike. 'I'll call you later.'

'Everything all right?' asked Robin, waiting until Strike had hung up until turning on the ignition.

'No,' said Strike, and as they set off up the road, he explained about Ted's stroke, and his Alzheimer's, and the burden Lucy was currently bearing, and the guilt he felt about not pulling his weight. In consequence, neither Strike nor Robin noticed the blue Ford Focus that pulled away from the kerb a hundred yards beyond the garage, as Robin accelerated.

The Ford's speed was often adjusted, which varied the

distance between it and the BMW, so that it was sometimes one, and sometimes as many as three cars behind them. Both detectives' minds were so preoccupied with their separate, joint, general and specific anxieties that both failed to notice they were, again, being followed.

117

K'an represents the heart, the soul locked up within the body, the principle of light enclosed in the dark – that is, reason.

The I Ching or Book of Changes

It was only as Robin approached Prudence's house that she registered, in some dim region of her mind, that she'd spotted a blue Ford Focus in her rear-view mirror at another point in the journey. She rounded the corner of Prudence's street, and the blue car drove innocently past. Preoccupied with the imminent meeting between Will and Flora, Robin immediately forgot it again.

'You'll like Prudence,' she said reassuringly to Will, who'd barely spoken during the journey. 'She's really nice.'

Will looked up at the large Edwardian house, shoulders hunched and arms folded, an expression of intense misgiving on his face.

'Hi,' said Prudence, when she opened the front door, looking understatedly elegant as ever in cream trousers and a matching sweater. 'Oh.'

Her face had fallen on seeing Strike.

'Problem?' he asked, wondering whether she'd expected him to call and apologise after their last, heated phone call. As he considered himself entirely blameless in the matter of identifying Flora, the idea hadn't occurred to him.

'I assumed it would just be Robin,' said Prudence, standing back to let them all in. 'Flora isn't expecting another man.'

'Ah,' said Strike. 'Right. I could wait in the car?'

'Don't be silly,' said Prudence, with a slight awkwardness. 'You can go in the sitting room.'

'Thanks,' said Strike. He caught Robin's eye, then headed wordlessly through the door to the right. Prudence opened a door on the left.

Like the sitting room, Prudence's consulting room was tastefully decorated in neutral colours. A few decorative objects, including jade snuff bottles and a Chinese puzzle ball, were arranged on wall shelves. There was a sofa upholstered in cream, a flourishing palm tree in the corner and an antique rug on the floor.

A pale and very heavy woman of around thirty was sitting in a low, black, steel-framed chair. Every item she wore was dark and baggy. Robin noticed the thin white self-harm scars on her neck, and the way she was clutching both cuffs of her long-sleeved top, so as to hold them down over her hands. Her curly hair was arranged to cover as much of her face as possible, though a pair of large, beautiful brown eyes were just visible.

'Have a seat, Will,' said Prudence. 'Anywhere you like.'

After a moment's indecision, he chose a chair. Robin sat down on the sofa.

'So: Flora, Will, Will, Flora,' said Prudence, smiling as she sat down too.

'Hi,' said Flora.

'Hi,' muttered Will.

When neither of them showed any further inclination for interacting with each other, Prudence said,

'Flora was in the UHC for five years, Will, and I think you were in for—'

'Four, yeah.'

Will's eyes were darting around the room, lingering on some of the objects.

'How long have you been out?' he shot suddenly at Flora.

'Um ... eleven years,' said Flora, peering at Will through her fringe.

Will got up so suddenly, Flora gasped. Pointing at her, Will snarled at Robin,

'It's a trap. She's still working for them.'

'I'm not!' exclaimed Flora indignantly.

'*She's* in on it, as well!' Will said, now pointing at Prudence. 'This place −' He looked from the Chinese puzzle ball to the antique rug, 'it's just like Zhou's office!'

'Will,' said Robin, getting to her feet, too, 'why on earth would I have gone undercover at Chapman Farm to get you out, only to lead you straight back to them?'

'They fooled you! Or, it's all been a test. *You're* an agent of the church too!'

'You found the plastic rock,' said Robin calmly. 'You saw the torch and the traces of my notes. If I were a church agent, why would I have been writing to outsiders? And how would I have known you'd find the rock at all?'

'I want to go back to Pat's,' said Will desperately. 'I want to go back.'

He was almost at the door when Robin said,

'Will, your mother's dead. You know that, don't you?'

Will turned back, glaring at her, his thin chest rising and falling rapidly. Robin felt she had no choice but to resort to dirty tactics, but it wrung her heart, nonetheless.

'You looked it up online, didn't you? *Didn't you?*'

Will nodded.

'You know how much I risked at Chapman Farm, by telling you that. You heard them talking about me after I left, and you found out my real name, and tracked me down to exactly where I should have been, at our office. I'm not lying to you. Flora was a church member, but she got out. Please, just sit down and talk to her for a bit. I'll drive you back to Pat's afterwards.'

After almost a full minute of deliberation, Will returned reluctantly to his chair.

'I know how you feel, Will,' said Flora unexpectedly, in a timid voice. 'I do, *honestly*.'

'Why are you still alive?' said Will brutally.

'I wonder myself, sometimes,' said Flora with a shaky little laugh.

Robin was starting to fear this meeting was going to do both parties more harm than good. She looked at Prudence for help, and the latter said,

'Are you wondering why the Drowned Prophet hasn't come for Flora, Will?'

'Yes, obviously,' said Will, refusing to look at Prudence, whose offences of possessing snuff bottles and antique rugs were apparently too severe for him to overlook.

'The Drowned Prophet kind of *did* come for me. I'm not supposed to drink on my meds,' said Flora, with a guilty glance at Prudence, 'and I try not to, but if I do, I start feeling like the prophet's watching me again, and I can hear her telling me I'm not fit to live. But nowadays I know the voice isn't real.'

'How?' demanded Will.

'Because she hates all the things I hate about myself,' said Flora, in a voice barely louder than a whisper. 'I know it's me doing it, not her.'

'How did you get out?'

'I wasn't very well.'

'I don't believe you. They wouldn't have let you go just for that. They'd have treated you.'

'They did treat me, kind of. They made me chant in the

temple, and gave me some herbs, and Papa J –' A look of disgust flickered across Flora's half-concealed face '– but none of it worked. I was seeing things and hearing voices. In the end, they contacted my dad and he came and picked me up.'

'You're lying. They wouldn't do that. They'd never contact a flesh object.'

'They didn't know what else to do with me, I don't think,' said Flora. 'My dad was really angry. He said it was all my own fault for running away and causing a load of trouble and not answering letters. Once we got home, he was really pissed off with me chanting and doing the joyful meditation. He thought it was me trying to stay in the religion ... he didn't understand that I couldn't stop ... I could see the Drowned Prophet standing behind doors and sometimes I'd see her reflection in the bathroom mirror, right behind me, and I'd turn around but she'd be gone. I didn't tell Dad or my stepmum, because the Drowned Prophet told me not to – I mean, I *thought* she told me not to ...'

'How d'you know it *wasn't* the Drowned Prophet?' said Will.

Robin was starting to feel that this had all been a terrible mistake. She hadn't dreamed that Will would attempt to re-indoctrinate Flora, and she turned to look at Prudence, hoping she'd shut this conversation down, but Prudence was merely listening with a neutral expression on her face.

'Because she stopped appearing, after I got treatment, but it was ages before I saw a doctor, because my dad and my stepmum kept saying I had to either reapply to uni or get a job, so I was supposed to be filling out application forms and things, but I couldn't concentrate ... and there were things I couldn't tell them ...

'I had a baby there and she died. She was born dead. The cord was wrapped around her neck.'

'Oh God,' said Robin, unable to contain herself. She was back in the dormitory, blood everywhere, helping to deliver Wan's breech baby.

'They punished me for it,' said Flora with a little sob. 'They said it was my fault. They said I killed the baby, by being bad. I couldn't tell Dad and my stepmum things like that. I never told anyone about the baby at all, until I started seeing Prudence. For a long time, I didn't know if I'd really had a baby or not ... but later ... much later ... I went to a doctor for an examination. And I said to her, "Have I given birth?" And she thought it was a very weird question, obviously, but she said yes. She could tell. By feeling.'

Flora swallowed, then continued,

'I spoke to a journalist after I left, but I didn't tell him about the baby, either. I knew the Drowned Prophet might kill me if I talked to him, but I was desperate and I wanted people to know how bad the church was. I thought, maybe if Dad and my stepmum read my interview in the papers, they'd understand better what I'd been through, and forgive me. So I met the journalist and told him some things, and that night the Drowned Prophet came, and she was floating outside my window, and she told me to kill myself, because I'd betrayed everyone in the church. So I called the journalist and told him she'd come for me, and to write the story, and then I slit my wrists in the bathroom.'

'I'm so sorry,' said Robin, but Flora gave no sign she'd heard her.

'Then my dad broke down the bathroom door and I got taken to hospital and they diagnosed psychosis and I got admitted to a mental ward. I was in there for ages, and they gave me tons of meds and I had to see the psychiatrist, like, five times a week, but in the end I stopped seeing the Drowned Prophet.

'After I got out of hospital, I went to New Zealand. My aunt and uncle are in business, in Wellington. They sort of made up a job for me . . .'

Flora's voice trailed away.

'And you never saw the prophet again?' said Will.

Angry at him for maintaining his inquisitorial tone after everything Flora had just told them, Robin muttered *'Will!'* but Flora answered.

'No, I did. I mean, it wasn't really her – it was my fault. I was smoking a lot of weed in New Zealand and it all started up again. I ended up in another psychiatric hospital for months, and after that my aunt and uncle put me back on a plane to London. They'd had enough of me. They didn't want the responsibility.

'But I've never seen her again, since New Zealand,' said Flora. 'Except, like I say, sometimes if I drink I think I can hear her again . . . but I know she's not real.'

'If you really thought she wasn't real, you'd have been to the police.'

'Will—' said Robin, and was ignored.

'*I* know she's real, and she's going to come for me,' Will continued, with a kind of desperate bravado, 'but I'm still going to turn myself in. So either you do believe in her, and you're scared, or you don't want the church exposed.'

'I *do* want them exposed,' said Flora vehemently. 'That's why I spoke to the journalist and why I said I'd meet you. You don't understand,' she said, starting to sob. 'I feel guilty *all the time*. I know I'm a coward, but I'm afraid—'

'Of the Drowned Prophet,' said Will triumphantly. 'There you are. You know she's real.'

'There are more things to be frightened of than the Drowned Prophet!' said Flora shrilly.

'What – like jail?' said Will dismissively. 'I know I'm going to jail, if she doesn't kill me first. I don't care, it's the right thing to do.'

'Will, I've already told you this: there's no need for either of you to go to jail,' said Robin. Turning to Flora, she said, 'We believe immunity from prosecution could be arranged if you were prepared to testify against the church, Flora. Everything you've just described shows clearly how traumatised you were by what happened to you at Chapman Farm. You had good and valid reasons for not speaking.'

'I tried to tell people,' said Flora desperately. 'I told my psychiatrists the worst thing and they said it was part of my psychosis, that I was imagining it, that it was all part of my hallucinations of the prophet. It's so long ago, now ... everyone will blame me, like him,' she added hopelessly, jabbing a finger at Will. Now that she wasn't holding her cuff over her hand, Robin glimpsed the ugly scars on her wrist where she'd tried to end her life.

'What things did you tell your psychiatrists?' said Will implacably. 'The Divine Secrets?'

Robin now remembered Shawna talking about Divine Secrets. She'd never found out what they were.

'No,' admitted Flora.

'So you weren't really telling them anything,' said Will scornfully. 'If you were convinced there's no Drowned Prophet, you'd have talked about all that.'

'I told them the worst thing!' said Flora wildly. 'And when they didn't believe that, I knew there'd be no point talking about the Divine Secrets!'

Robin could tell by the look on Prudence's face that she didn't know what these secrets were, either.

'You don't know everything I saw,' Flora said to Will, and there was a trace of anger in her voice now. 'You weren't there. I drew it,' she said, turning to Robin, 'because there were other witnesses, too, and I thought, if any of them had left, they might see the picture and contact me. Then I'd know *for sure* it was real, but all I got—'

'Was my partner,' said Robin.

'Yes,' said Flora, 'and I knew from the way he wrote he'd never been in the UHC. You wouldn't talk like that, if you had. "You really don't like the UHC, do you?" You wouldn't be that ... *casual*. Then I thought it might be someone from Deirdre's family, trying to goad me, and I felt ... so guilty ... so scared, I deleted my account.'

'Who's Deirdre?' said Will.

'Lin's mother,' said Robin.

For the first time, Will looked taken aback.

'Flora,' Robin said, 'can I tell you what I think you saw?'

Slowly and carefully, Robin described the scene in the temple she believed had taken place during the Manifestation of the Drowned Prophet, in which Deirdre had been taken out of the pool, dead. When she'd finished speaking, Flora, whose breathing was shallow and whose face was very white, whispered,

'How do you know that?'

'I worked it out,' said Robin. 'I was there for one of the Manifestations. They nearly drowned *me*. But how did they explain what had happened? How did they get away with telling everyone Deirdre had left?'

'When they took her out of the pool,' said Flora haltingly, 'it was still very dark. Dr Zhou bent over her and said, "She's all right, she's breathing." Papa J told everyone to leave, the younger ones first. As we were filing out, Papa J was pretending to talk to Deirdre, acting as if they were having a conversation, as though her voice was very quiet but he could hear it.

'But I *knew* she was dead,' said Flora. 'I was close to the stage. I saw her face when they pulled her out of the pool. There was foam on her lips. Her eyes were open. I knew. But you had to believe what Papa J and Mazu said. You *had* to. Next day, they gathered us together and said Deirdre had been expelled, and everyone just – they just accepted it. I heard people saying "Of course they had to expel her, if she'd displeased the prophet like that."

'I remember this boy called Kevin. It should have been his first Manifestation, but he was being punished, so he wasn't allowed to attend. He asked a lot of questions about what Deirdre had done to be expelled, and I remember Becca – she was a teenager, one of Papa J's spirit wives – hitting him round the head and telling him to shut up about Deirdre ... Becca was the one who made me ... who made me ...'

'What did Becca make you do?' Robin asked.

When Flora shook her head, looking down into her lap, Robin said,

'Becca made me do things, too. She also tried to get me into terrible trouble, hiding something stolen under my bed. I think she's nearly as scary as the Waces, personally.'

Flora looked up at Robin for the first time.

'Me too,' she whispered.

'What did she make you do? Something that might make you complicit in an awful situation? They did the same thing to me, sent me to look after a dying boy. I knew that if he died while I was with him, they'd blame me.'

'That's worse,' said Flora faintly, and Robin was touched to see genuine sympathy for her on Flora's face. 'That's worse than mine ... they *did* do it to make me complicit, I've often thought that ... Becca made me type letters from Deirdre, to her family. I had to make them up myself. I had to write that I'd left the farm but I wanted a new life, away from my husband and children ... so *obviously* Deirdre was dead,' said Flora in frustration, 'but Becca looked me in the eye and told me she was alive, and she'd been expelled, *even while she was ʽing me write those letters!*'

1044

'I think that's a big part of what they do,' said Robin. 'They force you to agree black's white and up's down. It's part of the way they control you.'

'But that's fraud, isn't it?' said Flora desperately. 'They made me part of the cover-up!'

'You were being coerced,' said Robin. 'I'm certain you'd get immunity, Flora.'

'Is Becca still there?'

'Yes,' said Robin and Will together. The latter wore an odd, arrested expression now; he'd followed the story of the fake letters closely.

'Has Becca ever increased?' asked Flora.

'No,' said Will.

Now, for the first time, he volunteered information rather than demanding it.

'Papa J doesn't want to, because he thinks her bloodline's tainted.'

'That's not why he won't let her have a baby,' said Flora quietly.

'Why, then?'

'He wants to keep her a virgin,' said Flora. 'That's why Mazu doesn't hate on her, like she does with all the other spirit wives.'

'I didn't know that,' said Will, very surprised.

'All the spirit wives know,' said Flora. 'I was one of them,' she added.

'Really?' said Robin.

'Yes,' said Flora. 'It started as the Loving Cure, and he liked it so much he made me a spirit wife. He likes ... he likes it when you don't like it.'

Robin's thoughts flew immediately to Deirdre Doherty, the prim woman who'd wished to remain faithful to her husband, and whose last pregnancy, she believed, was the result of Wace's rape.

'Mazu sometimes joined in,' said Flora, in a near whisper. 'She'd . . . sometimes, she'd help hold me down, or . . . sometimes he likes to watch her do stuff to you . . .'

'Oh God,' said Robin. 'Flora . . . I'm so sorry.'

Will now looked both scared and disturbed. Twice, he opened his mouth to speak, changed his mind, then blurted out,

'How d'you explain the things the prophet does at Chapman Farm, if she's not real, though?'

'Like, what kind of things?' said Flora.

'The Manifestations.'

'You mean, like, in the pool and in the woods?'

'I know they use little girls, dressed up like her, in the woods, I'm not stupid,' said Will. 'But that doesn't mean they don't *become* her, when they're doing it.'

'What do you mean by that, Will?' asked Prudence.

'Well, it's like transubstantiation, isn't it?' said Will. He might have been back on the vegetable patch again, lecturing Robin on church doctrine. 'The wafer they give you in communion isn't *really* the body of Christ, but it *is*. Same thing. And that dummy thing they make rise up out of the baptismal pool, it's just symbolic. It's *not* her, but it *is* her.'

'Is that one of the Higher-Level Truths?' Robin asked. 'That the little girls dressed up like Daiyu, and the dummy without eyes, *are* Daiyu?'

'Don't call her Daiyu,' said Will angrily. 'It's disrespectful. And no,' he added, 'I worked that stuff out for myself.'

He seemed to feel he needed to justify himself, because he said forcefully,

'Look, I know a lot of it's bullshit. I saw the hypocrisy, how Papa J gets to do stuff nobody else is allowed to – he can marry, and he gets to keep his kids and his grandkids because his bloodline's special, and everyone else has got to make the

Living Sacrifice, and the alcohol in the farmhouse, and the smarming around celebrities even though that's all supposed to be bullshit – I know Papa J's not a messiah, and that they do really bad things at that farm, but you can't say they haven't got *something* right, because you've seen it,' he said to Flora, 'and you have too!' he added to Robin. 'The spirit world's real!'

There was a short silence, broken by Prudence.

'Why d'you think nobody in the church ever admits they dress up little girls at night, and use a dummy to rise up out of the baptismal pool, Will? Because a lot of people believe they're literally seeing something supernatural, don't they?'

'Some of them might,' said Will defensively, 'but not all of them. Anyway, the Drowned Prophet *does* come back for real. She materialises out of thin air!'

'But if the other things are a trick . . .' suggested Flora.

'That doesn't follow. Yeah, OK, sometimes they're just showing us representations of the prophet, but other times, she genuinely comes . . . it's like, in churches, having a model of Jesus on the wall. Nobody's pretending it's *literally* him. But when the Drowned Prophet appears as a spirit, and moves around and everything – there's no other explanation for it. There's no projector, and she's not a puppet – it's her, it's really her.'

'Are you talking about when she manifests like a ghost, in the basement room?' asked Robin.

'Not just in the basement,' said Will. 'She does it in the temple, too.'

'Is the audience always sitting in the dark when that happens?' asked Robin. 'And do they sometimes make you clear the room before she appears? They made us leave the basement for a while before we saw her manifest. Is the audience always in front of her when she manifests, not sitting round the stage?'

'Yeah, it was always like that,' said Flora, when Will didn't answer. 'Why?'

'Because I *might* be able to explain how they do it,' said Robin. 'A man I work with suggested it could be an old illusion called Pepper's ghost. I looked it up. You need a glass screen, which is at an angle to the audience, and a hidden side room. Then a figure in the side room is slightly illuminated, and the lights on stage go down, and the audience sees the reflection of the supposed ghost in the glass, and it's transparent and looks as though it's onstage.'

Silence followed these words. Then, startling everyone in the room, Flora said loudly,

'Oh my God.'

The other three looked at her. Flora was gazing through her hair at Robin in what appeared to be awe.

'*That's it*. That's how they do it. *Oh. My. God.*'

Flora began to laugh.

'I can't believe it!' she said breathlessly. 'I've *never* been able to work that one out, it's always been the one that made me doubt . . . a reflection on glass – that's it, that makes total sense! They only ever did it where there was a side room. And if we were in temple, we all had to sit face-on to the stage.'

'I think,' said Robin, 'the temple at Chapman Farm was designed like a theatre. That upper balcony where members never sit, those recesses . . . I think it's been constructed to enable large-scale illusions.'

'You can't be sure of that,' said Will, who now appeared deeply uneasy.

'The Drowned Prophet isn't real,' Flora told Will. 'She's *not*.'

'If you honestly believed that,' said Will, with a trace of his former anger, 'if you *genuinely* believed it, you'd reveal the Divine Secrets.'

'You mean, the Dragon Meadow? The Living Sacrifice? The Loving Cure?'

Will glanced nervously towards the window, as though he expected the eyeless Daiyu to be floating there.

'If I speak about them now, and I don't die, will you believe she's not real?' said Flora.

Flora had shaken the hair out of her face now. She was revealed as a beautiful woman. Will didn't answer her question. He looked frightened.

'The Dragon Meadow is the place they bury all the bodies,' said Flora in a clear voice. 'It's that field the horses are always ploughing.'

Will emitted a little gasp of shock, but Flora kept talking.

118

In danger all that counts is really carrying out all that has to be done . . .

The I Ching or Book of Changes

Strike had been waiting in Prudence's sitting room for nearly three hours. Shortly after Prudence, Robin and Will had disappeared into the consulting room, he'd heard raised voices from behind the closed door, but since then there'd been no indication of what was happening in the meeting from which he'd been excluded. Prudence's husband seemed to be out for the evening. Both teenage children had made brief appearances, en route to the kitchen where they'd got themselves snacks, and Strike had wondered, while listening to them opening and closing the fridge, how odd they found the sudden presence of this hulking new uncle on the family tree and thought it possible they hadn't thought much about it. Happy families, he thought, didn't seem to brood on the significance and power of blood ties; it was only voluntarily fatherless mongrels like him who found it strange to see a faint trace of himself in people who were almost strangers.

In any case, whatever his half-niece and nephew's feelings about him, neither had offered Strike anything to eat. He didn't take it personally; as far as he could remember, offering food to adults he barely knew wouldn't have figured high on his list of priorities at their age, either. Half an hour previously, he'd sneaked into the kitchen and, not wanting to be accused of taking liberties, helped himself to a few biscuits. Now, still extremely hungry, he was thinking of suggesting to Robin that they stop off at a drive-in McDonald's on the way back to Pat's when his mobile buzzed. Happy to have something to do, Strike reached for it and saw Midge's number.

> Tash just texted me. She hasn't found the note. The robe was taken away before she got back to the massage place. Nobody's asked her about tapping on the window. What do you want her to do?

Strike texted back:

> Nothing. Police now know Lin's being held against her will there. Just cover the exit, in case they move her.

He'd barely finished typing when the door of Prudence's consulting room opened. His sister left the room first. Then came Will, who looked slightly shell-shocked.

'Is it all right,' he muttered to Prudence, 'if I use your bathroom?'

'Of course,' said Prudence. 'Down the hall, second left.'

Will disappeared. Now a large, curly haired woman dressed all in black emerged from the room, followed by Robin. Prudence had gone to open the front door, but Flora turned to Robin and said shyly,

'Can I hug you?'

'Of course,' said Robin, opening her arms.

Strike watched the two women embrace. Robin muttered something in Flora's ear, and the latter nodded, before casting a nervous look in Strike's direction and moving out of sight.

Robin immediately entered the sitting room and said, in a rapid whisper,

'Loads – *loads* of information. The Loving Cure – Papa J screws gay and mentally ill women, to cure them. The Dragon Meadow: they bury people who've died at Chapman Farm in the ploughed field, and Flora's certain the deaths aren't registered. But the big one's the Living Sacrifice. It—'

Will entered the sitting room, still looking vaguely disorientated.

'All right?' said Strike.

'Yeah,' said Will.

They heard the front door close. Prudence now entered the room.

'Sorry that went on so long,' she said to Strike. 'Did Sylvie or Gerry get you something to eat?'

'Er – no, but it's fine,' said Strike.

'Then let me—'

'Really, it's fine,' said Strike, who'd now mentally committed to a burger and chips. 'We need to get Will back to Qing.'

'Oh, yes, of course,' said Prudence. She looked up at Will.

'If you ever want to talk to someone, Will, I wouldn't charge you. Think about it, OK? Or I can recommend another therapist. And do read the books I lent Robin.'

'Thanks,' said Will. 'Yeah. I will.'

Prudence now turned to Robin.

'That was a massive breakthrough for Flora. I've never seen her like that before.'

'I'm glad,' said Robin, 'I really am.'

'And I think, you sharing your own experience – that was crucial.'

'Well, there's no rush,' said Robin. 'She can think over what she wants to do next, but I meant what I said. I'd be with her every step of the way. Anyway, thanks so much for arranging this, Prudence, it was really helpful. We should probably—'

'Yeah,' said Strike, whose stomach was loudly rumbling.

Strike, Robin and Will walked in silence back to the car.

'You hungry?' Strike asked Will, very much hoping the answer was yes. Will nodded.

'Great,' said Strike, 'we'll swing by a McDonald's.'

'What about Cedar Terrace?' said Robin, turning on the engine. 'Are we going to check whether Rosie Fernsby's there?'

'Might as well,' said Strike. 'Not a big detour, is it? But if we see a McDonald's, we'll do that first.'

'Fine,' said Robin, amused.

'Aren't *you* hungry?' said Strike, as they pulled away.

'I think I got used to less food at Chapman Farm,' said Robin. 'I'm acclimatised.'

Strike, who very much wanted to hear Robin's new information, gathered from her silence that she considered it inadvisable to dredge up everything that had happened in the consulting room with Will present. The latter looked exhausted and troubled.

'Have you heard from Midge?' Robin asked.

'Yeah,' said Strike, 'nothing new.'

Robin's heart sank. She could tell from Strike's tone that 'nothing new' meant 'nothing good', but in deference to Will's feelings, she forwent further questions.

They crossed Twickenham Bridge with its bronze lamps and balustrades, the Thames glinting, gunmetal grey, below, and Strike wound down the window to vape. As he did so, he glanced in the wing mirror. A blue Ford Focus was following them. He watched it for a few seconds, then said,

'There's—'

'A car following us, with dodgy number plates,' said Robin. 'I know.'

She'd just spotted it. The plates were fake and illegal, the kind that could be ordered easily online. The car had been moving steadily closer since they'd moved into Richmond.

'Shit,' said Robin, 'I think I saw it on the way to Prudence's, but it was hanging back. *Shit*,' she added, looking into the rear-view mirror, 'is the driver—?'

'Wearing a balaclava, yeah,' said Strike. 'But I don't think it's the Franks.'

Both remembered Strike's bullish assertion earlier that they'd stop and confront anyone who seemed to be tailing them. Each, watching the car, knew this would be exceptionally unwise.

'Will,' said Robin, 'duck down, please, *right* down. And hold on – you too,' she told Strike.

Without indicating, Robin accelerated and took a hard right. The Ford's driver was caught off guard; they swerved into the middle of the road, almost colliding with oncoming traffic as Robin sped off, first through a car park, then down a narrow residential road.

'The fuck did you know you'd be able to get out the other side of the car park?' said Strike, who was holding on as best he could. Robin was twenty miles over the speed limit.

'Been here before,' said Robin, who, again failing to indicate, now turned left onto a wider road. 'I was following that cheating accountant. Where are they?'

'Catching up,' said Strike, turning to look. 'Just hit two parked cars.'

Robin slammed her foot on the accelerator. Two pedestrians crossing the road had to sprint to get out of her way.

'*Shit,*' she shouted again, as it became clear that they were about to rejoin the A316, going back the way they'd come.

'Doesn't matter, just go—'

Robin took the corner at such speed she narrowly missed the central barrier.

'Will,' she said, 'keep down, for God's sake, I—'

The rear window and windscreen shattered. The bullet had passed so close to Strike's head he'd felt its heat: with blank whiteness where there'd been glass, Robin was driving blind.

'Punch it out!' she shouted at Strike, who took off his seat belt to oblige. A second loud bang: they heard the bullet hit the boot. Strike was thumping broken glass out of the windscreen to give Robin visibility; fragments showered down upon both of them.

A third shot: this time wide.

'Hold on!' Robin said again, and she skidded around the turn into the other lane, making it by inches, causing Strike to smash his face into the intact side window.

'Sorry, sorry—'

'Fuck that, GO!'

The passing bullet had flooded Strike's brain with white-hot panic; he had the irrational conviction that the car was about to explode. Craning around in his seat, he saw the Ford hit the barrier at speed.

'That's fucked them – no – shit—'

The crash hadn't been disabling. The Ford was reversing, trying to make the turn.

'*Go, GO!*'

As Robin slammed her foot to the floor, she saw a flashing blue light on the other side of the road.

'Where's the Ford? *Where's the Ford?*'

'Can't see—'

'What are you going *that* way for?' Robin yelled at the passing police car, which was going in the opposite direction. 'Hold on—'

She steered a hard left at speed into another narrow street.

'Jesus Christ,' said Strike, whose face had hit what remained of the windscreen, and who couldn't believe she'd made the turn.

'And again!' said Robin, the BMW tipping slightly as she took a right.

'They've gone,' said Strike, looking at the wing mirror and as he wiped away the blood trickling down his face. 'Slow down – you've lost them . . . *fuck*.'

Robin decelerated. She turned another corner, then steered into a parking space and braked, her hands gripping the wheel so tightly she had to make a conscious effort to let go. They could hear sirens in the distance.

'You all right, Will?' asked Strike, looking back at the young man now lying in the dark footwell, covered in glass.

'Yeah,' said Will faintly.

A group of young men were walking up the dark street towards them.

'You've got a crack in your windscreen, love,' said one of them, to hearty guffaws from his mates.

'*You* all right?' Strike asked Robin.

'Better than you,' she answered, looking at the cut on his face.

'Windscreen, not bullet,' said Strike, drawing out his mobile and keying in 999.

'D'you think they got him?' Robin asked, looking over her shoulder in the direction of the sirens.

'We'll find out soon enough. Police,' he told the operator.

119

Nine in the fifth place means:
Resolute conduct.
Perseverance with awareness of danger.

The I Ching or Book of Changes

'This is the fifth time we've spoken to the police about the UHC and suspicious activity around our office,' said Strike. 'I appreciate that you don't have all that information immediately to hand, I know I'm giving you a lot of back story you might think is irrelevant, but I'm not going to lie: I'd appreciate it if you stopped looking at me like I'm a fucking idiot.'

It was two o'clock in the morning. It had taken an hour for Strike's heart rate to slow to an appropriate rate for a stationary forty-one-year-old male. He was still sitting in the small police interview room he'd been taken to upon arrival at the local station. Having been asked whether he knew why someone might want to shoot him, Strike had given a full account of the agency's current investigation into the UHC, advised his interrogator to look up Kevin Pirbright's murder, explained that a gun-toting intruder had tried to break into their office a week previously and informed the officer this was the second time he and Robin had been tailed in a car in the last couple of weeks.

The sheer scale of Strike's story seemed to aggravate PC

Bowers, a long-necked man with an adenoidal voice. As Bowers became more openly sceptical and incredulous ('A *church* has got it in for you?') Strike had been provoked into open irritability. Aside from everything else, he was now exceptionally hungry. A request for food had led to the production of three plain biscuits and a cup of milky tea, and given that he was the victim of the shooting rather than a suspect, Strike felt he was owed a little more consideration.

Robin, meanwhile, was dealing with a different kind of problem. She'd finished giving her statement to a perfectly friendly and competent female officer, but had declined a lift home, instead insisting that Will be driven back to Pat's. Having seen Will into the police car, Robin returned to the waiting room and, with a sense of dread but knowing she had no choice, called Murphy to tell him what had happened.

His reaction to her news was, understandably, one of alarm and well-justified concern. Even so, Robin had to bite back angry retorts to what she considered Murphy's statements of the obvious: that extra security measures would now be necessary and that the police would need every scrap of information Strike and Robin could provide them about the UHC. Unknowingly echoing Strike, Robin said,

'This is literally the fifth time we've spoken to police about the church. We haven't been hiding anything.'

'No, I know, I get that, but bloody hell, Robin – wish I could come and pick you up. I'm stuck with this bloody stabbing in Southall.'

'I'm fine,' said Robin, 'there isn't a mark on me. I'll call an Uber.'

'Don't call an Uber, for Christ's sake, let one of the cops take you home. Can't believe they haven't nicked the shooter.'

'Maybe they have, by now.'

'It shouldn't be taking them this bloody long!'

'They radioed ahead to a couple of cars to try and cut him off, but I don't know what happened – either they didn't get there in time, or he knew a detour.'

'They must have him on camera, though. A316, bound to have.'

'Yes,' said Robin. She felt slightly jittery, perhaps a result of coffee on an empty stomach. 'Listen, Ryan, I'll have to go.'

'Yeah, OK. I'm bloody glad you're safe. Love you.'

'I love you too,' murmured Robin, because she'd just seen movement out of the corner of her eye, and sure enough, as she hung up, Strike emerged at last from his interview room, looking extremely grumpy.

'You're still here,' said Strike, cheering up at the sight of her. 'Thought you might've gone. Aren't you knackered?'

'No,' said Robin, 'I feel ... wired.'

'Getting shot at has that effect on me, too,' said Strike. 'What would you say to going and getting that McDonald's?'

'Sounds fantastic,' said Robin, slipping her mobile back into her pocket.

120

Forty minutes later, Strike and Robin got out of their Uber outside a twenty-four-hour McDonald's on the Strand.

'I'm having everything,' said Strike, as they headed to the counter. 'You?'

'Um – Big Mac and—'

'Oh, shit, what now?' growled Strike, as his mobile rang. Answering, he heard Midge's voice and a car engine.

'I think they're moving Lin. Tasha saw two men going into the office this afternoon. They were shown into the annexe, came out, left again. She didn't realise at the time they were police, because they were plainclothes – they drove in right past me, I should've realised they were cops, but honestly, they were both that well groomed, I thought they might be a gay couple having a getaway. I've been living in this car for the last three days and I'm knackered,' she added defensively.

'I know the feeling,' said Strike, watching Robin order.

'Next thing, Tasha's called in to see Zhou. "You appear to

have lost this, I hope it's not important." They'd found the note in the pocket of her robes. She acted innocent, obviously—'

'Fuck's sake, what's happening *now*?'

'I'm trying to tell you! Tasha thought she'd better clear out before she gets locked in an annexe too—'

'I'm not interested in Tasha!'

'Charming,' said the actress's voice in the background.

'Oh, for—' said Strike, closing his eyes and running a hand over his face.

'A plain van came out the front gates of the clinic ten minutes ago. We're *sure* Lin's in there. Three a.m.'s a bloody funny time to be driving vans around. Did I wake you up, by the way?'

'No,' said Strike, 'listen—'

'So we're tailing—'

'BLOODY LISTEN!'

Robin, the McDonald's servers and the other customers all turned to stare. Strike marched out of the restaurant. Once on the pavement he said,

'I'm awake because my car just got shot up, with Robin and me in it—'

'Wh—?'

'—and my information is the church has got guns, plural. This hour of the morning, it'll be obvious you're following that van. Give it up.'

'But—'

'You don't know Lin's in there. It's too big a risk. You've got a civilian with you – a civilian they know knows too much. Get the number plate, then go home.'

'But—'

'*Do – not – fucking – argue – with – me,*' said Strike in a dangerous voice. 'I've told you what I want. *Fucking do it.*'

Seething, he turned back, only to see Robin carrying two large bags of food.

'Let's have it in the office,' she suggested, keen not to draw any more attention to themselves inside the restaurant. 'It's only ten minutes up the road. Then we can talk properly.'

'Fine,' said Strike irritably, 'but give me a burger first.'

So they walked through the dark streets towards Denmark Street, Strike telling Robin what Midge had just said between large mouthfuls of burger. He'd already started on a bag of fries before they reached the familiar black door, with its skeleton-key-proof new lock. Once upstairs, Robin unpacked the rest of the food at the partners' desk. She still felt wide awake.

Strike, who'd soon devoured three burgers and two bags of fries, now started on an apple pie. Like Robin, he felt no desire whatsoever for sleep. The immediate past seemed to compress and extend in his mind: at one moment, the shooting felt as though it had happened a week previously, the next, as though he'd only just felt the heat of the bullet searing his cheek and watched the windscreen shatter.

'What are you looking at?' he asked Robin, noticing her slightly glass-eyed stare at the board on the wall behind him.

She seemed to withdraw her attention from a long way away.

'I didn't tell you what the third Divine Secret is, did I? The "Living Sacrifice"?'

'No,' said Strike.

'The UHC are child trafficking.'

Strike's jaws stopped moving.

'What?'

'Superfluous babies, mostly boys, are taken to the Birmingham centre where they're warehoused until they're sold. It's an illegal adoption service: babies for cash. Most of them go to America. Your friend Joe Jackson is in charge, apparently. From what Flora said, hundreds of babies must have passed out of the UHC by now.'

'Holy—'

'I should've realised there was something up, given how much unprotected sex they're having at Chapman Farm, because there are relatively few kids there, and nearly all of them looked as though they'd been fathered by Jonathan or Taio. Wace keeps his own bloodline and, of course, enough non-related girls to keep providing the church with future generations.'

Momentarily lost for words, Strike swallowed his apple pie and reached for the beer he'd got out of the office fridge.

'Will knew, because of Lin,' Robin said. 'When she got pregnant she was terrified Qing would be sent to Birmingham. Neither of them could understand why she was allowed to stay, so I have to assume Lin doesn't realise Wace is her father ... Strike, I'm really worried about Lin.'

'Me too,' said Strike, 'but Midge couldn't tail that bloody van through the night, and *definitely* not with her girlfriend coming along for the jolly.'

'That's not fair,' said Robin. 'You used to – I mean, obviously, I wasn't your girlfriend, but you let me do stuff in the early days when, technically, I was your temp. Tasha's worried about Lin too.'

'Investigation isn't a bloody team sport. So is it an open secret, this baby trade?'

'I don't know. Flora only found out when she was pregnant. One of the other women told her her baby was going to be sold for lots of cash for the glorious mission, but the baby died at birth. Flora was punished for that,' said Robin.

'Shit,' said Strike.

Whether or not Robin had intended her information to have that effect, Strike now felt guilty that he'd judged Flora Brewster so harshly.

'Robin, this is fucking massive, and you did it.'

'Except,' said Robin, who didn't sound particularly pleased, 'it's still hearsay, isn't it? Flora, Will and Lin have never been to the Birmingham centre. We haven't got a shred of concrete proof of the trafficking.'

'Emily Pirbright was relocated from Birmingham, right?'

'Yes, but given that she hasn't been allowed to leave Chapman Farm since I escaped, we might be waiting a long time for her testimony.'

'Abigail Glover was sent to Birmingham after Daiyu died, as well, but she never said a word about a glut of babies being kept there.'

'If Abigail wasn't ever pregnant, she probably thought all the kids belonged to people living at the Birmingham centre. Women seem to find out about it only once they're expecting ... we've *got* to get police in there,' said Robin, 'and *not* when the church is expecting it.'

'Agreed,' said Strike, now taking out his notebook. 'Fuck it, we've got the contacts, it's time to stop being so bloody polite. I say we try and get them all together, Wardle, Layborn, Ekwensi – Murphy,' he added, after a slight hesitation – needs must, he supposed – 'and lay it all on the line, preferably with Will and Flora present. D'you think they'd talk?'

'I'm ninety per cent certain Flora would, after tonight. Will ... I think he's still determined only to speak to the police once Lin's out.'

'Maybe bullets sailing a foot over his head will have sharpened his ideas up,' said Strike. 'I'll make those calls tomorrow ... later today, I mean.'

Strike ate a solitary cold chip lingering at the bottom of a greasy bag. Robin was again looking at the board on the wall. Her eyes travelled from the photo of rabbity-faced Daiyu to Flora Brewster's drawing of the girl without eyes; from the mugshot of twenty-something Carrie Curtis Woods to Jennifer Wace, with her eighties perm; from the pig-mask Polaroids to Paul Draper's timid moon face, and lastly to the note to himself Strike had written, which read, JOGGER ON THE BEACH?

'Strike,' said Robin, 'what the hell's going on?'

121

Six in the third place means:
Whoever hunts deer without the forester
Only loses his way in the forest.

The I Ching or Book of Changes

'Enough to bring down the UHC, if we're lucky,' said Strike.

'No, I mean the things that have been happening since I got out. Why are they simultaneously so slick, so hard to catch in the act, but also so incompetent?'

'Go on,' said Strike, because she was articulating something he himself had been wondering about.

'That couple in the red Corsa: were they *genuinely* tailing us? If so, they were lousy at it, whereas the Ford Focus – I know I messed up, not spotting them sooner—'

'No, whoever was driving that car was very good, and they also came bloody close to killing one or both of us.'

'Right, and whoever tried to break in here with the gun looked pretty efficient, and whoever murdered Kevin Pirbright has got clean away with it—'

'Whereas our green-eyed friend couldn't have been more obvious unless he'd held up a placard saying, "I am watching you".'

'And then you've got Reaney and Carrie, scared into suicide without even being face to face with the person . . . don't you feel as though we've got two different sets of people after us, one of them kind of a clown show, and the other lot really dangerous?'

'Personally,' said Strike, 'I think we've got someone after us who can't be picky about their underlings. They have to go with what they've got at any given time.'

'But that doesn't fit Jonathan Wace. He's got thousands of people who're absolutely devoted to him at his disposal, and whatever else you might say about him, he's got a real talent for putting people where they're most useful. He's never had a high-level defector.'

'There's that,' said Strike, 'and also the fact he'd have the ability to keep us under twenty-four-hour surveillance without ever repeating a face, whereas whoever's behind this seems to be watching us and following us at what seem fairly random times. I get the sense that they're only doing it when they can.

'You know,' said Strike, reaching for his beer, 'Wace absolutely denied he was following or watching us when I met him at Olympia. He would, of course, but I s'pose there's an outside chance he was telling the truth.'

'What if,' said Robin, thinking the thing out as she spoke, 'someone in the church is scared we've found out something Wace never knew about? Something he'd be really angry about?'

Both of them now looked up at the noticeboard.

'Going by who they're trying to stop us talking to, it's those Polaroids,' said Strike, 'because I doubt it's escaped your notice that the bullets only started hitting us once it looked as though we were heading for Cedar Terrace and, I strongly suspect, Rosie Fernsby. They didn't give a damn about Will, or they'd have tried to stop us earlier. It's possible they're banking on the fact he won't talk while they've still got Lin, in case she's the one who pays for it . . . in point of fact, she's something of a trump card for the church, isn't she? It's in their best interests to keep her alive ...

'No,' said Strike, reaching for his notebook and pen again, 'I still think Rosie Fernsby's the one in real danger. Someone's got to go to Cedar Terrace and warn her, if she's there.'

He made a note to this effect and set his pen down again.

Robin shivered. It was now approaching four in the morning, and while her brain was far too overwrought for sleep, her body felt differently. She was too busy staring at the picture of Daiyu on the noticeboard to register Strike taking off his jacket until he passed it to her.

'Oh ... are you sure?'

'I've got about five stone of extra padding, compared to you.'

'Don't exaggerate,' muttered Robin. 'Thank you.'

She pulled the jacket on: it was comfortingly warm.

'How did Wace react when you mentioned the pig-mask Polaroids?'

'Incredulity, disbelief ... exactly what you'd expect.'

Both sat in thought for a while, still gazing up at the board.

'Strike, I don't see why anyone would risk shooting us, purely because of those pictures,' said Robin, breaking a lengthy silence. 'They're horrible, and they'd definitely get tabloid coverage, but honestly, compared with what the church could be facing if we can get Will and Flora and maybe others to testify, those pictures would surely pale into – not insignificance, but they'd be just one more sordid detail. Plus, there's nothing in the pictures to show they were taken at Chapman Farm. It's deniable.'

'Not if Rosie Fernsby testifies, it isn't.'

'She hasn't spoken up in twenty-one years. Her face is hidden in the pictures. If she wants to deny it's her, we'll never be able to prove it.'

'So why's someone so keen to stop us talking to her?'

'I don't know, except . . . I know you don't like the theory, but she *was* there, the night before Daiyu died. What if she witnessed something, or heard something, as she was sneaking out of the women's dormitory to join her father and brother?'

'How far away from the kids' dormitory is the women's?'

'A fair distance,' admitted Robin, 'but what if Daiyu came into the women's dorm, after leaving the children's one? Or maybe Rosie looked out of her dormitory window and saw Daiyu heading for the woods, or a Retreat Room?'

'Then somebody else must have been with Daiyu, to know Rosie had spotted them.'

Another silence followed. Then Robin said,

'Daiyu was getting food and toys from somewhere . . .'

'Yeah, and you know what that smacks of? Grooming.'

'But Carrie said it wasn't her.'

'Do we believe her?'

'I don't know,' said Robin.

Another long pause followed, each of them lost in thought.

'It would make a damn sight more sense,' said Strike at last, 'if the last glimpse anyone ever had of Daiyu was her going out of that window. If you were going to drown a child in the early hours, why help them out of the window first? What if Daiyu didn't come back? . . . Or was that the point? Daiyu hides – or is hidden – somewhere after climbing out of the window . . . and another child gets taken to the beach in her place?'

'Are you serious?' said Robin. 'You're saying a different child drowned?'

'What do we know about the journey to the beach?' said Strike. 'It's dark, self-evidently – it must've been around this time of night,' said Strike, glancing out of the window at the navy blue sky. 'We know there was a kid in the van, because he or she waved as they passed the people on early duty – which, when you think about it, is suspicious in itself. You'd think Daiyu would've ducked down until they were safely off the premises if she didn't have permission for the trip. I also find it fishy that Daiyu was dressed in a distinctive white dress unlike any other at the farm. Then, after they left the farm, the only witness was an elderly woman who saw them from a distance and didn't know Daiyu from Adam anyway. She wouldn't have known which kid it was.'

'But the body,' said Robin. 'How could Carrie be sure it wouldn't wash back up? DNA would prove it wasn't Daiyu.'

'They might not bother taking DNA if Daiyu's loving mother was prepared to identify the corpse as her daughter,' said Strike.

'So Mazu's in on the switch? And nobody notices there's an extra child missing from Chapman Farm?'

'You're the one who's found out the church separates kids from parents and shifts them around the different centres. What if a kid was drafted in from Glasgow or Birmingham to be Daiyu's stand-in? All the Waces would need to do is tell everyone the child's gone back to where they came from. If it was a child whose birth was never registered, who's going to go looking?'

Robin, who was remembering the shaven-headed, closed-down children in the Chapman Farm classroom, and how easily they'd shown affection to a total stranger, now felt a nasty sinking sensation.

After another silence, Strike said,

'Colonel Graves thinks the witnesses who saw the van passing were set up, so the Waces could punish them and maintain the fiction that they didn't know about the trip to the beach. If it *was* a set-up, it was bloody sadistic. Brian Kennett: getting steadily sicker, no use to the church any more. Draper: low IQ and possibly brain-damaged. Abigail: the heartbroken stepmother can't bear to look at the stepdaughter who let her child drive off to a watery grave and insists on getting rid of her.'

'You think Wace would deliberately set up his elder daughter to be shut up naked in the pigsty?'

'Wace was supposed to be absent that morning, remember,' said Strike.

'So you think Mazu planned it all behind Wace's back?'

'It's a possibility.'

'But where did Daiyu go, if the drowning was faked? We haven't found any other family.'

'Yeah, we have. Wace's parents, in South Africa.'

'But that means a passport, and if Wace wasn't privy to the hoax . . .'

Strike frowned, then said with a sigh,

'OK, objection sustained.'

'I've got another objection,' said Robin tentatively. 'I know you're going to say this is based on emotion, not facts, but I don't believe Carrie was capable of drowning a child. I just don't, Strike.'

'Then explain "It wasn't a joke. It wasn't pretend. It was real. She wasn't coming back."'

'I can't, except that I'm certain Carrie believed Daiyu was dead.'

'Then—'

'Dead . . . but not in the sea. Or not with *her,* in the sea . . .

'You know,' said Robin, after another long pause, 'there might be an alternative explanation for the chocolate and the toys. Not grooming . . . blackmail. Daiyu saw something when she was sneaking around. Somebody was trying to keep her sweet . . . and that might tie back in with those Polaroids. Maybe she saw the naked people in masks, but unlike Kevin, knew they were real people . . . I need a pee,' said Robin, getting to her feet, Strike's jacket still wrapped around her.

Robin's reflection was ghostly in the tarnished mirror of the landing bathroom. Having washed her hands, she returned to the office to find Strike now at Pat's desk, poring over his attempt at a transcript of Kevin Pirbright's interview with Farah Navabi.

'I ran you off a copy,' said Strike, putting the still-warm pages into Robin's hand.

'Want a coffee?' asked Robin, dropping the pages onto the sofa to attend to in a few minutes.

'Yeah, go on ... *and she drowned, or they said she drowned*,' he read off the paper in front of him. 'So Kevin had his doubts about Daiyu's death, too.'

'He was only six when it happened,' objected Robin, switching on the kettle.

'He might not have had doubts *then,* but he grew up with people who might've let slip more than they let on at the time, and started wondering about it later ... and he says, *I remember funny things happening, things I keep thinking about, stuff I keep remembering*, and then, *there were four of them* – or that's what Navabi thought he said. It's not clear on the tape.'

'Four people in pig masks?' suggested Robin.

'Possibly, although we might be getting a bit too hung up on those pictures ... What else could it be? "More of them", "score of them", "sixty-four of them" ... Christ knows ...

'Then we've got *it was more than just Cherie* – he was slurring a lot, but that's what it sounded like ... then something about drinks ... then, *but Bec made Em, visible* and then *bullshit.*'

'But Becca made Emily lie about Daiyu being invisible?' suggested Robin, over the sound of the bubbling kettle.

'Got to be, because then Navabi says, *Becca made Em lie, did you say?* And Kevin says, *she was allowed out, she could get things* and *smuggle it in.*'

Robin finished making the two coffees, set Strike's beside him and sat down on the sofa.

'Cheers,' said Strike, still reading the transcript. 'Then we've got *let her away with stuff – didn't care about her, really – she had chocolate once and I stole some –* and *bully, though.*'

Robin had just found the part of the transcript Strike was reading.

'Well, *let her away with stuff* sounds like Daiyu ... and *didn't care about her, really* might well apply to Daiyu, too ...'

'Who didn't care about Daiyu?' objected Strike. 'Abigail told me she was the princess of the place.'

'But was she, though?' said Robin. 'You know, I saw a virtual shrine to Daiyu in Mazu's office and for a few seconds, I felt genuinely sorry for her. What could be worse than waking and finding out your child's disappeared, and then hearing she's drowned? But the picture other people paint isn't of a devoted mother. Mazu was happy to palm Daiyu off onto other people – well, certainly onto Carrie. Don't you think,' said Robin, warming to her subject, 'it's odd behaviour, the way Mazu's let this cult grow up around Daiyu? The drowning's mentioned constantly. Is that consistent with genuine grief?'

'Could be a deranged kind of grief.'

'But Mazu *thrives* off it. It makes her important, being the mother of the Drowned Prophet. Don't you think the whole thing feels ... I don't know ... horribly exploitative? I'm sure it felt to Abigail like Daiyu *was* her father and stepmother's little princess – she'd just lost her own mum, and her father had no time for her any more – but I'm not sure that was the reality.'

'You make good points,' said Strike, scratching his now heavily stubbled chin. 'OK, so we think *let her away with stuff* but *didn't care about her really* both refer to Daiyu ... So who was allowed out and able to get things and smuggle them in? Who did Kevin steal chocolate from? Who was the bully?'

'Becca,' said Robin, with such conviction that Strike looked up at her, surprised. 'Sorry,' Robin said, with a disconcerted laugh, 'I – don't really know where that came from, except there's something really weird about Becca's whole . . . *status*.'

'Go on.'

'Well, she seems to have been singled out *really* early by Wace as . . . I mean, if I had to pick out anyone who's treated like a princess, it would be Becca. I told you what Flora said about her being a virgin, didn't I?'

'You definitely didn't,' said Strike, staring at her. 'I'd've remembered.'

'Oh, no,' said Robin, 'of course I didn't. It feels like Flora told me that a week ago.'

'How can Becca be a virgin? I thought she was a spirit wife?'

'That's what's so weird. Emily's convinced Becca sleeps with Wace, which is why she never goes into the Retreat Rooms with anyone else, but Emily *also* told me Wace won't have kids with Becca. Shawna said that's because Wace doesn't want a baby with her, because her half-brother was born with so many problems. But *Flora* says all the other spirit wives know Wace isn't sleeping with Becca, and that's why Mazu doesn't hate Becca as much as she hates the rest of them. And honestly, that makes sense to me, because Mazu and Becca always seem – if not matey, there's definitely a sense of alliance.'

Another pause ensued in which both Strike and Robin drank coffee, reading the transcript, and the dawn chorus twittered ever louder beyond the windows.

'*Making allowances,*' Strike read under his breath. '*Bad t* – possibly *bad time . . . gonna talk to her . . .*'

'*She's going to meet me,*' said Robin, also reading. 'But who's "she"?'

'And did "she" turn up?' asked Strike. 'Or was "she" a ruse? Did he answer the door and find our masked gunman friend outside? Then Navabi says *is someone from the church going to meet you, Kevin?* and the by now exceptionally pissed Kevin says, *and answer for it.* So,' said Strike, looking up, 'which woman in the church had things to answer for, as far as Kevin was concerned? Who was going to "answer for it"?'

'Take your pick,' said Robin. 'Mazu – Louise – she dragged the family there in the first place – Becca—'

'Becca,' repeated Strike, 'who he connected with a plot, according to the writing on his bedroom wall . . .'

He dropped his gaze again to the transcript.

'Then Kevin goes off on a bit of a detour, starts talking about Paul Draper, or Dopey, as he refers to him here . . . *think was part of . . .* part of the plot? That fits, if Draper was one of the people set up to witness Carrie and Daiyu leaving.'

Robin was also reading the transcript again.

'*The pigs,*' she read aloud, 'and Navabi says *forget the pigs* and Kevin says he liked pigs . . . no *"he* liked pigs" . . . is that Draper?'

'Well, we know for sure it's not Jordan Reaney,' said Strike. '*I was in the woods . . . Becca told me off because, Wace's daughter* and *mustn't snitch.* And then Kevin mentions a plot again and *in it together.* So: a plot that involves Wace's daughter, and multiple other people.'

'Daiyu wasn't the only Wace daughter at the farm, remember,' said Robin. 'There was Abigail, Lin – any number of girls playing in the woods at Chapman Farm could have been fathered by Jonathan Wace. Most of the kids I saw in the classroom have got his or Taio's eyes.'

'*Always together,*' said Strike, reading again, 'which could mean Daiyu and Carrie – *if I'm right* – and *bution.* What's *bution*?'

'Attribution? Contribution? Distri—'

'Retribution!' said Strike sharply. '"Retribution" was written on Kevin's wall as well. And then he gets really incoherent. There's a gale blowing, an *ire* but *too wet* – no idea – *weird* – *threatened me* – *ran out of there* (I think, though possibly not) – *thought it was for punishment* – *Becca told me* . . . and then he went off to puke in the bogs.'

'Fire,' said Robin.

'What?'

'A fire, but it was too wet to catch, maybe?'

'You think someone was trying to burn something in the woods?'

'Someone *did* burn something in those woods,' said Robin. 'Rope.'

'Rope,' repeated Strike.

'There was a lump of charred rope near those stumps I told you about. The posts someone chopped down. They were in a circle – it looked pagan.'

'You think someone at Chapman Farm was conducting secret rituals in the woods?'

'Daiyu was supposedly doing secret magic with the big kids, don't forget. Oh, and we're also forgetting the axe. The one hidden in the tree, which Jiang says was Daiyu's.'

'Does it seem plausible a seven-year-old had her own pet axe?'

'Not really,' said Robin. 'I'm only telling you what Jiang said.'

Strike sat in silence for a few seconds then said, '*I* need a pee now,' and pushed himself to his feet with a grunt.

His first words on re-entering the office a few minutes later were,

'I'm hungry.'

'You've literally just eaten about five thousand calories,' said Robin in disbelief.

'Well, I'm doing a lot of brain work here.'

Strike refilled the kettle. The birds were singing more

loudly outside. The hour was fast approaching when Daiyu Wace had supposedly entered the sea at Cromer, never to be seen again.

'Why the same stretch of beach?' Strike said, turning to look at Robin. 'Why the hell was Daiyu – or whoever the kid was – taken to exactly the same stretch of beach where Jennifer Wace died?'

'No idea,' said Robin.

'And why did Jordan Reaney try and kill himself?'

'Again – no idea.'

'Come on,' said Strike bracingly.

'Well ... presumably because he was afraid of retribution,' said Robin.

'Retribution,' repeated Strike. 'Exactly. So what did whoever was on the phone threaten Reaney with?'

'I suppose ... being hurt in some way. Exposed as involved in something serious and criminal. Beaten up. Killed.'

'Right. But nobody's hurt Reaney so far except Reaney.'

Strike made two more coffees, passed one to Robin, then sat back down at Pat's desk.

'How's this for a theory?' he said. 'Reaney overdosed because he knew he'd be in deep shit once whoever phoned him realised he'd blabbed to me.'

'Blabbed what?'

'Good question. He was cagey about nearly everything. He did say he'd had to "clean up" after the Waces, and that things he'd done played on his mind ...'

'Maybe,' said Robin suddenly, 'he was supposed to destroy those Polaroids? Just the fact that they're still in existence might be what's got him in trouble?'

'Possible. Likely, even, given that those Polaroids definitely put the fear of God into him.'

Strike got up again and entered the inner office, reappearing with the noticeboard. Closing the dividing door, he propped the board against it and sat back down. For the longest time yet, the pair sat in silence, staring at the pictures, cuttings and notes.

'Some of this,' said Strike at last, 'has got to be irrelevant. People were there, but not involved. Things get misremembered. Accidents *do* happen,' he said, his gaze travelling yet again to Jennifer Wace.

Getting up again, he unpinned the picture of Kevin Pirbright's bedsit as it had been found on his death, and took it back to the desk to examine more closely. Robin was staring at the words 'jogger on the beach?' but Strike was now staring at one innocent little word on Kevin's wall, which he'd seen previously, and never thought about again. He looked up at the pig-masked figures in the Polaroids, and after several long minutes of staring at them, he realised something he couldn't quite believe he hadn't registered before.

He mentally backed away from his new theory to examine it in its entirety, and from every angle he surveyed it, saw it to be smooth, balanced and complete. The extraneous and the irrelevant were now lying discarded to one side.

'I think I know what happened,' said Strike.

And as he drew breath to explain, a quotation rang through his head that he'd heard recently from a man who had nothing whatsoever to do with the Universal Humanitarian Church.

'*And where the offence is, let the great axe fall.*'

PART NINE

Wei Chi/Before Completion

BEFORE COMPLETION. Success.
But if the little fox, after nearly completing the
crossing,
Gets his tail in the water,
There is nothing that would further.

> *The I Ching or Book of Changes*

122

At the beginning of a military enterprise, order is imperative. A just and valid cause must exist, and the obedience and coordination of the troops must be well organized, otherwise the result is inevitably failure.

The I Ching or Book of Changes

Of the many things that needed to be done before the agency could prove how, why and by whose contrivance Daiyu Wace had disappeared forever, Strike allocated one of the most important to Sam Barclay, whom he recalled from Norwich the day after the shooting, after Robin had gone home to catch up on some sleep. Both partners had agreed that the so far fruitless exercise of waiting for Emily Pirbright to appear with a collecting tin should now be abandoned, and the agency's efforts turned instead towards proving that the myth of the Drowned Prophet was entirely baseless.

'How far am I allowed to go, tae worm my way in wi' this guy?' asked Barclay, who'd just pocketed the name, address, place of work and photograph, all gleaned online by Strike, of the man who Strike wanted him to befriend, by whatever means necessary.

'Unlimited alcohol budget. Doubt he's into drugs. Milk the military. Big yourself up.'

'A'right, I'll get ontae it.'

'And be careful. There's a gun out there that's still got bullets in the chamber.'

Barclay gave a mock salute and departed, passing Pat in the doorway.

'I've called all these people,' she told Strike, holding in her hand a piece of paper on which Strike had listed the names and numbers of Eric Wardle, who was his best friend in the Metropolitan Police; Vanessa Ekwensi, who was Robin's; DI George Layborn, who'd rendered the agency significant help in a previous case, and Ryan Murphy. 'I've only been able to get hold of George Layborn so far. He says he could meet you Wednesday evening, next week. I've left messages with the rest of them. I don't see why Robin can't ask Ryan herself.'

'Because this is coming from me,' said Strike. 'I need to meet them all simultaneously, and lay out everything we've got, so we can hit the UHC as hard as possible, right when Wace and his lawyers aren't expecting it.'

'They still haven't found that bloke who shot at you two and Will,' grumbled Pat. 'Don't know what we pay our bloody taxes for.'

Blurry pictures of the Ford Focus with the fake plates had been appearing on various news channels all morning, with appeals to the public for any information. Though thankful his and Robin's names hadn't appeared in the press, Strike had had to take two cabs already that morning, and knew he'd need to hire himself a car for work purposes before the police were through with his own.

'Dennis just called, by the way,' Pat added. 'Will's feeling a bit better.'

'Great,' said Strike, who'd already endured ten solid minutes' grousing from Pat about the state of shock in which Will had been returned to her house in the early hours of the morning. 'Any news on him talking to my lawyer friend about immunity from prosecution?'

'He's thinking about it,' said Pat.

Strike suppressed any expression of frustration at what he considered Will Edensor's idiotic stubbornness.

Pat returned to her desk, e-cigarette between her teeth, and Strike rubbed his eyes. He'd insisted on walking Robin to her taxi at six o'clock, telling her it was imperative that neither of them took any more risks. In spite of their sleepless night, he hadn't been to bed: there was too much to think about, to organise and to do, and it must all be done methodically and stealthily if they were to have any chance of taking on the UHC without anyone else getting shot through the head.

His mobile rang and he groped for it.

'Hi,' said Robin's voice.

'You were supposed to be getting some sleep.'

'I can't,' said Robin. 'I came home, got into bed, lay there awake for an hour then got back up again. Too much coffee. What's going on there?'

'I've seen Barclay and I've called Ilsa,' said Strike, suppressing a yawn. 'She's happy to represent Will and Flora, if they're agreeable. Shah's on his way to Birmingham.'

Strike heaved himself up onto his feet and glanced down into the street again. The tall, fit-looking black man with green eyes had reappeared since he'd last looked, though on this occasion he was marginally better hidden than previously, in a doorway four along from the office on the other side of the street.

'We're still being watched,' Strike informed Robin, 'but only by the clown squad. He wasn't there when I went out to Cedar Terrace this morning.'

'*You* went? I thought we agreed neither of us was going to take stupid risks?'

'I couldn't send Shah, Barclay was still in Norwich and Midge was asleep. Anyway, it wasn't a risk,' said Strike, letting the blinds fall back into place. 'There was never going to be a safer time to go and talk to Rosie Fernsby than while police are hunting the shooter. Trouble with trying to kill people you're afraid know too much is, if you miss, you've not only handed them confirmation of their theory, you've made yourself a target. Anyway,' Strike continued, dropping back into his chair, 'Rosie-Bhakta was there.'

'She was?' said Robin, sounding excited.

'Yeah. She's bloody annoying, although maybe I'd've found her less so if I wasn't this knackered. Says she doesn't ever bother answering the landline because it's only ever for her mother – predictably, given it's her mother's house.'

'What did she say about the Polaroids?'

'Exactly what we expected her to say. She was quite excited to think she might be in danger, though. I've persuaded her to move to a B&B at Colin Edensor's expense.'

'Good. Listen, I'm worried about Midge going back to Chapman Farm—'

'She'll want to do it. She's constantly pissed off I don't let her do dangerous stuff. However bloody insubordinate she can be, nobody could call her a coward.'

Robin, who'd rolled her eyes at the word 'insubordinate', said,

'And what if they've put up cameras at the blind spot now?'

'Unless they're night vision cameras she'll be OK, as long as she's well covered and got the wire cutters. We've got to chance it. Without forensic evidence, we're going to be bloody hard-pressed to prove what happened . . .

'I've got Pat typing up a final report on Toy Boy, by the way. You'll like this: Dev caught him in the same hotel as Bigfoot, with another Eastern European girl.'

'No way.'

'Yeah, so I've passed those photos to the client. Toy Boy's seen his last Rolex. You and I will have to cover Hampstead while the others are working the UHC case. With luck, the clowns watching us will think we've lost interest in the church now we've been shot at.'

'I'm worried about Sam, though. What if——?'

'Barclay can handle himself fine,' said Strike. 'Stop worrying about him and Midge and concentrate on the fact that we're trying to take down a bunch of fuckers who're brainwashing thousands, raping people and selling kids.'

'I *am* concentrating on that,' said Robin crossly. 'For your information, I've spent the last six hours combing through every other Isaac Mills in the UK.'

'And?'

'And there are two more Isaac Millses who're the right age. One's a chartered accountant, the other's in jail.'

'*Very* promising,' said Strike. 'Which jail?'

'Wandsworth.'

'Even better,' said Strike. 'Won't be a long trip. What's he in for?'

'Manslaughter. I'm doing some more digging right now.'

'Great.' Strike scratched his chin, thinking. 'If he's the right one, you should visit him. Might require a lighter touch than I gave Reaney.'

He chose not to say that Mills was likely to fancy a visit from an attractive young woman far more than he'd want to meet a broken-nosed forty-one-year-old man.

'This is all going to take time to arrange,' said Robin, sounding worried.

'Doesn't matter. We do this properly or not at all. I'm trying to fix up a meeting with all our police contacts——'

'I know, Ryan just called me, he got Pat's message,' said Robin.

Then why the fuck didn't he call Pat? was Strike's immediate, ungracious thought.

'He can't do anything until next week.'

'Nor can Layborn,' said Strike. 'I might give them all a little kick up the arse, tell them my journalist contact is gagging to write a piece about the church and police apathy, and that I'm barely holding him off.'

'Would you mind not?' said Robin. 'Or not unless it's absolutely necessary?'

'You're the one who wants to speed things up,' said Strike.

And nobody made you start seeing that prick Murphy.

123

For the next fortnight, everyone at the agency was very busy, their efforts directed almost exclusively to proving Strike's theory about the fate of the Drowned Prophet.

Midge, who'd accepted with alacrity the possibly dangerous job of trying to get forensic evidence from the woods at Chapman Farm, returned safely and triumphantly from Norfolk. Given that the agency had no access to a forensics lab, the only hope of having her findings analysed would be in the context of a police investigation that hadn't yet started, if, indeed, it ever did. Everything she'd carried out of the woods at Chapman Farm was now wrapped carefully in plastic in the office safe.

After a week of hanging around various likely haunts, Barclay had successfully located the man whom Strike was so keen to have befriended, and was cautiously optimistic, given his target's fondness for drink and military anecdotes, that a few more free pints might see himself invited round to the man's home.

'Don't rush it,' warned Strike. 'One false move could set off alarm bells.'

Shah remained in Birmingham, where some of the activities he'd undertaken were illegal. In consequence, Strike didn't intend to share any of Dev's findings at the meeting with his and Robin's four best police contacts, which finally took place two weeks and a day after Strike and Robin had been shot at, on a Tuesday evening, in the useful downstairs room at the Flying Horse. Strike – who felt he was becoming increasingly profligate with Sir Colin Edensor's money – was paying for the room and dinner out of his own pocket, with the promise of burgers and chips to sweeten their contacts' sacrifice of a few hours of their free time.

Unfortunately for Strike, he was late for his own meeting. He'd driven to Norfolk and back that day in a hired automatic Audi A1. The interview he'd conducted there had taken longer than he'd expected, the unfamiliar car's pedals had been hard on his right leg, he'd hit a lot of traffic on the way back into London, and this, coupled with the stress of checking constantly that he wasn't being followed, had etched a slight scowl onto his face which he had to discipline into a smile when he reached the downstairs room, where he found Eric Wardle, George Layborn, Vanessa Ekwensi, Ryan Murphy, Robin, Will, Flora and Ilsa.

'Sorry,' Strike muttered, spilling some of his pint as he dropped clumsily into the spare seat at the table. 'Long day.'

'I've ordered for you,' said Robin, and Strike noted the look of irritation on Murphy's face as she said it.

Robin was feeling uneasy. Will, she knew, had been cajoled into attending by Pat and Dennis, the latter having told Will firmly that he was caught in a chicken and egg situation and needed to bloody well get himself out of it. Since arriving in the basement of the Flying Horse with Flora and Ilsa, Will, who looked pale and worried, had barely spoken. Meanwhile, it had required all Robin's cheerful chat and gratitude for her presence to raise the slightest smile from Flora, who was currently twisting her fingers on her lap beneath the table. Robin had already glimpsed a fresh self-harm mark on her neck.

Aside from her worries about how this meeting was likely to affect the two fragile ex-church members, Robin sensed undercurrents between Wardle and Murphy; the latter had become peremptory and curt in manner even before Strike arrived.

After some slightly stilted small talk, Strike introduced the subject of the meeting. The police listened in silence while Strike ran over the main accusations against the church, omitting all mention of the Drowned Prophet. When Strike said Flora and Will were prepared to give statements about what they'd witnessed while members of the church, Robin saw the knuckles of Flora's hands turn white beneath the table.

Food arrived before the police had had time to ask any questions. Once the waitress had left, the CID officers began to speak up. They were, as Strike had expected, starting from a position, if not of scepticism, then of caution.

He'd expected their muted response to the child trafficking allegations, given that neither Will nor Flora had ever been to the Birmingham centre which was supposed to be its hub. Nobody was disposed to challenge out loud Flora's statement, delivered in a quaking voice while staring at the table in front of her, that she'd been repeatedly raped, but it angered Robin that it took her own corroboration about the Retreat Rooms to wipe the doubtful expression from George Layborn's face. She described, in blunt language, her own close shaves with Taio, and the sight of an underage girl emerging from a Retreat Room with Giles Harmon. The novelist's name seemed unfamiliar to Layborn, but Wardle and Ekwensi exchanged a look at this, and both got out their notebooks.

As for the allegation that the church was improperly burying bodies without registering deaths, Robin thought that, too, might have been dismissed as an evidence-free claim, but for the unexpected intervention of Will.

'They *do* bury them illegally,' he said, interrupting Layborn, who was pressing a distressed Flora for details. 'I've seen it as well. Right before I left, they buried a kid who was born with – well, I don't know what was wrong with him. They never got him seen by anyone except Zhou.'

'Not Jacob?' said Robin, looking around at Will.

'Yeah. He died a few hours after you left. They buried him on the far side of the field, by the oak,' said Will, who hadn't previously disclosed this. 'I watched them do it.'

Robin was too distressed by this information to say anything except, 'Oh.'

'And,' said Will, 'we – I had to help—'

He swallowed and pressed on.

'—I had to help dig up Kevin. They put him in the field, first, but they moved him to the vegetable patch instead, to punish Louise – his . . . mother.'

'What?' said Vanessa Ekwensi, her pen hovering over her pad.

'She tried to . . . she went to plant flowers on him, in the field,' said Will, turning red. 'And someone saw her, and reported her to Mazu. So Mazu said, if she wanted to plant stuff on a Deviate, she could. And they dug him up and put him in the vegetable patch and made Louise plant carrots on him.'

The horrified silence that followed these words was broken by Strike's mobile buzzing. He glanced at the text he'd received, then looked up at Will.

'We've found Lin: she's been moved to Birmingham.'

Will looked stunned.

'They've let her out to fundraise?'

'No,' said Strike. 'She's in the church compound, helping look after the babies.'

He answered Shah's text, giving further instructions, then looked up at the police.

'Look, we're not stupid: we know you can't authorise or even guarantee a massive investigation like this, right now, tonight. But you've got two people here who are willing to testify to widespread criminality, and we're sure there'll be many more, if only you can get into those church centres and start asking questions. Robin's ready to go to court about everything she saw, too. There's going to be glory in this, for whoever takes the UHC down,' said Strike, 'and I've already got a journalist who's gagging to run an exposé.'

'That's not a threat, is it?' said Murphy.

'No,' said Robin, before Strike could say anything, 'it's a fact. If we can't get a police investigation without the press, we'll let the journalist have it and try and force one that way. If you'd been in there, as I have, you'd understand exactly why every day the UHC is getting away with it counts.'

After that, Strike noticed with satisfaction, Murphy said nothing more.

At ten o'clock, the meeting broke up, with handshakes all round. Vanessa Ekwensi and Eric Wardle, who'd taken most notes, separately promised to get back to Strike and Robin quickly.

Strike determinedly didn't watch Murphy kissing Robin goodbye and telling her he'd see her the next day, because she was taking over surveillance on Hampstead from Midge in an hour's time. However, Strike gained some pleasure from Murphy's clear unhappiness at leaving his girlfriend alone with her partner.

'Well,' said Robin, sitting back down at the table, 'it went about as well as could be expected, I suppose.'

'Yeah, not bad,' said Strike.

'So what happened in Norfolk?'

'I got an earful, as expected,' said Strike. 'They're definitely rattled. What about Isaac Mills?'

'No word yet. He might not fancy meeting me at all.'

'Don't despair yet. It's pretty monotonous in the nick.'

'D'you think you'll have to go back to Reaney?' asked Robin, as the waitress re-entered the room to clear away pint glasses and both detectives got to their feet.

'Maybe,' said Strike, 'but I doubt he'll talk until he has to.'

They climbed the stairs together, emerging onto Oxford Street, where Strike pulled out his vape pen and took a long-awaited lungful of nicotine.

'I'm parked up the road. There's no need to escort me,' Robin added, correctly guessing what Strike was about to say, 'it's still crowded and I definitely wasn't followed here. I kept checking, all the way.'

'Fair enough,' said Strike. 'Speak tomorrow, then.'

As he set off up the road, Strike's mobile buzzed again, now with a text from Barclay.

Still no invite

Strike sent two words back.

Keep trying

124

*The inferior man is not ashamed of unkindness
and does not shrink from injustice. If no advantage
beckons he makes no effort.*

The I Ching or Book of Changes

The second week of September passed without progress on the UHC case, and no word as to whether the church's accusation of child abuse against Robin was likely to result in her arrest, which meant she continued to suffer regular stabs of dread every time she thought about it. In slightly better news, both Will and Flora had been invited to give formal statements to the police, and, far more quickly than she'd expected, Robin received word that she'd been put on Isaac Mills' visitors' list.

'S'pose you were right: prison's boring,' Robin told Strike, when she called him from outside Hampstead's office to tell him the good news.

'Be interesting to know whether he's got any idea what it's about,' said Strike, who was walking away from Chinatown as he spoke.

'Anyone watching the office today?'

'No,' said Strike, 'but I've just followed a friend of yours to the Rupert Court Temple. Saw her from across the street when I was buying vape juice: Becca.'

'What, out with a collecting tin?' said Robin. 'I thought she was too important for that.'

'No tin. She was just walking along staring at the ground. She unlocked the temple doors and went inside and didn't come out while I was watching, which was for about half an hour. I had to leave, I've got Colin Edensor arriving in twenty minutes; he wants an update on Will. Anyway, very good news on Mills. This Saturday, did you say?'

'Yes. I've never visited a prison before.'

'I wouldn't worry. The dress code's fairly relaxed,' said Strike, and Robin laughed.

Having seen his 1999 mugshot, Robin hadn't supposed Isaac Mills would look more attractive or healthy seventeen years later, but she certainly wasn't expecting the man who shuffled towards her in the Wandsworth visitors' centre a few days later.

He was, without exception, the most pathetic example of humanity Robin had ever laid eyes on. Though she knew him to be forty-three, he might have been seventy. The small amount of hair he still possessed was dull and grey, and while his skin was bronzed, his hollow face seemed to have collapsed inwards. Most of his teeth were missing, and the few that remained were blackened stumps, while his discoloured fingernails scooped upwards, as if peeling away from his hands. Robin had the macabre thought that she was looking at a man whose proper setting was a coffin, an impression reinforced by the gust of rotten breath that reached her as he sat down.

In the first two minutes of their meeting, Mills told Robin that he never received visits and that he was waiting for a liver transplant. After this, the conversation stalled. When Robin mentioned Carrie – or Cherry, as she'd been when Mills knew her – he informed her that Cherry had been a 'stupid tart', then folded his arms and contemplated her with a sneer on his face, his demeanour posing the silent question, *What's in this for me?*

Appeals to conscience – 'Daiyu was only seven when she disappeared. You've got children, haven't you?' – or to a sense of justice – 'Kevin's killer's still walking around, free, and you could help us catch them' – elicited nothing at all from the prisoner, though his sunken eyes, with their yellow whites and pinprick pupils, remained fixed on the healthy young woman who sat breathing in his odour of decay.

Uneasily conscious of the time slipping past, Robin tried an appeal to self-interest.

'If you were to help our investigation, I'm sure it would be taken into account when you come up for parole.'

Mills' only reaction was a low, unpleasant chuckle. He was serving twelve years for manslaughter; they both knew he was unlikely to live long enough to meet a parole board.

'We've got a journalist who's very interested in this story,' she said, resorting in desperation to the tactic Strike had used on the police. 'Finding out what really happened could help us bring down the church, which—'

'It's a cult,' said Isaac Mills unexpectedly, a further gust of halitosis engulfing Robin. 'Not a fucking church.'

'I agree. That's what's got the journalist interested. Cherry talked to you about the UHC, then, did she?'

Mills' only response was a loud sniff.

'Did Cherry ever mention Daiyu, at all?'

Mills glanced at the large clock over the double doors through which he'd emerged.

Robin was forced to the conclusion that she had indeed been invited to Wandsworth to while away an hour of Mills' tedious, miserable life. He showed no inclination to get up and leave, presumably because he was enjoying the pathetic pleasure of denying her what she'd come for.

For nearly a minute, Robin contemplated him in silence, thinking. She doubted any hospital would ever be brave enough to put Isaac Mills to the top of a waiting list for a liver, because the newspaper-reading public would doubtless feel such a gift should go to a patient who wasn't an addict or a serial burglar and hadn't been convicted of several stabbings, one of them fatal. At last, she said,

'You understand that if you were to help this investigation, it would be publicised. You'd have helped put an end to something huge, and criminal. The fact that you're ill would be publicised, too. Some of the people trapped inside the cult have wealthy families, people of influence. Let's be honest – you haven't got a prayer of a new liver unless something changes.'

He glanced at her, his sneer more pronounced.

'You're not gonna get that cult,' he said, 'whatever I tell you.'

'You're wrong,' said Robin. 'Just because Cherry didn't drown Daiyu, doesn't mean she didn't do something nearly as bad. None of it could have happened without her collusion.'

By the tiniest tremor at the corner of Mills' mouth, she could tell he was listening more closely.

'What you don't appreciate,' said Robin, forcing herself to lean forwards, even though it meant getting closer to the source of Mills' disgusting breath, 'is that the cult centres around Daiyu's death. They've turned her into a prophet who vanished in the sea, only to come back to life again. They're pretending she materialises in their temple. Proof that she never really drowned means their religion's founded on a lie. And if you're the one who provides that proof, a lot of people, some of them very rich, are going to be deeply invested in you being well enough to testify. You might be their last hope of seeing their family members again.'

She had his full attention now. Mills sat in silence for a few more seconds before saying,

'She never done it.'

'Done what?'

'Killed Dayoo, or whatever her name was.'

'So what really happened?' said Robin, taking the top off her pen.

This time, Isaac Mills answered.

125

The way opens; the hindrance has been cleared away.

The I Ching or Book of Changes

Forty minutes later, Robin emerged from Wandsworth Prison in a state of elation. Pulling her mobile out of her bag, she noticed with frustration that it was almost out of power: either it hadn't charged properly at Murphy's the previous evening or, which she thought more likely given its age, she needed a new phone. Waiting until she was out of the vicinity of the stream of families now exiting the building, she called Strike.

'You were right,' said Robin. 'Carrie confessed nearly all of it to Mills, mostly whenever she got drunk. He says she'd always deny it when she sobered up, but basically, he's confirmed everything, except—'

'Who planned it.'

'How did you know?'

'Because she was still scared enough of them to kill herself twenty-one years later.'

'But Mills is very clear it was all a put-up job. Carrie faked the drowning, Daiyu was never on the beach. I know it's not enough, hearsay from a dead woman—'

'Still can't hurt,' said Strike. 'Will he testify?'

'Yes, but only because he's got hemo-something and thinks he might get a new liver out of it.'

'A new what?'

'Liver,' said Robin loudly, now heading for the bus stop.

'I'll get him one out of Aldi. Listen, have you seen the—?'

Robin's phone went dead.

'*Shit.*'

She hurried on towards the bus stop. She was supposed to be meeting Murphy at a bar in the middle of town at seven, but was now keen to find a way of speaking to Strike again, who'd sounded strangely keyed up before he got cut off. Unfortunately, she had no idea where he was. Speeding up, she tried to remember the rota: if he was at the office, or in his flat, she might have time to see him before going on to the West End.

The hour's journey back towards Denmark Street seemed interminable. Robin kept shuffling through different scenarios in her mind, trying to see possible routes to their murderer in the light of Mills' evidence, which confirmed Strike's theory and would add substance to whatever other testimony they could get. However, she still saw pitfalls ahead, especially if the plastic-wrapped objects in the office safe yielded nothing useable.

She and Strike had concluded during the sleepless night they'd spent at the office that there were four people, aside from Isaac Mills, whose combined testimony might reveal exactly what happened to Daiyu, even if the originator of the plan denied it. However, all had strong reasons for not talking, and two of them probably didn't realise that what they knew was significant. It was by no means certain they'd be able to take an axe to the roots of Jonathan Wace's dangerous and seductive religion.

A little over an hour later, Robin arrived in Denmark

Street, sweaty and dishevelled from haste, but on reaching the second landing her heart sank: the office door was locked and the lights were out. Then she heard movement above her.

'*What the fuck happened?*' said Strike, descending the stairs.

'What d'you mean?' said Robin, taken aback.

'I've been worried fucking sick, I thought someone had grabbed you off the fucking street!'

'My phone died!' said Robin, who didn't much appreciate this welcome, having just jogged up the street to see her partner. 'And I was in Wandsworth in broad daylight – *don't* start about guns,' she said, correctly anticipating Strike's next sentence. 'You'd have heard the bang, wouldn't you?'

As this was precisely what he'd been telling himself for the last sixty minutes, Strike bit back a retort. Nevertheless, finding it hard to shift gears immediately from acute anxiety to a normal conversational tone, he said angrily,

'You need a new fucking phone.'

'Thanks,' said Robin, now almost equally cross, 'I hadn't thought of that.'

A reluctant grin replaced Strike's scowl, though Robin wasn't that easily appeased.

'You were asking me if I'd seen something when I got cut off,' she said coolly. 'I haven't got long, I'm supposed to be meeting Ryan.'

Strike supposed he deserved that.

'Come up here,' he said, pointing towards his flat. 'They raided Chapman Farm at six this morning.'

'*What?*' gasped Robin, climbing the stairs to the attic behind him.

'A dozen coppers, Met and local force. Wardle's with them. He called me at two. Couldn't talk long, because they're still interviewing people. They've already released a severely dehydrated and traumatised Emily Pirbright from a locked wooden box in the farmhouse basement.'

'Oh no.'

'She'll be OK. They've taken her to hospital. It gets better,' said Strike, as they entered the attic. 'Shah's just seen roughly the same number of coppers entering the Birmingham centre. No word on Glasgow yet, but I'm assuming it's happening there, too.'

He led her through to his bedroom, a spartan place, like the rest of the small flat. The television at the foot of the bed had been paused on Sky News: a female reporter was frozen, open mouthed, in what Robin recognised as Lion's Mouth. Behind her was the entrance to Chapman Farm, which now had two uniformed officers standing outside it.

'Someone at the Met's leaked,' said Strike, picking up the remote. 'Said there'd be glory in it, didn't I?'

He pressed play.

'. . . already seen an ambulance leaving,' said the reporter, gesturing down the lane. 'Police haven't yet confirmed the reasons for the investigation, but we do know officers are here in large numbers and a forensic team arrived just over an hour ago.'

'Jenny, some have called the UHC controversial, haven't they?' said a male voice.

'Cautious,' said the smirking Strike, as the female reporter nodded, finger pressed to her earpiece.

'Yes, Justin, mainly in regard to its financial activities, though it must be said the church has never been convicted of any wrongdoing.'

'Give it time,' said Strike and Robin simultaneously.

'And, of course, it's got some very high-profile members,' said the invisible Justin. 'Novelist Giles Harmon, actress Noli Seymour – are any of them currently on the grounds, do you know?'

'No, Justin, we've had no confirmation of who's at the farm right now, although locals estimate there are at least a hundred people living here.'

'And has there been any official statement from the church?'

'Nothing as yet—'

Strike paused the news report again.

'Just thought you'd like to see it,' he said.

'You were right,' said Robin, beaming.

'Almost enough to make you believe in God, isn't it? I tipped off Fergus Robertson as soon as I heard from Wardle. I've given him a good few pointers as to where to get some scoops. Think it's time to turn up the heat on Jonathan Wace as high as we can. Got time for a coffee?'

'A quick one,' said Robin, checking her watch. 'Could I borrow a charger?'

This provided, and coffee made, they sat down at the small Formica table.

'Becca's still at the Rupert Court Temple,' said Strike.

'How d'you know?'

'She took the service today, which I got Midge to attend, wigged up.'

'I thought Midge was watching Hampstead?'

'Oh, yeah, I forgot – she got pictures of him with a bloke on the heath last night.'

'When you say "pictures"—'

'I doubt they'll be featuring on the family Christmas card,' said Strike. 'I'll let the client know on Monday, because he's home with her and the kids right now.'

'Go on about Becca.'

'She didn't leave at the end of the service. Midge is still watching Rupert Court, minus her wig, obviously. She's confident Becca's still in there. Doors locked.'

'Haven't the police been?'

'Presumably they're more interested in the compounds.'

'Is Becca alone?'

'Dunno. She could well be planning to make a break for it – unless she fancies taking the Stolen Prophet's way out, of course.'

'Don't say that,' said Robin, thinking of Carrie Curtis Woods hanging in the family garage. 'If we know where she is—'

'We do nothing – *nothing*,' said Strike firmly, 'until we hear from Barclay.'

'But—'

'Did you hear me?'

'For God's sake, I'm not a bloody schoolchild!'

'Sorry,' said Strike. The residue of his hour's anxiety hadn't yet dispersed. 'Look, I know you think I keep boring on about that gun, but we still don't know where it is – which is a pain in the arse,' he added, checking his watch, 'because we're on the clock, now the police have gone in. People are going to start arse-covering or making themselves unavailable for interview. They'll have an excuse for only communicating through lawyers now, as well.'

'D'you think they've got the Waces?' said Robin, whose thoughts had roved irresistibly back to Chapman Farm. 'They *must* have Mazu, at least. She never leaves the place. *God*, I'd like to be a fly on the wall when they start questioning her . . .'

Memories of people she'd got to know over her four months at the farm were revolving in her mind as though it was a zoetrope: Emily, Shawna, Amandeep, Kyle, Walter, Vivienne, Louise, Marion, Taio, Jiang . . . who'd talk? Who'd lie?

'I had bloody Rosie Fernsby on the phone at lunchtime,' said Strike.

'What did she want?'

'To go to a yoga class this afternoon. The glamour of being a hunted woman's worn off.'

'What did you say?'

'That she'd have to stay put and cleanse her own bloody chakras. She chose to take it as a joke.'

'Just as well. We do need her to testify.'

'What she's got to tell will take three minutes, if this comes to court,' said Strike. 'I'm trying to stop her getting bloody shot.'

Robin checked her watch.

'I'd better go.'

As she got to her feet, Strike's mobile buzzed.

'Holy shit.'

'What?'

'Barclay's done it, he's in.'

Strike, too, rose.

'I'm going to talk to Abigail Glover about Birmingham.'

'Then,' said Robin, as a feeling like fire flamed through her insides, 'I'm going to talk to Becca.'

'No, you're fucking not,' said Strike, pausing where he stood. 'Midge doesn't know who else might be in the temple.'

'I don't care,' said Robin, already heading for her phone. 'You realise she could be planning to head for San Francisco or Munich? Ryan, hi ... no, listen, something's come up ... I know, I've seen on the news, but I can't do dinner. Sorry ... no ... it's just a witness who might get away unless I see her now,' Robin said, meeting Strike's frown with a frosty look of her own. 'Yes ... OK. I'll ring you later.'

Robin hung up.

'I'm doing it,' she told Strike, before he could speak. 'She's not wriggling out of this. Not bloody Becca.'

'All right,' he said, 'but you go in with Midge, all right? Not alone.'

'Fine,' said Robin. 'Give me your skeleton keys in case she doesn't open up when I knock. I think this is going to be what they call closure.'

126

*In the royal hunts of ancient China it was customary
to drive up the game from three sides, but on the
fourth the animals had a chance to run off.*

The I Ching or Book of Changes

Robin parted from Strike in Tottenham Court Road, and
arrived in Wardour Street ten minutes later. It was swarming
with Saturday evening visitors to Chinatown, but she couldn't
see Midge. Her phone now charged sufficiently for at least one
call, Robin called the subcontractor's number.

'Where are you? Strike told me you were watching the
Rupert Court Temple.'

'I was,' said Midge, 'but Becca's left. I'm following her.'

'*Shit,*' said Robin, for the second time in as many hours. 'No,
I mean, it's good that you're still on her, but – is she alone? She
hasn't got a bag or anything, has she? Does she look as though
she's going on a trip?'

'She's alone, and there's no bag,' said Midge. 'She might just
be buying food. She's looking at her phone a lot.'

'I'll bet she is,' said Robin. 'Will you keep me posted on
where you are? I'm in the vicinity of the temple. Let me know
if she's on her way back.'

'Will do,' said Midge, and she rang off.

Deprived in the short term of her prey, frustrated and tense,

Robin moved out of the way of a group of drunken men. Fiddling with the skeleton keys in her pocket, she contemplated the red and gold creatures over the door of the temple: the dragon, the pheasant, the sheep, the horse, the cow, the dog, the rooster, and, of course, the pig.

127

Heaven has the same direction of movement as fire,
yet it is different from fire . . .

The I Ching or Book of Changes

It took Strike forty-five minutes to reach the fire station where Abigail was working that evening. It was a large, Art Deco building of grey stone, with the usual large, square openings below for the fire trucks.

Upon entering, Strike found a man in his forties scribbling a note at a desk in an otherwise deserted reception area. When Strike enquired whether Abigail Glover was currently on the premises, he said yes, she was upstairs. When Strike said his business was urgent, the fireman called upstairs on a wall-mounted phone, his expression amused. Strike wondered whether he had, again, been mistaken for one of Abigail's boyfriends.

She descended the stairs a few minutes later, looked disconcerted and irritable, for which Strike couldn't blame her; he, too, preferred not to be disturbed at work. She was wearing the regulation firemen's overalls, though without the jacket. Her black top was tight-fitting, and he assumed she'd been mid-way through changing when he'd interrupted her.

'Why're *you* 'ere?'

'I need your help,' said Strike.

'People norm'lly dial 999,' said Abigail, to a snigger from her colleague.

'It's about Birmingham,' said Strike.

'Birmingham?' Abigail repeated, frowning.

'Yeah. Shouldn't take long, but I think you're the only person who can clarify a couple of points.'

Abigail cast a look behind her.

'Earwiggin', Richard?'

'No,' said the man. He disappeared upstairs perhaps a little faster than he'd have done otherwise.

'All right,' Abigail said, turning back to Strike, 'but you're gonna 'ave to 'urry up, 'cause my shift's ended and I've got a date.'

'Fair enough,' said Strike.

She led him through a door to the right, which was evidently used for talks and meetings, because a number of steel-legged plastic chairs were stacked in corners. Abigail proceeded to a small table near a whiteboard at the far end, lifting down a chair for herself on the way.

'It's you, innit?' she said to Strike, over her shoulder. ''Oo's caused the shitstorm at Chapman Farm?'

'Ah, you've seen,' said Strike.

'It's all over the fuckin' news, 'course I 'ave.'

'I'd like to take credit,' said Strike, also picking up a chair and taking it to the table, 'but that's mostly down to my detective partner.'

'Did she get your client's relative out, before she torched the place?' asked Abigail, as both sat down.

'She did, yeah,' said Strike.

'Blimey. You don' wanna let *'er* go in an 'urry.'

'I don't intend to,' said Strike.

'It's gonna mean the press coming for me, though, innit?' said Abigail, looking tense as she pulled a pack of nicotine gum out of her pocket and put a piece in her mouth.

'Probably,' said Strike. 'I'm sorry about that.'

'When Dick called just now, I fort, "This is it. A journalist's come" ... go on, then. What about Birmingham?'

'We've found out your father was supposed to be taking Rosie Fernsby up to Birmingham the morning Daiyu disappeared, but he changed his plans.'

'Rosie 'oo?'

She wasn't at the farm long,' said Strike. 'Pretty girl. Dark, curvy – she was there with her father and twin brother.'

'Oh, yeah ... twins. Yeah, I remember them,' said Abigail. 'I'd never met twins before. I didn't know you could have boy and girl ones ... no fuckin' education,' she added bitterly. 'Like I told you before.'

'When we interviewed Cherie Gittins, she tied herself up in knots a bit about your father's whereabouts.'

'Found Cherie, didja? Bloody 'ell.'

'Yeah, she was married and living in the West Country. Anyway, she seemed to attach a lot of significance to the question of whether or not your father was at the farm when Daiyu disappeared.'

'Well, I dunno why she was confused. 'E was definitely there when the police come to say Daiyu 'ad drowned. I remember Mazu screaming and collapsin' and 'im 'olding 'er up.'

'When were *you* sent up to Birmingham, exactly?' asked Strike.

'Exactly? Dunno. After Daiyu's inquest.'

'Had there been any question of you going to Birmingham before Daiyu disappeared?'

'They prob'lly discussed it when I wasn' around,' said Abigail, with a slight shrug. 'Mazu wanted shot of me for years, and Daiyu dyin' gave 'er an excuse to do it. I din't give a shit, personally. I fort it'd probably be easier to escape from one of the other places, din't fink eiver of 'em would be as 'ard to get in an' out of as Chapman Farm, an' I was right.'

'Yeah, one of my operatives got into Birmingham without too much difficulty, on an out-of-date police ID.'

'Find anyfing interesting?'

'A lot of babies,' said Strike.

''Spect there *is* a lot, now,' said Abigail. 'No birf control.'

'How long were you at the farm, between Daiyu's disappearance and leaving for Birmingham?'

'Dunno. Week or two. Somefing like that.'

'And when you were transferred to Birmingham, did anyone from Chapman Farm go with you?'

'Yeah, bloke called Joe. 'E was older'n me an' 'e was one of my farver and Mazu's favourites. 'E wasn' going up there 'cos 'e was being punished, though, 'e was gonna be second in command in the Birmingham Centre.'

'And it was just you and Joe who were transferred that day, was it?'

'Yeah, 's far as I can remember.'

Strike turned a page in his notebook.

'You remember Alex Graves' family? Father, mother and sister?'

'Yeah, I told you I did,' said Abigail, frowning.

'Well, Graves' father thinks your father ordered Cherie Gittins to kill Daiyu.'

Abigail chewed her gum for a few seconds in silence, then said,

'Well, that's the sort of stupid fing people say, innit? When they're angry. Why's my farver s'posed to 'ave killed 'er?'

'To get his hands on the quarter of a million pounds Graves left Daiyu in his will.'

'You're shittin' me. She 'ad a *qua'er of a million?*'

'If she'd lived, she'd also have inherited the Graves family home, which is probably worth ten times that.'

'*Jesus!*'

'You didn't know she had that much money?'

'No! Graves looked like a tramp, I never knew 'e 'ad any money of 'is own!'

'Do you think a quarter of a million would be a sufficient motive for your father to want Daiyu dead?'

Abigail chewed her gum vigorously, still frowning, before saying,

'Well ... 'e'd've liked the money. 'Oo wouldn't? But of course 'e didn' fuckin' tell Cherie to do it. 'E wouldn't've wanted to upset Mazu.'

'Your father sent you a message, when I met him.'

'You've *met* 'im?'

'Yeah. He invited me backstage after his Olympia rally.'

'An' 'e sent *me* a message?' she said incredulously.

'Yeah. "Popsicle misses you."'

Abigail's lip curled.

'Bastard.'

'Him, or me?'

''Im, obviously. Still tryna ...'

'To ... ?'

'Tug the 'eartstrings. It's been twenny fuckin' years an' not a fuckin' word, an' 'e finks I'll fuckin' melt if 'e says fuckin' "Popsicle".'

But he could tell she was disturbed by the thought of her father sending her a message, even if it was difficult to tell whether anger or pain predominated.

'I can understand why you don't like the idea of your father drowning people,' he said. 'Not even Daiyu.'

'What d'you mean, "not even Daiyu"? Yeah, she was spoiled, but she was still a fuckin' *kid,* wasn' she? An' what d'you mean *"people"*? 'E didn't drown my muvver, I toldja that last time!'

'You wouldn't be the first person who found it hard to believe their own flesh and blood could do terrible things.'

'I've got no fuckin' problem believin' my farver does terrible fuckin' fings, fanks very much!' said Abigail angrily. 'I was *there,* I saw what was fuckin' goin' on, I know what they do to people inside that fuckin' church! They did it to *me,* too,' she said, thumping herself in the chest. 'So *don'* tell me I don' know what my farver is, because I fuckin' do, but 'e wouldn't kill members of 'is own—'

'*You* were family, and as you've just said, he did terrible things to you, too.'

''E didn't – or not . . . 'e *let* bad stuff 'appen to me, yeah, but that was all Mazu, an' it was mostly when 'e was away. If that's all about Birmingham—'

She made to stand up.

'Just a couple more points, if you don't mind,' said Strike, 'and this first one's important. I want to ask you about Becca Pirbright.'

128

Through repetition of danger we grow accustomed to it. Water sets the example for the right conduct under such circumstances . . . it does not shrink from any dangerous spot nor from any plunge, and nothing can make it lose its own essential nature. It remains true to itself under all conditions . . .

The I Ching or Book of Changes

Robin had now stood waiting in Wardour Street for nearly an hour. Midge had texted ten minutes previously that she was waiting for Becca to emerge from a chemist's. Wardour Street was still full of people entering and leaving Chinese restaurants and supermarkets. The red and gold lanterns swung gently overhead in the breeze as the sun sank slowly behind the buildings.

Robin was banking on Midge giving her due warning that Becca was on her way back to the temple, so she could find a less obvious place to watch, but the longer Robin waited, the more the little battery life in her phone was leaking away.

She was afraid that if Becca spotted her, she'd turn tail and run. It might be better, she thought, to be waiting in the temple when Becca returned. That, after all, was Becca's place of safety and her final destination; it would be far harder for her to refuse to talk there than in the street. After a few more moments of indecision, Robin texted her intention to Midge, then headed into Rupert Court.

None of the people walking up and down the narrow passage paid her the slightest attention as she removed the skeleton keys from her pocket. This, after all, was London: each to their own business, unless it became so noisy, violent or otherwise bothersome that passers-by felt duty bound to intervene. It took Robin five goes to find a key that would unlock the temple doors, but finally she managed it. Having slipped inside, she closed the doors quietly behind her and locked them again.

Becca had left the temple lights on their lowest setting, doubtless to make it easier for her to navigate when she returned. The place was deserted. The gigantic cinema screen facing Robin was black, which gave it a faintly forbidding look. The Disneyesque hand-holding figures that ran around the walls had blended into the shadows, but the ceiling figures were dimly visible: the Wounded Prophet in orange, with the blood on his forehead; the Healer Prophet in his blue robes, with his beard and serpent-wrapped staff; the Golden Prophet in yellow, scattering jewels as she flew; the Stolen Prophet in scarlet, with his noose around his neck; and lastly the Drowned Prophet, all in bridal white, with the stylised waves rising behind her.

Robin walked up the scarlet-carpeted aisle to stand beneath the image of Daiyu, with its malevolent black eyes. It was while she was still looking up at the figure that Robin heard something she hadn't expected, and which made the hairs on the back of her neck stand up: the screaming of a baby, somewhere inside the temple.

She turned swiftly, trying to locate the source of the sound, then headed towards the stage. To the right of it was a door so well camouflaged in the gold temple wall that Robin hadn't noticed it during the services she'd attended, distracted, no doubt, by the images of Gods, and of the church's charitable work, shown onscreen. Robin felt for the flush pull handle and tugged.

The door opened. There was a staircase beyond, leading upstairs to what Robin knew were sleeping quarters. The baby's cries grew louder. Robin began to climb.

129

The fate of fire depends on wood; as long as there is wood below, the fire burns above.

The I Ching or Book of Changes

'So,' said Strike, pausing in his note-taking to read back what Abigail had just told him, 'in the two or three weeks you spent at the Birmingham centre, you definitely don't remember any eleven-year-olds being transferred from Chapman Farm?'

'No,' said Abigail.

'That tallies with my information,' said Strike, 'because my operative in Birmingham made enquiries about Becca Pirbright. They know who she is, because she's a big shot in the church now, but they said she'd never lived there as a child.'

'What's it matter wevver she ever lived in Birmingham?' said Abigail, perplexed.

'Because that's where her brother and sister believed she'd gone, after Daiyu disappeared. Becca returned to the farm three years later, and she was changed.'

'Well, she would be, after free years,' said Abigail, still looking puzzled.

'But you can't remember the Pirbright kids?'

'No, they must've been a lot younger than me.'

'Becca was five years younger.'

'Then we'd've missed each uvver in the dorms.'

'Dark,' Strike prompted her. 'Reasonably attractive. Shiny hair.'

Abigail shrugged and shook her head.

'Their mother was called Louise.'

'*Oh,*' said Abigail slowly. 'Yeah ... I remember Louise. Really good-looking woman. Mazu 'ad it in for 'er the moment she arrived at the farm.'

'Did she?'

'Oh yeah. It was all bruvverly love an' not bein' possessive an' shit, but Mazu fuckin' 'ated all the women my farver was shagging.'

'Was he calling them spirit wives in those days?'

'Not to me,' said Abigail restlessly. 'Listen, can you get to the point? Only I've gotta meet Darryl an' 'e's pissed off at me at the moment 'cause 'e finks I'm not givin' 'im enough attention.'

'You don't seem the type to be bothered by complaints like that.'

''E's very good in the sack, if you must know,' said Abigail coolly. 'Is that it, then, on Becca and Birmingham?'

'Not entirely. I'd have asked Cherie to clarify the next couple of points, but unfortunately I can't, because she hanged herself hours after I interviewed her.'

'She ... wha'?'

Abigail had stopped chewing.

'Hanged herself,' repeated Strike. 'It's been a bit of a feature of this case, to tell you the truth. After I went to interview Jordan Reaney, *he* tried to kill himself, too. I'd shown both of them –'

He slid his hand into his coat pocket, extracted his mobile and brought up the pictures of the Polaroids.

'– these. You can swipe right to see all of them. There are six.'

Abigail took the phone and looked through the pictures, her expression blank.

'Are those the kinds of pig masks you were made to wear as punishments, by Mazu?' asked Strike.

'Yeah,' said Abigail quietly. 'That's them.'

'Were you ever forced to do anything like this?'

'*Christ,* no.'

She pushed the phone back across the table, but Strike said,

'Would you be able to identify the people in the pictures?'

Abigail drew the phone back towards her and examined them once again, though with obvious reluctance.

'The tall one looks like Joe,' she said, after staring for a while at the picture in which Paul Draper was being sodomised.

'Did he have a tattoo?'

'Dunno. I was never in the Retreat Rooms wiv 'im.'

She glanced up at Strike.

'S'pose your partner found out about the Retreat Rooms, did she?'

'Yes,' said Strike. 'D'you think this happened in one of them?'

'No,' said Abigail, dropping her gaze to the phone again. 'The place looks too big. Looks more like a barn. There was never no one takin' photographs or nuffing in the Retreat Rooms, no group stuff, nuffing like this. It was s'posed to be "spiritual", what you did in there,' she said, her mouth twisting. 'Jus' one man an' one woman. An' *that,*' she said, pointing at the picture of the small man being sodomised, 'was right out. My farver an' Mazu didn' like gays. They both 'ad a fing about it.'

'Can you identify any of the others? The smaller man?'

'Looks like Dopey Draper, poor sod,' said Abigail quietly. 'The girls, I dunno . . . s'pose that *could* be Cherie. She was blonde. An' the dark one, yeah, that could be Rosie whatever-'er-name-was. You didn't get many chubby girls at Chapman Farm.'

'Can you remember anyone having a Polaroid camera?' asked Strike, as Abigail pushed the phone back across the table to him.

'No, it weren't allowed. No phones or cameras, nuffin' like that.'

'The original Polaroids were found hidden in an old biscuit tin. Long shot, I know, but can you remember anybody at the farm having chocolate biscuits?'

''Ow d'you expec' me to remember chocolate biscuits, all this time after?'

'It'd be quite unusual to see biscuits at the farm, wouldn't it? With sugar being banned?'

'Yeah, but ... well, I s'pose someone in the farm'ouse could've 'ad 'em, 'idden ...'

'Going back to where your father was, when Daiyu disappeared: there was a man seen on the beach by witnesses, shortly before Cherie emerged from the sea: a jogger. He never came forward when the story of the drowning hit the press. It was dark, so the only description I've managed to get is that he was large. Did your father like jogging?'

'Wha'?' said Abigail, frowning again. 'You fink 'e pretended 'e was going to Birmingham, ordered Cherie to drown Daiyu, then gone jogging on the beach to check wevver she was doin' it?'

'No,' said Strike, smiling, 'but I wondered whether Cherie or anyone else at the farm ever mentioned the presence of the jogger on the beach when Daiyu disappeared.'

Abigail frowned at him for a moment, chewing her gum, then said,

'Why d'you keep doin' that?'

'Doing what?'

'Sayin' Daiyu "disappeared", not "drowned".'

'Well, her body was never found, was it?' said Strike.

She looked at him, her jaws still working on her gum. Then, unexpectedly, she slipped her hand into the pocket of her work trousers and pulled out her mobile.

'Not ordering a cab, are you?' said Strike, watching her type.

'No,' said Abigail, 'I'm tellin' Darryl I might be a bit late.'

130

*. . . flowing water, which is not afraid of any
dangerous place but plunges over cliffs and fills up the
pits that lie in its course . . .*

The I Ching or Book of Changes

Robin was standing very still in the dimly lit upper floor of
the temple. She'd been there for nearly five minutes. As far as
she could tell, the baby, which was now silent, had been crying
in a room at the very end of the corridor, which would look
onto Rupert Court. Shortly after the baby's wails had ceased,
she'd heard what she thought was a television being turned
on. Somebody was listening to a news report about the goings
on at Chapman Farm.

'. . . can see from the aerial picture, John, a forensic team is
at work inside a tent in the field behind the temple and other
buildings. As we reported earlier—'

'Sorry to interrupt you, Angela, but this just in: a statement
has been issued to the press on behalf of the head of the UHC,
Jonathan Wace, who's currently in Los Angeles.

'"Today, the Universal Humanitarian Church has been
subject to an unprecedented and unprovoked police action
which has caused alarm and distress to church members living
peacefully in our communities in the UK. The church denies
any and all criminal wrongdoing and strongly deplores the

tactics used by the police against unarmed, innocent people of faith. The UHC is currently taking legal advice to protect itself and its members from further violations of their right to religious freedom, as guaranteed by Article 18 of the UN Universal Declaration of Human Rights. There will be no further statement at this time.'"

As far as Robin could tell, the room with the television was the only one that was occupied. Its door stood ajar, and the light from the screen spilled out into the corridor. She began to move carefully towards it, the sound of her footsteps masked by the voice of the journalists.

'. . . started here in the UK, didn't it?'

'That's right, John, in the late eighties. Now, of course, it's spread to the Continent and North America . . .'

Robin had crept to the door of the inhabited room. Hidden in shadow, she peered through the gap.

The room would have been entirely dark but for the television and the moon-like lamp outside the window, which hung from the ceiling of Rupert Court. Robin could see the corner of what looked like a carry cot, in which the baby was presumably now lying, the end of a bed with a blue counterpane, a baby's bottle on the floor and the edge of what looked like a hastily packed holdall, from which some white fabric protruded. However, her attention was fixed upon a woman who was kneeling on the floor with her back to the door.

She had dark hair, tied back in a bun, and wore a sweatshirt and jeans. Her hands were busy with something. When Robin looked at the woman's reflection in the window, she saw that she had a book open in front of her and was rapidly counting out yarrow stalks. A white object hung on a black cord around her neck. Only when Robin focused on the reflected face did her heart begin to pound violently in her chest. With the familiar fear and repugnance she'd have felt on seeing a tarantula creeping across the floor, she recognised the long, pointed nose and dark, crooked eyes of Mazu Wace.

131

As water pours down from heaven, so fire flames up from the earth.

The I Ching or Book of Changes

The room had become steadily darker as Strike and Abigail talked. Now she got to her feet, flicked on a light, then returned to the detective and sat back down.

''Ow can she still be alive? That's crazy.'

'Just for the sake of argument,' said Strike, 'let's say your father and Mazu wanted to put Daiyu beyond the reach of the Graves family, to prevent them getting a DNA sample from her and proving she was Alexander's daughter, rather than your father's. Aside from the fact that Mazu wanted to keep her daughter, the quarter of a million would have reverted to the Graves' control if they got custody.

'What if your father and Mazu faked Daiyu's death, with Cherie as a willing accomplice? Let's say, instead of drowning, Daiyu was removed from the farm long enough to have credibly changed her appearance. She then came back three years later under a different name, as a child who'd supposedly gone to Birmingham to be trained up as a future church leader. Memories grow vague. Teeth can be fixed. Nobody's sure quite how old anyone is, in there. What if your father and Mazu passed Daiyu off as Becca Pirbright?'

ROBERT GALBRAITH

'Come off it,' said Abigail. ''Er sister an' bruvver would've known she wasn' Becca! 'Er *muvver* would've known! People don't change that much. They'd never 'ave got away wiv that!'

'You don't think people can be so brainwashed, they'll go along with what the church elders tell them? Even if the counter-evidence is staring them in the face?'

'It would've come out,' insisted Abigail. 'Daiyu would on'y've been – what? – ten when she got back? I'll tell you this for free: Daiyu would *never've* kept 'er mouth shut about 'oo she really was. Pretend to be some ordinary kid, instead of Papa J an' Mama Mazu's daughter? No way.'

'But that's the thing,' said Strike. 'Becca *wasn't* treated like an ordinary kid when she came back – far from it. She was fast-tracked to the heights of the church while the rest of her family were kept as dogsbodies at Chapman Farm. She's the youngest Principal the church has ever had. Your father's also made her a spirit wife.'

'Well, there you bloody are, then!' said Abigail. ''E'd be committing fuckin' *incest* if 'e—'

'Ah,' said Strike, 'but here's where it gets interesting. Becca seems to have become a spirit wife around the time your half-brother Taio started showing a sexual interest in her. Robin's also got it on good authority that Becca's still a virgin.

'Now,' said Strike, to the clearly incredulous Abigail, 'I don't know about you, but I don't buy the story that your father picked out Becca as a future church leader when she was only eleven, so four separate theories occur to me, to account for why she was treated so differently from everyone else.

'One reason could be that your father's a paedophile, and separating Becca from her family was his way of ensuring he could have sexual access to her.'

''E's not a paedo,' said Abigail. 'Not . . . not a proper one.'

'What d'you mean by that?'

1126

''E's not too fussy about age of consent, as long as they're – you know – well developed, like that Rosie. Long as they look like women. But not eleven-year-olds,' said Abigail, 'no way. Anyway, Becca wouldn't still be a virgin if 'e was fucking 'er, would she?'

'I agree,' said Strike. 'That explanation doesn't cut it for me, either. So if your father's interest in Becca wasn't sexual, we're left with three possibilities.

'Firstly: Becca's really Daiyu. That can only be proved, obviously, if we get a DNA sample from Mazu. But there are objections to that theory, as you point out.

'So we move on to the next possibility. Becca's not Daiyu, but she *is* your father's biological daughter, and with Daiyu gone, she was trained up to take her place.'

''Ang on,' said Abigail, scowling. 'No, 'ang on. Louise already 'ad kids, she brought 'em to the farm wiv 'er. Becca wasn' born there.'

'That doesn't necessarily mean she's not your half-sister. Nor, come to that, does Daiyu being born before you and your father went to live at the farm mean Daiyu wasn't his child, either. You told me last time we met that your father moved around a lot when your mother was alive, and he's done a lot of roaming around since going to live at the farm, as well. I think it's naive to imagine that the only place your father has sex with other women is at Chapman—'

'*Daiyu wasn' my fuckin' sister.* She was Graves an' Mazu's kid!'

'Look,' said Strike calmly. 'I know you want to believe your father sincerely loved your mother—'

'He fuckin' did, all righ'?' said Abigail, now growing pink again.

'—but even men who love their wives have been known to be unfaithful. Were you and your parents on holiday in Cromer when your mother died, or were you living in the vicinity?'

'Living,' said Abigail reluctantly.

'Don't you think it's possible your father and Mazu had already met, and started an affair, before your mother drowned? Isn't it plausible he took you off to live at Chapman Farm so he could be with his mistress and have both his kids under the same roof? He'd hardly admit as much to his grieving daughter, would he?'

Abigail's face had reddened. She looked angry.

'The same applies to Louise,' said Strike. 'He could have fathered all her kids, for all you know. Business trips, interviewing for jobs, delivering luxury cars, overnight stays in different cities . . . I know you'd rather think your father's promiscuity and infidelity started at Chapman Farm, but I'm trying to find out why Becca was singled out in a way no other eleven-year-old has been, before or since, and one very obvious explanation is that Jonathan Wace fathered her. He seems to value his own bloodline.'

'You could've fooled me,' snapped Abigail.

'When I say "value", I'm not suggesting this is a case of ordinary love. His aim seems to be to propagate the church with his own offspring. If one or two leave he probably thinks of it as a sustainable loss, given that the classroom at Chapman Farm is full of his descendants.

'But there's a simple way to prove all of this, or rule it out. I've got no authority to force DNA samples out of your father, Mazu or any of the Pirbrights, but if *you* were prepared—'

Abigail stood up abruptly, looking distressed, and walked out of the room.

Confident she'd return, Strike remained where he was. Taking out his phone, he checked for texts. One of them would have pleased him immensely, had he not read the second, and felt anger mixed with panic.

132

Water flows on uninterruptedly and reaches its goal:
The image of the Abysmal repeated.

The I Ching or Book of Changes

The television in the upstairs temple room was no longer showing footage of Jonathan Wace or Chapman Farm. Instead, the presenter and two guests were discussing the likelihood of Britain formally leaving the EU in early 2017. Mazu paused in her manipulation of the yarrow stalks to mute the television, then continued counting.

She soon finished. Robin watched Mazu's reflection stoop to make a last note on a piece of paper on the floor, then turn the pages of the I Ching to find the hexagram she'd made.

'Which one did you get?' said Robin loudly, stepping into the room.

Mazu jumped to her feet, her face ghastly white in the dim light cast by the television screen.

'How did you get in here?'

'I've gone pure spirit,' said Robin, her heart beating so fast, she might just have run a mile. 'The doors flew open for me, when I pointed at them.'

She was determined to seem unafraid, but it wasn't easy. Her rational self insisted that Mazu was ruined, her power gone, that she cut a pathetic figure in her baggy sweatshirt and her dirty jeans, yet some of the terror this woman had inculcated over months remained. Mazu stood before her as the demon of fairy tales, the witch in the gingerbread cottage, mistress of agony and death, and she stirred in Robin the shameful, primitive fears of childhood.

'So what's the I Ching telling you?' Robin said boldly.

To her disquiet, the familiar tight, false smile appeared on the woman's face. Mazu ought not to be able to smile at this moment; she should be cowed and terrified

'"*Tun/Retreat,*"' she said quietly. '"*The power of the dark is ascending.*" It was warning me you were walking up the stairs.'

'Funny,' said Robin, her heart still hammering. 'From where I'm standing, the power of the dark seems to be in freefall.'

As she said it, the light from the television momentarily brightened, and she saw the reason for Mazu's confidence. A rifle, hitherto in shadow, was leaning up against the wall just behind her, within easy reach.

Oh, shit.

Robin took a step forwards. She needed to get closer to Mazu than a rifle barrel's length, if she was to have any chance of not getting shot.

'If you make an act of penitence now, *Robin* –' This was the first time Mazu had ever used her real name, and Robin resented it, as though Mazu had somehow made it dirty, by having it in her mouth '– and as long as it's given in a true spirit of humility, I'll accept it.' The dark, crooked eyes glinted like onyx in the gloom of the room. 'I'd advise you to do so. Much worse will happen if you don't.'

'You want me to kiss your feet again?' said Robin, forcing herself to sound contemptuous rather than scared. 'Then what? You'll drop the child abuse charges?'

Mazu laughed. Robin had never heard her do so before,

even during the joyful meditation; a harsh caw erupted from her mouth, all pretence at refinement gone.

'You think that's the worst that can happen to you? *Daiyu will come for you.*'

'You're insane. *Literally* insane. *There is no Drowned Prophet.*'

'You'll find out your mistake,' said Mazu, smiling. 'She's never liked you, Robin. She knew all along what you were. Her vengeance will be—'

'Her vengeance will be non-existent, because she isn't real,' said Robin quietly. 'Your husband lied to you. Daiyu never drowned.'

The smile vanished from Mazu's face as though it had been slapped off. Robin was close enough now to smell the incense perfume that didn't mask her unwashed smell.

'Daiyu never went to the sea,' said Robin, advancing inch by inch. 'Never went to the beach. It was all bullshit. The reason her body never washed up is because it was never there.'

'You are filth,' breathed Mazu.

'Should've kept a closer eye on her, shouldn't you?' said Robin quietly. 'And I think you know that, deep down. You know you were a lousy mother to her.'

Mazu's face was so pale, it was impossible to know whether she'd lost colour, but the crooked eyes had narrowed as her thin chest rose and fell.

'I suppose that's why you wanted a real Chinese baby girl of your own, isn't it? To see whether you can do any better on a second att—?'

Mazu wheeled round and snatched up the gun, but Robin was ready: she seized Mazu around the neck from behind while trying to force her to drop the rifle, but it was like wrestling with an animal: Mazu had a brute strength that belied her age and size, and Robin felt as much revulsion as rage as they struggled, now terrified for the baby, in case the gun fired accidentally.

Mazu twisted one bare foot around Robin's leg and succeeded in toppling both of them, but Robin still had her in a tight grip, refusing to let her pull free or far enough away to shoot. With every ounce of her strength, Robin managed to flip the older woman over onto her back and straddled her as they both struggled for possession of the rifle. A torrent of filthy curses issued from Mazu's lips; Robin was a whore, trash, a demon, a slut, filth, shit—

Over the screams of Yixin, Robin heard her name shouted from somewhere inside the building.

'HERE!' she bellowed. 'MIDGE, I'M HERE!'

Mazu forced the rifle upwards, catching Robin on the chin, and Robin drove it back down, hard, on the woman's face.

'ROBIN?'

'HERE!'

The gun went off; the bullet shattered the window and blew out the lamp outside. Robin heard screams from Wardour Street; for a second time, she rammed the rifle down on Mazu's face, and as blood spurted from the woman's nose, Mazu's grip loosened and Robin succeeded in wrenching the gun from her grasp.

The door banged open as Mazu raised her hands to her bleeding nose.

'Jesus Christ!' shouted Midge.

Panting, Robin scrambled off Mazu, holding the rifle. Only now did she realise she was holding part of the black cord of Mazu's pendant in her hand. The mother-of-pearl fish lay broken on the floor.

Behind Midge, holding two Boots bags, was Becca Pirbright. Aghast, she looked from Mazu, whose hands were clasped to the nose Robin sincerely hoped she'd broken, to Robin, and back again.

'Violence, Mazu?' whispered Becca. 'In the temple?'

Robin, who was still holding the rifle, let out a genuine laugh. Becca stared at her.

'Can someone do something about that baby?' said Midge loudly.

'You do it,' Robin told Becca, pointing the rifle at her.

'You're threatening to shoot me?' said Becca, dropping the bags and moving to the carry cot. She scooped up the screaming Yixin and tried to soothe her, without much success.

'I'm calling 999,' said Midge, phone in hand.

'Not yet,' said Robin. 'Just cover the door.'

'Well, I'm telling Strike you're all right, at least,' said Midge, rapidly texting. 'He's *not* happy you came in here without back-up.'

Robin now looked Becca in the eye.

'It was you I came for.'

'What d'you mean, "came for"?' said Becca.

She spoke as though Robin was unspeakably impertinent. No matter that she'd interrupted attempted murder, or that press were swarming at the gates of Chapman Farm, or that police were raiding the church – Becca Pirbright remained what she'd always been: utterly convinced of her own rectitude, confident that everything, even this, could be put right by Papa J.

'You're already facing child abuse charges,' Becca said contemptuously, ineffectually trying to quell Yixin's screams by jiggling her. 'Now you're taking us hostage at gunpoint.'

'I don't think that's going to wash in court, coming from the person who colluded in covering up infanticide,' said Robin.

'You're unbalanced,' said Becca.

'You'd better hope psychiatrists find *you* are. Where were you for three years, after Daiyu died?'

'That's no business—'

'You weren't in Birmingham. You were either in the

Glasgow centre, or some rented property where Jonathan Wace could keep you well away from other people.'

Becca's smile was patronising.

'Rowena, you're an agent—'

'It's Robin, but you're damn right, I'm your adversary. Do *you* want to tell Mazu why you're the only virgin spirit wife, or shall I?'

133

Nine at the top means . . .
One sees one's companion as a pig covered with dirt,
As a wagon full of devils.

The I Ching or Book of Changes

The door behind Strike banged open again. Abigail, now divested of her fireman's apparel and wearing jeans, marched towards him with a leather bag slung over her shoulder, grabbed her vacated chair, dragged it into the centre of the room, then clambered up onto it. Tall as she was, she had no difficulty in reaching the smoke alarm in the middle of the ceiling. With one twist, she'd taken off the lid and pulled out its batteries. Having replaced the lid, she jumped down off the chair and rejoined Strike at the table, pulling a pack of Marlboro Golds out of her bag. She sat down and lit one with a Zippo.

'Is that allowed, in a fire station?' he asked.

'I don't fuckin' care,' said Abigail, inhaling. 'All right,' she said, blowing smoke sideways, 'you can 'ave DNA, if you want, an' compare it to this Becca's, but if she's still in the church, I don' see 'ow you're gonna get it.'

'My partner's working on that right now,' said Strike.

'I was finkin', upstairs.'

'Go on,' said Strike.

'What you jus' said, about all what Daiyu was gonna get, from Graves' will. That 'ouse. You said it was worf millions.'

'Yeah, it must be,' said Strike.

'Then the Graves lot 'ad a motive to get rid of 'er. Stop 'er gettin' the 'ouse.'

'Interesting you should say that,' said Strike, 'because that thought occurred to me, too. Daiyu's aunt and uncle, who'll inherit if Daiyu's dead, have been doing their best to stop me investigating her disappearance. I went to see them in Norfolk the other day. It wasn't a happy interview, especially after I told Phillipa I'd seen her at your father's Olympia meeting.'

'The fuck was she doing there?'

'Something had clearly rattled her enough to make her desperate to speak to your father. Phillipa left a note for him, backstage at Olympia. I asked whether they'd received an unexpected, anonymous phone call recently, which spurred her into action.'

'Wha' made you ask that?'

'Call it intuition.'

Abigail flicked ash onto the floor and kicked it away with her foot.

'You'd get on wiv Mazu.' She affected a malignant whisper. *"The divine vibration moves in me."* What was this phone call about?'

'They didn't want to tell me, but when I suggested that someone had called to say Daiyu's still alive, Phillipa gave herself away. Turned white. You can see how a phone call like that would put the fear of God into them. No more family mansion for *them,* if Daiyu's still breathing.

'And I have to say,' added Strike, 'Nicholas Delaunay ticks quite a few boxes for me, as Kevin Pirbright's killer. Ex-marine. Knows how to handle a gun, knows how to plan and execute an ambush. The person who murdered Kevin was pretty slick.'

Abigail took another drag on her cigarette, frowning.

'I'm lost.'

'I think Kevin Pirbright worked out the truth behind Daiyu's disappearance before he died, and that's why he was shot.'

Abigail lowered her cigarette.

''E knew?'

'Yeah, I think so.'

''E never said nuffing to *me* about Daiyu.'

'He didn't mention it being an odd coincidence, Daiyu dying exactly where your mother did?'

'Oh,' said Abigail. 'Yeah. 'E *did* say somefing abou' that.'

'Possibly Kevin only put it all together after he'd approached you,' said Strike.

'So 'oo called these Delaunay people?'

'Well, that's the question, isn't it? I suspect it was the same person who called Jordan Reaney to find out what he might have let slip to me, and who called Carrie Curtis Woods, and tipped her into suicide.'

Strike's mobile buzzed, not once, but twice, in quick succession.

'Excuse me,' he said. 'Been waiting for this.'

The first text was from Barclay, but he ignored it in favour of Midge's.

Robin safe. Got Becca and Mazoo shut in temple.

Immensely relieved, Strike opened Barclay's message, which comprised two words.

Got everything.

Strike sent two texts of his own back, returned his mobile to his pocket, then looked again at Abigail.

'I said there were four possibilities, to explain Becca's strange status in the church.'

'Listen,' said Abigail impatiently, 'I'm sorry, but I told Darryl I was gonna be late, not that I was never gonna turn up.'

'Is Darryl the tall, good-looking black guy with green eyes? Because I know he wasn't the fat guy driving the red Corsa. That was your lodger, Patrick.'

The pupils of Abigail's dark blue eyes enlarged suddenly, so that they became as opaque as Strike had seen her father's.

'I had to keep you talking,' said Strike, 'because there were things that needed doing while you were well out of the way.'

He paused to let her speak, but she said nothing, so he continued,

'Would you like to hear some of the questions I've been pondering, about Daiyu's drowning in the North Sea?'

'Tell me what you like,' said Abigail. She was striving to look unconcerned, but the hand holding her cigarette had begun to shake.

'I started small,' said Strike, 'by wondering why she'd drowned exactly where your mother did, but the deeper into the investigation I got, the more unexplained things started cropping up. Who was buying Daiyu toys and sweets in her last few months at the farm? Why was she wearing a white dress rather than a tracksuit when last seen alive? Why did Carrie strip to her underwear, if they were only going in for a paddle? Why did Carrie run off to poke at something at the water's edge, right before the police arrived? Who was the second adult, who was supposed to be in the dormitory the night Carrie helped Daiyu out of the window? Why did your father spirit Becca Pirbright away from the farm, after Daiyu vanished?'

Abigail, who'd already ground out her first cigarette under her heel, now took out a second. Having lit it, she blew smoke into Strike's face. Far from resenting this, Strike took the opportunity to breathe in some nicotine.

'Then I started thinking hard about Kevin Pirbright's death. Who gouged some of the writing out of his bedroom wall, leaving only the word "pigs", and who stole his laptop? Who was Kevin talking about, when he told an undercover detective he was going to meet a bully and "have things out" with them? What exactly did Kevin know – what had he pieced together – such that he deserved a bullet through the brain?

'Now all of those things, separately, might have explanations. A junkie could've stolen his laptop. The kids in the dorm might've simply forgotten the second person in charge the last night Daiyu was seen there. But added together, there seemed to be a hell of a lot of unexplained occurrences.'

'If you say so,' said Abigail, but her hand was still shaking. 'But—'

'I haven't finished. There was also the question of those phone calls. Who called Carrie Curtis Woods, before my partner and I visited her? Whom did she call back, after we'd left? Who phoned Jordan Reaney, from a call box in Norfolk to throw suspicion on the church, and put him in such a state of fear and alarm he tried to overdose? Who were those two people terrified of, and what had that person threatened them with, that made them both decide they'd rather die than face it? And who called the Delaunays, trying to make them scared Daiyu was still alive, to throw a red herring in my path, and make them even more obstructive?'

Abigail blew smoke towards the ceiling and said nothing.

'I also wanted to know why there's a circle of wooden posts in the woods at Chapman Farm that someone once tried to destroy, why there's an axe hidden in a nearby tree, and why, close by the destroyed ring, somebody once tried to burn some rope.'

Abigail gave a little convulsive jerk at the word 'rope', but still said nothing.

'Maybe you'll find this more interesting with visual aids,' said Strike.

Once again, he brought up the pictures of the Polaroids on the phone.

'That's not Joe Jackson,' he said, pointing. 'That's Jordan Reaney. That,' he said, pointing at the blonde, 'is Carrie Curtis Woods, *that's* Paul Draper, but *that*,' he pointed at the chubby dark girl, 'isn't Rosie Fernsby. That's *you*.'

The door behind Strike opened. A bearded man appeared, but Abigail shouted *'Fuck off!'* and he withdrew precipitately.

'Military-level discipline,' said Strike approvingly. 'Well, you learned from the best.'

Abigail's irises were now two near-black discs.

'Now,' said Strike, 'you *had* to identify the tall guy and the dark girl as Joe Jackson and Rosie, because Carrie had already pulled those names out of her arse when she was panicking. None of you realised any of those Polaroids were still hanging around, and none of you expected me to have them.

'For a frankly embarrassing length of time, I kept asking myself who took those pictures. Not everyone in them looks happy, do they? It looked as though this had been done for punishment, or in service of some sadist's kink. But finally, I saw what should've been obvious: there are never all four of you in one shot. You were all taking pictures of each other.

'A little secret society of four. I don't know whether you enjoyed sticking two fingers up at the spirit bonding nonsense, or liked fucking for the fun of it, or were just passing on the lessons you'd learned from Mazu and your father, about the pleasures of compelling other people to participate in ritual humiliation and submission.'

'You're fucking cracked,' said Abigail.

'We'll see,' said Strike calmly, before holding up the picture of Draper being sodomised by Reaney. 'The masks are a nice touch. Extra level of degradation, and also a bit of plausible deniability – you'll have learned the value of that from your father. I note that you come out of this particular sex session pretty well. Fairly straightforward sex and a bit of vanity posing with your legs open. Nobody's forcibly sodomising *you*.'

Abigail merely took another drag on her cigarette.

'Having realised that you were taking pictures of each other, the obvious question is, why were the other three participating in what doesn't seem to have been completely pleasurable for them? And the obvious answer is: you had all the power. You were Jonathan Wace's daughter. Because I don't buy the Cinderella crap you've been feeding me, Abigail. I'm sure Mazu disliked you – stepdaughter, stepmother, that's hardly uncommon – but I think, as Papa J's firstborn, you had a lot of leeway, a lot of freedom. You didn't get to be that weight on the usual diet at Chapman Farm.'

'That's not me,' said Abigail.

'Oh, I'm not saying I can *prove* this girl's you,' said Strike. 'But Rosie Fernsby's very clear it's not *her*. You tried to stop us talking to her, not because she was in these pictures, but because she wasn't. And she remembers you clearly. She says you threw your weight around a lot – "porky" was how she described you, by strange coincidence. Naturally, she'd have been especially interested in you, because you were the daughter of the much older man she'd convinced herself she was in love with.

'It was pretty stupid of you to tell me Mazu made people wear masks while crawling around on the ground. Obviously I understand where you got the idea, and that you were trying to add a nice flourish to your depiction of her as a sociopath, but nobody else has mentioned pig masks used in the context of punishment. It's important not to use incriminating things in their wrong context, even in service of a cover story. Many a liar slips up that way. Signposts to things you might not want looked at.'

He paused again. Abigail remained silent.

'So,' said Strike, 'there you are at Chapman Farm, throwing your weight around, with three vulnerable people at your beck and call: a juvenile criminal who's hiding from the police, a boy who was mentally sub-par even before you helped kick the shit out of him, and a runaway girl who was never going to trouble Mensa.

'As Papa J's entitled firstborn, you were allowed out of the farm to buy things: chocolate, little toys, a Polaroid camera, pig masks – biscuits, if you fancied them. You could pick and choose, within the constraints of Mazu's iron regime, which was probably more stringent when your father wasn't around, what jobs you preferred. You might not have had the option to lie in bed all day eating biscuits, but you could decide whether – to take a random example – you wanted to share childcare duty overnight with Carrie, and who you wanted on early duty with you, in the morning.'

'All of this,' said Abigail, 'is specker – specla—'

'Speculation. You'll have a lot of time on your hands in prison, serving life. You could do some Open Univ—'

'Fuck you.'

'You're right, of course, this is all speculation,' said Strike. 'Until, that is, Jordan Reaney realises he's up to his neck in the shit and starts talking. Until other people who remember you at Chapman Farm in the eighties and nineties come crawling out of the woodwork.

'I think you and Daiyu were *both* spoiled and neglected at Chapman Farm, with a couple of important differences. Mazu genuinely detested you, and abused you during your father's absences. You were grieving the loss of your mother. You were also obsessively envious of the attention your only remaining parent showed towards your bratty stepsister. You wanted to be Popsicle's pet again and you didn't like him cooing over Daiyu – or, more accurately, the money she was worth. You wanted retribution.'

Abigail continued to smoke in silence.

'Of course,' said Strike, 'the problem you had inside Chapman Farm – as, indeed, you've had outside it – is that you couldn't pick the people who were best for the job, you had to take what you could get, which meant your obedient pig-mask lackeys.

'Daiyu had to be lulled into a false sense of security, and kept quiet while it was happening. Bribes of toys and sweets, secret games with the big kids: she didn't want the treats or the attention to dry up, so she didn't tell Mazu or your father what was going on. That was a kid who was starved of proper attention. Maybe she wondered why her big sister—'

'*She wasn't my fuckin' sister!*'

'—was suddenly being so nice to her,' Strike continued, unperturbed, 'but she didn't question it. Well, she was seven years old. Why would she?

'Reaney supposedly oversleeping the morning Daiyu disappeared smacked of collusion the moment I heard about it – collusion with Carrie, at the very least. You bought soporific cough medicine or similar, in sufficient quantities to drug the rest of the kids, on one of your trips outside the farm. You volunteered yourself and Carrie for dormitory duty, but you never showed up. You were waiting outside the window, for Carrie to pass Daiyu out to you.'

Abigail had begun to shake again. Her handsome head trembled. She tried to light a fresh cigarette from the stub of the old one, but had to give up, resorting to the Zippo again.

'The idea of the faked drowning is obviously to provide

a cast iron alibi for the murderer – or murderers, plural. Did you or Reaney actually do the deed? You'd have needed two people, I expect, to stop her screaming and finish her off. Then, of course, you needed to dispose of the body.

'Paul Draper got in trouble for letting the pigs out, but that wasn't an accident, it was part of the plan. Some of those pigs were smuggled out into the woods and put into a pen constructed of posts and rope. My partner informs me pigs can be pretty vicious. I'd imagine it took all four of you to get them where you wanted them, or did Dopey have particular pig expertise you called into service?'

Abigail didn't answer, but continued to smoke.

'So you'd corralled the pigs in the woods . . . and someone, of course, had got hold of a hatchet.

'What did Daiyu think was going to happen, once you'd led her off into the trees, in the dark? Midnight feast? Nice new game you had for her? Were you holding her hand? Was she excited?'

Abigail was now shaking uncontrollably. She moved the cigarette to her lips, but missed the first time. Her eyes were jet black.

'When did she realise it wasn't a game?' said Strike. 'When you pinned her arms to her sides so Reaney could throttle her? I don't think the hatchet can have come into play until she was dead. You couldn't risk screams. It's very quiet at Chapman Farm at night.

'Have you ever heard of Constance Kent?' Strike asked her.

Abigail merely stared at him, trembling.

'She was sixteen when she stabbed her three-year-old half-brother to death. Jealous of her father preferring him to her. It happened in the 1860s. She served twenty years, then got out, went to Australia and became a nurse. Is that what the firefighter stuff was about? Trying to atone? Because I don't think you're completely conscience-free, are you? Not if you're still having nightmares about hacking Daiyu to pieces so the pigs could eat her more easily. You told me you "hate it when there's kids involved". I'll bet you do. I'll bet it brings back worse bloody memories than *Pirates of the Caribbean.*'

Abigail was white. Her eyes, like her father's, had become as black and empty as boreholes.

'I give you credit for the lie you told Patrick after he heard you screaming in your sleep, but once again, your lie gives something away. A whip, used on Jordan Reaney. You remembered that, and you associated it with Daiyu's death. Was he whipped because he should have been supervising Draper? Or because he'd failed to find the lost pigs?'

Abigail now dropped her gaze to the table top, rather than look at Strike.

'So: Daiyu's dead, you've left Reaney to clean up the last of the mess, with instructions to set the pigs free once they've eaten the body parts, and to destroy the makeshift pen. You hurry off for early duty. You'd picked your companions for that morning carefully, hadn't you? Two men who'd be exceptionally easy to manipulate. "Did you see that, Brian? Did you see it, Paul? Carrie was driving Daiyu! Did you see her wave at us?" Because, obviously,' said Strike, 'the thing in the passenger seat – which had to be wearing the white dress, because Daiyu had worn her tracksuit into the woods – couldn't have waved, could it?'

Abigail said nothing, but continued to smoke, her fingers trembling.

'It took me far longer than it should have done to realise what was in that van with Carrie,' Strike went on. 'Especially as Kevin Pirbright had written it on his bedroom wall. *Straw.* All those straw figures, made annually for the Manifestation of the Stolen Prophet. If Jonathan Wace's daughter wants to have some fun crafting with straw in a barn, who's going to stop her? Wouldn't have taken nearly as long to construct a miniature version, would it?

'Carrie's careful to let herself be seen in Cromer, carrying the figure in the white dress down towards the water in the dark, because it's important to establish that she and Daiyu actually went to the beach. I interviewed the Heatons, the couple Carrie met on the beach, after she came back out of the water. They bought the whole thing, they never suspected there was no child; they saw the shoes and the dress and believed Carrie – although Mrs Heaton had her doubts about whether Carrie was genuinely distressed. She mentioned a bit of nervous giggling.

'I didn't twig about the straw figure when Mr Heaton told me the van was covered in "muck and straw". Didn't even catch on when his wife told me Carrie had run off to poke at something – seaweed, she thought – when the police turned up. Of course, the sun would've been coming up by then. Bit weird, for a clump of wet straw to be lying on the beach. Carrie would have wanted to break that up and throw it back into the sea.

'Ever since the Heatons told me she was a champion swimmer, though, I've wondered whether that was relevant to the plan. It was, of course. You'd need to be a powerful swimmer to get right out into deep water, deep enough to make sure you weren't going to send all that straw straight back to the beach, keep your head above water while you untied it, and stay afloat while you broke it all apart. Genius plan, really, and a very accomplished bit of business from Carrie.'

Abigail continued to stare at the table, her cigarette-holding hand still shaking.

'But there were a few slip-ups along the way,' said Strike. 'Bound to be, with a plan that complicated – which leads us right back to Becca Pirbright.

'Why, when Becca's sister told her she'd seen Daiyu climbing out of the window, did Becca come up with a cock and bull story about invisibility? Why, when Becca's brother said he'd seen you trying to burn something in the woods – I presume Reaney didn't do the job of destroying the pig pen thoroughly enough, and you wanted to finish the job, even if it was raining – did Becca insist he shouldn't snitch? Why was Becca helping you cover everything up? What could have convinced an eleven-year-old to keep quiet, and keep others quiet, when she could have run straight to your father and Mazu with these odd stories, and gained their approval?'

Abigail now raised her eyes to look at Strike, and he thought she wanted to hear the answer, because she didn't know it herself.

'If ever anyone manages to de-programme Becca, which might be impossible by now, I think she'll tell quite a strange story.

'I don't think Becca's first impulse, on hearing what her brother and sister had witnessed, would have been to go to her own mother, or to the church Principals. I think she'd have gone straight to Carrie, who she seems to have worshipped as the only mother figure she'd ever really known. Becca's sister told my partner that Becca would have done literally anything for Carrie.

'I think Carrie panicked when she heard there were witnesses to Daiyu going out of the window and you burning rope in the woods. She'd gone along with the fake drowning because she was terrified of you, but I think she hoped, even while she was enacting the plan, that the thing wasn't really going to come off. She might have hoped you'd set her up for a practical joke, or that you'd get cold feet when it came to actually killing your stepsister in the woods.

'I think, when Becca kept going to Carrie with odd little

bits of information she'd gleaned from her siblings, and maybe strange happenings and behaviours she'd picked up on herself, Carrie panicked. She knew this clever little girl must be shut down and persuaded that every anomaly, every inexplicable event, has an explanation – an explanation that must be kept secret, because she was worried that if you found out Becca knew a bit too much, she'd be the next child to get chopped to bits in the woods.

'Now, what do we know about Carrie?' said Strike. 'Good swimmer, obviously. Runaway. Has been indoctrinated for the previous two years in all the mystic crap at Chapman Farm. Loves kids, and is loved back.

'I think she cobbled together some story about Daiyu's spiritual destiny to explain anything weird Becca and her siblings might have noticed. I think she fed Becca a line about Daiyu not being really dead, that the things she or her siblings had witnessed had mystic explanations. She encouraged Becca to come to her with anything else she'd heard or noticed, so Carrie could tie them in with her nonsense story about dematerialisation and resurrection, in which she'd played her own pre-ordained part, and I think she told Becca all of this was going to be their special secret, as the Blessed Divinity wanted.

'And Becca bought all of it. She kept silent when Carrie told her to, she shut her siblings down, she gave them pseudo-mystical explanations, or told them off for being grasses. Which means, ironically, that the myth of the Drowned Prophet began, not with your father or Mazu, but out of a teenager's imagination, in service of covering up a murder and silencing a kid who was a danger to all of you.

'And after the inquest was over, Carrie did a flit, changed her name and tried to forget what she'd colluded in and tried to cover up. I suspect it was at *that* point that the heartbroken Becca went to your father and told him the whole story. If

I had to guess,' said Strike, watching Abigail closely for her reaction, 'your father took you aside at some point, probably after he'd talked to Becca.'

Abigail's lips twitched, but she remained silent.

'Your father must've known you should've been in the dormitory that night, and he definitely knew you were on early duty that day and saw the truck pass. He might've asked what you were burning in the woods. He'll have already noted the strange coincidence of Daiyu dying exactly where his first wife did, as though someone was trying to rub his face in it, or even cast suspicion on him. Because he should've been on his way to Birmingham with a fifteen-year-old girl when Daiyu "drowned", shouldn't he? Whether the police brought him in for questioning about taking an underage girl he'd only known a week on a road trip, or about infanticide, it wouldn't look very good for a church leader, would it?

'No, I think your father suspected or guessed that you were behind Daiyu's disappearance, but being who he is – an amoral narcissist – all he really cared about was hushing it up. He'd just been handed the story of Daiyu ascending to heaven through the divine vessel of Carrie Gittins and he definitely didn't want his daughter banged up on suspicion of murder – very bad for business. Much better to accept the supernatural explanation, to comfort his distraught wife with this mystic bullshit. Bereaved people will clutch at that kind of stuff, or there wouldn't be any bloody mediums. So your father strings Becca along; he says, yes, he knew all along Carrie wasn't a bad person, that she was merely helping Daiyu fulfil her destiny, and how clever of Becca, for seeing the truth.

'Then he, too, does a bit of expert grooming. Perhaps he told Becca that it had been foreseen that she would come to him as a divine messenger. Maybe he told her the spirit of the prophet lived on in her. He flattered her and groomed her exactly as you groomed Daiyu – but without the ending of the pigs and the axe, in the woods at night.

'You were shunted off to Birmingham to keep you out of sight and out of trouble, and Becca was secreted somewhere safe, somewhere you couldn't get at her, where your father indoctrinated her so thoroughly into obedience and chastity and unquestioning loyalty that she's become a very useful tool for the church. I think she's been kept in a state of virginity for no other reason than that Wace doesn't want her getting too close to anyone but him, and also because she's the one woman he doesn't want Mazu getting jealous of – because Becca's the keeper of the biggest secrets. Becca's the one who could testify that the supernatural explanation for Daiyu's disappearance came from Carrie, not your father, and she could also tell a story of how expertly Wace fed her vanity, to keep her from ever talking. From what Robin found out at Chapman Farm, Becca might well have moments of lucidity, but it doesn't seem to overly trouble her. I don't think there's a more committed believer in the UHC than Becca Pirbright.'

Strike now sat back in his chair, watching Abigail, who now looked back at him with a strange, calculating expression on her pale face.

'Are you about to say that's all speculation, too?' asked Strike.

'Well, it is,' said Abigail, her voice slightly hoarse, but defiant, nonetheless.

She dropped her third cigarette to the ground and lit a fourth.

'Well, then, let's move on to more provable matters,' said Strike. 'Kevin Pirbright, shot through the head a few days after he told someone he was going to meet the bully from the church. A Beretta 9000 firing bullets at my car. A balaclavaed figure, padded out in a man's black jacket, trying to smash its way into my office with the butt of a gun. Those phone calls, and the resultant suicide attempts. A phone call made to the Delaunays from the same mobile used in the call to Carrie, telling them Daiyu's still alive, trying to drag them into the frame of suspicion and to derail my investigation.

'My conclusions are as follows,' said Strike. 'The person behind all of this has access to a motley selection of men to do her bidding. She's either sleeping with them, or stringing them along so they think she will. I doubt any of them know what they're doing it for: possibly I'm a jealous ex-boyfriend who needs watching. They can't keep my agency under surveillance all the time, and nor can the woman giving the orders, because they've all got jobs.

'I further conclude that the person directing operations is themselves fit, strong and addicted to adrenalin – the escape from Kevin Pirbright's bedsit, the attempted break-in of my office, the tailing of my BMW by the blue Ford Focus, the shooting. That person is more efficient than any of her under-lings and doesn't mind narrow escapes.

'I think this person is clever and capable of hard work when it's in her interests. She kept tabs on Paul Draper, Carrie Curtis Woods and Jordan Reaney – although possibly me telling you Reaney was in the nick put you onto his current whereabouts.

'But I don't think Reaney told you about the Polaroids. I thought he must have done, initially, but I was wrong. Reaney knew he'd fucked up, though. His reaction had told me those Polaroids were even more significant than they looked. You threatened to turn him in for Daiyu's murder if anything he'd said or done led to you, and he panicked, and overdosed. Reaney's got more of a conscience than you'd think from his CV. Like you, he still has nightmares about chopping up that child and feeding her to the pigs in the dark.

'The reason I know Reaney didn't tell you about the pictures is Carrie wasn't expecting them. The killer hadn't been able to forewarn her, which meant she had to come up with a story on the spot. She knew she mustn't identify you or Reaney, the two killers, so she pulled two names out of thin air. I note, too, that it was only after Carrie blabbed to you about the Polaroids that the masked gunman turned up at my office and tried to break in. You weren't after the UHC file. You were after the pictures. Trouble is, in tracing Carrie, you missed a boyfriend and a name change between Chapman Farm and Thornbury. Isaac Mills is still with us, and he's prepared to testify about what Carrie confessed to him when drunk.'

A sneer twisted Abigail's mouth again.

'It's all hearsay an' specker—'

'Speculation? You really think so?'

'You've got fuck all. It's all fuckin' fantasy.'

'I've got the axe Jordan Reaney hid in a tree, an axe that's been the subject of a lot of rumours among the kids at Chapman Farm. Your half-brother thought it had something to do with Daiyu. What had he overheard, that made him think that? Forensics have moved on a lot since the mid-nineties. It won't be hard to pick up even a speck of human blood on that axe. I've also got a sample of earth from the middle of those broken posts. All a lab will need is a few bone fragments, even very small ones, and Mazu's DNA will confirm their identity.

'Now, you might well say, "even if Daiyu was murdered in the woods, how d'you prove it was me?" Well, one of my detectives has been at your flat with your lodger tonight. You'd have done better to kick Patrick out when you said you would. A useful dogsbody, I'm sure, but thick and mouthy. My detective found Kevin Pirbright's laptop hidden inside a chair cushion in your bedroom. He found the bulky black men's jacket you borrowed from Patrick to murder Kevin Pirbright and to try and break into my office. Most importantly, he's found a Beretta 9000 stinking of smoke, sewn up inside a cushion on your bed. Strange, the things a firefighter might find in a burning flat, when they've finished dragging junkies out of harm's way.'

Abigail's mouth opened, but no sound came out. She remained frozen, with the cigarette between her fingers, as Strike heard a car pulling up outside the fire station and watched the driver get out. Evidently, Robin had acted on his instructions.

'This,' he said, turning back to Abigail, 'is Detective Inspector Ryan Murphy of the Metropolitan Police. I wouldn't make too much trouble when he arrests you. He was supposed to be having dinner with his girlfriend tonight, so he'll be in a bad mood already.'

EPILOGUE

T'ai/Peace

No plain not followed by a slope.
No going not followed by a return.
He who remains persevering in danger
Is without blame.
Do not complain about this truth;
Enjoy the good fortune you still possess.

The I Ching or Book of Changes

134

Evil can indeed be held in check but not permanently abolished. It always returns. This conviction might induce melancholy, but it should not; it ought only to keep us from falling into illusion when good fortune comes to us.

The I Ching or Book of Changes

The long lawn sloping down to the Thames behind Sir Colin Edensor's house had gained a number of brightly coloured objects since the last time Strike and Robin had seen it. There was a red and yellow car large enough for a small child to sit in and propel themselves along with their feet, a miniature goalpost, a blow-up paddling pool decorated with tropical fish and a quantity of smaller objects, one of which was a battery-powered bubble machine. It was this that was attracting the delighted attention of the white-haired toddler who was now answering to the name Sally rather than Qing, and two dark-haired little boys of around the same age. Their shrieks, shouts and laughter carried into the kitchen as they attempted to catch and pop the stream of bubbles issuing from the purple box on the grass.

Four adults were supervising the toddlers, to make sure they didn't stray too close to the river at the foot of the garden: James and Will Edensor, James' wife Kate and Lin Doherty.

Inside the kitchen, watching the group on the lawn, sat Sir Colin Edensor, Strike, Robin, Pat and her husband Dennis.

'I can never,' said Sir Colin, for the third time, 'thank you enough. Any of you,' he added, including the Chaunceys in his glance around the table.

'Nice to see them getting on,' said Pat in her baritone, watching the re-christened Qing chasing bubbles.

'What happened when James and Will met for the first time?' asked Robin, who didn't want to seem too nosy, but was very interested in the answer.

'Well, James shouted a lot,' said Sir Colin, smiling. 'Told Will what he thought of him, in about fifteen different ways. Funnily enough, I think Will actually welcomed it.'

Robin wasn't surprised. Will Edensor had wanted to atone for his sins, and with immunity from prosecution guaranteed, and the Drowned Prophet proven to be a mirage, where else was he to get the punishment he craved, but from his older brother?

'He agreed with every word James said. He cried about his mother, said he knew nothing could ever make right what he'd done, said James was justified in hating him, that he understood if James never wanted to have anything to do with him again. That rather took the wind out of James's sails,' said Sir Colin.

'And they're going to live here with you?' asked Strike.

'Yes, at least until we can sort out proper accommodation for Lin and little Sally. With the press milling around and so on, I think it's best they're here.'

'She'll need support,' croaked Pat. 'She's never been in charge of the kid all by herself. Never run her own house. Sixteen, it's a lot of responsibility. If you found her something round my way, I could keep an eye on 'em. My daughter and granddaughters would muck in. She needs other mothers round her, teach her the ropes. Get together and moan about the kids. That's what she needs.'

'You've done so much already, Mrs Chauncey,' said Sir Colin.

'I was her age, near enough, when I had my first,' said Pat unemotionally. 'I know what it takes. Anyway,' she took a drag on her e-cigarette, 'I like 'em. You brought Will up very well. Good manners.'

'Yeah, he's a nice lad,' said Dennis. 'We all did stupid things when we were young, didn't we?'

Sir Colin now took his eyes off the group on the lawn to turn to Robin.

'I see they've found more bodies at Chapman Farm.'

'I think they're going to be finding them for weeks to come,' said Robin.

'And *none* of the deaths were registered?'

'None except the prophets'.'

'You don't want coroners involved, if you've been refusing people medical help,' said Strike. 'Our police contact says they've got three skeletons of babies, presumably stillbirths, out of the field so far. There'll probably be more. They've been on that land since the eighties.'

'I doubt they'll be able to identify all the remains,' said Robin. 'They were recruiting runaways and the homeless as well as wealthy people. It's going to be a big job tracing all the babies who were sold, as well.'

'It beggars belief that they got away with it for so long,' said Sir Colin.

'"Live and let live", isn't it?' said Strike. 'If nobody wants to speak out, and with the charity work there as a smokescreen, plus all the useful celebrity idiots . . .'

The previous fortnight had seen a multitude of front pages devoted to the UHC in both broadsheets and tabloids. Fergus

Robertson was busy morning and night, sharing inside details nobody else knew. It was he who'd ambushed an outraged Giles Harmon outside his house in Bloomsbury, he who'd first broken the news of the alleged child trafficking and he who'd doorstepped the MP who was a church Principal, who'd been suspended by his party pending investigations into substantial undeclared donations he'd received from the UHC. The packaging multimillionaire, too foolish to have hidden behind his lawyers, had made several injudicious and unintentionally incriminating comments to the press jostling outside his offices. Mazu, Taio, Jiang and Joe Jackson were in custody. Dr Andy Zhou's arrest had caused a flurry of statements from wealthy women who'd been cupped and hypnotised, massaged and detoxified, all of whom refused to believe the handsome doctor could have done anything wrong. A carefully phrased statement had also been issued by Noli Seymour's agent, expressing shock and horror at the findings at Chapman Farm, of which Noli had naturally had no suspicion.

Jonathan Wace had been arrested while trying to drive over the border into Mexico. He was smiling in the gentle, self-deprecating way Robin knew so well in the photograph that showed him handcuffed and being led away. *Father, forgive them; for they know not what they do.*

The temple at Chapman Farm had been thoroughly searched by police, and the means by which illusions had been conducted had been leaked to journalists, along with photographs of whips and the box. The various bodily fluids that lingered in the mattresses and bedding of the Retreat Rooms were being tested and the Chapman Farm woods were cordoned off. The axe and soil Midge had stolen had been handed to the police, and Wardle had called Strike with the news that the thigh bone of a young child had been dug up close to the rotting wooden posts. Evidently the pigs hadn't managed to consume all of Daiyu Wace before Jordan Reaney had to get back to bed, and Abigail Wace reach the yard in time to watch the truck bearing the straw figure pass, in the dark.

Meanwhile ex-church members were coming forward in increasing numbers. Guilt and shame had kept them silent, sometimes for decades, but reassured by the possibility of immunity from prosecution for their own coerced actions, which ranged from administering beatings and helping bury bodies illegally to failing to secure medical assistance for a fourteen-year-old who'd died in childbirth, they were now ready to find catharsis in testifying against the Waces.

But there were still those who saw no evil in anything that had been done. Danny Brockles, the ex-addict who'd travelled the country with Jonathan Wace to extol the merits of the church, had been interviewed. All evidence of wrongdoing, he said, sobbing, had been planted by the agents of the Adversary. The public needed to understand that satanic forces were behind this attempt to destroy Papa J and the church (but the public seemed to understand no such thing, judging by the angry and indignant comments posted online beneath every article on the UHC). And Becca Pirbright, who remained at liberty, had twice appeared on television, composed and personable, calm and charming, disdainful of what she termed lurid, scaremongering and sensational reporting, denying all personal wrongdoing and describing Jonathan and Mazu Wace as two of the best human beings she'd ever known in her life.

Robin, watching Becca at home, found herself again thinking of the church as a virus. She was certain many, if not most, members would be cured by this eruption of revelations, by the evidence that they'd been thoroughly hoodwinked, that Papa J was no hero, but a conman, a rapist and an accessory to murder. Yet so many lives had been destroyed . . . Robin had heard that Louise Pirbright had tried to hang herself in the hospital to which she'd been taken upon release. Robin could quite see why Louise preferred death than to have to live with the knowledge that her foolish decision to follow Jonathan Wace into his cult twenty-four years previously had led to the death of two of her sons, and total estrangement from both of her daughters. Emily, who'd been found unconscious in the box when police entered the farm, had been sent to the same hospital as Louise, but when offered a meeting with her mother by well-intentioned medics, had informed them she never wanted to see Louise again.

Murphy was inclined to be triumphalist about the church's demise, but Robin found it hard to celebrate. Murphy and Strike kept telling her that the child abuse accusations against her would be dropped any day now, but she'd had no word to that effect. Even worse than her personal fear of prosecution was her dread of the church reforming and rebuilding. When she said as much to Murphy, he'd told her she was too pessimistic, but watching Becca smiling on television, clearly unshaken in her belief in the Lotus Way, Robin could only hope that the world would watch more closely and ask more questions, when the next five-sided temple appeared on a piece of vacant land.

'And what about the Waces?' Sir Colin asked Strike, while the children on the lawn continued to chase bubbles.

'Confidentially,' said Strike, 'Mazu hasn't spoken a word since her arrest. Literally not a word. One of our police contacts told us she won't even talk to her own lawyer.'

'Shock, do you think?' said Sir Colin.

'Power play,' said Robin. 'She'll continue to act as though she's the divine mother of the Drowned Prophet until her dying breath.'

'But surely she knows, now . . . ?'

'I think,' said Robin, 'if she ever allowed herself to accept that Daiyu was murdered, and her husband knew all along, and made sure to get her killer out of the way to safety, it would drive her out of her mind.'

'And has Abigail confessed?' Sir Colin asked Strike.

'No,' said Strike. 'She's like her father: brazen it out as long as you can, but her boyfriends are turning on her. Now they've realised they might be accused of being accessories to attempted murder, they can't wait to get off the sinking ship. Confidentially, one of her fireman colleagues saw her pocketing the gun and ammo when she found it in a burned-out drug den. He says he assumed she was going to hand them over to the police. 'Course, he'd have to say that – he's married, and he doesn't want it to come out that she was sleeping with him, as well.

'Reaney's currently denying he knows anything about axes and pigs, but a guy who was in the men's dormitory that night remembers Reaney sneaking back inside, in the early hours. Reaney was in his underwear: he'd obviously had to get rid of his bloody tracksuit somewhere. Then he accused everyone of nicking it, when he woke up.

'I think Abigail will be found guilty of Kevin's murder, and for trying to kill Robin and me, and I think she and Reaney are both going to be done for Daiyu's murder.'

'Abigail must be seriously disturbed,' said the compassionate Sir Colin. 'She must have had a dreadful childhood.'

'A lot of people have dreadful childhoods and don't take to strangling small children,' said the implacable Strike, to nods of agreement from Dennis and Pat.

Strike was thinking of Lucy as he spoke. He'd spent the previous day with his sister, accompanying her to view two prospective nursing homes for their uncle. Afterwards they'd had a coffee together in a café, and Strike had told his sister about Mazu attempting to kill Robin in the Rupert Court Temple.

'That evil bitch,' said the horrified Lucy.

'Yeah, but we got her, Luce,' said Strike, 'and the baby's back with her mother.'

Strike had half-expected more tears, but to his surprise, Lucy beamed at him.

'I know I nag you, Stick,' she said. 'I know I do, but as long as you're happy, I don't care if you're not – you know. Married with kids, and all that. You do wonderful things. You help people. You've helped *me,* taking this case, putting that woman behind bars. And what you said about Leda . . . you've really helped me, Stick.'

Touched, Strike reached out to squeeze her hand.

'I s'pose you're just not cut out for the whole settling down with one woman thing, and that's OK,' said Lucy, now smiling a little tearfully. 'I promise I'll never go on about it again.'

135

*. . . if one is intent on retaining his clarity of mind,
good fortune will come from this grief. For here we are
dealing not with a passing mood, as in the nine in
the third place, but with a real change of heart.*

The I Ching or Book of Changes

A week after they'd visited the Edensors, Strike, with a
heavy heart but a sense of obligation, agreed to meet Amelia
Crichton, Charlotte's sister, at her place of work.

He'd asked himself whether he was truly honour-bound to
do this. The UHC case had mercifully relegated Charlotte's
suicide to the back of his mind, but now that it was over – now
that the shattered lives and suicides were being tallied, and the
storm which had caught these people up had passed, leaving
them broken in an unfamiliar landscape – he was left with
his own personal debt to the dead, one he didn't particularly
want to pay. He could imagine optimistic souls telling him
that, much like Lucy with regards to Leda and the Aylmerton
Community, he'd find some kind of resolution in this meeting
with Charlotte's sister, but he had no such expectation.

No, he thought, as he dressed in a sober suit – because
military habits of proper respect for the dead and bereaved
are hard to overcome, and however little he liked Amelia or
the prospect of this meeting, he owed her this, at least – it

was far more likely that Charlotte's sister was the one who'd achieve resolution today. Very well, then: he'd give Amelia satisfaction, and in doing so, offer Charlotte one more chance at a clean sucker punch via her proxy, before they were finally done.

Strike's BMW, from which the police had now dug out a bullet, remained in the repair shop, so he took a taxi to Elizabeth Street in Belgravia. Here, he found Amelia's eponymous shop, which was full of expensive curtain fabrics, tasteful ceramics and chinoiserie table lamps.

She emerged from a back room on hearing the bell over the door ring. Dark-haired like Charlotte, she had similar hazel-flecked green eyes, but there the resemblance ended. Amelia was thin-lipped, with a patrician profile she'd inherited from her father.

'I've booked us a table at the Thomas Cubitt,' she told him, in lieu of any greeting.

So they walked the short distance to the restaurant, which lay just a few doors down from the shop. Once seated at a white-clothed table, Amelia asked for two menus and a glass of wine, while Strike ordered a beer.

Amelia waited for the drinks to arrive and the waiter to disappear again before drawing a deep breath and saying,

'So: I asked you to meet me, because Charlotte left a note. She wanted me to show it to you.'

Of course she fucking did.

Amelia took a large swig of Pinot Noir and Strike a similarly large slug of his beer.

'But I'm not going to,' said Amelia, setting down her glass. 'I thought I had to, immediately after—I thought I owed it to her, whatever . . . whatever it said. But I've had a lot of time to think things over while I've been in the country, and I don't think . . . maybe you'll be angry,' said Amelia, taking a deep breath, 'but when the police were done with it . . . I burned it.'

'I'm not angry,' said Strike.

She looked taken aback.

'I . . . I can still tell you, broadly, what she said. *Your* bit, anyway. It was long. Several pages. Nobody was spared.'

'I'm sorry.'

'What for?' she said, with a trace of the acerbity he remembered from their prior acquaintance.

'Sorry your sister killed herself,' said Strike. 'Sorry she left a letter you're probably finding it hard to forget.'

Unlike Sir Colin Edensor, who'd been born working class, and unlike Lucy, whose childhood had been unclassifiable, Amelia Crichton didn't cry in public. However, she did press her thin lips together and blink rather rapidly.

'It was . . . horrible, seeing it all written down, in her handwriting,' she said in a low voice. 'Knowing what she was about to do . . . but, as I say, if you want me to tell you what she said about you, I can, and then I'll have done what she asked – more or less.'

'I'm pretty sure I know,' said Strike. 'She said, if I'd picked up the phone, it would all have been different. That after all the pain and abuse I doled out to her, she still loved me. That she knows I'm now having an affair with my detective partner, which started days after I walked out on her, proving how little I valued our relationship. That I've fallen in love with Robin because she's biddable, and unchallenging, and hero-worships me, which is what men like me want, whereas Charlotte stood up to me, which was the root of all our problems. That one day I'll get bored with Robin and realise what I've lost, but it'll be too late, because I hurt Charlotte so deeply she's done with life.'

He knew just how accurately he'd guessed the contents of Charlotte's note by Amelia's expression.

'It wasn't just you,' said Amelia, now with a softer and sadder look than he'd ever seen on her face before. 'She blamed everyone. *Everyone.* And only a single line about James and Mary: "Show them this, when they're old enough to understand." That's the main reason I burned it, I can't ... I couldn't let ...'

'You did the right thing.'

'Ruairidh doesn't think so,' said Amelia miserably. Strike only vaguely remembered her husband: a Nicholas Delaunay type, but ex-Blues and Royals. 'He said she wanted it kept, and I had a duty to—'

'She was full of drink and drugs when she wrote that letter, and you've got a duty to the living,' said Strike. 'To her kids, above all. In her best moments – and she had them, as we both know – she always regretted the things she'd done when she was high, or angry. If there's anything beyond, she'll know she shouldn't have written what she did.'

The waiter returned to take their food order. Strike doubted Amelia wanted food any more than he did, but social convention meant they both ordered a single course. Once they were alone again, Amelia said,

'She was always so ... unhappy.'

'Yeah,' said Strike. 'I know.'

'But she wouldn't ever ... there was a – a *darkness* in her.'

'Yeah,' said Strike, 'and she was in love with it. It's dangerous to make a cult of your own unhappiness. Hard to get out, once you've been in there too long. You forget how.'

He drank some more of his rapidly diminishing pint before saying,

'I once quoted Aeschylus at her. "Happiness is a choice that requires effort at times." Didn't go down well.'

'You did Classics as well?' said Amelia, mildly surprised. She'd never shown much interest in him as a human being while he'd been with Charlotte. He'd been a misfit, a ne'er-do-well of mongrel breeding.

'No,' said Strike, 'but there was an alcoholic ex-Classics teacher in one of the squats my mother took me to live in. He used to drop pearls of wisdom like that, mainly to patronise us all.'

When Strike had told Robin the story of this man, and how he, Strike, had stolen his Classics books in revenge at being condescended to, she'd laughed. Amelia merely looked at him as though he were talking about life on some faraway planet.

Their salads arrived. Both ate quickly, making forced conversation about the congestion charge, how often each of them got into the country and whether the Labour Party could win a general election under Jeremy Corbyn. Strike didn't ask whether Charlotte had genuinely had breast cancer, though he suspected, from the absence of any mention of it from Amelia, that she hadn't. What did it matter, now?

Neither ordered pudding or coffee. With perhaps equal relief, they rose from the table barely three quarters of an hour after sitting down.

Back on the pavement, Amelia said unexpectedly,

'You've done wonderfully well with your business. I've been reading about that church . . . it sounds the most dreadful place.'

'It was,' said Strike.

'You actually helped out a friend of ours, recently, with a nasty man who was taking advantage of his mother. Well . . . thank you for meeting me. It's been . . . thank you, anyway.'

She looked up at him uncertainly, and he bent down to allow her to give him the standard upper-class farewell, an air kiss in the vicinity of each cheek.

'Well – goodbye and – and good luck.'

'You too, Amelia.'

Strike heard her sensible heels tapping away on the pavement as he turned to walk away. The sun slid out from behind its cloud, and it was that, surely, and nothing else, that made Strike's eyes sting.

136

*Confucius says . . . Life leads the thoughtful man on
a path of many windings.
Now the course is checked, now it runs straight again.
Here winged thoughts may pour freely forth in words,
There the heavy burden of knowledge must be shut
away in silence.
But when two people are at one in their inmost hearts,
They shatter even the strength of iron or of bronze.*

The I Ching or Book of Changes

'Oh, good,' panted Robin, entering the office pink-faced, at speed. She'd just half-run along Denmark Street. 'He's not here yet – Ryan, I mean.'

'He's dropping by, is he?' said Pat, typing with her e-cigarette jammed between her teeth as usual, and looking pleased at the prospect of seeing the handsome Murphy.

'Yes,' said Robin, taking off the jacket she didn't need on such a warm September day. 'He's picking me up, we're going away for a couple of days and I'm really late – but so's he.'

'Tick him off for it,' said Pat, still typing. 'You might get flowers.'

'Pretty shady behaviour, Pat.'

The office manager removed her e-cigarette from between her teeth.

'Know where *he* is?'

'No,' said Robin, who was now reaching for an empty case folder on the shelf. She understood Pat to be referring to Strike, who the office manager usually called 'he' when he wasn't around.

'Meeting *her* sister.'

'Whose sister?'

'Charlotte's,' said Pat in a loud whisper, though it was only the two of them in the office.

'Oh,' said Robin.

Deeply interested, but not wanting to gossip about Strike's private life with their office manager, Robin took down the folder and rummaged in her bag.

'I'm only back to file these notes. Could you tell Strike they're in here when he gets back, if I'm already gone? He might want to look over them.'

Robin had just met the agency's newest client, a professional cricketer, at his Chelsea flat. She'd expected the interview to last an hour, but it had gone on for two.

'Will do. What's he like, then, the new bloke?' asked Pat, e-cigarette between her teeth. The man in question was tall, blond and good looking, and Pat had evinced a certain disappointment that he wasn't going to have his preliminary interview at the office, but at home.

'Er,' said Robin who, in addition to not gossiping about Strike behind his back, also tried not to criticise clients in front of Pat. 'Well, he didn't like McCabes. That's why he's come back to us.'

In fact, she'd found the South African cricketer, who Strike had called an 'arsehole' after one phone conversation, an unpleasant combination of arrogant and inappropriately flirtatious, especially as his girlfriend had been lurking in the kitchen all through the interview. He'd given the impression he took it for granted that he was the best-looking man Robin had seen in a long while, and had made it clear he didn't consider her entirely unworthy of notice. Robin had to assume the stunning brunette who'd seen her out of the flat at the end of the interview either took him at his own valuation, or enjoyed the gorgeous flat and the Bugatti too much to complain.

'Is he as handsome in person?' asked Pat, watching as Robin placed her notes inside the file, then scribbled the cricketer's name on the front.

'If you like that sort of thing,' said Robin, as the glass door opened.

'Sort of thing's that?' asked Strike, entering in his suit, his tie loosened and his vape pen in his hand.

'Blond cricketers,' said Robin, looking round. Her partner looked tired and downtrodden.

'Ah,' grunted Strike, hanging up his jacket. 'Was he as much of an arsehole in person as he was on the phone?'

Seeing as the not-bitching-about-clients-in-front-of-Pat ship had now set sail full speed out of the harbour, Robin asked,

'How bad was he on the phone?'

'A good eight point five out of ten,' said Strike.

'Then he's the same in person.'

'Fancy updating me before you leave?' said Strike, checking his watch. He knew Robin was due to take some long-overdue leave today. 'Unless you need to get going?'

'No, I'm waiting for Ryan,' said Robin. 'I've got time.'

They entered the inner office and Strike closed the door. The board on the wall that so recently had been covered in the UHC pictures and notes was empty again. The Polaroids were with the police, and the rest had been added to the case file, which was locked in the safe, pending its use in the forthcoming court case. Jacob's body had now been identified, and the accusation of child abuse against Robin had at long last been dropped; the weekend away with Murphy was at least partly in celebration of this fact. Even Robin could see how much happier and healthier she looked in the mirror, now that this weight had been lifted off her.

'So,' said Robin, sitting down, 'he thinks his estranged wife is having an affair with a married *Mail* journalist, hence the stream of scurrilous stories the *Mail* have had on him lately.'

'Which journalist?'

'Dominic Culpepper,' said Robin.

'Married now, then, is he?'

'Yes,' said Robin, 'to a Lady Violet somebody. Well, Lady Violet Culpepper, now.'

'Should be juicy, when it breaks,' said Strike, unsmiling. Depression was radiating from him as the smell of cigarette smoke had, before he'd embarked on his health kick.

'Are you all right?' Robin asked.

'What?' said Strike, though he'd heard her. 'Yeah. I'm fine.'

But in reality, he'd called her into the inner office because he wanted her company as long as he could get it. Robin wondered whether she dared ask, and decided she did.

'Pat told me you were meeting Charlotte's sister.'

'Did she?' said Strike, though without rancour.

'Did she ask to see you, or—?'

'Yeah, she asked to see me,' said Strike.

There was a short silence.

'She wanted to meet me right after Charlotte died, but I couldn't,' said Strike. 'Then she closed up shop and went off to the country with her kids for a month.'

'I'm sorry, Cormoran,' said Robin quietly.

'Yeah, well,' said Strike, with a slight shrug. 'I gave her what she was after, I think.'

'What was that?'

'Dunno,' said Strike, examining his vape pen. 'Reassurance nobody could've stopped it happening? Except me,' he added. 'I could've.'

Robin felt desperately sorry for him, and knew it must have shown on her face, because when he glanced up at her he said,

'I wouldn't change anything.'

'Right,' said Robin, unsure of what else to say.

'She called here,' said Strike, dropping his gaze back to the vape pen in his hand, which he was turning over and over. 'Three times, on the night she did it. I knew who it was and I didn't answer. Then I listened to the messages and deleted them.'

'You couldn't have known—'

'Yeah, I could,' said Strike calmly, still turning the vape pen over in his hand, 'she was a walking suicide even when I met her. She'd already tried a couple of times.'

Robin knew this from her conversations with Ilsa, who scathingly categorised Charlotte's various suicide attempts into two categories: those meant to manipulate, and those that were genuine. However, Robin could no longer take Ilsa's estimation at face value. Charlotte's final attempt had been no empty gesture. She'd been determined to live no longer – unless, it seemed, Strike had answered the phone. The suicide of Carrie Curtis Woods, no matter that Robin now knew she'd been a collaborator in infanticide, would be a scar Robin bore forever. How it felt to know you might have prevented the death of somebody you'd loved for sixteen years, she had no idea.

'Cormoran, I'm sorry,' she said again.

'Feel sorry for Amelia and her kids, not me,' he said. 'I was done. There's nothing deader than dead love.'

For six years now, Robin had longed to know what Strike really felt for Charlotte Campbell, the woman he'd left for good on the very day Robin had arrived at the agency as a temp. Charlotte had been the most intimidating woman Robin had ever met: beautiful, clever, charming and also – Robin had seen evidence of it herself – devious and occasionally callous. Robin had felt guilty about hoarding every crumb of information about Strike and Charlotte's relationship Ilsa had ever let fall, feeling she was betraying Strike in listening, in remembering. He'd always been so cagey about the relationship, even after some of the barriers between them had come down, even after Strike had openly called Robin his best friend.

Strike, meanwhile, was aware he was breaking a vow he'd made himself six years previously, when, fresh from the rupture with a woman he still loved, he'd noticed how sexy his temp was, almost at the same moment he'd noticed the engagement ring on her finger. He'd resolved then, knowing his own susceptibility, that there would be no easy slide into intimacy with a woman who, but for the engagement ring, he might willingly have rebounded onto. He'd been strict about not letting himself trawl for her sympathy. Even after his love for Charlotte had shrivelled into non-existence, leaving behind it a ghostly husk of pity and exasperation, Strike had maintained this reserve, because, against his will, his feelings for Robin were growing deeper and more complex, and her third finger was bare now, and he'd feared ruining the most important friendship of his life, and trashing the business for which both had sacrificed so much.

But today, with Charlotte dead, and with Robin perhaps destined for another engagement ring, Strike had things to say. Perhaps it was the delusion of the middle-aged male to think it would make any difference, but there came a time when a man needed to take charge of his own fate. So he inhaled nicotine, then said,

'Last year, Charlotte begged me to get back together. I told her nothing on earth would make me help raise Jago Ross's kids. This was after we – the agency – found out Jago was knocking his older daughters around. And she said I needn't worry: it'd be shared custody now. In other words, she'd palm the kids off on him, if I was happy to come back.

'I'd just handed her all the evidence a judge would need to keep those kids safe, and she told me she'd shunt them off on that bastard, thinking I'd say, "Great. Fuck 'em. Let's go and get a drink."'

Strike exhaled nicotine vapour. Robin hadn't noticed she was holding her breath.

'Always a bit of delusion in love, isn't there?' said Strike, watching the vapour rise to the ceiling. 'You fill in the blanks with your own imagination. Paint them exactly the way you want them to be. But I'm a detective ... some fucking detective. If I'd stuck to hard facts – if I'd done that, even in the first twenty-four hours I knew her – I'd have walked and never looked back.'

'You were nineteen,' said Robin. 'Exactly the same age Will was, when he heard Jonathan Wace speak for the first time.'

'Ha! You think I was in a cult, do you?'

'No, but I'm saying ... we've got to forgive who we were, when we didn't know any better. I did the same thing, with Matthew. I did *exactly* that. Painted in the gaps the way I'd have liked them to be. Believed in Higher-Level Truths to explain away the bullshit. "He doesn't really mean it." "He isn't really like that." And, oh my God, the evidence was staring me in the face, and I bloody *married* him – and regretted it within an hour of him putting the ring on my finger.'

Hearing this, Strike remembered how he'd burst into her and Matthew's wedding, at the very moment Robin had been about to say 'I do'. He also remembered the hug he and Robin had shared, after he'd walked out of the reception, and she'd run out of her first dance to follow him, and he knew, now, there was no turning back.

'So what did Amelia want?' said Robin, bold enough to ask, now that Strike had told her this much. 'Was she – she wasn't blaming you, was she?'

'No,' said Strike. 'She was carrying out her sister's last wishes. Charlotte left a suicide note, with instructions to pass on a message to me.'

He smiled at Robin's fearful expression.

'It's all right. Amelia burned it. Doesn't matter – I could've written it myself – I told Amelia exactly what Charlotte wrote.'

Robin worried it might be indecent to ask, but Strike didn't wait for the question.

'She said that even though I was a bastard to her, she still loved me. That I'd know one day what I'd given up, that I'd never be happy, deep down, without her. That—'

Strike and Robin had once before sat in this office, after dark and full of whisky, and he'd come dangerously close to crossing the line between friend and lover. He'd felt then the fatalistic daring of the trapeze artist, preparing to swing out into the spotlight with only black air beneath him, and he felt the same now.

'—she knew I was in love with you.'

A stab of cold shock, an electric charge to the brain: Robin couldn't quite believe what she'd just heard. The passing seconds seemed to slow. She waited for Strike to say 'which was her spite, obviously,' or, 'because she never understood that a man and a woman could just be friends', or to make a joke. Yet he said nothing to defuse the grenade he'd just thrown, but simply looked at her.

Then Robin heard the outer door open, and Pat's indistinct baritone, greeting someone with enthusiasm.

'That'll be Ryan,' Robin said.

'Right,' said Strike.

Robin got to her feet in a state of confusion and shock, still clutching the cricketer's folder in her hands, and opened the dividing door.

'Sorry,' said Murphy, who looked harried. 'Did you get my text? I was late leaving and traffic's bloody gridlocked.'

'It's fine,' said Robin. 'I was late back myself.'

'Hi,' said Murphy to Strike, who'd followed Robin into the outer office. 'Congratulations.'

'What for?' said Strike.

'The church case,' said Murphy, with a half-laugh. 'What, you've already moved on to some other world-shattering—?'

'Oh that,' said Strike. 'Yeah. Well, it was mostly Robin.'

Robin took down her jacket.

'Well – see you Monday,' she said to Pat and Strike, unable to meet the latter's eyes.

'You taking that with you?' Murphy asked Robin, looking at the folder in her hands.

'Oh – no – sorry,' said the flustered Robin. 'This belongs here.'

She set the folder down beside Pat.

'Bye,' she said, and left.

Strike watched the glass door close, and listened to the pair's footsteps dying away on the metal stairs.

'They make a good couple,' said Pat complacently.

'We'll see,' said Strike.

Ignoring the office manager's swift, penetrating look, he added,

'I'll be in the Flying Horse if you want me.'

Picking up his jacket and the folder Robin had left, he departed. Time would tell whether he'd just done something foolish or not, but Cormoran Strike had at last decided to practise what he'd preached to Charlotte, all those years ago. Happiness is a choice that requires an effort at times, and it was well past time for him to make the effort.

ACKNOWLEDGEMENTS

My deepest gratitude as ever to my wonderful editor (and fellow cult aficionado) David Shelley. I promised you a cult book, and here, at last, we are.

A very big thank you to Nithya Rae for her superb copyediting, especially for catching date and numerical slip-ups.

To my fabulous agent, Neil Blair, who was one of this book's early readers, thank you for all your hard work on my behalf, and for being such a good friend.

Thank you as always to Nicky Stonehill, Rebecca Salt and Mark Hutchinson, who provide endless support, wise guidance and many laughs.

My gratitude to Di Brooks, Simon Brown, Danny Cameron, Angela Milne, Ross Milne, Fiona Shapcott and Kaisa Tiensuu: I say it every time, but without you, there could be no books at all.

Lastly, to Neil Murray, who really didn't fancy a book about a cult, but who likes *The Running Grave* the best of the series: see? I always know best – except on the many occasions when you do x

CREDITS

READ
CORMORAN STRIKE
BOOK 1

'Reminds me why
I fell in love with
crime fiction in the
first place'
Val McDermid

'A scintillating novel'
The Times

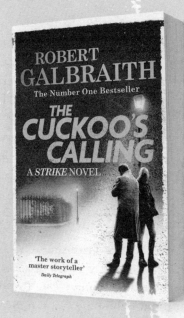

When a troubled model falls to her death from a snow-covered Mayfair balcony,
it is assumed that she has committed suicide. However, her brother has his doubts,
and calls in private investigator Cormoran Strike to look into the case.

Strike is a war veteran – wounded both physically and psychologically – and his
life is in disarray. The case gives him a financial lifeline, but it comes at a personal
cost: the more he delves into the young model's complex world, the darker
things get – and the closer he gets to terrible danger . . .

A gripping, elegant mystery steeped in the atmosphere of London – from the
hushed streets of Mayfair to the backstreet pubs of the East End to the bustle of
Soho – *The Cuckoo's Calling* introduces Cormoran Strike in the acclaimed
first crime novel by Robert Galbraith – J.K. Rowling's pseudonym.

READ

CORMORAN STRIKE
BOOK 2

'Galbraith has pulled
off a thoroughly
enjoyable classic'

Peter James

'A superb and
polished thriller . . . an
ingenious whodunit'

Sunday Mirror

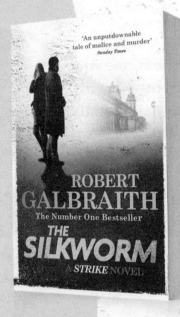

'An unputdownable
tale of malice and murder'
Sunday Times

**ROBERT
GALBRAITH**

The Number One Bestseller

**THE
SILKWORM**

A STRIKE NOVEL

When novelist Owen Quine goes missing, his wife calls in private detective
Cormoran Strike. At first, she just thinks he has gone off by himself for a few days
– as he has done before – and she wants Strike to find him and bring him home.

But as Strike investigates, it becomes clear that there is more to Quine's disappearance
than his wife realises. The novelist has just completed a manuscript featuring
poisonous pen-portraits of almost everyone he knows. If the novel were published it
would ruin lives - so there are a lot of people who might want to silence him.

And when Quine is found brutally murdered in bizarre circumstances, it becomes a
race against time to understand the motivation of a ruthless killer, a killer unlike any
he has encountered before . . .

**A compulsively readable crime novel with twists at every turn, *The Silkworm*
is the second in the highly acclaimed series featuring Cormoran Strike and his
determined young assistant Robin Ellacott.**

READ

CORMORAN STRIKE
BOOK 3

'Strike is a compelling
creation . . .
this is terrifically
entertaining stuff'
Irish Times

'As readable and
exciting as ever'
Daily Telegraph

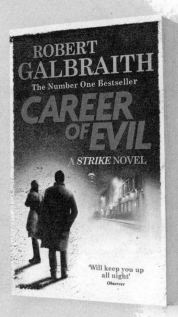

When a mysterious package is delivered to Robin Ellacott,
she is horrified to discover that it contains a woman's severed leg.

Her boss, private detective Cormoran Strike, is less surprised but no less alarmed.
There are four people from his past who he thinks could be responsible – and Strike
knows that any one of them is capable of sustained and unspeakable brutality.

With the police focusing on the one suspect Strike is increasingly sure is not the
perpetrator, he and Robin take matters into their own hands, and delve into the dark
and twisted worlds of the other three men. But as more horrendous acts occur,
time is running out for the two of them . . .

A fiendishly clever mystery with unexpected twists around every corner,
Career of Evil **is also a gripping story of a man and a woman at a crossroads
in their personal and professional lives.**

READ
CORMORAN STRIKE
BOOK 4

'Come for the twists and turns and stay for the beautifully drawn central relationship'
Independent

'An obsessive reading experience'
Observer

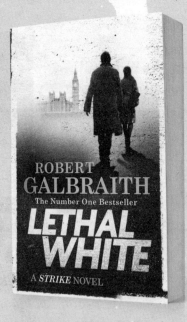

When Billy, a troubled young man, comes to private eye Cormoran Strike's office to ask for his help investigating a crime he thinks he witnessed as a child, Strike is left deeply unsettled. But before Strike can question him further, Billy bolts from his office in a panic.

Trying to get to the bottom of Billy's story, Strike and Robin Ellacott – once his assistant, now a partner in the agency – set off on a twisting trail that leads them through the backstreets of London, into a secretive inner sanctum within Parliament, and to a beautiful but sinister manor house deep in the countryside.

And during this labyrinthine investigation, Strike's own life is far from straightforward: his relationship with his former assistant is more fraught than it ever has been – Robin is now invaluable to Strike in the business, but their personal relationship is much, much more tricky than that . . .

Lethal White is both a gripping mystery and a page-turning next instalment in the ongoing story of Cormoran Strike and Robin Ellacott.

READ
CORMORAN STRIKE
BOOK 5

'An ambitious,
immersive mystery'
Heat

'Confident,
utterly gripping,
niftily plotted'
India Knight

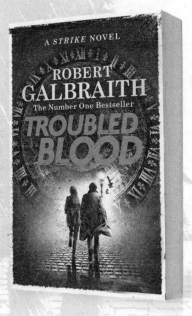

Private Detective Cormoran Strike is visiting his family in Cornwall when
he is approached by a woman asking for help finding her mother,
Margot Bamborough – who went missing in mysterious circumstances in 1974.

Strike has never tackled a cold case before, let alone one forty years old. But despite
the slim chance of success, he is intrigued and takes it on; adding to the long list of
cases that he and his partner in the agency, Robin Ellacott, are currently working on.
And Robin herself is also juggling a messy divorce and unwanted male attention,
as well as battling her own feelings about Strike.

As Strike and Robin investigate Margot's disappearance, they come up
against a fiendishly complex case with leads that include tarot cards,
a psychopathic serial killer and witnesses who cannot all be trusted. And they
learn that even cases decades old can prove to be deadly . . .

**A breathtaking, labyrinthine epic, *Troubled Blood* is the fifth
Strike and Robin novel.**

Help us make the next generation of readers

We – both author and publisher – hope you enjoyed this book.
We believe that you can become a reader at any time in your life,
but we'd love your help to give the next generation a head start.

Did you know that 9% of children don't have a book of their
own in their home, rising to 12% in disadvantaged families*?
We'd like to try to change that by asking you to consider the role
you could play in helping to build readers of the future.

We'd love you to think of sharing, borrowing, reading, buying or talking
about a book with a child in your life and spreading the love of reading.
We want to make sure the next generation continue to have access
to books, wherever they come from.

And if you would like to consider donating to charities that help
fund literacy projects, find out more at www.literacytrust.org.uk
and www.booktrust.org.uk.

Thank you.

 hachette
CHILDREN'S GROUP

little, brown
BOOK GROUP

*As reported by the National Literacy Trust